Mr Marvellous Ride

TRACY KASABOSKI

Rabbit Rock Press

Rabbit Rock Press

Mr Isbister's Marvellous Ride

AN ENTRY FOR THE
Stephen Leacock Award
FOR HUMOUR FOR
2025

Co-Authored with Kristen den Hartog

The Occupied Garden: A Family Memoir of War-Torn Holland

The Cowkeeper's Wish: A Genealogical Journey

For my sisters and my mother.

And to the memory of my father.

Intrepid travellers, all

Chapter 1
ALICE AND THROCKMORTON

Through the tall parlour window, hung with decades-old velvet drapery and several layers of simpering lace, a watery sun glinted on the glass of the greenhouse in the spacious garden belonging to Mr Roderick Throckmorton Isbister, of Sowerby Grange. Barely glimpsed through the wall of hollyhocks, hawthorn and elder, its whitewashed panes were visible from Mr's vantage point, seated as he was across the breakfast table from his wife, but it wasn't the greenhouse itself that drew Mr's stealthy glance. Beyond that structure sat the true object of his guarded attention, a small wooden shed that had seen better days, one door nearly off its hinge, a bit of rot punking the floorboards, and a well-tracked mouse trail hollowing a plank in the wall. As Mr Isbister sat opposite Mrs on this pale morning in 1922, his heart beneath his brocade waistcoat lurched happily at the thought of the secret ensconced in that ramshackle building.

Mrs Isbister's squawk made him jump, and he realised he'd been holding his toast aloft, forgotten. He lowered it to his plate with surreptitious guilt. "I have it on good authority," she said, "that you have taken to dabbling in the arts." As she spoke, she peered at him, her gaze travelling over her spectacles and down her long nose and skewering him neatly, somewhere between the tidy mound of his well-fed tummy and the narrow bones of his under-worked shoulders. The word arts might well have been rotten fish, or smelly socks, or philanthropy, such was the curl of distaste in her voice. R. Throckmorton Isbister made an effort not to squirm, and was fairly certain he'd managed to look only mildly uncomfortable.

It was true that what had begun as mere peeks into glossy books about the *avant garde* art world had blossomed into a bit of an obsession for Mr Isbister; that if Mrs Isbister were to look carefully she might indeed see cerulean oil paint beneath the fingernail of his left pinkie, and vermilion pastel smudged on the pad of his right index digit. The odour of turpentine was caught in his slender moustache, but Mrs Isbister

1

would never have occasion to notice *that*, he knew with stalwart certainty. If, he told himself, in his mind drawing his backbone even more rigidly upright, she were to look beyond the press of the linen on the breakfast table between them or the crisp of the toast on its scalloped plate or the scald of the tea in the china pot, she might have noticed a shine in Mr Isbister's eye reminiscent of the one that had been there on the eve of their wedding, and that had not been there since, or, in fact, for very long on the night itself. Could he have turned the hands of the clock back he would surely have set them to the morning of that fateful day, well prior to the hour of the deed itself, and, armed with the knowledge of the misery of his future, would have turned his nose in the direction of the door and followed it, out, as it were, and away. Not for the first time he imagined his escape: one long foot placed in front of the other and taking him down the lane that led to the village, through it to its outskirts, then over hill and dale till he reached the seaside, there to shed his coat-tails and abandon his cuff-links, set a knife between his teeth and sail into the sunset, marvelling at both his luck and the hue of water and sky.

"Have you been – painting?" Mrs Isbister continued, the utterance causing her mouth to shrivel as if she'd tasted a lemon. R. Throckmorton wondered how it was that a woman with so lengthy and lean a nose could at the same time have such a round and vapid face. The one did not complement the other; indeed, Mrs Isbister seemed a conglomerate of mismatched parts: a wide bottom and tiny feet, small hands at the ends of dimpled arms, an extra chin that hung like a beard between pinched ears. Despite her wide face she had a curiously narrow forehead, a result, Mr Isbister felt certain, of winding her hair too tightly into an otherwise girlish chignon at the nape of her neck. Of the body parts beneath the full skirts and stiff jackets he could only surmise – he'd never seen them and had no particular desire to, although if he dredged memory their wedding night of some twenty-five years ago surfaced, the events therein as murky and suspect as effluvia on stagnant water.

It wasn't that the attractions of the fairer sex eluded him. On the contrary. Despite his ineligible state he was not immune to the pungent aroma of the serving girl's armpit when she placed his dinner before him nights, nor were his eyes blind to the pink of her ankle as she hung laundry in the yard. There was nothing carnal about his relations with the girl – he couldn't even recall her name – but there was a gnawing guilt that had to do with imagination. Her various bits frequently sprang to his mind whilst thumbing through his art book and enjoying a titillating ogle of Venus' ample buttocks and Hélène Fourment's bunions and dimpled knees and – goodness – her bared bosom. He often had to put the book away on account of what he was certain was his extraordinarily high colour; he kept the volume tucked beneath his mattress – on hindsight perhaps not the best location, since the maid may have had occasion to find it when changing the sheets on his bed.

The more he thought on it, lips firmly sealed against any reply and eyes hedgingly evasive, the more convinced he became that the girl must have turned the book over to his wife, hence these pointed questions. Pinned as he was by Mrs Isbister's glare, he could not give in to his urge to scissor to his room and check, though mustering outward calm was agony. He realised he was sitting on his hands like a schoolboy evading the strap, and he furtively extracted them, flexing his fingers, pointedly not looking there lest his wife's gaze follow. They were so obviously the hands of a painter: slender, long, hairless, lightly stained – but more than that, and a greater secret, even, was that they were the hands of a tinkerer. Or would be, given what he had recently hidden in the toolshed. He stretched his lips in what he presumed was a smile, although perhaps grimace was more accurate – and countered her attack with equal acerbity.

"Painting? I?" His tone warned of heightened indignation, R. Throckmorton Isbister felt quite sure. He would have shaken his jowls but he had none. He eyed hers somewhat enviously.

She frowned, and leaned across the table. Her nose seemed to grow, her glasses to shrink. "Mr Isbister," she said to her husband in a scolding tone. "I have it on good authority."

He frowned back, tremulously, although he'd hoped not. What, pray, could she have against such a pursuit? Indeed, the noblest of men collected art. Admittedly, he knew what her objections were. She voiced her poorly informed convictions loudly and unabashedly about most topics, and so he was privy to her distaste of the people she referred to as "painters." Most were lewd men who lived in Paris, den of sin, existing in poverty and obscurity until they died. The more he thought about what could have precipitated her accusation, the more he felt sure she had seen his book. And although the volume featured more than plump naked thighs and budding bosoms, one chapter was in fact a treatise of the naughty Rococo period, wherein even the clothed subjects enticed. Mr Isbister would have hastened to make the defense that he had not chosen the volume for that reason, no. He'd purchased it rather hastily, in fact, on one of his clandestine visits to the Lesser Plumpton School of the Arts where various art books were for sale in the lobby. He'd chosen it randomly, and, upon perusal in the privacy of his sitting room, thought it a most titillating selection. But while *he* enjoyed its content, Mrs would most emphatically not, and so, sitting across from that inquisitor now, Mr Isbister decided that his best response to her volley would be a muddying of the waters, so to speak. He mustered courage, his voice coming forth sharply.

"You have it? Have what? Have what, madam? I?"

Was it his use of the word "madam" that caused her to contract into her chair? That precipitated the sinking of her neck into her shoulders? While Mr and Mrs Isbister addressed one another with the titles that denoted them partners in a marriage, however reluctant, they used the terms sir and madam only in moments of anger or extreme disappointment. Neither cared to mention that as husband and wife they'd uttered one another's given names but once; he mumbling "Alice" as he groped beneath the sheets on their wedding night, still anticipating bliss, she squawking "Throckmorton!" on the same night, damping his expectations. Since then, they'd drawn back more or less comfortably, Mr to his apartment and Mrs to hers, the parlour and dining room their shared space in the house, never again descending to the familiarity and embarrassment of Throckmorton and Alice.

Mr Isbister understood advantage when he saw it. He rose, the bones of his knees a-tremble (he detested conflict). His long feet angled toward the door. His hips swivelled in their sockets. His eyes itched to lay their gaze upon his book – not to ogle the bloated blue-grey thighs of some Rococo demoiselle. Merely he wished to reassure himself that the volume was still there, tucked beneath his mattress, delectable pickle between bread. Then perhaps he might chance scuttling to the garden shed, although venturing there in daylight was to court discovery. He blinked rapidly at his wife while her neck remained submerged, and coasted on the masculine supremacy society awarded all husbands. "I shall be in my room," he announced. "Or out for a walk." He should have turned and left then, spun on his heel and withdrawn, point made. If he had, his superiority might have remained intact. Instead, momentarily enjoying himself, he made an error in judgement and kept talking as he headed for the door, his tongue glib. "I might be in India, come to think of it, sitting on a cashmere rug and chatting with a maharajah, or perhaps in Canada, riding with the Mounties and finding their man. Or I shall be in China, supping China tea, or in Kenya, on safari, hunting down elephants –!"

Mrs Isbister pounded the flat of her hand on the dainty table and the biscuits rattled on their saucers. Tea spilled from a cup. She stood, and in girth, there were two of her to Mr Isbister's one. From the corner of darting eyes he noticed the serving girl – the one with the ankles and the fragrant armpits – peer at them from the hallway. Mrs Isbister did not see.

"Mr Isbister, I am quite distraught!" she cried, nostrils flaring, her face dangerously red. "Have you or have you not been taking *art* classes?" The word *art* wobbled in her throat like phlegm, and for half a moment Mr Isbister thought she might expectorate, the better to dispel the distasteful utterance. He had not quite cleared the doorway, and now balanced mid-step on the ball of one slender foot, pinned by guilt. He *had* been considering art classes, even if he'd not yet plucked up the courage to actually attend. But how had she known? Had she discovered the red-jacketed pamphlet outlining the various courses on offer at the Lesser Plumpton School of the Arts that had made its way into his pocket on his last visit to the lobby of the building that housed the school? Had someone seen him, perhaps, and reported him slinking through the doors of the once elegant if decaying structure? It was true he'd gone there on more than one occasion, curious and deliciously excited by the smell of oils and turpentine and the idea of nude models perched on cloth-draped stools, or reclining on divans, limbs arranged just so to best catch the light. Of course, he'd happily paint apples if that was on offer at the lessons, and expected one would have to work up to nude models, but the idea was titillating nonetheless, and he'd wondered, standing in the lobby, if he might someday become another Fragonard. For the time being, though, he was no one. If he had any artistic talent, it was as yet unproven and untried, and he could reply with complete confidence to his wife's accusatory question that no, he had not been taking art classes. Just as he had not followed through as thoroughly as he'd have liked on his curiosity about plants, though he had drawn plans to enlarge the greenhouse and had read up on soils and the need for a proper watering system. Mrs hadn't been opposed entirely to that interest; she thought the pursuit of gardening a pastime not without its rewards, for she always wanted floral sprays for her tables, and there was a cost to that if one did not have prolific gardens. She had encouraged his horticultural endeavours, not immediately understanding that Mr's curiosity lay more in the botanical direction, with a nod to fungi – *marasmius rotula* was his favourite, with its little wheel-like discs suspended on unbelievably delicate and thready stalks – and wetland species, neither good for decorating indoors because of their swampy odours and short lives. For a while he'd been excited, his long nose in *The Illustrated Handbook of English Botany*, sharing the Latin for Greater Bladderwort – *utricularia vulgaris* – at the dinner table, and explaining that sundews, a common and incidentally pretty fenland plant were in fact carnivorous. Inevitably, his interest in the more conventional of plant life waned, and the greenhouse plans found the dustbin. He tried to sneak out in his wellies, pocket guide to wetlands in his coat, looking forward to poking about amongst rotten logs and old stumps, but Mrs had soon realised that her interpretation of this current fascination of her husband's was rather different from his, and she began to round him off at the door, pointing to the hoe and the yard and directing: this bed will be for coral gladioli, and this for pink hollyhocks, and this for fat white peonies. Mrs salivated over the possibility of placing first in the village's annual horticultural competition, and Mr found himself with tool in hand, and little time to spare for his woodland walks amongst the mushrooms. A neighbour grew some scented Queen Anne roses that Mrs coveted, and she harangued him over tea until he scuttled down the road and begged a cutting. She plucked the greenhouse plans from the bin and he erected the addition, whitewashing the glass with slow and reluctant swabs of the brush. It wasn't greenhouses, per se, that he objected to, he said aloud but in hushed tones, standing in the silence of the building. In fact, he had some interesting and unusual samplings already on the go, and he'd designated a corner of the greenhouse to experiment with something exotic like the fascinating *amorphophallus titanum* – translated (blushingly) as "giant, misshapen penis," or, more colloquially and more politely, the corpse flower. He'd read of the plant in a botanical journal, how the strange specimen from the rainforests of southeast Asia flowered but rarely, though when it did emerge from its swollen underground tuber it did so with stunning impact, thrusting its flower-bearing spike through a ridged crimson and cream collar, and emitting a scent reminiscent of rotting meat. R. Throckmorton Isbister had been besotted, and even more convinced that the cultivation of hothouse pansies was not for him. He placed a mail order for one, and once it arrived and joined his other endeavours – among them a *crassula perforata* that looked like a stack of tiny buttons, and a well-established rosette of *aeonium* – then his whitewashing brushstrokes would be enthusiastic and anticipative.

"You may not leave until you give me an answer!" Mrs Isbister cried, and Mr, still paused in his exit, heard several things in her tone that decided his reaction – shock that he would depart in the midst of her inquisition, not to mention breakfast; anger that he had spoken to her so flippantly and nonsensically; and confidence that he would do as she directed, whether replying to her question or planting pansies. And despite the bravado that had propelled him to the door a moment ago, his shoulders slumped. The *amorphophallus titanum* that had, for an invigorating instant, bloomed inside him, went flaccid, and withered on its stalk. He did not want to be harangued for non-existent art classes, or be the object of her wrath for avoiding the planting of pansies. He noticed the maid, still hovering, and saw her raise plump fingers to her mouth to cover a titter. She thought him a fool, no doubt. As ever, he was unmanned. He would answer, and affirm Mrs' role as head of the Isbister household.

He pivoted slowly on the ball of that poised foot, and turned back to the red-faced Mrs, whose bosom heaved in her bright yellow morning gown. His brocade waistcoat had ridden up on the compact bulge of his tummy and he tugged the fabric down, gathering his slight dignity. He could feel the expectant indignation of Mrs from across the room, and behind him, the cheek of the peeping maid. His reply was awaited. He held his hands out in front of him, fingers splayed, noticing the smudge of vermillion on his thumb, but also a narrow rim of black grease beneath one fingernail. He remembered the garden shed and the secret it held, and his internal corpse flower throbbed ever so slightly. Gently defiant, he said, "I'm sorry, my dear, I've forgotten the question." Then he departed, passing the maid, who giggled and dipped a curtsey. It was a small victory, but R. Throckmorton Isbister gripped it firmly.

Chapter 2
THE TRUSTY TRIUMPH

Two weeks earlier, Roderick Throckmorton Isbister had gotten a wee bit squiffy at the Pig and Whistle, one of the village of Watton Hoo's three pubs. Mr Isbister wasn't a tippler, habitually; in fact, he was more a totaller, as in tea. But on the rare occasion he enjoyed a pint, he felt it apropos to give his best effort to the imbibing of the local publicans' various brews.

On this particular day, Mr had begun the afternoon at the Pig and Whistle, where several of the locals tipped their flat caps to him, and bought a round. For the last number of years the talk had been mostly of the war, of course – but never with any gusto, and that had thinned as the village limped into the new decade. During the war, those who'd had boys serving went to the pub to forget their worries, and maybe throw a game of darts. Few had wanted to think about the raging battles across the Channel, or admit their fear of the telegram delivery boy on his bicycle. War'd be over soon anyway, and no mistake, had been the mantra. Except from then to now had been a long road. Mr, beyond his best years and not a candidate for a soldier even at the start of the war, and having no children of his own, had found that a bob of the head went a long way when the topic came up in company of the pub's patrons. And while he enjoyed a tilt or two in the safety of his own imagination, sword brandished or rifle aimed, heroism a-rage, in the here and now he was content to do battle with nothing more than his wife's tongue. The armistice had brought some euphoria, but it was a short-lived gasp, like the toot of a horn rather than the full song. The locals, for the most part, had looked up and glanced round, then hunched again over their pints.

Mr Isbister had dropped in at the pub after a particularly trying day in the greenhouse: three panes of glass had been broken, and no one, not maid nor cook nor the dustbin boy would own up to the crime. Secretly, Mr suspected Mrs of the deed. She didn't venture often to the

9

greenhouse, but once he'd come across her in the confines of the glass structure, growling and swatting with a long stick at an errant butterfly that she was sure was eating the leaves of her young camellia plants, recently acquired by mail order. He did not question her as he did the other three, but he swiveled an eyeball in her direction, suspicious.

The Pig and Whistle, or Hock and Toot as it was affectionately referred to by those same regulars, had thick stone walls and plank floors that were warped with the wear of many centuries. The publican, Nate Darby, told anyone who would listen that the Darby family, and men of the name Nate Darby in particular, had been publicans at this establishment nigh on three hundred years, give or take. Mr Isbister, whose family went back in these parts not at all, given that Mrs owned their house and grounds, gave the man his due, raising his glass. "P'raps this pub ought to be called The Pig and Darby," he declared genially. A disapproving silence fell. A cricket chirred from a corner. Mr's eyes made the round of hostile glares, and he swilled his pint, setting it down on the bar. "No, then," he said, and teeth showed again, conversation resumed, and Nate Darby refilled his glass. "On the house," he told Mr, then leaned across the gleaming wood between them and said, "You're not a local; you couldn't have known."

Relieved, Mr bought a round, and then a second. Another patron reciprocated, and someone else shouted "Pasties, all 'round!" An arm was slung round his shoulder. The savoury pasties appeared, piping hot and spilling onion and shredded beef, and Mr wondered foggily why anyone would ever need, or want, to go home, when everything was here, at the Pig and Whistle. A barmaid sat on his knee. It occurred to him she looked a lot like his house maid, she of the covered mouth, a-titter.

He made a friend. Two, if you counted the publican, Nate Darby, who kept refilling his glass. He became "Roddy," and wondered how it was he'd never met many of the men of the village before, having lived here, albeit somewhat secluded at a local house of privilege, for so many years. Stephen Vanson shook his hand, several times, and told him about living in Merthyr Tydfil, a Welsh city of sin and corruption and wickedness. "I was bogged down with the worst of men," Stephen confessed, eyes fixed blearily on the glass in front of him, his shoulders hunched over the bar. "Went to jail, I did. For thieving. And well deserved. Robbed a shop owned by a widow, three of us blokes. Worst luck, we had. Copper happened by just as we struck a light trying to see what the bloody hell we were thieving. Raised the alarm and we were all caught straightaway. Would've gone worse on us than it did, but for the widow's own mercy. She spoke up for us in court, and I thank her to this day, I do, and have vowed to be a better man." His face swung up to meet Mr's, and his red-rimmed eyes followed a second later. He grinned lopsidedly. "Want to buy a motorcycle?"

It was the moment of Mr Roderick Throckmorton Isbister's undoing.

"A motorcycle?" he queried, working to force his tongue to shape the words over the effects of so much ale. His chin wobbled uncertainly over his neck.

"She's a beauty. You can have her for a pittance," Stephen said, his long, earnest face angling towards Roddy's raised brows. "Bought her on a whim, but she's too much a novelty for the missus, riding in the sidecar. Can't stand the wind, she says. Thinks it'll ruin her hat." He guffawed, and poured the remnants of his foamy ale down his throat. "'Tender, please!" he called, gesturing to his and Roddy's glasses. Roddy's chin dipped towards the bar, but his brow furrowed, considering the exotic idea of a motorcycle. Raffish. Jaunty. He eyed the barmaid across the room, the one who looked like his serving girl, and inhaled, wondering if her armpits held the same dusky odour, picturing her in the sidecar.

Before the evening was out, Roddy had bought a motorcycle, a Triumph "Trusty," 550 cc, four horsepower machine with a wicker sidecar. Green stripes and leather helmet included. No additional charge. He thought it a wonderful purchase, but cautiously, cognizant of the amount of ale he'd imbibed alongside his new friend Stephen, and, truth be told, how little he knew about motorbikes, wheeled the contraption home, and hid it beneath an oiled canvas sheet in the old garden shed behind the greenhouse. In the morning, nursing a rather large head and avoiding the beady eyes of Mrs Isbister, he snuck outside and erased the tyre tracks from the path.

*

11

Now and again, Mrs Isbister went out. One afternoon, shortly after his purchase of the motorcycle and well before their disagreement at breakfast, Mr had watched as Mrs stood in front of the hall mirror, smiling at her reflection and sliding rather lethal-looking pins through her hat, an elaborately decorated straw affair with bobbing flowers and other things that bounced and jiggled. Earlier, she'd announced that she was attending a meeting of the Horticultural Society in the village, but her spirits seemed rather higher than such an event would normally warrant, or so Mr thought. Still, question not lest ye be questioned, was Mr's current motto, and he said – calmly, he hoped, though his voice might have squeaked – "enjoy your day, my dear," and closed the door after she left.

The motorcycle had been on his mind all morning, and he'd been eager to try sitting on it, to tinker with it, hear it run. He'd had no chance to visit the shed prior to this day, and he was beside himself with anticipation. He stood by the long parlour window and parted the lace just slightly, watching the decorated contrivance that was his wife's hat woggle along on the other side of the laurel hedge, then elevate as she climbed into the waiting pony trap, and jerk forward as cart and hat, with wife upon and below, departed. Before Mr dropped the lace curtain, one yellow petunia waved.

The moment Mrs Isbister was out of sight, Mr Isbister had sped to the garden, slowing as he neared the back of the greenhouse. He glanced over both shoulders, half expecting Mrs to have doubled back to check on him, but there were no gaudy baubles visible in the laurel. The shed door creaked as he pushed it open, and his heart thundered to see the shape of the machine beneath its cloak of oiled tarpaulin. He stepped inside, and the pungency of gasoline and rubber and metal assaulted his nose. He lifted the canvas, and there she was. A beauty, as his pub pal had declared. Stephen had included a motorcycle manual with the sale, and Mr fished it out of the leather satchel strapped to the back, running his hand over the gold lettering on the front cover: *The Motor-Cyclist's Handbook, A Guide to Driving and Maintaining Your Trusty Triumph.* On the inside cover there was a photo of the author seated on his machine, and Mr Isbister pictured himself in a similar pose – the casual, insolent slouch, one foot on the ground, the other on the foot-peg, the machine slung effortlessly between his legs. The author wore a strapped leather cap like the one Stephen had given him, and his goggles were pushed up high on his forehead. "*Phoenix*" – the author's motorcycle pen name – stared out of the plate with a confidence that seemed to Mr Isbister to say, 'I am a man of this young century; Adventure is my middle name.'

Mr Isbister parked himself on an upturned bucket and put his nose between the covers, swooning his agreement with the very first words: "It has been said, with truth, that an inherent love of things mechanical finds a more or less definite place in the character of every Englishman…" He read on in a low mutter, his finger tracing the words. "To own a motorcycle is, in effect, to own a private locomotive, capable of transporting the rider up hill and down dale for long distances, with a rapidity impossible with any other class of vehicle of the same size and weight." He nodded enthusiastically, and wriggled his buttocks more firmly onto his bucket seat. "The delightful sensation of free-wheeling down a long and easy grade on a pedal cycle – an experience which most of us frequently enjoy – is reproduced, with a motorcycle, on the level, up steep hills, and indeed, in every stage of progress, calling for no effort on the rider's part, and requiring no particular skill in order that good results may be obtained." Mr was thrilled with that reassurance, and read on. So passed the better part of an hour.

A tit mouse running over his foot startled him from his bookish stupor, and he sprang from his perch on the bucket, hastening to the shed door to confirm his solitude. Thankfully, it remained intact. He closed the handbook and set it on the upturned bucket. There'd be time enough later for reading. Right now, he wanted to hear the old girl purr, and he slung his leg over the saddle and gripped the handlebars. He put his foot on the kick-starter, turned the gas lever as Stephen had demonstrated the day of the purchase, and jumped, delivering his full weight to the pedal. The pistons pumped, and the Trusty sprang to life, a puff of exhaust clouding the air. He shut it off quickly, dismounted and stuck his head out the door. Had anyone heard? But nothing moved on the paths. The way was clear. He turned back to the motorcycle, his hands clasped together in adoration. She was incredible! He climbed onto the bike again and restarted it, this time squeezing the gas lever and admiring the pop-pop-pop of the engine. He reached behind and pulled the goggles out of the satchel, fastening the buckle at the back of his head. They were a bit snug and his eyes bulged behind the round lenses, but R. Throckmorton Isbister was too excited to notice slight discomfort. With the motorcycle still on its stand and the little engine putt-putting away, he leaned over the handlebar, imagining the road ribboning before him, and the wind on his face.

Sometime later, thinking the hour must be growing late, he reluctantly shut the machine off and replaced the heavy tarpaulin, tucking in the edges with tender fingers. He pocketed the goggles and the handbook, anticipating wearing one and perusing the other in the comfort of his apartments of an evening, and he exited the shed, pulling closed the door. He stood blinking in the afternoon light, the endearing putter of his Trusty Triumph ringing in his ears, daydreams of a countryside adventure playing in his mind, and began to notice that the day held both a dappled sunlight that teased the colours out of the veronica and phlox, and an odd bluish haze that shrouded the granny's bonnets and the pinks. With a guilty start and a sniff he realised that the haze was the Trusty's exhaust hanging low amongst the Isbisters' garden foliage, and, horrified to think that Mrs would be arriving home any minute to notice both the smell and the smog and thus discover his secret, he grabbed up a piney bough from the refuse pile and waved it, running through the garden's paths to disperse the blue fog.

The Triumph had him, without a doubt. As he leapt and cavorted, his imagination ran unfettered, and he saw himself on the motorcycle, goggles buckled, an ivory scarf, perhaps, fluttering from his neck. Green hills rolled by, and low stone walls, and children cheered, while ladies threw flowers. *Phoenix*, the name, was spoken for, but there was no reason he, R. Throckmorton Isbister, should not adopt another equally intrepid moniker. *Chimera*, maybe: a beast equal parts lion, serpent and goat. He made a throaty goatlike noise – "meh-eh-eh," – but stopped short when he heard a giggle.

It was the serving girl. She stood by the far corner of the greenhouse, nearest the laurel hedge that sheltered the garden from the gravelled drive. On the far side of the hedge, he saw now, his wife's hat was bobbing, headed, it would seem, from the pony trap that had just ferried her home from her Horticultural Society meeting, to the front door.

"Sar?" said the maid, and jerked her head over her shoulder towards the bobbing hat. "Mistress." She grinned at her feet, insolent, but dipped a curtsey, respectful.

Embarrassed, annoyed, grateful, Mr dropped his branch and dusted his hands as if to indicate that he'd been engaged in important yard work. Brushing and whatnot. The removal of cobwebs. He plucked at his suspenders in what he hoped was a show of masculine authority, and nodded, expecting her to understand the gesture as a dismissal, but she stood on the path like a chess piece, a conundrum. She blocked his way, and he felt a moment's flutter that she knew his secret and intended to give him away. But the questions of whether she did or didn't, would or wouldn't, piffled as the dustbin boy appeared, wheeling his cart. The maid turned, giving room, and Roderick Throckmorton Isbister, man of the house, strode by her, tilting his chin ever so slightly up, feigning purpose. As he passed first her, distracted, and then the dustbin boy, oblivious, he touched his pockets to reassure himself of the goggles and handbook. Yes, still present.

Chapter 3
THE STINK OF SMELLY SOCKS

As Mr Isbister had expected, Mrs was not about to let the matter of the art dabbling go unaddressed. At dinner, she broached the subject a second time, but with the jab and cross of what she saw as his neglect of the greenhouse. Although he'd called a fellow in to replace the mysteriously broken panes of glass, the job was apparently not up to snuff, for Mrs now complained that one pane was loose, and rattled when the door was opened. Mr paused. He'd prepared a parry to her anticipated thrust on the subject of art, but the greenhouse complaint threw him a-kilter. Had he been inclined to gnash his teeth, he would have.

As it was, he was feeling rather more congenial this evening, since the morning's discord – unsettling though it had been at the time – had given him what he'd felt was license to don his wellies and take a defiant walk on one of his favourite paths, a pungent affair of spongy detritus that wound along the black and tumbling waters of a creek, sheltered beneath mossy branches of wych elm and drooping crack willow. Spider webs abounded, hung with incredible delicacy among the leaves and grasses, and while Mr appreciated their gossamer beauty, his eyeballs were trained rather lower, hoping for a glimpse of the delicate Lilac Bonnet mushroom – *mycena pura* – with its phosphorescent gills, or perhaps even the elusive Red Raspberry Slime, which, Mr had read, took up residence on rotting stumps and thereupon enjoyed a mobile phase during which it proceeded to engulf and consume its host.

Alas, he saw neither specimen, but the lack was of no consequence. The woodland jaunt had served, as ever, to buoy his spirit, enough, as it turned out, that he felt only mild puzzlement when he turned suddenly on the footpath, intending to begin his return journey, and spotted Stephen Vanson, his pub acquaintance and seller of the Trusty Triumph, on the trail behind him. It was a secluded trickle of a track, rarely used, so it was odd indeed to meet another tromping its length, but that fact did not immediately occur to Mr Isbister.

Stephen hailed him first. "I say, Roddy, and that's a coincidence, eh? Both out adventuring, same time, same place." He grinned as he advanced, and stuck out his hand.

Roddy – Mr – shook it, and such was the other's charmingly wide smile and ready words that he did not wonder at Stephen's lack of suitable attire. Where wellies were in order for a swampy walk, Stephen wore plain shoes, now mud-caked, and had not thought to at least tuck his trouser legs into his socks to save the laundry bill. He wore a vest and shirtsleeves, with no jacket, though the day was fresh and called for one.

"Had a go on that motorbike yet, Roddy? She's a beauty, and no mistake. Miss her, I do, just like a lady friend – well, maybe not quite that, eh?" He guffawed at his own humour and gave Mr a dig in the ribs, and Mr offered a chuckle. Then, with the skill of a theatre muse, Stephen fixed a frown upon his handsome face, and stuck out his bottom lip. He dug his hands into his trouser pockets and toed the duff of the footpath, putting Mr in mind of a chastened child.

"Listen, here's the rub, mate. I know I sold her to you fair and square and all, but the missus was set to clout me when I told her the bargain price. You been bilked, she shouted. Come at me with her dishrag, all whacks and slaps. I know 'tis a said and done deal, and I've no right to come begging a fairer price – you're cannier than I, is all, and made a wily purchase. But if you could see your way to adding a bit o' jam to the pot, well, it'd go a long way towards me marital harmony, if you take my meaning." He glanced up at Mr, and perhaps seeing confusion on Mr's face – for Roderick Throckmorton Isbister had never been taken by anyone, himself included, as canny or wily or, goodness, a bilker – Stephen gave an elaboration.

"Between you and me, Roddy, I'm short on funds and one of me little ones is not quite up to dick. Needs some medical treatment, and it costs a wad. I didn't say before, 'cause I don't want pity, and 'tis no-one's concern but mine and me missus, but the sale of that bike was to pay for the child's care, and I let the old putt-putt go too cheap, and that's the sad fact."

Mr Isbister was taken aback. A sick child, by golly. His heartstrings were sufficiently tugged, and though he wasn't a stupid person, and saw his way to a glimmer of suspicion that he was being duped, of greater concern was that should Stephen's tale be true, Mr, by declining to sweeten their already completed transaction, might be solidifying a reputation as someone who would take advantage of not only a man of lesser circumstance than himself, but of a poor, sick child. There was no further debate in his mind. He made agreement with Stephen Vanson and they shook on it, Stephen rather heartily.

"I've got some tools I could part with as well – spanners and whatnot. Handy when you're a motorcycle man, by crumb, and that's you now, eh, Roddy? Come by the Hock and Toot, mate, we'll share a pint and top up the purchase price on that machine and haggle on the spanners. A fair price for a fair man. I'm in the pub most nights, just look for me!" And with that toodle-oo, Stephen vanished back the way he'd come, his shoes leaving wet prints in the spongey litter that quickly filled with water. Mr Isbister stood looking after him, an uneasy niggle inside him. In the end he shrugged it off, choosing instead to feel a certain noble purpose attached to his purchase of the motorcycle.

At dinner that evening, Mrs wore a large-skirted gown in an unnatural shade of green, patterned in a dizzy of vines and swooping floral curlicues that drew one's eyes on a journey that near spun them in their sockets. Mr seldom took note of Mrs' attire, but one could not help but be aware of this creation. It was rather an abomination, indeed an insult to the world of horticulture that she purported to revere, although he rather doubted that she would agree to such an assessment. He did not wonder at her choice for long, for soon into their repast she pinioned him with his neglect of the greenhouse.

"It cannot continue, Mr Isbister," she said after her initial tirade. "My chrysanthemums have very basic needs, and they are not being met. Your inattention is causing my gladioli to wilt." She peered at him over the lamb, congealing in its sauce, and he tried to ignore the grey bit of meat stuck to her chin that had been missed by the swipe of her napkin. "To wilt, Mr Isbister," she repeated, her frown puckering her brow and giving additional girth to her jowls.

Tonight he would not rise to her bait. "I have tended them, my dear, most tenderly," he replied, and smiled at his small witticism. He focused on a green bean, sawing at it with his knife and putting the morsel carefully into his mouth. He chewed, avoiding her skewering gaze, but aware she had not shared the humour of his response.

"Your tenderness, then, leaves something to be desired," she countered flatly. That comment brought his eyes back to hers where they danced together in a mutually accusing glare. Mr, to his disappointment, was the first to look away. He returned to his beans, dissecting a second green pod.

"I have it on good authority," she continued, ignoring Mr's cringe at the phrase, bringing, as it did, their morning's disagreement to mind, "that the ingredients in an artist's paints –" she glanced pointedly at his fingers, though he'd washed thoroughly and knew there was no offence there, "can include substances that are poisonous. Arsenic. Lead, even."

He chewed his bean thoughtfully, but said nothing. From experience he knew that silence was better than rejoinder. She would have her say, and, usually, her way.

"Were you, as I believe, to be in fact trying your hand as a *painter*, that is to say, *dabbling in the arts* –" there again, the stink of smelly socks in her words, "I would appreciate it," careful enunciation here, and a piercing glare he could feel but would not meet, "if you would desist, in deference to the life of my dear flowers. In fact, Mr Isbister, I must insist."

R. Throckmorton Isbister swallowed his well-mashed bean, and slowly set down his cutlery. He blinked several times, carefully considering his response. His knee-jerk was to rebuff her demand, and return to the morning's disagreement. She might be master of this house in almost every way, but *he* – he was the husband! But then he considered the motorcycle hidden in the potting shed, the crooked walls of that structure tucked behind the very greenhouse she required him to frequent, and saw that in pleasing Mrs in regards to her chrysanthemums and other floral endeavours resident in that same greenhouse, he was in fact giving himself the perfect alibi for his disappearances. All he need do was traipse through the house now and again with soiled hands and a petal or two in his wiry hair, and she would be no more the wiser.

He swiveled his head and attempted pleasantry with a smile that came out rather more reptilian than he would have wanted, but there it was. She was clever, he knew, and suspicious, so an easy capitulation would not work to his favour. And yet, he had not admitted to her accusations of artistic interests, so how could he make such an agreement as she demanded? He suspected trickery woven in to her request. He picked up his fork and knife and separated a piece of lamb, popped it in his mouth and chewed pensively. He was gratified to notice that she awaited his response almost politely. Goodness.

"My dear," he said, once the lamb had been swallowed and his lips smacked, "I cannot agree to your request that I desist in my participation in that which it has not yet been determined that I have, in fact, participated in." Mrs blinked, and frowned, perhaps trying to sort out his jumble of words. Mr quickly continued while in happy possession of her momentary confusion. "However, I hereby assure you that your flowers and greenhouse will receive my utmost care and attention." He smiled again, and reached for the salt cellar, sprinkling a pinch on his boiled potato. "And may I say, Mrs Isbister, that your gown this evening is most becoming. A true testament to your horticultural passion, I'm sure." He speared a chunk of salted potato and ate it, feeling rather pleased with himself.

Mrs Isbister, for her part, eyed him with obvious mistrust, but without a sure reason for her misgivings, turned her attention to her own plate, and tucked into her overlarge portion of lamb and sauce.

Chapter 4
THE CHESHIRE CAT

It wasn't terribly late, but Mr was by habit an early to bed sort of fellow, content to seek his pillow once the moon got up, which, depending on the season, could be five o'clock on a winter's night, or eleven in early summer. This eve was something in between, summer in its dog days, and yet Mr Isbister, search though he might, could not find the cradling arms of Morpheus. He tossed and turned and rolled until the sheet encased him entirely, mummy-like, and in the end he fell with a thump onto the rug. As he struggled to free himself, a faint tap-tap came at his door, and he froze in mid contortion, trapped in the bedding. Surely not she – Alice – after all these years, seeking to be wife to his man?

The tap sounded again, timidly. "Sar?" came the query through the keyhole, sotto voce. Mr recognised the maid, and froze in his sheet. What did *she* want, and at this hour?

"Sar?" again, wheedling. "It's me, Elizer. Can I come in, sar?"

Eliza – that was her name? And in? In? To his innermost chamber? His *sanctum sanctorum*? To what end? R. Throckmorton writhed in his sheet, seeking release. Should he be flattered? Frightened? What would a man of the house do? He was conscious that beneath his swaddle he wore a rather faded, striped nightshirt with a stain or two, and beneath that naught but a bare bottom. Bright spots appeared on his cheeks.

"Go away!" he hissed, rolling across the rug. The sheet, it seemed, was determined to cling on, and he imagined he understood something of what the lunatic felt, buckled into his strait jacket.

"Sar, I've a message from Mr Vanson." This time her voice came like a buzzing horn, her lips pressed with a relentlessness to the aperture.

"Who?" he returned, with a wheeze.

"Mr Vanson, sar, Mr Stephen Vanson, what sold you the motorcycle," was the reply.

The sheet came loose, and Mr floundered amongst its flaps, aware that his bare posterior was at least momentarily exposed. Was she peering through that same keyhole? He disentangled himself while at the same time wondering how in blazes his maid – whom he now knew to be called Eliza – had known he'd acquired a motorcycle from Stephen Vanson, of the village. He thought back to the day by the shed, when she'd warned him of Mrs' return from the Horticultural Society meeting. She must have ventured into the shed after he'd gone, and surmised, or perhaps, more worryingly, made inquiries.

He reached the bedroom door, and opened it just a crack, his eyeball to hers.

"Can I help you?" he inquired, somewhat ridiculously. For of course she had stated her business already, and clearly. A message, she'd said, from Stephen Vanson, Mr Isbister's motorcycle co-conspirator.

"I've a message, sar," she repeated, nonplussed, her eye still pressed to the gap, blink blink. "Mr Vanson do request the pleasure of your company at the Pig and Whistle this even', for to complete certain transactions as were previously agreed." She grinned, and he saw, not otherwise noticed before, that she had a rather large gap between her two front teeth.

"I'm abed," he said, indignant.

"But y'aren't, sar," she countered, and bobbed a belated apology. "Y'are here, at the door, and afore that, flounderin' on the floor. 'Tis a ways from the bed, 'struth." She shrugged and smiled like a Cheshire cat, tit-tat, and he was unpleasantly reminded of his wife.

"Alright, I'll come," he said. His tone was gruff and grumpy, but in truth he was chuffed. The night had promised to stretch long, otherwise. He closed the door on her roving eyeball, and dressed in a trice. Trousers, shirt and vest, sensible shoes. No tie, no jacket, no gloves or other gentlemanly accoutrements. When he was done and had pulled open the door she was there, her maid's uniform replaced with a village girl's attire – plain dress, sack coat, a straw hat of gaudy decoration not unlike his wife's bobber and waver, crowning red curls he hadn't noticed before. She dipped a curtsey and turned, leading the way.

The house was quiet – Mrs was abed, as he'd been, alone in her apartments. The various lamps were already extinguished – like many others of the rural persuasion they'd not yet paid the cost for electrification, or indeed trusted the invention – and the only light as they threaded the passageways was the maid Eliza's candle, fluttering in its sconce. Mr had a sudden premonition of adventure, and stifled his own Cheshire grin. Once through the garden door, Eliza paused. She glanced first one way, then 'tother, then turned to Mr Isbister with a saucy look. "Let's take the Trusty," said she, her eyes glittering. His heart leapt, and he needed no further persuasion. He paused long enough to grab his goggles, then he led the way to the shed, bold as brass in the candlestick moonlight. Eliza helped him throw off the tarpaulin, and, certain he appeared every inch the *Phoenix* – nay, the *Chimera* – he straddled the seat and jumped on the kick-starter. The engine caught and chugged.

It was his first chance at driving the motorcycle, and he'd had no practice. But Eliza was a game companion, chortling good-naturedly when he stalled the machine right off the stand and then twice drove her into the laurel hedge when he did get her mobile. Both times Eliza helped to extricate the Triumph, then hopped back into the wicker sidecar with enthusiasm, and cheered him on.

"No matter, sar, you'll get the hang of it by and by," she said, by way of encouragement, straightening the straw bonnet that had been knocked askew by Mr's incompetent handling of the machine. And, surprisingly, he did find the knack of it, and before long they were putting along the lane, goggle-eyed Mr at the controls of the Trusty, Eliza the maid ensconced beneath a lap rug in the sidecar, an unlikely pair.

It wasn't a particularly late hour if one was a pub-goer, and the lights of that establishment were in full blaze, bleeding through the cracks of the shutters. As they arrived Mr Isbister misjudged the brakes and ran the Trusty into the hedgerow, but Eliza merely laughed and said that was thrice in one night. "She do seem to like a good rub amongst the bushes," she added, climbing out of the sidecar and again straightening her hat. Mr Isbister sprouted bright spots on each cheek, for he thought the comment rather ribald.

They entered the Pig and Whistle together, a mistake, Mr supposed, belatedly, for what speculative things might this press of people whisper about Mr Isbister from Sowerby Grange in company of his maid at the local pub? To add fodder, owing to their chilly but exhilarating night ride, and, in Mr's case, his reaction to Eliza's bold comment, both wore pink complexions, wind-mussed hair, and a sparkle in their eyes as if they'd been up to something naughty. The pub's patrons – mostly old men and women on account of the recent war – looked their way, brows raised, but their interest was fickle, and the din of voices continued unabated. Mr realised he still wore his goggles strapped to his head, his eyes bug-like behind the lenses, and grinned sheepishly to no one in particular as he removed them and tucked them into his vest pocket.

Stephen Vanson hallooed from a table tucked into a far corner, and Mr, with Eliza at his heels, made his way there, weaving through the almost tangible smell of pipe smoke, cooked meat and spilled ale, zigzagging around benches and stools and the occasional patron who reared up to call for a refill. At Stephen Vanson's table Mr and Eliza shared the one narrow bench left vacant in the vicinity, and if it was a tad cosier than was appropriate, elbow to elbow, as it were, Mr was feeling something akin to blithe, and didn't mind. He looked around happily, unaware that the goggle imprint upon his skin gave him the look of a startled owl.

"Lizer," said Stephen smoothly, nodding to the maid. She returned the nod, and her red ringlets bounced. Stephen motioned for the barmaid's attention, and said, "What'll it be, Roddy? My treat."

"Half pint, if you will," Mr replied genially, "but please, I'll buy."

"Well, never eye a gift horse, and all that," said Stephen by way of acceptance, and as the barmaid approached, he called out for a pint and another half and a gin toddy "for the lady." Fleetingly it occurred to Mr to wonder how Stephen knew what Eliza – Lizer, as he'd called her – might choose for a quencher when he'd not asked her, but Eliza didn't seem to think it odd. There was no time to consider the matter extensively, for Stephen was leaning across the table, offering Mr a cigarette from a silver case. As he declined, enjoying himself, "Not my poison, heh, heh," he caught a glimpse of letters – initials? – that were not SV engraved in fancy scrollwork on the lid, but the case was quickly snapped shut and pocketed, and Mr forgot about it as the barmaid plunked a tankard of foamy ale in front of him.

The three sat amiably, sipping, and Mr tapped his toes to a tune being played at another table by a fellow with a tin whistle. Eliza's chin rested in her upturned palm, but her red head wagged to the music in complement to Mr's toe tapping. In another life, he found himself thinking, eyeing her, red spots again blooming on his cheeks, he might have asked her to dance. He reached for his mug and found it empty. Stephen called for another round, and Mr missed the glance he and Eliza exchanged. She stood, and touched Mr's arm in a gesture he would have found excessively familiar at home. Here, though, he inhaled as she bent towards him. "Be right back, sar, don't be leavin' without me, now." And he chuckled, for the night, surely, was young. The barmaid, he noticed, had brought him a full pint this time, and considering how easily the last one had slid down his gullet, he thought that a time-saver, and clever.

"So, Roddy, you're enjoying the Trusty?" Stephen asked in his well-oiled voice, edging his stool nearer to Mr's bench.

"Goodness, yes," Mr enthused, after a large swallow of his ale. It was thirsty work, riding motorbikes and rubbing elbows with the working man. "Tonight was my first outing. Exhilarating! Just capital!"

Stephen smiled. "Glad to hear it. I miss her, as I told you. Fair hurts to think about it. But you'd promised to sweeten our deal, soothe the ache, so to speak…."

"How fares your boy, if I may ask," Mr Isbister said, sobering with concern. His pint was gone already, and he felt the glow of it. Stephen signalled for another.

"He'll be better with treatment," Stephen replied gravely. "At least that's the hope of the missus and me. But time is of the essence for Johnny, I'm sure you can appreciate, and the missus, well, she's impatient to see it done."

"Of course, of course," Mr Isbister said hurriedly, mortified now that he'd not thought to attend to the matter of the cash in a more timely fashion. That he had not brought it embarrassed him, for the anticipation of the ride here rather than the ultimate purpose of it had been foremost in his mind. He hung his head, and the bald spot on his crown caught the lamplight.

"Have you got it then? I did send word," Stephen said, and Mr Isbister, with his face drooped over his pint in misery, did not see the flicker of impatience pass over Stephen's chiseled features.

"To my shame I do not have it on my person," Mr admitted. The ale, to which he was not overly accustomed, lent him uncharacteristic familiarity, and he glanced up at Stephen and grasped the other man's long-fingered hand. "But you shall have it forthwith! Tomorrow I shall visit my banker and make a withdrawal, and it shall be for twice the amount agreed to. Twice! We shall have your little one fit as a fiddle before you can say Jack Robinson."

"You're a king among men, Roddy," Stephen said with an admiring shake of his head. He gently extracted his fingers from Mr's grip, and wiped at an invisible tear. "The missus'll be putting you in her prayers, an' no mistake." The two men sat in companionable silence, sipping.

A short while later Eliza returned, pressing past him to the other side of their shared bench. He shivered, smelling lemons, and for a shocking moment thought of his one grope beneath the sheets all those years ago, hoping for marital bliss. He glanced surreptitiously her way, and wondered that he'd never noticed how blue were her eyes, how fair her skin. He took a large gulp of his depleted ale – was it his third? his fourth? – and stifled a burp.

"What've I missed?" she asked, smiling widely. She downed the remains of her gin in a single neat swallow. Mr stared at her admiringly, thinking the gap in her front teeth most becoming.

"You've missed a fellow at his best and most generous," Stephen said expansively, and called to the barmaid, "Two pints, Ivy, and another white satin for my darlin' sister!"

Mr Isbister, bleary from the drink but lucid enough, blanched, and croaked, "Eliza's your sister?" He wasn't sure why, but he felt deceived, suspicious, and not a bit rattled. Why hadn't she said?

Eliza glared at Stephen, a look that could have been a snarl. Stephen grinned lazily, and turned his hatchet-like cheekbones to Mr.

"Lizer'n me don't always see eye to eye, 'struth. Some days a fella'd be forgiven for thinkin' she'd like to pretend I ain't here at all."

That declaration didn't seem to sit any better with Eliza, and she sat in sullen silence, her arms crossed over her chest. When her gin arrived, she threw it back in two swigs and called for another. Mr, cognizant of the fact that he had already drunk too much yet loathe to be wasteful (the habits of wartime rationing ingrained), swallowed his ale. He didn't quite know what to make of this revelation – the dubious

Stephen and the fair Eliza – his maid – siblings, but suspected there was something cautionary in it.

Stephen talked, his voice the only one at the table. The night had aged and the pub was now standing room only, men elbow to elbow at the bar, and over the general din, Mr heard only snippets of Stephen's monologue – some joke about a neighbour, and a lot of ha ha ha from Stephen's mobile mouth – but the evening, generally, Mr Isbister decided, had taken a turn downhill. When he finished what was likely his fifth or sixth glass of beer, he put what coin he had on the table, more than enough to pay the bill, and stood, wobbling a little, and pulled his goggles from his pocket. He'd gone a bit sour on Stephen Vanson.

"We'll have to take our leave now," he said politely to Stephen. He fastened his goggles onto his head, and wondered if they were foggy or if the trouble was his somewhat drink-bleared eyesight.

Stephen stood, and shook his hand. "Thank you again, Roddy. It's a load off, if you know what I mean. How's about we make a date to meet up here tomorrow night then, eh?"

But Mr was not so inclined. Bug-eyed behind the lenses of the goggles, a comic look that was not synchronous to his mood, he told Stephen that he would send word with Eliza – *his sister* – when their next meeting would be. And goodnight. Eliza lingered, promising to follow in a minute.

Outside, Mr breathed the still night air. He felt his faculties somewhat less impaired now he was removed from the warm drowse of the pub, but he was by no means cock-sharp. He eyed the Triumph with trepidation, and climbed aboard. Several kicks of the starter later, he slumped in mute frustration upon the saddle. She would not go. He envisioned a long walk home, and wondered if the morning sun would arrive there before he did. He tried again, and again, and when his foot slipped and he scraped his ankle against the pedal he had a sudden uncharacteristic flare of temper, and jumped off the bike and kicked the tire.

"Let me, sar," said Eliza, appearing behind him. Embarrassed, but not knowing what else to do, he stepped back as she hiked her skirt, climbed onto the motorcycle, turned the gas lever – which he realised belatedly he'd forgotten to do – and easily sparked the Triumph to life.

"Hop in," she called over the putt of the engine, motioning towards the wicker sidecar, and Mr, to his further shame, did just that, with no argument or protestation. He pulled the rug up over his lap, turned his head lest he be tempted to ogle her ankle, and got comfortable. As Eliza steered the bike onto the lane that would take them home, he promptly fell asleep, his goggles askew, but still fastened to his head.

Chapter 5
THE BLINK OF HER BLUE, BLUE EYE

For days after his visit with Eliza to the Pig and Whistle, Mr Isbister sulked in his rooms. He told Mrs he had a touch of the ague, and remained in his nightshirt, supping on broth and biscuits. Eliza, hair tucked up beneath her mopcap, delivered the food, but he wouldn't allow her into his apartment. They exchanged food trays but no words through a crack in the door. He lazed about, sprawling on the bed, then in an armchair, then lying on the floor and considering the floral pattern in the ceiling's elaborate plasterwork.

Despite his brooding he had not forgotten his duty to Stephen Vanson's boy, whatever neglects to his own hygiene he might have made. A comb he'd seen no use for, nor tooth powder, though in truth the fuzz of his head and fur of his teeth became less an indulgence after the second day and he'd relented. Before then, in fact the day after his singularly humiliating visit to the Pig and Whistle, he'd kept his promise and, nursing a rather large head and sporting bloodshot eyes, took the pony and cart to the bank in Lesser Plumpton where he kept a small account for pocket money, rather separate from the account in Bristol that Mrs held charge of, and made the requisite withdrawal. He then retained Eliza's services in delivering the funds to her brother, and went promptly to bed. Stephen sent a note of thanks, left by Eliza on his dinner tray. *Dear Roddy, me and the Missus ar gratfull fur yore ginerossity. Our sun Charly will sherly suffer noe more thanks to the treetmint. Yors truly, and with much respeck, Stephen P. Vanson.* Mr tossed the note on his bedside table.

By day, dressed in plaid slippers and wrinkled nightshirt, kept snug by a nubby old cardigan, Mr perused the guidebook for the Trusty. He read about carburetors and throttles and tyre pressure, and he studied the diagrams and charts. He recalled that Stephen had promised to sell him tools, but if or when that was now likely to happen, he would not yet speculate. His current reclusive state could in part be laid at the door of that fellow; he returned repeatedly in his mind to Stephen's callousness towards Eliza, and, his own irrational irritation that Stephen had turned out to be her brother, and tossing that fact out as if it were a great joke. Further, he was miffed (there was no other word for it), with Eliza for her part in not mentioning the relationship, and then, if he was honest, for her surprising competence with the Trusty, demonstrated most ably by starting the motorcycle when he could not. And! adding insult to injury, driving it home whilst he snored in the sidecar. He supposed he should be grateful but was instead, to his shame, embarrassed, unmanned, made small.

When he tired of *The Motor-Cyclist's Handbook*, he got up from his wing-back chair to shuffle around the room, stretching his arms over his head and working the crick out of his neck. His bottom frequently fell asleep, and he considered how that might be, one part of his anatomy a-snooze whilst the rest of him was awake. He mulled other numbing questions, such as why the toes on his left foot were longer than the toes on his right, and why one's stomach gurgled equally with hunger and satiety. He examined the swirling pattern of the carpet until he felt almost sick, and then took a nap on his bed backwards, his slippered feet resting on the pillow.

For variety, and, were he to admit it, less polite reasons, he thumbed through his art book, which he'd been relieved to discover still resided beneath his mattress. But the paintings therein failed to inspire him as they once had, and he wondered how he'd not noticed before the great number of models, clothed and otherwise, with red hair, or who owned various bodily bits that were strangely Eliza-like. This one's chin, that one's wrist, the other's pink ankle. Even a fruit bowl brought her to mind, lemon scented, as he recalled, with a whiff of gin and perspiration. Inappropriate, he scolded himself, and put that book away too, when he felt over-warm.

On the fourth day of his seclusion, a tap came at his door shortly after breakfast. Mr was slumped in his wingback chair, contemplating the stain of jam on his nightshirt, added this morning whilst devouring his toast. It joined the one he'd made yesterday – marmalade – and another from some other meal, beef gravy, he thought.

"Sar?" Eliza's voice reached him through the keyhole, and he sighed. He hadn't the energy for conversation. In fact, he'd thought about returning to bed, for the day was overcast and dull, and a shroud might be just the thing.

"Excuse me, sar, it's me, Elizer," she said. And he felt a quick petulance. Of course it was she. Who else would it be that called him "sar" in that less than polished whinge? He felt immediately ashamed. R. Throckmorton Isbister had never been a snob. He rose, and went to the door, parting it a crack.

There she was on the other side. She wore her mopcap, but her hair was not tucked demurely beneath it as was usual. Instead it fell in riotous red glory. Such dishabille was improper – a dereliction, he felt quite sure, of convention. And yet something in his chest gave an odd pit-patter, and he gripped the doorknob as she leaned in towards him.

"Is Mrs about?" he squawked, his eyeball scanning the hallway beyond her.

"No, sar, she's gone out," Eliza replied. Mr felt sure she pushed ever so slightly against the door as if to gain entry. He thought of his many-spotted nightshirt and his state of unwash and held firm. "She did send me to say, sar, that you're to skiver in your rooms no more. She be sick of it." She grinned, showing her tiny pearl teeth with the gap in the centre, and Mr Isbister, despite the message, felt a slight weakness at the knees. "You're to be up and at it, says she, in time for dinner this eve. You've a guest coming. Your new neighbour, Colonel Someone-or-Other."

Mr frowned. He disliked directives from Mrs, though she gave them all the time and he found life easiest when he complied. It occurred to him the exact wording of the order had most likely been altered along the way as "skiver" was not a term he'd heard Mrs Isbister use in the past. He harrumphed anyway, indicating his displeasure in what he was certain was gruffly man-of-the-house. The message was delivered but Eliza continued to stand on the other side of the door. Mr too remained pinioned to the crack.

"Sar –" she said, just as he said "I believe –" and they tittered.

"You first," said she, smiling, and he thought he might fall through the gap in her teeth and be swallowed up.

"Very well," said Mr. "I feel I owe you a debt of gratitude for – er – steering us home the other evening. It must have been a task indeed to so quickly learn how to maneuver that great beast of a machine. I myself have only just got the mastery of it, and you, of course, are but a girl, and small."

"Aw, no," Eliza responded with a shrug of her shoulder. "I've driven plenty o' bikes. The Trusty's a peach, an' no mistake. It were me pleasure, sar. I'd run you about any time."

He didn't quite know how to respond, for the idea of driving about on the motorcycle with – goodness – his housemaid was rather vellicating, although he'd prefer not to be in the sidecar. He knew such a thought was despicable, for he was a married man of a certain class, while she, well, she had red hair, and…other attributes. He swallowed.

"And you, Eliza? What did you wish to say?" he asked, smiling expansively. His mood was suddenly restored. If she were going to apologize for her somewhat callous brother he would reassure her on that score – the events of four nights ago were now forgiven and forgotten, snuffed out by the blink of her blue, blue eye.

"Just that I'm to bring you hot water, sar. Fer your tub. Dinner's at eight, and you're to be scrubbed and presentable. And wear the burgundy vest, she says, with the buttons polished."

"She does?" he asked, momentarily taken aback. Mrs had never, in all their years together, directed his wardrobe.

The housemaid's eye slid sideways, avoiding his. "No sar, 'struth she did not. But 'twould be my recommendation, if you were to ask. Burgundy vest, striped shirt and collar, green frock coat. Unless there be stains, then change the frock to the brown. Sar."

She bobbed a curtsey and disappeared, and Mr closed the door. Whistling, he went immediately to his armoire to search out the burgundy vest and inspect the green coat.

Chapter 6
ONE WOLF OR TWO

Mr Isbister's mood had been quite improved by Eliza's visit. After recommending his wardrobe for his wife's dinner party she'd seen to his tub, dragging the big copper vessel into the middle of the room and filling it, one bucket at a time, with hot water she hauled up from the kitchen. (The addition of modern plumbing was something Mrs, not being the one to haul the water, considered unnecessary. It ranked with equal lack of importance alongside electricity.) Still clad in his days-old nightshirt and ratty slippers, Mr remained out of sight behind a delicate Chinese paper privacy screen, and when Eliza had placed soap and towel next to the tub and backed out of the room after the last bucket was dumped, he bared his less than muscled bod and immersed himself. He soaked and soaped until he was prune-like, then climbed out and dressed in the suggested attire. Polished cufflinks and a watch fob completed his toilette, and with his narrow feet encased in the shoes she had left outside his door, shined, he made his way at the appointed hour to that part of the house shared with Mrs Isbister.

It seemed the guests were already arrived, for as he approached the closed door of the parlour he could hear male voices, and Mrs' rarely used laugh. Hovering nearby was Eliza, and she stepped out from behind a large potted fern, wringing her hands in a strangely nervous gesture.

"Sar!" she called to him in something akin to a stage whisper. "I need to speak with you –" but before she could say more, the parlour door swung open, and Mrs stuck her head out and spotted them.

"Ah, there you are," she said to Mr. "Hahaha," she honked, surely for the benefit of the guests in the room behind her. She reached a hand out to Mr, and he wondered if she actually intended that he take it. Her colour was high, he saw, and he thought he smelled something floral. Was she wearing scent? Already the evening felt surreal. He stumbled forward.

"What are you about, girl?" Mrs hissed past him at Eliza. "You're to be serving, not gawping!" She turned, ushering Mr before her into the parlour, lit most elegantly with flickering gaslight and candles.

Two men sat on the cushioned settee, and stood as Mr Isbister entered the room. Mrs swooped past him, her girth in a voluminous purple gown momentarily blocking one of the guests as she hastened to make introductions. Mr shook the hand of the first fellow, a short man with bulk equal to Mrs Isbister's own, a ruddy complexion and thick mutton-chop salt and pepper whiskers. He wore a frock coat over his waistcoat and a striped shirt; indeed, his outfit was not unlike Mr's own, somewhat dated, ensemble.

"Lieutenant-Colonel Barks, Mr Isbister, 54th Division, retired," the man said in a voice as big as he was round, pumping Mr's hand as he spoke. "Gallipoli and Egypt, don't you know. Bit hard of hearing on account, but not complaining, not complaining."

"Delighted to make your acquaintance, Lieutenant-Colonel," Mr said, and extricated his hand from the fellow's thick grip. He turned to the second visitor, and felt his jaw drop, for this man was surely none other than Stephen Vanson, albeit wolf-like in his sheep's clothing.

"Captain Plucky," Stephen said in a nasal, upper-crust accent unlike the one Eliza's brother used. He gripped Mr's hand, and his eyes danced as he met Mr's shocked stare. "Though of an entirely different theatre than my esteemed colleague here. 58th London, and the shrapnel wounds to prove it." He cocked a chiseled brow at Mr, reached up to smooth his oiled and parted hair, and grinned above his fashionably tight suit and purple paisley tie. "As I was saying to Barks on the way over, we retired officers are a dime a dozen these days, all but came out of the woodwork once the war finished and all the messy bits tidied up, eh wot? And much obliged to your missus, too, for allowing an extra guest to push in uninvited."

Mrs, beaming from guest to guest, chortled, and clasped her small hands together in front of her tremendous bosom. "Not at all, Captain Plucky, not at all! It's an honour, of course. Why, I was commenting to Throckmorton just the other day that it's high time we entertained again, now that a decent interval has passed. The war, you know, put paid to our social engagements."

Mr was thoroughly agape, taking in Stephen's button-top spats and short, drainpipe pants. What game was this? Should he call the fellow out? And yet how could he, for then he'd have to explain how he knew the man, and the fact of his ownership of a motorcycle would come to light, and who knew what Mrs' reaction to such a revelation might be? Mr supposed he must look like a simpleton, and closed his mouth. Before him, the chap he knew as Stephen Vanson sat back, relaxed, every inch a London man, and Mr could credit neither Stephen's transformation nor the reason for it, or indeed the fact that Mrs was pretending they had ever entertained, and had called him Throckmorton. The evening was just begun and he already wished it was over.

"The Lieutenant-Colonel and the Captain were just explaining a rather interesting conundrum that has occurred, and their excellent solution!" Mrs Isbister declared. "Why I do believe if these two had been in charge of diplomacy the war might have ended much sooner!" She beamed at her guests, and her jowls were like an extra smile. At that moment, Eliza appeared in the room bearing a tray of drinks. Her usual mopcap was gone, Mr noticed, but her red hair was pinned and tucked and otherwise made to behave beneath a less moppy type of headdress. Mr watched her suspiciously, looking for signs that she knew what was afoot, but she moved inconspicuously amongst the occupants of the room, avoiding eye contact. "Cocktails," Mrs told the Lieutenant-Colonel, who selected a glass with a look of puzzlement on his face. "American, apparently. Highly irregular, but some of the ladies at my Horticultural Society meeting say it's the thing up in London."

"As a Londoner myself, let me assure you, your ladies are correct," Stephen Vanson – Captain Plucky – said, accepting a glass from the proffered tray and skilfully ignoring Eliza, the maid, his sister. Mr took a glass and sipped, tasting a boozy mixture of bitter and sweet. "Westminster politicians serve cocktails most regularly at dinner parties, don't you know," continued Captain Plucky, sipping and smacking his lips. He grinned, and added, "They're delicious but potent, and a person, having swallowed a glassful, is then eager to swallow most anything at all!"

Lieutenant-Colonel Barks and Mrs Isbister laughed, a great cacophony of noise that had them both apparently weak-kneed, for they leaned towards one another with unseemly familiarity. While Mr shared in the mirth at Stephen's joke, he was certain his eyes conveyed his disapproval of their proximity, would Mrs only look his way. She did not, though, instead placing her girlish fingers on the Lieutenant-Colonel's arm.

"How droll, don't you agree, Lieutenant-Colonel," said she to Barks. Mr Isbister felt sure she simpered. He didn't think he had ever seen his wife act coyly, or with flirtation, and he found himself rather aghast at the behaviour.

"Ahem," he said, but no one noticed.

"Dear lady," Barks said, patting Mrs Isbister's fingers with his own great paw, "with your husband's kind permission, please call me Woody. Short for Woodward."

Mr Isbister thought his brows might be touching his hairline – or the place where it had once been located. What manner of fellow was this Woody Barks chap, that he would take such liberties and upon so short an acquaintance! Mr had been Mrs' husband for more years than he cared to count, and the number of times he had heard his given name on his wife's lips could be tallied on one – maybe two – hands, yet this fellow was swanning in with the subtlety of a torpedo. But no one noticed Mr's glower. Despite asking his permission, the good Lieutenant-Colonel Woody Barks never once looked his way. His eyes, above his ridiculous mutton chops, were only for Mrs, and she – blushing! – bid him call her Alice!

At that moment, Eliza reappeared to announce that dinner was ready, and Mr had no chance to either give or deny permission to the Lieutenant Colonel's effrontery. Instead, he followed glumly behind his wife and her newfound friend, and played escort to the dapper Captain Plucky.

At table, he ruminated and muttered over both men. Woody Barks – ridiculous name – and Captain Plucky. Plucky indeed, he snarled to himself, attacking his lemon oyster with severing cuts of his knife. In his mind, he rehearsed several challenges to the man, fraud that he surely was, but couldn't quite summon the courage to verbalize any of them, in part because Eliza was in and out of the room, her face pale with – what? Fear? Unease? Distress? He noted particularly that neither she nor Plucky exchanged so much as a glance, an omission that served to irritate Mr further yet. He wanted confirmation of her disapproval of this charade. His displeasure, however, went un-noted, or, perhaps worse, ignored, not only by Eliza but by his dinner companions. The Lieutenant-Colonel and Mrs Isbister hee-hawed and tittered and patted one another's hands through four exhausting courses, and Captain Plucky tucked food away like he was storing it for the winter, pausing only now and again to burp delicately and pat his mouth with the linen napkin. Between courses he talked, relaxing against the chairback and casually flicking the napkin, as cocky as if he were the host of the evening, and not a guest, imposter, charlatan. Mr's mood, already rather foul, disintegrated further when he burnt his lip on the gammon soup, but with gentlemanly aplomb he kept his irritation in check, allowing Captain Plucky his head as he used up the air with his verbiage. What little oxygen was left over when Plucky paused, Woody Barks easily expropriated, and Mr, never an avid conversationalist, nodded and mhmm'd in the appropriate places, while giving the lion share of his attention to his jellied eel and wishing both men gone. The conversation was banal; war stories or gossip about the acerbic Lady Astor and her wit: "I married beneath me. All women do." Mrs guffawed at that, and Mr avoided her pointed gaze.

But then Mrs spoke in a new, coquettish voice she had dredged from someplace, and Mr's ears perked up. "Tell again, Woody, how you both came to be residing next door. I'm sure Throckmorton missed the story, and it's so incredulous I would love to hear it again myself."

Mr continued to slurp his eel, but murmured with a hopefully not stony smile, "Yes, do tell us. An incredulous story, you say? My." Captain Plucky had the decency to move slightly in his seat, and Mr chose to deem it a squirm. Rightly so, he felt sure. Rightly so.

"Incredulous it is, Throckmorton," said Woody, "Enough to make a stuffed bird laugh, I say." Mr kept his face in his eels lest his annoyance show. Throckmorton, indeed. When had that invitation to familiarity been made?

"They've rented Natterjack Hall," said Mrs to Mr, jumping in, and, turning back to Barks, added, "It's so lovely to have neighbours again after all these years. The fellow who used to live there was rather odd – "

"Harold Guppletwill," Mr interjected, defensively. "A great man. OBE, you know. A member of both the Royal Geographical Society and the Royal Zoological Society. Very knowledgeable. An expert on the natterjack toad, hence the name of his house. Cute little devil. Small, but with a phenomenal vocal range."

"The esteemed Guppletwill, or the toad?" Captain Plucky asked, drawing snorts of laughter from Mrs Isbister and Barks. Mr forced a pinched smile and remained mute. Eliza, in the midst of whisking plates away, caught Mr's glance and as quickly looked askance.

"Goodness, can't think when I've enjoyed an evening so much," said Mrs, beaming all around and dabbing mirth from her small eyes. She gave a sudden start, and two spots of colour appeared on her cheeks. Mr's eyes narrowed. Was the bold Lieutenant-Colonel, not content to merely pat-pat his wife's arm, making footy advances beneath the shroud of the table cloth? If he was, he gave nothing of his clandestine activity away, and he met Mr Isbister's stare with an expansive grin.

"So yes, Natterjack Hall," Barks continued. "I gather this Mr Guppletwill, toad expert though he might have been, moved on –"

"Is," said Mr Isbister flatly. He smiled to soften the interruption, though he suspected the look may have come across as bared teeth. "Toad expert though he *is*. And yes, Harold went to the Amazon jungle. To research, among other things, the habitat of a giant toad that reportedly grows to twelve inches, weighs an astounding six pounds, and has toxic skin." His admiration for the man and his work was reflected in his tone, and the dinner guests looked amused. Mr Isbister decided not to add that he had itched to go along.

"Well, he *did* seemingly disappear," said Mrs in a conciliatory tone. "He went away in 1914, just before the war. That's eight years ago. It almost seems a lifetime."

"Indeed," said Lieutenant-Colonel Barks, returning Mr's grimace with a lift of his substantial whiskers. "Anyway, Natterjack Hall became available one way or other. I merely answered a "to let" advert in the Times and wrote to the address supplied, and Bob's your uncle, as they say."

"But that's not the interesting part," chimed Captain Plucky, leaning forward, his eyes sparkling mischievously. "I had also answered and applied to an advertisement, although in the Herald, and apparently Bob is uncle to us both!" He and Barks and Mrs Isbister shared a chortle, while Mr, puzzled, looked from one to the next.

"Are you saying the agent let Natterjack Hall to both of you at the same time? Well, how can that be?" he asked.

"Doesn't matter. Some sort of odd duck thing, I expect. Left hand, right hand, wot? We'll get the kinks worked out eventually, deposits paid and all, but in the meantime, we've decided to share," Lieutanant-Colonel Barks said, beaming around the table. "Natterjack Hall's got plenty of room for two bachelors with a lot in common – retired military men, similar habits and vices, hehe." He waggled his brows at Mrs. "We've compared."

"Indeed we have," Captain Plucky agreed. "Apart from our military backgrounds, we both like a round of backgammon and can be rather competitive over croquet."

"True, true," confirmed the Lieutenant-Colonel. "We agree Scotch whisky over Irish, don't mind a cigar now and again, and we both admire the odd duck's art collection – he had quite an eye for botanicals."

"Prints, of course, little value," Captain Plucky added. "But lovely. A contrast, perhaps, to the ugliness of toads et cetera."

Mr sniffed. He didn't think toads ugly. Rather he thought them *interesting*. He said nothing, for he found himself pleased that the two men appreciated Harold's botanicals collection. Harold had been – still was, Mr felt sure, wherever he currently resided – rather proud of it, in his modest way. Botanicals, Harold had mused to Mr on more than one occasion, were the perfect marriage of art and science. One informed the other. The drawings were concise, both scientifically and botanically, but with an emphasis on beauty and aesthetics. Harold had framed the prints in categorical groupings; specifically, Mr recalled one of grasses and sedges, another of ferns, pepperworts and horsetails, and a third of so-called exotics, of which was paramount a rendering of the magnificent corpse flower: *Amorphophallus titanum*.

Mrs sniffed too, and Mr glanced her way, noting her pursed lips and wrinkled nose. Art was her least favourite topic, and her guests had unintentionally struck that sour note. She pat-patted Lieutenant-Colonel Barks's hand, somewhat sharply.

"Surely *art*, though, is, at least generally speaking, unseemly," she said.

"Unseemly?" the Lieutenant-Colonel replied, his whiskers drooping. "In what way?"

Mrs spluttered, and blinked her eyes in rapid succession. "I have it on good authority," she said – and here Mr was tempted to grin, but did not – "that painters – *artists*, if you will – are licentious sorts, given to all manner of depravities." Her voice dropped to a harsh whisper, her eyes shriveled to obsidian beads. "An over-indulgence in drink, the frequenting of bawdy houses. One painter I heard about was a *dwarf*," she added, leaning into the table to share this abomination.

"Dwarf, eh?" said Lieutenant-Colonel Barks, patting Mrs' hand consolingly. "I knew a dwarf once. Met him in Singapore. Capital chap. Led me quite the dance, I'll admit. Poor directions, uncles and cousins. Won't say too much in polite company, wot, but he was a decent sort, once we'd agreed to parameters." He chuckled, and smoothed his mutton chops.

"Army life," said Captain Plucky, exchanging knowing glances with the Lieutenant-Colonel. "Julio Quint was the name of the dwarf I knew. Met him in Paris. Funny fellow, great sense of humour. He wasn't a painter. Businessman might be a more apt description. Truth be told, he did frequent his share of brothels – sorry to say, in polite company." He winked at Mrs, who dimpled and appeared to forgive him.

"Well," she said. "Well."

Banter followed; a somewhat trivial discussion that included Lieutenant-Colonel Barks' opinion – shared with Captain Plucky – on the merits of certain classical painters, but all in all the slant of the conversation greatly improved Mr's mood, and when Eliza entered with a tray of puff pastries and chilled dessert wine, he did not try to skewer her with a look. Instead, he considered the odds of finding art allies in such unlikely guests, and thought that perhaps there was something to be salvaged of the evening, and concessions made, despite the question mark that was Captain Plucky. Not that he'd excuse the fellow's deception, but to use a military analogy – a nod to the two supposed military men present – one must pick the timing of one's battles. For the first time that evening Mr Isbister smiled around the table, and raised his glass of chilled dessert wine.

"I must say, lovely to meet you gents. On behalf of Harold, may I just add that your appreciation of his botanicals is most gratifying. He was rather proud of them." His voice quavered slightly with the mention of Harold, dear friend. "1922 may yet go down as a good year. Here's to victory, and its many fronts."

"Hip, hip," said Captain Plucky. Lieutenant-Colonel Barks chuckled, and clinked his glass against Mrs'.

Chapter 7
NATTERJACK HALL

The morning after the dinner party, Roderick Throckmorton Isbister woke early. There'd been rain overnight, nothing heavy, but it had set the frogs to singing, and Mr lay abed and found himself thinking about Harold Guppletwill. He and Harold had been kindred spirits, he'd always felt. Their interests had meshed and they'd spent many a day in company slopping through marshes in their wellies and exclaiming over various amphibians, or selecting samples of this lichen or that plant. To look at them one might be forgiven for thinking they were brothers: Throck and Harold were both small men with balding pates and roundish tummies and a curiosity about the natural world. Newts, insects, lichens, fungi, all these things stirred their hearts, but Harold's true passion was toads and frogs, and in particular, the natterjack toad, after which his house was named. The natterjack was elusive, but known to inhabit the warm, shallow pools of the local marshes, and Harold, though forever searching, had yet to find a colony. His quest was more than mere curiosity. Harold was, in fact, a true scholar, a learned man with scientific papers to his credit, laboratory and field experience, and membership in related royal societies. Mr Isbister, by contrast, was a simpler fellow, if no less interested.

When Harold had announced his last expedition, travelling to the rain forests of the Amazon in search of the giant cane toad, Mr had been, yes, jealous. He admitted that only to himself, for in truth he was ashamed of the emotion, and wished he'd felt nothing more than excitement on his friend's behalf. It was a wonderful opportunity for Harold, Mr Isbister well knew, and so he pent up his envy, saying only, as he shook Harold's hand on the day of his departure in April, 1914, that he wished he was going along as his research assistant. But Harold had one of those, a young up-and-comer and a student from Oxford, and so he'd given Mr Isbister a wistful smile and said, "Keep an eye out for the natterjacks, Throck. And when you find them, take notes."

Eight years had passed. Mr had had not a postcard. He'd written once to the Royal Zoological Society and once to the Royal Geographical Society, as he couldn't recall which society was funding the expedition, and twice to Harold's employer, Oxford University, to inquire after Harold, but had received no reply. Eventually, and to his shame, he gave up. But while he had ceased to make inquiries, he had not stopped believing that Harold Guppletwill would turn up one day, suitcase in hand, full of tales of his adventures, and that Harold and he would resume their field trips and their shared pursuit of the shy natterjack toad.

In the meantime, Mr found it oddly comforting to think that Harold's house was occupied, albeit by a portly military man in what would seem to be romantic pursuit of Mr's wife, and a charlatan who was either scamming the military man or scamming Mr Isbister himself. In spite of that, Mr felt surprisingly chipper this early morning. Better, in fact, than he'd felt in a while. He considered why that might be, and decided that it was the dinner party that had brought him out of his days-long funk. Admittedly, the evening hadn't begun well. The Lieutenant-Colonel's boldness with his wife had been puzzling, and Stephen Vanson's odd duplicitousness – which remained a query – more so, but the company of the men, their jokes and perhaps most of all their frank support both of the arts and of the physically different in the face of Mrs' aversion had all conspired to improve his mood tenfold. Whatever game was afoot with Stephen Vanson would soon make itself obvious, Mr Isbister felt sure.

He threw back the counterpane and slid his feet into the plaid slippers that he'd left set at just the right angle next to his bed and shuffled to the window, scratching his nethers on the way. Beyond the curtains the day was dull, but his mood was bright, and he stretched and cracked his bones and washed in last night's cold water, then dressed and went down to breakfast.

It was apparently the maid Eliza's day off, so said the cook who plunked a boiled egg and a plate of toast onto the table next to the pot of tea. Mrs had a headache, she added, so Mr would be breakfasting alone. Mr hummed to himself as he swirled strawberry compote onto his warm toast, thinking that the day was shaping up very well indeed. He decided as he munched happily that a walk in the woods might be just the thing, what with Mrs indisposed and unlikely to question his whereabouts, and he'd no sooner brushed the crumbs from his shirt and wiped a smear of yolk from his chin than he was drawing on his wellingtons and pulling on his jacket and heading out the door.

He took his favourite path, the one that meandered along the creek bank and where he'd often spied the delightfully interesting jelly ear fungus that did indeed bear an uncanny resemblance to the human ear, lobes and all, hanging from the branches of the wych elm. This route was the same one he'd been following the day Stephen Vanson had chanced upon him, and begged extra funds for his young son. Mr Isbister wondered how the little fellow fared, and if he'd had his treatment. Charley was his name, Stephen's letter had said. Mr paused in a particularly wet spot, brown water swirling round his boot. At the pub hadn't Stephen called him Johnny?

He extracted his boot from the sucking muck, and squelched on. Perhaps he'd misheard. Before long he came to a fork in the path. Straight ahead and he'd eventually arrive at the place where the path petered out, and where the creek burrowed underground, leaving behind shallow pools that Harold declared ideal natterjack territory. Harold had heard them sing now and again, at night, loud and clear as a bell chime, and each time, for days after, he and Mr Isbister had kept watch near those pools, seated on a fallen log in companionable silence. The natterjack remained elusive, however, and eventually, with Harold's impending departure, the men had abandoned their vigil.

The fork to the right led to Harold's house, Natterjack Hall, and today Mr Isbister followed it for the first time since Harold had gone away. The track was much overgrown, in spots almost disappeared, but Mr knew the way instinctively, and he traversed it in almost joyous nostalgia. Damsel flies took flight as he pushed through tall grasses, and a spiny little hedgehog scurried to its burrow when Mr tripped over a root and startled it. Squirrels chucked, alerting their kind of an intruder, and a lop rabbit, long ears dragging the ground, hopped out of his way on the path. Soon, the steep roof of Natterjack Hall could be seen through the trees, and Mr Isbister stopped short of exiting the woods, his presence disguised by foliage.

The house looked much the same. Thick ivy crawled up the wall, and the gardens had been tended. Mr Isbister supposed there was a hired man doing the upkeep, probably engaged by the same estate agent that had let the place to Lieutenant-Colonel Barks and Captain Plucky. On the front step Harold's enormous bronze toad sat where it always had, its throat swollen in perpetual croak.

The door next to the casting opened suddenly, and Mr shrunk low as Eliza emerged from Harold's house. Her bright hair was unmistakable, and the same straw hat she'd worn to the Pig and Whistle was balanced on her head. On her heels came Stephen Vanson, dressed in striped shirt and trousers, his sleeves rolled casually to mid forearm. Mr could hear the rumble of his voice but couldn't make out the words, though it was obvious that this was an argument. Eliza threw a retort over her shoulder as she kept walking, but Stephen reached out and grasped her elbow, pulling her to a halt. She shook him off and continued down the drive, marching in the direction of the village. Stephen leaned against the door frame and watched her go, and when she was out of sight, went back inside the house and closed the door.

Mr Isbister stood in the woods for a moment. Should he visit? Go and knock boldly upon the door, uninvited? It wasn't the thing done, of that he was well aware, but doubtless Stephen Vanson or Captain Plucky or whoever he truly was set little store by conventions. Perhaps he could get the man to explain his duplicitousness, confess the ruse, as it were. He threw off the willow branch that was tickling his ear and tromped toward the front door, decided, but as he stopped in front of it, prepared to knock, the door opened again and Stephen appeared, jacketed and with a hat on his oiled hair. The two men startled at the sight of one another, but Stephen recovered his composure more quickly.

"Roddy!" he said with what seemed to be a forced grin. He glanced quickly behind him into the dark hallway and pulled the door closed. "Out for a stroll, then? Just happened by? Sorry, old chap. Woody's not at home, and I'm on me way out. Nice of you to come. Give me best to the missus." He tipped his hat and stepped sharply past Mr, and before Mr could gather the wherewithal to object, or indeed say anything at all, he was gone, headed down the drive at a brisk trot.

*

If Mr thought to follow and catch the man up, there was certainly no chance in his wellingtons, a boot much better suited to a gardener's slow pace than to the tip-tap of the fast-stepping Vanson-Plucky. Mr did follow to the end of the drive, but the fellow had disappeared, as if into thin air. His attempt at a confrontation scuppered, Mr opted to walk the village road back to Sowerby Grange. Perhaps on a straightaway section of the road he'd spy his quarry, and hail him. In the meantime, the road was a change of pace, a gravelled, narrow affair that was in fact little more than a lane. It mounted every hillock and circled every boulder as it wound its way through the countryside, carrying travellers on a meandrous U from Lesser Plumpton to Watton Hoo, and points in between. Tall trees lined its path, their branches shading and overhanging the roadway, and beyond the trees, on the side opposite the acreage occupied by Natterjack Hall and neighbouring Sowerby Grange and the tangled forest between them, pastureland spread in undulating greenery. Behind sagging and often non-existent fences, mud-grubby sheep munched on onions scattered for their gastronomic pleasure. Mr, clumping along in wellies much better suited to mucky trails than to hard-packed surfaces, soon regretted his decision to take the road. Used for centuries by pedestrians and horse-drawn carts, it was usual to find the way blocked by gaggles of aggressive geese, or by a farmer leading a few cows, or by a confused jumble of sheep baa-aa-aaing, minus their shepherd. But in these post-war days of modern invention, it was also frequented in ever-increasing numbers by motor vehicles speeding pell-mell around the curves, leaving a choking dust in their wake. This very thing happened as Mr Isbister trudged the downside of a dip. Luckily he heard the roar of the engine before he saw the machine appear, and he jumped into the ditch, landing alongside a cow that stood munching placidly on ryegrass. The auto sped by, spitting gravel, and the cow, unperturbed, turned its big head to Mr, and regarded him with long-lashed brown eyes.

By the time Mr Isbister arrived home to Sowerby Grange he'd encountered two speeding automobiles, been chased by an angry goose, and smelled of cabbage, having begged a ride on a brassicas-laden wagon. His mood was hardly cheerful, and it was even less so when, pausing by the back kitchen entrance where it was his habit to leave his muddy wellingtons, he saw Mrs Isbister in the greenhouse, clucking over Lieutenant-Colonel Barks.

In no mood to be hospitable, he stomped towards them, pulling up short at the last minute when he spied, beyond the whitewashed glass, the door of the shed where his Trusty was hidden, ajar. His heart leapt. He scuttled to the shelter of the laurel hedge. His eyes flicked nervously from his wife and her mutton-chopped companion to the sagging door of the garden shed. Had someone been inside? Why? When? Had the Trusty been discovered? Was it still there!?

It seemed forever but eventually Mrs Isbister and the Lieutenant-Colonel exited the greenhouse, all hahahas and hohohos, tucked together like sycamore seeds. They wandered, absolutely meandered, as if they had not a care in the world, and Mr, to his embarrassment, yearning to check the shed but needing to be sure they would not circle back and catch him, slunk from shrub to bush, following them. Finally, they emerged onto the back lawn, where he saw a table set with tea for two. "Woody" held the chair out for Mrs, and Mr could hear her laughter all the way across the lawn to his hiding place, and watched as she sat, spreading her already voluminous yellow day dress in a rather old-century pose. When the biscuits were shared and the tea poured and pinkies raised on both sides, Mr Isbister scuttled to the shed.

The door was closed. Had he imagined it open? Or had someone happened along – the dustbin boy, perhaps, or Eliza – and closed it? He tiptoed up the path and through the overgrowth of thistles and stinging nettle and, taking one last glance around to be sure no one was watching, pulled open the shed door. The Trusty was there, the bulky shape of her at home beneath the canvas tarpaulin, safe and sound. Mr Isbister breathed a sigh of relief and sat down upon the upturned bucket, suddenly weary from the day's excitements. He realised he was sweating and wiped his brow with a handkerchief drawn from his coat pocket. The handkerchief smelled of lemons, and he thought of Eliza. His placid and unremarkable life had become erratic and unpredictable, and he wasn't at all sure he was enjoying it. But…there was this fascinating machine, and he'd had almost no chance to ride it. He lifted a corner of the tarpaulin, releasing the motorcycle's pungent odours: grease and oil and gasoline, rubber and metal.

That night the dinner hour seemed interminable. Cook served again, and Mr was reminded that it was Eliza's day off. Mrs barely spoke – a good thing, if unusual – but she hummed while she ate and giggled softly at some humour to which Mr was not a party – both behaviours serving to give Mr rather a bad headache. Mrs had second and then third helpings, and Mr, ever polite if nothing else, felt he could not excuse himself while she still ate, and so he sat, watching her many chins wobble as she chewed, wondering what on earth Lieutenant-Colonel Barks saw in his wife that he simply did not.

Finally, she pushed herself back from the table, dabbing at her lips with her napkin and smiling almost stupidly at her plate, as if she could see Lieutenant-Colonel Barks's mutton-chops reflected in the congealed gravy. Mr a-hemmed, and when she glanced up he seized the chance to excuse himself and bid her goodnight. In his room he paced, returning again and again to the window and peering down into the dark garden, the shape of the tool shed beyond the greenhouse barely discernible in the gloaming. When the house settled and lights were extinguished, Mr exchanged his dinner jacket for a warm tweed and wrapped a scarf around his neck. He tucked the leather helmet and goggles into his pocket, and tip-toed through the quiet house, meeting nary a soul on his way to the Trusty's hiding place. Once there, he removed the tarpaulin, pocketed the matchbox he'd stashed under a pot for lighting the motorcycle's headlamp, and backed the bike through the propped door, which he then made sure to close and latch. He pushed the Trusty through the garden paths and past the laurel hedge, a feat in itself with the sidecar attached, down the rather long drive to the point where it curved and he could no longer be spied from the house. He was really quite winded by then, so he climbed into the wicker sidecar for a breather, pulling the lap robe across his knees to ward off the chill night air.

He'd no sooner rubbed his hands together beneath the lap robe's woolen warmth than he heard running footfalls on the gravel behind him, and he twisted in horror. He'd been caught! But even as he turned in guilty fear the rational part of his brain knew it could not have been Mrs. She would not have run with such dainty steps. Indeed, she would not have run. And sure enough, it was – not Eliza, as he'd thought, hoped? – but the dustbin boy, hallooing in a whispering shout.

Gracious. Did everyone know his secrets?

"Mr Isbister, sar!" the boy – Tommy? Timmy? – rasped. He panted to a stop beside the wicker sidecar where Mr sat, looking ridiculous, he was sure, with no driver at the motorcycle's controls. "I were asked to give you this," said the boy, his breath pluming white in the cool night air. He held out a folded scrap of paper.

Mr Isbister took it, eyeing the boy, although the bright moon cast shadows, and he couldn't see the lad's face. He unfolded the message, and saw an address scribbled there. 24 Dilly Lane, Lesser Plumpton. Why did that strike a bell? He glanced back at the boy.

"What is this?" he asked, holding up the paper.

"Dunno, sar," the boy replied.

"Who gave it to you?" Mr pressed.

"Me sister, sar."

"Your sister," Mr Isbister said flatly. "Who is your sister, young man, and why might she be passing me notes?"

"Lizer's me sister, sar," said the boy, his tone suggesting Mr should know this obvious fact. "Yer housemaid Lizer. And I dunno."

"Eliza's your sister?" Mr repeated. He shook his head, crumpling the note. "The girl has brothers coming out the woodwork. Very well, then, boy, what might I find at 24 Dilly Lane in Lesser Plumpton, were I to venture there?"

"Dunno, sar," the boy replied. "But I know the way. I could take you, like."

Mr smoothed the paper over his knee, peering at the writing as if it might share a clue. A silence hung as he considered. He'd been going to take the Trusty for a little joy ride anyway, why not all the way to Lesser Plumpton, get a real feel for what the old girl could do? The night was fine and clear, the moon almost day-bright, and, truth be told, the idea of possibly meeting Eliza at the end of the drive was more than appealing.

"What's your name, young man?" Mr asked, stuffing the note into his jacket pocket.

"George, sar," the boy said. "Shall I drive, sar? I know how—" He was already moving eagerly towards the driver's seat.

"Most emphatically not!" Mr Isbister said, throwing off the lap rug and scrambling out of the sidecar. Memories of his previous humiliation as a sidecar passenger were still rather raw. "You may come along for the ride, Master George, but I shall do the driving."

Mr paused to light the acetylene headlamp (George helped, being more familiar with the contraption), and they swapped places, George climbing into the seat Mr had vacated, and Mr slinging a leg over the Trusty's seat. He thought of Phoenix and his oh-so-cocky perch on the Triumph in the guide book, and, imagining himself such a one, secured his leather helmet and goggles and tugged on his driving gloves. His white silk scarf with his initials embroidered on one end – RTI – stirred in the slight breeze. He kicked the bike over, and the old girl started with ease as if she looked forward as much as he to a moonlit jaunt through the countryside. He glanced at George, tucked into the sidecar beneath the lap rug, and the boy grinned back at him. Mr pressed the throttle and the Trusty jumped forward eagerly, heading down the drive with a perky little pop-pop-pop.

Chapter 8
THE GREEN FAIRY

Mr Isbister didn't visit Lesser Plumpton often. The largest of a string of villages nestling the banks of the River Windrush, it did rather bustle, being a market town, and Mr avoided busyness as a rule, although it did house the Lesser Plumpton School of the Arts where he'd purchased his book on Rococo Art, and where he'd not long ago aspired to lessons. Funny, he thought, cheerfully guiding his motorcycle along the moonlit lane, how one's focus could get nudged off its axis without one realizing. The development of any artistic talent he might have seemed far less important recently than exploring on his Trusty, and becoming a good driver. He swerved to avoid a frog that jumped before the beam of his headlamp, but the machine remained under his careful control. His inner Phoenix – nay, Chimera - applauded. Mr grinned into the wind.

The way to Lesser Plumpton took Mr and young George along the very route he'd walked earlier that day when he'd made his return from Natterjack Hall. He readily recalled the livestock, and here and there at a bend in the road his headlamp caught the blinking gaze of sheep, and an occasional cow. Mr thought of the bovine he'd shared the ditch with, and hoped the beast had at last been led to a shed where she might pass the night in safety.

Other than the fenced animals, they saw no one on the thin ribbon of a road. Now and again Mr glanced at his passenger, wondering if the lad might doze off given the late hour, but George remained alert, the lap rug pulled to his chin. It was a cozy ride, Mr knew from experience; in fact, piloting the motorcycle was rather a tough job in comparison. One's arms grew tired, and he hadn't dressed warmly enough. His leather helmet kept his ears snug, and his driving gloves shielded his hands, so that was something, although a thicker jacket was called for, and a woolen scarf rather than the fluttering silk would have been more the ticket.

As they neared Lesser Plumpton the trees thinned out and houses appeared more frequently, fronting the road. Low stone walls lined the shoulders, and eventually they came to a crossroad. Mr slowed the bike, checking for cart or motorized traffic, and glanced down at George.

"Which way to Dilly Lane, young man?" he called over the noise of the Trusty.

"Straight on, sar," George called back.

And so they went, Mr steering the motorcycle through the village's narrow streets, quite pleased at his demonstrated prowess. Of course, there was neither traffic nor pedestrians, but there were kerbs, and bumpy cobbles. When at last they turned onto Dilly Lane, Mr realised he knew precisely where they were: at the end of the street was the grand old building housing the Lesser Plumpton School of the Arts. At George's direction, he stopped in front of it.

"This place?" Mr asked, puzzled. He pushed his goggles onto his forehead and rubbed the red rings around his eyes. "I've been here before, but never paid much heed to the address," he said, more to himself than to George, who had climbed out of the sidecar and was standing with the rug around his shoulders. George held his hand out, palm up, as if expecting payment.

"I'll watch her for you, sar," George said, nodding towards the Trusty, and then at his still empty palm. "Whilst you go in."

"In?" queried Mr.

"In, sar," George said, jerking his chin towards the carved doors of the Lesser Plumpton School of the Arts.

"But – it's so late," Mr said, baffled. "Surely there are no exhibits open? No art classes in session?"

"No, sar," said George impatiently. "But there's a show on, and I was to bring yer. There's a seat reserved. Give the name o' Roddy at the door, I were told."

Mr frowned at the brick facade of the building, and in the silence of the street he heard the faint sound of music and laughter from beyond the closed doors. Roddy. Was this some Stephen Vanson trickery?

"Go on, sar, or you'll miss the act," George said, giving him a light push towards the door. "I'll put out the headlamp."

Mr took a step towards the door, but George's fingers plucked his sleeve.

"Sar? I'll be watchin' the Trusty?" he asked, his hand held out for a coin. "And puttin' out the headlamp, like I said."

Mr paid, then pulled open the door to the Lesser Plumpton School of the Arts and entered the lobby. The sound of jaunty piano music and crowd laughter assailed his ears. He glanced behind him, and George waved. The door closed.

Mr stood on the plush of the carpet. He'd never visited in the evening, and the school looked different with the gaslights casting a glow. The shelves from which he'd selected his book on Rococo art were locked away behind ornately carved panels and the high counter where the day attendant usually sat was empty but for a billboard upon an easel. "Grandest Night of the Season!" it read. "Tonight! Annual Benefit in Support of the Lesser Plumpton School of the Arts." Then on a third line, "Local Talent in True Music Hall Tradition!" There was more in smaller print, but the music had picked up again, and Mr drifted toward a doorway over which was hung a thick dark curtain. He stepped through it into velvety blackness, and as he stood blinking, just making out a cavernous room filled with the backs of people's heads and a gaslit stage beyond, someone tugged his sleeve.

"Here for the show, gov?" the fellow asked, and Mr, a man of no great stature himself, looked down at a dwarf with a tidy, pointed beard and wearing evening dress of white tie and tails.

"Er, indeed," Mr answered. "I'm to say 'Roddy,' I believe."

"Eh?" asked the man, seemingly hard of hearing over the piano, which had begun to pound out a lively tune.

"Roddy, sir. I'm to say Roddy," Mr Isbister said, bending towards the man and increasing his volume.

"Roddy! Ah, yes, why didn't you say? Evening's half over, gov, but you'll still catch an eyeful. This way, Roddy." The fellow turned on his heel and led off through the throng of seats, and Mr followed to an empty one in the second to front row, left of centre stage. The little man departed with a flourish and a bow, and Mr pardoned and excused himself past several already seated patrons and took his place. What the dickens was this all about, he wondered, not a little thrilled with the evening's unexpected adventure.

The pounding piano music, it turned out, was an introduction to a pantomime called Puss in Boots, in which an actor in heavy makeup, musketeer boots, a foppish hat and a bushy cat's tail proceeded to convince the receptive audience, clapping and cheering throughout the number, of the authenticity of a tale about a wily cat who tricked and deceived his way to wealth and power, while gaining the hand of a princess for his penniless master. The costumes were exquisite, the music and dance lively, and Mr was enthralled. His was one of the loudest voices to shout "Bravo!" when the pantomime finished and the actors bowed.

A juggler came next, tossing flaming torches into the air and catching them with a skill that left Mr's jaw agape, and that was followed by a fellow who walked on his hands and back-flipped his way across the stage. A comic duo performed, and Mr found himself laughing with abandon, and nudging his neighbour who was chuckling with equal mirth.

Then the man who'd ushered Mr to his seat climbed onto the stage. He thanked the audience for coming, and for their support of the Lesser Plumpton School of the Arts, and introduced the final act of the evening: "Miss Eliza Vanson."

Mr gasped and clasped his hands in anticipation. His eyes shone.

She appeared then, Eliza, dressed in a demure, old-fashioned gown with flounces on the long skirt and full, puffed sleeves. She had a large red bow atop her head, and her hair curled in girlish ringlets over her shoulders, and from his vantage point so close to the stage Mr could see that she wore the same heavy stage makeup the other performers had worn, her eyes kohled and her lips rouged. It was not unbecoming. If she saw him there in the second row, brimming with admiration, she did not let on, instead smiling shyly at her audience and twirling a parasol like some Edwardian lady from a decade past.

The audience hushed. Mr was enthralled – and exceedingly warm. Eliza, he knew, had a strange effect on him. It was most inappropriate, but also rather exciting. He pulled out his handkerchief to dab away the moisture on his forehead, and realised with some embarrassment that he'd sat the night through with his leather helmet on his head, and with his goggles pressing his brow. He glanced sheepishly at his neighbour, but the fellow was staring in anticipation at Eliza, who began to sing, softly and demurely. Mr forgot his helmet and goggles.

"*A sweet Lesser Plumpton girl you see*" – someone in the audience hooted –,

"*A belle of good society.*
I'm not too young, I'm not too old,
Not too timid, not too bold,
Just the kind you'd like to hold."

There were more hoots from the audience, and Mr felt his cheeks redden. He glanced around furtively. Was anyone looking pointedly at him?

The piano's polite tinkle became a crescendo, and Mr's eyes nearly popped as Eliza tossed aside the parasol, drew up her prim skirts to reveal bright red stockings and – goodness! – a black garter, and launched into a rousing version of the song's chorus: "*Ta-ra-ra-boom-de-ay, ta-ra-ra-boom-de-ay!*"

The whole audience sang in unison, and Mr's embarrassment faded. This was good fun! He sang along, though not sure of the words, and swayed from side to side with his seatmates. Several more verses followed, and after each one a boisterous rendition of the chorus. When she finished the song she bowed, gave a last cheeky show of her garter, and sashayed off stage and out of sight to the clapping, shouts and whistles of the audience. The curtain fell, the audience rose, and the room thinned out until Mr Isbister sat alone, still mesmerized by the evening's entertainment. At last, the stage lights were extinguished and only the dim glow of the wall sconces remained.

"Mister," the small man who'd seated him called from the doorway. "Show's over. Time to go."

Mr roused himself. At the door he paused and dug in his pocket for a coin, presenting it to the fellow whose white tie was now loosened in anticipation, perhaps, of further disrobing.

"For the fund, if you please," Mr said magnanimously, giving a little bow.

"Admission were twice that," said the other flatly. "Grandest night o' the season, as the billing foretold. And weren't that final number something?"

Mr blushed, and rooted in his pocket for a second coin. "Of course, of course," he said, handing it over. "A grand entertainment all round. Spectacular job. Never seen better." In fact, he'd never been to a music hall or viewed any show of the sort he'd watched this evening, so that was a truth, at least. He wondered fleetingly what Mrs would say to such a spectacle, and shuddered to think.

The dwarf pocketed the coins and was already walking away. "Night, gov!" he called over his shoulder, and Mr exited the Lesser Plumpton School of the Arts, pulling on his driving gloves. Eliza stood there, beside the Trusty, her elaborate white stage costume replaced with a long sack coat and a snug-fitting cloche hat. She looked rather ordinary, and Mr felt his tummy flip-flop.

"Capital job on the song," he said, approaching her and the bike. "Quite appealing. I had no idea…" Close up he saw that she still wore the heavy makeup, and it was hard to find her features beneath the distraction of the over-black eyes and the pouting red mouth. But then she grinned, and he saw the familiar gap between her front teeth, and he smiled back.

"'Tis kind of you to say," she said. "I'm happy you came. I weren't sure you would."

Mr chuckled. "Well, young George was rather mysterious about the whole thing, and I'm fast discovering I can never turn down the chance for adventure. Who knew I was such an intrepid soul, eh?" As he spoke, he realised that in fact he'd always had an adventurer's spirit. Hence his wistfulness over Harry Guppletwill's research trips. Convention, marriage, his own timidity, if he was honest, had left it suppressed.

"Well then, sar, if you're up for a bit of fun there's a party for the cast of the show in a flat round back of the School. That's where Julio lives. Caretaker by day, master o' ceremonies, and, if I dare share his secrets, cock o' the heap by night." She smiled again, and Mr a-hemmed and fussed with the cuff of his glove. He wasn't sure what a cock of the heap was, or did, or who Julio might be, although the name, unusual as it was, rang a bell. Nevertheless, here was a chance for a bit more adventure, now he'd whet his appetite. His only hesitation was the Trusty, left unattended on the street at this late hour, but when he voiced that worry the lap rug stirred in the sidecar, and George's tousled head appeared.

"Still on duty 'ere, sar," George said in a sleepy voice. "Extra coin in it, figger?"

Mr glanced at Eliza, who laughed and shrugged a shoulder. "Always a game one, our George," she said, and started off down a narrow walk that led to the rear of the building. Mr, quite sure a lad as young as George should be home abed but equally sure he wanted to follow Eliza into the darkness, paused only a moment before tossing George another coin.

*

Julio was the dwarf who'd ushered Mr to his seat, and who, at the end of the evening's entertainment, had taken his coin and prodded him for another. His flat, a large space with a private entrance at the rear of the building that housed the Lesser Plumpton School of the Arts, was unlike anything Mr had seen. Eliza called it bohemian, whatever that meant. There was fabric everywhere, rippling veils of sheer silk and flowing chiffon in rich hues that hung from the ceiling and fluttered against the walls. The furniture was low and thickly cushioned, encouraging languorous poses and the stretching of limbs. Pungent Turkish tobacco smoke filled the air, and its haze and the low lights from candles and guttering oil lamps made it difficult to see. A gramophone played music that Mr thought was likely American; there was a tootling clarinet and a wailing trumpet and a toc, toc, toc noise that might have been someone beating a metal cup with a stick. Mr didn't understand its appeal, but Eliza, flinging off her coat, tapped her toes and wiggled her elbows to the confusion of it. Others danced too, and Mr stood in the midst of them feeling excruciatingly awkward, and wondering if it would be awfully rude of him to back out the way he'd come, and go home.

"Not a dancer, then, gov?" Julio appeared next to him, and handed him a drink. Mr smelled something oddly like licorice, and looked at the glass of green liquid dubiously.

"Absinthe," Julio said, watching him. "It's French. The French are good at everything alcoholic, I always say. Everything gastronomic too, come to think of it. And if you believe the stories about old King Bertie who visited France rather regularly, they're good at a few less savoury pursuits as well." He chuckled, and rocked up and down on the balls of his feet. Mr suddenly recalled where he'd heard the name Julio – from Stephen Vanson, Captain Plucky, in relation to Paris, and brothels. He took in the fellow's tidy appearance – his neatly trimmed beard, his ruddy-coloured hair precisely oiled and parted. Mr took a hesitant sip of the absinthe, and then another. It wasn't half bad.

"Interesting drink, absinthe," Julio continued, sipping from his own glass and watching his guests as they laughed and cavorted and lounged. "Distilled from a maceration of anise, wormwood, fennel and, I believe, sometimes sage or tarragon."

"It's rather good," Mr said, sipping again. His gaze rested on Eliza, who was arm in arm with a dark-skinned fellow, performing some sort of wanton dance move, feet flying.

"It is rather good," Julio agreed. "A word of caution though, my country friend. It's highly intoxicating. Some say it weakens one's moral and physical fibre. The painter Van Gogh cut off his own ear after prolonged use of the stuff, and some people blame Oscar Wilde's decadence on an over-indulgence in absinthe."

Mr's brows shot all the way up to the red mark on his forehead made by the overlong wearing of his helmet. Oscar Wilde, as everyone knew, had been jailed for indecent acts. There'd been quite a to-do about it in the papers at the time. Mr hadn't paid the scandals much attention, but he certainly knew of some of the fellow's work. *The Importance of Being Earnest* he'd thought quite droll, although *The Picture of Dorian Gray* he'd avoided. When *Dorian Gray* was first published, he recalled, critics had branded it immoral and profane. Mr had thought it best to steer clear. Of Van Gogh and his demons Mr was well aware. He frowned at the glass in his hand, half gone now.

"I recall a painting I saw once," Mr said to Julio. "Or rather, I saw a print of it in a book. It was called *The Absinthe Drinker*." He'd seen it in an art book on one of his browses through the School's collection. He warmed to the topic. Art remained one of his passions. "Edgar

Degas, I believe, was the artist. A rather melancholy work. The subjects were a man and a woman seated at a table. Before them was a green drink just like this," he lifted his glass. "And on their faces a look of incredible lethargy and hopelessness."

Julio chuckled. "Have you seen the painting by Viktor Oliva? It too is called *The Absinthe Drinker*. I saw it once in Paris, hanging in some gallery. And I thought, there is the work of a man who has known the effects of this liquor – hallucinogenic, addictive, perverse even. Oliva painted an image of a man in a café, a half-drunk glass of absinthe before him. And as do the couple in the earlier Degas piece, this man wears an expression of abject melancholy. Abject. Seated upon the table, tempting his gaze, is a naked and translucent female, representative, of course, of the effects of absinthe. The so-called green fairy of raffish allure."

"Raffish - good gracious," said Mr, sipping.

"Indeed," said Julio. He clinked his glass against Mr's, and drank, then wandered away with a mischievous backward glance.

Mr watched the dwarf go. What a strange and interesting fellow he was. Mr looked down at his glass of green liquor, and wondered if any of what the man had said was true. Hallucinogenic? Should he pour the stuff in one of Julio's many potted plants? It tasted rather nice, though, and after all, what harm could one drink do? Mr sipped again, and decided to wander through the crowd.

He spied several of the actors from the Puss and Boots number. The man who'd played Puss still sported the nearly thigh-high boots, and had kitty-cat whiskers glued to his nose. He wore rather tight satin trousers and had a braying laugh, and as Mr shuffled past, trying to be unobtrusive, Puss nodded to him and winked. Mr pretended interest in his absinthe, swirling the green liquor in his glass and tossing back the last measure. He moved on, setting his empty glass on a table filled with a collection of both empty and full glasses, and picked up another. Why not, he thought, throwing care to the wind. He'd never been amongst so motley a crew, so uninhibited a group, and he found it strangely empowering. He sipped the second drink, but found it disappeared rather more quickly than the first. Courting danger, he took a third from the tray, promising himself he would take only the smallest sips. He already felt rather unsteady. Julio passed by, grinning, and trailed his fingers over Mr's arm whilst holding fast to a tall, slender man wearing a long plaid skirt. Another fellow swirled past in a risqué costume of netting and differently sized black polka dots strategically placed to cover various indecencies. Mr, befuddled, raised his absinthe and sipped. What a crazy, wonderful, wanton place the world could be, he thought. He leaned back against a billowing curtain and stumbled, finding it hollow. He set his empty glass on a table. Perhaps he'd had enough.

Someone turned up the volume on the gramophone, and Eliza appeared, fanning herself with her hand. A few damp tendrils of hair clung to her brow, and he caught a whiff of perspiration. It was not an unpleasant odour, coming from her. He smiled at her, although somewhat blearily.

"Are you enjoying the party, sar?" she asked. She had to lean rather close and raise her voice, such was the noise level of the room, what with the music, the loud talk and laughter, and the stomping and shuffling of the dancers' feet.

"Oh yes," he replied, nodding vigorously in case she could not hear him. "Lovely people. Julio and I had a rather interesting chat." He was almost shouting, and still wasn't certain she understood what he said, for she smiled vacantly and grasped his hand as a particularly lively song blasted from the gramophone.

"Dance with me!" she cried. He protested that he only had left feet, but allowed her to drag him to a spot amongst the other dancers, and, the last of his inhibitions all but erased, found himself copying Eliza's wiggles and stomps. Such was his exuberance that at one point, the other dancers took notice and backed into a circle, clapping and cheering him on as he whirled and cavorted like he'd been born for the music hall stage.

When the song ended, he collapsed, laughing, onto a nearby heap of cushions. Eliza fell beside him. He closed his eyes, intending only to catch his breath. He thought Eliza's head might be resting on his chest, and it was a rather nice feeling. Despite the noise and the music and the smoke and the laughter, he fell asleep with his mouth open, the bald spot on the top of his head shining in the light of the lamps.

Chapter 9
SOMETHING TO IT

Mr's fear was that Mrs should find out. That someone, somewhere, would hear of his foray into the world of performers and let slip a comment, or march straight to Sowerby Grange and tell her she'd married a scoundrel. He would be brought low, and shamed. After laying abed a full day to recover from his ghastly headache and his dry and foul-tasting mouth, he gingerly climbed out from beneath the blankets, having no idea how he'd arrived there but finding himself fully clothed and with a smear of black kohl and red rouge across his shirt. With gentle probing of his bruised brain he recalled the events of the previous night: the note delivered by George, the dustbin boy who'd turned out to be another of Eliza's brothers; the pleasant night ride to Lesser Plumpton; the delightful music hall show at the School of the Arts, and Eliza's number – ta-ra-ra-boom-de-ay! They'd gone to a party afterwards, something he should never have agreed to. He remembered the dwarf, Julio, and the strangely delicious liquor – absinthe, the man had called it, as he'd regaled him with tales of its poison. Mr shuddered.

They'd danced, he and Eliza. With abandon, if he hadn't imagined the whole thing. And everyone had watched and applauded. He groaned with the recollection. Goodness, he'd danced with his maid! And then, and then – he frowned. The more he thought about it, the more he remembered what fun the whole thing had been. It was completely inappropriate, yes, to dance with one's maid, and he had no idea how he'd gotten home, but at the end of the day, if he was honest, he would only be brought low and shamed by his own drunkenness, not by dint of the company he'd kept. If Mrs found out, he was prepared to accept her disappointment, and when the opportunity arose, he intended to apologize to Eliza for his unseemly behaviour, and send a similar note to Julio.

He felt much better when he'd changed out of his rumpled clothing and eaten the sandwich left next to his bed. Eliza's doing? Such

61

a caring soul. She must have made his excuses with Mrs, and it occurred to him that such behaviour must not become a habit. He squiffy in his bed, Eliza covering with his wife. In his many years he'd never been one to overindulge – well, not often, anyway. The recovery was most unpleasant.

It was around the dinner hour, he suspected, and he decided to venture to the dining room and see if he might end the day with a semblance of normalcy. He combed the tufts of his grey hair, using water on a wayward piece that refused to lay flat, then gave up on it and put on a tie. Mrs would appreciate the effort, he felt sure. He'd almost reached the dining room when Eliza appeared, headed in the same direction and balancing a tray. They stopped a few feet from one another, and Eliza, glancing around almost guiltily, bobbed a curtsey. It might have been the low light of the room, but Mr thought he could still see traces of kohl round her eyes.

"I need to speak with you," he whispered.

"I'm sorry, sar," she whispered back. "I never should've taken you round to Julio's. It were all my fault."

"Nonsense," he replied, wondering with a sinking stomach what she was referring to that was her fault. He couldn't remember anything after the dancing. "How did we get home?"

"I drove," she said. "George helped me get you in the sidecar, and then he squeezed in beside you for the ride home. It were he put you to bed."

"George?" Mr said, thinking of the boy's small stature.

"Well, I 'elped 'im," she said with a shrug. "And you bein' on the smallish side o' things, we managed."

He didn't know whether to feel insulted or embarrassed or grateful, but he had no chance to speak further, for the door of the dining room opened, and Mrs poked her head out. Her face fell when she saw him.

"Oh," she said flatly, her eyes travelling over him with distaste. "You're up. We were told you were ill, and wouldn't be joining this evening."

Mr glanced quickly at Eliza but her eyes were downcast and she had stepped away from him, waiting to be given access to the room beyond. He looked at his wife, and saw she was wearing a shoulder-baring gown of plum taffeta that he didn't recall seeing before. Her grand bosom, which he also could not recall ever seeing, was pushed into view by some female manipulation beneath the garment, he supposed, and the dimpled flesh heaved up and down with each breath. He watched the expansion and contraction of her overly exposed chest with an awe that Harold Guppletwill's scientific mind might have appreciated, and a relief that he had, many, many years ago, escaped its smothering.

"We?" he asked, drawing his gaze up to her over-pink face. He suspected there was more to this evening than a simple dinner for one.

"The boys are here," she said, simpering over her shoulder. "From next door. Woody, and Captain Plucky."

"Oh," he said. "And I have not dressed for the occasion."

"You haven't," she agreed.

"Perhaps I shall go and change," he said.

"But are you well enough?" she asked, making an attempt to sound concerned for his health.

"On second thought, no," Mr said, touching his forehead. He really did not relish an evening in company with the two "neighbours," and Mrs at her most giddy. "I do have rather a headache. Will you pardon me, my dear, and make my excuses to the lieutenant-colonel and the – er – captain?"

"Of course, of course," Mrs said, positively beaming her delight at his decision. "Probably best. We've got drinks already, and the table is set for three." Her gaze flicked to Eliza, still standing to one side with the tray of nibbles in her hand. "Well, go in, girl. Don't just stand there. This is a private conversation." Eliza scurried past her, avoiding Mr's eyes, and Mrs rolled hers, commenting to Mr after Eliza was gone, "Strange girl. This morning at breakfast she looked like she'd painted herself. Black eyes, and bright red lips. And yawning as if she'd stayed up all night. I had a word with Cook about her, but Cook says she's a good worker, and would be hard to replace if I were to dismiss her."

"Indeed," said Mr suavely. Secretly he was shocked at the idea that Mrs would consider firing Eliza, and he realised for the second time that day how highly he'd come to regard her – Eliza, not Mrs.

"Well, goodnight, Mr Isbister," said Mrs, her attention drawn by male laughter in the room behind her. Mr felt a flash of irritation.

"Goodnight," he replied, somewhat frostily. "Oh, and Mrs Isbister, please direct the maid to bring a tray in my room. I may have a headache, but I do still have an appetite." He turned on his heel and walked away, pleased at the double entendre that would have slid right past more than just his wife's exposed bosom.

*

Mr went directly from his encounter with Mrs to the tool shed to check on the Trusty. As promised, the bike was there, snug beneath her tarpaulin. Even the matches Mr used to light her headlamp had been put back under its pot; young George must have checked his pockets lest the box fell out. There was not a speck of dust on her, which meant the boy had likely cleaned her up after their dusty ride, and the lap rug had been neatly folded and stored on the seat of the sidecar. All in all, George had done a fine job, and Mr made a mental note to give him a coin for his troubles, on top of the ones he'd already paid for his services the past night. Nursemaid, after all, had not been part of their agreement.

Mr left the shed, closing the door and latching it. He checked the greenhouse; all was as it should be, despite Mrs and the lieutenant-colonel's recent interest in its contents. He stood beneath its roof for a while, enjoying the earthy, rooty scent, the silence, and the darkness, with only the moon for light. Such utterly peaceful moments often brought thoughts of Harold Guppletwill, and he wondered if the moon was as bright in whatever part of the world he lingered. It occurred to him that his friend had been often on his mind of late, more so than during the last several years when war had been raging across the channel. Then, there'd been little room for worries of Harold. War news and its local impact – village boys fighting and dying, and even some of the young ladies, gone to nurse – seemed to devour every scrap of energy and attention left to those not directly engaged. But now, now Harold came again to the fore, and Mr missed his friend with renewed poignancy, and wondered if they would meet again.

He sighed, and left the cloistered warmth of the greenhouse. As he paused to latch the door, he heard in the far distance a sudden loud, rasping, rolling croak: errr...errr...errr, and his heart leapt. The natterjack toad! How well he recalled its distinctive song, and how that sound brought him to those days spent with Harold in dogged pursuit of that amphibian quarry. It was apropos, he thought, standing on the pea gravel outside the greenhouse in the evening's gloaming, that he should hear the natterjack call just as his thoughts had turned so wistfully to Harold. He drew a deep, satisfied breath through his nose, and nodded. There was something to it, he thought. Something to it indeed.

A footstep crunched on the path's gravel, and he looked around. Someone was there in the shadow, watching him, and he frowned into the darkness.

"Who is it?" he challenged. "Show yourself."

Young George stepped into view and doffed his flat cap.

"'Tis me, sar, George," he said. "I weren't spyin' on yer. I were avoidin' yer, really. Passin' through, saw yer out here, gawping up at the moonlight and thought, what the dickens is 'e doin' now? Best not interrupt, like."

Mr scratched his head. What was he to make of that, and not take offense? He supposed he had looked rather odd, standing in silence in the dark, staring up at the sky. But after all, it was his garden – well, Mrs' – and he had every right to stand and gawp if that was what took his fancy. This was George, though, who'd looked after the Trusty so well the previous night, and with whom he'd shared the sidecar, an ordeal that can't have been pleasant for George.

"Hail, George," Mr said in a friendly tone, lifting his hand in greeting. Perhaps he could ease the boy's opinion of him. "Did you hear that furious croaking noise just now? An amphibious serenade, it was. Music to the ears! A treat one is not often privy to."

"Sar?" said George, furrowing his brow.

"That, young man, was the natterjack toad. A rarity in these parts, indeed in much of old England, and a toad with amazing vocal abilities. A very good friend of mine studied them. In fact, his home is named after them," said Mr, proudly.

"Oh, I know the place, sar," said George eagerly. "Natterjack Hall. Me brother Stephen –" he stopped, snipping off the words as surely as if he'd severed them with a pocketknife.

"What of your brother, young Master George?" Mr pressed. "He's not truly a captain, is he? And how has he come to be residing at Natterjack Hall, and using a different name? I confess I am quite a-muddle."

George toed the path's pebbles. In the darkness, Mr could not see his face, but he was certain of the boy's discomfort, and he felt some guilt. Still, he let the silence stretch and grow brittle, hoping for an answer. George, though, had been well coached, or so it would seem.

"I don't know nuffink 'bout that, sar," he said. "Or toads. Stephen *were* in the army, though. He told me stories 'bout ridin' a Trusty and collectin' 'omin' pigeons from big wicker towers – important work, that, an' dangerous. I fink he should of got a medal but Lizer says they don't hand 'em out willy nilly." He sounded a bit resentful, but whether of the fact of the unawarded medal or Eliza's opinion Mr couldn't be sure.

Mr found himself wondering if he'd misjudged Stephen Vanson, despite his duplicity. Motorcycles, homing pigeons and wicker towers did sound quite exciting. Perhaps the fellow had been involved in some sort of espionage during the war. It would go a way to explaining his chameleon-like abilities. To George he said, lamely, "Possibly the requisite medals are in the post. Likely an oversight."

George shrugged, and both man and boy fell silent. Crickets chirred in the long grass growing next to the greenhouse, and in the distance, an owl hooted. Suddenly, George tilted his cap back on his head and leaned towards Mr, his face in all its earnestness visible in the blue moonlight. "I know somefink about the other gent, though. Colonel Whatsit."

"Lieutenant-Colonel Barks?" said Mr, fearing he sounded eager. Gossip was never to be encouraged, of course, but under the circumstances, how could one not wish to hear a whisper about the esteemed military man who'd insinuated himself into Mrs' favour?

"Yeah, him. He gets letters, lots of 'em. Sometimes he reads 'em soon as they're delivered, right then and there on the front step, all frowns and furrows, so not happy news, I'd wager," George glanced over his shoulder as if checking for eavesdroppers, then added, "I waylaid the postman once on his way to the Hall. Tried to be friendly-like, figgered maybe he'd let me see one of them messages but he got on 'is high horse, him an' his livery, and told me it was a hangin' offence, stealin' someone's mail." George rolled his eyes. "Pfft. I bopped 'im on the nose for callin' me a thief. I weren't plannin' to steal, just to look. 'Sides, they don't hang people for thievin'." He paused, seeming uncertain. "Do they?"

"Well, no, but, George, one should not go about punching the postmen," Mr said, keeping his tone light to cover his shock at the boy's admissions. Pilfering and fisticuffs, goodness. He eyed the lad, sizing him up. Ten years old, maybe. Shrewd for his years, definitely. He supposed he shouldn't be too surprised at the boy's actions. He was Stephen Vanson's brother, after all, even if he seemed a decent young chap.

"He weren't really a post*man*," George said, his lip thrust forward in a pout. "He had pimples and all. Weren't much older'n me."

"Well, that's different then," Mr said, but saw that the sarcasm slid right past George. Silently chiding himself for his nosiness, he asked, "Did you, then? See one of the letters?"

"Well, when I bopped the fella, he fell off his bike and his sack of mail spilled out in the road. Course I helped him gather 'em up – not that he appreciated it – and I might've slipped one into me pocket. Odd, though, it were addressed to *Major* Barks, not colonel, or whatever he says he is." George shrugged. "Anyway, I had a read, then delivered it meself. Shoved it under the door at Natterjack Hall."

"And?" prompted Mr, his own guilty curiosity goading him on.

"I couldn't make head nor tail of what it said," George told him. "It were nothin' but nonsense. Gibberish, like. And the handwritin' all crabbed and blotted, like someone cried on the paper. But when you figure where it come from, I guess that's not strange. Cane Hill, was the postmark."

"Cane Hill?" repeated Mr. The name was a query.

"Cane Hill," George said again, his tone suggesting that Mr should know it. "A sanny. An asylum. Cane Hill Lunatic Asylum. A place where they put the nutters."

"Ah," said Mr, and though he understood what George was telling him, in fact he understood nothing at all. Did Lieutenant-Colonel Barks have a relative or friend at this lunatic asylum? Someone, perhaps, who'd known him long before he'd earned a promotion to the esteemed rank of lieutenant-colonel? And, at the end of the day, did Mr, as a mere neighbour and acquaintance, and ignoring the fact of the fellow's rather irregular attentions to Mrs Isbister, have any right to know? It was odd, he supposed, but oddities seemed to swirl about him these days, and Mr did not like the intrigue.

Chapter 10
AN AGGRESSIVE OLD CURMUDGEON

Mr returned to his rooms after his encounter with George. He'd hoped to see Eliza, apologize properly for his behaviour at Julio Quint's, perhaps query her about what Stephen Vanson's game might be, for surely there was a game, but she did not appear. Instead, his dinner, cold, was waiting on a tray. He ate it, thumbing through the Trusty's manual, but he was distracted, his thoughts returning to George's revelations, such as they were, about the esteemed Barks. The man's business was his own, of course, but he was living in Harold's house, and paying more than appropriate attention to Mrs, and for those reasons he decided he would ask Eliza about the lieutenant-colonel, with whom her brother lived, expecting she might have some insight. He returned to his manual, waiting for Eliza to collect the dishes, but she did not come, and he fell asleep in his chair. Sometime in the night he rose, undressed and crawled into bed, and in the morning, the tray was gone, and a jug of warm water had been left for washing, along with a sliver of soap and a soft towel.

He lay abed for a long while. His drapes had been pulled open, and his window unlatched, presumably by Eliza when she'd brought his soap and water. From the yard beyond came the happy trill of larks and robins. The sun was out. It was a fine day. He decided on a bit of greenhouse work, but before he went down to breakfast, he wrote Eliza a note, and left it beside the water pitcher, where he knew she'd find it.

Dear Eliza, he wrote. *Please accept my profuse apologies for my behaviour at your friend Mr Julio's flat (I'm sorry, I realise I don't know his last name). It was kind of you to invite me to the evening and I am ashamed if my actions were less than gentlemanly.* He read what he'd written, frowning over the last line, then added, to clarify, *dancing with abandon, sleeping on the floor etc.* He considered asking her to convey his regrets to Julio as well, but that, he knew, was a task any gentleman would feel duty bound to complete in person, and directly to the fellow himself. Not to mention such a visit would require another evening jaunt on the Trusty, no small incentive in itself.

Downstairs, there was toast and marmalade and beans and boiled egg and a pot of tea. Mrs did not appear. Nor did Eliza. Mr hummed contentedly, enjoying the solitude. He lapped up his soft egg, liberally doused with pepper, and helped himself to an extra spoonful of marmalade. Then, with no one to comment, he spooned a second egg from the bowl and sliced it, laying the perfect little ovals onto a second slice of toast. The morning was moving along rather swimmingly.

When he'd finished, he patted one or two stray dribbles of yolk from his chin and dusted toast crumbs from the happy mound of his tummy. So far, his morning had been one of perfection: his every need met and with no evidence of the complications of servant or wife or neighbours. Outside, a fine sun beamed. His wellingtons beckoned. Mr pushed back from the table and set aside his napkin, leaving the remnants of his repast to be tidied by his invisible housemaid. Life as it should be, he felt quite sure.

For much of the morning Mr Isbister puttered in the greenhouse. It was warm there. The punky scent of peat and loam and compost wrapped around him like a blanket, and the pungent green smell of new leaves was almost soothing. Snug in his long, rubberized apron, his hands encased in pliable cotton gloves that were soon as damp as the soils he tended, he plucked and thinned and trimmed and trowelled and watered. Then he got down to more serious business and grafted and pruned and transplanted. During one particularly satisfying manoeuvre, scuttling a spiny *alluaudius* from its birthing pot to a more permanent home in a big earthenware crock, Mr smiled to realise he was egging the process on with a rendition of "ta-ra-ra-BOOM-de-ay!" Various images flitted through his mind: red-stockinged ankles, an endearing tooth gap, and a blue eyeball pressed to the open crack of his door. He giggled.

"Throckmorton!" boomed a voice behind him, and he startled, dropping his trowel. Turning, he saw Woodward Barks, his broad belly near bursting the buttons of his polka-dotted waistcoat. Mr wondered how long he'd been standing there. Overhead, beyond the greenhouse's glass roof, a cloud slid across the sun, and the sparkle inside the greenhouse dimmed.

"Lieutenant-Colonel," Mr said, making an effort to sound at least somewhat welcoming. He rubbed at an itch on his nose with the back of his glove, and immediately suspected he'd smeared dirt there. He sighed under his breath.

"Please, Throckmorton, Woody to friends," the Lieutenant-Colonel said, chiding him. "I may have an impressive rank and of course the fact of my years in a position of command does render many a man awestruck, but surely we're past all that deference and homage claptrap by now?"

Mr wasn't sure how to reply to that, so he made a non-committal noise, blinked, and rubbed his nose again, belatedly remembering the soil caked on his glove.

"What've you got there, Throckmorton? Looks a bit – unfriendly, what with all those nasty spines. Puny little leaves, too. Have you watered it? Not a plant man myself, but your Mrs has shown me her peonies – proud of them, wot? She's sweet on the pink ones, but then, you'd know that, given that pretty much every flowering thing out there is of the pink variety." He guffawed and waved a hand towards the garden beyond the greenhouse, and Mr frowned. Barks was right. The gardens' pink sameness had been a sore point for Mr, but Mrs, with her Horticultural Society membership, had trumped his objections, and so past the whitened glass of the greenhouse windows, theirs was a garden awash in various shades of pink. Dark pink roses, pale pink peonies, rather harsh pink petunias, and the purple-pink cottage pinks. There were other colours here and there, but in the main it was a veritable plethora of pink. Not that pink wasn't lovely. But, as Harold Guppletwill often said, quoting the poet William Cowper, variety is the very spice of life that gives it all its flavour. No wonder Mr instinctively preferred the overgrown paths and bramble-choked trails of the woodlands. There, at least, was diversity. And here, in the greenhouse. He stooped and retrieved his trowel, and in an attempt at regaining his footing and proving to the brash Barks that he was neither intimidated nor in awe of him, he gestured to the lethal-looking spined succulent he'd just repotted.

"This, Woody, is an ocotillo plant, of the genus *alluaudia*. Native to Madagascar," he began. He'd been about to explain that his friend and neighbour, Harold Guppletwill, had brought several specimens home from a trip there, and before leaving for the Amazon, had asked Mr to look after them. A delicate task, as the plants were completely out of their element here in the damp English climate. It took some skill, Mr had been about to point out, to coax such a prehistoric looking specimen to thrive – all spiny stalk and hoary thorn and tiny discs of succulent greenery.

Woody, however, interrupted.

"Ah – Africa! The Dark Continent, as the Victorians referred to it, on account of what little they knew of her mysterious interior. Livingstone and Stanley and all that. I myself have rather fond memories of Africa – Egypt, specifically. Mind you, sand was not one of them." He hahaha'd at his own humour, his mutton-chop whiskers moving up and down as if mechanically activated. Mr was put in mind of a wooden soldier figurine Mrs owned, the jaw of which was operated by a clever lever in the back.

"Anyway, Throckmorton old boy, I just came by to invite you and Alice for dinner Saturday next. I will send a card round, do it proper and all, but I wanted to give you an informal by the by. Bit of a to-do, and all. It's my birthday. I always do it up big. One should celebrate the fact of oneself, don't you think?" His chops moved again with the judder of his laughter. Mr offered a grimace that he hoped could pass as pleasant. Woody pushed open the greenhouse door, and Mr had just turned back to the spiny thorns of his ocotillo when Woody cried, "What the devil!" and stepped quickly into the garden. Mr set down his trowel and hurried after him, peering from the doorway.

On the path that led from the laundry yard a big black billy goat stood, drawn up short by the Lieutenant-Colonel's charge into his path. He was unusually large, as goats go, and clamped between his teeth and hooked onto one of his long, pointed horns was a yellow dress Mr recognised as belonging to his wife. He knew it well as she wore it often. He suspected it was a favourite. There were pink flowers embroidered on the hem and dainty yellow buttons sewn down its wide bodice. The goat's eyes, Mr noticed, were a match with the dress for colour, and the big billy stared flatly at the man blocking his way, and pawed the pea gravel with his hoof. Woody Barks crouched aggressively into what Mr supposed was a wrestling stance, spreading his thick thighs and flexing his ham fists.

"Stay back, Throckmorton. This fellow means business," Woody growled. Mr, still paused in the greenhouse doorway, wondered if Woody referred to himself, poised to attack, or the animal, with similar intent. Either way, he disliked the outcome. He suspected that this was Amos, a billy goat known in the countryside around Watton Hoo and Lesser Plumpton as an aggressive old curmudgeon. People told stories in the pubs of big Amos and his escapades. Every now and again he escaped his pen and went on a rampage, chasing geese and trampling flower gardens and creating havoc until he could be rounded up and returned to his owner. Mr suspected the old goat knew his days were numbered, and these capers were simply his last-ditch effort at a life under his own direction.

The standoff was broken by the sudden appearance on the scene of Mrs Isbister, who, coming round the corner and seeing her dress in possession of a billy goat, shrieked and ran towards the animal, waving her arms. Close behind her came young George and another, older boy, perhaps sent to catch the wayward animal. They too yelled and broke into a sprint. The goat, startled by the shouting and running figures, turned towards them and reared up on its hind legs, pawing the air with its front hooves. Mrs, closest, screamed in fright and put her arms up to save herself. The goat spun again and was off, flying at a gallop past the still crouched Barks, with George and his companion in pursuit.

Mrs, bosom heaving, jowls a-swing, turned on the men in a fury. "That beast has my dress!" she cried. "And you stand here! Both of you! You, in your apron —" she gestured dismissively at Mr "and you, with your supposed battlefield bravery!" She shook her jowls at Woody. Then she burst into tears, burying her face in her hands.

Barks, with an alarmed glance over his shoulder at Mr, stepped hesitantly forward and patted her shoulder. He beckoned urgently to Mr, who approached his wife with equal reluctance. The two men stood awkwardly alongside her, sharing in their disinclination to the task of attempting comfort to an angry, sobbing woman. Invariably one said the wrong thing, or made the wrong gesture.

To Mr's relief, George re-appeared through a gap in the laurel hedge, yellow dress held aloft. "Got it, missus!" he cried triumphantly, and Mrs, shaking off Woody's feeble pats with a contemptuous swat, swiped angrily at her tears. She thanked George with an imperious nod, took the muddied dress and exited the garden, bellowing for Eliza to fetch the laundry tub.

Woody and Mr eyed one another with frowning commiseration. Woody reached into his vest pocket and pulled out a silver flask. Uncapping it, he took a swig and passed it to Mr, who likewise tossed off a shot, the burn of strong Scottish whisky a balm for the nerves. He passed it back to Woody who absentmindedly handed it to George, fellow martyr.

"Did we do something wrong?" asked Woody with a lift of his thick brows. He took back the flask before George could imbibe, capped it, and returned it to his pocket. Then he hooked his thumbs in his braces and frowned.

"The goat did," said George wisely, hooking his thumbs into his own braces, a mime and a hero.

Chapter 11
CHARADES

For a short while after the billy goat incident, Sowerby Grange returned to the rhythm it had known prior to the arrival of Lt Colonel Barks, or Stephen – Captain Plucky – Vanson, or Mr's acquisition of the Trusty, or his friendship with Eliza. For a few days things were the way they used to be, not idyllic, by any means, but the way that he and Mrs had gotten on for the two and a half decades they'd been married. Shared meals, mostly. Separate everything else. He to his books, greenhouse, walks in the woods, and imaginary discussions with Harold Guppletwill on topics of interest; she, presumably, to her Horticultural Society meetings, and whatever else occupied her time. There was no mention made of the goat, and Mrs, feelings soothed, wore the yellow dress, mended and washed, Mr supposed, by Eliza. He and Mrs ate together, exchanged pleasantries of the day, talked about the weather, then went their separate ways until the next repast. Eliza served. Mr did not meet her eye. He noticed her pungent arm pits but made a point of not thinking about them when he was alone. His art book remained in its lair beneath his mattress, and Mrs did not revive the subject of his dabbling.

He wasn't sure why it seemed important to revert to that earlier reality. The goat incident felt somehow traumatic, as if the goat's appearance in the garden that afternoon was a portent that the world as he knew it was about to implode. Fearing such a thing and what it might mean, he'd retreated into the safe cocoon of his life as R. Throckmorton Isbister, unfulfilled, unappreciated, unloved. He even considered selling the Trusty, but decided he couldn't go that far, not yet. It was a dull week, and by Saturday, he found himself wondering how he'd survived so many years of monotony. Despite his fear of the unknown and the augury he'd earlier envisioned and thought to avoid, he knew that his life on its current trajectory could not continue.

Barks had indicated that his dinner party was to be an occasion of note, so Mr dressed accordingly. Crisp white shirt and tie, gold cufflinks, a tuxedo jacket with peaked lapels and pressed pants. Shoes polished. He was pleased that he'd made the effort when Mrs appeared in watered blue silk and wearing a fur stole. She placed her gloved hand in his and they made their way to the pony cart. Mr thought of the Trusty, and an exciting midnight romp in such clothes, but a glance at Mrs' pinched features reminded him of the reality of their union. Mrs would not enjoy such an adventure. At least, not with him.

Natterjack Hall was well-lit. Young George met them in the driveway – Mr supposed his services were for hire equally – and led their cart away to be looked after along with the other vehicles Mr could see tucked around the side of the house: one or two other pony carts, but also a racy mint green AC motor car, an elegant Sunbeam two-seater, and a pretty red Morris. Impressive, it would seem, the people Woody Barks knew. He didn't see a motorcycle, but he and George exchanged a gleaming eye, and Mr suspected the lad was thinking of the Trusty, same as him.

After seeing George in the driveway Mr had expected to find Eliza taking coats and serving drinks, but a plump, dark-haired girl whom Mr thought he might have seen in the Puss and Boots production at the Lesser Plumpton School of the Arts fundraiser dipped her knee at the door. Mr wondered with momentary strangulation if she'd been at the after-party, and seen him asleep on the floor. He avoided her gaze and handed over his outer coat. Mrs kept her fox stole, as was fashionable, and barely acknowledged the girl. They went through to the parlour where the rest of the guests had gathered, drinks in hand. A footman – gracious, at Natterjack Hall amongst the botanicals! – paused with a tray of drinks, and Mrs accepted a pink frothy creation, while Mr took an amber measure of what appeared to be plain old Scottish whisky. No absinthe tonight, he promised himself with a grimace, though in fact there was none on offer.

Sipping his whisky, glancing around, Mr saw Woody Barks separate himself from a knot of guests and make his way towards them. He wore his dress uniform, buttons a-gleam and tall black boots polished, and even Mr could not help but be impressed. Mrs, he noted, nearly swooned, and clutched Mr's arm, which he thought rather indecorous. He supposed she had forgiven Woody, as she seemed to have forgiven him, for his inadequacies in dealing with Amos the goat. As the lieutenant-colonel arrived at their side Mrs tittered happily and strolled away with their host without a backward glance. Mr sipped his drink and watched them go, feeling surprisingly little more than annoyance at being thus ignored and abandoned. He turned and moved off in the opposite direction, pausing to mingle with a haha here and hoho there, eventually taking up a spot next to a potted palm.

"Good evening, sar," came a voice at his shoulder, the words almost whispered, and he turned to see Eliza, although not the Eliza his wife would recognise. Her eyes were painted with black kohl, not theatrically and with exaggeration as they'd been for her stage number at the Lesser Plumpton School of the Arts, but subtly, with smoky edges that gave her a rather melancholic appeal. She wore a skull-fitting cap of some sparkling gold fabric beneath which her red curls lay in long ringlets, and a thin-strapped dress of a similar material that hung, tube-like, over her slender frame, not quite reaching the ankles that Mr had ogled on more than one occasion. He could see her shoes; not serviceable flats but dainty cream leather with a heel that made her rather a bit taller than Mr. Overall it was quite a becoming ensemble, Mr supposed, but probably not something one would find tucked away in the bureau of a serving maid. As usual, where Eliza was concerned, he didn't quite know what to think, and was surprised to feel irritation.

"'Tis me, sar, Eliza," she said, keeping her voice low, and grinned, revealing the gap in her front teeth.

Mr took a second, bracing sip of his whisky, and straightened his back, hoping he hadn't appeared to be gawking. "I see that," he replied, somewhat frostily. "You look nothing like her, though. Do all these people know you're my maid?" The question felt immediately mean, but it was too late to take it back.

Her grin slid to a frown. "If you're worried about Mrs Isbister recognizing me, she just swanned past me without battin' an eye. And the rest of 'em? Well, I never met most of these people. They're Lieutenant-Colonel Barks's friends. A few, like me, are here at me brother's invitation."

"Of course, of course," he said, nodding his head but refusing to meet her eyes. "Your brother – whatever his name is." His annoyance with Stephen Vanson and that one's as yet unexplained masquerade was getting the better of him in the moment, he knew, even as he inwardly chastised himself for his rudeness. Surely none of it was her fault?

"He ought to explain that," she acknowledged.

"He ought," Mr said in a clipped tone.

"For tonight, though, could we just enjoy the party?" she asked, giving him her most winning smile. "I had a peek at the table cards. We're seated next to one another at dinner. We might as well get on, don't you think?"

Mr harrumphed, but as ever was won over by either her logic or her presence. Together they circulated through the room, pausing near little clusters of people and joining in conversation here and there when they were acknowledged. Mr spotted Stephen – Captain Plucky – dressed stylishly and with his dark hair oiled and parted as precisely as if he'd used a ruler, but he moved, as they did, from group to group, staying just beyond them and never within greeting distance. Mr wondered if that was intentional. He also noticed that his wife and Woody seemed to have disappeared. Perhaps he was showing her the garden. Harold had a wonderful collection of bronzed insects and amphibians there, of which the greatest was the natterjack toad perched at the front door. And though it bothered Mr that Stephen Vanson avoided him and that Woody Barks had appropriated his wife – inappropriately – Eliza clung to his arm, which went a long way to making up for both those transgressions. That she transformed so completely into this – well, say it – pulchritudinous being gave him a moment's pause, and indeed it also flickered through his mind that she was as talented a mime as her chameleon-like brother. But there was an evening to get through, amidst company he might not otherwise enjoy were it not for her presence, no matter her incarnation.

"Eliza!" cried a familiar voice, and Mr saw Julio, the dwarf from the Lesser Plumpton School of the Arts approaching through the milling guests. A tall, overly angular woman in an exotic turban-style headdress had her hand draped over his shoulder as if afraid she might lose track of him. Julio was dressed not unlike Mr in white tie, and, spying Mr alongside Eliza, his grin widened.

"Roddy! Lovely to see you again, although when last we crossed paths you were – shall we just say, less alert?" he grinned, and Mr, mortified, glanced around, though no one appeared to have heard, or be paying them any heed.

"Mr – er –" Mr began, and faltered, realizing he had no last name to call upon for Julio. And despite their previous acquaintance, and the fact that Julio had felt no need to stand on formality, it was the thing done, to use a last name until invited otherwise.

"Quint," Eliza supplied, giving Mr's arm a surreptitious squeeze that Julio noted pointedly.

"Please," Julio said, holding up his hands. "I am Julio. Surely two who have experienced the charm of the green fairy together as we have are on a first name basis." He grinned and raised his brows at Mr and the woman beside him laughed, a surprisingly manly sound. Without being obvious Mr peered a little closer, and noted the woman's overly bony wrists and bobbing Adam's apple. And was that the faintest of stubble on the woman's upper lip? It was quite possible, Mr surmised, that she was in fact a he. He'd heard of such things, but in his buttoned-down world had not seen it firsthand.

With an effort he drew his gaze back to Julio. "Regarding our last – crossing of paths, as you put it, I fear I owe you an apology," Mr began bravely, resisting the urge to glance at Julio's friend and to reach up and run a loosening finger round his overly restrictive shirt collar.

"Nonsense," Julio interrupted. He turned to his companion, who appeared to be listening with bored disinterest. "As Maggie here would agree, anything goes at the house of Quint."

"Hello, Magnus," Eliza interjected, smiling and touching Maggie's arm. That one returned the smile, revealing large, square teeth behind painted lips, and Mr suddenly recollected Julio at the cast party in the company of a tall man in a long plaid skirt. He thought it likely that Maggie/Magnus was one and the same.

Just then, a gong sounded, the call to dinner, and the four acquaintances followed the other guests to the dining room, where a long table had been elegantly set with Natterjack Hall's finest china and impeccably polished silverware. The chandeliers sparkled overhead, and the wall sconces were lit with white tapers. Mr, forgetting for a moment that Mrs was somewhere in the press of people, was pleased to feel Eliza's hand tucked into the crook of his arm. He was certain he escorted the loveliest woman present, and flushed with the pleasure of the thought. They found their seats next to one another, as Eliza had said, and Mr held out her chair with gentlemanly aplomb.

It was a very long table, seating at least thirty guests, placed in the traditional Victorian custom of man, woman, man, woman. To Mr's right was an elderly matron with a tiara. To Eliza's left, Julio. Across from him, almost obscured by one of the enormous floral sprays set at intervals down the length of the table, sat Stephen Vanson – aka Captain Plucky. Mr was not letting up where Stephen was concerned, no matter how pleasant his sister. He tried to catch his eye to glare, but Stephen was occupied with pulling out a chair for the lady to his left, while keeping up a steady stream of banter in what Mr had come to think of as his "London man" accent.

Woody and Mrs entered the room through a different door from the rest of the guests. Mrs' colour was rather high, Mr noted shrewdly, feeling the corners of his mouth pull down into a frown. He watched as Woody took the chair at the head, first seating Mrs to his right, she all a-beam and a-titter. Spouses were not usually next to one another at dinner parties such as this, so Mr had not expected to sit with his wife, but the place to the host's right was usually reserved for someone of special importance. That Mrs had been given that honour could be construed as simply a nice gesture towards a friendly neighbour, Mr supposed. He looked round the room to see if any brows were raised, or if there were knowing glances being exchanged, but it appeared no one else noted anything untoward in the seating arrangements. Mr watched Mrs fan herself with girlish coyness as Woody leaned to whisper something, and the two of them laughed, sharing a look, and it occurred to Mr that there was something of the young Alice there, the one he'd groped beneath the sheets on a murky wedding night umpteen years ago, and whom he'd not seen since. It was happiness he was witnessing, he thought, staring. Something he rarely saw at home. She glowed. Her hair, wound into its usual chignon, appeared less tightly pulled, the texture softer, the colour not so lacklustre. Her cheeks were flushed rather than ruddy, and the jowls wreathing her jaw managed to seem perky instead of mopey. Mr looked down at his empty plate, considering his feelings. There was some jealousy; she was *his* wife, after all; and some embarrassment. No man wants to be cuckolded so blatantly. With surprise he decided his feelings could best be described as bland, and he realised he did not begrudge her obvious happiness with the bold Lieutenant-Colonel Barks. Instead, he was perhaps disappointed, not with the fact of their almost non-existent marriage, *that* was nothing new, but with himself for being the kind of person others felt they could ignore. Somewhere in there was a lesson to himself, and he vowed to give it a good bit of navel-gaze in short order.

The dinner was long: six courses, though in the more formal days before the war Mr had sat through twelve, so he wasn't bothered. He avoided glancing towards the end of the table but it was difficult to ignore Woody Barks' loud voice and louder laugh, and Mrs' chiming in. Conversation followed the old custom of so many minutes spent talking with one's neighbour to the left, then so many to the right. Usually, guests took their cue for the change in banter from the lady of the house, but there currently being no one formally in that role, Barks himself led the company through dinner. Unfortunately for Mr, in more ways than one, Woody preferred to converse with Mrs, sitting on his right. That meant that all the other male guests were to chat similarly with their neighbour to the right, and for Mr, that was a dowager called Mrs Smilton, or was it Stilton, who dribbled her soup and smacked her lips. Mr found next to nothing in common with Mrs Stilton/Smilton, and she seemed to be hard of hearing, so most of what he said met with little or no response.

Now and again, though, Woody at the head of the table recalled his duty and turned to the person on his left. The rest of the male guests followed suit, and Mr, to his relief, got a few moments with Eliza. She, with Julio on her other side, often turned to Mr with laughter on her face, and he made an effort to appear as jovial.

"Are you enjoying the evening?" he asked her on only his third chance at conversation. They were already on the salad course, which meant that dinner would soon be over, and the ladies would retire while the men remained behind and smoked. At least, that was the way things had been done before the war, and Woody Barks did seem to be a man for whom traditions held some sway.

"Oh, indeed, sar," she said, batting her smoky eyes his way. "Julio is always so full of tales. A body could listen to him all night and never get bored."

"No," said Mr, agreeing, but sourly. The evening had taken a downward turn, and little green horns of jealousy sprouted. He, after all, was so boring he couldn't even keep his own wife. He scowled at the food on his plate, and poked at it with his fork.

"I got your note," she said, her voice low. It took Mr a moment to glean her reference, but then he remembered. Of course. The note he'd left on his tray, confessing regret for his behaviour at Julio Quint's party. He a-hemmed into his napkin. "Truth be," Eliza continued, "I don't see the need for an apology. It were all in fun, were it not?"

"I – I suppose it were – I mean, it was," he replied hesitantly, shrugging. "It's just not done, is all."

"What's not done? Fun?" she asked, smiling, but obviously puzzled.

"Well, fun of that sort," he said lamely. "What we did…"

"We didn't do nothing I wouldn't do again," she replied, turning to her salad and selecting a tomato.

"Sleeping on the floor?" he said, blanching.

"Even that," she said, tilting her chin. Then, curses to Woody Barks, they were changing again, and Eliza's attention returned to Julio and his witticisms. Mr turned reluctantly to Mrs Stilton/Smilton, but she'd fallen asleep over her iceberg lettuce. The dessert course couldn't come soon enough.

*

There was smoking after the meal, and brandy, but if Mr had thought he might corner Stephen Vanson – Captain Plucky – for a word he was mistaken. The captain regaled several of the other male guests with tales of his war exploits, something that might have been a gloomy subject, but left to the charismatic captain, was all but a comedy show. If any of them felt Captain Plucky had given himself a platform they didn't let on, laughing and chortling and sucking on their cigars, happy to be entertained. Mr half expected them to launch into a chorus of Tipperary, and be done.

At the far end of the table the lieutenant-colonel was not to be outdone, and had his own group of toadies hanging on his every word. The air was thick with the smoke from the cigars, and ash littered the tablecloth. Mr hoped they had a good laundress, for Harold's sake. Mr, not a cigar smoker by choice, did on occasion partake of a cigarillo when on offer, and that was his choice this evening. Julio, he noticed, made the same selection. Together, neither enthralled with the war tales of their hosts, they puffed in relatively companionable silence, although Throck's method of smoking was unconventional, and did not involve inhaling the vile stuff. At length, out of simple curiosity and not because he felt the need for words, Mr turned to Julio.

"Have you lived in these parts long?" he asked.

Julio blew a few smoke rings and smiled. "A few years. Not long, in the grand scheme. I've been around. Paris, before the war. Snuck away before things got horrible. I ran an establishment there, then another when I landed in London."

"Indeed," Mr said. He sipped his brandy and decided not to ask what Julio meant by establishment. "And how did you end up in Lesser Plumpton?"

"Needs must, my dear Roddy," Julio replied evasively, grinning. He sucked on his cigarillo, and blew a stream of smoke, disturbing the already blue air. He eyed Mr, as if considering whether to share more, then said, "A friend was in a bit of a bind, and I helped out, part of which entailed coming here. An opportunity presented itself, and … Fanny's your aunt, as young Stephen would say." He raised his brows at Mr, his grin mischievous.

"Speaking of Stephen –" Mr began, but then Woody at the end of the table tapped on his glass with a spoon to draw the company's attention, and it was time to go through to join the ladies. Mr gnashed his teeth, stubbed out his barely smoked cigarillo and tossed back his brandy.

In the drawing room a game of charades had been organised, and Mr found himself part of a team that consisted of himself, Eliza, Julio, Maggie, Stephen/Captain Plucky, and another female guest who was quickly introduced to Mr, although he never did catch her name. Mrs, he noticed, was on Woody's team, no great surprise, and on account of his rank as host, Woody took the lead, standing before his guests as they clapped, his hands raised.

"For those of you who've never played, charades is a French game –" The guests interrupted with good-natured boos and hisses. Even post-war, who loved the French, after all? Woody, grinning, held up his hands again to quiet the catcalls. "Never mind that. In the English version –" cheers this time – "we play in teams, and every time your team correctly guesses the charade as enacted by their fellow member, they earn a point. The actor may not speak or make any noise, he simply mimes the challenge on the card he has drawn. And there's a time limit, so if the gong sounds and your team hasn't yet figured out the charade, you get nothing. At the end of the evening, whichever team has the most points, wins."

"Wins what?" someone called. Woody smiled, and his eyes locked, momentarily, oddly and almost challengingly, on Mr's.

"Something special," he said, his smirk evasive. He held up his hands again, quelling more questions. "Enough! Let the game commence!"

Someone passed a bowl, and each team selected a folded paper to determine order of play. Mr's team, calling themselves, in laughing self-deprecation, the Misfits, drew a 1, so they were first up. Mr huddled with his fellow members, but uncertain of the game as he'd never played, he let the others determine strategy. It was decided that Eliza would start, she having some stage experience, and Mr nodded his agreement, for what it was worth. She bounced up, put her hand in a second bowl proffered by a footman, and withdrew their team's challenge. She frowned over it for a moment, then at Julio's call "time's ticking," she shrugged and crouched on the floor, her knees bent to her elbows, a difficult manoeuvre in a cylindrically shaped dress such as she wore. Her shoulders were hunched and her hands splayed on the carpet, and Mr immediately thought of a frog, but unsure, glanced over at his fellow team members.

"Frog!" called Stephen, confident. Eliza gave a small shake of her head and, still in her crouched pose, made a sort of lumbering hop. Mr frowned in puzzlement. Surely she was just that – a frog.

"Frenchman!" Julio called, and the room erupted in laughter.

"Ten seconds!" called Woody. Eliza gave an exasperated toss of her head and looked straight at Mr. Still in her froglike pose, she opened her mouth wide, as if in a yell, and Mr knew intuitively what she was trying to mimic.

"Five seconds!" Woody interjected, heightening the tension.

"The natterjack," Mr said, almost stumbling over the words in his sudden certainty. "It's the natterjack toad, of course."

Eliza jumped up, fists in the air like an Olympic runner first through the finish line, and their team, suddenly realizing they'd won the round, though not quite certain how, capered and cheered, and clapped Mr on the back.

"Round one to the Misfits for correctly guessing the word 'toad'," Woody cried good-naturedly, and the guests' focus turned to the next team. Eliza flopped onto the thickly cushioned sofa next to Mr, and beamed. He stared at the gap between her teeth, feeling happy.

"Natterjack toad, eh Roddy? Rather specific," Julio said, leaning across Eliza to grin at Mr. "How you got *that* out of whatever Eliza was doing is a story the two of you will have to share one of these days." He laughed and sat back, turning his attention to the charade that had the floor.

The game went for several rounds, and when the points were tallied, the Misfits were tied with their host's team, the Imperiums. The room had become a bit rowdy, Mr noticed, not without excitement. Several of the ladies had doffed their gloves, and one or two white ties had been loosened. Mr himself kept his knot tidy, the proximity of Eliza tonight and the recent memory of his green fairy adventure ensuring his caution. For the final, deciding match, the time allotted for each team to correctly guess their charade was halved, and the pressure was indeed on. Mr moved to the edge of his seat, eager to do his part as a member of the Misfits. It would be Eliza again, pantomiming, he thought. She was their best weapon. But to his horror, Stephen reached over and tapped him with one long finger.

"You're up, Roddy," he said.

"What? I? No, no, no…" Mr protested. First, he would not be a good mime. Second, he detested the limelight. Third, he would fail, and let down his team, and that must not happen.

"It's the rules, Roddy," Julio said, adding his prod. "We've all had a go. Now it's your turn. Do us proud, gov."

Eliza gave him a gentle push paired with an encouraging look, and Mr, knees a-quiver, stood up and faced the room. The laughing, boisterous crowd now seemed to cackle at him, a hyena pack sensing prey. He saw Woody's eyes on him, and though that one was smiling in a friendly enough way through his fat whiskers, Mr couldn't help notice that he sat alongside Mrs on a settle for two, and that one arm rested on the seatback behind her. Nothing improper, Mr acknowledged, but passively possessive. Sick with embarrassment and certain of his own inadequacy, knowing he was about to fail, Mr accepted the piece of paper presented by the expressionless footman and opened it. 'Floor,' it read.

Silence fell over the assemblage. Mr made a small noise that was fear, but might have been construed by the more optimistic as a giggle. Floor, he thought to himself, standing upon one. And yet, he had learned, the rules did not allow one to simply point to the object one was supposed to describe by mime and gesture. He wished said floor would simply open and swallow him.

"Half the time, Roddy," Stephen warned. "Make a move."

Mr grimaced. More pressure was precisely the thing he did not need. How did one mime a floor? He made a stomping gesture with his foot, trying to indicate solidity and something beneath one, but that only brought cries of "dance!" and "tantrum." He frowned, scouring his brain, trying to think of another tactic. Perhaps a more architectural approach was in order. He traced an uncertain box shape in the air, adding the peak of a roof.

"House!" called Eliza, encouraging.

Mr shook his head, and redrew the house shape, emphasizing the straight line at the bottom that indicated the floor and the word they needed to say.

"Home?" Julio asked.

"River!" cried Stephen's lady friend. "A river in front of a house!"

"Ten seconds!" Woody called from across the room.

Mr's heart sank even further than it already had. He suspected it was in his boots. Then, suddenly, a wild idea came to him and he looked at Eliza, catching her gaze and holding it. Making his best effort at theatre, he mimicked waltzing with an invisible partner, then sank to the carpet and closed his eyes, laying his head upon the pillow of his hands with a satisfied smile. He wondered if she would put it together with his drawing of a house and understand.

"Time!" cried Woody, and Mr got to his feet. There was clapping, but the Misfits had lost. He sat on the sofa next to Eliza, and despite the backslapping of his team mates, and words of reassurance that he'd done well in spite of the loss, he was disappointed.

"What was the word?" someone among the guests called. And before Mr could reply, Eliza said, "floor," and shrugged. "It were obvious, but we weren't quick enough." There was laughter and chatter, and opinions expressed on how one might otherwise articulate the word, and in the midst of it, Eliza gave Mr a knowing glance, and added quietly, "It were rather clever, actually. I might've got it with five more seconds." Stephen leaned in, interrupting the moment, and said to the team at large, "We've still got a chance. If Woody's team doesn't get their challenge either, then we do it again."

Mr, relaxed now that he was no longer in the spotlight, watched with incredulity as Mrs rose, her colour high, and dipped a little curtsey to her team. In the many years he and Mrs had been wed he was certain she had never played a game even remotely like charades. He also would have maintained that the woman he was married to would have steadfastly refused to take part in such silliness, play-acting in front of guests and with everyone hooting and hollering. *Charades*, he would have thought, would have come out of her mouth just the way *art* had, as though accompanied by the taste of fish gone off. Yet there she stood in her billowing blue gown, fox stole long discarded with the warmth of the room, delivering her rendition of a swan – for that's what their team's challenge word turned out to be – with all the grace of a capable actress. Woody, guessing the word correctly, got to his feet and gave Mrs an ovation, and she, blushing, took a bow.

"Do you think that was fixed?" Stephen asked no one in particular, clapping along with everyone else but watching Woody and grinning slyly.

"Team Imperium!" Woody cried, rising with his team mates. "Outside! Outside! Our prize awaits! Everyone, join us!"

The footman gathered wraps and cloaks. It took some time before everyone had been helped into their outer wear and had pulled on their gloves, and Mr, with Eliza, was among the last to emerge from the front doors of Natterjack Hall onto the moonlit and lantern-lit gravel of the drive. It was impossible, at the back of the clustered guests, to see what was causing the commotion of oohs and aahs, but then through a parting, Mr saw headlamps and heard the noise of an engine.

"A charabanc!" someone cried. "What fun!"

And someone else said, "And a motorcycle. Exciting!"

Mr heard the unmistakeable pop pop pop of a Triumph, and pushing to the front of the crowd, saw Woody Barks in helmet and goggles, seated on Mr's own Trusty. Mrs, looking both frightened and excited, was squeezed into the sidecar with a somewhat manic grin on her face, and Mr's cozy rug was pulled up to her round chin. Next to the motorcycle, a shiny topless charabanc idled. The other members of the Imperiums had already taken up their seats in the long vehicle, and there was room for more – room, in fact, for all of Woody's guests. They began piling in, exclaiming their excitement, but Mr, frozen in place at the raw nerve of Woody, who must have somehow stolen the Trusty from Mr's shed for the occasion, and at his further audacity in stealing his wife at the same time, and further yet at Mrs' happy collusion in this utter overrunning of Mr's dignity as a man and a husband, shouted loudly, and pointed his finger at Woody and Mrs.

"No!" he yelled, livid. "I forbid it! Get out of that Trusty right now!" His face, he felt sure, was bright red with anger, his eyes popping like a madman's. He stalked forward, shaking off Stephen bloody Plucky's staying hand. The other guests, slow to notice the commotion, were still laughing and chattering as they claimed seats in the long, open autobus, but as they settled, they nudged one another, pointing to Mr and his shuddering wrath.

"You have no right!" Mr shouted, the words directed at Woody, for after all, that one had stolen his motorcycle. But of course, Mr's ownership of the motorcycle was a secret. He kept it hidden in a shed so the very woman who was now seated in it, enjoying it, and gaping at his outburst, would not discover her husband's deceit. Instead, it appeared that Mr was in fact displaying almost insane jealousy, and that likelihood seemed further confirmed when Mr screeched, "I will not stand for this!"

Woody, calm as a lieutenant-colonel used to battle, waved the charabanc on, and gunned the Trusty. "Calm down, Throck. It's just a motorcycle ride. We'll be back by midnight!" He pressed the throttle and steered the machine down the lane. Mrs' shriek of delight and fright echoed into the night air.

Mr stood, trembling, both shocked at his own outburst and outraged at Woody's blatant theft of his motorcycle. Blanching, aghast, the Trusty now out of sight in the dark, he turned back to Natterjack Hall. Eliza stood there, alone. Stephen, Mr supposed dully, must have hopped on the charabanc and gone for a ride with the rest who didn't care that Woody Barks was a liar and a thief and a wife-stealer.

"He stole my Trusty," he said to Eliza, lamely. He felt like crying, but knew that would never do. He, and she, would be most awfully embarrassed were he to do that.

"I don't think he did, sar," she answered. "He borrowed it, is all. An' he probably don't even know it's yours."

Mr frowned, puzzled. "What do you mean?"

"I think probably Stephen took it, borrowed it. For the party, like. For a lark. For Lieutenant-Colonel Barks to have a bit o' fun."

"He did?" Mr asked, his anger renewed, and re-directed.

"'Twould be just like our Stephen," she said apologetically. "He don't have a good sense of right and wrong, I'm afraid. He wouldn't've done it out o' meanness, you see, but out of friendship. For Woody."

"He had no right," Mr said petulantly.

"He hadn't," Eliza agreed. They stood in silence for a moment, the moonlight and the driveway's lit lanterns casting a shallow glow. "I'm cold," she said.

Mr sighed. His anger had deflated, and he was left with a bereft sort of emptiness. He looked at Eliza, shivering in her thin dress, and no wrap to warm her. He shrugged out of his own coat and put it around her shoulders.

"Mrs Isbister and I came in the pony cart. Shall we find it, and George, and go home?"

Chapter 12
MISFORTUNES

Two days later, the Trusty was back beneath its oiled tarp, snug in the toolshed behind the greenhouse. Eliza had assured Mr of its eventual return, and, trusting her, he'd waited, although not patiently, checking almost hourly until on the second day after the party, he'd noticed tyre tracks on the path next to the greenhouse, and there she was. He pulled back the tarp and checked her from stem to stern, so to speak, but there were no new scratches or dents. He tightened a nut or two, oiled the chain and checked the petrol, then gave her a good and lusty polish. Outside, he used a pine branch to sweep away the tell-tale tread marks on the garden path, and retreated to the greenhouse to putter and pot and ruminate on the misfortunes of life.

Mr had not come across Mrs since the party. She'd been indisposed, Eliza reported, back in her role as housemaid, and Mr, sniffing disdainfully, chose not to care. He took his meals in his room, and spent his waking hours in the greenhouse or with his nose in a book, passing time. Repeatedly, his thoughts got the better of him, and he found himself re-reading paragraphs, the words trotting by incomprehensibly, or digging up and subsequently repotting the same cutting of a plant, with no idea as to why he'd done it. What occupied his mind, he came to realise, was a bigger question involving the meaning of life. Was he destined to simply while away the years in domestic unhappiness, clocking time, as the working man put it, never following a dream or having an adventure or caring about someone more than he cared about himself? He wasn't a young man. He had grey hair – what wiry bits were left of it – and wrinkled skin and his feet smelled when he pulled off his wellies. Was this – and in his mind's eye he waved a hand in an expansive gesture that took in his current lacklustre surroundings – as far as his life would reach? The thought that it might be sent him to his room, and into his marmalade-stained nightshirt, contemplating, yet again, the paisleys of his carpet.

The only time there was much lucidity to his thinking was when he was walking the woodland path that wound beneath the overhanging branches of trees and edged the brook between Sowerby Grange and Natterjack Hall. Harold Guppletwill had named the wild tract of land Whortleberry Wood on account of the many bushes of that variety growing along the banks of the creek, and Mr smiled fondly, recalling the two of them with mouths made blue by the plant's delicious berries. There'd been much laughter in those days, but serious discussion too, and although Harold was the Oxford scholar, he had seemed to value Mr's opinions and observations, and when they were together, Mr certainly felt every measure Harold's equal. His memories of those times were most poignant within Whortleberry Wood, and, walking there, smelling bog rot and fungi and moist greens, he recalled Harold's voice and his whisper of a laugh. "We're two different pods," Harold had said to him once, after a particularly excellent afternoon of conversation and genial argument, "but we're both peas."

The sights and smells of the wood and the cathartic memories the path invoked never failed to improve Mr's mood, and a day spent in morose contemplation of his bedroom slippers could always be rescued by a walk along the brook. This was his occupation one evening, just before dusk, a couple of days after the return of the Trusty. He'd decided, earlier, that the only one suffering from his reclusive behaviour was himself, so he'd put on his favourite corduroy jacket, elbows shiny from wear, popped his flat cap over the equally shiny bald spot on his head, tugged his wellies over thick socks that he'd snugged up over his worn and faded trousers, and went out into Whortleberry Wood. He paused just long enough on his way by to check the shed door and found it secure; he'd installed a hasp and a padlock since the theft. He was taking no chances with Stephen, who had difficulty, it was now proved, with honesty and possession.

Mr exited through the old iron gate, promising himself yet again that he would repair its broken hinge and shore up its anchoring post. He didn't mind such chores, relished them in fact, or once had. Lately the Grange and her upkeep didn't hold much interest for him. Whether or not the gate hung crooked or the flagstones on the path to the laundry yard were loose or the glass in the roof of the greenhouse rattled seemed inconsequential. Once, he'd have made notes in a tidy little journal about things that needed doing, or had been done, either by him or the man Friday from Watton Hoo Mr called upon for odd jobs. Now, he couldn't seem to think straight unless it was to daydream about the motorcycle in the shed, or to picture his life as any but the one he had.

He walked on, enjoying the squish of damp on the spongy path. The yellow limestone of Sowerby Grange had long disappeared from view, and in Whortleberry Wood, daylight was making a slow and regal exit, shrouding the flora and fauna in a soft mantle of gold. Insects sparkled, and spider webs hung like gossamer lace. Bees fat with pollen droned past, lazy in the sweet evening air. The further the sun sank, the more intense became the gilding, so reeds transformed into shards of amber, branches were burnished copper, and green leaves shimmered emerald. If Mr had believed in a realm of fairies he might have thought he had stumbled upon one, such was the wood's other-worldly beauty.

Had Harold been there, they might have argued over which artist best would do justice to this splendour. Mr, traipsing the path, smiled to imagine it. Given Harold's propensity for botanicals and the detail and simplicity of scientific drawing, Mr suspected he might be inclined toward Arthur Rackham, whose drawings for *The Fairy Tales of the Brothers Grimm* and *Peter Pan* and other classics had earned him a well-deserved reputation as a master illustrator. Mr himself felt sure the English painter John Simmons was the man for the job. Mr had once perused a book at the Lesser Plumpton School of the Arts that had focused on Simmons' watercolours of ethereal scenes, and Mr thought his capture of the glow and glitter, his attention to detail and, as the book had described it, his "blurring of boundaries" was a perfect match for the magic he was seeing in Whortleberry Wood this night. Harold might even concede, Mr thought, imagining his friend's indulgent chuckle.

The sun had almost completely sunk away, and the golds and coppers were fast fading. The path Mr walked, squelching in his wellingtons, was rather dark now, and he stumbled more than once over rocks and roots he could not see. Just as he'd decided to turn back, he heard a noise on the track in front of him. He peered into the evenfall, certain something was there but unable to make out a shape. Despite the stillness of the wood with which he was familiarly comfortable, he felt a small shiver of fright. Fairies and magical creatures, fantastical as they were, did not scare him; rather, he was wary of more flesh and bone adversaries. Boars and wolves had been gone from these parts for more than 300 years, but rogues, rascals and footpads surely lurked. Vagabonds and nomads of the more harmless sort also roamed, and since the war's end many an unemployed ex-soldier had knocked at Sowerby Grange's kitchen entrance with a crutch or a look of melancholy, begging a bowl of broth. Sowerby Grange never turned anyone away, and on that score Mr and Mrs agreed.

The shadow on the footpath moved and grunted, and Mr, grasping a stick, peered into the darkness, and called, "Who's there?"

Through the murk came a snort and a thunder – hooves, he realised at the last moment, leaping off the path and out of the way of Amos, the deranged goat. As the creature ran past him, eyes yellow and wild, Mr marveled at the size of him, and saw that the animal again had a garment flapping from his horns. Underwear, this time. Longish, and flannel, the rear hatch a-flutter. Mr hoped they weren't his own, or if they were, they did not have his name stitched into the waistband.

When Amos' hooves could no longer be heard thudding down the track and Mr's heart had stopped pounding, he began the walk back to Sowerby Grange. Despite his encounter – benign, after all – with Amos the goat, he was reluctant to leave Whortleberry Wood. The thought of returning to the musty carpets and silence of his rooms inside the house gave him no pleasure, and when the white walls of the greenhouse hove into view, the toolshed beckoned from the tangle of briars and nettles behind it, and like metal to a magnet he went there and sat on the doorstep. The evening had grown damp and the air heavy. Moisture had begun to cling to the hedges of the garden, and the path he'd just come down that led from Whortleberry Wood was now invisible, hung with tendrils of mist. It was one of those nights, he thought, his whimsical side winning out over the sensible, when things happened.

As if on cue, Stephen Vanson appeared round the corner of the greenhouse, and although Mr was startled by his sudden appearance in the darkness of the yard, he suspected Stephen was even more surprised to encounter Mr, for he jumped back like a boy caught pinching a biscuit.

Both men recovered quickly, and Mr said testily, "If you've come to steal my motorcycle again I've put a lock on my shed."

Suave Stephen missed only a beat or two before replying with a chuckle, his slick London accent tucked away in a pocket in favour of the West Country burr he'd had when Mr first met him. "Aw, Roddy, no 'arm done, eh mate? 'T'were Woody's day, an' all. I think we did 'im proud." He sat on the doorstep alongside Mr, gave him an elbow and grinned. "Your Mrs were a game bird. I hadn't pegged 'er for the sort."

Mr scowled, refusing to be coddled. Stephen Vanson had more to answer for than theft, although that in itself was plenty. And whether or not Mrs had giggled her way into tomfoolery was beside the point, and also not Stephen Vanson's concern.

"The lieutenant-colonel. Does he know who you are?" Mr asked. Best to come at him full bore, he thought, give him no chance to squirm his way out of honest answers.

Stephen laughed and shrugged. "'E knows I'm Captain Plucky, 58th London. We've exchanged a war story or two. Mine are authentic, in a roundabout way. Dunno 'bout 'is."

"I think you take me for a fool," Mr said, his tone surly.

Stephen gave a derisive snort. "I rode motorcycles in the war. Did I ever tell you that? One of me fellow riders, an American bloke, used to say "every man is a damn fool for at least five minutes each day. The wise fella don't exceed the limit." He chuckled and shook his head. "He died, that 'un. Gangrene. Bloody awful way to go. Sliced 'imself tryin' to open a tin o' beans. Guess 'e should've timed 'imself."

Mr didn't know how to respond to that, so he sat in silence. *Had* Stephen been in the war? The man was an utter conundrum, at best. At least, he was a charlatan.

"Tell you what, Roddy me 'ansum," Stephen said. "Let's roll out the Trusty and take a prowl down the pub. 'Tis a fit night for it." He nudged Mr in the ribs, and grinned. Mr could see the white of his teeth shining in the darkness. "I'll tell you all about me troubles, if it's a tale you're after," Stephen said, coaxing. "Where me mother was born, an' all."

Mr eyed him suspiciously. Nothing Stephen said or promised was ever completely honest, but maybe this was a chance to get the truth of a few matters out on the table, so to speak. Had he been duped when Stephen sold him the Trusty? Had there ever been a sick child? How had Stephen come to be living at Natterjack Hall, and most importantly, what was his game?

"Alright, then," Mr agreed, standing up and brushing dirt from his trousers. "I'm up for a story or two." He retrieved the key for the shed lock from beneath an upturned pot, making a mental note as he opened the door that he'd have to find a new place to hide it, or keep it on his person if he didn't want Captain Plucky to come borrowing again. Stephen helped him pull off the tarp, and held the door wide while Mr backed the bike carefully through the opening. Together they pushed the Trusty through the garden and down the lane, and when they were out of sight of the house, Mr dug his helmet and goggles out of the satchel and tugged them on.

"Light the headlamp, if you please," he directed. He intended to take charge of this evening from the outset. Stephen Vanson might be a slick character, but he'd find he was no match for Mr on his toes. Mr harrumphed to himself, and started the bike.

Stephen suggested the Pig and Whistle in the village of Watton Hoo, the local where Mr had first met Stephen, and where the two of them had made the deal on the Trusty. It was also the place Mr had gone with Eliza that first time, and where, to his shame, she'd had to drive them home. Squaring his jaw, asserting himself, feeling contrary, Mr instead turned west towards Lesser Plumpton, a stretch of road with more twists and turns and hills than its eastern counterpart. Stephen, looming large in the sidecar, went gamely along with the decision. Never mind that Mr wasn't familiar with pubs in Lesser Plumpton, and when they arrived in the village he had to ask Stephen for directions.

They parked outside an establishment called the Cock and Bull, and Mr eyed Stephen dubiously, wondering if there was some double entendre in his choice, and he intended feeding Mr a lot of made-up stories. But the pub looked welcoming enough. Its lights were bright and its shutters were glossy red, and the metal sign that swung over the entrance boasted its name in tidily painted letters. They entered, and as they did several heads turned. Quite a few of the patrons nodded and tipped caps, knowing Stephen it would seem. That one slung his arm familiarly over Mr's shoulders, as if they were close mates, and Mr couldn't see how he could shrug it off without appearing an ass.

"Coupla pints, Biddy, love!" Stephen called to the barmaid, and steered his captive towards a booth in a corner. There, Stephen released him, and they sat on opposite sides of a rectangular plank table, shiny with many years' worth of elbow rubs.

"Do you frequent all the locals?" Mr asked, sourly. It annoyed him that no matter where he met Stephen Vanson it seemed to be his home turf, and people knew and liked him.

"I do me best, Roddy, mate," Stephen answered, and grinned at the barmaid as she plunked two pints of a dark and foamy brew in front of them, then swaggered away, tossing a look at Stephen over her shoulder.

"I'm not your mate," Mr said petulantly.

"Now that makes me sad," Stephen said, but the flash of his teeth said otherwise. He took a long drink of his beer, and leaned back on the settle, a man at ease with his world. Mr didn't touch his pint. There were things he needed to say and things he needed to be told, and he wasn't about to let drink muddle his thinking. But Stephen, quicker to the mark, began talking before Mr could organize his thoughts.

"I were never a Captain in the war. I admit the lie. Take that one on the chin. But I were there, fightin' fit an' all that. Well, I weren't exactly fightin'. Not in the trenches like those poor buggers with their rotten feet and their typhoid, and wrestlin' the rats for rations. I were a despatch rider. Had a Triumph Trusty motorcycle just like the one I sold you. No sidecar, mind. But she were a lovely little machine, as dear to me as a horse to a cavalryman, I reckon. We went through thick and thin, me and that Trusty. She carried me through bombed out roads, dodging and swerving the craters like she were born to it, and odd times she got bogged down in the mud – and it were awful stuff, thick as glue – I hauled 'er out. I'd've put her on me back if I'd had to." He seemed to get misty-eyed, and Mr, caught up in the narrative despite his wariness of Stephen's ability to charm, watched for signs of fakery.

"At first it were a bit of a lark. Me an' some o' the other blokes figured we were in for a grand time. Tipperary, top of our lungs. Most of us thought that, when it started out. Bunch o' cheerful Charlies, we were.

But it don't take long before the noise of the shelling an' the sight o' the earth explodin' in bits all around you sets you straight. I had a mate, Humphrey – we called him Humper, you don't want to know why – got blown to smithereens when he drove over a land mine. Weren't nothin' left of him 'cept bits of his motorcycle. Another pal we named Pupper on account of his hailing from Houndsditch and havin' a bit of a hangdog face, he caught a bit of flying shrapnel in the head. I were just fifty yards behind him when it happened, and I can tell you there were bits of him left over but nothin' much you'd want to see. Don't get me wrong here, Roddy, I'm not sayin' we didn't have a laugh and a good tumble down the sink now and again. Fact is, if you didn't, you'd go starkers. But a piss-up and a visit to the local brothel didn't stop you wonderin' every time you drove out, is it my turn? Is today me last?"

Stephen paused, stared into his glass, then took a long swig of his ale and Mr, stumbling over the references, was nevertheless drawn into the tale with a kind of horrified fascination. People talked about the war of course, but he'd never heard stories like this. He didn't realise he was leaning forward, and had all but forgotten to be suspicious of Stephen's theatrical capabilities. He, too, lifted his glass, but remembered to take just the smallest sip. When Stephen summoned the barmaid for another pint, Mr declined. His was still quite full.

"Anyway, not to be morose, because for the most part us despatch riders had a good gig compared to them poor sods at the front. When I were first told I were bein' assigned to the pigeon carrier service I thought, well damn, there goes me chance at impressin' the ladies when I get back to ol' England. Picture it: me, 'ansome bloke, smart uniform, lookin' right dapper on me Trusty, then damn if they don't strap this big wicker box – twenty-eight bloody inches square – onto your back and load it up with a bunch o' birds, cooing and burring as they do, 'cept you can't hear 'em over the noise of the bike. Ever try drivin' a machine with a basket o' birds on your back? It strangles you, not a word of a lie, an' it winds you some fast. It's like you ran a mile instead of drivin' one. Takes a bit, I can tell you, to get the feel of it, the balance an' the weight an' whatnot."

He paused to sip his pint, and Mr, his imagination captured, asked, "And then what did you do, once you had a load of pigeons?"

"Took 'em to the front, o' course," Stephen replied, wiping foam from his lip. "They're carrier pigeons, so you deliver 'em up to the front lines or wherever the sergeant tells you they need 'em, and they fly right back to where they come from. But first, see, the officers at the front write messages on scraps o' paper and attach 'em to the bird's leg, so the birds're actually messengers deliverin' vital information – troop movement, battle outcomes, things the generals in command might need to know in a hurry. Or they'd use 'em for urgent requests – artillery support, maybe, or more tins o' bully beef." Stephen grinned at that last, and winked. He held up his empty glass to summon Biddy from across the room with another. She brought two, and Mr realised he'd finished his as well. "It were the time o' me life, Roddy. Horrible, but important, know what I mean? Don't get me wrong, I'm glad it's over, and I'd never want to do it again, but it was excitin', and frightenin', and it were good to feel that somethin' you did mattered. A lot. Not to mention, them birds and the messages they carried saved the army's bacon more times 'n I can count."

"Not to mention their despatch riders," Mr said, with a nod. He had a new respect for Stephen, and, sipping his beer, for the bike outside. "Do you think it was ever used in the war – my bike, I mean?"

"Could be, Roddy, could be," Stephen replied. "She's a fine machine, war service or no. If you've regrets about buyin' 'er I could find a quick sale for 'er on your behalf. Maybe just a small commission for the service."

"I've no intention of selling," Mr answered sharply. "Nor of lending, had I been asked."

"I explained 'bout that," Stephen said, but had the grace to look a bit sheepish.

"I don't think you did, actually," Mr said petulantly. He got no further, for just then a woman approached their table. She was tall and sharp-featured, with lips painted into a harsh red rosebud, and wiry hair of an unnatural colour. Her eyes were darts, fixed on Stephen with a hard glare Mr found alarming. He drew back instinctively, sliding his mug of ale with him, far from her.

"Ah, Stephen, a sight for me own sore eyes," she said in a surprisingly husky voice. She flapped her lids, and Mr, withdrawing yet further, noticed Stephen smiled in his predatory way and leaned towards her, seemingly oblivious to the dislike in her gaze.

"Poppy, how're things?" he said, his own voice gone dusky. Mr watched this peacock dance, and suspected he was seeing two of a kind at work. "You're a long way from London town."

"That I am, love, that I am," Poppy replied. She squeezed herself onto the seat beside Stephen, and cast just a perfunctory glance at Mr. Mr looked away, happy in this instance to be neither greeted nor acknowledged. "I come lookin' for you, dear, but you're a hard one to track down." She glanced at the almost empty pint in front of Stephen, and he, taking her meaning, signalled to Biddy to bring three more. Mr, to his chagrin, realised he'd downed his second nervously, without noticing.

"When I saw you sat here in the very pub I was aiming to have a drink I thought what a chance, it's like fate sent me out this even'," she said.

"Fate, was it? 'Tis a fine thing to have such on your side," Stephen said blandly. His eyes met Mr's and flicked away. Mr, with an intuition he felt he did not normally possess, thought that Stephen was not too happy to see this woman, and did not believe her story of a chance encounter.

Stephen was watching the woman from beneath hooded eyes, his handsome mouth pulled into a thin line. Poppy of the bottle brush hair seemed not to notice. She toyed with the glass of ale, drinking in dainty sips. When it seemed she was content to sit in silence, Stephen, for whom a gap in conversation was an unnatural thing, said, "This is me friend Roddy Isbister, Poppy." He nodded towards Mr. "Poppy Kellow, Roddy."

Mr nodded politely. Poppy gaped at him.

"Isbister? From Sowerby Grange? *That* Isbister?" she said indelicately, her eyes running over Mr, sizing him up, perhaps checking for a pocket watch, or some sign of authenticity. He wanted to squirm, but managed not to. He wondered how a Londoner like her knew of Sowerby Grange, and the name of its occupants.

"No," said Stephen, giving Mr an imperceptible shake of his head, although he needn't have been concerned that Mr would want to share his identity with this odd and forward woman. "Roddy's an old friend from Bristol."

"Bristol, eh?" Poppy said, and her eyes raked Mr again as if for confirmation. Whether she found it or not, she sniffed, and said scathingly, "Might as well be dead, livin' in Bristol."

Mr offered a weak smile and contemplated the foam on his ale. He considered nodding to the lady, rising and taking his leave, abandoning Stephen to her company, but decided that if he was anything he wasn't mean. He'd have to remain, and wait it out.

Stephen gave an audible sigh. "How's your brother, Poppy?" he asked, and Mr sensed from his reluctant tone that it was a question he'd been avoiding asking.

"Poor to worse, since you're askin'," she replied, shaking the frizz of her head. "His foot pains 'im somethin' awful." Tears appeared in her wide eyes, and she sniffled, although Mr felt sure she was demonstrating rather than actually feeling distress. He glanced at Stephen, whose sardonic expression confirmed Mr's opinion.

"And a little more money would help ease it, you're thinkin'? You're a wonderful sister, Poppy, looking out for your brother like you do," Stephen said, surprisingly sweetly.

"Ah, you know, Stephen, I does what I can. As for the money, if you've any to spare, Stephen, me friend, it'd go a long way," she replied, and touched his hand. "His medical bills, you know. And whatnot."

"It'll take some doing, Poppy," Stephen said, frowning and shaking his head, oozing charm.

"Charlie's a wreck, Stephen. The pain's some dreadful." She leaned forward, and in a conspiratorial whisper said, "'E's been takin' a tincture, but I'm sure it's laudanum. Or worse."

When Stephen only shook his head in commiseration she grimaced, and Mr sensed exasperation as she pressed her shoulder to Stephen's, forcing him gently against the wall, and said, her tone coy, "Come on, now, Stephen. You know our Charlie. Gots a few dangerous friends, 'e do, what want to come after you in the night, bricks and bats, talk o' knives, even. Crazy stuff. Windin' 'im up. I said to 'im, I said, don't do nuffink rash, Charlie. Stephen'll 'elp out, like 'e promised."

"And so I did, love, so I did," Stephen said. His tone was smooth, but Mr, with his gawping spectator's eye, saw the subtle change in Stephen's face, from calm and unruffled to tense, with a hard gaze and a clenched jaw. He understood that Stephen was livid, and he wondered that Poppy did not notice, although perhaps she did and didn't care. She seemed a tough nut, and not a little scary.

Poppy finished her drink and eyed Stephen baldly. "Shall I tell 'im you'll be in touch, then? That you're bringin' 'im some more money? Edge him away from them blokes 'e keeps listenin' to?" She waited, watching him with a flat, steady gaze. Only when he gave a curt nod did she stir from her seat, but not before pulling a card from her pocket and sliding it towards Stephen. It was a calling card, Mr saw, similar to the ones ladies used to announce themselves when visiting for tea. This one had a black background and a gold elephant emblazoned on its front. Stephen's face, Mr noticed, hardened further. "Just a little reminder," Poppy said. "To help you do the right thing. Elephants never forget, Stephen, so think of that." She smoothed her rumpled coat and smiled somewhat smugly at Mr. "Nice to meet you, Roddy Isbister, not of Sowerby Grange." Then she smirked at Stephen and said, "Say hello to Ellie and the boy." And she walked away.

Stephen watched her exit the pub, then he slumped in his seat, looking defeated. He stuck out his bottom lip in a way that made him appear a petulant child, and Mr supposed he'd just witnessed a bit of blackmail at work. He wondered if Ellie and the boy she'd referred to were Stephen's wife, perhaps, and son. He asked Stephen what the woman had meant by the motorcycle pot, suspecting it had something to do with his own Trusty. Stephen frowned into his glass for a while, then sighed heavily and met Mr's gaze.

"That woman and her money grubbin' brother'll be the ruin o' me, I swear on me mother's grave. The Trusty I sold you belonged to Charlie, Poppy's brother. I won her – the Trusty, not Poppy –" a lightning-fast grin flashed across his face and was gone – "fair and square in a poker game."

"You what?" Mr interjected, appalled. The Trusty, stakes in a poker game? What kind of fool bet a motorcycle on the turn of a card? He shook his head. He couldn't credit it.

Stephen seemed not to hear him. "Charlie's an ex-army man, same as me, but 'e's a lush and a bit of a bumbler. Can't seem to get things on track, and if it hadn't been me what took the Trusty off 'im it would've been another. I felt sorry for 'im, but all's fair in love and war, as they say, and what's a good poker game if not one or t'other?" He sipped his ale, and drummed his fingers on the table, and Mr sensed he was sorting out the tale, and how to tell it. Maybe even what to tell.

Mr prompted him. "So, if you won the bike in a gamble, why do you feel you owe him – because it's obvious you do." He paused, then pressed, "Did you cheat?"

"Of course not!" Stephen replied indignantly. He didn't meet Mr's gaze, however, and instead drained his ale and signalled to Biddy the barmaid. Mr, seeing he too had finished his beer, asked for cordial. In Stephen Vanson's company it was never wise to be in one's cups.

"I ran over 'is foot and broke it," Stephen muttered finally. "The damn fool. He jumped in front of the bike as if to stop me takin' it, but bloody 'ell, I'd won the thing. I wasn't about to let 'im hold me up. I didn't mean to run 'im down, but 'e threw 'imself into me path, and bam! I 'it 'im. Well, 'is foot. He screeched like a buzzard until every bloody window in the street had a face in it. I got 'im into the sidecar and sped off, and, well, once out the street where it happened we came to a gentleman's agreement on the matter."

Mr raised his brows, wondering what, exactly, that meant, but Stephen was already obliging with select details. He didn't say precisely how the agreement came about, but the short of it seemed to be that Stephen, appropriating the role of good Samaritan, recognised that he'd taken the Trusty off a fellow in need – fairly, mind – and to make what small amends might be reasonable, decided to sell and give the man a cut of the proceeds.

"He being a fellow ex-serviceman and all?" Mr asked, endeavouring to keep the scepticism from his voice.

"Something like that," Stephen said evasively. The black card with the gold elephant sat on the table in front of him, and he stared at it, frowning.

"What is that?" Mr asked, gesturing to the calling card.

"It's an elephant, Roddy, come on," Stephen replied, rolling his eyes. He picked up the card and stuffed it in his jacket pocket.

"Do you know what it signifies? Or why this Poppy person gave it to you?" Mr persisted.

"Nope," said Stephen with finality. His gaze was flat and unyielding. If he knew, Mr saw, he wasn't about to share.

They sat for a few minutes more, sipping their drinks in silence, an unnatural state for Stephen, Mr felt sure. He considered what Stephen had revealed of his agreement, if it could be called that, with Poppy's brother, and wondered if it was in fact blackmail. Such a lot about Stephen seemed underhanded and shady. Mr thought back to his own first meeting with him at the Pig and Whistle when he'd bought the Trusty, and then their subsequent encounter in Whortleberry Wood, when Stephen had mentioned – or perhaps invented – the name of his sick child. Mr frowned.

"Does your Charlie like elephants?" Mr asked slyly, sipping delicately at his cordial. It had been flavoured with rosehips, which gave it a rather unmanly pink hue. He wished he'd chosen lime.

"My Charlie?" said Stephen, obviously puzzled.

"You did tell me you had a son named Charlie," Mr said, twirling the last bit of pink sediment in his glass. "Although if memory serves you also told me you had a son named John. Maybe you have one of each?" He fixed Stephen with what he intended to be a sneer of cynicism, but which he suspected came off as merely curled lips.

Stephen laughed and drained his beer. "Maybe I do, Roddy me lad, maybe I do." He stood, signalling to the barmaid and tossing some coins on the table. "I've had enough of the Cock and Bull, Roddy. How 'bout you?" And without waiting for a reply, he headed for the door, lifting a hand to those who called out their farewells. Mr was left to scramble after him, and despite being sure he'd gotten the upper hand, he felt like a chastened boy.

*

There were several more pub stops that night while Stephen and Mr engaged in an odd dance of evasion and misinformation. Hoping to get to the bottom of a number of oddities – how Stephen came to be a tenant at Natterjack Hall, if he'd known Woody Barks prior to sharing that residence with him, what the elephant card meant and whether or not he was married to someone named Ellie, and had a son called Charlie, maybe, or John – Mr left off the cordial with its cloying sweetness, and imbibed in rather more glasses of porter than he'd intended, but he was not alone in his overindulgence. Stephen seemed to be working from his own end, both on pints and on queries for Mr – who'd inherited Sowerby Grange, then, Mr or Mrs? And if Mr had not known Woody Barks prior to his arrival at Natterjack Hall, had Mrs? Despite their growing inebriation neither man had given up whole truths, Mr decided, staring into his yet-again-empty glass as he sat inside The Maid and the Miller pub – or was it the Fine Fettle? Liars' Arms, more like. The night had grown much longer than he'd anticipated. Whilst trying to pry certain truths one from the other, he and Stephen's conversation had veered into the realm of art (Stephen could never be called a patron), suffrage (Stephen was a big proponent of the Representation of the People Act of 1918 which gave the right to vote to all men over the age of 21), and turnips, of all things, which Mr detested and Stephen loved, boiled, with butter. It then somehow turned to dreams and aspirations, and Stephen talked of the stage, and moving pictures.

"I think I could really be someone in that world, Roddy," Stephen told him earnestly, and Mr's head bobbled. Yes, he thought Stephen probably could. "You seen anything with Douglas Fairbanks? Or Charlie Chaplin? Extraordinary! An' I've got more in the looks department than either o' them chaps, do say so meself. Music Hall's fine for people like Lizer. She's got a talent, no question. But I – I can live and breathe meself into a part, an' that shows on the screen." He eyed Mr. "What about you, Roddy? If you 'ad your druthers?"

Mr sighed, and rested his chin on his palm, contemplating the smoke-filled air above Stephen's head. He chuckled, thinking of the day he'd told Mrs that he'd be in China, supping tea, or in Canada, helping the Mounties get their man. He'd been joking in a not funny way, but if he was honest, his words weren't far off the mark. To Stephen he said, "I'd be out of here, no question. I'd be on a research trip to the Amazon jungle, perhaps, assisting my good friend, Harold. But barring that rather out of the question fantasy, I'd simply ramble, I suppose. Go on an adventure. Seek new places. Discover."

With questions and queries unresolved and dreams hanging in the air, the publican called out "Time, gents!" and Stephen and Mr drained the remainder of their porter and rose, admittedly on wobbly legs. In the street, the Trusty sat waiting, and the men stood side by side, eyeing the machine, a momentary awkwardness between them after sharing private aspirations. Then Stephen slung an arm across Mr's shoulders.

"I should drive," he said, pressing his forehead against Mr's ear, not in an intimate gesture, but out of a rather drunken effort at standing up straight.

Mr chuckled and stumbled, his own insobriety giving him license to believe he was perfectly capable of piloting the Trusty, and earlier embarrassments in that regard clouding his better judgment. "No," he told Stephen with a confidence he felt but which was not warranted, "she is my motorcycle, I will be her coxswain! Climb aboard, friend!"

And so it happened that Mr was driving the Trusty Triumph along the road from Lesser Plumpton towards Watton Hoo, between which villages lay Natterjack Hall and Sowerby Grange. Stephen was lounging in the sidecar beneath the cozy rug when a creeping mist began to spread across the fields and over stone walls and into the narrow gravel roadway. At first it was a thin fog, and nothing debilitating, but before very long it was thick and cloying, its fingers inching into every crevice and bump on the road. It deadened even the happy little putt-putt of the motorcycle's engine, and made the already dim light of the acetylene headlamp even fainter. Now and again the mist shredded, and they drove through a clear patch, but it very quickly closed ranks so that Mr wasn't entirely sure which side of the narrow road he drove on. In his drunken indifference he decided that as long as they were still clipping along in a more or less straight line and hadn't found a ditch, things were going rather swimmingly. He began to sing the song Eliza had performed at the School of the Arts' fundraiser, marveling at the acoustic effect the fog had on the sound.

"Ta-ra-ra-boom-de-yay!" he warbled. The bike hit a pothole and swerved. Stephen bounced in the sidecar, and laughed, calling over the noise of the engine, "Atta boy, Roddy. Keep 'er between the lamps and the posts!" Mr pressed on the throttle, stepping up the speed a notch. He pictured himself a true Chimera, legendary motorcycle hero. "Ta-ra-ra-BOOM-de-yay!" he sang, and Stephen joined in.

Out of nowhere a figure appeared in the grey fog directly in the path of the Trusty. Whether a more sober man might have avoided the collision was debatable, certainly a more sober man would have been driving with greater caution on such a night. But these points did not cross Mr's mind until after the event. Now, he plowed full speed into whatever – whomever – loomed before him, and if there was a sound Mr would have described it as a muffled whomp. He caught a wild-eyed glimpse through the swirling fog of a bit of yellow fabric, and a shoe, maybe, flying through the air. The bike came to a wobbling halt, put-putting as if nothing at all had happened. Mr, his heart thumping in fright and shock, sat transfixed on the seat of the motorcycle. What had he done? Had he hit someone?

Stephen sprang from the sidecar as the bike came to a stop. He disappeared into the fog in the direction the body had flown. Mr thought he heard sounds from the ditch, moaning perhaps, but he could see nothing, and wanted to see nothing. His hands felt glued to the bars of the Trusty, his feet to her pedals. In his mind's eye he saw the yellow fabric, and knew with horrible certainty that it was Mrs' favourite day dress. Fingers of fear closed around his throat. Had he killed his wife?

"Stephen?" he called, his voice thin and quavering. Time stood agonizingly still. What was Stephen doing? What was he finding in the ditch? Mr knew he should move off the bike and go and see for himself the chaos he had wrought, see if there was assistance to be offered, but he couldn't convince his limbs to stir. Then Stephen appeared through the mist, running a hand through his hair. In the pale light afforded by the Trusty's headlamp, his face was a sickly shade of puce and his eyes were bloodshot. His lips were pressed together in a hard line.

"It's bad, Roddy," he said.

"It is?" Mr said. He thought he would cry. "Is it – is it – I saw the dress…"

A flicker of something crossed Stephen's face.

"It is," he said. He bowed his head. Mr sat in shock. He was a murderer. "They'll hang you, Roddy," Stephen continued, shaking his head sadly. "Dangle you from a gibbet. Stretch yer neck till yer eyes pop.

It's a disgustin' thing to do to a man, but there it is." He shrugged apologetically.

"Dear God," Mr stammered. "Dear God."

"Don't know as there's much help in *that* quarter, given what's 'appened," Stephen said. He glanced over his shoulder towards the ditch. Mr's eyes followed, but the fog was complete. Not even a scrap of the dress could be seen.

"What should I do?" Mr said. He felt like he would throw up.

"I know what I'd do in your shoes," Stephen said. "Go on the lam. Do a runner. Make a dash for it."

"Run?" Mr repeated stupidly. He couldn't think straight, and his head hurt. Running seemed like the absolute wrong thing to do. "Surely I should turn myself in. Confess. Bring Alice's – remains – somewhere?" Mrs' name felt foreign on his tongue, and the idea of her lying there in the ditch made his insides go all a-muddle.

Stephen threw back his head and laughed, the sound flat inside the fog's blanket. "I think you'd best go 'ave a look." He jerked his head in the direction of the ditch, grinning, and Mr wondered if he'd gone a bit mad from the drink, or the crash, or both. But he took courage and climbed off the bike and inched his way through the veils of fog.

Would there be blood? Would her head be twisted at an impossible angle, or would she just appear to be sleeping, Mrs in repose? He could see not even a foot in front of him, and he wondered if he'd somehow missed the body. He was about to call out to Stephen when his foot caught and he tripped, falling on top of the corpse in its heap of yellow fabric. He scrambled back in horror, then noted the black horns, spotted coat and yellow eyes of Amos the goat. What he'd taken for a shoe was in fact a hoof. Mr sat on the grass, staring at the dead goat wrapped in Mrs' dress, and succumbed to an odd mix of laughter and shuddering sobs. He'd killed Amos the goat. A sad thing, but at least he wouldn't hang for it.

Chapter 13
THE CUSHION OF A WELL-KNITTED SOCK

The fact of his responsibility for the death of Amos the goat had a sobering effect on Mr, and dampened his aspirations of wandering at large. For a day or so after the incident he laid low, choosing to potter in the greenhouse or peruse his art book of an evening, the Trusty abed in the shed. Of Mrs he saw neither hide nor hair, a phrase he chuckled over in a macabre way, given her awful presence, however intangibly, on the night of Amos' demise. This decision to eschew company was made all the easier by Mrs' continued indisposition, a state which at first he did not question. She had a bit of the ague, he supposed, or was sniffly. He thought it likely that in truth she was simply avoiding him, and any difficult questions he might put to her regarding her behaviour on the night of the lieutenant-colonel's party – riding in motorcycles, for example. What she could not know, of course, was how hypocritical it would be for him to ask such a thing, when the motorcycle was in fact his, and he had ridden in it numerous times with their maid, their dustbin boy, and most recently, the man she knew as Captain Plucky.

Eliza was equally elusive. He encountered her only once or twice over the course of several days; she served him dinner on the first day in relative silence, and surely was about the house, since his bed was made and water left for his ablutions. On the second day he was served by cook, as it was Eliza's day off, but she was back on the job on the third, by which time Mr had grown a tad weary of solitude, and went so far as to voice his concern for Mrs' health and continued absence to Eliza at dinner.

Beneath her mopcap Eliza looked startled. She bobbed a curtsey and reached to straighten his plate of chip and egg, a flusterish gesture that made Mr frown in puzzlement.

"I'm sorry, sar, I thought you knew," Eliza said, avoiding his gaze. She arranged the salt cellar and brushed some crumbs from the tapestried tablecloth. "Mrs isn't here, sar."

"Not here?" Mr repeated, balancing his knife carefully on the rim of his plate, decorated with the Sowerby family crest. He'd never liked the china with its prancing stag and chevrons and laurel leaves; he thought it pretentious. Similarly, the silverware, with its curling S embossed on the handle. There were limitations and expectations in those trappings, he had always felt, certain he neither met the expectations nor embraced the limitations. He was fairly confident Mrs would have agreed.

"No sar," Eliza confirmed. "She left a couple of days ago, sar. To visit an aunt, I believe. In – er – Bristol?" She frowned, as if unsure.

"Bristol? An aunt? What aunt? Well, what the dickens – why wasn't I told?" he was annoyed, more by the fact of her uncommunicated departure than by her actual absence, if he was honest. He regretted directing his irritation at Eliza, but there it was.

"I'm sorry, sar, I thought you knew," she said again, and bobbed a second curtsey.

"It's not your fault," he said, contrite, and somewhat embarrassed by his snappishness. He poked his cooling egg with his fork. "Did she say how long she'd be gone?"

"No sar. She did take three cases, though, sar, her hat box and her fox stole, so I expect she'll be a while," Eliza replied.

"Indeed," muttered Mr, frowning. Odd behaviour, he thought. In all their years of marriage Mrs had never gone away, except for family funerals, in which case Mr had invariably accompanied her. The only time she had gone alone was when her uncle in Limpley Stoke had collapsed, and she'd been summoned by his daughter, who couldn't seem to cope. Mr hadn't seen the sense of traipsing along, an extra body as it were, and most likely in the way. He'd stayed home, and spent hours in Whortleberry Wood, poking in the mud. Harold had joined him, and they'd had their lunches together sitting on a rock in the wood, munching on bread and cheese and sour pickle. It was the most enjoyment Mr had had since, or almost. There were a few occasions recently that gave it good run.

Eliza said, "Ahem," softly, and Mr glanced at her. He'd almost forgotten her presence, actually, and wondered why she was still standing there. Hovering, really, watching the play of his features. He was doubly annoyed.

"What is it?" he snapped, and felt badly for his obvious irritation, but there it was.

"Umm, she also took a pair of wellingtons, sar. And socks."

Mr gaped at his maid. Wellingtons? Socks? Whatever for? Mr hadn't even been aware that Mrs owned a pair of socks, let alone wellingtons. One went with the other, of course, for rubber boots were dashed uncomfortable without the cushion of a well-knitted woolen sock. Mrs invariably wore dresses and, presumably, stockings beneath – thin, pale things he'd seen limpid on the laundry line. Thick, serviceable woolen socks would never fit into the dainty footwear Mrs wore, and which occasionally he'd seen poking out from beneath her voluminous skirts. No, never, in their years of living under the same roof, had Mrs appeared in boots or socks. He steepled his fingers, thinking.

"As her maid," Mr began delicately, aware that the question he was about to ask was *in*delicate, and that he was also asking her to break what amounted to a confidence, even if her discretion had not been expressly requested, "you may be aware of just when, and perhaps how, she came by such items as socks and wellingtons?"

"Oh, yes, sar," said Eliza, with another quick bob. "They came a few days ago. Delivered from a London store, sar. Beeton and Beadle on the box."

Mr turned his gaze to the congealed yolk of his egg. A suspicion that was most ungallant had begun to form in his mind, and he wondered if the sneer in his thoughts was present on his face, the result of his expectation that Woody Barks was behind the gift of the wellies, as well as Mrs' subsequent "visit" to a Bristol aunt. Although the thought was uncharitable in that it could be completely unfounded, and shocking, if it were true, nonetheless there it was.

"Did this – delivery – occur before or after Lieutenant-Colonel Barks' birthday affair?" he asked. He took a careful pinch of salt from the cellar and dropped it on his egg, then stabbed the cold morsel with his fork and ate it, savouring, in a hair-shirt sort of way, its unpleasantness.

"Day of, sar," she answered. "She were chuffed when it arrived. Seemed to be expecting it. There were a note enclosed, but I didn't read it."

Mr's eyes, beady, no doubt, flicked quickly to Eliza. "Of course you didn't," he said in an admonishing tone. He sniffed. Maids, of course, read anything that was left lying around. He wasn't born yesterday. "But did she share its contents? Read it to you, perhaps?"

"We-ell," Eliza said, evasively, "She wanted to try 'em on right away. Had me help her, as they were a bit of a squeeze. She were like a little girl, sar, all giggles and blushes. I asked her if she were goin' walkin' in Whortleberry Wood, like you do, sar, but she said gracious no, she were goin' on a holiday with a friend. An adventure, she said, and she sighed like this, sar." Eliza mimicked a lovestruck maiden, posing with her hands clasped to her chest and flapping her eyelids. A year ago Mr would have had a hard time imagining Mrs in such context, but his world had gone topsy-turvy, and nothing he thought he knew for certain was that anymore.

"And when she left? Did anyone pick her up?"

"Dunno, sar, it were me day off," she replied.

"Ah, I see," Mr said. He was aware that his tone was curt and clipped, but he was exerting great effort to appear calm and rational, when in fact he wanted to shout "How dare she!" and perhaps throw the salt cellar, maybe stamp his foot. He gestured to the plate of now-limp chips and half-finished egg and said, "You may clear," and she did, and left him to sit there, ruminating.

*

For probably an hour Mr sat in the same spot in the parlour, frowning at the carefree sprinkle of salt and pepper, tossed there haphazardly when he'd been Mr Roderick Throckmorton Isbister of Sowerby Grange, with his wife of twenty-five years, indisposed, mind, reposing in her chambers elsewhere in this mausoleum of a rural country house. Such a short time to pass, and yet here he was, still the same named fellow, but instead a man made foolish by his own inadequacies, his own willingness to coast like an automaton through a life he had neither wanted nor enjoyed for quite some time. It wasn't that he begrudged Mrs her happiness – well, perhaps a tad – but her finding that happiness and acting upon it meant he looked a fool, indeed *was* a fool for not acting in his own best interests, as she had obviously had no trouble doing just that. He drummed his fingers on the soiled tablecloth. What did one do in the face of one's wife's suspected infidelity, her obvious preference for another, indeed her disdain for the very institution he had hitherto considered unimpeachable? She had not been happy, that much was clear, as she had seemingly run off with Woody Barks, but neither had he been exactly joyous in their matrimonial co-existence. The difference was that he had been, well, complacent, while she – she, apparently, had not. A devilish voice whispered from his shoulder that in fact that wasn't true. Who had been sneaking off to buy motorcycles, and who had danced with, and slept with (albeit not in the carnal sense) his maid?

Beyond the thin lace curtains Mr could see that the moon was up. Night had fallen. From the corner of his eye he noticed that the parlour door opened more than once; Eliza, peeking round, checking on him. The thought was surprisingly satisfying. He tried not to consider where Mrs was at this moment, or what she might be doing, although in truth he did not insert himself into the scenario as some kind of wronged cuckold. Instead it was a matter of wounded pride rather than jealousy. Other than a wish for things to have been different from the very outset of their marriage, he didn't actually mind the idea of Mrs in the arms of her lover, if that's what was happening somewhere, someplace. Truth be told he very much did not care what she did; rather he needed to decide what this turn of events meant for him, and what he would now choose to do.

The clock struck ten before he roused himself and quit the parlour. He didn't return to his rooms, but instead went to the back of the house where he tugged on his wellingtons and donned a jacket, and headed for the stillness of Whortleberry Wood. The moon was full, and there was a chance he could hear the natterjack toad this night. And while he told himself that was what he hoped for, in fact if the toad had uttered its distinctive croak, Mr would likely not have heard it. He trudged the path in complete distraction, noting but not appreciating the way the silver moon lit the leaves of the white willows, and though he had not consciously taken the fork that led to Natterjack Hall, he suddenly found himself there, standing on the step beside the big bronze toad. There was light beyond the drawn curtains, so someone was at home. Mr stood for a while, deciding whether to knock, then took the proverbial bull by the horns, and rapped on the door.

After a few moments, a pointy-nosed maid answered, peering into the darkness where Mr stood.

"Yes?" she inquired, her brows lifting. Her mouth did not follow suit.

He stepped forward into the light, noticing as he did the muck caked onto his boots. Not the attire of a gentleman caller, though what gentleman called at his time of night, and without invitation?

"Good evening," he said, drawing himself up, tugging on his cuffs, doing his best to appear respectable. "Is the master of the house at home?"

"Which one?" the maid asked, frowning confusion.

"Either will do," Mr replied, attempting a pleasant tone, but not certain he succeeded. Even to his own ears his voice had a snarling edge. He noticed that the maid inched the door to, and positioned herself slightly behind it, as if to affect a barricade. He wondered if he appeared threatening in some way.

"Well, neither's here," she said curtly, and made to close the door.

More annoyed by the answer than he cared to admit, Mr put his foot out, wincing as the door jammed against it. He grimaced, and might have growled, and saw that the maid had now hidden herself behind the door to gape out at him through the boot-wide opening. Her eyes were round saucers.

"No need to be hasty," Mr said. "Just a question or two, good lady, and I shall be on my way. No need to fear –" This last admonishment was accompanied by a shove on the door, not the best choice of actions, Mr acknowledged in hindsight, since the door was then jerked open by a rather large and burly footman minus his usual expressionless façade. That one put his beefy hand on Mr's narrow chest and thrust, and Mr found himself sprawling next to the bronze toad, and the door slammed shut. He heard the bolt slide home, and seconds later, the face of the lantern-jawed footman and that of the maid appeared in the parlour window. They scoured the dark, searching for him, but Mr was already slinking towards Whortleberry Wood, nursing a scraped elbow.

*

He could never afterwards be sure at what point he'd arrived at his chosen course of action, whether he thought things through on his trudge back through the Wood, or if the plan, such as it was, had been arrived at purely spontaneously the moment he'd stopped at the old iron gate. Nonetheless, he'd paused on the wooded side of that metaphoric and actual barrier, and had been suddenly cognizant of his choice. His heart was thumping, not with fright or over-exertion, though in truth the walk back through Whortleberry Wood had been a challenge in the dark, and he'd scared up a creature or two. Rabbit, perhaps. Or hedgehog. No, what he felt was not a fearful thing, nor even excitement, at least not in the giddy, heady sense of the word. Rather he decided it was more like affirmation – the way one feels when one has made a choice, and the right one.

The iron gate creaked as he pushed it open, old metal hinge on old metal post, but to Mr's ears the sound was a happy squeak rather than a tired groan. It was a bon voyage kind of noise. A farewell salute. He was leaving. After twenty-five unhappy years in this place – Sowerby Grange – he was moving on. Where would he go? He didn't know. It didn't seem important. But, for the first time ever, Roderick Throckmorton Isbister would be following his heart. No holds barred. No commitments, no responsibilities. He latched the gate and stood for a long while, staring back at Whortleberry Wood, unaware that the moonlight silvered the bare dome of his pate. He thought of Harold Guppletwill in that moment, wondering if Harold would ever return here, and if he did, would he think of his old friend? Mr sighed and smiled. The thought of Harold, he realised, no longer stirred an envious yearning. He was about to have his own adventure. And just as he turned his back on the Wood, the loud, unmistakeable croak of the natterjack toad pierced the night air.

"Bloody hell, what was that?"

Mr jumped, startled both by the toad's exuberant noise and the unexpected female voice coming to him in the dark. He squinted, and saw Eliza standing a few feet away on the garden path. She wore the shapeless sack-cloth coat she'd had on the night of her performance at the Lesser Plumpton School of the Arts, and a cloche hat of some unremarkable colour pulled down over her red hair.

"I'm leaving," he said, drawing himself up as if to defend his decision.

"I'm coming," she replied, then smiled, revealing the gap between her two front teeth.

Chapter 14
SKULKING BEHIND THE PROVERBIAL BUSH

Alice Millicent Sowerby wed Roderick Throckmorton Isbister on a rained-out day in March, 1897, and though the weather was not remarkable, the bridegroom's slight stature and even slighter fiscal worth were – at least to those who gossiped behind gloved hands.

Alice knew they whispered about the groom, and she herself was somewhat dismayed when she met him, even then thinning of hair and with a mound of a tummy. He had narrow shoulders and a weak chest and exceptionally long and narrow feet, she noticed, if no one else did, and a little round ball on the end of his nose that he rubbed with his thumb when deep in thought. He was some ten years her senior, thirty-five to her twenty-five, but that in itself was not unusual. If she'd held out any hope at all it would have been that she and her marriage partner might at least share some similar interests. Something to discuss over the dinner table, if nothing else. However, on making his acquaintance, she discovered they had very little in common. He took almost no interest in the Grange, her childhood home, and though initially it appeared that they might find a meeting of minds over plants and flowers, it was soon obvious that while she preferred showy cultivars – roses, peonies, carnations – he preferred weedy things that should be discouraged, even if just for their horrid names: wound-wart, ragged robin, skullcap. He had an annoying curiosity about what he called "nature"; by which she eventually understood he meant swamps and silly things like frogs and whatnot. Why anyone would find bogs and stench and slimy creatures interesting she could not fathom. Their attempts at conversation failed utterly. Their attempt at other – intimacies – was equally disastrous. Alice realised within the first few weeks of her union with this small, insignificant man that she had made an awful mistake.

There was nothing for it, of course. R. Throckmorton Isbister had been proposed as a suitable candidate for marriage by her father's solicitor and old friend, Sir Barnabas Henshaw, who, with paternal concern, had explained the conditions of her deceased father's will to her in his Bristol office. The two men, her father, Sir Templeton Sowerby, and Sir Barnabas, had served together in India, solicitors both, and widowers, with some important positions in the British government there. She didn't know exact details. Suffice to say the two men had worked in the colonial office for many years, *sans famille*, as it were, and been rewarded for their service with a knighthood conferred at a joint ceremony, soon after they retired and returned to England. Alice, left from a very young age in the care of a governess at Sowerby Grange, barely knew this man – her father – who moved in and took charge of every aspect of her life when she was 19. The governess, who'd been next to a mother, was paid a handsome bonus, thanked and dismissed. The cook was replaced. Maids whose work hadn't been up to snuff, as Sir Templeton put it, were also let go. Alice was heartbroken, but not just by the changes wrought by the return of her long absent father. Alice had been in love. Madly, deeply, unreservedly in love with a military man who, she knew, loved her back. Sir Templeton, unimpressed by and unsympathetic to his daughter's declaration of commitment to a man already embarked upon a military career that had sent him off to Africa, had snorted his derision and told her to forget the fellow. The match wasn't on, were his words.

But Alice had continued to write to her dear heart, as she called him, her Woody. And Woody, Woodward Barks, yes, he, the same, had written back, albeit less and less frequently as the years passed. Before long his letters to her ceased, and her more recent ones came back in the post in a large clump, which was when her father understood there'd been correspondence between them despite his express forbiddance of the relationship. He was less than pleased, but he'd come to know the headstrong nature of his daughter, and so he took it upon himself to explain to her his objections to the military fellow, citing his advanced age (Woody was some fifteen years her senior), his obvious commitment to pursuing a military career abroad (Sir Templeton had made inquiries and learned that the man had risen quickly through the ranks and was by all accounts a most dedicated soldier), his postings to all manner of uncivilized places full of veiled people and unpleasant food. Such a life,

Sir Templeton told Alice, was not one he would choose for her, given their own history, father and daughter, of a lifetime spent apart.

Alice didn't care, and boldly told her father she would wait for Woody. One day, she knew, he would come back. He'd promised, and she believed him. She might have crossed her arms stubbornly. Sir Templeton played his trump card then, and informed his daughter that this so-called beloved was less interested in her than she in him, given that he'd married a woman in Tripoli. He delivered this news flatly, with the sensitivity of a fish.

Alice was devastated. She locked herself in her room at Sowerby Grange. Food was delivered on a tray and left in the hallway on a small table placed next to her door. She devoured every crumb but did not appear. For months she lived this way, seen by almost no one, eating, sleeping, reading novels like Bleak House and Wuthering Heights, and re-reading the letters Woody had sent in the early days. My pudding, he'd called her, my steak and kidney pie. Her father, from whom, after all, she'd come by her stubborn streak, made no effort to placate her or bribe her out of what he saw as her petulance and self-indulgence, and carried on with life as if his daughter had not made herself a recluse. When she did finally appear, many pounds had been added to an already rather rotund physique, and though he saw with displeasure the double chin that had blossomed beneath her once sweetly round face, he refused to comment on or acknowledge the result of her sulkiness. And while they were still barely speaking to one another, he died of a stroke.

Alice was twenty-four. Woody, her darling soldier, was gone from her life, and she was alone. Sir Barnabas Henshaw summoned her after a suitable period and read first her father's will, bequeathing Alice all his worldly possessions, including Sowerby Grange, the family seat. He then read the codicil, and Alice discovered that he'd amended his generous gift with the most unkind stipulation. She might inherit Sowerby Grange only providing she wed a suitable man by the age of twenty-five who was not Woodward Barks, and who was approved by her father's solicitor, Sir Barnabas himself, with parameters and characteristics previously communicated to him.

Which somehow, eventually, and on the cusp of Alice's twenty-fifth birthday, culminated in her unhappy union with one Roderick Throckmorton Isbister.

Throckmorton, as he preferred, was an acquaintance of Sir Barnabas. Unmarried, unambitious, unremarkable and unassertive, he was a quiet and mild-mannered fellow who seemed rather content with his uninteresting life as a country gentleman, living in a small stone cottage belonging to one of Sir Barnabas' clients, in a village on the edge of the Cotswolds. Throckmorton's family had come from money but he'd been the younger son of the younger son of the younger son, and nothing of his family's slight wealth had come his way, nor did he seem to mind. But he had proper manners, and understood a gentleman's role in society, and could be counted on to be unobtrusive and bland, and make polite conversation in the right company. Sir Barnabas thought him ideal for young Alice, the responsibility for whom had begun to feel like an albatross round his neck. If she didn't marry as her father had decreed in his codicil, whose problem would she be, he wondered? He couldn't simply abandon the woman, homeless and alone. And how would he actually get her out of Sowerby Grange, if it came to that? R. Throckmorton Isbister seemed the perfect solution for all concerned.

While Alice wasn't keen, she understood that she had no choice. Throckmorton, on the other hand, needed convincing. He was perfectly happy as a lacklustre gentleman getting by on his own, puttering, as it were, in his garden, going for long walks in swampy places, poking about for unusual mushrooms and whatnot. He didn't see the need for a wife, of all things. In fact, the whole idea as proposed by Sir Barnabas sounded a bit horrifying. He said as much, in his hedging, evasive, hand-wringing way, and was quickly shaken loose of the notion that he might have a choice when Sir Barnabas baldly threatened his eviction from the village cottage, and even, nastily, suggested that he could affect the cessation of the meagre allowance he lived on, provided by a distant cousin who, truth be told, cared very little what might become of him, if he even knew he existed. Throckmorton, taken aback, asked for time to mull it over, and Sir Barnabas gave him one week. There was really no question as to the outcome.

Gallop ahead twenty-five years and one arrived at the current situation of Alice and Throckmorton, neither a happy participant in their matrimonial state, but neither with much of an alternative. Until, one day, a letter arrived, unremarkable, unobtrusive, just a plain letter like so many others that were delivered the width and breadth of the country on any given morning. It was post-marked London, addressed to Alice Sowerby of Sowerby Grange. The maid brought it on a tray to Mrs' bedchamber, where the lady of the house was taking her Sunday prerogative of having a bit of a lie-in. She eyed the letter as she sipped tea and nibbled biscuits, wondering who might be writing to her from London, of all places, where she knew no one. And even more curious, using her maiden name. It was hotel stationary, she saw, noting the discreet crest in one corner of the envelope. She slit it open after licking jam from her butter knife and unfolded the enclosed note, fixing her spectacles onto her nose.

Dear Miss Sowerby, it read. *I hope this letter finds you, and if it does, that if finds you well. It is many years since we corresponded, and many more than that since we last saw one another, and I do hope you'll forgive an old soldier who has not for a moment stopped thinking of you.*

At this point, Mrs gasped, and clutched the letter to her substantial bosom, feeling her heart thunder beneath the creamy paper. Woody! She read on.

I am home now, in England, having been fortunate in my career and having risen through the ranks with, if I do say so myself, more than my share of good fortune and strategic postings. I am now Lieutenant-Colonel Woodward Barks, retired, and at your service.

Mrs lowered the letter with a trembling hand. Woody, a lieutenant-colonel. She pictured him in a smart uniform, buttons gleaming. He'd cut a fine figure, she knew, and pressed her hand to her suddenly warm cheek. Could she see him? How? When? And what would she tell Mr?

I hope you will forgive my boldness if I call you by the name that has been etched upon my lips all these years, and write what is in my heart, dear Alice! I cannot help it, and I find I cannot stop my pen. And yet I must, for I know not what is in your heart. I will be at this London address awaiting a response from you. If I hear nothing then I shall expect you have found contentment elsewhere, and though I shall be a broken man, I will nonetheless be glad for your happiness, even whilst pining for those heady days of our youth, when all was possible between us.

I remain ever yours faithfully etc, etc, Lt.-Col Woodward Barks, your Woody.

Mrs wrote him back. Immediately. Well, what else could she do, after all? Simple courtesy dictated that she at least respond; no one with any degree of breeding would disagree. After her initial shock and excitement she calmed herself, took stock, and considered her options. The impulsive young girl inside her matronly frame wanted to hop the first train to London and find him, her Woody, her soldier, fling herself into his arms and rejoice that life had given her this incredible second chance. The married matron understood that she could not do that, at least not without understanding the situation exactly. After all, there'd been talk of a wife. In Bombay. Or was it Poli-something? And there was Mr Isbister to consider, at least somewhat. So she wrote Woody back, coyly, flirtatiously, but also scoldingly.

Dear Lt-Col Barks. How lovely to have a letter from you, after so much time. I am delighted, of course, to hear of your successful career. I am sure such accomplishments as you have enjoyed have been personally gratifying for you.

For many years I thought of nothing but you, and, like you, longed for the heady days, as you call them. But circumstance, and a lack of correspondence from you, forced my hand, and I am wed these twenty-five years, not miserably, but not happily either. What of your own situation in that regard? Word reached me prior to my succumbing to the matrimonial state of your own union occurring in someplace foreign.

Yours as once was, Alice Sowerby, now Isbister (Mrs).

Woody's reply came lightning fast, and Mrs was taken aback. He professed his continued, undying love for her, and vowed that had never changed. Indeed, there'd been a wife, but she was no more, and had never been to him what Alice herself had been. No meeting of the minds, he wrote, as they'd had. No thinking, feeling, doing as one person the way he and Alice had done. It had never been his intention, he professed, to stop writing, but the post had been unreliable in some of the godforsaken places he'd been. Sometimes even paper had been hard to come by. He'd been a soldier, after all, immersed in life and death struggles and as an officer with rather important responsibilities, if he did say so himself, had been at the whim of political agendas beyond his own manipulation. The army, he told her, cared nothing for the love of Alice and Woody, and he'd had to accept that or fail at his duty.

Mrs, reading his words, glowed with anticipation, reassured. He loved her still, had never stopped! Could she see him? What would it be like to be in a room with him again? She recalled his robust personality, so unlike Throckmorton's, the way his voice boomed and seemed to shake the walls. She shivered. He was widowed, but she had a living, breathing husband, which, she noted, he had pointedly not mentioned. She could meet him, but should she do it clandestinely, skulking behind the proverbial bush, or openly, sharing – what exactly? That Woody was the love of her life? That she'd wanted to marry him once upon a time? That just knowing he lived and breathed and was here, in England, made her knees go weak? And while she considered all these things, prepared to proceed slowly and with care, Woody – devil-may-care Woody, the dear – promptly got down to it, so to speak, discovering the availability of Mr Guppletwill's residence next door (the large house named, ridiculously she thought, after a frog), letting it, and moving in. She'd been shocked to receive his card stating his new residency, so close, and asking her to call around. She wondered that Mr did not notice her exceptionally high colour as she read it, the pink dewiness that spread, she was sure, from her forehead to her bosom in a tell-tale blush of excitement. Right away, on the pretext of attending a Horticultural Society meeting, she pinned on what she hoped was her most flattering and girlish hat, the one with the bobbing petunias, so pert, and went post-haste to Natterjack Hall, aware that as she did, she was setting something in motion that could not be stopped.

Chapter 15
HOT AIR BALLOONS AND OTHER CURIOSITIES

Once, Alice's governess, Miss Martha Dudley – Muddy, to Alice – had taken Alice to a village in Sussex called Bramber. Muddy said it was a holiday, but it was apparent even to young Alice, twelve at the time, that Muddy was there on her own family matter. In retrospect, Alice supposed Muddy had had little choice but to bring her along when word arrived that her sister's husband, an aspiring taxidermist, had gone a little loopy, shedding his clothes and running stark naked through the streets of Bramber, shouting about kittens in knickers and gambling rats. Alice, listening at keyholes and not above a good snoop through Muddy's things, understood that Muddy's brother-in-law had been hoping for a job as apprentice to a local taxidermist, a man named Walter Potter, proprietor of an establishment known as Mr Potter's Museum of Curiosities. For some reason, he'd been rejected. Neither he nor Muddy's sister could explain why, but Alice, with the fresh and clear vision of youth, saw immediately that any man who acted like a raving lunatic could never have withstood a job stuffing dead animals and dressing them in human clothing. Which is exactly what Mr Potter of the Museum of Curiosities did.

Upon first arrival in Bramber, Alice's nosy curiosity had focused on the brother-in-law, prone in his bed, dosed with chicken soup and not a little brandy. Muddy comforted her long-suffering sister who hovered at his bedside, spoon feeding him and making sympathetic noises. To Alice, the brother-in-law appeared merely self-indulgent and insipid, and she quickly lost interest in spying on him round the clucking figures of Muddy and her sister. Left for the most part to her own devices, Alice wandered the village and soon discovered Mr Potter's Museum, the source, apparently, of the brother-in-law's ills. Alice put a white gloved hand on the door and pushed her way in.

A bell tinkled, announcing her arrival, but the room she entered was empty of people; no fellow browsers or curators to direct her gaze.

The place smelled odd; a faint mix of turned meat, must and mothballs that made Alice wrinkle her nose in distaste. She assumed the taxidermy displays throughout the museum were the cause. There were stuffed animals of every shape and sort, posed in odd dioramas that mimicked human pastimes: guinea pigs on their hind legs, engaged in a cricket match complete with spectators beneath a refreshment marquee; rats, representative of the lowest class, cavorting in a tavern, about to be raided by police; bloated toads frolicking in a park on swings and see-saws. Alice failed to see the charm of the creations, particularly the toads, which didn't have the soft fur of the other creatures to make them at least somewhat appealing. She moved on to glass cabinets displaying a variety of what the polite world would call freaks: a two-headed lamb, a four-legged chicken. For want of this, she thought, Muddy's brother-in-law had gone mad?

They stayed two weeks, and Alice was glad when Muddy decided she'd done all she could, and it was time to go home to Sowerby Grange. Alice had never been outside of the Cotswolds, save for occasional trips to Bristol when she'd been almost too young to recall, and so the train rides had been exciting, the countryside sliding past in a blur. But while she'd enjoyed the adventure, as she saw it, to Bramber, Sowerby Grange was where she wished to be. There, everything was familiar, and belonged to her, and so she put her foot down when Muddy wanted to journey to Bramber now and again to see her sister, and decreed there'd be no more holidays. Even when Mr Isbister entered her life they did not travel. There were short visits to Bristol, of course, now and again. Business mainly, the odd meeting with Sir Barnabas to sign this or that, nothing she understood or cared about. Only once, mere weeks into their unfortunate union, had she and Mr gone on an outing together, and then it was just up the road to Watton Hoo. He had called it an adventure, eyes a-gleam. She later pronounced it a completely foolhardy and terrifying act of utter recklessness, but it was early days in their marriage, and she was making an effort.

A fair had come to Watton Hoo, and the newlyweds had taken the pony cart over and strolled the grounds. There was a tug of war on the village green that drew a large hooting crowd. Men whose local was the Pig and Whistle Pub were pitted against those who patronized the rival Stag's Antlers. Mr paused to watch, his thumbs hooked into his braces. He wore a happy grin on his face. Mrs rolled her eyes. She wandered towards the sampling tables, drawn by the competing cries of a butcher peddling his savoury sausages, "Try them while they're hot!" and a woman flogging her gooseberry tarts "No better pastry in the whole of Gloucestershire!" Mrs ate two tarts, to test the claim, then to keep the butcher happy, swallowed a few morsels of meaty goodness. She complimented the tart maker and the butcher and placed orders with both vendors for delivery to Sowerby Grange. She moved on, licking her lips, wiping a dribble of grease from her chin and thinking that the day was going rather well after all.

Then Throckmorton had appeared at her elbow, his face shining with excitement.

"My dear, come with me!" he cried. "It's the most wonderful thing!" And, curious, she'd followed him through the press of people to an open field where an enormous silk balloon of orange and blue stripes hovered above the ground, tethered to the green by thick ropes. Beneath it, sitting firmly on the ground but connected, it appeared, to the balloon by smaller ropes, was a large wicker basket. A man with a purple top hat, oddly circus-like with its silver trim, bustled about inside the basket, tightening knots and periodically pulling on a lever over his head that caused a contraption there to belch flames up inside the balloon. Mrs gaped. She'd never seen anything like it.

Later she tried to recall how it was she'd come to agree to climb into the thing alongside Throckmorton. She'd certainly felt none of the excitement he obviously did, his eyes as round as saucers and with a silly, almost lunatic grin on his face that made his ears stand out slightly from his head. Instead, her knees had gone weak and she'd protested, hanging back. She could not go up in that thing. It wasn't seemly, let alone safe. But as Throckmorton dragged her forward, in his eagerness paying no heed to her objections, the crowd began to cheer, and people reached out to touch her arm. "Godspeed, Mrs," one fellow said. "Do us proud," came another, and then the worst, "Never knew a Sowerby to shrink from a challenge, miss. Well done." She'd eyed the shimmering balloon, swallowing her fear, and let Throckmorton boost her into the basket.

The man in the purple top hat was a foreigner, Mrs realised with a sinking feeling once she'd climbed aboard the balloon. Muddy used to say with a zealous glint in her eye that every Briton worth their salt knew you couldn't trust a foreigner. This one wore a frock coat that matched his hat, sported an enormous poufy bow tie, and his fingers glittered with rings. When Mr tried to engage the man in conversation, asking what Mrs felt sure were annoyingly technical questions, the fellow grinned beneath his pencil-thin moustache and replied, *"Sì,"* and continued to shout in some unintelligible language at several men, presumably his crew, who were working to free the tethers anchoring the balloon to the ground. He moved here and there inside the basket, checking the progress outside, and Mrs thought it wise to stay out of his way. Mr, on the other hand, hung almost obsessively on the balloon master's every motion, occasionally inserting eager comments punctuated by hand gestures into the mix, and grinning like the proverbial village idiot. He'd get them both thrown overboard, Mrs thought, then decided that that would be a good thing if it happened now, before they were off the ground. But then the basket lurched, and lifted, and there was a great cheering from the crowd, and Mrs, feeling the sausages she'd eaten earlier come precariously close to surfacing, experienced the absolutely terrifying sensation of floating. Gripping Mr's arm, she peered over the side of the basket, and watched the ground recede.

What surprised her most was the silence. Apart from the occasional roar of flame when the balloon master reached up to pull a lever on the contraption above their heads, the groan of the ropes and the creak of the basket, there was absolute silence. Mrs' fingers were white from gripping the basket's rim, and when she looked straight down she felt dizzy and sick, but Throckmorton, who seemed somehow to be successfully conversing with the purple-suited foreigner, told her to look out, not down, and then, with only minimal terror, she was able to appreciate the beauty of a bird's eye view. As they skimmed seemingly effortlessly over the land, Mr pointed out the steeple of the church in far-off Lesser Plumpton, and moments later, Sowerby Grange itself, and she had to admit her pleasure as they floated above its roofs, circling around over the wood that separated her home from neighbouring Natterjack Hall, and heading back towards Watton Hoo. Below them, ponds reflected the sky, woodlands huddled thick and dark, and farms and pasturelands lay like a patchwork quilt of browns and golds and yellows and greens.

"What a marvel," Mr said reverently, leaning out over the basket's rim. "I shall never forget this. Never." He pumped the balloon master's hand, then turned back to the vista and released a whoop of pure joy.

*

If she was honest, Mrs thought back to that day's adventure with pride, and not a little self-congratulation. She'd been afraid, and yet she'd climbed aboard that flying machine and had done her part as a member of one of the area's leading families. If not for Throckmorton, the day would not have happened, and she acknowledged that with a dip of her triple chin. But she also knew, revelling in the homage the crowd paid her after the balloon had landed, that the people cheered a Sowerby, she, Alice – not an Isbister. And, she told herself, preening, she deserved their praise.

There were parallels, Mrs recognised, between that day all those years ago, and this, though a crowd cheering as she sped off in a motor car on a clandestine assignation with her dear Woody was not one of them. Rather it was the way she'd felt during the balloon ride – queasy excitement, heart-stopping thrill, outright fear, and a lack of confidence in her ability to command her own faculties – that was mirrored as she glanced at Woody, his grey hair combed by the wind, his big hands encased in driving gloves, adeptly handling the wheel. She could barely believe she was here, next to him, in an automobile no less, travelling at such a speed, much faster than the motorcycle ride on the night of his birthday. The car – a Morris, she thought he'd called it, borrowed – hit a bump in the road and bounced, and while she reached out to grab onto something, he laughed loudly and patted her hand. She was beginning to understand that Woody would require things of her that she'd never have agreed to, had anyone else asked, and she found that slightly alarming, but at the same time tantalizing. He was impulsive and effervescent, and challenged her thinking on so many things. Take art, for example, although she had not changed her mind in *that* regard. Her lips drew together in a tight pinch. How was it that a military man such as Woody, his life spent strategizing and battling and roaming about with sabres quelling uprisings and whatnot, came to have opinions about *art*? And defend them in public? She glanced at him, admiring the largeness of him, his nose more bulbous than she remembered from their youth, his eyes crinkled from years spent squinting into the hot sun of other lands. What *had* they talked about in their smitten youth, she tried to recall? Not art. People change, she supposed… after all, she had wellingtons and thick socks packed in her case. They hit another bump in the road and she held onto her hat. Woody chortled.

*

The Morris, slightly muddied, pulled in at a lovely little limestone inn late in the afternoon. They'd driven roads that wound through some spectacular scenery, gorges and cliffs and hills that would have been stunning, Alice thought, if enjoyed at a more leisurely pace. She thought it likely her fingers had made permanent grooves in various surfaces of the Morris's interior, and she hoped that the owner of the car, when it was returned to him, wouldn't be overly cross with Woody for the effect of his passenger's faint-heartedness on the dashboard.

The inn was tucked into a narrow street in the sleepy village of Nookey Hollow, its name, the unimaginative Nookey Hollow Inn, stencilled in curling letters on a metal sign that swung over the entrance. Now that their journey was at an end, she felt suddenly nervous and rather girlish, or at least, more so than usual, for Woody had that effect on her no matter what. He came around to her side of the car and handed her out, more of a haul, really, for she was neither little nor spry, and after sitting so long felt as if she'd become permanently attached to the seat. But Woody was gracious, as ever, and pretended not to notice, giving her his arm once she was upright. Together they swept through the front door of the building, Woody calling out in his booming voice, "Good afternoon, Nookey Hollow, we have arrived!"

An eager landlord appeared, tall and cadaverous but with fleshy lips that seemed to Alice as if they must be perpetually wet. He drew his long-fingered hands together, tap tap, and bid them welcome, introducing himself as Mr Coddle, and indicating the line in the guest register where Woody should sign. The men made amiable conversation, something about caves and barrows and cheddar, of all things, but why the men should talk about cheese in the context of rocks Alice had no idea. In fact she barely heard their words as she watched Woody sign the register: Lieutenant-Colonel and Mrs Barks. She gave a nervous titter, suddenly over-warm and faint. Goodness, what had she gotten herself into? Fearing collapse, panting slightly, she clutched Woody's arm. The pen in his hand smeared the vellum and the landlord frowned.

"My dear, are you unwell?" Woody asked, turning to her with concern. Without waiting for a reply, he said to the landlord, "We've had a long drive and Mrs Barks needs to lie down. Please lead the way, my good fellow."

Her heart a-thunder and her knees weak at the horrifying idea of sharing a room with a man, dear heart or no, Alice, now known as Mrs Barks, leaned heavily against Woody, now known as her husband, and with almost funereal solemnity, followed Mr Coddle up a narrow staircase to the second floor of the Nookey Hollow Inn.

Chapter 16
WHAT HAPPENED AT NOOKEY HOLLOW

Three days hence, Alice, Mrs Barks, she as was Mrs Isbister, as was Alice Sowerby, sat before the dressing table in her room at the Nookey Hollow Inn, delicately applying powder to her nose, then her shoulders, then to her substantial bosom, lifted into almost celebratory status by a rather snug corset. On the bed lay the gown she would wear to dinner that night: a brilliant peacock blue trimmed with green ribbon, and next to it her fox stole. In the corner, by the door, lay her wellingtons, a pair of rather manly trousers she would once never have believed she'd be caught wearing, and her discarded socks, the cushion of which she had been extremely grateful for these last few days. All were muddy. The socks smelled. One of the inn's maids would collect the lot and have them pristine for the morning, when she and Woody were planning one last adventure into the Mendip Hills, wherein this quiet little village lay, a stone's throw from Wells and its beautiful cathedral.

Mrs Barks studied her reflection in the triple-paned mirror, each of the three angles sharing something different. In the left glass, a cheeky dimple appeared when she smiled. Had it always been there? And in the right, a prettily plump brow, though until now she'd never considered this her best side. Full on, her appraising stare found an intrepid adventurer, a clever conversationalist, and a tantalizing temptress all at once. This, then, was Alice Barks.

Where had this person come from? Alice wondered. She laughed to think of the trembling, naïve soul who'd nearly fainted in the lobby, and who'd been led as if to her demise to this room three days ago. She needn't have worried. Woody, darling Woody, had understood. In fact, she'd come to realise, he had his own trepidations. She rested her chins on clasped hands and recalled the afternoon of their arrival.

She and Woody had followed the landlord upstairs, she fully trembling, not realizing Woody was also undone. The landlord had stopped at the top of the second landing, slotting a key into the lock of the first door.

"The lady's room," he said, bowing slightly as he flung open the door. There'd been flowers in a vase on the bedside table. "And the gentleman's." He turned to unlock a second door across the hall, told them dinner was at eight, and departed.

Alice had stood, gaping into her room, realizing that Woody had booked two rooms, one for him, and one for her, despite their pretence at being a married couple. She thought her heart would burst with gratitude, and that she might cry.

"Are you alright, my dear?" he'd asked with concern. His palm, now that she thought about it, had been a bit clammy where it touched her hand. She, not trusting her voice, had merely nodded.

"I'll knock at eight," he said, backing into his own room. He was frowning with concern, and obvious uncertainty. "See if you feel up to dinner."

And that was all.

Dinner had been served in the inn's small but well-appointed dining room. A fire had been lit in the hearth, white cloths covered the tables, and candles gave the room a soft glow. There were several other guests enjoying the inn's ambiance, but Woody made no effort to engage anyone else as Alice knew he so liked to do. Instead, he gave his full attention to Alice. They were the last ones to leave the dining room at the end of the evening, having eaten, drunk champagne and stared into one another's eyes until the landlord yawned loudly from the doorway, not so subtly eyeing the clock on the mantle. Leaning together, they'd climbed the stairs, and just as Alice had made up her mind, her heart a-thunder, to invite him into her room, he pat-patted her hand, kissed her cheek, and said goodnight. Alice was surprised, but pleasantly. His gentlemanly restraint knew no bounds.

Woody rapped on her door in the early morning, suggesting she wear her socks and wellies and the other little gift he'd arranged for her – it was in her case – and meet him downstairs at half eight. Curious, not a little scandalized, somewhat embarrassed, she appeared wearing his gift of corduroy trousers and a wool jumper, and was relieved when he stepped forward, similarly dressed, and with a wide, approving smile cried, "Wonderful!"

The inn provided walking sticks, and Woody had a canvas knapsack on his back and a map in hand, and though he refused to say what the day's adventure was, Alice surmised they'd be going on foot. She was exceedingly grateful for the steadiness the stick leant her as they took a path into the rocky, green hills above the village.

Physicality was not Alice's strong suit. She was rather more full-figured than most women, with small feet that did not readily support such a large body for extended periods of time. Sitting was more her thing. Several years ago she'd commissioned a photograph, a rather regal image if she did say so herself, in which she'd posed, seated, in a stiff taffeta gown with full leg-o'-mutton sleeves and tiny buttons that began at her neckline and buried themselves somewhere in the shadows of her substantial bosom. The photographer, a small twit of a man who reminded her of Mr, and for whom she'd felt immediate dislike, suggested a portrait type of image, a head and shoulders shot that would fade round the edges using an effect that was, he assured her, exceedingly popular, particularly with ladies of a certain – er – size. Alice had very nearly ordered him out of her house, but instead, in a voice that dripped disdain, said she wanted a head-to-toe photograph of her entire – she used that word – figure, seated to emphasize what she called her impressiveness, then fixed him with a scornful stare that came through in the finished image. She loved the photograph, if not the photographer, and had hung it, elaborately framed, over the mantle in the parlour.

Woody and Alice marched the hills for the better part of the morning, meeting the occasional fellow hiker and exchanging a nod, though few words. Alice doubted she could have managed more than a hello anyway, so winded was she by the exertion of trekking the rock and root-strewn paths. Woody puffed too, perhaps, she dared venture, even more than did she. Like Alice, he could never be called compact. And, she'd noticed, where in their youth he'd had a barrel-chested type of physique, that barrel had slipped to a more central location. And though in Alice's view that did not make him less attractive, it was not a body type conducive to tromping about the countryside. He was better on a horse, or behind the wheel of a motor car. She wondered, but didn't ask, why he'd chosen such a holiday, but trusted that he had his reasons.

Near midday they came across a boy fishing in a stream, and sat upon a rock to watch him cast and reel, cast and reel. Insects buzzed across the caramel surface of the water, and small eddies appeared and disappeared. Alice and Woody sat side by side, Alice wheezing and fanning herself, Woody harrumphing, face bright red with exertion. He took out a handkerchief and mopped his brow, catching her eye as he did so and chuckling sheepishly.

"Not as young as I used to be, har har," he said. "Hope that doesn't put you off." He frowned in mock seriousness, and Alice's heart went pitter patter. Dear Woody. Though he made light she could see that he was uncertain of her opinion of him, of his virility, though the word, even unspoken, made her blush. She wondered if he was blind that he couldn't see how she adored him, and how much *she* was struggling to impress *him*. Suddenly this holiday in the wilds made sense, and she leaned forward impulsively, about to kiss him.

But Woody got to his feet at that moment, not noticing her amorous intent, and strode toward the boy who was joyously reeling in a small trout.

"Way to go, lad!" he cried in his booming voice. "That's a nice bit of lunch you've got yourself there. Any more in the creel?"

The boy grinned and opened the lid on the little wicker basket beside him on the grass, showing off his morning's catch. Woody peered inside, and Alice watched from a distance as the two chatted, overlarge Woody and the skinny boy. She smiled as Woody tousled the lad's head, and gave him a light punch in the arm. Then Woody had the rod, and the boy was showing him how to angle the line into the swirling eddies, just so, and Woody chortled like a youngster himself as he cast and reeled and tried to hook a fish.

Alice reclined on the rock, enjoying the warmth of the sun on her face. Her feet hurt and her back ached, her knees were throbbing and she was rather sweaty under her mannish corduroy and bulky jumper, but she was happier than she'd ever been. She was hungry too, and she wondered what Woody had stored in the canvas knapsack he'd left beside her on the rock. She considered opening it and helping herself, but figured that would be presumptuous. She decided to wait for him, and closed her eyes, folding her arms behind her head to cushion it. Funny, she thought, how when you took one of the senses out of the mix the rest seemed heightened. She could better hear the gurgle of the water, the chirp of some bird, the noise the reeds made as the light breeze strummed them. She could hear snippets of conversation between Woody and the boy: "me da says I'm a born fisherman, mutter, mutter, mutter," and "no doubt in my mind, lad, muzzle, muzzle, muzzle." There was laughter, and more mutter/muzzle, and then Alice heard, or thought she heard, Woody say in a tone of regret "...take my son fishing, murmur, murmur, murmur."

She sat upright. My son? Had she heard right? Woody had never mentioned a son, children. She frowned, then saw that he was calling to her, beckoning her over. She rose from the rock and went forward, hoping her smile was not as wooden as it felt.

"The Mrs," Woody said to the fisher boy, by way of introduction. The boy, freckled beneath his battered straw hat, bobbed his head. To Alice, Woody said, "Give it a go, my dear, it's rather a hoot," and he handed her the rod.

The boy coached her, as he'd done with Woody, but Alice heard not a word. She grasped the handle of the fishing rod, noticed the hook tied to the end of the line, and sent it into the water with a mighty snap of her wrist, all the while thinking about what Woody had said, or not said, and, if he *had* said it, what it meant. He had a son? Did have, or had had? Living, or dead? When? Where? Why had he not mentioned him?

The rod in her hand gave a tug, and instinctively she tugged back, feeling the line go taut.

"You've caught one!" cried the boy.

Alice blinked at him uncomprehendingly.

"By gum, she's a natural!" shouted Woody. "Haul him in, my dear! Let's see what you got!"

To the shouts and whoops of Woody and the boy, Alice reeled and hauled and fought the fish on the end of the line, and eventually landed a huge trout. The fish flopped on the grassy bank, and the boy did a strange kind of celebratory dance, hooting and cavorting along the water's edge.

"Cor, I ain't never seen one this big out o' this river!" he cried, pausing in his wiggles to bend almost reverently over the glistening fish body, his hands upon his knees. The boy's eyes, Alice saw, were as big as saucers. He added wistfully, "Sure wish I could show me da."

Of course, Alice gave the fish to the boy, and he went on his way as the happiest of children, turning to wave to Alice and Woody at least three times before disappearing out of sight. Alice wanted to ask Woody about the mention, or not, of a son, but courage eluded her. Such a question could ruin the holiday. There was nothing for it but to partake of their picnic lunch, and they ate it there by the river, cold sausage and meat pasties and a block of cheddar cheese that Woody, smacking his lips and licking his fingers, told her was locally made. He produced a bottle of beer to share, but Alice declined, already concerned about having to go behind a shrub. Woody had no such qualms. Before they started back to the inn, he excused himself and went for a short walk out of sight of Alice, but not far enough that she couldn't hear the splatter and dribble of what she assumed, wrinkling her nose, was urine. Amid the sounds he broke wind more than once, and punctuated the business with satisfied groans and grunts and huffs. At first Alice was shocked by his base bodily functions – what kind of man relieved himself within earshot of a lady? But when he reappeared, smiling innocently and adjusting his belt, she told herself his behaviour was merely indicative of the level of intimacy they now shared, like a true man and wife, inseparable, and with no secrets. Yet even as she thought it, she was reminded of the shred of a sentence she'd overheard earlier "…take my son fishing…" Was there a son? And why, if there were no secrets, had he not said?

After they got back to the inn Alice had pleaded a headache and took a tray in her room at dinnertime. Over a delectable repast of lamb kidneys and bread pudding and turnip mash slathered in onion gravy Alice agonised over whether to approach Woody about what she thought she'd overheard. One moment she'd decided she'd ask him, just point blank as the saying went. The next she'd talked herself out of it, fearing ruining their romance. That there was a romance she had no doubt. True, there'd been no stolen kisses, no hesitant touching or tentative gropes, but there was anticipation of those things, Alice felt sure.

The next day, charmed by Woody's boyish concern for her welfare and by the posy he brought to her door in the morning, she'd assured him she was quite recovered. Was she up for another day's adventure, he'd asked, eager above his mutton-chops. And she, peeking round a partially open door, ignoring the groan and protest of her aching body and dreading another day traipsing around the countryside with a stick had chirped, "Happily!" and been rewarded when he said, "No trousers today, Mrs Barks. Regular attire. We'll be taking the car into town."

They'd driven in to Wells, parked the Morris, and wandered through the medieval streets. Alice had decided to put the possibility of a son out of her mind and enjoy the few days she and Woody had together, and had been glad not to be climbing hills and tripping over rocks and worrying about peeing behind bushes. The cathedral in the centre of the town was a glorious old pile of stones, or, as the landlord Mr Coddle had described it, an exquisite example of Gothic architecture. "Note the spectacular outer façade boasting some 300 statues," he'd said, following them to their car, his precise, long legged steps putting Alice in mind of a stork. "And the jousting clock! You must see the jousting clock. Every quarter hour a little mechanical fellow – the *jacquemart* – strikes a set of bells, and jousting knights appear to chase one another above the clock face." Mr Coddle had clasped his long fingers together in adoration.

"It sounds impressive, Mr Coddle," Alice had said, smiling politely and allowing Woody to hand her into the car's narrow seat.

"Oh, it is, Mrs Barks, it is," Mr Coddle replied. "If you take one thing away from your visit, madam, it will be the sight of that clock, I guarantee it."

The clock was quite something, Alice had to agree. The *jacquemart* was delightful, sitting high on a perch in the north aisle of the cathedral, sporting a rather French moustache and curling hair. Indeed, at the quarter hour, Alice and Woody witnessed the little fellow – Jack Blandifers, by name – strike his bells, two with hammers, and two with his heels, at which point the knights burst from the clock's workings and jousted, knocking one another from their horses. Woody threw back his head and laughed at the sight, the booming sound echoing round the transept and drawing looks from every quarter. Alice squeezed his arm and shushed him, and they hurried out of the cathedral's silence, giggling like children.

From the cathedral they ventured to the neighbouring Bishop's Palace, where swans paddled the moat and called for their dinner by ringing a bell that dangled above the green water. It was a romantic place, with flowers growing out of cracks in the centuries old stone walls, acres of gardens for strolling, and benches in quiet alcoves. Alice and Woody paused frequently at such locations throughout the afternoon, Alice with cramping calves, creaking joints and pinching corns. She suspected that Woody was no less ragged from the previous day's outing, judging by how heavily he took a seat beside her at each stop. They enjoyed an early dinner at a pub that had been recommended by a local, and drove back to Nookey Hollow in amiable silence, too tired to talk. Alice thought she'd never been so content.

On their third morning, Woody had planned another early start. Alice decided that it must be part of a military man's world and done without second thought, all this rising with the sun and being chipper at so ungodly an hour. Stifling a yawn as she met Woody in the dining room for a plain breakfast of porridge and jam, she considered that the only thing missing was the bugle.

She wasn't sure what the day would bring. As with their other escapades, Woody had been close-lipped. But she had been advised to wear her trousers and jumper and wellies again, and bring her walking stick, so she was prepared to traipse the hills and knew she would need plasters on her corns again tonight. These outdoor ramblings were not her cup of tea, but she'd be with Woody, and eyed him adoringly, ruddy cheeked above his full whiskers, a bit of porridge stuck just there below his lip.

The Nookey Hollow Inn had supplied a guide for today's excursion, the landlord's son, Alice presumed, for he was tall and gaunt like that man, although had a less fleshy pair of lips, and introduced himself at Tim Coddle. Despite the name he did anything but, setting a brisk pace that had Woody and Alice exchanging encouraging glances, but not much in the way of banter, given that they were both breathless.

Their trek wasn't long this time. They clumped down the main street of the village, quiet in the fresh of the morning. The only sound was that of the milkman, doing his rounds in a pony cart, the glass bottles clinking in their crates. He tipped his cap and Tim Coddle nodded, and they continued until they reached an overgrown path that skirted a hillside, precarious and rock-strewn. Coddle had a key to the locked gate, and Woody and Alice followed him through. He locked it behind them, and led the way forward. He'd not so far proved to be much of a conversationalist, but he spoke now, telling them to watch their step on the right. Alice, breathing hard, looked down the steep incline along which they walked, and thought that went without saying.

Before very long the path curved and they stood in front of a gaping rock maw in the hillside. Alice wondered if this was Nookey, the hollow for which the village was named. Chill air wafted from the darkness, but it was a fresh, almost metallic smell, and Alice thought she could hear water dripping. She glanced at Woody, but he was watching Tim Coddle with an eager look as the fellow pulled a lantern from the pack he'd worn on his back, and crouched to light it.

They were going *in* there? Alice blinked hard, and swallowed nervously.

"Surely there are bats in caves?" she said, thinking the men mad for expecting her to venture inside such a place.

"Yarrup," said Tim Coddle. She assumed that was a yes. Her eyes were wide as she grasped Woody's sleeve, drawing his attention.

"We can't go in there," she said, adding a tremulous smile to soften her words, which came out sharply, and in a bossy tone that would have been rather familiar to Mr, back home.

"Normally that's true," Woody conceded, misunderstanding her objection and appearing not to notice her snappishness. "But Coddle knows the landowner, and at my request made a special arrangement to take us in. Exciting, eh?"

Alice said nothing, but Woody didn't notice her reluctance. Coddle had his lantern lit and made another noise that may or may not have been a word, and led the way toward the cave opening. Woody, lifting his thick eyebrows and shooting Alice a gleeful grin, followed, beckoning her after him. Alice hesitated, then as the two men disappeared into the cave opening, gave an exasperated hiss and hurried to catch up.

Inside, the air changed. It was cold and still, and sounds from outside – bird calls, cow bells, the breeze on leaves – disappeared. All was silent in the cave when they stood still, except for the distant plonk, plonk of water dripping somewhere beyond the lantern's yellow glow. When there was a noise, the scuff of a boot on the stone floor, the huff of Woody or puff of Alice or another unintelligible word from Coddle, the sound was magnified, and echoed. The three shuffled along, Alice following Woody following Coddle, who held up the brass lantern and lit the way. Alice could see damp, grey rock walls warped by who knew what forces into porcelain-smoothness, wobbling ridges, and pitted craters. It was beautiful, really, if the idea of being underground and in the near dark wasn't so terrifying. Up ahead the lantern swung, casting long yellow light with teasing irregularity. Alice glanced behind, and saw they'd come far enough and perhaps rounded a bend or two so that the daylight, their point of entry, could no longer be seen. She shivered, and tripped on a loose stone. Coddle muttered something, and Woody glanced over his shoulder at her with a smile she thought was meant to be encouraging, but, in the overwhelming shadow, appeared menacing.

"Not far to go, my dear," Woody said, and though he spoke in a voice exceedingly quiet compared to his usual volume, his words bounced and echoed off the rock walls, and Alice thought she heard a squeak and the rustle of wings overhead. Up ahead Coddle muttered again. Alice cringed, but kept moving. Not far to what? The threesome crouched low as the passage grew narrow and the bedrock closed in around them. Alice grasped the hem of Woody's jumper and they followed Coddle like ducks in a row. What manner of place was this? And why had Woody thought she would enjoy tromping into what seemed the very centre of the earth? Or had he? Perhaps his intention all along had been to frighten her. How well did she know him, really, after all these years? The young girl she'd been was certainly no more. Perhaps the same was true of him, a military man who'd lived long in uncivilized countries, had committed who knew what unspeakable acts in the name of sovereign and country. Perhaps his sole intention here was something heinous and sinister, and Coddle, too, was in on it.

But then the tunnel opened into an enormous cavern, and Alice saw that they stood on a flat ledge that jutted out over a pool of luminescent green water. Coddle's lamplight reflected on the pool, and played like wafting silk on rock walls made golden, and that towered above them. Alice gaped, astonished. How could she have doubted her dear Woody? This was a palace the like of which no queen had ever seen, and *he* had brought *her* here. There were glistening stone icicles hanging from the ceiling of the cavern, and below them, seemingly growing out of the rock bed, formations that looked like stacked china plates, waxy white and milky. In places the rock appeared pleated, like a well-made skirt. In others it was a myriad of small chips, as if a bevy of workmen had hit it with chisels. It was magical. Like something in a fairy tale. Alice turned to Woody to say just that when suddenly Coddle's light went out, and the cavern was plunged into utter, complete, total darkness. Someone, not Alice, screamed, and there was a splash as someone, not Alice, landed in the water. Alice planted her small feet, determined to grow roots through the bedrock, put her hands out in front of her and called plaintively into the blackness, "Woody?"

There was a great deal of spluttering and coughing, sure signs that whoever had fallen into the water was at least still alive. After a moment, Coddle's lantern again flickered to life, and Alice saw that it was indeed Woody struggling to climb out of the pool of water, which she now saw was no more than waist-deep. Coddle was as apologetic as a near non-verbal fellow can be, grunting more than usual and peering with obvious concern at the bedraggled Woody, whose whiskers really looked rather comical drooping wet. His woolen jumper and trousers sagged sympathetically, and Alice put a hand to her mouth to stifle the laughter that burst forth, a reaction entirely due to shock, she was sure.

*

One advantage to small fingers, Alice knew, was that it was easy to fasten one's gown when one had a row of thirty or so buttons running the length of one's bodice. And ten more on each sleeve. The effect of so many little cloth-covered fasteners was, Alice thought, tidy elegance, a sort of nod to fastidiousness and good taste all at once. The detail of the tiny buttons, married with the stunning peacock blue fabric and the accent of green ribbon trim meant the gown, if she did say so herself, could not have been more becoming. Alice smiled triumphantly and placed a large feather, dyed in the same brilliant blue as her gown, into her upswept hair and stood back to take stock, finding a piece of herself in each of the three panes of the dressing table mirror. Absolutely magnificent.

According to the small mantle clock it was just past eight, but Woody had not yet rapped. She wondered what was taking him. He'd said he would collect her for dinner at eight, and he was usually militarily punctual. Perhaps he'd taken a nap when they'd returned to the inn after their morning adventure in the cave and had overslept. She certainly had dozed, and she wasn't the one who'd fallen headlong into the cold waters below that stone ledge. She pressed a hand to her bosom as she recalled the terror when Coddle's lamp went dark, and then the further horror at the sound of that splash. If she was honest, her immediate fear was that it had been Tim Coddle who'd fallen into the pool, because, really, how then would she and Woody find their way alone out of the cave in the dark? But happily – well, somewhat – it had been Woody that had mis-stepped. A humiliation, certainly, but surely he'd have recovered by now. Alice paced the room, not wanting to sit lest she put a crease in her gown. It would be a shame to mar such perfection before Woody got a look.

When the clock donged the half hour Alice decided to go down to dinner alone. Perhaps she'd misunderstood, and Woody was even now waiting for her in the dining room, enjoying a Scotch whisky and glancing periodically at his pocket watch. She tapped on his door as she went by just to be sure, but there was no answering call, so she descended the stairs, swept across the lobby in her peacock finery and entered the dining room unaccompanied – an improper thing, to be sure, but this entire tryst had been that, so what was one more transgression?

Woody wasn't there. Her heart gave a small pitter-patter of uncertainty, and she glanced around, not sure what to do. Other diners looked briefly at her, but only, she thought, because she stood there so indecisively. She lifted her chin and went to the table she and Woody usually shared near the back of the room, and with a view outside. A waiter hurried over and drew back the chair for her, apologizing for not attending to her the moment she came in.

"Lieutenant-Colonel Barks, madam? Will he be joining you?" the waiter asked.

"Of course," Alice replied, with perhaps more indignation than she intended. "I expect he's just running a little late," she added, smoothing the wrinkle from her tone, and the fellow bustled away.

She sat for a good quarter hour, enduring the darting glances of the waiters, and the curious looks she began to draw from the other diners as time passed and she continued to sit alone. Fleetingly, she wondered if he'd been more upset at her laughter in the cave than he'd let on, and was repaying the humiliation by making her wait. She sipped her cordial. Woody enjoyed wine but she found the taste sour and unpleasant. She kept her back straight and her shoulders square; good posture, like good diction, were two important hallmarks of the well-bred. That much at least she had learned from dear Muddy. She cast her gaze out the window, avoiding eye contact with anyone in the room, and frowned, noticing that the Morris was not parked in the place where they'd left it yesterday upon their return from Wells. The car was a blaring red colour, not at all to Alice's taste, but also not easy to miss, and Alice was certain of the spot where it should be parked because it was alongside a large flowering thistle, and its prickly spines had snagged Alice's jumper when she'd exited the car. They'd gone nowhere by automobile since, so where was the Morris?

"Ahem." Mr Coddle, the landlord, stood at her table, looking a bit sheepish.

"Yes?" Alice said, apprehensively, and annoyed.

Mr Coddle glanced around the dining room, and Alice sensed that he was feeling embarrassment, and suspected with a sinking feeling that it was on her behalf. His already long face drooped.

"Mrs Barks, might we – er – speak, as it were, in the lobby?" he asked. She noticed he was wringing his hands. She felt a warm flush creep over her, this one rather unlike the florid sensation Woody's nearness inspired. Mustering every bit of dignity, she smiled graciously as if nothing at all was wrong and rose slowly, allowing Mr Coddle to pull back her chair and lead the way out of the dining room. From the corner of her eye, she saw people whisper behind their hands. Someone snickered. In the lobby Mr Coddle handed her a folded piece of paper.

"My apologies, Mrs Barks, to have caused you the discomfiture of sitting alone in the dining room. I was to give you this note earlier but I was unavoidably detained with a bit of a crisis in Room 6. I have not been privy to its contents but I can say that the lieutenant-colonel asked me to convey his regrets and to make arrangements for a train for you in the morning." He bowed and started to withdraw, then paused.

"One last and rather indelicate item, madam," Mr Coddle said, looking pained. "There is the matter of the account – the, er, bill, Mrs. Barks. The lieutenant-colonel left in such a hurry, he didn't settle, I'm afraid."

Alice gawped at the man, barely comprehending. Was he saying Woody was gone? And he hadn't paid the bill? Her mouth fell open and at the same time the note dropped from her gloved hand. Mr Coddle's unhappy gaze followed it, and he appeared about to retrieve it, maybe press it back into her palm. Instead, he took a step backwards, seeming to sense that something was rather hugely amiss, and had the good grace to slink away.

Alice stared at the folded message lying on the carpet. What had happened? What had gone wrong? She could feel a muscle twitching in her cheek, and suspected her face had erupted in blotches, a reaction indicative of both anger and shock. What possible excuses could be written in that message, she wondered. And would she choose to believe them? She clenched her teeth. What a naïve and ridiculous woman she was, to have so readily fallen for the charms of a man she really only barely knew. For the first time in days she thought of Mr Isbister. When she arrived home tomorrow, he would be as obtuse as ever, potting about in the greenhouse or sniffing out frogs in the swamp, perhaps even unaware she'd left. She wanted to cry, but she equally wanted to scream. She snatched up the note and stuffed it inside her glove. She'd read it in her own good time, or not at all. She hadn't yet decided.

As she marched towards the staircase the bright feather she'd tucked so happily into her hair a scant hour ago, hoping to impress Woody, dislodged, and sagged in front of her face. Not breaking her stride she reached up and plucked the feather out, pausing just long enough to stick it into an urn, where it bobbed, a gaudy misfit among the fern fronds.

Chapter 17
NEVER BEEN TO THE SEASIDE

There were no wistful over-the-shoulder glances, no tugs of nostalgia, no regrets of any kind as Mr Isbister climbed onto his Trusty and rode off into the night, although admittedly, the departure hadn't been entirely smooth.

He had paused long enough to stuff a canvas haversack with necessities – extra socks and a pair or two of smalls, an undervest, spare trousers and his well-worn flat cap. He'd included his straight razor and shaving brush, his toothbrush and tooth powder, and several nice large hankies. Hankies were a staple, really. You never knew when one might come in handy, or what part of one's body might require its use, in a pinch. Apart from those few items, he had had the foresight to think of money, a necessity for the purchase of petrol, oil and food, and ducked into his bedroom to gather what coins and bills he could find tucked haphazardly into trouser pockets and bureau drawers. All in all, it came to a tidy enough amount; no need to pilfer the little strongbox which Mrs kept in a locked desk in the drawing room. It contained a wallet embossed with the Sowerby crest, and she always kept a fair sum in its kid leather pocket, but it was her household fund, and Mr was nothing if not gallant. He left it untouched. At the last minute, he gathered some books, envisioning leisure time with feet up. *The Illustrated Handbook of English Botany* wasn't to hand, which was a loss, but he retrieved his art book from beneath his mattress, and his motorcycle manual from the bedside table. This was it, after all. He wasn't coming back.

He donned several layers of clothing, knowing from experience that riding on the motorcycle at night, even in summertime, could be a chilly prospect, so when he trundled downstairs with his haversack in hand, he was sufficiently clad in serviceable trousers held up by a pair of suspenders, a button-down shirt, a striped jumper of woolen knit, and a corduroy jacket. His only moment of difficulty came when he spied his mud-caked wellingtons. Those, like his botany book, he would miss. He felt a catch in his throat, and almost brought them along – but, no, they were impractical on the bike. They would have to remain behind. He was resolved.

He stepped outside into the garden and stopped, experiencing yet another pang. Across the way, the greenhouse glowed in the moonlight like a milky beacon, summoning him. He decided he couldn't leave without a last visit, and set his haversack on the ground, his walk to the greenhouse door almost processional. As he opened it, the loose pane of glass rattled in the ceiling, and he chided himself for never having gotten around to fixing it. Inside, the greenhouse's earthy warmth hugged him like a friend, and he wandered amongst the plants, briefly touching those leaves that allowed it, and favouring the spiny ones with a tender smile. Next to Whortleberry Wood, this place had been his sanctuary, and he wouldn't soon forget it.

"I'll not be back," he said aloud, "but you'll be alright." The plants sat in what seemed like expectant silence, like good children hoping for a treat. He paused, and an idea came to him. He returned to the house and retrieved his muddy boots from the cloakroom, then re-entered the greenhouse, and set the wellingtons inside the door next to the watering can. He nodded. Better.

When he exited the greenhouse he saw Eliza standing by the privet hedge. She waved, and Mr grabbed up his haversack and headed her way. No turning back now.

*

The sidecar was roomy enough to stow Mr's haversack and Eliza's bag – a sturdy one, Mr noted approvingly, made of stout Brussels carpet. Eliza had also brought along an extra rug, and convinced Mr that the old canvas tarpaulin he'd used to cover the Trusty might also come in handy, and together they'd folded it and placed it beneath the sidecar's button-tufted cushion, additional padding but also some shelter, should they have need of it. It had been Eliza, too, who'd hauled the little oil can and the empty petrol container from the shed, and Mr, strapping them onto the back of the bike, nodded to himself, admiring her practicality. They hadn't yet left the drive and he was already wondering how far he'd have got without her.

His pocket watch (not the gold one engraved with the Sowerby family crest, a gift from Mrs on some occasion or other, and given not out of affection but because it was the thing done, but his own plainer version, owned since he was a young man), told him it was midnight, as fitting a time as ever to embark on such an adventure. His leather helmet was snug on his head, and he pulled his goggles down to protect his eyes. Eliza, he saw, had her own pair, though where and how she'd come by them he had no idea. They glanced at one another through the thick glasses and nodded, and Mr, butterflies in full flight in his stomach, gave Eliza a thumbs up signal and gunned the bike. The Trusty gave an excited putt-putt, then coughed and died.

"What the dickens?" said Mr. This was not exactly the start he'd pictured. The butterfly flutter in his stomach became the panicked flapping of moths.

"Try it again," Eliza advised calmly, snug beneath the lap rug. "Use the priming cock."

Yes, of course, the priming cock. He smiled sheepishly, and wondered if Eliza had read the bike's manual. This time, the Trusty lived up to its name. He steered her down the drive and out onto the road, on a whim turning left towards Lesser Plumpton instead of right towards Watton Hoo.

They hadn't discussed, and Mr hadn't thought even to himself, what their destination would be. They simply drove, casting periodic giddy glances at one another, breathing the scented night air, and marveling at the way the white moonlight gave everything a sort of bone china gleam. They putt putted through Lesser Plumpton, heading roughly north and west through the Cotswolds. At each crossroads Mr slowed the Trusty and turned to Eliza, and with neither choosing to shout over the noise of the bike's engine, their consultation on direction was a simple matter of a head jerk, a thumbs up or down, or a shrug. Fate was cast to the wind, and depended upon which name on the fingerposts most appealed. So when they came to the first crossroad, Eliza chose Gormley Green over Twiggly End with a shrug, and at the next Mr opted for Rothsbottom rather than Upper Swine with a grin.

Eliza sang. The noise of the engine drowned her out for the most part, but snippets came to him on the wind. Something about being the only boy and girl in the world. He liked the idea that she felt emboldened enough to burst into spontaneous song, and his heart skittered lightly at the idea that she might sing such words in reference to the two of them. The only boy and girl in the world. What a splendid idea. He glanced at her, saw her red hair tugged by the wind, her hat pinned down by her goggles and one hand on the top of the hat, holding it in place. She sang lustily, and unselfconsciously, as if hardly aware of the words. She only once glanced his way, her gaze sweeping him but not singling him out as she took in the countryside around them that was lightening as dawn began to break in the sky at their backs. The song was not for him – well, perhaps the music was for him, for both of them, but the words intended no special meaning. He chided himself, but light-heartedly, for foolishly even entertaining such an idea.

Eliza tapped his arm and signalled that she wanted him to pull over. He drew the motorcycle to the side of the road, tucking her up against a low stone wall skirting a field and turned off the motor.

"I think the old girl needs a break," he said to Eliza, patting the Trusty's gas tank. Eliza climbed out of the sidecar and stretched her limbs.

"She sure does," she replied. She grinned at Mr, who stumbled to apologize, assuring her he hadn't meant Eliza.

"Never mind, sar," she said cajolingly. "Both old girls need a break, so if you don't mind looking the other way I've a need to visit the other side of that stone wall."

Mr, catching her meaning, pinked and obediently turned his head, while Eliza went behind the wall and relieved herself. Truth was, he had to take care of the same business, though the idea of such a thing in the presence of a lady made him not a little embarrassed. Still, there was nothing for it. He went a little further along the wall to spare her the immodest sound of his tinkling, and when he returned he saw she'd unstrapped the petrol can and was refilling the tank. He dug through his satchel and came up with one of his enormous hankies, offering it that she might then wipe her hands. What a team they made, he thought.

Eliza was rummaging through her own bag, the large Brussels carpet one, and produced a flask of tea, two boiled eggs and some biscuits. How clever of her to bring food, Mr thought, and said so. He hadn't realised how hungry he was, but after all, it was a new morning, and this, then, was breakfast. He was surprised that he wasn't tired, and in fact, still felt rather exhilarated by the idea of escape and adventure. He and Eliza munched side by side, leaning on different parts of the bike, and Mr said, "I wonder where we are, exactly." Eliza then produced a map from her bag and Mr chortled. She was the best fellow adventurer he could have wished for, he thought, and told her. They spread the map on the flat top of the stone wall, and traced their journey so far, laughing at the zigzag route they'd taken through the night, choosing their direction on whims, and seeing how far they hadn't come. Mr, tapping his lip, said, "Perhaps we ought to choose a destination." They leaned in, as if expecting some locale to make itself plain.

"I've never been to the seaside," Eliza offered, running her finger along the coastline on the map.

"Nor I," said Mr.

"There are several," Eliza said.

"Several?" Mr echoed.

"Seasides," she replied, looking doubtful. Mr peered at the map again, seeing only one long snaking coastline, but assuming that what she actually meant was that one could choose the seaside at any number of places; Somerset, perhaps, on the Bristol Channel, or Devon, even, a little further afield.

"Land's End," he said, blurting it out. The end of the country, unless one took a boat. Another whim. It was becoming a habit.

"Gosh, I love that name," she said.

"Then Land's End it is," Mr said expansively. Luckily, their haphazard nighttime journey had sent them roughly south though they'd departed initially on a northerly route, and they plotted a way to the next village, towards that spit of land at the tip of Cornwall. Then Mr folded the map into a tidy rectangle, Eliza packed up the remains of breakfast and they stowed their bags in the toe of the sidecar.

"You drive," said Mr, gesturing to the Trusty's seat, and Eliza, grinning widely, hiked her skirt and climbed aboard. Mr settled into the sidecar, pulling the rug up over himself, and before Eliza started the motor he leaned over and tapped her arm.

"One more thing," he said, blinking through his goggles. "Call me Throck."

"Yes, sar," she replied, blinking through hers, and the Trusty sprang to life.

*

It is an amazing thing to witness the world come awake, and this, the first morning of what Throck hoped would be a delightful journey, was no different. Cocks bantered about, and presumably crowed (though Throck couldn't hear them over the noise of the motorcycle), long before what he had always thought of as morning. That time when one's eyes fluttered open to find the sun well up, or, if cloudy, daylight at least routing every shadow, and the aroma of kippers and toast and a nice pot of tea, perhaps, wafting. As Throck and Eliza travelled the narrow lanes from one village to the next, through woods and alongside plowed fields, over bridges and under tunnels, he considered something he'd never actually thought about before – that morning arrived in the wide outside world hours before it ever arrived in his narrow indoor world. By the time the sun actually lifted above the horizon its light had already crept forth, and barnyard animals, birds, scuttling hedgehogs and slinking foxes rose too with that early dawn. Traffic in the form of milk carts and hay wagons and other farming conveyances appeared next, and then working-class men in their flat caps and women with baskets over their arm, and sometime after that a morning arrived that Throck recognised, peopled by more smartly dressed citizens, getting about for one reason or another, or tucked in their houses, reading newspapers and making lists. Throck was a little embarrassed to be a part of that last group, missing out on hours of time, taking for granted that precious thing one could never get back.

They putt-putted until about mid-day, taking turns at the controls of the Trusty, one driving while the other dozed or simply took in the sights. Eliza, he noticed, liked to wave when they saw people, and invariably, they waved back, whether in response to her exuberance or the unusual sight of a motorcycle and sidecar careening down their quiet country lanes. Throck was completely enamoured of the machine and the way it carried on up hill and down dale, never a groan or a squeak or a complaint, as long as it had its petrol and its squirt of oil every five miles or so. It bumped over cobbled streets as happily as it swerved along dusty cart tracks and gravelled roads, and when they stopped at a small market town somewhere south of Bristol, Throck gave it a good rub-down with one of his hankies, restoring its metal gleam.

It was important to get out and move about, Throck decreed, citing cramped legs if one was riding in the sidecar, and sore arms, if one was at the controls. Eliza agreed, though Throck noticed that she seemed unhampered by such afflictions. With the Trusty having its own well-deserved rest, parked in the market square of a little town called Chew Crumpet, Throck performed a few deep knee bends accompanied by some hoo-haas to keep the lungs perky, and generally stretched his legs. A few women with baskets over their arms gave him a wide berth. Eliza scampered off to visit the shops, mentioning the need to replenish supplies, although to Throck's mind, they hadn't really used anything other than some oil and petrol and a boiled egg or two. Still, ladies must be humoured. He took a seat on a bench next to the Trusty and relaxed, enjoying some sun.

He may have dozed, but he came awake with a start as an automobile, garish red and moving at a dangerous speed, careened into the square, the horn sounding with repeated duckish burps. Pedestrians jumped out of the way and Throck sprang to his feet, agape. What kind of lunatic drove a motor vehicle in such a manner? The car sped past him, the tyres slipping on the cobbles, and just as Throck raised his fist to shake it at the driver, he recognised Woody Barks. In a second that seemed to last a full minute and move as slowly as a snail, their two sets of eyes, as round as plates, connected. Throck saw panic in Woody's. He wasn't sure what Woody saw in his.

Then he was gone. The red car disappeared down the very road Throck and Eliza had just travelled, trailing the noise of the horn behind it. Throck's mouth hung open. Woody. In a car. Without Mrs. What did it mean? He sat back down on the bench, frowning. He may have made a colossal error in his assumptions.

Eliza returned shortly. She'd bought some sausage and a roll of bread and a bottle of beer, she said, and did he see the red Morris go flying past? The keeper of the shop she'd been in had said they ought to send the constable after the fellow and stop him before he hit someone.

Or hit an animal. An image of dead Amos the goat flitted through Throck's mind, but only momentarily. There were other things right now to worry about.

"It was Woody," Throck said.

"What?" asked Eliza.

"Woody. It was Woody. Woody Barks," Throck said. "Lieutenant-Colonel Barks." He was still frowning. Woody's flapping mutton-chops and the round O of his mouth between those unmistakeable whiskers was stuck in Throck's mind. That and the look of alarm he'd seen in Woody's eyes. What did it mean, he asked himself for a second time. To Eliza he said, "Mrs Isbister wasn't with him."

"Oh," said Eliza. She remained still, clutching her paper-wrapped parcels, seemingly uncertain what to do or say. After a few moments she asked, "Do you want to go back, then?"

"Back?" Throck repeated.

"Home, sar," Eliza said, her tone soft but slightly exasperated.

"No. Well, I don't know," Throck said. He felt a bit squirmy inside. Was it guilt?

Eliza sat down on the bench beside him and gazed at the parcels in her lap. Her shoulders seemed to slump, and Throck considered what it would mean to Eliza if he decided they should return home. She would have no job, he supposed. Mrs wouldn't agree to keep her on, given the circumstances, although it was hardly fair. But fair didn't play into things very often in life, or so it seemed to him.

Yet even apart from what might happen or not to Eliza if they went home, he didn't want to go back to Sowerby Grange. That, he decided, was the squirmy part. He should, perhaps, return. An honourable man would. An honourable man would not have left in the first place. No, that wasn't quite true. An honourable man would have stood his ground twenty-five years ago and refused to be bullied into accepting a life he hadn't needed or wanted. An honourable man would have gone and lived in a tent, if it had come to that, after the solicitor, Sir Barnabas Henshaw, had arranged his eviction. Well, that's what he was going to do now. The honourable thing. And live in a tent, perhaps. Better late than never.

"You should go home, then," Eliza said, interrupting his thoughts and rising from the bench. She went to the sidecar and hauled out her big Brussels carpet bag, slung it over her shoulder. "I won't be going with you, sar, so's you know. I'll make me own way from here. But good luck to you, sar. It were a nice ride."

Throck leapt up off the bench. "No!" he cried, so loudly that people bustling about the market square paused and gawked in their direction. "No," he said again, more calmly this time. He stared at his feet for a moment, and twisted his goggles in his hands. His mind seemed blank but for that one single word. He repeated it, with finality, "no." Then he took a deep breath, grasped the carpet bag from Eliza's shoulder and put it back in the sidecar. "I believe it's your turn to drive, Miss Vanson."

She hesitated, searching Throck's face. Then she shrugged and smiled, exposing the gap in the front of her teeth. "Elizer, sar" she said. He felt something skitter happily inside himself.

"Throck," he replied, bowing, and they both laughed.

They threaded their way on the Trusty, Eliza driving, Throck in the sidecar, meandering through the town until they came to its outskirts. There, at a fork in the road, a fingerpost indicated two choices. If they went left, they would head towards a place called Nookey Hollow. They shared a giggle at the name. They consulted their map, saw that Nookey Hollow was a village in the Mendip Hills, and not in the direction they needed to go. They took the right fork, and continued on, the day sunny and warm and wonderful.

Chapter 18
HAVING A BIT OF TROUBLE

The rain poured down as if the sky felt the need to dispense with every bit of moisture it held. It battered the canvas of their makeshift tent – the Trusty's oily tarpaulin – making an awful racket and seeping in round its edges, so rivulets ran in tiny torrents through their shelter. The motorcycle shared the space with them, making an effective wall with which to support one edge of the tarpaulin. A couple of sturdy sticks stuck into the ground held up the other side. Throck and Eliza huddled beneath the canvas on the lap rugs, and shared the bottle of beer she'd purchased at the last town.

The storm had caught them by surprise. They'd been on their merry way, Eliza singing while she drove and Throck taking his turn to wave to people walking on the road. Most did not wave back at him, he noticed, the way they did when Eliza did the waving, but he opted not to be discouraged. He was intensely happy now that his adventure was back on track, and he'd chosen not to think about Woody and/or Alice – selfish, perhaps, but there it was. From now on he would live in the moment, concentrate on the here and now, consider tomorrow when it arrived.

Suddenly, though, the here and now had begun spitting fat raindrops. Throck had not been sure how many miles they'd covered since departing Chew Crumpet, but the day had waned and the sun had begun to sink off to the west before they'd realised a storm had snuck up behind them, making an emergency stop necessary. At the first spot that looked hospitable – a small clearing in an otherwise rocky and hilly area – they'd pulled over and figured out how to rig the tarp for shelter before the clouds opened completely and the rain pelted down.

"This is quite nice, really," Throck said, feeling expansive. The tarpaulin smelled of oil, the rug he sat on was acting more like a sponge than a cushion and soaking up the seeping water, and he had to speak rather loudly to make himself heard over the incessant hammer of the rain. But he was warmish, was sipping beer alongside a red-headed girl, and together they had a map that laid out a million possibilities. What more could a fellow want?

"Harold Guppletwill and I used to sit in the rain," Throck said, reminiscing, passing the bottle to Eliza. "Well, not teeming rain, of course, and not beneath a tarpaulin like this. If Harold was on the hunt for something – the natterjack, always, of course, but he looked for other things too, newts, for instance – we often found ourselves sitting on a rock in a light shower." Throck shrugged and smiled. "A little rain never hurt anyone."

"And did Mr Guppletwill ever find his newt?" Eliza asked, returning the bottle to Throck.

"Oh, yes," Throck replied. He took a swig of the beer and handed it back. "Cute little fellows. One of them sat for an hour on a rock while Harold made a sketch of it. Posing, or so it seemed. Quite astounding, really."

"And yourself, sar? Were you agog o'er newts too?" She was rummaging in her bag as she asked, and when he didn't reply straightaway, she looked up to see he'd fixed her with a reproving eyeball and a frown. She amended with reticence, "Throck, I mean," then pulled forth bread and cheese and passed some to Throck, who munched contentedly. This was dinner, he thought with pleasure, though nary a plate in sight.

"Most things Harold studied I found interesting," Throck replied. "Harold would have it no other way. To know Harold was to be utterly engulfed by his enthusiasm for his studies. One couldn't help but share his zeal. I admit to a great envy but also great admiration of Harold's chances to do wonderful things for the world of academia. He was a clever, clever man – *is* a clever man. I refuse to accept that he will not one day come back."

"If you're that certain, 'twill be," Eliza said with quiet conviction.

They sat in silence a while, then she said, "You're a clever man too, Throck. You could discover newts on your own, happen you took a notion."

Throck gave a small laugh, embarrassed but pleased by the compliment. He knew he wasn't dull-witted by any stretch of the imagination, but he wasn't Harold's peer in the academic sense. Goodness. To steer the conversation away from an awkward discussion of the quality of his intellect, he said, "Newts have a certain charm, I'll admit, but fungi are my own personal fascination. So many shapes and colours and sizes and habits. They're everywhere, if people would just notice." He glanced around and grinned, pointing out a smattering of small orange discs sprouting just there beneath the sidecar. "Cowpat gems, if I'm not mistaken. Fresh-laid dung is a favourite for them, so we'll have to watch our step when we move the bike." He took another bite of cheese, a delicious sharp cheddar with a faint hazelnut flavour, and chewed pensively, then added, "*Marasmius rotula* – collared parachute to the lay person – is my favourite."

"I know," said Eliza.

"You do?" Throck said, looking at her in surprise.

She shrugged and reached into her seemingly bottomless carpet bag, pulling out a small well-thumbed volume which Throck instantly recognised. It was his copy of *The Illustrated Handbook of English Botany*. His face shone as he glanced from Eliza to the book and back again.

"The corner o' the page on – rotunda, or whatever it is, is turned down. And there's scribbles, and all manner o' doodles," she said by way of explanation. "I saw the book in the drawing room when I were gatherin' items to bring along with us. I thought you'd want it."

Impulsively, Throck leaned over and hugged her like an exuberant child receiving the very best toy for Christmas. She laughed. He felt like a character out of Dickens – Bob Cratchit in receipt of the turkey. Such a heart she had, to think of him that way. *He* hadn't considered *her* when he'd rushed about stuffing socks into his haversack. He promised himself, without saying anything aloud, that he'd be a more thoughtful travel companion in the days ahead.

By the time the rain began to let up it was thoroughly dark out, and Eliza and Throck decided a journey through the night with puddles aplenty to dodge, while perhaps being in the spirit of adventure, was an unnecessary discomfort. The rain could start again, and then where would they be, trying to resurrect the tent or find some other shelter in the dark in the wet. With full bellies and no pressing need to move on, they curled up where they were, Throck wrapped in his rug and Eliza in hers, and slept.

*

In the early morning Throck came gradually awake. Bundled cocoon-like in his rug, sensing an uncomfortable wetness that was due, he was sure, to the tumultuous downpours of the night previous and nothing embarrassing, he opened his eyes. Eliza was already up, he saw, and for a moment he remained silent, watching her, she unaware of his scrutiny. Who was she, this extraordinary young woman who sang music hall ditties at the top of her lungs while driving a motorcycle through rather challenging terrain, and then, upon halting, produced food and books from her bag like a magician, and proceeded to charm him with her cleverness and ingenuity? In all his many years he had never met anyone quite like her, she of the tangled red hair and sweet smile and plain words. She sat in profile, and he noticed she had a pencil and seemed to be writing on a piece of paper.

"Good morning," he said.

She started almost guiltily, and crumpled the paper into her palm.

"Making a list?" he asked.

"Something like that," she replied. The paper and pencil went into her pocket, he saw, and she held out a hunk of sausage. "Breakfast?" she said. "I wondered if you might be going to sleep all day. Cocks crowed ages ago."

Throck struggled upright, still wrapped in his rug, and took the sausage. Munching it, he saw that she had the map spread out. "Have you been plotting out the day's route?"

"I have," she said. "And it's a long way to Land's End. It's in Cornwall. Did you know?"

"I did know," Throck replied. He swallowed the sausage and accepted the apple she handed him. "Too far, do you think? We can change our destination, if you like."

"I don't see that we're in a hurry for aught," she answered with a lift of one shoulder. "It's just – I knew someone once what moved to Devon. It's on the way."

"Ah," said Throck. "A friend? Perhaps you'd like to visit?"

"No. We had a falling out," Eliza said evasively, then smoothly changed the subject by directing Throck's attention to the map, where she'd pencilled in a route that took them as far as Wellington, near the Blackdown Hills. "If it don't rain today I reckon we can make it there. Happen it's a nice place, I hear."

"From your – someone?" Throck asked, teasingly. He didn't mind that she didn't want to share the details of the friend, he told himself. But he was curious. She hardly ever spoke of her past.

Eliza, however, pointedly ignored the question, and didn't so much as glance at him as she packed up their things – the map, the damp rugs that she shook free of grass and what clots of mud would come off, the empty beer bottle that she stoppered and stowed in her carpet bag, and the remains of the sausage that she wrapped in its butcher paper and tucked away for later. Then she gestured for Throck to take an end of the Trusty's tarp and they folded it in what Throck sensed was less than amiable silence, and tucked it back beneath the sidecar cushion.

"I'll take first go, shall I?" Throck said jovially, attempting to lighten the mood.

"Suit yourself," Eliza replied, and climbed into the sidecar.

Throck stood beside the bike. He caught sight of himself in the small rear-view mirror fastened to the handlebar, and saw that what little hair he owned was sticking out at angles from his head, and his cheek held the imprint of the buckle from his haversack, which he'd used as a pillow. He looked troubled, his lower lip jutting slightly, his eyes creased with concern. Not the face of an intrepid adventurer, sallying forth in pursuit of the mysteries of the world, or for now at least, the curiosities of Cornwall. Best to clear the air, he thought. No sense dragging a big anvil of discord around with them. The Trusty couldn't bear it, and neither could he.

"I apologize," he said, making a small bow. "I should not have asked about your Devon acquaintance. It was not my business or my place." Eliza looked down at her hands, folded in her lap. "Perhaps we need parameters. Boundaries, if you like. Things we must not do or say. Would that be a good idea?"

He waited. He shifted from one foot to the other. Eliza appeared to be thinking. A fellow lumbered into view on the road, driving a gaggle of muttering geese before him. Throck nodded. The fellow said "A'right," and continued past.

"We don't need such rules," Eliza said from the sidecar. "I'm just a little grumbly this morning. I'll come 'round."

She threw him a bit of a smile and that was enough for Throck. He preferred the pleasant to the un, and if Eliza said she'd come around, that was all he needed to hear. Onward and forward. He straddled the bike and kicked the starter, and though he spun the tyre in the mud, he got enough traction to get them out onto the road and on their way.

*

On the side of the road near the village of Stoke Bumbley, a fellow in a dapper white suit was stopped by his car, tinkering with the motor. Throck pulled over to ask if the man knew which town nearby might have a chemist shop that sold petrol so they could replenish their dwindling supply. The Trusty was on her last few gulps, and they'd nothing left in the can Eliza had brought from the shed. The fellow, deep in concentration, apparently didn't hear the Trusty putt in behind his vehicle, and when Throck walked up to him and tapped him on the shoulder the poor man banged his head on the lifted bonnet.

"What the devil," the man cried, turning towards Throck and rubbing his head. He was a tall man with what the ladies might call a handsome face: the hard blue eyes hawkish above a sculpted jawline. He scowled at Throck, whose friendly how-do-you-do smile slipped crookedly. The hand he'd held out to shake was not taken, and Throck let his drop to his side.

"Apologies," said Throck. Then, attempting friendliness again, "Having a bit of trouble?"

"No," growled the man. "What does it look like?"

Throck paused. Was the man using sarcasm, or was he really not having trouble? And how could he, Throck, just delicately reverse from this rather unpleasant dialogue and drive away? Would that be impolite? Would it matter? Well, of course it would matter, he chided himself. One should always avoid appearing rude or discourteous, even when on the receiving end of such behaviour. It truly was what set the gentleman apart from the boor.

Eliza appeared at his side just then, and Throck noticed the fellow's scowl faded and he stood a little straighter. He lifted his pork pie hat to her and said, pleasantly, "Afternoon, miss."

"Hello," she replied. "Nice car you've got there. My brother had one. It's a Bentley, isn't it?"

"Ha. You've got an eye," he said. Throck supposed that meant the car was indeed a Bentley, since if he'd been referring to Eliza's rather startlingly blue eyes, he'd likely have used the plural.

"Did it overheat?" she asked, peering past him at the steam leaking from the engine. "I recall my brother had to change his radiator core once. A nuisance, to be sure, but it fixed the problem. Or so he said."

The man narrowed his eyes at Eliza, as if suspecting her of espionage. "Your brother said, did he? Ha." He glanced over his shoulder at the engine behind him, as if it too was guilty of some sort of collaboration. Throck, for his part, was beginning to understand that 'ha' did not necessarily indicate humour in this man's vocabulary.

"I have some water with me," she said. Then by way of explanation when the fellow didn't seem to follow, added, "To top up your radiator so you can get on your way. Until you can fix it."

He harrumphed. "Were you in munitions?" he asked.

"During the war," she acknowledged.

"Birmingham?" he asked.

"Slough," she replied.

Throck watched this rather cryptic exchange and wondered when might be a good time to jump in and ask about the petrol. Eliza, though, had things well in hand, and had dug out the tea flask, refilled with water at the last village, and was pouring the water into what presumably was the radiator. Throck wasn't sure about such things. The Trusty, thankfully, was not so complicated.

"We were wondering where we might buy some petrol," Eliza said as she re-stoppered the flask and offered up one of her smiles.

"Yes, not easy to find a chemist," the man said, succumbing in a small way and turning up a corner of his mouth. But it as quickly drooped again and he glared at the Bentley's radiator as if it was sure to double-cross him and overheat yet again. In an angry tone he added,

"Bentleys are far superior to any other vehicle, of course. Can't credit why this one's giving me a headache. Trouble is, one can't find a decent automobile repairman for love or money, even though everyone's out of work. Lazy sods, you ask me. And as for finding petrol – well, outside of a market town you'll be hard pressed."

Eliza smiled sympathetically. Throck, having studied her smiles in depth, knew there was also impatience behind that sweet demeanour. She leaned towards the fellow and touched his sleeve ever so lightly. "Ah, but you're one of the lucky ones," she said, as if sharing a secret. "Driving a Bentley. Smooth as silk they are, or so my brother always said."

"No quarrel with that," the man agreed, although his surliness was unabated. "Selling up was a poor choice on his part. Why did he sell, then, if he thought it was so great? Probably couldn't find a mechanic. Ha."

"Could never find a chemist," she answered. "Just like us." She smiled again, persuasively, Throck thought. He wondered if there was any truth in this tale of Stephen and a Bentley, or if it was all bunk. Or – a second thought – had Eliza yet another brother?

The fellow laughed, though Throck didn't really understand what was funny. He tapped his chin as if something had just occurred to him, and a great gold ring on his forefinger glinted in the sun. To Throck it looked like a signet ring, with some sort of bird on it. "I'll tell you what," the man said. "I don't know where you can find a chemist, but I've got a full tank of petrol right here. Seeing as how your brother was a fellow Bentley man, we might be able to make a deal." He patted the Bentley and cocked a brow at Eliza. Throck frowned. Was the fellow leering? And what did he mean by make a deal?

If the man was leering, Eliza seemed unperturbed. She took a step forward and looked up at him, cocking her own brow. "Why, thank you, Viscount Dempsey." She emphasized his name. "A Bentley man can always be counted on to be honourable, least that's what my brother says. Quart of water for an overheated Bentley in exchange for a quart of petrol for a thirsty Triumph seems a fair trade. Thoughtful of you to suggest it." She smiled and Throck watched, not quite sure what had passed between Eliza and this fellow – gracious, was he really a viscount, and how did Eliza know it? – but aware that she seemed to have gotten the upper hand. The only worry now, he thought, was how they would syphon the gas from the man's car but then, goodness, there was Eliza, drawing a length of rubber hose from her carpet bag. Throck's jaw fell open but he had the good sense to close it and remain in the background. This, undoubtedly, was Eliza's triumph to savour.

Chapter 19
OTHER PEOPLE'S KNOW-HOW

The petrol from the Bentley man carried them to the Blackdown Hills, an area of graceful beauty. Gentle was a word that came to mind, or tranquil, Throck decided, but not tepidly or insipidly. Straddling the border between Somerset and Devon, the woodlands in the Blackdown Hills were fragrant with wildflowers, streams sparkled in secluded dells, and villages were come upon unawares, tucked away behind hedge-banks and reached by winding lanes that the Trusty, and so Throck, thrilled to. Throck was enamoured – or would have been had Eliza shared his sense of excitement.

She, instead, seemed melancholy. Almost despondent, as if she were being led to her doom and not visiting the loveliest of places. Throck, at the helm of the motorcycle, glanced so often at her with concern he almost drove the bike off the road. He decreed it was time to stop and set up camp for the night, though it was just late afternoon. Because they had daylight and time and favourable weather, they were able to do a proper job of constructing their shelter, and Throck learned a thing or two from Eliza as she directed the cutting of whippets and a ridge pole, then showed him how to stick the withies into the ground in two opposite rows and bend their tips into the holes she chiseled in the ridge pole. Two more withies placed at one end helped sturdy the structure. It was a bender tent, she told him as they laid their canvas tarpaulin over the framework. Used by the gypsies up Birmingham way. Throck beamed. He, living like a gypsy. It was a story for Harold, to be sure.

Once the tent was set up, they hung their rugs from a tree branch to air them out. They'd been stowed damp after the previous night spent in the rain on the side of the road, and were rather musty and muddy. They hung clothing as well, though not their smalls. Despite sharing their days and sleeping side by side, at night modesty must needs be paramount, Throck was sure they would both agree. Once that was done

Throck thought they might eat. His belly rumbled and he wondered what other edibles Eliza might have stored in her voluminous carpet bag. He got out the botany handbook and settled down by the babbling stream near their tent, his back against a tree, assuming Eliza would call him for sustenance. Ah, leisure was a fine thing.

Eliza, though, had other ideas.

"Sar," she said hesitantly, then immediately, and with an apologetic smile, revised that. "Throck, I mean. We've settled in rather nicely. Happen we might stay on here a day or two? Poke about." She nodded towards his book, now cover up on his lap. "You might search out some mushrooms and whatnot."

Throck waited, sensing more to come. She still did not seem her old self. The gap in her teeth was not appearing as frequently as it should, nor did the light in her blue, blue eyes.

"I were wondering if you might allow me to take the Trusty for a bit? Visit the market at that last town we passed, buy a few things. Cheese, bread. A packet o' tea." She shrugged, and, like someone requesting a concession they don't expect to receive, added "I could get us another bottle of beer."

Throck smiled. "Beer. Well, of course you must. And cheese would go a long way with that." He closed his book. "I could go with you, if you like. For company." But even as he said it, he sensed she did not want him along. Perhaps it was something to do with her melancholic mood.

"You'd just be sitting on a bench waiting while I shop," she said. "Wouldn't you rather stay here with your book?"

Throck nodded, and smiled, though in truth had no desire to be alone, even in the midst of the Blackdown Hills. He enjoyed Eliza's company, his fellow adventurer. He liked knowing she was nearby. But he said what she wanted him to, and waved her towards the bike. "You're astute and intuitive, dear Eliza. A couple of hours to doze and poke about, as you say, will be just the thing. Let me give you some money for the beer and the food."

She drove off down the leafy lane, her big carpet bag stowed in the sidecar. As she disappeared out of sight Throck experienced a pang of concern, and an intuition that all was not well. What if she didn't come back?

*

He told himself worrying was unproductive. He tried to read but found his gaze insisted on straying to the lane down which she'd disappeared. Instead of relaxing he paced around their little campsite and tried to distract himself by identifying various plants and flowers along the stream's bank. A usually enjoyable pastime but, as with reading, one on which he could not concentrate the longer the day stretched and Eliza did not return. As the afternoon grew old, he wandered a bit further along the stream, looking for a diversion, and came across a magnificent old clapper bridge, its smooth shale slabs laid end to end over low stone piers. Forgetting for a moment Eliza's absence, he admired the simplicity of the construction, and considered the building of it centuries ago, the men and ox and carts employed for days in the activity, and the eventual celebration of its completion. What would those same men say, he wondered, to the knowledge that ages on – hundreds of years even – some lonely fellow past his prime and lacking much of a purpose in life would stand upon it in silent tribute to their skill? Perched at its centre, he gazed upstream in the direction of the little camp. They'd chosen a very picturesque location, and now that the sun had begun to sink the light was such that insects, hovering above the sparkle of the stream, appeared like suspended bits of molten silver, and water droplets, clinging to small reeds at the shore, were pearlescent. The leaves of the trees, in their full summer splendour, rustled very gently on a breeze that was almost imperceptible. Just enough to stir the scent of flowers and water and remind one of the beauty of the world at large.

In the distance, and through the gently swaying greenery, Throck could see the bender tent in its little clearing by the water. He'd wanted to ask Eliza how it was she knew how to make a gypsy tent, but her melancholy and her previous sensitivity to questions had stayed his query. As his eyes rested on the tarped shelter, he thought he saw some movement, and he shielded his eyes against the sunset. Was Eliza returned? He hadn't heard the Trusty. He strained to see and gave a shout when he recognised the long, striped face of a badger. He started to run back along the clapper bridge, yelling and waving his arms, and the badger, alarmed, scuttled off through the underbrush. When Throck arrived at the bender tent his heart was thundering. He lifted the flap of the tarp and saw what the badger had been after. Eliza had left food behind: bread, cheese, sausage, but she'd also left him a box of matches, presumably so he could start a fire when it got dark. He slumped onto his knees, puffing hard from his sprint, but also dismayed. It appeared she had not any intention of returning that night. Or perhaps at all.

*

Since she'd left him a gift of the matchbox, he decided he may as well try to get a fire going. It would stave off a bit of the desolation of being alone in a wood, and it might be cheery to cook some of the sausage, make a proper dinner of it. He turned the box of matches over in his palm, wondering if there were instructions for starting a fire in the woods, though truth be known he hadn't the skill to light the hearth fires at Sowerby Grange either. If there was one thing this so-called adventure was teaching him, it was how very much he had relied on other people's know-how as he coasted through life, feet up on a stool, a cushion beneath his backside.

He knew one needed dry items to burn, so sticks, presumably. A good variety was not hard to find in the woods, and he gathered some, dumping them in a little heap on a flat rock not too far from the tent. A non-burnable surface on which to light one's fire was important, he surmised, if one did not wish to burn the woods down around one's ears.

The sticks assembled, Throck lit a match and held it beneath one of them, but before the stick caught the match burned out, singeing his fingers. He tried again with greater success, but the flame he managed fizzled without doing much burning. Something was clearly wrong in his pyre design, or perhaps these were not flammable sticks, and he needed a different species. He tried not to let frustration overwhelm, but he did feel on the verge of a yell, or even a sob. Buck up, he chided himself. It was not yet dark, and there was still a chance, though admittedly appearing more remote with each passing hour, that Eliza would return. But even that thought was humbling. He should be able to do this without her.

A thought came to him. Paper! Paper was a good burnable substance. And he had not one but three books with him: his treasured botany book, the manual for the Trusty, and his rather large and clumsy art book. Of the three, the art book was the biggest indulgence, and in a life or death situation (which admittedly this was not yet, he reminded himself) that tome would be the first to be sacrificed. He stumbled to the tent and retrieved the book, dashing away a tear as he tore and crumpled the frontispiece and the index. Perhaps that was all he would have to give up. He stuffed them beneath the sticks and reached for the matches.

"Evenin', young'un," came a voice, deep, but mellow, like thick honey.

Young'un? He? Throck twisted around to see a man decidedly older than he standing behind him with a sparse white beard, straggling grey hair and a large nose shot through with veins, bordering on purple. He wore a shirt in the full-sleeved style of a century past, baggy-kneed breeches tucked into much worn boots, and he carried a long gun under one arm. A brace of plump wood pigeons hung from his belt.

Throck was perhaps staring, because the odd fellow seemed to think him daft, and made another attempt at a greeting. "You all roit?" He shifted the gun, and the movement spurred Throck to recall his manners.

"Hello!" Throck responded, keeping an eye on the man's weapon. He scrambled to his feet and brushed dirt from his palms and smiled, making a belated attempt at politeness. "Can I help you?"

"Hmmm," replied the visitor, glancing round. He appeared to think that maybe he ought to be the one doing the helping.

Throck, unsure of the protocol when armed guests happen upon one's campsite, gestured round the clearing, as if to offer the fellow a chair. "Welcome," he said, although it came out as more of a question than a greeting.

"'Aving a bi' of a campout, then?" the man asked, looking pointedly at the tent and the unsuccessful fire. "Down from London, 'appen?"

"Yes – that is, no, not London. From the Cotswolds, actually. Just en route, as it were."

"On a root?" the fellow repeated with a frown, but did not pursue. He nodded at the sticks Throck had collected for his fire. "'Appen ye're not 'avin' much luck there."

"No," Throck agreed sheepishly. "The sticks don't seem to want to catch."

"Ye need some proper tinder," the visitor said, propping his gun against a tree. "A bit o' yer old man's beard an' some tree gum an' ye'll be roit as rain." He turned and walked off, indicating as he went that Throck should follow him. Throck hastened to comply, and the fellow led the way downstream and across the clapper bridge, Throck giving a last worried glance back at the clearing, though the evening was growing so dark he could barely make out the tent. Was it a bad idea to follow this strange man on a hunt for someone's beard and gum from a tree?

They didn't venture far. The huntsman, if that's what he was, paused by a knobby spruce tree, and nudged Throck to make sure he was paying attention as he used a stick to scrape globs of gooey sap from a wound in the tree's bark. From another tree nearby he harvested drapes of lichen that Throck knew as *usnea longissima* and which did indeed resemble a scraggly beard. Tutor to pupil, the fellow showed Throck how to combine the resin and the lichen into what seemed to Throck to be a hoary dollop of goop. They concocted several sticky balls – Throck had one stuck to just about every finger – and then made their way back to the clearing. The huntsman brought along a goodly supply of dry spruce sticks, as if skeptical of the quality of Throck's previous collection.

The visitor introduced himself as Mungo Large, and seemed to want to take Throck under his wing. Rearranging the kindling Throck had earlier attempted to light, he added the dry spruce sticks he'd gathered and showed Throck how to place the spruce-lichen balls in strategic locations throughout the pile.

"Now hold yer match to them balls," Mungo Large said, encouraging, "and watch 'er go."

Throck obeyed, and indeed the gum and lichen balls blazed effortlessly, and quickly ignited the dry spruce sticks, which in turn began to char and then burn the heavier wood Throck had gathered. He sat back on his heels, grinning like a school boy, and held his hands out to the crackling warmth. Mungo hunkered down beside him and slapped his brace of pigeons on the ground next to the fire.

"Hungry?" he asked, and Throck noticed that when he grinned he had a gap between his teeth not unlike Eliza's. The smile was quickly swallowed by the whiskers, though, and even so, there was no time for wrenching reminders of runaway companions. Mungo drew a blade that looked as if he'd forged it himself, and nudged Throck to attention, unnecessarily, for who would not have their eye on a man just met and wielding a knife. Mungo demonstrated the cleaning of the pigeon, inserting the point of the knife just there, at the base of the first bird's breast, and Throck watched closely as he made a small incision, then inserted a finger into the wound and peeled back the bird's skin, feathers and all. A cut here and there at the wing joints, a little tug, and a soon-to-be-tasty breast of pigeon was ready for the flame.

Mungo handed him the bloody knife. "Your turn, young'un."

Throck accepted the blade with more than a little hesitation. He'd never stuck a knife into a creature before, living or dead. But he doubted Mungo Large would countenance squeamishness, or allow him a bite of succulent bird if he did not do his share, so, his belly rumbling, his tongue sticking out of the corner of his mouth, he attempted the cleaning of the second bird. All in all it went rather well, although Mungo helped with the final yank. When the deed was done and the breast slapped down alongside its mate, Mungo said approvingly, "Yep."

Mungo then used his blade to whittle a sharp end on a green stick and threaded the pigeon breasts onto the skewer. He pulled a small paper packet from his pocket and sprinkled what appeared to be dried herbs onto the birds, then handed the skewer across the fire to Throck, with a nod.

"Me own special blend," he said. "Rosemary and lavender and salt o' the sea. There'll be some tasty morsels." He leaned back on his elbows, watching critically as Throck turned the meat over the fire. "Roast 'em slow, that's the way. Turn 'em even, like. Happen we'll have ourselves a fine little feast o' them pigeons."

"You're a generous man, Mr Large," Throck said. Without him, Throck was fully aware, he'd likely not have had this fire, and certainly would not have eaten much more than cold sausage and what was left of the cheddar, and almost definitely he'd have had no company at all in the darkness of the Blackdown Hills.

Mungo pulled a metal flask from somewhere and unstoppered it, taking a long swig. "'Tis human nature," he said in his timbred voice, "sharing, helping. Man has done it since time began, and will do, I reckon. Not a thing to remark on, really." He shrugged and drank again, then passed the flask to Throck.

It was a stiff liquor, and unfamiliar. Its obvious potency put Throck in mind of the absinthe he'd drunk with Julio Quint, though the flavours were not similar. He tried to hand the flask back but Mungo waved him off. Throck took another swallow, savouring the taste. Sweet but strong, with a hint of something like almond. He felt decidedly at ease, and sipped again. A woodsman's life was becoming more appealing by the minute.

"Don't burn the birds," Mungo said. This time he accepted the flask, took a good long pull and smacked his lips. "Portuguese," he said to Throck, indicating the container. "Happen I know a few sailors down Torquay way. Not all vessels put in at London docks. Least not straightaway." He grinned and winked.

The pigeons smelled delicious. The scent wafted as Throck turned them. His mouth watered and his stomach rumbled. He wondered how much longer before they could indulge.

"Were you a sailor once, then?" he asked by way of conversation, continuing to turn the pigeons on their spit.

"I've been on a ship or two in me youth," Mungo acknowledged. "'Twere never me thing, though, the sailing life. All that ocean. Blue or grey water and not much of anything else. The woods, now there's where me own heart lies. Four seasons, each with different colours and smells. And the birds." He nodded to the pigeon. "I'll take a roast squab o'er a fish any day o' the week. And speakin' o' which, those birds'll be ready for the tasting, young'un. Pull that spit off the fire."

They tucked into their dinner with gusto, and Throck thought he'd never eaten anything so delicious. The juice from the bird dripped down his chin, and for a fleeting moment, and not unhappily, he thought of Mrs, and how much she enjoyed her food, the evidence of it very often on her face. Copying his companion, he ran his sleeve over his mouth, and smacked his lips.

Mungo passed the flask, and they shared the Portuguese liquor between them. When it was done, Mungo brought out another, and

Throck retrieved the sausage and cheese from the tent and, chuckling like school boys, they indulged in a second course.

"Where ye headed then, young'un?" Mungo asked later, leaning back against a rock. He pulled out a pipe and began to stuff its bowl.

Throck, belly full and more than a little bleary-eyed from the liquor, lounged against his own rock, and replied with a wave of an arm, "Land's End."

"Ah, that grand spit at the end of the civilized world," Mungo said. "A jumping off point to be sure."

Throck knitted his brow, puzzling over Mungo's words. Was it a jumping off point? Or a destination in itself? He'd thought the latter, but maybe he'd been wrong. He and Eliza hadn't discussed what came after Land's End, if anything.

"When I were a young'un, younger'n you, mind, I ran off like ye. Packed up me kit and took off, I did. Jus' like that. Left the Mrs behind and away I went. Me 'n' 'er'd had our days, I figured, and we were good and sick of each other. She couldn't wait to see the backside o' me, and I couldn't wait to show it to 'er. So away I went, all the way to the tip o' Scotland. John o' Groats, 'appen."

"John o' Groats," Throck said. "I've heard of it. A curious name."

"Curiouser and curiouser," Mungo said, lifting one eyebrow. "Found out when I got there that the town – if ye can call it that, all 300 or so souls of it – were named for a Dutchman called Jan de Groot who used to ply a ferry twixt the town and some islands thereabouts."

Throck pursed his lips in contemplation. "So John o' Groats is a corruption, of sorts, of the Dutchman's name, I take it?"

"'Tis a fact," Mungo said, confirming with a nod. "But that don't make it curious. What made it curious was the translation o' Groot, as they told it me." He peered at Throck over a tipple from the flask. "Groot means large! Large! Me own name!" He slapped his thigh and laughed. "It felt like fate, Throck. Like I were meant to be there."

Throck smiled happily. "What happened, then? Since you're here and not there? If it was fate, I mean."

Mungo nodded, and sighed. "Well, I spent some time wanderin' the few lanes thereabouts, and climbin' the sand dunes, and in me meanderin' I met up with a lassie name o' Ismay whose man were off t'sea. She taught me a thing or two 'bout the place, not least o' which were that most o' the men, her own included, go off on their fishin' boats for days at a time, leavin' their women a little lonely." Mungo grinned and waggled his brows. "We had a grand ol' time, me and Ismay. But come home those fishermen do, an' by time the boats were sighted and Ismay were lookin' askance me feet took it upon theirselves to get a little itchy. The place might be *called* Large, but it's only that in its dreams, and I guess I weren't really done wanderin' anyway. Some commiseratin' soul told me John o' Groats weren't the end o' the world, so I got on a ferry and went as far as I could. The Orkney Isles, then the Shetlands." He stared into the glow of the fire, his eyes reflecting the embers, and Throck thought he saw more than that in their depths – fragmented images of faraway places, memories of people met by chance and circumstance. Intangible treasures. Mungo brushed impatiently at one eye, and Throck wondered if he'd shed a tear.

"I don't regret a minute of me travels, young'un," Mungo said. "I've seen and done things most people could only imagine, and I've learned things that I do believe have made me a better man. I've had me share o' scrapes and dodgy situations, but I'd brought along the tools of the traveller's trade – curiosity, respect and good humour – and made proper use of 'em." He leaned forward and tossed another piece of wood on the fire, sending tiny sparks skyward. "After the Shetlands I hopped a fishing boat for Norway, all towerin' mountains and dark forests and narrow waterways they call *fjords* that open to the sea. I tell ye, young'un, ye've never seen the like." He shook his head as if to emphasize the incredibility of the place. "I worked on a timber gang in Norway, and spent a few months trying me hand at silver mining. Met a lovely girl named Siri who liked havin' an Englishman about the place, but before long I had the pangs, stronger than the ones I were feelin' for Siri even. I left and headed south, and eventually made me way home." He threw Throck a wide grin. "Not to the wife, mind. That ship sailed. But it were time to close the circle. And I missed these 'ere Blackdown Hills."

Throck doubted *he'd* ever want to go home again, but nodded anyway, understanding. The more he thought on it, the more certain he became that the open road – open seas, even, though that was a more daunting prospect – were in his own future. With or without Eliza, if need be. The men sat in silence a while, and the mood seemed to have turned broody until Mungo, all but lolling on the ground, propped himself up on an elbow and changed the subject.

"Did I tell ye," he asked, his tone light, "about the time I were in the Olympic games?" He nodded. The flask of Portuguese liquor went back and forth. "True story. It were Paris, turn o' the century. I were a shoo-in for the win. Guess what the event were?" He raised himself up and leaned towards Throck, who was also happily lolling, lulled by his full belly and an excess of drink.

"Live pigeon shooting," Mungo said, not waiting for Throck to respond. "One competitor at a time, ye stand at the ready with your rifle, and then whoosh, they let 300 of the buggers go at once. The sky goes black with pigeons, and ye've got to shoot and kill as many of the birds as ye can. Bit of a blood bath, 'struth, and a mess o' feathers and guts after, so not a favourite with the squeamish."

"Goodness," Throck said, doing his best to keep up. He looked at Mungo out of one eye. The flask went back and forth some more. He wondered how many of them Mungo had tucked in his various pockets. Flasks, that is, not pigeons.

"I didn't win, case ye were rootin' for me," Mungo said. "I'm a crack shot but couldn't match the Belgian who took the gold. Twenty-one birds he killed. They billed the sport as *tres aristocratique*. Maybe that's why I didn't win. Not an aristocrat, me. Just a huntsman."

He fell silent, staring at the fire's embers, thinking, perhaps, of faded glories. Across from him, Throck too had grown pensive, but his thoughts had nothing to do with huntsmen or aristocratic Olympians. He was thinking of Eliza, with her blue, blue eyes and her red hair. What had happened to her? Why had she left? Where had she gone, and, most importantly, would she come back? He thought about Mungo's girls, Ismay and Siri and who knew how many others, left in the wake of his itchy feet. Had Eliza felt the same affliction?

An owl hooted, and the dying fire cast Mungo and Throck in a flickering bronze light. Both men slept, Mungo with his rifle beside him, Throck with his head on a rock.

Chapter 20
A BOLD ADMISSION

Throck's coming awake was a slow and painful process. At first consciousness his eyelids fluttered, and through the slit of them he confirmed that there was indeed daylight beyond their mantle. The same affirmation roused a dull hammering in his skull and he groaned, turning in search of some more comfortable position. He then came sluggishly to the realization that he'd been asleep on a rock, and with Herculean effort, roused his limbs and crawled to the bender tent. Inside it was dark and there was the relative comfort of his rug. He curled up and returned to the land of Nod. His last thought before drifting back to sleep was of damning the Portuguese and their liquor, and though they'd not been present on this particular foray, he likewise cursed the French and their absinthe.

He dreamt he heard the Trusty putter into camp, and the dream was so vivid he could smell the motorcycle's exhaust. He could smell bacon too, oddly, and imagined the dull clank of a pot, and even, with great clarity, Eliza's voice.

"Sar," she said, softly. He grumbled and rolled over. Her voice was nice to hear, even if it was a dream version, but he really did not want to be disturbed at this moment. Sleep felt paramount. He burrowed further into his rug.

Her voice came again, more insistently, "Sar!" and was accompanied by the sensation of being shaken. His brain clunked unpleasantly in a skull without padding.

"G'way," he muttered, and struck out with his arm, coming in contact with something solid before the cocooning rug was ripped from his body. He came abruptly awake, blinking, and saw Eliza, holding his rug in one hand and her nose with the other.

"That's a fine good morning," she scolded. "You might have blacked me eye." She tossed the rug back on top of him and left the tent, calling over her shoulder, "There's bacon and tea if you'll drop the fists."

Throck crawled from the tent. On his hands and knees he surveyed the clearing where, yes, it was coming back to him, the night before he'd learned not only to start a fire with a bit of tree gum and some lichen, but how to clean a dead pigeon and cook it to perfection on a spit.

"Is Mungo still here?" he asked, after clearing the cobwebs from his throat. Looking around, though his eyes were bleary, he could see the answer.

Eliza was bent over a small tin pot that contained the tea, Throck presumed, for a goodly steam rose from it. She used a cloth – one of the handkerchiefs from his haversack – to grasp the handle, and poured some of the dark liquid into a tin cup, which she handed to him. He didn't ask where the pot and cups had come from. Time for details later. He sipped gratefully at the hot liquid, closing his eyes to savour it.

"Who might Mungo be, that he ought to still be here?" she asked. Her tone was a little sharp, it seemed, though he couldn't think why. It was she, after all, who had some explaining to do. She handed him a tin plate with some bacon and scrambled egg, and, sharp tones aside, he thought he might faint with the pleasure of the smell. Food, and tea, just the thing on an off kilter morning.

"Mungo's a friend," Throck answered, his reply deliberately evasive. "Kept me from starving." He was coming around, regaining his senses as it were, and taking back the role of the injured party. She, after all, had abandoned him, and stolen his Trusty.

Except here she was, cooking him breakfast.

"Starving, were you?" she said, with an arch of her eyebrow. "There were sausage and cheese in the tent." She sat down beside him and they munched the food silently, staring into the embers of the small fire. He wanted to ask how she'd started it, and to tell her about the tree gum and lichen, but of course there were other topics more important to be dealt with first.

"You came back," he said.

"You thought I wouldn't?" she asked.

"Well, it did seem a long shopping trip," he replied.

She said nothing, and poured more tea into his tin cup. The bacon was delicious. Almost as good as the pigeon the night before, but he did not share this observation. When they'd finished their meal she took the dishes and the little pot down to the stream and gave them a scrub, using sand as an abrasive. Throck joined her, one of his large hankies at hand, and dried them. The sun was out and there was a bit of a breeze, and the reeds on the far bank of the stream moved languidly. Throck sat back on his haunches and lifted his face to the sun, its warmth balm to a man feeling the after-effects of an overindulgence in Portuguese liquor. He'd expected to be left to it, but instead Eliza sat beside him, and turned her face upwards as well, eyes closed.

For quite a long time they sat in a silence that at any other time Throck would have described as companionable, but which today he sensed held a thread of tension. There were things that needed saying, but his earlier attempt at conversation having been rebuffed, he was hesitant to be the one to initiate a beginning. After years of living with Mrs he was good at avoiding conversations he did not want to have, but not so good at starting ones he did. After a while, when it seemed Eliza would say nothing, he plunged in.

"We are less than a week into our journey, and it would seem we have come to an impasse of sorts," he said.

"An impasse?" she repeated, puzzled.

"At the risk of raising your ire yet again, I feel I must point out the facts as I see them," Throck said, forging on. "You, indicating a need to shop for supplies, took the Trusty with my happy blessing. That, I have no quarrel with."

"But I didn't come back right away," Eliza said.

"You did not," Throck affirmed, a modicum of indignation creeping into his tone. "In fact, I wondered if you intended to return at all."

"Did it not cross your mind that I might have had an accident?" she asked defensively. "Or that the motorcycle might have broken down?"

"No," he replied firmly. And when her look challenged him, he added, "You left me the matches. And food."

She pouted slightly at that reply, and he could sense her continued reluctance at sharing her secret. She picked up a pebble from the stream bank and inspected it, turning it between thumb and fingers. She sighed, and tossed it into the water.

"I went to see George's mother," she said.

"George's mother?" Throck repeated. "Your mother, you mean?"

Eliza gave a hiss of exasperation. It was obvious she did not want to tell this story, but Throck was determined not to let her off the hook, so to speak, on this one. She had nearly deserted him and stolen his motorcycle because of it, and if they were to continue to be – whatever they were – he felt he had a right to hear it.

"George isn't me brother," Eliza said, nodding when Throck lifted his brows. "He belongs to a friend of mine, Nancy Gladwell, as was Grimshaw. Well, she used to be a friend, anyway. Not sure she is now."

Throck pictured young George, small for his age, but a clever lad, and wily. He'd known a thing or two about the Trusty, Throck remembered fondly, and wasn't above reading other people's mail or gadding about in the dark. He was like Eliza in many ways, so Throck was mystified by this admission.

"Nancy and me shared a flat in one of the Peabody Buildings in London before the war, on Webbers Row, it were, in Southwark. We did odd sorts for a bob – but by night we were music hall performers, singing and dancing and the like, only Nancy were better'n me. She could hit a high note like no one, and she were dimpled and pretty and liked to laugh. She had a following, had Nancy. Always a crowd vying for a smile, or something more. She used to bring admirers to the flat now and again. One of the most frequent visitors was me brother Stephen, and for sure Nancy were right sweet on him. I think he used to find it funny that I'd have to make meself scarce. I sure wasn't laughing, but Stephen were ever a ladies' man, and Nancy had a mind of her own."

"Goodness," said Throck, shocked by such a bold admission. He glanced sideways at Eliza, but she had her eyes on the gurgling stream, and seemed determined not to look at him as she talked.

"When it come obvious that Nancy were – you know, in the club – well, it were quite a pickle. She couldn't work. No one wants to hire a woman in that condition, either before the babe comes or after, even in the music hall business, unless you work at the lowest sorts of establishments. When I pressed, she admitted that Stephen were likely the father, but being as she couldn't be completely sure, and Stephen being Stephen, he wouldn't marry her. Any other admirers she'd had, the ones who'd pledged undying devotion even, well they disappeared in a hurry. But I were her friend. Despite her choices, I were her friend, and I said I'd stand by her."

Throck, watching her, saw a steely look in her blue eyes he'd noticed before, though less obviously. Shocked by her tale so far, he nonetheless found himself admiring that determination, and in his heart he cheered her brave choice.

"I took any jobs going, nights at music halls when I could get 'em, and by day whatever was going. The best of it was maid's work at some of the middle class houses on the other side of the river. I did what I had to to put food on our table and pay the rent. Little George were a happy baby, and the cutest thing y'ever saw.

"When the war started it were a blessing, though it may shock you to hear me say it. George were four year old by then, and, well, maybe not at first, but eventually, there were good work available. Lots of work. And few men for the jobs. So women – I – worked in factories. They were good paying jobs, and more hours than there were girls, so I gave up whatever I'd been doing before. With George grown older and off at school part of the day, Nancy figured out she could pay a little girl to look after him while she worked and still come out ahead in her pay, so she took a job as well, and so it went for all the years of the war.

"But then, Nancy being Nancy, she found someone new. Bert Gladwell by name. A nice bloke, she said, though I never met him. He weren't a soldier. Bad heart or something. Worked in a telegraph office, I think. All the same, we argued about him. I said she needed to tell him about George, she said she couldn't, or she'd lose him. One day a couple of years into the war – George were five or six – she didn't come home from work. I were some angry, thinking she'd gotten up to her old ways, but when she didn't show up the next day either I went by the factory where she worked and asked some of the girls if they'd seen her. They told me she'd quit. Said she was getting married, and had moved to someplace called Hemyock, in Devon, with her bloke."

"And she left George behind," Throck said, shaking his head at the callousness.

"She did," Eliza said, her tone harsh. "A little boy, but old enough to understand. It broke me heart. I made up a story about how she loved him but had to go away. Weren't no matter, I said, we were family anyway, like brother and sister, and as long as you have that you've got no worries. But now I had to figure out what to do. I thought about saying George was me son, and that his da had been killed. After all, there were plenty of genuine war widows. But there were also lots of girls putting that sort of a story out there. I didn't want to be suspected of being one of them, so I chose a different lie. I got a job in Slough, and me and George moved to new lodgings where no one knew us and I said he were me brother, and all were well for a while."

"For a while?" Throck asked, sensing more to the story.

"The war were ending, weren't it?" Eliza said. "Soldiers were coming home and wanting their jobs back. Factory work – munitions, anyway – was slowing down. The factory in Slough were retooling to make car parts, and I didn't want to go back to London and me old life, so when I saw a notice in a newspaper advertising for a maid at Sowerby Grange, a nice long ways from where anyone knew me, I applied."

"And here we are," said Throck.

"And here we are," Eliza repeated.

"Except," said Throck, slowly, "we don't get here from there." He turned towards her on the stream bank. He anticipated that she might think his words unkind, but he thought it best to get them out there. "Haven't you gone and left George, just like his mother did?"

"No, I haven't," Eliza said indignantly, twisting to meet his challenge. "He's got Stephen, and Julio. And I wrote to him when we left. I posted the letter at Chew Crumpet. There's a big difference between what I did and what Nancy did."

"Perhaps," said Throck, unconvinced. He believed her when she said that she wrote because he recalled her secretive scribbling, but he remained skeptical of her reasons for coming along on this trip. He'd thought, perhaps naively, that she'd wanted an escape the same as he. Now it seemed there'd always been another motive. "Did you tell George the reason you were going on this journey was to meet up with his mother?"

"Of course not," she said angrily. "That were never me reason. How was I to know that would happen? I didn't plan it. I saw the name of the town where she lives on the map, is all, and thought I might try to see her, tell her about George."

"And to do that you needed to steal my motorcycle? Why not just admit what you wanted to do? It says very little for your faith in me."

At that, Eliza fell silent. He stole a glance at her, and saw she was frowning and staring at the water. After several long minutes she looked over at him, and he, meeting her gaze, was taken aback yet again by the brilliant colour of her eyes. They could set one off one's axis, if one weren't careful.

"I'm sorry. It seemed easiest not to have to explain things from me past," she answered. "And I suppose I feared what you'd think." She picked up another pebble and tossed it into the stream, waiting, it seemed, for Throck to say something, or to indicate somehow that he forgave her. He did forgive her, of course he did, but he let a bit more time pass before he tossed his own pebble, and then another, and then a third. Before long they were laughing, and competing over who could throw their stone the furthest, and at some point Eliza paused and turned to Throck with a smile. "I were always coming back," she said. And Throck, glad of that, decided that there was time enough later to press for more details about her visit to Nancy.

*

The tension of the morning eased after that, and Throck and Eliza agreed that another day spent camped out by the stream in the Blackdown Hills might be just the thing. Eliza sorted the provisions she'd purchased, boiling the eggs and cooking the rest of the bacon so they'd have food at hand when they resumed their journey. Not that there was any hurry, she said over the pan, and Throck smiled indulgently. He found himself picturing what it would be like to have a little cottage somewhere, to bustle in a kitchen together, bumping elbows, or to sit and share a pot of tea whilst talking of dreams and adventures. He blushed at such whimsy, and told himself he did not necessarily mean with Eliza, ho ho, she was younger of course, and likely hoped for someone, well, else. Besides, he planned to wander, perhaps become a soldier of fortune, an argonaut or an Odysseus. No room at all for a cozy life.

Throck told Eliza about Mungo and regaled her with some of his tales, and in the afternoon they walked to the clapper bridge and across it, following the footpath to a pool of calm water where Eliza suggested they enjoy a swim. The afternoon was warm, but Throck blanched. A swim? Naked? Or, just as horrifying, in his smalls? Of course he was thinking mainly of Eliza's reputation, he said in protest, but did not say that he was also loathe to display his own less than stellar physique, what with its wrinkles and sags and unsightly tufts of grey hair here and – er – there. But Eliza laughed and said her reputation couldn't be compromised if there were no one about, and besides, they were both in need of a wash. Throck, colouring, supposed that in the absence of a proper tub of warm water and a bar of soap and a private room, a swim in a pond would have to suffice. All the same, he was relieved when Eliza directed him behind one bush while she disrobed behind another.

Discreetly, and mindful of the other's modesty, each made a point not to look as first one, then the other, emerged from behind their respective shrubs and entered the pool. Once in the water, however, submerged to the neck beneath its relative cover, a playfulness took hold, and they splashed and ducked and dove and laughed aloud. Throck couldn't recall the last time he'd enjoyed himself so thoroughly, and thought how far they'd come from their initial relationship of maid and master.

Later, dressed in damp clothes and walking in single file across the clapper bridge towards their camp, Throck broached the subject of Nancy, and what had happened when Eliza found her.

"Well, she were stunned," Eliza said over her shoulder. "Her mouth hung open and she went all white, but her husband Bert were there too, so weren't much for it but for her to play along, make me out to be long and lost and all that. But with a look she warned me to say nothing of George, and I didn't. Least not 'til her man were out of the room." She stepped off the last of the bridge's stones, a wobbly slab that teeter-tottered, and turned back to Throck, offering him a steadying hand. She didn't let go as they walked along the stream path, and Throck, completely distracted by the feel of her hand in his, was hard put to concentrate on her words. It occurred to him that no one had ever held his hand before. Not even Alice.

"He did seem a nice man, her Bert, just as Nancy had said all them years ago. He helped her cook dinner, and he put their two little uns to bed so we could catch up, and then, after inviting me to stay the night seeing as it'd got quite dark, he went off to the pub. All were pretty civil up 'til then."

"Was she angry that you'd come?" Throck asked, making an effort. He was acutely aware that her hand was cool, her touch light, nothing at all to it, and yet... His palm was growing moist and hot and he feared that she would soon let go and wipe her hand on her skirt.

"Not so much angry, but scared," Eliza said. "I could see it in her eyes the whole time her Bert were in the room. Pleading with me not to give her secret away." She snorted. "As if I would do that after all I'd already done for her."

"Indeed," agreed Throck. He stumbled over a root and Eliza tightened her grip of his hand.

"I come right out and asked her, now she was settled, did she want her Georgie back? A boy should be with his mother, most times. I told her he was a good lad, a bit on the small side but healthy, and clever as a whip. I said he'd done some schooling and could read and write and do his sums, stuff like that."

"And he knows his way around a motorcycle," Throck put in, glancing at Eliza with a grin. He'd already begun to grow comfortable with the hand-holding, even if he wasn't sure of its intent.

"He does, our George," Eliza said fondly, grinning back. "But Nancy started to cry. Said how would she explain George to her Bert, and her other two little'uns, not to mention her friends and neighbours? It were too late to give out that she'd been widowed during the war, and besides, that claim, as I said before, had been spun aplenty.

"I told her I hadn't come to threaten or make trouble, but since I were nearby I wanted to give her a chance, in case things had changed for her and she regretted what she'd done.

"Mayhap that weren't the right choice of words, because she stood then, like she were playing the part of a ladyship in a tragedy, and she looked right down her nose at me and said George was as much me brother Stephen's problem as he was hers, and if he had no regrets o'er the boy then neither did she. She wasn't turning me out in the night, she said, as if 'twere a kindness, but first thing in the morning she expected me gone. And she took herself off to bed, just like that. Left me to climb under the blankets Bert had laid out for me on a pallet on the floor, and that were the end of it. I woke before anyone else and left without seeing her again."

"Well, perhaps it's for the best," Throck offered. "If she doesn't want him he's better off with people who do."

"You're right," she said, giving his hand a lighthearted swing. "When she spoke I felt badly for George all over again that his mother didn't want him, but I doubt he even remembers her. 'Tis me and Stephen and Julio he knows as family, even if Stephen won't own up to his responsibility. But whether George knows Stephen as father, or brother, or something else, he knows he's loved, and in the end, what more does a body need?" She smiled, and Throck smiled back, then tripped on another darned root.

*

Throck was in his rug and Eliza in hers, both curled up and asleep even before the sun had completely dropped beyond the trees. Perhaps it was the swim, or the warmth of the day or the bit of a feast they'd had for their dinner – sausage and potato warmed in the pan Eliza had bought in Hemyock along with the tin plates and cups. Whatever the reason for their early doziness, Throck found himself wakened by a plaintive voice calling softly from outside the tent.

"Young'un? Young'un?" Twice summoned, Throck struggled to an elbow as the owner of that familiar voice, Mungo Large, poked his grizzled head through the bender tent's flap. "Y'awake, young'un?" he buzzed in a loud whisper.

Throck sat up. Dragging his rug with him, he exited the tent, ushering Mungo before him, while behind him, he heard Eliza stir and murmur sleepily, "Throck, is someone there?" He let the flap fall, not because he didn't want Mungo and Eliza to meet, but because he knew if the tables were turned, and he'd been woken from much-longed-for sleep by one of Eliza's new-met acquaintances, he'd have been grateful to have been allowed to return to his slumber.

"Sorry, Throck old boy," Mungo said, waggling his brows. "Got yourself a lovely in there, have ye? Far be it from me to interrupt. I were passin', is all, an' thought to wag the tongue a bit, share me chicken, if ye were of a mind." He held up a plucked bird by its feet, its wrung neck dangling.

"I haven't got a lovely," Throck said indignantly, eyeing the fowl dubiously. He recalled his part in the cleaning of the previous night's pigeon, a squeamish business, although with a delicious reward. Chickens, presumably, would be subject to similar indignities.

"Eh?" said Mungo, with obvious confusion. His gaze moved past Throck at that moment, and he smiled widely and made a courtly bow. Throck glanced over his shoulder to see Eliza emerging from the tent, her red hair tousled, blinking against the evening light. He felt his cheeks go hot.

"How d'e do, missus?" Mungo said. "Mungo Large, it'd be, makin' your acquaintance. Friend o' Throck's here." He nodded towards Throck who stood dumbly by, and when that one made no introductions he shrugged as if to suggest there was no accounting for a fellow's manners, no matter how gentlemanly they otherwise appeared.

"Eliza Vanson," Eliza said, sticking out her hand, and Mungo shook it.

"I were passin', an' thought to share me chicken," Mungo said, hoisting the dead fowl.

The bird's wobbling head did not faze Eliza. She smiled prettily and said, "How kind, Mr Large, sar. Shall I clean it?"

Mungo grinned and threw a pointed glance at Throck. "Please, call me Mungo." He handed Eliza the bird. "And by all means, missus, if ye've no trouble doin' the honours. She'll be a roit tasty one, I'm sure."

"But we've eaten," Throck blurted. For some reason Mungo's presence made him feel defensive. Perhaps it was Mungo's assumption that Eliza and he were – something other than they were. He neither wanted to clarify that nor defend it, nor even really think about it in any concrete way. As soon as the words left his mouth he regretted them, especially given Mungo's wounded look and Eliza's frown.

"I can be on me way, if ye'druther," Mungo said, ducking his head. For a big man, Throck thought, he did an excellent impersonation of a pouting child.

"Don't mind Throck," Eliza said, turning away with the bird and glaring at Throck through narrowed eyes. "He's still half asleep, most like. He's not usually so rude."

Throck murmured a shamefaced apology, and scuffed his boot on the ground. Under his breath he said petulantly, "we did have sausage and cheese."

Eliza took herself off to clean the bird, accepting Mungo's large knife to perform the job, while Throck and Mungo built up the fire, their conversation limited to "pass me that stick," and "thanks." When the fire snapped and crackled, illuminating the little campsite which had grown dim with the sinking sun, Mungo and Throck sat on the ground across from one another. They could hear Eliza down by the edge of the stream, her ministrations causing the occasional splash. Throck supposed she was rinsing the poor creature as she gutted it or skinned it, similar to the preparation of the pigeons

After a length of awkward silence Mungo leaned forward and nudged Throck.

"Is she yer missus?" he hissed. "I didn't mean ter interrupt."

"You didn't," Throck hissed back. "And she isn't."

"Happen I can make a hasty exit," Mungo offered, "if, ye know, ye want ter be about things."

Throck blanched. "No," he said, indignation plain in his tone.

"Keep yer shirt on, young'un," Mungo replied, holding up a hand. "How were I to know she were yer sister?"

"She isn't!" Throck retorted. Goodness, must the fellow press so!?

"Isn't what?" asked Eliza, appearing out of the gloaming with the pink body of the headless chicken in one hand, Mungo's knife in the other.

"Isn't...squeamish," Throck said, improvising. He tossed a glare at Mungo and waved a hand toward the naked chicken. "Where'd you learn to do *that* in the streets of Southwark?"

"Southwark, is it then?" Mungo put in, getting to his feet and taking the bird from Eliza. "I ventured through that part o' London on more'n one occasion. Knew a pretty betty there name o' Margaret Ellen. Liked the bottle more'n was good for 'er, but she 'ad a way with a bird." He turned the chicken around, inspecting Eliza's efforts, and nodded. "Commendable job. It'll benefit only from the application of me own special blend of 'erbs – of which Throck here is familiar."

Throck dipped his head in agreement. "Pleasantly," he said, glad that the conversation had steered away from whether Eliza was or was not his "missus," whatever that term meant to Mungo. He'd rather not have to define their relationship at all, thank you very much, particularly after the rather confusing events of the last day or so.

Eliza fetched the tin pan she'd cooked the bacon in that morning, and offered a bit of the fatty leftovers, which she'd wrapped in butcher paper.

"Ah, a woman after me own heart," Mungo said. With his big hands he cracked the chicken's bones so it would lay flat in the pan, and Throck concealed a wince; who knew the food one consumed went through such horrors before appearing on one's plate as a delectable morsel? Then Mungo and Eliza worked in unison, adding some bacon and herbs, a cup of water fetched from the creek, and some potatoes Mungo pulled from his pocket. Mungo set the pan on the red coals and sat back to share a satisfied smile with his fellow cook. "A match made in heaven, I'm sure. Margaret Ellen would be proud."

"How is it, sar," Eliza asked after they'd shared the tending of the bird for a while, "that you travel with chickens, and potatoes, and herbs even, at the ready?"

"And last night, pigeons," Throck interjected, with a lift of his brows.

Mungo laughed. "Last night, as I explained to Throck at the time, I were passin' after a bit o' huntin'. I happened to have shot me a couple o' plump pigeons, and it seemed the neighbourly thing to do to share 'em with this lonesome lad." He nodded in Throck's direction. "They turned out roit tasty, wouldn't ye agree, Throck?"

Throck nodded.

"Today, happen I were visitin' me daughter. She's a farmer, damn foin one, though 'er man's a wastrel and good for naught. She lives just there, beyond the pool t'other side o' the clapper bridge and behind the 'edgerow, so I were passin', ye might say. Agin."

Thock and Eliza's eyes met and as quickly parted, and Throck supposed she was thinking the same as he, that they'd been in their smalls in that very pool, right next to Mungo's daughter's farm. Anyone might have seen them frolicking.

"Whene'er I visit 'er she sends me 'ome with a hen or two. Odd times a pie, if I come by on bakin' day. Lucky man, I," Mungo finished. He poked at the chicken in the pan and it responded with a sizzle, and Throck smelled the herbs Mungo had added, and the crisping potatoes. It struck him that, simple food though this was – and the pigeon the night before, and even the plain sausage and cheese and boiled eggs – it somehow tasted better than anything he'd been served on a china plate, his napkin at hand and Mrs across the table.

The chicken took much longer to cook than the previous night's pigeons, but Mungo's stories filled the space and passed the time. Despite his declared attachment to the Blackdown Hills, it seemed that Mungo had spent much of his life away from them. He'd lived in Marrakesh, he said, where he'd learned the Moroccan method of tanning leather – the secret was apparently pigeon poop and the ash of the Argan kernel – and from that city he'd ridden a camel into the vast golden sands of the Sahara Desert. Mungo's description of the long-lashed camels, the rippled dunes, and the relentless sun was so vivid that Throck wiped sweat from his brow, then realised he was sitting too close to the cookfire. In Portugal, Mungo went on, where he'd first sampled that same liquor he and Throck had shared the night before, he'd lived with a family in the Algarves region, and spent his days helping to harvest olives from a tree that was said to be more than 2000 years old. Eliza's eyes were wide, and Throck felt a twinge of something he recognised as envy. He recalled his rant the day Mrs had tried to skewer him on suspicion of dabbling in the arts – perhaps he'd be in India, he'd threatened, sitting on a cashmere rug and chatting with a maharajah. He smiled ruefully. Mungo, it seemed, had lived that life and was now returned to tell the tales.

When the chicken was ready and shared amongst the three diners, Throck ate his portion in silence, savouring flavours that had surely been conjured by his stoked imagination: sweet clove and mellow almond, tangy lemon and sharp olive. Mungo and Eliza chatted while they ate, talking about Southwark and the seedy Borough, of all places, as if anything of interest ever happened there. Throck glanced over at the Trusty parked next to the little bender tent, and wondered if it could carry him far enough away.

Chapter 21
DEAR FRIENDS

The weather remained warm and the days took on a lazy quality, and Throck felt as if he were in a dream, or perhaps had been transported to one of those John Simmons paintings he so admired, where the air was slightly golden and time stood still. Although the more sensible part of him knew they should be pressing on – the Blackdown Hills, after all, was not their destination but a stop along the way – he felt content in the limbo of the place, and he sensed that Eliza did too. They did nothing much; swimming in the pond when the afternoon sun was high and warm, or dozing streamside, Throck with his *Handbook* upon his chest, Eliza thumbing through the Trusty's manual, which, to Throck's amusement, she found more interesting than the pictures in the art book. The days passed idyllically, and from wisps of boyhood memory came a line from *A Midsummer's Night's Dream*, required reading from Throck's grade-school days. *I know a bank where the wild thyme blows, where oxslips and the nodding violet grows.* Eyes closed, the burble of the stream in his ear, Throck barely noticed as the hours rolled slowly on like boyish, carefree somersaults in slow motion.

Mungo visited each day, and Throck and Eliza came to look for him as the sun sank low, lighting the damselflies that flitted over the stream and turning the reeds at the water's edge russet. He always brought an offering – vegetables from his daughter's garden, a nice bit of ham with mustard, a bottle or two of beer, or fresh bread and sweet butter, and then settled in to share a meal. Mungo and Eliza took turns preparing and serving, and Throck noticed, to his shame, the flush of a smile on Eliza's face the first time Mungo served her, and it occurred to him a likely fact that few were the times she'd sat as a guest, another doing the work that had always been hers to do. It would behoove him, he thought to himself, to take a page from Mungo's book and learn to be less the master and more the companion where Eliza was concerned. She, after all, had shown herself his equal or his better at almost every opportunity so far, and be damned to the mores of the Mrs Isbisters of the world.

They'd been camped for a week when the weather turned, and though the clouds edged in almost surreptitiously, more veil than heavy blanket, Throck felt as if a spell had been broken, or some magical enchantment lifted, silly as that sounded. The drone of bees was gone from the day, and the stream, which before had sparkled in the sun, now reflected only leaden sky. Eliza noticed the change too, he thought, for she bustled about, gathering and sorting things that had become strewn, while he checked over the Trusty, cleaned the spark plug and topped up her oil and petrol from the storage cans. Unspoken, it seemed, they'd agreed it was time to move on.

Late in the afternoon, they heard a conveyance making its way along the path. A pony and cart, by the sound, and they glanced at one another, turning to wait for it to appear through the trees. No one, so far, had come this way but Mungo, and he timed his arrival closer to the dinner hour, when the fire was burnishing its coals and the sun was on the wane. When the contraption came into view Throck saw a lone woman at the reins, wrapped in a homespun shawl, a felt hat crammed on her head. The hat shadowed part of her face, but Throck could see a full roundness there that might once have been considered pretty, and dimples though she wasn't smiling. He sensed Eliza stiffen beside him, and with sudden certainty he knew this was Nancy, George's mother. He also knew that he would not allow this woman to mistreat Eliza again, and though he had no doubt Eliza could hold her own he pressed his lips together, squared what shoulders he had and stepped forward. He resisted the urge to flatten the wires of his grey hair, or to brush at the dirt on the knees of his pants. Instead, he eyed the woman with what he hoped was a steely gaze, and said, "Good afternoon. Mrs Gladwell, I believe? To what do Miss Vanson and I owe this unexpected – er – pleasure?" His smile was thin, and he intended his eyes to be hooded, though what the woman actually saw was questionable. In fact, she looked right past him at Eliza, and pulled something from the pocket of her skirt.

"I'm not here to say I'll take 'im," she said without preamble. "I gots a new life, an' I won't put tha' in danger, not even for little Georgie

Pie." She leaned forward in the seat, glancing around though Throck couldn't think who she thought might overhear. "Them elephants have a long reach, Lizzie, you know it. But Devon's far, an' I gots a new name. 'Sides, Georgie's done a'right fer 'imself. You said. 'E's a grown boy, an' 'e don't need 'is muvver anymore."

It seemed to Throck she was convincing herself, not repeating anything Eliza had told her, but he stayed silent, understanding that this was an apology of sorts, or at least an attempt to mend their differences. He wondered fleetingly what she meant about elephants, but then the woman shoved the item she'd pulled from her pocket towards them, and Throck stepped forward to take it. It was a photograph, yellowed and a little cracked, and Throck saw that it showed Nancy in her younger days, laughing, her mouth open wide, leaning on the arm of an equally mirthful fellow that Throck recognised immediately as Eliza's brother Stephen. He passed the photograph to Eliza who'd said nothing at all, but she glanced at it as she took it, and then looked back at Nancy.

"If 'e wants to know someday who 'is mum and dad are, you can show 'im that," Nancy said. "But if 'e shows up at my door I'll turn 'im away. Blame's got two 'eads, know what I mean? And I ain't takin' no chances." She flicked the reins and turned the little cart around, and drove out of sight through the trees.

*

Mungo arrived as he always did, late in the day and close to the dinner hour. He'd brought pigeons – two braces this time – and the gift of a gooseberry tart from his daughter's kitchen. Throck was pleased to see him, and not just because of the usual gift of food. In the morning he and Eliza would be pulling up stakes, so to speak, and venturing onward, and, as he told Mungo, they hadn't wanted to miss saying a proper goodbye. As enjoyable as their time in the Blackdown Hills had been, Throck told him, it was Mungo's own tales of wonder and adventure that spurred them to return to that dusty trail.

"The wide world, my friend – or more immediately, Land's End – awaits!" Throck cried, waving his arm in an expansive gesture. From the corner of his eye he saw Eliza eye him dubiously, and he wondered if he'd overdone his goodbye speech. But Mungo, on receiving the news, was understanding.

"Can't argue with the yearnings of the wanderlust," he said, nodding. "'Appen I've felt it often enough meself to know the pull of it. It'll be hard comin' by this way and not findin' ye both, I don't mind sayin'."

He fell to doing the honours with the pigeons, but Throck noticed that his usual stream of words was more a trickle, and the subject of Throck and Eliza's departure was not broached again while he cooked, threading the birds onto sticks and turning them patiently over the fire in the method he'd coached Throck on several nights earlier.

The news, however one chose to take it, did not hamper anyone's appetite, and the three ate with gusto, licking their fingers and smacking their lips like children with Christmas candy. As the evening progressed Mungo returned to form, sharing yet more anecdotes from his journeys, his ruddy face shining above his beard in the glow of the firelight. Despite the steady flow of words, Throck sensed something wistful in Mungo's voice. He wondered if Mungo was feeling melancholy over the fact of their parting of ways, recognizing that he himself was experiencing the same, now the decision had been made. Mungo was easy company, good company, in fact, and he filled any awkward spaces with his deep mellow voice, talking on and on, and yet not seeming to monopolise attention. He was a font of knowledge, a natural entertainer, and reminded Throck of Harold Guppletwill in a way he could not quite put his finger on. A good soul, perhaps. Or a kindred spirit. Certainly, there were no physical similarities; Harold and Mungo were as different as a beetle and a bird. Despite knowing Mungo such a short time, Throck knew he would keep the memory of him in the same pocket of his life where Harold resided, next to his heart.

When the fire died to embers and the night grew old, Mungo rose to leave. He shook Throck's hand with a big, firm grip and clasped Eliza's more gently, and called them dear friends. And so they were, Throck supposed, for all that they'd only recently met. There was a lump in his throat he didn't mind admitting to as he watched Mungo Large walk off with a backhand wave.

*

The Trusty had sat idle too long and took to the narrow, winding roads like a swallow winging on a breeze. Oxeye daisies and harebells blurred white and purple in the ditches as the Trusty sped past, Throck at the controls and Eliza, goggles pinning down her hat, singing some ditty at the top of her lungs. Throck grinned beneath his snug leather helmet, loving the day, but when a bug hit his teeth he spat out the crunchy mess of it and resolved to keep his mouth shut.

They had only just come down out of the Blackdown Hills when a meeting of several roads caused some confusion, and Throck pulled the Trusty off to one side. There should have been a fingerpost here, he was sure, indicating the town of Ottery St. Mary at one of these forks, but if it had existed it was gone now, and he wasn't sure if he should take the road to the extreme right, or the road only slightly right, or the one ahead. Most assuredly, he felt, the correct road was not either of the left ones, or the one down which they had just come. Eliza dug in her carpet bag for the map, and they spread it out to ponder.

Just then a woman happened along, small and wiry and with a wizened brown nut of a face. She had a frayed straw hat with a yellow flower perched atop her grey hair, and she pushed a barrow cart filled with brown pottery jugs that clinked and rattled. She would have lumbered past them without so much as a greeting, but Eliza stepped into her path with a smile, and said, "Good afternoon, ma'am. I wonder if you'd know which road goes to Ottery St. Mary?"

The woman stopped and set down the barrow. She flexed her fingers and rolled her shoulders and gave a huff, as of impatience, and tipped back the straw hat. Throck saw that her eyes, red-rimmed and rheumy, pointed in different directions, and he wondered if she was fixing Eliza or himself with her hard stare.

"If ye're hopin' to see the flaming tar barrels ye're either too late or too early," she said with obvious annoyance. She shook her head, muttering, "Everybody's lookin' to see the damn tar barrels. Anyone'd think we were a zoo out here, animals in cages." She added in a mocking voice, "Let's go watch them crazy people in Ottery St. Mary run around with flaming tar barrels on their shoulders. That'll be a fun treat."

"Tar barrels?" asked Eliza, braving the eyeball.

"Tar barrels," the woman repeated, loudly, as if Eliza were either stupid or hard of hearing. "Guy Fawkes night they light them tar barrels and hoist 'em up on their shoulders and run round town till they can't stand it no more. Been doin' it in Ottery for 400 years. Ye sayin' ye never heard of it? I find that hard to believe when every damn toff from Bodmin to Wells comes to watch it each year. Turned parts hereabouts into a bloody joke, it has. People show up here in the middle of the summer thinkin' men run around Ottery any given night o' the week with a flaming barrel on their back. Idiots." She spat into the dirt.

"Oh," said Eliza. She glanced over at Throck and gave a slight shrug of her shoulders. Throck stepped forward with the map.

"Actually, madam, we're on our way to Land's End, and trying to follow our map. But we're not sure which fork to choose here. The fingerpost seems to have disappeared." He smiled, and held out the map but she brushed it aside and glared at him with one rheumy eye.

"Do I look like a fingerpost?" she said. The flower on her hat waved back and forth in happy opposite to the scowl she wore on her face.

"No, madam, my apologies," Throck said with a small but impatient sigh. They were getting nowhere, and he decided it would be best to simply let the old woman go on her rather unmerry way. He and Eliza would do as they'd done in the Cotswolds, and pick a road at random. They had no schedule, after all. He turned back to the Trusty. Eliza had already climbed into the sidecar. "We're sorry to have bothered you," he said over his shoulder.

"Get down off your high horse, Mr," the woman said, stepping in front of the motorcycle. "We might make a bargain." She folded her arms across her chest and indicated the barrow cart. "That there cart's a heavy load, and I've to walk it all the way into Ottery. I do it weekly, mind, so it's no great hardship but here's you come along like a little present."

Throck and Eliza exchanged a puzzled glance.

"One o' you strong'uns push this here cart into town for me, t'other gives me a ride in that contraption ye got. Fancy a ride in one o' them things, I do. Seize the moment, as they say." She thrust her face towards Throck in a challenge, and he, instinctively, drew back.

Eliza hopped out of the side car.

"I'll push your barrow, ma'am," she said. "Mr Isbister here'll drive you into Ottery. Tell me where to meet you, as I don't know the lay of the place."

Throck climbed off the bike, not to be outdone. "No, no, no. I'll push the barrow into Ottery. You drive the lady here on the motorcycle."

"I'm the younger," Eliza countered.

"But I'm the man," Throck countered, aware as he said it that it was really no argument at all. They stood, Eliza and Throck, head to head like two cantankerous rams, and then the old woman, who'd climbed into the Trusty's sidecar while they argued, said, "You're both damn fools, even if ye didn't know about the tar barrels. You, push the barrow," she pointed at Throck. "You," she indicated Eliza, "drive the motorcycle. I've a fancy to have a ride in one of these things and I've a fancy it be driven by a girl. It'll make a double good story."

Obediently, Eliza climbed onto the motorcycle and Throck hefted the handles of the barrow. They set off down the far-right fork towards Ottery St. Mary with a plan to meet at the tumbling weir, wherever that was, although the old woman assured Throck that anyone in town could direct him. He'd be glad of the restfulness of the place once he arrived, she promised. The Trusty putt-putted away, and the woman, holding her hat with its dancing flower, chortled her glee. Throck, before long, was alone on the road in the dust, his arms already aching with the weight of the cart and its little brown jugs.

Chapter 22
HUMILIATIONS

On the train ride from Wells back to Lesser Plumpton, and then on the short ride via hired trap to Sowerby Grange, Mrs perfected the story she'd tell Mr once she arrived home. Prior to her departure she'd put it out there with the maid Eliza that she'd been called away to a sick aunt in Bristol, so the foundation for the lie was already laid, and maids always gossip. All that needed doing was embellishment, and knowing how scant was Mr's attention to anything Mrs said, it was likely, Mrs figured, that she could say pretty much anything and he would nod his balding head, sprinkle a bit more pepper on his egg, and accept it.

Uppermost in her mind – much higher, actually, than soothing any doubts Mr might have about the reason for her absence – was Woody's callous desertion of her at Nookey Hollow. Try as she might she could not fathom it. Had they – and here she blushed just to think of it – consummated their tryst she might have considered that he'd simply used her for his own base needs and, once satisfied, discarded her. But in fact he'd been a perfect gentleman until he'd disappeared and left her with the bill. She went hot all over every time she thought of the embarrassment of it. On the train, she'd read the note he'd left, but it was barely legible let alone comprehensible. *I'm sorry*, he'd scrawled. Well, what was she to make of *that*? She was prepared to concede that there might have been an emergency – but she could not fathom what could possibly have been so urgent that he couldn't have paused to tell her in person, to pay the bill, to save her from such abject humiliation. She felt again the crushing embarrassment of sitting in the dining room at the Nookey Hollow Inn, waiting like a fool for someone who wasn't coming.

The hired man who drove Mrs home from the train station was kind enough to unload her luggage, as no one stepped out of Sowerby Grange to greet her. Mr, she supposed, would be engrossed with some cutting or other in the greenhouse – he was interested in the most unpleasant plants, all spines and needles and odd smells. She'd as soon have tipped the lot of them into the dustbin. Just as likely, he'd skipped breakfast and gone straight out to the woods to poke around and get muddy. He may not even have realised she'd been gone for several days, such was his singular focus when it came to those woods. The thought of coming back to life with him and all his oddities pressed down on her, and she had to chide herself sternly to lift both her chins and square her substantial shoulders and push bravely forward.

She paid the driver, and when he stood waiting expectantly, she pried another coin out of her purse and tipped him. Everyone, these days, wanted something extra, she thought with a sniff, as if they weren't paid well enough for the simplest of jobs. She closed the front door, and stood looking around at the dark hall. The house was almost tomb-like in its silence. She wondered if it was the maid's day off, or if she'd find the girl sleeping somewhere, shirking her duties. She turned to the hall mirror to unpin her hat, and saw reflected an overweight woman of a certain age, the mouth hard with disappointment, the eyes devoid of spark. It was a face no longer lovely, though just a day ago Woody had made her feel as if she was. She thought of the image of herself in the triple-paned mirror in the room at the Nookey Hollow Inn, and remembered the brightness of that woman's eyes, the expectation there. That woman had had the excitement of a peacock blue dress lying across her bed, and anticipation of the night ahead stirring her blood. That woman had not yet been discarded and humiliated by the man she loved.

Mrs laid her hat on the table below the mirror, but as she turned towards the parlour, she stumbled over one of the cases and fell with a crash onto her hands and knees, crying out as she went down. The stupid man, to leave them there in the middle of the floor! And to think she'd tipped him! Pain drilled through her wrist and she rolled into a sitting position on the floor, and in a fit of temper kicked at the offending case, then burst into tears. She sat sobbing, clutching her injury, and wishing the floor would swallow her.

"Missus?" came a small voice.

Mrs blinked back her tears and glanced around. The dustbin boy, she could never remember his name, stood in the doorway that led to the parlour, a feather duster in his hand and a red polishing rag stuck into his belt.

"What are you doing here?" Mrs said, her tone acidic, but there it was. She was angry to have been found crying on the floor like a child, and *by* a child, no less.

"Um, cleaning, missus," the boy replied. One lock of dark hair flopped down over his forehead, and Mrs was reminded of someone, though in her distraction she couldn't think who.

"Well, where's the maid, and why isn't she doing the cleaning?" Mrs snapped. She wanted to get to her feet to try to regain some semblance of dignity, but with her girth, and now an injured wrist, she feared she could not manage it without assistance, and most certainly this bony little boy could not help her.

"Dunno, missus," said the boy, evasively. "Gone, I think."

"Gone? What do you mean, gone? Is it her day off?" Her wrist was throbbing now, and making Mrs that much more cross. She scowled at the child, all skinny arms and legs and big eyes.

"Dunno, missus," the boy repeated, and glanced around, as if wondering how he might escape. But instead of running off, he set the feather duster on the table beside Mrs' hat and approached her, taking her by the elbow, and pulling her good arm around his neck.

"What on earth –!" Mrs cried as the boy hoisted her off the floor with a grunt and steadied her to her feet. He leapt away from her then, as if fearing she might cuff him, and grabbed up the feather duster.

"Well, my goodness," said Mrs, starting to dust off her skirt and then wincing at the pain in her wrist.

"I can bandage that for ye, missus," the boy offered. "And I know somefink what's good for the pain."

"Hmphf," said Mrs, pushing past the boy into the parlour and crossing the room to sit with a huff on the settle. The boy, who'd followed, hovered, part scared rabbit, part capable servant. Mrs rested her head against the back of the settle and closed her eyes. It would not do to cry again, so she said curtly, "Get the bandages then. And be quick about it. No lollygagging."

"Set your wrist upon this pillow, missus," said the boy, darting forward to fix a cushion beneath the sore limb. "So's the blood don't pool." Then he went to the sideboard and withdrew a bottle of brandy from the lower cupboard. It occurred to Mrs to wonder, with pinched lips, how a dustbin boy knew where the liquor was kept, but for now she said nothing, and with a nod of her head, accepted the glass of brandy he brought. She was not in the habit of indulging in such vices as brandy, a man's drink, surely, but at the moment she was grateful for the effect it would have, and she sipped it slowly while the boy scampered away after the bandages.

He wrapped her wrist with a surprisingly gentle touch, and it seemed a good snug fit of a dressing. Mrs, lazy and languid with the effects of the brandy, put her head back on the settle and dozed. She did not feel the boy position a footstool beneath her feet, or see him bring a light blanket to cover her against a chill, or, when the day grew old, pull the heavy drapes and light a lamp. When she awoke later in the evening she was surprised to see him still hovering, and did not argue when he gave her his arm and helped her upstairs to her room. There, she saw, a light dinner had been laid, her bed had been turned down, and her cases had been unpacked and put away. The maid must have returned, Mrs thought, smiling in spite of things, pleased that some small part of her life had righted itself. She settled into a winged back chair, her feet upon a stool and her bandaged wrist resting on a cushion, her food on a tray before her, and said imperiously to the boy as he backed out of the room, "Send the maid up when you go down, young man."

He paused, blinked at her, and replied, "Ain't no maid, missus. Nor cook, neither. There's only me."

*

Mrs slept in her clothes, corset and all. As uncomfortable as that was, she could not bring herself to ask the dustbin boy's help in undressing. And sending for Mr, assuming he'd remembered to wander home from his jaunt in the woods, was equally unthinkable. The boy had thoughtfully left her the bottle of brandy, and after a second and then a third snifter of the stuff, she found she had few cares about her state of dress, and fell upon the bed in what was, truth be told, a stupor.

When she woke in the morning her face was pressed into a puddle of drool on the pillow, and her wrist and head throbbed in unison. After several attempts she forced one eye open and saw a steaming pot of tea and a plate of scones and jam on the table next to her bed, and, once she convinced her leaden limbs to move and managed to flop onto her back and wedge herself upright, she tucked in, and was much restored.

Later, well aware that she wore yesterday's travel dress, sweat-stained and dusty, she smoothed the skirt as best she could and tidied her hair, although working with only one hand made success rather difficult to achieve. Then she ventured downstairs to find Mr and try to discover what had happened to their staff, cook and maid, in her absence. For caution's sake, in her mind she ran through her story of the sick aunt in Bristol, lest Mr have queries.

She need not have bothered. The house was empty. She walked through every room, even the kitchen, and though she found things pin-neat and scrubbed cleaned, there was no sign of Mr, nor of the cook or the maid, as the dustbin boy had said. Neither was he present that she could see, and so she ventured outside, thinking to check the greenhouse. But even there, silence yawned. Mrs stood in the middle of the structure, looking around at the benches with their potted plants, and simply could not fathom where everyone had gone. The plants appeared well cared for, and several of Mr's vegetative monstrosities had blossomed, if you could call the strange growths and protuberances flowers. She sniffed at one, a fat-leaved thing with spiky edges that had produced a large but lovely single bloom, but it really had no smell at all. What was the point, she thought with a shake of her head, in flowers that don't smell, and plants so spiky and spiny one fears for one's safety when nearby?

The greenhouse door opened behind her then, and she turned, expecting Mr, but instead the dustbin boy stood there, wearing, strangely, Mr's wellingtons, too big for his small feet, surely, and riding up over his knees. He tipped his flat cap to her, and set down the watering can he'd carried with him.

"Mornin', missus. D'ye need yer bandage changed?" the boy asked.

"No. Yes," said Mrs, in a flap. "Not right this minute." The fact of the boy in Mr's wellingtons was unsettling, and she looked at the child in confusion. "Where's my husband?"

"Gone, missus," the boy replied, tilting his chin as if in defiance. "Same as everyone else."

"Except you," Mrs said, and the laugh that escaped her was shrill, silly even. She felt as if she'd come, like a different Alice, down a rabbit hole, or perhaps, more probably, through a looking glass, although this place was most assuredly not a Wonderland. But where were the people she'd left behind when she'd ridden off with Woody in the red Morris Minor? She took a deep breath and steadied herself against one of the potting benches.

"Do you know where Mr Isbister has gone?" she asked. "Or anyone else, for that matter?"

"The cook quit," the boy answered plainly. "Said there weren't no one to cook for, an' since no one said when they were comin' back, or if they were comin' back, she left. She said she were owed her wages, and there weren't no one to pay 'er, an' she weren't workin' fer free. She said."

Mrs supposed that were true enough, and the fault was partly hers. She hadn't spoken to cook before she left on her trip, but she'd assumed Eliza, the maid, would have made things at least somewhat clear. Mrs would never have intentionally overlooked cook's pay packet, but in the excitement of her trip to Nookey Hollow, more than one thing, it seemed, had ended in disarray.

"And my maid?" Mrs pressed.

"On 'er way to Land's End," he answered. That lock of hair fell across his forehead again, giving Mrs pause. She frowned, momentarily diverted by that same earlier niggle of recognition. Who did the boy remind her of? She shrugged off the distraction and focused on his reply.

"Land's End," she repeated. "How very odd. Do you know why she's gone there?"

"To have an adventure?" the boy replied, but with an upturn to the statement that made it a query, as if Mrs might know the answer as much as he himself. "Missus, can I change yer bandage? Make yer some tea, mayhap? Or perhaps yer wantin' a bath, now that ye've had a good sleep after yer travels." Silence hung between them for a moment, and then the boy crossed his arms and said baldly, "I'm all ye've got, missus. Fer now."

Mrs stared mutely at the boy. How could it be that everyone had deserted her, and that she was left with this urchin, eager and earnest though he seemed. Could he run a household? Could she rely on him? Could she trust him? And, paramount, could she live down the shame of needing a skinny little boy to help her out of her corset?

*

Mrs' mood began to improve in lockstep with the healing of her wrist, a relatively quick affair, given the fact that it was merely a light sprain, or so the dustbin boy said. She'd put the conundrum of Woody's abandonment to the side rather successfully, she told herself, taking the lifted chin approach, but of Mr there'd still been no sign, and she had begun to wonder if she ought to contact the police. It was not unusual for Mr to wander off during the day – even, she knew, to go wandering at night – but to have just disappeared off the face of the earth surely meant something was amiss. She considered her options, and decided that, while she detested the idea of inquiring at Natterjack Hall lest Woody be back in residence, it was surely her wifely duty to ascertain that Mr wasn't in fact there too, or that the boys next door did not have some word of him, and knew where he'd gone.

She didn't have to go next door in person though, she reminded herself. That was the joy of having servants. She called the dustbin boy to the parlour – he'd become her man of all work, and a reliable fellow he was proving to be – and instructed him to go around to Natterjack Hall and ask after Mr Isbister. See if the gentlemen, Captain Plucky or Lieutenant-Colonel Barks, knew of his whereabouts.

"I'll have to see the police if they've no word at Natterjack Hall," she said, her back to the boy who stood in the doorway twisting his cap in his hands. As she spoke, she unlocked the desk drawer and rummaged for the strongbox, intending to give the lad a coin for his extra trouble. But when she flipped open the lid, the box was empty. She stared at it, frowning. There'd been a goodly sum in there before she'd left for Nookey Hollow, contained in a brown leather billfold and a matching change purse, one thick, the other a-jangle, both embossed with the Sowerby crest. She always kept the strongbox topped up with funds. Her bank was in Bristol, and visiting there was most inconvenient.

"Ain't no need to go next door, missus," the boy said, drawing her attention away from what she thought was surely evidence of a theft.

She turned to look at him, sensing some reluctance in his voice, as if he were about to confess something. Her eyes narrowed. Had he stolen the money from the strongbox? What did he mean, no need to go next door?

"Mr Isbister bought a motorcycle a while back. With a sidecar. It's been gone from the shed as long as he's been gone from the house." He looked at her, holding her gaze expectantly, and Mrs saw that he was waiting for her to connect the various dots of information he'd shared over the past couple of days and draw a conclusion. She remembered the motorcycle she and Woody had ridden out on the night of his birthday celebration, and she recalled Mr's fury, so unlike him. The motorcycle, then, must have been his, and Woody, bold, audacious Woody, had "borrowed" it. If she hadn't been so stunned by all she was putting together she'd have laughed out loud at the comedy of it. She turned back to the empty strongbox as another thought occurred to her. One corner of her lip curled, and not prettily.

"Might he be travelling to Land's End?" she asked, arching a brow. She thought of the evening of her dinner party, Mr and the maid conversing in the corridor, the abrupt way they'd ceased talking when she'd appeared, the maid jumping back and casting her almost-kohled eyes to the floor.

The boy shrugged. "Might be," he said evasively.

Mrs closed the strongbox and locked the desk drawer. Land's End. On a motorcycle. With the maid. She stood stock still, thinking. The boy remained in the doorway, hesitant. What to do now? She'd been left. Deserted. Passed over by not one but two men. She drummed her fingers on the desk surface, and turned back to the boy with a steely look in her eye.

"Thank you for telling me," she said. "But I ask you to tell no one else. If you must say anything at all about Mr Isbister's absence, say he has gone to visit a sick relative. In France, maybe, or no, let's say Scotland. Remote Scotland. They have a bracing climate, and if I have to send him somewhere, even in pretense, I'd rather imagine him as uncomfortable as possible."

"You might choose Canada, then," the boy offered. "I hear it gets ruddy cold there, beggin' yer pardon, missus."

She gave him a reptilian smile. "Yes, so I've been told. And horribly hot in the summer. But if Mr turns up suddenly, or is spotted somewhere by people who know him, then that story loses credibility, as one cannot simply pop across the ocean as easily as one can ride a train to Scotland. Do you see? I am doing this to protect myself, young man, and my reputation. No, Scotland it is, but the most craggy and barren part of Scotland, in a kilt, sleeping amongst sheep, and in bad weather."

The boy grinned and nodded, and Mrs watched him go. The boy thought she was joking, but there was nothing at all funny about any of this. She was angry at everyone: at Woody for humiliating her, at Mr for the insult he'd paid her by leaving, and at the maid for having the audacity to go with him. She tucked the fact of the missing money away, undecided as to accusing one or both of them of theft.

Chapter 23
THE SOBER LIGHT OF DAY

The letter from Woody came with the morning post a week after Mrs arrived home.

She was breakfasting in her room, that singular privilege of married women everywhere – well, monied married women – when the boy knocked on her door and said the post had arrived.

"Entrée, George," Mrs called, licking the raspberry cream tart from her fingers – where had the boy come by such delicious pastries? She'd learned the boy's name on their second day together, after he'd begun to help her with her corset, and after they'd come up with the plan about Mr's absence. It seemed only right that she know the boy's name, Mrs told herself, given their new level of intimacy. The door to her apartment opened and George advanced, bowing as he held out a silver tray with the contents of the morning mail.

"Thank you, George dear," Mrs said. "Set it there please. You may take the breakfast things. I fear I've rather eaten a half dozen of those tarts – where on earth did you purchase them?"

"I baked 'em meself, missus," George answered. "Ain't no special knack to it, really. You just need the best cream, an' that's down to good wanglin'."

"Wangling! Goodness," said Mrs, smiling. "Sounds downright American!"

George grinned, and backed from the room with Mrs' tea tray, which weighed a good deal less than when he'd brought it in.

Mrs reclined on the pillows of her bed and closed her eyes. She breathed slowly in and out, enjoying the feel of a full belly and considering how young George had come to be her stalwart, her knight, if you will, in shining armour. There was no job the young boy would not undertake. Indeed, after her initial reluctance, he'd shown himself indispensable by helping her dress and undress like a true lady's maid, always averting his gaze; he'd washed her smalls, tucking lavender into her drawers; he'd fetched her bathwater, cooked her meals and run hither and thither at her beck and call, showing up even that last girl, Eliza, whose blue, blue eyes Mrs had always thought somewhat bold.

She reached for the mail from the tray George had left, and sorted through it, a collection of the usual envelopes – except for one. She dropped the others and held it before her, fingers trembling, recognising immediately the bold stoke of the handwriting on the paper. It was from Woody, postmarked London. So at least she knew he was not next door at Natterjack Hall. Somehow that was encouraging. She tore the letter open with both dread and eagerness.

Darling Alice, it read.

Forgive me, dear heart. I left you, despicably. I had no choice. Please let me explain to you in person. When you hear my reasons you will, I hope, understand, and, I beseech you, forgive me. I am arriving on the London train on Tuesday. I beg you to see me.

Love conquers all, my dear heart, I believe that.

Yours devotedly, Woodward Barks, Lt-Col, Retd.

Mrs set the vellum down on the coverlet, a frown upon her face. Woody, coming here again. And to explain. What reason could there possibly be for his awful desertion? Should she see him? Give him the chance he asked for? He certainly didn't deserve any chances. Since the revelation of Mr's abandonment on top of Woody's, Mrs had been feeling decidedly unforgiving. The milkman, unlucky enough to meet Mrs on the doorstep one morning, received a scolding about the late hour of his delivery. The poultry farmer, who'd been kind enough to bring eggs to Sowerby Grange where usually his customers came to him, was told in no uncertain terms that there'd been bits of straw stuck to the eggs last time, and could he please ensure that did not happen again. Even the butcher in Watton Hoo had felt Mrs' wrath, however indirectly, when the joint of beef George procured for their Sunday dinner was poorly marbled. She'd written the butcher a terse note expressing her displeasure, and George, delivering it, had come home with the butcher's profuse apologies, and a packet of his best sausages, gratis.

The only one who could do no wrong, it seemed, was George. For all intents and purposes, he ran the household at Sowerby Grange. In fact, there was no other. Despite his young years, George cooked, baked, cleaned, scrubbed, shopped, gardened, laundered, swept, watered and whistled through the days, and when he was not hard at one of those chores, he was drawing a bath for Mrs, or helping her into or out of this gown or that, even fixing her hair and helping to choose her jewelry. One must keep up appearances, after all. He was a boy-of-all-work, a lady's maid, a housekeeper, cook and gardener, and was also fast becoming a dear companion. Often, especially in the evenings, that loneliest time of the day, Mrs called him to her sitting room, and they talked, or read books, or Mrs played the small upright piano, so different from the big square instrument that sat unused beneath a brocade cover in the drawing room. George taught her a ribald song or two that made her laugh out loud – *A week or two ago, by accident don't you know, I tore me Sunday breeches right behind!* and *We don't mind the colour of yer tie, old man love me, you're a swell. But there's one thing about yer we don't like. Yer 'at don't fit yer very well!*

One evening, as Mrs sat alone in the dining room enjoying a delicious dinner by candlelight, a thought occurred and she rang her little bell, summoning George from the kitchen, where he also ate alone. He came immediately, still chewing, and Mrs told him to fetch his plate and sit with her. It seemed silly, she told him as he drew up a chair and grinned at her over the polished rosewood table, that they should eat alone, she to the tick of a clock, he to the tick of a cooling stove. And thereafter, once George had cooked and served, he sat at Mrs' right, and the two unlikely companions ate together.

A light tap came at Mrs' bedroom door, and George poked his head in.

"Ready for your day, missus?" he asked, as he did every morning after she'd indulged in tea and tarts. Behind him in the hallway he had a bucket of hot water ready for her ablutions, and a folded towel hung over his arm.

Mrs, though, didn't answer. Her cheerfulness of an hour ago when she'd sung the praises of the raspberry cream tarts had evaporated. Oh, she heard him, but she was still frowning at the letter from Woody, and wondering what she ought to do. She picked it up again and re-read it, and this time, her heart gave a little pitter-patter at the words darling, and dear heart, and devotedly. She couldn't not see him, really.

After she'd made her decision Tuesday couldn't come fast enough. With poor George's help she tried on every dress in her armoire, the peach satin – too girlish; the grey silk – too sombre; the blue print with yellow buttons – too, what? Frivolous? Gay? Flippant? The trouble was she didn't know what Woody was going to say, and therefore she didn't know what sort of occasion this would be. In the end, surrounded by mountains of fabric, and with only a day to make up her mind, she collapsed in a shuddering, sobbing blob of nerves, unable to make any decision at all.

George patted her back and told her not to think about it anymore, it was time for tea. He told her to come down in half an hour, and to close her eyes for a few minutes first, and rest.

"It's only a dress, missus," he said, before he closed the door. "The gent's not comin' here for silks or satins."

*

Tuesday morning came. Mrs decided on a floral day dress in hues of pink. The colour of optimism, she told George, pasting on her best smile.

Tuesday afternoon followed. There was no word from Woody. Mrs' smile began to slip. George challenged her to a game of backgammon in the garden. Mrs had been tutoring him, and he was getting rather good. So passed several hours. Tea-time arrived, then dinner. Mrs changed into a dress of ecru lace, with fat pink ribbons, keeping the nod to optimism, though she no longer felt its buoyancy. At each sitting she ate enough for three people, and George told her she was as jumpy as a cat in a room full of rocking chairs. The comment was intended to make her laugh, she knew, but all she could manage was a faint-hearted grimace. After dinner, with the sun on the wane and casting the trees outside in burnished copper, he counseled brandy, but Mrs, uncharacteristically, asked if he'd accompany her on a stroll in the garden, and so they went.

They were an odd sight: Mrs, as wide as three of young George, clinging with obvious fragility to the boy's arm, the skirt of her ecru lace dress nearly swallowing his legs as they walked side by side on the garden path. Mrs sighed frequently, and huffed with the exertion of the walk after consuming so much food. George, addressing the sighs rather than the huffs, about which he could do little, responded with consoling words, "there, there, missus, just wait," or "tsk, tsk, missus, it'll all come right in the end."

And then suddenly Woody appeared, a-wash in the golden glow of the evening light. George spotted him first. Standing beneath the rose arbour, he was wearing the impressive dress uniform he'd worn at the birthday party at Natterjack Hall, all polished buttons and shining black boots and gold braid. His mutton-chop whiskers bristled remarkably, and he had a dress sword in a scabbard at his side that glinted, reflecting the sunken sun. George said "cor…" in admiration, prompting Mrs to look up.

What happened next, and indeed in the many hours that followed, Alice could never relay with accuracy. Nor would she want to. But in the secret recesses of her mind, she revisited the night time and again – George's discreet disappearance, Woody stepping forward to catch her as she swooned, she and Woody entwined in one another's arms, his apology, her happy tears, a bit of clinging and groping and a kiss, and eventually, ultimately, the bliss of union, though no vicar had spoken any words. And lying beneath the covers in her big, previously unshared four-poster bed, Alice listened to Woody snoring beside her, and wondered what story he'd tell her come morning when they finally spoke of serious matters, and a small voice inside her head asked if she'd been too quick to forgive.

*

She woke to the steady thrum of rain on the windowsill, and, for once not minding the gloom, Alice stretched languidly, happily. Yesterday was a blur of fraught emotion: fear that Woody would not come, elation when he did, and finally, the ecstasy of their final intimacy. She flushed to think of it. When he'd appeared in the garden last night after that day of frayed nerves all she could think about was the joy that flooded through her. Nookey Hollow's humiliation had seemed unimportant. There'd been no mention of what she'd come to think of as the Nookey Hollow Matter, and although at least once he'd tried to speak of it, she had closed her eyes and boldly kissed him, sealing his silence, big body pressed to big body. Not now, she'd said, a wanton temptress, eyes a-flutter, bosom heaving. She'd never felt such abandon, nor had her heart ever been so full. Even now, in the sober light of day and without knowing what he would say when he finally explained, she was not sorry for last night.

She rolled and reached for Woody across the wide bed and found the space empty. She sat up, and glanced around the room, called his name, voicing it in a dovelike coo. Was he there, standing behind the heavy drapes, contemplating their blissful union as he stared out at the rainy morning? Sitting in the big chair in the shadows, watching his lady love sleep? No. She looked about for any evidence of him – his discarded uniform coat, the puddle of his trousers, the flop of his tall leather boots, but the room was empty of any sign that he had been there. She turned back to the pillow beside her, and yes, it held the imprint of his head, and there – grey hairs on the white cotton, so he had not been a dream, or a figment of her overwrought imagination. And yet, her heart sank, her gut clenched. Despite her thoughts of moments before, her bravado that she was not sorry for the night just past, doubt engulfed her. *Should* she be sorry? What kind of woman was she to have let a man breach the well-fortified walls of her chastity, and without being sure of him, without knowing beyond all doubt that he loved her, had not meant to hurt her, and would find a way for them to be together?

A light rap came at her door, and George poked his head in.

"Mornin', missus," he said with his usual cheerfulness. The door opened at the prod of his toe, and he entered, bearing a breakfast tray. A teapot steamed, and she could see a platter of treats. One cup, one plate, one knife, one napkin. Was this George's way of being discreet, and of not jumping to conclusions based on what he might or might not have seen or heard last night? Or indeed, this morning? Maybe he'd witnessed Woody's departure, and had a message from him? But George said nothing except, "warm treacle tarts this mornin', missus, and fresh strawb'ries wiff clotted cream. Fit for a queen, if I do say so meself." He placed the tray beside the bed, drew open the curtains, and departed.

Wednesday passed much like Tuesday, although with less optimism in its beginnings. Whether consciously or not, Alice dressed to reflect her mood – a sombre grey skirt of railroad striped jacquard, and a plain white blouse, adorned with a brooch bearing the Sowerby crest. She patted the piece as she pinned it on, and lifted her chins, and caught

George's eye in the mirror as he stood behind her holding a light shawl at the ready.

"Bring on all comers, eh, missus?" he said, and grinned.

She smiled back. "Quite right, George. Quite right." She smoothed her hair and then her skirt, and let George place the shawl over her shoulders.

He did not come Wednesday, but in the late afternoon, just when Alice was beginning to despair, he sent a note. George delivered it with her tea, and he'd placed her spectacles alongside the cream vellum on the tray. Alice ate the bacon butty well slathered in brown sauce first, and then, requested a second. She would need fortification for the reading of the note. She eyed it, and the familiar heavy flourish of Woody's penmanship, with trepidation and hesitation. What if it was a farewell message, a string of words chosen to soften the blow of his departure, but to deliver the fact of it nonetheless? She left the note on the tray and pushed back from the table, dabbing the corners of her mouth with a spotless white napkin.

At dinner, George propped the still unopened note next to the salt cellar, and she eyed it with a flare of her nostrils, as if it were a bug, or some other unwanted and unwelcome intrusion. George ate at her right, as always, and she noticed his eyes flicking to her more frequently than usual, as if gauging her level of fragility. She was touched by his concern, but annoyed that Woody could unbalance her so. She should just read the damn note and get it over with. In the middle of consuming her liver and onions, potato mash still untouched, she set down her knife and fork with a clatter and ripped open the envelope, aware of George watching her. He chewed slowly in a bovine sort of way, that lock of hair flopped over one eye.

My dear Alice, it read,

Forgive me, darling, but this is harder than I'd thought it would be. You and I are star-crossed, I fear. I do not know if I can bring myself to burden you with my troubles, but until I find that courage we cannot be together. I will remain at Natterjack Hall for the time being while I consider my prospects. You must never think, my love, that I regret anything that has happened between us. Never! Indeed it has only made me love you all the more, and for that reason I must think carefully on the choices I will soon have to make.

Yours forever, Woodward Barks, Lt-Col, Retd.

Alice set the note on the table and picked up her knife and fork. She cut a triangular piece of liver, pushed limp onion onto it with her knife, and put the morsel in her mouth. She chewed, swallowed, repeated, and when she had finished her meat, she moved on to the mound of potatoes, lifting fork to mouth like an automaton until her plate was clean. Then she dabbed her lips with her napkin, nodded to George, stood and left the room. If she'd glanced over her shoulder as she exited, heading for her bedroom, she'd have seen George watch her retreating form with a wrinkle of concern on his brow, and then she'd have seen him pick up the note she'd left behind, read it, and tuck it into his pocket with a frown.

Chapter 24
EGLANTINE AND SERHAN

Thursday was the day the Horticultural Society met, and Alice – Mrs –
put on her straw hat with the nodding silk flowers (her favourite), and
George drove her to Watton Hoo in the pony trap. George seemed to
have appointed himself her guardian, and truth be told she rather enjoyed
his doting. It was a bit like having a son, she supposed, or a grandson
perhaps. At her age, any chance of her becoming a mother in the
biological sense was surely past, not that she had ever aspired to the role.
Mothering, she expected, would not have been something she was suited
to. All that neediness. All those sticky fingers. Most mothers, she'd
noticed, seemed rather harried, pulled taut like an overstretched wire.
And then there was the unpleasant smells of children, and their frenzied
busyness. She was quite content to have skipped that occupation in her
youth, and equally happy to have George in substitution now, reaping
the benefits, as it were, without having invested the stock.

All of that Mrs thought only in the most peripheral sense as she
and George jiggled along in the cart towards Watton Hoo. More
prominent in her mind was Woody and his pang of a message. What
burden of trouble he could be referring to she did not know, but she'd
overheard him mention a son to that fishing boy. Was the child dead?
Alive? Was he the trouble? And if so, why couldn't he tell her? After the
initial – to use a crude analogy – gut punch of his letter, Alice had found
herself feeling a bit cross and impatient with the whole thing. He simply
needed to find a spot of courage, surely not a difficult thing for a retired
lieutenant-colonel, a military man who had supposedly toiled for decades
in the queen's and then king's and then a second king's service, and in
the most inhospitable of outposts. Not a job for a handwringer.

She'd determined to carry on as normally as possible, so she
shoved Woody and his secrets out of her mind and alighted at the church
of St Mary Hoo, pressing some coins on George above and beyond what
he'd need for his household shopping, and telling him to treat himself to

a lemon ice and be back for her in an hour. The meetings, held in a room in the basement of the church, did not usually run much longer. As George flicked the reins and the pony cantered off, a couple of Mrs' fellow Society members hailed her, hurrying towards her from across the street.

"Mrs Isbister! Hallo!" cried one. The other waved a gloved hand. Mrs smiled stiffly. These two, Ada Mellows and Ida Meake, were sisters, bone-thin and square-jawed, but talkative sorts prone to gossip. The behind-the-hands titter amongst the rest of the Society members was that the two women were the exact opposites of their married names, neither one mellow or meek. Ha ha. Mrs, of course, did not condone such idle chatter, neither the prattle relentlessly dispersed by the Mrses Mellows and Meake, nor the jest at their expense.

"We missed you at our last meeting, Mrs Isbister," ventured Ada Mellows, her pale brows raised expectantly as if Mrs were obliged to account for her absence.

"Have you been unwell? Someone mentioned that poor Sowerby Grange looked to be near deserted, and yet here you are!" said Ida Meake. Both sisters smiled, but it was a predatory curl of the lips, and Mrs resisted the urge to peek round their skirts for a glimpse of swishing tail.

"And yet here I am," Mrs repeated, and returned their smile with a chilled version of her own. "Have I missed anything monumental?" she asked. The three women turned as one and walked up the steps of the church.

"Nothing at all," said Ada Mellows smoothly. At the doorway she gestured Mrs ahead of her into the church, and added to Ida behind Mrs' back but well within her hearing, "Although I wonder what *we* might have missed...." Mrs glared at the women over her shoulder, but the sisters ignored her, and shared a wolfish grin.

Inside the basement meeting room, the three ladies found their seats. It appeared they were the last arrivals, and Mrs took the only available spot, unfortunately next to the Mrses Meake and Mellows at the back of the room. The chair groaned horribly as she lowered herself onto it, and several ladies looked over their shoulders with concern.

The podium at the front of the gathering was hung with the Watton Hoo Horticultural Society banner, cream satin with a gold fringe, embroidered with a border of laurel leaves and with a pink floral spray in the centre. One of the original members had designed the crest and sewn the standard, and before the war, the ladies were to have had enameled brooches made for each member, replicas of the Society's banner. The war and its more pressing concerns had put that item in abeyance, but with a gradual return to more normal life, the pins had reappeared on the agenda, and were the first item of business today, introduced by the Society's president, Mrs Lettice Beasley.

Mrs Isbister, normally an active and interested member of the Society, and who'd served on more than her share of committees in the past, now to her chagrin found she could not keep her attention on the business at hand. Try as she might to stay focused on Mrs Beasley's authoritative voice detailing the costs of having the pins designed and cast and enameled, her thoughts instead wandered, and somehow Mrs Beasley's voice deepened to Woody's, and his face replaced hers there at the front of the room. *"Darling Alice,"* came the words, muffled as through a downspout, *"Dearest heart."* She shook herself and her chair creaked ominously. Ladies twisted again to look at her.

"Of course, payment for each member's pin would necessarily be collected at the outset..." Mrs Beasley was saying, and Mrs sniffed and struggled to clear her head, but Woody had found a purchase and would not leave. *"Never think, my love, that* ...the order will be placed straight away once payments in full have been collected." Mrs blinked and coughed discreetly into her glove. She fumbled in her reticule for a handkerchief, and dabbed at the moisture that had sprung up on her forehead. Her armpits felt embarrassingly damp. Next to her, Mrs Mellows and Mrs Meake tittered softly.

Somehow, Mrs hung on through the first half of the meeting, and at the break, partook of tea and biscuits, Hettie Carbunkle's delicious raisin buns, and other baked delights. She circled the room, greeting this colleague and that, exchanging pleasantries, and with the fortification of several plates of the dainty pastries thought she was quite herself again, Woody's unnerving intrusions surely at bay. But then, as the second half of the meeting was about to begin, and seating herself again in the narrow chair – why did they make them so frail – she overheard Ida Meake say to Ada Mellows, "Did you hear? That lieutenant-colonel who rented the old Guppletwill place has a lady friend?"

Mrs' heart began to thunder and she felt herself again go hot all over. Someone knew about her and Woody?

Ida went on, "Oh yes, a sweet young thing, apparently. No more than twenty-five if she's a day. A foreigner, though. Dark hair, and eyes like chocolate. Can you credit it? And him – dashing, I'll grant you, in an old-fashioned sort of way, I mean really, mutton-chop whiskers? – but he's old enough to be her father!"

A noise like a choked frog escaped Mrs' throat and spots danced before her eyes. The room swam, and she thought she could hear laughter, and then a voice much deeper than the sisters', Woody's, she was sure, came down that long pipe, *"You and I are star-crossed, I fear."*

And then she collapsed. When she awoke, she was on the floor, broken bits of the rickety chair beneath her, and Mrs Lettice Beasley was waving smelling salts beneath her nose.

*

Mrs was silent on the ride home in the pony cart. George had been summoned and had rushed to her side, and she'd leaned on him as if she were one hundred years old, and frail. After assuring the buzzing Society ladies that she did not want the doctor, she let George escort her from the basement of St Mary Hoo. As distraught as she was, both from the gossip she'd overheard and from embarrassment at fainting and crushing her chair, it did not escape her notice that George led her with authority through the press of women, saying as they went, "Back, ladies, please, mind yer parish pick-axes!" Several women sniffed, but Mrs supposed it was George's tone rather than his words that caused the reaction. Mrs suspected that they, like she, had no idea what a parish pick-axe was in George's world, but it didn't sound complimentary.

In the cart, George kept up a lively banter, putting a humourous spin on his encounters of the day in an obvious attempt at getting Mrs' mind off her troubles, though of course he couldn't have known the cause. Mrs appreciated his effort, listening with half an ear. It was always a bit of a tonic, being in George's company, although today, she was sure, it was going to take rather a large dose. She closed her eyes, and George told her about the butcher, who'd had a bit of raw meat of which he'd seemed unaware stuck to his forehead. "Like a sticker stamp it were, missus, a sign of 'is callin'. I weren't about to suggest he peel it off."

"Quite so," Mrs murmured, giving a small smile in spite of herself. George continued, relaying how the green grocer had slid on a bit of rotten lettuce and went – begging yer pardon, missus – arse over tea kettle, which served 'im right, George said, for tryin' to short old Missus Quark a penny on 'er change. Mrs sniffed, her eyes still closed. "Indeed," she commented.

And round by the Hock and Toot pub, George went on, a man had given chase to a hairy old pig, and the porker'd gotten the better of him. "The pub's patrons what'd come outside with their ale to watch 'im go, said the pig escaped from 'is pen on account o' the look o' bacon in his owner's eye."

In spite of herself, Mrs chuckled and opened her eyes. "And did the man catch his pig?" she asked.

"Not while I were watchin'," George replied, his eyes on the road but his grin wide. "I heard tell there were more than a bit o' grease on that old porker's backside, so even if the fellow does catch 'im up it ain't likely he'll hold onto 'im. Sounds like a prank to me, missus. I wonder what the fellow did to deserve it." The cart hit a bump and jarred Mrs' hat crooked. She reached up to fix it and George said, "Sorry, missus, bump in the road. Sometimes there ain't no avoidin' 'em, but we carry on, eh?"

Mrs eyed him, wondering how a wise old man had ended up in the body of a small young boy.

*

The day after the disastrous Horticultural Society meeting, Mrs came to a decision. George encouraged her, prodding her to take the bull by the horns and stand up for herself. From his words she understood that either he had intuited, in his canny way, the origin of her problem, or, just as likely, he had read the letter from Woody. Surprisingly, she found she didn't mind. George, she felt sure, was stalwart, and had her best interests at heart. So, after some deliberation, she told George to hitch up the pony cart. Ignoring the fact that it was impolite to visit without first sending a card, she put on her most becoming visiting outfit, a lovely grass green with black piping and collar, and instructed George to take her round to Natterjack Hall. If Woody was indeed ensconced there with a lady love, young or otherwise, she must know it, and must confront the issue head on.

George was handing her down from the cart in the driveway of Natterjack Hall when the front door burst open and Woody himself ran out of the house. A flung shoe whizzed through the open door after him, and walloped him in the back as he spotted Mrs and George before him. He drew himself up short.

"Good God. Alice!" he said, obviously shocked at the sight of her. He made a hasty bow, and picked up the fallen shoe, as if placing it behind his back could erase the odd scene she and George had just witnessed.

"Woody," Mrs said coldly. She looked him up and down, as if evaluating his worth and finding him lacking.

"Who's this?" came a voice, female and biting, and Mrs looked past Woody to see a most beautiful young woman standing in the doorway to Natterjack Hall, presumably the thrower of the shoe. She was tall and willowy and graceful, with wavy black hair cut into one of those short, modern, and outlandishly boyish styles that showed off a long, slender neck and a determined jawline, and she glared out of large dark eyes that arrowed each of them, she, George, and Woody, in turn. Beside her, George said, "Cor…" in admiration, and Mrs might have too if she hadn't been indignant.

"Who's this?" Mrs said, not to be upstaged, although she supposed she knew who it was, recalling the Mrses Meake and Mellows and their church basement gossip. Woody's lady love. The reason he had deserted her. Well, it certainly appeared he'd gotten himself a hot-tempered mistress, even if she was a beauty, and far too young for him.

But then a third player entered the scene. Pushing past the woman in the doorway was a young man of about the same age, and with the same beauty, albeit in a manlier version. The same lofty height, the same dark hair, the same everything, really. They seemed a matched set, except the young man had an open, friendly smile and came down the steps to offer his hand. Mrs took it, and allowed the fellow to press his lips to her glove. How civil, Mrs thought, and returned his smile in spite of herself.

"Please forgive us, Mrs…?" he said, drawing her and George past the statue that was Woody and the icicle that was the young woman and into Natterjack's front hallway.

"Isbister. And this is my companion, George," Mrs replied. George gave her an encouraging look, and they followed the young man into the drawing room.

"Mrs Isbister, George, lovely to meet you both," said the young man affably. "I am Serhan, and the lady with the bad manners on the front step is my sister, Eglantine. I call her Egg, but she hates it. Actually, I call her Egg *because* she hates it." He laughed, and Mrs felt a wiggle of familiarity that she couldn't quite place. The three of them, George, Serhan and Mrs perched, George and Mrs on the settle, Serhan on an upholstered chair.

"I do apologize for visiting unannounced," Mrs said. "I'm usually much more observant of conventions."

"Not at all, not at all," Serhan said. He leaned towards her conspiratorially, "To be quite honest, I'm not bothered by conventions, myself. In fact, I rather abhor them." He smiled again in that charming way so that Mrs, who usually would have been offended by such an admission, for in her world conventions were paramount, found herself smiling back, and nodding. "My sister, however, is a strict conventionalist, if there's such a word. If a thing's not done, then it's simply not done, and woe betide the poor sod – brother, most often as not – who has committed the faux pas." He laughed that familiar laugh again, and Mrs decided she'd never met so engaging a young man. One could relax in such company. She felt her own tension ease slightly, but then over Serhan's shoulder she saw Woody and the haughty Eglantine appear in the doorway, and her smile drooped. Serhan glanced from Mrs to Woody and back again, seeming to comprehend that something was amiss.

"It would seem, Mrs Isbister, that this is not a social call?" he said smoothly, the intonation suggesting a question, but not one that required a response. "Nor one, I surmise, intended for me or my sister." He rose, bowing politely to Mrs and George who had also gotten to their feet, and went to the doorway where he took Eglantine's elbow, and although she scowled, she let him lead her out of the drawing room. Over his shoulder, Serhan said to Mrs, "Lovely to meet you, Mrs Isbister. Do come again."

Mrs and Woody stood eyeing one another across the room, and Mrs wondered if he could see how she trembled. She had both feared and longed for this meeting, and it was doubly fraught after their recent night spent in – *flagrante delicto*, to be delicate. Beside her, George asked in a whisper, "Missus? Should I go?" She nodded, and George, reluctantly, followed Serhan and Eglantine from the room.

Woody turned to close the doors after the boy and remained standing where he was, his hands on the knobs, his broad back to Mrs. She could see the rise and fall of his shoulders, and after several long and uncomfortable moments, heard an odd hiccup of a noise, and she realised he was sobbing. Aghast, she stood frozen in place. How did one react to the sight of a grown man crying, a man who has wronged you, and deserves none of your pity, surely, and yet a man whom, in spite of yourself, you cannot help but love? She thought of George's wise words about carrying on, and took a hesitant step in Woody's direction.

"Perhaps I should not have come," she said, her tone gentle.

"Perhaps not," he replied in a strangled voice.

The words felt like a slap. Mrs drew herself up in indignation. How dare he dismiss her, when she, the wronged party, offered the proverbial olive branch!

"Then step away from the door, you cad, and I will leave you to your temptress!" she bellowed. "I hope she throws the other shoe at you, or a boot even!" She charged towards the door in full steam, but Woody turned and blocked the way, his big face bright red, and wet with tears.

"Temptress?! Where did you get such a preposterous idea? She's my daughter, Alice!" he cried, his voice a boom of volume. And as Mrs gaped, he continued in a softer tone, "And Serhan is my son. Twins, in case you hadn't noticed. Blood of my blood, flesh of my flesh. Serhan is rather like me, I fancy. Eglantine less so. Both of them have the look of their mother."

Words overheard by the stream in Nookey Hollow came back to her, something about taking his son fishing. She'd wondered about it then, and since, and indeed at Nookey Hollow had agonized over it, but hadn't asked lest it ruin the holiday. Perhaps she should have done, and they'd not be here now, in the midst of such awful discord. She said meekly, "You have children? You never said…"

"I intended to," Woody replied. "In truth, I was afraid." His whiskers drooped, and his wide shoulders sagged. He looked like a pillow with the stuffing coming out. Mrs, despite being the aggrieved, wanted to comfort him but held back, sensing yet more to this story.

"Why?" she asked. Surely if he loved her, they should have no secrets. Or was that naïve? A sentiment from a cheap novel?

"Their existence is – complicated," Woody replied. A lame answer, she thought, and insulting to his offspring. But she reigned in her judgment and asked, "Are they why you left me at Nookey Hollow?" That wound was fresh in her voice.

"No – well, yes. They, or rather, Eglantine, summoned me," Woody replied. He was reluctant, Mrs could see, but she was not about to make this confession easy for him. He owed her truthfulness, at least.

"So you deserted me, and went running," Mrs said.

"I had to," Woody said dully. "My – my wife had escaped from the Cane Hill Lunatic Asylum."

Mrs gaped. There was a humming in her ears and for a moment she thought she might faint again, like at the Horticultural Society meeting, although this time, at least, she was not seated on a rickety chair too slender for a child's bottom.

"Your wife?" she repeated hoarsely. The day was getting worse by leaps and bounds. She had a headache above her eyes, and she needed to sit down. She stumbled to the settle and collapsed, touching a gloved hand to her temple. "But you said she'd died."

"I admit the lie," Woody said dejectedly. He'd followed her across the room and now sat heavily in the chair vacated by Serhan. He rubbed his big hands over his face, pressing the skin this way and that, and his eyes, when they alighted again on Mrs, were red. "It's the bald truth that she's been dead to me these many years, since the twins were young and I had no choice but to put her in that place. For all intents and purposes, I have been a single man, a widower, for even before she was committed to the asylum she was a mocking copy of the woman I'd married in Constantinople years ago." Woody looked at Mrs with anguish, and despite the horror of what she was hearing, part of her wanted to reach out, gather him into her embrace and tell him everything would work out in the end. Instead, she sat mutely.

"I want you to know, Alice dear, that I did my best by Defne – Daphne, as she came to be known once we'd moved to England. But it became impossible. As I said, I was living away for months, even years at a time owing to the demands of my career, and perhaps it was my absence that contributed to her spiral into madness. At first it was small things. The children seemingly terrified of being out of sight of the other, for example, something I chalked up to their being twins. But then there was their fear of the downstairs closet, and the way they'd cower when Defne came into the room, and the odd way she wanted to hug them at the most unusual times. In the middle of dinner, or in the park whilst strolling. Once I came home on leave and found she'd gone away and left the children with a neighbour. The poor woman was distraught. She had four children of her own, and had no idea where Defne had gone. Out to buy kippers for tea, she'd said, but never came back.

"It escalated from there. I can't begin to tell you the awful things she did, the frightening behaviour. She was deranged, and most times the episodes occurred while I was away and she was here, in England, at once a mother and a monster. I had to leave again, but this time I put the children in boarding school. They were young, but of an age to be admitted, and I do credit the strength of those institutions for the children's general stability in the face of their rather dark first years. Defne I committed to a sanatorium – Holloway first, for a short stay, hoping she'd improve. And then Cane Hill, when the doctor wrote that things had gone downhill. It was the greatest relief, I admit, when the doctor agreed that she was incurable, and would need to live there for the remainder of her days.'"

"Goodness. I had no idea," Mrs said, a hand to her bosom, trying but failing to imagine a life spent in an institution, or, just as bad, a life tethered to someone committed. Poor, dear Woody. She frowned, puzzling over the information she'd just taken in. Ever pragmatic, she was already ferreting out solutions to the dilemma of Defne Barks. "You married her in Constantinople. That's a foreign place…India, isn't it? Or

Egypt? Couldn't she have stayed there? Could she go back? Her family could look after her."

"She's Turkish," Woody replied. "When we married, her family disowned her. She was the daughter of a prominent man in Constantinople, and he was incensed over the match. He tried to stop us marrying; in fact, her entire family tried to stop it, and even once the deed was done, our lives were in jeopardy. Knives and back alleys, that sort of thing. Constantinople, I have no doubt, is still a dangerous place for me. For her safety, I brought her to England, and the twins were born here, in London. I tried to do my best for them, but I think they would say they have not had overly happy lives."

Mrs – Alice – pulled a handkerchief from her reticule, for Woody's face had again crumpled, and his shoulders shook. She leaned across the space between them and wiped his tears with her handkerchief, but that released a flood, and the only thing for it was to clasp his big body to hers, and hold on for dear life. What they would do now, Alice had no idea.

Chapter 25
I WERE NEVER HAPPIER

The tumbling weir of Ottery St Mary was indeed easy to find, once one asked, but inevitably, Throck discovered, a question was asked in return, or rather, a query with an accusatory tone. It happened twice, once when he first entered the village proper, pushing the old woman's barrow after his trek of several miles, and sought assistance, and again when he'd followed the original directions to the corn mill and adjoining brush factory, but still could not spot a weir.

"Weir's just there, behind the mill wall," one of the millworkers told him, a kerchief across his face to guard against the corn dust that hung thick in the air. The fellow pointed to a narrow lane that curved around behind the four-storey brick building, then the man's eyes drifted suspiciously to Throck's wheeled burden. "Heyup, what're you doin' with Minnie Small's barrow?"

After he'd explained, yet again, that he was trundling the pushcart at that same lady's request, and was to meet her at the weir, the workman shrugged and turned away. "'Appen it ain't none o' *my* business," he muttered, by his very tone suggesting otherwise. Throck hefted the jug-laden barrow and carried on, groaning under the weight of it, and ruminating on the fact that Minnie Small, if that indeed was the woman's name, should bear such a moniker when she was, given the load of the barrow, instead rather mighty. Mungo Large might have appreciated the irony, Throck thought with a chuckle, and then chuckled again, for that itself was funny in a way, Large and Small.

Before he saw it, he could hear the running water of the weir, and once arrived, he realised that instead of the more usual dam-like structure he'd been expecting, this instead was circular hole in the midst of a pond, and the water flowing gently over its rim resembled sluice down a plughole. He set the barrow on its pegs, grateful to have finally arrived at his destination. It was a peaceful spot this, in spite of the noise and dust of the mill; on Throck's right the factory's red brick back wall reflected in the still water, and cast a shadow that darkened the pond, while off to his left the narrow channel of the leat was edged with swaying daylilies and irises and the slender, drooping, lushly purple spikes of a buddleia shrub, the so-called butterfly bush that, true to its name, was hosting a bevy of those delicate insects, attracted, perhaps, by the plant's honey-like scent. Throck sat down amongst the flora, and rested his head against the barrow handle. Just a few moments' doze was all he required. No burden at all in such a setting. Then he would look about for Eliza and Minnie Small.

He hadn't intended to fall soundly asleep, but he must have because he awoke with a start and a splutter when Minnie poked him in the chest. Her wrinkled face hovered inches from his, and he saw wiry hairs sprouting from her chin. Her right eyeball glared at him through the lens of his goggles, while her left held a bead on the mill.

"Goodness," said Throck in a voice raspy with sleep. His gaze moved towards the red brick wall of the mill where her left eye was trained, involuntarily checking to see what the old woman was looking at. She poked him in the chest again, and he, still sleepily disoriented, crabbed backwards, but the barrow blocked his retreat, and rocked precariously. The crockery jugs clinked.

"Careful with my cider! I hope for your sake none got stolen while you were sleepin' like a dunderhead," Minnie scolded. She straightened and stepped over Throck to inspect the jugs, and seemed to find all in order.

"Throck, meet Minnie Small," Eliza said, and Throck, his wary gaze on that feisty lady, glanced around to see Eliza standing off to one side where he hadn't noticed her. The Trusty rested a few feet behind her, and it occurred to Throck fleetingly that he must have been completely unconscious when they arrived, for he'd heard nothing of the motorcycle's little engine. No wonder Miss? Mrs? Small was worried about her jugs.

"Minnie's son has a small farm outside the village. He makes this cider, and Minnie sells it for 'im," Eliza explained, nodding towards the barrow.

"Small & Smaller, we're called. Best cider you'll find this side o' the Blackdown Hills," Minnie said, her tone and her eye challenging

Throck to gainsay her. "Anyway, 'bout time you got here. Lizzie and me were about to send the watch out after you. You won't never make a barrowman, take's you that long to trudge a coupla miles, there's a truth."

Throck wasn't about to argue. Barrowman was not a job he intended to pursue. Nor would he correct the woman over Eliza's name, since it seemed Eliza herself was letting it stand. He got slowly to his feet, every muscle in his neck and arms protesting, his poor feet feeling as flat as paddles. He eyed the Trusty, wondering if he could make it as far as her sidecar. He'd have to ask Eliza to drive. He doubted he could manage the bike's controls with his every appendage aching like a sore tooth. Minnie Small peeled off Throck's goggles and helmet and shoved them towards him, then hefted the handles of the barrow. Throck attempted a weak smile and opened his mouth to bid her farewell. Not to be uncharitable, but he found Minnie Small rather alarming, like a grandmother gone a bit off, and he was looking forward to the open road, just him and Eliza. Preferably with him asleep in the sidecar. The day had indeed sunk away, and had the look of early evening, with the sun beginning to slant in the sky. They might do a night drive, as they had that first night of their adventure.

"Let's go then," Minnie said over her shoulder. She was already pushing the cart down the path alongside the leat, and Throck noticed how smoothly the barrow moved with Minnie at the handles. Eliza was astride the Trusty, and Throck climbed gratefully under the rug of the sidecar. He was about to call out a weak goodbye, lovely to have met you, ta-ra etc, when Eliza leaned over and said, "She's invited us to stay the night at 'er cottage. It were kind, and I didn't know how to say no." She shrugged apologetically, gunned the Trusty and putted after Minnie, who was already turning the corner at the end of the lane. Throck groaned, and wondered if the ladies would take it amiss if he opted to sleep in the sidecar.

*

Minnie Small's little cottage teetered on the bank of the River Otter, just at the edge of the village of Ottery St Mary. Low-walled and with a haphazardly thatched roof, it squatted in the midst of a stone-fenced yard filled with the implements of Minnie's trade: several barrows in various states of repair, stacks of cider jugs stencilled with the Small and Smaller name, a couple of large wooden tubs, a variety of bungs and syphon hoses and a rubbish heap that seemed to consist mainly of broken crockery bits. Grass and weeds grew tall, and woven through the debris and vegetation were narrow paths that looped almost playfully this way and that, and seemed to have no rational destination. Several of the trails sloped all the way to the water, the mud of the riverbank smoothed as by many bottoms making a slide of it. Children, Throck wondered, glancing around but seeing no telltale signs of little ones. Perhaps Minnie herself, then, finding a playful way to take a bath? Both seemed highly unlikely.

Eliza called from the doorway of the tiny house, and Throck turned from his contemplation of the waterside yard. Though he was no Mungo Large, he had to duck to clear the lintel, but once inside the cottage he saw it was spacious enough, with a flagstone floor and exposed rafters and beams supporting the roof's thatching. A ladder at one end of the room led to a small loft, where, Throck presumed, Minnie slept. The walls in the main area of the house were whitewashed, which brightened what otherwise would have been a dim interior, and shelves lined every wall, filled with books and bric-a-brac: miniature tea cups painted with otters, tiny sculptures of otters, little gilt-framed oils of otters, otter shaped lamps and a hinged metal tin that said 'Otter put it in here.' Throck raised his brows and said, "Goodness," but the ladies, chatting in what served as a kitchen, were paying him no heed. He turned to watch them, Eliza smiling and helping as Minnie brewed tea in an otter-shaped tea pot and laid some cold fish pies on a cloth embroidered with grinning otters.

"Lived here me whole life," Minnie was saying as Throck tuned in, "Right here in this very cottage. Couldn't ever see meself anywheres else, I don't mind sayin'. I'm happy here. And there's them what'd miss me were I to leave." She said this last with a softening of her tone that was almost sentimental.

Trying to join in, Throck said in a friendly tone, "Your son?"

Minnie scowled at him. "Pfft. Good fer nothin'. More like his father than a little bit. Never appreciated the charms o' this place, an' when he were old enough to know his own mind he moved o'er to the farm to live with his da. Wanted to learn the brewin' business, he said, 'cept his da were a wastrel and died never showin' him a thing. So guess who had to teach 'im?" One of Minnie's eyeballs skewered first Throck, then Eliza. "I did, that's who. What he learned, he learned from me. An' now he's a master brewer round these parts, no doubts there, but he's still good fer not much. Who treks the roads with the barrow and drums up sales? Who figgered out about customer loyalty and givin' the bleeders what they want when they want it? Who figured out Small and Smaller could be a goin' concern in the cider world, and the joke on him? Not that one."

"Oh," said Throck, accepting a proffered fish pie. What else could one say, really?

Minnie's eyeball measured him with an up and down wobble, then, as if concluding he was decidedly uninteresting, turned back to Eliza. Throck bit into his pie, happy to be ignored. Minnie was more than a little intimidating.

"Tell me more, now, Lizzie, about growing up in Southwark – London town," Minnie said, her brown nut of a face visibly softer when turned on Eliza. "I can't think what it must be like in such a big city. Is't all vice and wickedness? Purse thieves on every corner? 'Tis what you hear."

Throck, munching, turned to Eliza, curious. Why had he not thought to ask her such a question, he chided himself. Oh, he'd been to London once or twice, and knew a bit of what the polite parts of the city were like. But what had it been like for her, growing up there, south of the Thames with its rough streets, stinking factories and crumbling tenement buildings? A place you read about in *The Illustrated Police News* or in *The Times'* report on The Old Bailey criminal court proceedings, or in a Dickens novel. Companions on the road should know certain things about one another, surely.

Eliza sipped her tea, obviously discomfited to be the focus of attention. She smiled awkwardly, and glanced almost apologetically at Throck before turning to Minnie. "Vice and wickedness, as you say, there is aplenty, and thieves too, no mistake. But there were – still are, I'm sure – kind-hearted souls who'd give you a morsel o' food when it was all they had for themselves, and who'd give you a place to sleep if you found yourself out in the cold and starin' down the workhouse door."

"And were you, then, starin' down the workhouse door?" Minnie prodded – rudely, Throck thought, his gaze on Eliza anxious. He wanted to tell her not to answer. He doubted many would choose to admit to being low enough in their life to have needed the workhouse, and suspected it would be a source of some embarrassment. Mrs, he recalled, had felt rather strongly that "those types" as she'd put it, must lie in the beds they'd made. He remembered replying that circumstance often beyond one's immediate ability to change, and not choice, was the more likely reason for the majority of admissions to such a place. His heart hurt for Eliza, pinioned here by Minnie's boldness, but selfishly, he hesitated to object. He too wanted to hear her answer.

"I don't know," she said with a shrug. "I were very young when my mother died – she called me Lizzie too – and I suppose if a friend of my mother's hadn't taken me in I would've been sent to Hanwell, or another of the schools for paupers. So I'm grateful, indeed, for Gin-Gin, and her good heart."

"Gin-Gin?" Minnie said, leaning across the table in her eagerness to hear more of the tale. Throck wanted to flick the pastry crumbs that hung on her chin, but suspected she'd take unkindly to the move. He was as curious as Minnie, but prided himself on his restraint. "What kind of name is Gin-Gin?" Minnie persisted. "Was she a drunk?"

Eliza gave a short laugh, and Throck watched her carefully. If he were more of a man, he scolded himself yet again, he'd jump in here and rescue her. To his shame, he let her continue. "She were a drunk, yes," Eliza said, lifting her chin as she spoke, and fixing not Minnie, but Throck, with the steady gaze of her blue eyes. "But she were also a brilliant music hall performer. Gin-Gin Geneva was her stage name. She used to take me along when she were working, and I'd sit backstage and watch her. She had a voice that few could match, and a gift handling the audience. They'd cheer for 'er, and shout out that they loved 'er. After the performances she'd get herself a bottle of gin and we'd stop at the fish 'n' chips shop on the way home to Lant Street, and we'd burrow into the blankets, she with her gin and me with me food, and we'd sing all her show tunes 'til one of us fell asleep – usually her."

"You poor dear," said Minnie, still bent forward, enthralled.

"I were never happier," Eliza countered, and that blue gaze pinioned Minnie Small as Minnie had pinioned her. Then her eyes moved back to Throck and softened, he thought, and she flushed as she added, "Until now." Throck smiled, holding her gaze, feeling like he'd won a prize.

*

Minnie Small clambered into her loft some time later, and was quickly snoring, the noise rebounding off the cottage's walls. Before retiring she'd made up a pallet on the floor for Eliza, and Eliza climbed beneath the blanket gratefully, no doubt exhausted from the day and the story she'd been goaded into telling. Throck had been waved to a chair. He'd never slept sitting up, and suspected that after the night was done, he still would not have accomplished such a feat. He shifted this way and that, unable to find a position conducive to sleep, and after what felt like hours, he rose with a groan, his neck cricked and arms still protesting the day's work, and went outside to visit the privy he'd spied earlier over by the fence.

The sky overhead was spangled with millions of stars. He paused, awestruck, looking at the swath of their diamond-like sparkle against the inky backdrop of the night, and wondered how it was he'd never noticed such astronomic beauty before. Was the night sky less vivid at Sowerby Grange, he wondered, or, even, in the Blackdown Hills? He supposed the glow of the campfire had something to do with his not noticing, and in the case of Sowerby Grange certainly, there was the overhang of the trees in Whortleberry Wood, and the prevalence of fog at night, and his tendency to be ensconced in his bedroom with only the swirls of a plaster ceiling overhead. Here, the air was crisp and clear and the heavens wide open, and while he felt small beneath this majesty, he also felt incredibly honoured to have been given the gift of such a sight.

A movement on the path drew his attention from the celestial glitter. He heard rather than saw something scuttle through the weeds – a patter of little feet on hardpack and the hush of swaying grass – and he peered into the darkness, but could see nothing. Then, in his peripheral vision, he noticed movement on yet another path – and there, ahead of him, more swishing of the vegetation. Whatever the thing was, it was small and furry and rather quick on its feet, and Throck stood stock still, alarmed. He heard a splash down by the river, and another, then squeaking noises that reminded him of a child's toy, and he realised to his horror that Minnie Small's yard was swarming with creatures. Suddenly one of the animals was directly before him on the path and Throck gaped. Otters! The animal rose onto its thick hind legs, hissed and bared its teeth and lunged aggressively, and Throck had just enough time to take note of its rather sharp claws before he turned and ran for the nearest shelter, the little privy next to the fence, pursued by the beast, he felt quite sure.

He stayed in the outhouse all night, listening to the otters cavort in Minnie's yard, sliding in and out of the river that flowed so placidly alongside. They squeaked and growled and pipped amongst themselves, but Throck was not fooled by their cuteness. He saw the beady eyes, whiskered mouths, tiny round ears and claws of a predator, and thought it more than likely that they preyed on helpless frogs and turtles. He slept eventually, but dreamt of Minnie Small, confusing her with the otters. When Eliza tapped on the privy door in the morning, he scrambled awake, mustered what dignity he could and exited, apologizing if he'd taken too long with his daily. He did not look at her as he passed by, but went straight to the Trusty and busied himself checking the oil and refilling the petrol tank, unaware that he had the impression of an outhouse plank upon one side of his face. Of the otters, there was no sign.

*

Neither was Minnie Small in evidence that morning, and so there was no chance to ask her about her otters, but that's what they were, Throck felt sure. *Her* otters. He put two and two together: the myriad of well-worn paths through her garden, the location of the little fenced cottage right upon the bank of the River Otter, and Minnie's collection of otter trinkets, and was confident that she would agree they were *her* otters. Come to think of it, Throck mused, she looked a bit otter-like herself, with her small brown face and her chin whiskers. As a man who identified with frogs and turtles and other otter comestibles, it was no wonder he and she had not exactly hit it off.

Eliza had kindly said nothing about the fact he'd slept in the privy, and Throck pretended he'd fooled her on that account. The only discussion they had before resuming their travels was which way to go, and for that, they consulted their map. Minnie had apparently left early with her barrow to start her deliveries, but Eliza shared her advice, which was to take the high road straight through to Penzance, and stay off the smaller roads like the one on which they'd met, and which, in Minnie's opinion, were for carts and barrows, not high-speed machines like the Trusty.

Throck laughed when Eliza shared Minnie's words. "High speed machine? The Trusty? How fast did you get the old girl going, anyway?"

Eliza shrugged. "Fast enough, I suppose, to impress Minnie Small," she answered. "But she pushes a barrow cart all day and has never even been on a bicycle, let alone anything with a motor. The only chance she ever had for a ride in any kind of machine were back in her younger days, when she were invited up to – I forget – some royal society or other to give a lecture. It would've meant a train ride to London, but she didn't go."

"A royal society? She told you that?" Throck said, and heard the scoff in his voice.

Eliza nodded. "She did." Her gaze was steady, and Throck could see she believed the story, even if it sounded far-fetched to him. A woman like Minnie Small, lecturing? Pshaw.

Moderating his tone so it was devoid of the skepticism he felt, he said, "What might she have been lecturing on, then? Did she say?"

"Otters," Eliza replied. "She knows a thing or two about 'em, it seems, and even years back had quite a reputation as an expert."

Throck turned sheepishly to the map, and pretended to study it closely.

"Well, well," he said, and nodded.

Chapter 26
SLOE GIN AND EMMETS

The high road, as Minnie had called it, was straight and well-surfaced for the most part, but it also had more traffic than they'd seen on their cart track and back lane meanderings. Two lorries and a car passed them in the span of an hour. The car whizzed past, spraying gravel and filling the road with dust, while the lorries trundled by, overtaking the Trusty with a honk and a wave and an equal quantity of dust. Throck, taking his turn at the bike's controls, lifted a hand in return, motorist to motorist, as it were, though in fact he was sorely tempted to make a different sort of gesture. He was truly thankful for his goggles; at least his eyes were protected even if he had grit in his teeth. It was true that one could make good time on such a road, if that was one's intent, and in what seemed no time at all they had travelled the distance from Ottery St Mary to nigh on Bodmin, at the end of the windy and rock-strewn moor, and Eliza tugged at Throck's sleeve and signalled that she wanted him to pull over.

"I'm tired and hungry and there's too much dust," she said when he'd stopped the bike in the shelter of some trees. "Might we find a place to rest a while? I don't like this high road. It doesn't feel…adventuresome – at least not in a good way."

Throck had to agree. If he looked anything like she then he was coated in a layer of dirt, his cheeks were raw from the wind, and his eyes were a little wild, like a dog in a room full of cats. They paused long enough to swill a bit of cider, a parting gift from Minnie Small, washing the parch from their throats, then climbed back upon the Trusty and trundled down the first narrow lane that led off the moor. This was a rocky place, spare and almost devoid of any vegetation save tall grass and wild flowers, but there was a small wood in the distance, and it was there that the lane led, tapering until it reached the shade of the trees and then quickly becoming almost too narrow for both the Trusty and its sidecar. Once or twice the bottom of the sidecar scraped, or was hung up entirely, and Eliza had to hop out, both to lessen the weight and to direct Throck over the myriad boulders. The closeness of the trees and the rocky path made turning around impossible, but Throck doubted they would have made that choice anyway, their exchange of grins as they overcame yet another rocky hurdle confirmation of their shared opinion that this, indeed, was adventure. They pressed on.

Before long, the trail they were following crested a hill and took a downward slope through the trees, and Throck noticed bright green moss on the boulders and a decided wetness to the ground. Over the quiet putt-putt of the barely moving Trusty, he heard rather than saw the distinctive chortle of rushing water, and he glanced at Eliza, who'd been walking behind the bike, lessening its load and pushing to help it over the occasional overlarge rock. She, too, had heard the sound, and as they reached the foot of the hill, Throck paused, slowing the motorcycle to a stop.

"Should we investigate?" he called over his shoulder to Eliza, but she was already bounding off the path and disappearing through the wall of green foliage, calling back "Of course!"

Throck turned off the Trusty's engine, feeling a pinch of envy at the ease with which she plunged into escapades. Would he ever be so intrepid?

He followed, pushing his way through the leafy branches that slapped at his face, and tripping over ropy roots that seemed to lift off the forest floor just as he stepped over them. The ground beneath his feet was spongy, and he slid more than once in mud, but there was no rotten, marshy smell to this place. In fact it smelled fresh and lush and quenching, and when he finally came in view of the water, he saw that it was in fact a waterfall tumbling perhaps twenty feet off a ledge of flat rock and collecting in a pool below. There, in the middle of that pool, Eliza was already swimming, her garments hung on a bush at the water's edge.

"Come in, Throck! It's cold, but wonderful!" she called, and ducked her head beneath the dark water.

Eager to rid himself of the dust of the road, confident that Eliza would turn her back to allow him his modesty, Throck stripped down to his smalls and arranged his clothing tidily on a shrub next to hers, then leaped into the water with a yell. It was chest deep, and cold, indeed, but exhilarating, and he paddled his way across the pond to join Eliza, his bunioned feet slip-sliding over the rocky bottom. Each time he neared her, though, Eliza laughed and backed away until she stood directly beneath the waterfall, its spill cascading onto her head and over her shoulders. She stretched out a hand to him, smiling through the water curtain, but Throck hesitated. He disliked water pouring on his head. Sometimes the water got in one's ear canal and was stuck there and wouldn't come out, and for days one had that annoying gurgle in one's ear drum. Water pouring with such force upon one's head was rather unnatural, he thought, and a bit wild. But Eliza was laughing, her eyes sparkling, the water running over her limbs like liquid silver, and so he plunged forward, cares to the wind, and they stood there, the two of them, beneath the thundering force of the waterfall, Throck's few gray hairs plastered to the dome of his head, Eliza's abundant red shrouding her like a veil.

*

After their swim they found a nearby clearing where there was dry ground, and pitched a makeshift tent using the old tarpaulin as they'd done on their first night, with the Trusty as a wall, and sticks to prop the other side. The evening, when it drew down, was pleasant, and without rain, unlike that first night, and Eliza started a small fire that they sat beside, cooking a bit of sausage and potato and sipping Minnie Small's cider. Throck again was struck by how content he felt. How absolutely at peace.

"What were you like as a boy?" Eliza asked suddenly, poking at the embers of the fire with a stick and sending sparks into the sky.

"I?" Throck said, surprised by such a question. He frowned, considering. What *had* he been like as a boy? Small and unimportant came to mind, not so different from what he was now, as an older man. He'd been an only child, born to much older parents, and he'd lived a quiet country life, except for a long and unpleasant stint at boarding school. The answer struck him with certainty. "Lonely," he said, and shrugged.

She held his gaze, and after a moment, nodded, attending to her prodding of the embers.

"That's sad," she said.

They sat in silence for a while. Then Throck, fearing she might be contemplating the tragedy of his life and hoping to change her train of thought, said, trying for a light tone, "What of you, Eliza? Surely better, living with Gin-Gin, your saviour."

Eliza looked at him steadily, unsmiling. "I were never lonely. Never that. Gin-Gin were kind to me. Like you." She contemplated the flickering fire, then looked again at Throck, and his heart felt full with the trust he saw in her eyes. She added, peering across the flames, "There are things I did, though, that I'm sorry for. Things I'd do over, or do differently. One day I'll go back. To Southwark. To the Borough. To make amends."

"Amends? Whatever for?" Throck asked, puzzled.

But Eliza yawned widely, and either did not hear or pretended not to.

"I'm for bed," she said, rising and turning toward their makeshift shelter. "We should start early," and as she ducked beneath the flap of the tarpaulin, she added, "Goodnight, sar."

Thock poked the dying embers with a stick. Sir, she'd called him, again. He'd thought they'd gone beyond that. He sat for a long time alone under the night sky, watching the orange glow fade.

*

The morning was grey and overcast, and a light rain dampened both clothing and spirits. Neither Throck nor Eliza broached the subject of Southwark, or the peripheral conversation, and all of the previous day's lightness of being seemed to have vanished. Without discussion Throck drove, and Eliza burrowed into the sidecar, and once they cleared the woods in which they'd camped, an open trail was theirs for the riding. They were headed, Throck thought, roughly southeast, and sure enough, before long, the Trusty crested a bony hill and came in view of the vast grey undulating sea.

He steered the motorcycle along a coastal path meant more, he was sure, for horse traffic or pedestrians than for motorcycles, but as the land was wide open and windswept, it mattered little. Here there were no encroaching trees, and although there were plenty of boulders, the path wound around them rather than over them, and he guided the Trusty without difficulty. Eliza dozed, or at least remained buried beneath a double layer of rugs. Throck wiped the rain from his goggles now and again, forging eastward along Cornwall's spiny coast, keeping the wild sea to his left, noticing as he drove the way the water dashed itself against the ancient rocks. It seemed a battle that had played itself out over millennia, and would continue that way unchecked, with no winner and no loser. At the occasional knoll he could see the path's track tracing the jagged coastline like an unfurled ribbon, and he pressed on through bracken and heather made salty by the sea spray that washed the cliffs. He glanced periodically at the hump of rugs that was Eliza, wondering if he should wake her for this first glimpse of the seaside that she had been so excited for, but decided there would be many miles yet of riding alongside the seemingly unending ocean, and she likely needed her sleep. He thought about what she'd said the night before, about making amends for something, or to someone, in Southwark. The woman Gin-Gin Geneva? He blushed at the name, picturing a blowsy woman in overtight curls and with overmuch flesh on view, perhaps sporting net stockings, or worse, pantaloons and a corset. Yes, he'd seen those sorts of pictures, to his shame; one or two of the locals at the Hock and Toot had passed round some cabinet cards with risqué photos of music hall madams and painted film stars. They'd had names not unlike Gin-Gin's: Saucy Suzanne and Betty from Brest were two he recalled, printed on the cards in a curly-queue typeface. Despite the stiff wind off the sea Throck reached a finger to his collar to loosen his scarf.

He stopped the bike to top up the petrol, and Eliza stirred from her nest, appearing dishevelled and disoriented from beneath the rugs. She blinked, squinting against the daylight even though, to Throck's more accustomed gaze, it was a dull and dark day. He thought she might comment excitedly about the sea, shifting so restlessly off to their left, but instead her eyes travelled inland, over Throck's shoulder, and Throck saw them widen as she cried, seeming to come fully awake, "What's that?!"

He turned to look, and saw up on the slight rise in the near distance, several enormous upright columns of black stone, standing perhaps twice the height of a man. Throck had seen monoliths like these before, but never in such a moody location, with the roiling grey sky as a backdrop, and surrounded by a skirt of tall grasses bent low in the sea breeze. His rational mind knew them for large rocks, although it was true some folk attached magical properties to such stones, and he conceded he had no idea how the unnatural formations might have been created, or indeed placed. As he stared at the pillars, he found himself imagining them as ancient beings, or otherworldly, perhaps, inhumanly tall and broad-shouldered, with rock faces that frowned down upon mere mortals chancing to pass below. Come no closer, they might have warned; bow to us, revere us, and pass on.

Eliza seemed to hear a different message. While Throck straddled the seat of the Trusty, immersed in his imaginings, she scampered up the rise and approached the stones, running her hands over the lichen-covered surfaces and exclaiming. She went from one to the next and the next, touching and peering and occasionally throwing Throck a smile of wonderment over her shoulder. "Aren't they amazing?" she called, almost dancing as she moved between them. The wind had become stiff, and tugged at her clothing with a force. He, below on the track, eyeing the standing stones with trepidation though of course he knew they were nothing more than rocks, shouted over the howl of the wind, "Come back. We should be getting on."

And just as he spoke, Eliza cried out, and disappeared.

Throck blinked. One minute she'd been there, prancing among the stones like some druid maiden of old, her red hair whipped by the wind, and the next she was gone. His heart in his throat, he leapt off the motorcycle and scrambled up the hillside. The standing stones were even taller as he reached them, and loomed over him, seeming to bend menacingly towards him. The wind was fierce, and roared as it passed amongst the rocks. If Throck had been wearing a hat it would have been plucked from his head and sent sailing into the grey sky. His shouts were tossed with the same disregard.

"Eliza! Eliza!" There was panic in his voice. Now that he was up here, on the hillside amongst the towering stones, he saw that indeed she had disappeared, as if from the face of the earth. The pillars formed a rough circle perhaps twenty feet in diameter, their surfaces weathered and spotted with crusty orange lichen. Throck flung himself from one stone to the next, calling out, angered by the way the wind thinned his voice when he most needed it to be strong. Overhead, terns wheeled in the leaden sky, and Throck wasn't sure if they helped him with their cries, or hindered, and mocked him. He stopped to shake his fist at them, and when he turned back to his quest, saw the gaping hole in the ground almost beneath his feet. Eliza was there, peering up at him from a dark, rocky crevice, the entrance to which was nearly covered over by the long tussocky grasses. There were smudges of dirt on her face and dried grass stuck in her hair, and her hand, when she reached up to him, was scraped and bloody. He tugged her free of the burrow with a strength he'd not known he possessed, and when she was again above ground relief flooded through him. They collapsed to their knees in the centre of the ring of stones, gasping for breath with the effort of the extrication. The wind lifted Eliza's hair into the air, and Throck's jacket flapped like the wings of a bird. Eliza laughed, a crack of sound that was close to a sob, and cradled against her chest the arm Throck hadn't tugged on. "Bloody 'ell," she said, "I think I've broke me wrist. And maybe me ankle."

*

Because of Eliza's injuries Throck steered the Trusty into the first village they came to, following a path down off the clifftops. Portluce's streets were steep and narrow, its buildings whitewashed and so close to the bricked lanes that it was all Throck could do to avoid scraping the sidecar against walls. He pressed hard on the brake to counteract the downward slope of the grade, and though he passed several curious citizens from whom he might have asked directions to the local surgery, he could not stop the motorcycle until he came at last to the cove itself, a horseshoe inlet filled with bobbing fishing boats. The sandy beach held stacks of what Throck surmised were crab and lobster pots, crafted of bent withies or woven rope, and the air, understandably, was pungent with the odours of fish and seaweed. Gulls soared overhead, filling the sky with their shrilling.

Even before he could climb off the Trusty a fellow approached, scratching beneath a knitted wool beanie with one hand and under a rumpled and much-stained twill smock with the other. He was a smallish man, Throck saw, his own size, if he was honest, but this man had a wiry body that bespoke a kind of working man's strength that Throck certainly did not possess. Nor did this Cornishman own the rounded tummy that Throck had, although, if Throck did say so himself, that mark of a soft life was fast disappearing the longer he spent on the road. Nevertheless, he felt decidedly the lesser being as he got off the motorcycle, stuck out his hand and offered a smiling, "Hello."

"A'right," the man replied. He shook Throck's hand, but said nothing more. His gaze, travelling over Throck, then the motorcycle with Eliza tucked beneath the rugs in the sidecar, and back to Throck, held only mild curiosity, as if nothing much could surprise him. Further back on the beach, Throck noticed, a small crowd of locals had gathered, presumably to gawk at the oddity in their midst: Throck, Eliza and the Trusty with her sidecar.

"Is there a doctor about?" Throck asked. "My friend here has hurt herself falling down a burrow."

"Burrow, eh?" the man repeated, lifting grizzly eyebrows. He peered at Eliza more closely, his eyes almost as vividly blue as her own. "Wotcher doin' fallin' down a burrow, me lover?"

The endearment, if it was that, gave Throck pause. Whatever did the fellow mean, being so forward with a lady he'd only just met – hadn't met, actually, not formally, anyway. But he checked any offense he'd been ready with, thinking of Mungo Large who'd called him young'un, after all, when he was not. And, for that matter, Stephen Vanson, who, on the day he'd sold Throck the Trusty, had called him 'ansum, a thing he also could never claim to be.

"Well, it wasn't on purpose, I can promise you that," Throck said, tempering his ill-humoured words with what probably appeared a disingenuous smile. Dash it all, they needed a doctor, not a grilling. "Is there someone hereabouts who could have a look at my friend's injuries?"

"Your friend is she now?" The man's tone was skeptical. "Fell down a burrow, you say?" He frowned and scratched again beneath beanie and smock. Throck felt his patience grow thinner.

"Yes, a burrow. She fell down a burrow while exploring some monoliths not far from here," Throck said. There was exasperation in his voice now, and he heard Eliza say warningly, "Throck…"

"Best stay away from the monoliths, 'specially the likes o' you emmets, come from afar. Never know when you might stumble down a burrow," he said, and Throck gave a low hiss of impatience. The fellow ignored him, and said to Eliza, "Can you walk, me lovely?"

"She needs to see a doctor," Throck repeated stubbornly. He was more than slightly annoyed with this fisherman's plodding persistence, and almost pushed past him, intending to find someone else in the village who could direct him, when the man's next words drew Throck up short.

"I be the doc hereabouts." He ignored Throck's open mouth and went to the sidecar, bending towards Eliza. "You've a scrape or two on your face, I can well see. That's an easy enough tidy up."

"I've hurt me ankle, and me wrist throbs something awful," Eliza said to the fellow. Throck thought she looked a bit grey, as if she might be sick to her stomach.

"Best get her up to me surgery," the doctor, if that's what he was, said to Throck. The man eyed the Trusty and the somewhat battered sidecar dubiously, and said, "If you can coax this contraption the ways up yonder," he gestured towards the snaggle of whitewashed houses that hugged the steep-sided inlet, "betwixt us we can see about prying the maid out of it."

Throck scowled at him. How did he know Eliza was his maid? Had been. But no, of course, that's not what the man meant, he realised. Feeling decidedly cantankerous, and disliking the fisherman/doctor though there was no time to explore why, he climbed onto the Trusty, restarted her engine, and gunned it unnecessarily, causing a backfire that drew a frown from Eliza and turned more than a few curious heads from the crowd assembled on the beach.

*

As it turned out, Eliza had sprained both her wrist and her ankle. Nothing a bit of ice and elevation wouldn't cure, so the doc said. When Throck was allowed in to see her (he'd been made to wait outside for what seemed an unreasonably long period of time), he found her looking much improved and resting on a comfortable looking settle in a low-ceilinged but bright room with windows that looked out over Portluce's sheltered bay. It was a picturesque place, Throck could admit, and thought it probably was rather lovely on a sunny day, the water a-sparkle and the fishing boats bobbing.

Eliza smiled at him as he bent to get through the low doorway. A plate of something that looked like oat cakes sat on a table nearby, and she waved him to it, supposing, correctly, that he'd be as hungry as she. He took one and munched, mindful of crumbs, and perched on the edge of the settle to look over her care. Her wrist and ankle had been tidily bandaged, and her foot was propped on a stool. With her free hand – as luck would have it, her writing hand – she was penning a letter on stationery Throck supposed had been provided by the good doctor. All, indeed, seemed very well.

"I'm writing to George," she told Throck, setting down the pen. "I haven't had a chance since I posted the last one, and as we're to be here a few days I thought I'd use the time to send another."

"Well, good," said Throck, nodding. He took a second cake. "I like George. Say hello from me." He paused, and added, "If you think it's appropriate." Then he gestured to the bandaged wrist and ankle, and said, "A few days, then, is it? I suppose I should ask about for an inn."

"No need," said the doctor, and Throck looked up to see the man standing just inside the doorway. He glanced past Throck to Eliza, and the especially warm smile he turned on her faded as he looked back at Throck. "It's all arranged. You'll kip here on the settle, and the patient –" he threw Eliza another indulgent smile "– will stay with me sister Loveday close across the way." He held up a hand as Throck opened his mouth to protest that such an arrangement was surely an infringement. Throck, as was his nature, was being polite, but in truth he did not relish the idea of separating from Eliza, or worse, of staying here with the doctor, who, he sensed, disliked him mutually. He eyed the man, still in his stained fisherman's smock, for goodness sake. (He chose to ignore the fact that he himself still had his pants tucked into his socks.) Did the fellow have any actual medical training? But the moment the thought popped into his head he retracted it, hearing the pinch of Mrs' voice overlaid upon it. So far removed from her, was he now to become her? He drew himself up, vowing to do better, and muttered his thanks to the doctor.

*

Throck insisted on seeing Eliza well settled in Loveday Quick's white walled cottage, and the doctor, whose name, Throck learned at last, was Pascoe Bonny, hadn't exaggerated when he'd said she was close by. The small door to Loveday's house banged against the small door to the doctor's if they stood open at the same time, and if a window was left ajar in both houses, one could have a conversation with a person in the other cottage without rising off the settle. Throck supposed such a feature would make for good neighbours, but then, thinking of Woody Barks, wondered what would happen if it didn't.

Loveday Quick was short like her brother, with a frizzled cap of tight colourless curls and a body as round and solid as one of the melons Throck had once upon a time grown in the greenhouse at Sowerby Grange. She had a houseful of children that she herded about with plump hands, a sharp wit, and small, darting eyes that missed nothing, from the youngest attempting to plug his or her nose with dried bean seeds to the oldest prying boldly into Eliza's large carpet bag almost before it was set upon the floor. Throck was rather alarmed by the busyness of the place with its swarming little people, and stood in the doorway fearing entry. Eliza, though, was soon showing off her bandages to the curious eyeballs, and smiling with Loveday in that sisterly fashion Throck had noticed women could have with one another when they chose. With all the bustle of a clucking hen Loveday settled Eliza in a chair and shooed the children away, though they swarmed back within seconds, and Throck, standing forgotten in the doorway, could see that everyone was already enamoured of Eliza, and he had no cause here for concern. He waved from the stoop, though no one saw, and turned back across the way to Pascoe Bonny's house.

The doc – the moniker he himself used and which did indeed suit the man better than doctor, Throck admitted – was tugging on a pair of wellingtons that reminded Throck, longingly, of his own. Throck stood uncertainly in the passageway between Loveday Quick's house and the doc's, and wondered what he should do with himself. It was late afternoon, he supposed, although with the leaden sky it was hard to be sure. From this vantage point, partway up the bay's steep incline, he could see the grey sea, choppy and foaming. Far out on the water, he thought he could see small boats, their sails stiff, moving through the waves.

"Them there're the pilchard boats," the doc said, coming to stand beside him and following his gaze. "They're not out for the pilchards today, though. Sea's too rough to spot the shoals." He nodded over Throck's shoulder, and Throck turned to see a squat, wooden building, not more than a shed, really, keeping a lonely vigil on a nearby clifftop. "See up there on that hill? That there's the huer's hut. Huer'll keep watch on the calm days, look out for the pilchards to come in, and when 'e spots 'em, he'll raise the hue and cry, and then you want to see boats launch some quick."

"Oh?" said Throck, curious. He'd eaten salted pilchards once or twice in his day, and knew the little silver fish were a staple in this part of the country, but he had no knowledge at all of the ins and outs of the industry. He'd assumed a fisherman just got in his boat on any given day at any given time and took his luck as it came. "That's a job, then? Huer?"

"Oh, aye," said the doc. "Important job, huer. Me grandfather were a huer. Damn fine one, too. Huer spots the shoal comin' in – she looks like a great dark cloud out in the water, but as she comes and comes you can soon see the fish leapin' and playin' on the surface, hundreds and thousands of 'em at a time – and the huer gives his cry." The doc turned and fixed Throck with a bald stare. "But once that shoal's been spotted and the men've taken to their boats and set out to sea, then the huer's job really becomes vital."

"Oh?" Throck said again. "More important, even, than spotting the shoal in the first place?"

The doc scowled at him, as if he'd asked a stupid question, or a trick one, mayhap.

"Boats're out on the water, fetching about for the fish, see? 'Cept it's the huer, like some god on high, what can see the shoal, whether it's going to swerve left or right or zigzag, mebbe. So he takes a coupla gorse branches or whatever's to hand and waves 'em, just so, directing the fleet, y'see, tellin' 'em where them crazy pilchards're heading, and once the boats are ranged in place, pilchards embayed and nets at the ready, he signals again, and the nets are shot." He nodded, squinting out at the churlish sea. "'Tis a sight to behold, to be sure, and another when the men come ashore with their catch."

Throck, imagining the scene the doc described, said, perhaps more wistfully than he actually felt, "I've never been on a boat."

The doc made a chuffing sound that might have been a laugh, and started down the steep hill towards the beach. "Then you 'aven't lived," he said over his shoulder. "We'll remedy that in the morning. You can help me haul the crab traps. Come along. We've dinner to collect."

*

Throck and the doc traipsed over thick mats of fishy smelling blackish-green vegetation – bladderwrack, the doc called it, and told Throck it was quite edible, and healthy, but for today they'd stick to shellfish.

"They're shore to be tasty," said the doc, and Throck glanced at him, wondering if that was seaside humour, or simply the man's dialect. If it was meant to be funny, the doc was deadpan, and Throck shrugged and followed him obediently through tide pools, feeling the seawater squish into his shoes and wishing, fervently, for his wellingtons. Every now and again the doc bent and plucked up a few shells to throw into the bucket he'd tasked Throck with carrying, and Throck would peer at the bounty, noting black shells and blue shells and white shells of various shapes and sizes.

"Mussel," the doc would say as the shell clattered into the bottom of the bucket, or "cockel," or "clam." The sea, it seemed, gave up her edibles to more than just fishermen. Throck, a fan of oysters particularly, with lemon, presumed this fare would be as tasty, and looked forward the reward. The find of the day was a fat purple-backed lobster that added significant weight to the pail, and that wagged its rather ominous looking pincers at Throck weakly. He felt sorry for the creature, but thought it best not to voice the opinion. Fishermen, if they were anything like farmers, would find sentiment over a crustacean as mawkish as a farmer would over a chicken.

When they'd finished scavenging, as the doc called it, they retraced their steps over the bladderwrack and wet sand and slippery rocks and climbed back up the steep hill to the doc's surgery. The upper half of his sister Loveday Quick's split door stood open, and the doc rapped, calling through the opening while he worked his boots off. Throck too removed his wet shoes and socks, and stood in his bare feet, noting with slight embarrassment that the skin was as white and puckered as a fish's belly, and his toenails needed a good clipping.

Loveday appeared and whisked away both the bucket of shellfish and Throck's shoes and socks, which she said she'd dry by her kitchen stove. Throck thanked her, but she bustled off without a backward glance, as if drying wet socks was nothing she wouldn't do for any visitor. The doc beckoned him opposite, through the door to the surgery, and the men went into the front room with its view of the cove below, and settled down in comfy chairs, each with a glass of sloe gin in hand, and sipping.

"So, go ahead," said the doc in the forthright manner that continued to put Throck on edge, "tell us where you and the maid were headed before she tumbled down the burrow."

"Eliza and I," Throck replied, emphasizing her name, "were on our way to Land's End."

"What for?" asked the doc bluntly. "Amn't nothin' there of interest. A bit of rock, a view of the sea. Nothin' you can't see here in Portluce, or anywheres along the coast, for that matter."

"Oh," said Throck, suddenly unsure. Nothing there? Perhaps they should rethink their plans. He resolved to discuss it with Eliza, but in the meantime, he answered, truthfully, "Eliza noted it on our map, and liked the name." He paused, and then added, "We're on an adventure," as if that explained it.

"Hmpf," said the doc, and sipped his gin, his eye on Throck appraisingly. "Sounds like something a couple of emmets'd do."

"Emmets?" asked Throck, annoyed. He had a suspicion the term was not meant to be flattering. What right had this man to pass judgement on what he and Eliza might choose to do, or where they might decide to go? He considered getting up and leaving this fellow to his unpleasant company, but his wrinkled bare feet were propped on the man's footstool, and he was rather comfortable, and hadn't finished his drink.

"Strangers. Outsiders. Definitely not Cornishmen," replied the doc, clarifying the term off-handedly. He stood and took Throck's half-empty glass to the sideboard, refilling it and his own with the ruby red sloe gin. He handed Throck's back to him, and with a swift change of subject, asked, "Is the maid your – well, what is she, exactly? You seem oddly met."

Throck's indignance at such a forward question was immediate, but then he thought of Mungo, who hadn't this man's acerbic personality, and yet he, too, had wondered at the dynamic of his and Eliza's relationship. He supposed, were the tables turned, that he might also be curious, although he would never be so bold as to ask. Still, he swallowed his irritation, and after a moment's consideration, replied simply and honestly, "She's my friend."

"Friend," repeated the doc, nodding. "Well, that's better'n if she were your enemy." He didn't laugh, or smirk, or even smile, but Throck was beginning to understand that Pascoe Bonny was a bit of a dry-wit, and this was meant to be funny. Softened up by the second glass of sloe gin, Throck gave an obligatory chuckle.

"You're not married, then," the doc continued, drumming his fingers on his knee.

"To Eliza? No," Throck replied. He almost added that he did have a wife, back in the Cotswolds, but caught himself in time. No sense complicating matters unnecessarily. He stared into his glass, avoiding the doc's eye.

"'Tisn't seemly," Pascoe Bonny said tersely.

"There's nothing unseemly about it, in fact," Throck countered defensively. He understood the man's position, indeed he did; it was one that most of society would take, feeling themselves completely justified in judging another person's choices. He himself might even have leaned towards such disapproval had he not met first Harold Guppletwill, whose curiosity and humility had indeed inspired Throck's viewpoints, and second Eliza herself, who took a similarly modest and open approach to her fellow man. "Eliza and I are travel companions. We're sharing an adventure that is in every way respectful and unimpeachable, and – and – well, I won't defend myself to you."

"Amn't concerned about you," Pascoe responded drily, swirling his gin. "But 'tis my duty to inquire after such as she, as any upright folk should. Wouldn't be proper if I didn't."

Throck's cheeks and the dome of his head, he was sure, were bright red, but he said nothing further other than to suggest that the doc, to allay his concerns, pose his queries to Eliza who would, undoubtedly, reassure him. The answer seemed to satisfy the doc, and after a bit of broody silence and a few more sips of gin, the conversation resumed, steered from Eliza's precarious virtue to fishing, and before long, the men were summoned for dinner. Throck's belly had begun rumbling at the wonderful smells drifting over from Loveday's kitchen, and he was all but rubbing his hands together in anticipation of the meal. Following the doc's lead, he padded into Loveday's warm and noisy kitchen on bare feet, hoping he didn't give offence with their nakedness, and wondering if his socks would yet be dry – and where his haversack with the extra pairs had disappeared to.

*

Dinner was a delicious repast of the fruits of the afternoon's scavenging, but there was no chance for Throck and Eliza to have words on their own to discuss their plans. In fact, there was no chance for words between them at all. He and Eliza sat at opposite ends of Loveday's long table, Eliza at Loveday's right, Throck at Pascoe's, with Loveday's clamouring children ranged in between, and there was a general din of clattering tableware and chattering Quicks. Loveday appeared to have made an effort for the occasion. Throck noticed her wiry hair pampered with a black bow, and she wore a bracelet of unusual dark pearls. He commented on the piece, wondering where in the world one might find black pearls. Loveday and Pascoe fixed him with identical flat stares, and then Pascoe said that Loveday's no-good husband was a mariner, and had brought them from "some God-forsaken place – Tahiti, or Fiji. Someplace where they don't wear proper clothes."

"Ah," said Throck, wishing he hadn't asked.

"He don't come around these parts anymore, so good riddance," Pascoe said tightly. To Loveday he said, "Don't know why you keep puttin' that thing on."

"It's pretty," she replied, and brother and sister pinched their lips in identically stubborn grimaces. Loveday passed a basket of bread, and dinner resumed.

The children, a product, presumably, of the absent pearl-gifting mariner, were oblivious to the adult discussion and took no notice of the mention of their father. Nor did it seem any great thing to Pascoe or his sister that the children climbed beneath the table and onto Eliza's lap, for neither mother nor uncle made any effort at restraint. Rather, the children romped with their doting approval, and Throck was irked by what he considered their hijinks. He told himself it was his lack of experience with children, but catching Eliza's glance now and again as dinner progressed, he thought he detected her own annoyance at having the little beings bounce on and off her lap at will, careless of her bandaged wrist, or climb beneath the table to cause mischief. One of the young Quicks had been so bold as to tug on Throck's bare toes, and almost involuntarily Throck had kicked out and struck home. The child had surfaced crying, and tucked itself onto its mother's lap where it was petted until the sobs subsided. No one, thankfully, asked what had caused the mite's tears, nor did the child report, but when it had finished its wailing, it was let free to climb and cavort again. Throck awaited retaliatory mischief from beneath the dinner table, but none came. He was careful not to wiggle his toes and bait the fish.

Despite the undisciplined children the meal was delicious. And after the shellfish melee Loveday served up a strawberry pie, and at long last every child sat still for the length of time it took them to devour their generous slice. Throck was relieved by the relative silence, if not by the noisy slurps and burps and smacking of lips. The children really had no manners at all, Throck thought, hearing Mrs Isbister in the thought, but for once feeling certain this was a topic on which they might have agreed. Taking the opportunity that the lull in noise and activity provided, Throck turned to the doc and asked when he thought Eliza would be well enough to travel.

"Travel?" said the doc through a mouthful of pie, pastry crumbs ringing his lips. "You can see she's got her arm in a sling, man, and a bandaged ankle. You said she shares the driving?" His tone was incredulous, as if Throck had just posed a completely ridiculous idea.

"Well, yes, but —" Throck began, intending to explain that of course he would not expect Eliza to do any driving until she had healed, but surely she could ride in the sidecar in comfort?

"Out of the question," the doc said with a decisive shake of his head. "A spell of rest and relaxation are what this young lady needs, not traipsing around the countryside on the whimsy of some old fool."

"Old fool?" Throck began indignantly, incredulous at the doc's words. But the children had finished their pie and had again begun to ride roughshod over the evening, and Throck felt another tug at his toes beneath the table. He set down his fork and knife with a clatter and said, "Now see here!" although whether this was directed at the mischievous prankster playing with his feet or Pascoe Bonny wasn't quite clear.

Loveday clucked as she cleared the table, and called over her shoulder, "Don't be ticklin' old Mr Isbister, children, he's a bit tetchy." To Throck, steaming at the table while Loveday's brood clamoured about him, she said, "You and Pascoe run along now to your pipes, or whatever it is you men do, and leave me to clean up. Eliza here needs to get some rest."

Throck glowered round the room, but Loveday was busily banging pots and pans and the doc had arisen from the table and was bending over Eliza, checking the bandage on her wrist and mumbling questions that Throck couldn't hear over the din of the children and Loveday's clatter. Eliza did catch his eye across the doc's shoulder and gave him an apologetic smile, and he felt his anger ebb. Perhaps the doc was right, he thought with a sigh. She did look somewhat wan. He was champing at the proverbial bit rather selfishly, he supposed, and apparently Eliza still needed to recuperate. He made a promise to himself to do better, and with a small wave to Eliza, followed the doc out of the house. It appeared they'd be enjoying the pleasures of Portluce a while longer.

Chapter 27
A PROPER GOOD TRIUMVIRATE

True to his promise, or his threat, depending on how one looked at it, the doc woke Throck early to go fishing – or crabbing, if that was the correct term. Throck rolled off the settle in the doc's front room where he'd actually enjoyed a rather refreshing sleep, and pulled yesterday's grubby trousers over his smalls, making a mental note to find his haversack when they returned. In his angst at dinner the previous evening, he'd forgotten all about asking Loveday for the return of his shoes and socks, or if she'd seen his haversack, although with annoyance it occurred to him that he shouldn't have had to ask for his own possessions. The doc loaned him a pair of rubber boots, heavier than he was used to, and a bit large, and tossed him a twill smock similar to the one the doc seemed to live in, and Throck felt a true Cornish fisherman. Such jaunty attire did not change the fact that Throck's experience of boats was limited, to say the least. He'd been pushed out of a row boat once or twice in his days at boarding school, although the water had been only knee-deep, and he'd fished a few times, pole and line, with Harold Guppletwill on a pond not far from Watton Hoo, but he'd never been in a boat the size of the doc's crabber, nor ever set to sea.

The doc's small lugger had a sail, but the choice this morning was to row. Throck wanted to ask why but the doc was snapping instructions, and Throck already felt like he was in the way no matter where he stepped, and he felt doubly clumsy in the too-big boots that also leaked. He paid grave attention, understanding without being told that obeying the captain of any skip contributed to all hands staying above water, and he did his best, he thought, in light of the fact that he wasn't entirely sure what the forward thwart was, or what one should do when commanded to trim the boat. Thankfully, the breeze was light and the sea calm, and once he conquered his fear of the idea of being afloat on such an immense body of water, he was exhilarated by the fresh sea air, the vast horizon, and the thrill of hauling on the ropes and landing a withy basket with a crab inside. More than once he looked for Eliza to share the exhilaration, but she, of course, was not present, and his verbal description of the morning's adventure would have to do.

As it was, there would be no such chance. Instead, he almost drowned.

He was helping to haul in the last of the doc's crab traps, tethered as they were on what seemed to Throck to be fathoms of rope, but in fact was, according to the doc, merely seventy feet, and his arms felt as if they'd stretched to twice their normal length. Sweat was dripping from his brow, and the weighted trap he pulled on seemed as if it must contain a 200-pound man rather than a crusty little Brown crab or two. The doc had turned away to fuss with one of the already hauled traps balanced on the gunwales, when a wave rocked the boat and Throck lost his balance. With a startled cry he pitched overboard, tumbling headfirst into the salty sea. Water went up his nose, and he must have somersaulted, the borrowed rubber boots pulling him down, the rope he'd been hauling on tangled round his flailing body, and suddenly he was right way up again but still underwater, peering upwards through the sea to the doc's face staring back at him over the lugger's gunwales with an expression as stony as a gargoyle's. Throck struggled with what seemed to him a superhuman effort, but the rope hampered his movements, and the heavy boots dragged like lead weights. He opened his mouth, fishlike, certain he was a goner, wondering why the doc, peering through the water, looked to be making no move to rescue him. This was the end, then. Tugged to the bottom of the sea in a pair of wellingtons too big for his feet, wearing a Cornish fisherman's smock though he was far from a fisherman, and with no socks. An embarrassing way to go. And, worst of all, no chance to see Eliza again, to thank her for her companionship, and to tell her he bequeathed her the Trusty –

The doc's hands grasped him suddenly, the wiry strength Throck had noted before serving to pop Throck corklike out of the water. Spluttering, coughing, gasping for air, he lay in the bottom of the lugger, sea water pouring from his boots. The doc said nothing at all, for once, just grasped the oars and started to row back to Portluce's sheltered cove. Throck remained curled on the wooden floor of the boat, wondering if indeed the doc had hesitated to rescue him, or if it was Throck's own panic that had made it appear so. Either way, crabbing, it seemed, was over for the day.

*

There were no words exchanged between Throck and the doc, either on the row back to shore or on the walk from the beach to the surgery. A couple of fishermen on the beach eyed Throck, soaking wet from head to toe, and the doc, dry as a pin, and grinned. The doc greeted them with a stoic "A'right," but kept walking. For Throck's part, he was too exhausted and shaken to form a sentence, and he hadn't the energy to contemplate with any enthusiasm the reason for the doc's silence, or why it had taken him so long to decide to save him, if in fact that was what had happened. After seeing Throck home, the doc closed the window shutters, darkening the front room where Throck's makeshift bed was, and retreated from the surgery, leaving Throck to rest. An uncharacteristically tactful gesture, Throck thought, peeling off his wet things and scrambling beneath the blankets on the settle. It had been an unpleasant morning, to say the least, but on a positive note his haversack had appeared, and sat on the floor next to the settle, along with his dry socks and shoes. Oddly, his art book lay atop the shoes, and if he thought it rather an invasion of his privacy that someone had felt bold enough to rifle through his haversack and then, even more strangely, to leave the evidence of having done it, he had no energy to consider the implications. Instead, he fell quickly asleep, the shutters blocking out the light and the noise of the surf. He snored through the remaining daylight hours, and dreamt, of all things, of standing beneath the waterfall with Eliza, rivulets of fish coursing over their heads.

When he woke it was to a dark room. He blinked, orienting himself to his surroundings, then rose and opened the shutters to see the cove twilit, the sky purpling as the sun sank somewhere behind Portluce. The sea was still and dark, a sleeping dragon, Throck thought, its very changeability part of its beauty. Despite his near drowning in those waters, this was an undeniably stunning vista, and Throck tucked the sight into his growing store of memories. A day would come, he knew, when this marvellous ride would be at an end, and memories would be precious. Increasingly, he feared Land's End would indeed be an ending.

Shrugging off such gloomy thoughts, he turned back into the room and saw, to his utter delight, that a bath had been left for him, the water still warm. He slid into it gratefully, humming one of the tunes Eliza sang – *If you were the only girl in the world, and I were the only boy* – happy to soap away the smell of the sea and the salt that had crusted onto his skin. It was the first bath he'd had in days, he realised, other than splooshes in ponds and waterfalls, and the warmth, though tepid, was delicious, the soap delightful. He took his time about the ablutions, and when he was done and had dressed, he found a plate with a cold dinner left on the small table by the window. He didn't wonder that he hadn't been woken in time for dinner, and instead saw it as consideration of his day's ordeal. When he finished the food, he went next door to return the plate, supposing that the doc must be there with Eliza and Loveday Quick and her brood. But when he knocked, and was bid enter, only Loveday was in the kitchen, up to her elbows in soapy water. The children must have been already abed, he supposed, glad of the fact. Of the doc and Eliza there was no sign.

"Heard you had quite a tumble today," Loveday said. She hadn't paused in her washing, or even turned to look at him when he came in. Her tone, it seemed, was chilly, though he couldn't think why.

"Bit of a mishap," Throck acknowledged. He remained standing by the closed door, not having been invited to one of the painted chairs tucked into the long table. "Thank you for the food," he said, holding out the plate. Loveday accepted it with suds on her hands, but said nothing. "And thank you for the bath, as well. It was very much appreciated, after so many days on the road, not to mention my dunking." He chuckled, trying to add some levity, but Loveday harrumphed, and there was much of the doc's brusqueness in the sound. He wondered what he'd done to rile her. "Is Eliza about?" he asked, getting straight to it. There was no point in continuing with pleasantries if the conversation was going to be one-sided.

Loveday set down her wash rag and looked at him. Her small eyes were like the ball-peens of a blacksmith's hammer, and he could see dislike quite plain on her face. He was a little taken aback, but then she smiled, and the crease of her round apple cheeks disguised her obsidian gaze. She gestured for Throck to sit, and she pulled out a chair next to him, her legs spread wide beneath her dress to accommodate the girth of her large stomach. Throck was reminded of Alice, but harsher, and without that one's dignity and sense of propriety.

"Mr Isbister," Loveday began, a heave to her words as if what she had to say were a terrible burden. "Eliza do be a lovely girl. Sweet, and I daresay, innocent. But you must see, surely, that 'tisn't seemly, you traipsing her round the countryside on that – contraption – getting up to all sorts –"

"Now see here –" Throck objected, indignant, thrown akilter by what felt like an attack.

"No, you see," Loveday interrupted, the ball-peens in full view again. She leaned her bulk towards him, effectively barricading him in his chair with no route of escape. The tight curls of her hair framed her head like a woolly helmet. Instinctively, Throck drew back, alarmed by the threat of her. Loveday continued. "The doc and I think it best if you just travel on without the maid. Eliza has seen the folly of your little adventure, an' knows it be in her best interest if you just go along on your way. She do miss her folk, an' has written to 'em. They be comin' for 'er."

"What? What folk? That can't be true. Where is she? Let me speak to her," Throck said angrily.

"She's resting, Mr Isbister," Loveday said firmly. "Doc's orders. Her folks're comin' to get her, take her back home, so don't get yourself all uppity 'bout truth and things you know nothin' about. I'd say time they gets 'ere, you'd best be gone, you know what's good for you."

"I don't believe you. I demand to see her." Throck's head was spinning. What nonsense was this? But he thought of the letters he'd seen her writing as they'd travelled, and doubt reared its head. She'd said she was writing to George, but what if she'd actually been writing to Stephen? What if she truly did not want to continue their journey? Wouldn't she have felt she could tell him herself? In exasperation he pounded his small fist on the table, eliciting a hiss from Loveday, and a noise from the doorway. Throck looked up and saw the doc standing there, his arms folded across his fisherman's smock.

"Throck," the doc said, drawing out the name warningly. "Let's do be civil now. Amn't nothin' you can do about situation. Loveday found the lewd book you carry – all them unseemly pictures in it – and together with the girl 'erself we've decided 'tis best that you be travellin' on alone. An' that there's a kindness towards you."

"What?" Throck cried, his head twisting from the doc to Loveday and back again. "That's ridiculous! It's an art book, and there's nothing lewd about it." He flushed, knowing full well that such a statement could be argued.

The doc continued, unabashed. "Fisherfolk be good people, Throck, but they knows when something's vulgar, and they knows how an anchor rope can twist round a boot needs be." Throck's blood ran cold and he thought of the doc's impassive face staring over the gunwales as he'd thrashed in the water, drowning. The doc continued, "It's been arranged – girl's family'll come to claim 'er, and if you're still here when they arrive it might take some convincin' for them not to send you off to Bodmin Jail for kidnap. Havin' such a book in your possession'll make you no friends wi' the magistrate hereabouts."

Throck's heart was pumping with the shock of the doc's insinuations, and with a bravado he did not feel, he said, "Bring Eliza here. I don't know where you've come up with this craziness, but she and I are travel companions, each of our own free will. As for her family, if anyone's a charlatan or a cad it's her brother!"

Loveday raised her brows, rose and returned to her washtub, but not before she and the doc exchanged a pitying look that only served to rile Throck further. Released from Loveday's proximity, he stood, a wildness taking hold of him that felt completely surreal, and he wanted to laugh, but madly. With some part of his brain he thought of a passage from *Alice's Adventures in Wonderland*, a novel he'd read this past winter in quieter times, his toes stretched to the fire, in which the heroine of the tale had a conversation with a Cheshire cat: "But I don't want to go among mad people," she'd said. And the cat had replied, "Oh, you can't help that. We're all mad here. I'm mad. You're mad." "How do you know I'm mad?" Alice had asked. And the cat had answered, "You must be, or you wouldn't have come here."

Throck considered his options, which were few. He glanced toward the narrow stairway that presumably led to bedrooms above, but to get to it he'd have to go round the long table and pass both Loveday and the doc, neither of whom would allow him access, he was sure. He considered shouting, again, but that had not brought Eliza so far, and there'd been raised voices aplenty, so she was either locked in an upstairs room or had indeed decided to forego the rest of their adventure. Perhaps there was even family, as Loveday and the doc claimed, coming to get her. What did he truly know of her intentions, really? But no, he shook that thought off. Eliza Vanson, free spirited and braver than most, had had no second thoughts, was not cowering upstairs waiting to be rescued from him – him! – and had not written to family to come and get her. He simply did not believe it.

He drew himself up. Loveday and the doc's eyes were on him. Neither tried to stop him as he walked to the door. The doc moved aside, and said, "Best you go tonight. I've put your things there, by the contraption you rode in on. An' no hard feelings. 'Tis best for the maid, just as sure as you're no fisherman."

Throck stalked past him without a word or a glance, and ducked through the door into the night air. The Trusty sat where he'd parked it two days ago, his haversack resting against one wheel. He tried the door to the doc's house, thinking to check that none of his scant possessions had been left behind, but found it locked. He turned to the Trusty, and any who saw the expression on his face could have read the determination there: this was not over.

*

Throck drove the Trusty out of Portluce and up onto the grassy moorland under a sky gone inky dark and spangled with stars. The moon was high and afforded some light, and it was just as well, since Eliza had the matches in her carpet bag, and Throck had no way of lighting the Trusty's headlamp. He putted slowly along the cart path, and though it was hard to tell which part of the darkness was cliff edge and which part crashing sea, he could easily discern the white ribbon of the path before him. He was heading east, but he could just as soon have turned west, or driven in circles. He had no intention of leaving the immediate area without Eliza, or without first determining that it was, in fact, Eliza's wish for him to go on alone. Such a decision would be awfully disappointing, were it true, but one he would also endeavour to respect.

How he would discover Eliza's mind on the matter, he did not know. Riding back into the village was out of the question. In such a small place it was likely most people knew he'd been driven from the doc's house; it was also rather likely that they either suspected or had been told something other than the truth, and believed him, at best, to be some lecherous debauchee, and at worst a maniacal abductor. People would be on the lookout, he figured, for a small, crazy fellow with wild eyes and a balding pate and driving a motorcycle, so he'd have to re-enter the village on foot, disguised, or sneak in under cover of dark. With no means of disguising himself – he doubted pulling a rug over his head or wearing a cloak of bracken would go unnoticed – darkness it would have to be.

But not tonight. Tonight, the doc and Loveday would surely be on tenterhooks, wondering if he would return, listening for every creak and groan and investigating. Throck wouldn't have put it past the doc to have come up on the cliff to look around, make sure he'd travelled on. And so he did, reluctantly.

He'd driven about half an hour along the winding cliffside path, long enough to ensure the doc and any foaming-at-the-mouth fishermen he might have recruited, up from Portluce on foot, would not have followed, when he noticed what looked like a small campfire up ahead. He drew the motorcycle to an abrupt stop. In the dark, with no light but from the heavens, it was easy to spot the amber glow, off the path, it seemed, by a few hundred feet and set in the lee of what appeared to be some sort of building. He turned off the Trusty's engine, his heart beginning to thump. Would the campers have heard him coming? With the pound of the surf so close by it was possible they hadn't. Should he approach, or try to sneak past, pushing the bike? Would they be friend or foe? Who camped out on the high moors of Cornwall, unless maybe gypsies, or ne'er do wells. Gypsies, he reasoned, would have their own caravans, and surely travelled in numbers. That left brigands, bandits, outlaws. He hesitated, swallowing nervously, then he thought of something Mungo Large had said about dodgy situations and being armed with the tools of the traveller's trade: curiosity, respect and good humour. He decided to approach and take his chances.

He pushed rather than drove the Trusty, the better to hail and be hailed, the only noise over the rush of the sea the small squeak the old girl had developed in the sidecar's wheel. As he neared the little campfire, he could see that what he'd thought was a building was in fact the crumbled remains of an old stone and cob-built cottage, all but two of its walls returned to rubble. Next to the fire was the inert shape of someone lying wrapped in a blanket.

"Hallooo, friend!" he called, thinking a cry from a ways off was better than approaching to stand over top the fellow, and perchance frighten him into a drastic reaction. But the figure did not stir, so Throck tried again, raising his voice, but again there was no response. A thought struck Throck. What if the fellow was dead? What then? What would he do about *that*? Prop the body in the sidecar and drive on to the next fishing village? And would there be an inquest then, and blame apportioned? And what if they decided that Throck was somehow responsible for his death up here on the lonely moor, and none to speak for him? What then? In a last desperate move, he squeezed the bulb of the Trusty's horn – meep, meep – and to his great relief the lump gave a rumbling cough and stirred, glancing around to see what had pulled him from his slumber.

Throck pushed the Trusty forward, calling out again, "Hallooo, friend!" and this time the fellow threw off his blanket and got to his feet, peering in Throck's direction, and by the light of the meagre fire Throck beheld none other than Mungo Large. Friend indeed!

"Well, I'll be damned," Mungo cried, lunging forward and clasping Throck in a bear-like embrace. "Young'un! I were sure ye'd be far on to Land's End by now, all agog at yon boundless sea!"

"You don't know how glad I am to see you!" Throck said. He almost wept, and was surprised by the surge of emotion. In the turmoil of figuring out what to do about Eliza whilst driving along the cliff in the dark he hadn't realised how utterly alone and, yes, frightened he'd felt without her. But now here was Mungo. All would be well.

"Sit, young'un, sit!" Mungo was saying. "Let's get these 'ere flames dancin', though as ye can see, firewood's at a premium in these parts." He gestured around at the undulating, grass-capped landscape, near barren of trees but for gnarled, twisted hawthorns and spiny gorse.

He threw a few thin sticks onto the coals, and, tinder dry, they caught quickly, and the fire leapt, giving light. Mungo reached for a satchel on the ground and pulled out a bottle. He unstoppered it and handed it to Throck without a word, and Throck took a grateful swig, recognizing the faint almond of the Portuguese liquor Mungo had shared with him back in the Blackdown Hills. He recalled the hangover, too, but tonight thought it a price he'd pay in exchange for some of its numbing effect. He took a second gulp and then a third, and he sensed Mungo watching him, waiting, perhaps, for the liquor to do its work. Throck handed the bottle back to Mungo with a nod of thanks.

"So, tell me what's gone wrong, then," Mungo said at last. "Ye've the look of a sheep dog what's been left in the barn. Where's Eliza?"

Unburdening, Throck proceeded to tell Mungo Large everything that had happened since they'd parted ways: Eliza falling into the burrow in the stone circle and spraining her wrist and ankle, then the ride to Portluce into the care – or clutches – of the oddball doctor Pascoe Bonny and his sister Loveday Quick with their opinion that Throck and Eliza's companionship was "unseemly." Finally, Throck related the standoff in Loveday Quick's kitchen, and his subsequent banishment from the village, which meant that Eliza was left behind, a prisoner, he was sure – or, as the doc and his sister claimed, a maiden awaiting rescue by her outraged family.

Despite what Throck saw as the seriousness of his sorry tale, Mungo laughed out loud. Shaking his head, he reached for his pipe and thumbed some tobacco into it, then lit it and puffed, the sweet smell of its smoke mingling with the more acrid of the campfire.

"Here's what I be thinkin'," Mungo said after a moment of contemplating the fire and sucking on his pipe. "Our young friend Eliza be no easy mark, and she sure as hell be'nt a damsel in distress, no matter what some bony doctor says."

"Bonny," Throck muttered, tasting the name like rancid mutton. "Pascoe Bonny."

Mungo spoke on. "So, if her family's comin' to get her, let 'em come. Matter o' fact let 'em arrive d'reckly, straight to little Portluce off the train from London to Truro, knockin' on the bony doc's door and whiskin' the poor maid home." He licked his thumb and smoothed his wiry brows, and combed his fingers through his beard. "Reckon I'll have to tidy up a bit, mayhap shave me face hair if I'm to pass as a member of a respectable girl's fam'ly. I grant ye, respectable amn't a word people find on their tongue when describin' Mungo Large."

"You?" said Throck, gaping. "You'd go get her? Just walk into the village and – and –"

"Why not? It be a genius idea, do say so meself. Unless she has in fact written to 'er brother, which ye say, likely not, then who's to gi'e me a challenge? I'll have our girl sprung before ye can say Jack Robinson."

Throck considered. He could drive Mungo to the edge of the village, staying out of sight to be sure not to give the game away. Mungo would walk down to Loveday Quick's door, purporting to be Stephen Vanson, her brother, to whom, he would claim, Eliza had written at an earlier opportunity, since any letter she might have posted from Portluce would only just be arriving up in London. He'd knock, demand to see his sister, and Eliza, seeing Mungo on the doorstep, would know Throck wasn't far off. He gave a chortling laugh. It was a perfect plan. He stuck out his hand and Mungo passed him the Portuguese liquor.

*

"I never asked," Throck said after a time, "how you come to be camping out here in the middle of Cornwall, and travelling by bicycle, no less." For indeed Mungo's little campsite included a well-oiled BSA Roadster propped against one of the walls of the crumbling cottage. Throck had owned a BSA bicycle himself once upon a time, long before becoming a motorcycle man, so he was familiar with the machine, built by the Birmingham Small Arms Co. Ltd., and billed as "the bicycle that lasts a lifetime." A good choice for an intrepid adventurer, if one couldn't own a Trusty.

"Well, I'll tell ye, that'd be down to you, young'un. I weren't followin' ye, per say, but I did ask after ye here and there, and ye weren't hard to track, really. Dashin' fellow on a motorbike with a red-haired lovely ridin' shotgun, as the Americans say." Throck gave a pleased little pfft at the description of him as dashing. "Truth is, I come to realise after meetin' up with the two of ye that I missed that nomad's life, out on the road, distant horizons an' all that. Round about home, if ye can call it that, weren't no one interested in me tales of far-off places. Locals at the pub'd find a reason to slide off their stool if I started in on the finer points of ridin' camels, or the nuances of bartering in Marrakesh. They thought I never noticed. I might be a big man, Throck, but I still bruise. Even me daughter took to rollin' 'er eyes." Mungo shrugged and tossed a pebble. "So, I said me farewells to the lass – again, though she's used to her old man blowin' with the wind and I think she were glad to be shut of me. Then I hopped on me old BSA and Bob's your uncle, as they say. I'm on me way to Penzance. Figurin' to catch the ferry over to the Scillies." He looked into the flames and the lines on his face softened. "I met a girl once, Celestine were her name. Blackest eyes y'ever did see, with little sparkles in 'em, as heavenly as her name implies. Yep. Anyway, she were from the Scillies; told me at the time that if I hadn't been there I hadn't lived." Mungo chuckled. "But don't they all say that? I've come to reckon it be code for 'I'd like to see yer again, sweetheart,' and you know me, Throck. I don't like to disappoint."

"I doubt you ever do, Mungo," Throck replied with a smile.

"You and me wife'd disagree there," Mungo said, returning the grin.

They sat in easy silence for a while, contemplating the fire. They'd polished off the liquor, but the bottle had been only half full, so the mood was mellow rather than raucous, and Throck poked at the embers, sending sparks into the air. As always, lately, he was thinking of Eliza, and wondering if, in her mind, the end of the road, the end of their shared journey, would be Land's End. The idea made him rather melancholy, and cryptically, he said to Mungo, "How do you know if you've got the measure of a person? I mean, the truth. What if someone is really good at lies, and you're really good at gullibility?" Mungo frowned and looked uncomfortable. Throck continued, "She took my bike and was gone all night. I thought she wasn't coming back." Mungo raised his brows and kept his gaze focused on the fire. "When she showed up the next day, she said she'd gone to see a friend. She did, but I don't understand why she didn't say, before she left, I mean." He gave the embers a hard poke and his stick broke. He tossed it into the flames.

"It felt like a betrayal. And now I find myself wondering about a lot of things."

Mungo nodded slowly. "Trust is important, young'un."

"I know," replied Throck, jutting out his lip. "But that doesn't make it easy. I just wish I knew where we stood. Where she sees our travels together ending. For me, it's not at Land's End, although it's feeling more and more like an ending."

"Then, I say you come out and ask her," Mungo said. A moment later, he asked, "When I go to pry 'er out o' that place tomorrow, d'ye think she'll be glad to see me?"

Throck hesitated for just a moment. "I hope so," he said. But if he was honest, he was not at all sure she would.

*

Throck hardly slept, burrowed in his rug on the other side of the fire from Mungo, and in the morning was eager to put Mungo's plan into action. But Mungo counselled patience, convincing him to wait until late in the afternoon to make plausible his tale of having come by the London train, and then by hired cart across country from Truro. While they passed the time, Throck loaned Mungo his straight razor so he could shave his straggling white beard, and indeed its removal took years off his face. He combed his thin hair and knocked the dents out of his old felt hat, and when he at last decreed that it was time to go, they strapped the BSA onto the back of the Triumph and Mungo squeezed into the sidecar alongside the jug of Minnie Small's cider, Throck's haversack, the rugs and tarpaulin, the cans of petrol and oil, and Mungo's own thankfully scant baggage, and putted their way back along the cliffside track towards Portluce. In sight of the huer's hut on the westernmost edge of the rise just above Portluce, Throck brought the Trusty to a stop and Mungo climbed out of the sidecar. Without a word he nodded confidently to Throck and touched the brim of his hat, then set off at a jaunty pace in the direction of the village. Throck and the Trusty took cover behind a thick stand of vanilla-scented broome and hunkered down to wait. The day was calm and sunny, and bees busied themselves amongst the yellow flowers of the broome and the oxeye daisies and the spiky blue heads of sheep's-bit. The sea beyond sparkled. Several hours went by. Throck whiled away the time thumbing through the Trusty's manual. Given the different varieties of plants he'd seen in this part of the country he would have preferred to peruse his botany book, but it was in Eliza's bag. He wasn't in the mood for the art book. So he read up on the Trusty's magneto, discovering that if water were to get into it, say, by driving through an absurdly large puddle, he might experience loss of spark, and thereby a stopped engine. In which case, he read, he'd have to dry out the magneto by removing the pick-up, wiping the slip ring, and Bob, as Mungo would say, should then indeed be one's uncle. There were diagrams in the manual, at which Throck peered, and he felt fairly confident that with the few spanners he'd brought along he could manage drying out the magneto should he ever have need to. Or, preferably, he could avoid absurdly large puddles.

Throck's belly rumbled, and for the first time since the night of his departure from Sowerby Grange he pulled forth his pocket watch – a useless effort since it hadn't been wound and read ten o'clock, and either way you looked at it, whether ante or post meridiem, it was incorrect. Had it been two hours – more, less – since Mungo had disappeared down the road into Portluce? He peeked around the broome but the landscape was empty. No Mungo, no limping Eliza. Where were they? He sighed and for the third or fourth time that day, pushed last night's doubts to the back of his mind. She'd come. She would.

He fished in his haversack for one of his large handkerchiefs and began to polish the Trusty. He'd been neglectful of late and the salt air was dulling her shine. As he gave the motorcycle the once over, he thought about what Stephen Vanson had told him about the motorcycle's possible past as the steed of a despatch rider in the war, and he wondered if this old girl might have witnessed a French countryside bombed beyond recognition and pitted with craters, a sea of mud and blood, or so he'd read. Bikes like the Trusty were mechanical heroes – heroines – Throck reckoned, and he rubbed with vigour, whistling a song that the papers said had been the marching mantra of the troops – *It's a long way to Tipperary, it's a long way to go*. He paused when his arm grew sore, and he stuffed the handkerchief into his pocket and leaned against the sidecar, turning to stare out at the cerulean sea. Dreamer that he was, he imagined himself afloat upon the waves – not in a fishing boat like the doc's, chock-a-block with tripping hazards and crowded with crab pots, but on a big ship, a steamer on its way to the Scillies, where Mungo was heading, or to France maybe. Or on one of those enormous ocean liners en route to Canada, or further still…South America, New Zealand, the South Pacific. Inevitably, when his thoughts turned to reveries of the waiting wide world, he thought of Harold Guppletwill, disappeared into the jungles of the Amazon. What wonders had he seen? Where was he now? Had he found his giant cane toad?

A tern cried, and then again, drawing Throck's attention away from the wavering horizon. When it called a third time, he realised it was calling his name, and that it was no tern, but Eliza!

He stepped out of the cover of the shrubbery and saw her, hobbling slightly, arm in arm with tall Mungo. She waved her free arm in an arc when she saw him, and his heart jumped with joy. At last! He ran towards them across the open grassland, laughing and shouting her name, and when he reached them, he pulled up short, grinning happily from her to Mungo and back again. How could he have doubted her?

"Here you are!" he cried.

"Here she be!" echoed Mungo, not a little boastfully.

"Oh, Throck," said Eliza, and stepped forward to hug him.

*

Spirits were high all round that night as the three shared the campfire in the lee of the crumbling cottage, but an intuitive soul might have felt an undercurrent of expectancy, and seen that questions remained unasked and unanswered between Throck and Eliza about what had gone wrong in Portluce, and what it meant for whatever was to come. But first, the friends munched on fish pies supplied, in clucking fashion, by Loveday Quick, who'd concerned herself that it was a long ride to Truro by cart, and where on earth would Eliza and her brother get something to eat? But before Loveday had become motherly, she'd put herself up like a wall between Mungo and Eliza, grilling Mungo as if she worked for Scotland Yard, and summoning the doc from across the way before she'd allow Mungo to duck his head and cross her stoop.

"They're a pair, them two," Mungo said, shaking his head and popping the last of the pie into his mouth. "Thought I might have to resort to a bit o' pushin' and shovin' just to get to see the lass." He nodded towards Eliza who had cloaked herself in her rug, her face and a bit of red hair all that was visible in the firelight. "Seemed to feel themselves guardians o' some moral 'igh ground, wherein the two of them be judge an' jury both. In the end, though, that's what worked in me favour. People like them what think a young lady don't know her own mind also think 'er brother's 'er keeper, see, so as long as I were aggressive, they were always going to hand 'er over, believin' me, after all, to be 'er brother."

"In the end," repeated Throck. "But not at first?" His eyes skittered to Eliza now and again as Mungo talked. She hadn't said much, but at least she had eaten, and smiled when their eyes met.

"Well, they give me the once over, no question," Mungo replied. "Mayhap me fine vintage and ill-favoured countenance gave 'em some doubts that such a one could be brother to so fair a young miss as Eliza. But I took to me role, Throck, I did. I could've been on the stage. Missed me callin'. Standin' there with them two self-righteous barmers tryin' to deny me the right to see me own sister, well, I don't mind tellin' ye I had a little display o' temper that had them changin' their tune right quick." He chuckled, and paused for a swig from the jug of Minnie Small's cider that was making its rounds. He nodded towards Eliza. "Young miss did her part, happy as a lark to see me when they fetched her into the kitchen. Clever one, she is, catchin' on straight away that it must've been you, Throck, what sent me. Anyway, the doc and his sister wanted to follow us up onto the bluff to make sure the cart met us for the return trip to Truro, but I put paid to that idea. Told 'em no cart boy were goin' to go back on his promise to a London man like me, or 'e knew I'd come find 'im, and make 'im answer."

Throck and Eliza exchanged a smile at the idea of Mungo being taken for a London man; indeed, Throck thought, Mungo Large seemed of no place at all, and everyplace at once. He was grateful, and said as much. Despite Mungo's tale, questions remained that only Eliza could answer, and Throck decided it was best to ask them and be done than have them hanging about like an unwanted relative at a garden party. He plunged in.

"What I can't understand," he said, turning to Eliza, "is how the whole sorry mess came about in the first place. How, exactly, did Loveday Quick and the doc decide you needed rescuing from *me*? And why, when I stood in Loveday's kitchen demanding to see you, didn't you appear? Surely you heard me shouting?"

There was a decided edge to his words, and no one spoke for a few moments; the only sounds were the crash of the sea and the crackle of the fire. Mungo looked uncomfortable, and his eyes slid from Throck to Eliza and back again. Eliza looked as if she might cry, but then she seemed to square her shoulders and lift her chin.

"It's my fault, I suppose," she answered, pinioning Throck with her blue stare, her face aglow in the firelight. "At first, Loveday seemed a kind soul, and reminded me som'at of Gin-Gin, only without the booze. At one point I may've said how Portluce were charmin', and how I'd love to stay, but I were meanin' it as a politeness, not a wish. She saw me writin' me letter to George on that first day, and inquired, and I told her I were writin' to me brother, that I had family what I missed, in London and other places, that there were people I longed to see – which is true, Throck, I've told you before how I've a yearning to go back to Southwark. Soon after that I found meself sleeping the day away. When he first treated me, the doc gave me a tincture he said was for the pain, but perhaps he then fixed it stronger and slipped it into my tea, because when you came for me last night I heard you, but thought I were dreaming. I couldn't raise me head off the pillow for love nor money."

"Bleedin' nutters," Mungo interjected, shaking his head. Throck's gaze remained on Eliza, who momentarily closed her eyes. When she opened them again, they rested on Mungo, and she smiled.

"I were never so glad to see someone," she said earnestly. "I thought Throck had left me behind, as Loveday were quick to claim. I'd be better off, were what she said. And if me family didn't come, I could stay with 'er, two pearls in an oyster, were how she called us. I thought Land's End and me days of adventuring were over." She shuddered and reached out, one hand to Mungo, the other to Throck, and hung on. "Thank goodness for you, my friends."

*

After such comments it hadn't seemed necessary to broach the subject of what might come after Land's End, so in the morning Throck said nothing and helped Eliza into the sidecar while Mungo hopped onto his BSA Roadster. They'd agreed to travel together to Penzance, despite

Mungo being on a bicycle and Throck and Eliza on a motorcycle, so Throck maneuvered the Trusty along the coastal path at bicycle speed, waving now and then to a grinning Mungo who rode ahead and looked repeatedly over his shoulder at Throck and Eliza as if fearing they might disappear. It was hard pedalling for Mungo. He was a big man whose sheer size created stiff resistance for the sharp easterly wind that had blown up sometime overnight, and which hampered forward progress even for those lucky enough to be piloting a motorized unit like the Triumph. When they paused to rest Throck offered, courteously, to trade places and let Mungo try his hand at the Trusty, but Mungo, gracious fellow that he was, declined. Throck was grateful, for he doubted he would have had the strength or stamina to make any headway at all driving the BSA.

Because they drove at a snail's pace Eliza was able to spread their map upon her lap, tucking it below the sidecar's body and out of the wind, and Throck noticed her satisfied smile as she traced the route to Land's End. He thought of what Mungo had said about trust, and what Eliza herself had said when they'd rescued her, and put his worry over endings to the back of his mind. He supposed he was altogether too much a fretter, a thing he'd have to work on changing.

At Mungo's signal they stopped for lunch and another much-needed break in the shelter of a wooded area. The wind had slackened somewhat but the sky remained gloomy and threatened rain, although so far it had held off. The three shared food – Eliza pulled hard cheese and jam tarts from her bag of bounty, as Throck had come to think of her carpetbag – the tarts another gift from Loveday, while Mungo unwrapped a waxed cloth that held tasty morsels of cooked rabbit, which brought about reminiscences of their time together in the Blackdown Hills.

"We were an intrepid trio," Throck said, and everyone agreed.

They travelled an hour more before they had to stop again, this time when the chain came off Mungo's BSA. Mungo's thick fingers had trouble fishing the thing out from where it had jammed behind the sprocket, so it was Eliza's dainty digits that came to the rescue. Throck handed his friends a handkerchief to wipe the black from their hands, and Mungo said "'Tis no hardship at all havin' the two of ye along on me travels. 'Appen we do make a proper good triumvirate.'"

"A proper good triumvirate," repeated Throck, and an idea struck him – a perfect solution, if he did say so himself, to the worry of Land's End being an ending. Impulsively, eagerly, he blurted, "Eliza and I will come along to the Scillies! Take a bit of a detour. Add a leg, as they say." Mungo's face, he saw, mirrored his own happy grin. "We'd be just like the three musketeers, all swashbuckle and hurrah! And besides, when one has seen the edge of one cliff, one has seen them all."

"No!" Eliza interjected vehemently. She scowled at Throck. Silence fell. "It's nothing to do with you, Mungo," she added apologetically, and Mungo mumbled something about it being just an idea worth pondering before he slunk quietly way, finding more to tend to on the BSA.

Eliza turned back to Throck. "Land's End were always where we were going," she said, disappointment thick in her voice. She looked wounded and Throck felt his stomach clench. The few drops of rain had become a light patter, and one landed on her cheek like a tear.

"It was indeed our original destination," Throck agreed. "But when one is on an adventure, one's plans sometimes deviate. It's the nature of the thing." He heard the curtness in his tone.

"Well, you speak true when you use the word one," Eliza retorted. "There were two on this adventure in the beginning. And those two were going to Land's End."

"And then what?" asked Throck crossly. "I don't want Land's End to *be* the end."

"All things come to an end, Throck," said Eliza with a small shake of her head. "Even adventures." She turned away and gathered up the few things they'd used to work on the BSA, handing them to Mungo. No one said anything further or even looked at one another, and the once intrepid trio mounted their various steeds, motorized and otherwise, and continued towards Penzance in a gently falling rain.

Chapter 28
OFF ONE'S ONION

Alice retreated to Sowerby Grange and spent her days in what George referred to under his breath – though she heard him plainly – as a funk. He catered to her as ever, and they dined together in the evenings, but she sensed the boy watching her like one might a jack-in-the-box, albeit a cheerless one, expecting it to pop its lid at any moment.

And though she couldn't explain to George, she had no intention of letting her emotions get the better of her. Instead, she was carefully considering not just her options, but Woody's story, going slowly and methodically over each detail he'd revealed and giving it the sniff test, as with cracked eggs, to suss out any rot. She did not rush in her deliberations, nor did Woody pressure her. In fact, after she'd departed Natterjack Hall, leaving Woody sobbing into her handkerchief, she'd neither seen nor heard from him, nor from his rather unnerving children which, for the time being, suited her quite well.

The young man Serhan she thought she could make allowances for. He seemed an amiable sort, with a sense of humour and some decency, even if he'd claimed to be unconventional. What could he mean by that, she wondered? The other one – Eglantine – well she was another matter. How a genial, caring man such as Woody – or at least, the Woody she thought she knew – had fathered such a disagreeable, hot-headed miss she could not credit. It was highly probable, Alice decided, that the unpleasant twin was a copy of her mother in more than looks. As for the revelation that Woody's wife was alive and an inmate – albeit an escaped one – of a lunatic asylum, gracious, it seemed there was no end to the warps and wefts of the life of Lieutenant-Colonel Woodward Barks.

It was George's idea – or was it, she couldn't recall exactly – to spy on the occupants of Natterjack Hall, although she preferred to call George's undertaking an observation. The word spy sounded nefarious, and rather underhanded. George, thumbs tucked into the armholes of the waistcoat he'd taken to wearing (one of Mr's, she suspected), called himself Paul Pry, and grinned. Alice sniffed and called him Cheeky.

He took to the task with a relish that in normal circumstances might have given her pause. He never said when he was going or indeed if he was going, he just disappeared and reappeared, and, usually at the dinner table, made a report. Not that there was much to tell. Woody, it seemed, had become a recluse, and George saw him only enough to know that he hadn't popped his clogs, as George put it, and had grown rather a lot of hair. His whiskers, which Alice adored, had become a full, straggling beard, and his usually neatly combed grey locks stood out from his head, unkempt and uncared for. He looked, George told Alice, leaning towards her conspiratorially, "like a nutter. Off 'is onion, as if they didn't have one too many o' those in that family already." Alice frowned, thinking George's comment maladroit, but also disturbed by the idea of an unhinged Woody. She considered venturing round to see for herself, but it was too soon. She hadn't yet decided how she felt about Woody's circumstance, and he, obviously, hadn't felt compelled to pressure her. Which, on the one hand, she appreciated; on the other, a measure of forlorn wooing might go a long way to persuading her in his favour.

Of the twins, there was more to tell. The young woman, Eglantine, apparently spent a great deal of time lounging in a chair in the garden, doing very little. George spoke of her with awe in his voice that Alice found annoying, but she confined her opinion to a snort, wanting his information more than she wanted to curtail his admiration. His descriptions were pathetically poetic – she had, in George's view, eyes as big and brown as a squirrel's, lips the colour of crushed huckleberries, and languid limbs "like they don't have no bone in 'em." When Eglantine appeared outside, she invariably wore a floppy wide-brimmed hat that George, with his unlikely but indisputable knowledge of women's fashion thought was "worth a few bob." Alice, having heard enough of the fashionable Eglantine Barks, interrupted.

"And the brother, Serhan, what of him?"

"He paints, mostly," George replied around a mouthful of grilled lamb and mashed potatoes.

"Paints?" Alice repeated, her lips puckered with the sour smack of the word, causing George to glance up from his meal and look around. "As in *art*?"

"Well, I suppose, missus," George shrugged, resuming his forking of food. "I were shankered down in the woods, weren't I, so I couldn't rightly make out what he were doing exactly. But he had one o' them stands for the picture to sit on –"

"An easel," supplied Alice, frowning.

"And he were dabbing at the picture with a brush," finished George. "Maybe he were paintin' his sister. She's somethin' to look at, sure enough."

"Yes, well," sniffed Alice. An artist. Things just seemed to get worse.

"There's more, missus," George said hesitantly, sensing Alice's disapproval of something he'd said. "Should I go on?"

Alice gave an impatient wave of her fork. She wasn't annoyed with the boy, or even with his admiration of the hostile Eglantine. Rather she was angry – such a base emotion – at the cruel joke life seemed to be playing on her. Tempting her with the reappearance of the love of her life only to discover he had children – one of them unpleasant, the other an artist – and worse, a wife. It was all such a complicated muddle. She forced a smile. "Please, do."

"Cap'n Plucky's come back," George said, puffed up with what he obviously felt was the importance of his news. "And 'e's got a car." The last word was stuffed full of admiration, and in spite of her dull mood, Alice smiled indulgently. She often forgot how young George was, all agog over the toys and trappings of men. Truth be told, she'd forgotten about Captain Plucky. He just seemed to fade away in the midst of the confusion over her and Woody's return from their – er – sojourn to Nookey Hollow. She hadn't actually given him a thought, or inquired as to where he might have gone. "I wonder what the haughty Miss Eglantine will make of the debonair Captain Plucky," she said, imagining a thrown shoe or two.

"Couldn't rightly say, missus," George replied, "but they seemed to hit it off alright." He snickered. "I saw 'im kiss her in the garden under 'er hat. The two of 'em had to come up for air like drownin' folk."

271

Heavens, what next, thought Alice. The world had indeed gone off its axis.

*

Several days later George served tea at the usual time, laying out the Belgian lace tablecloth and presenting a pot of Earl Grey and a delicious medley of darling little Scotch eggs, petite cress and cucumber sandwiches, and buttery scones lashed with Pimm's-soaked fruit and whipped cream. Alice clapped her hands in a tidy gesture of appreciation. In these hard-bitten days it was nice that George took such pains to coddle her. As she tucked in, selecting only three scones rather than four, mindful that this was tea, and dinner was still to come, she eyed George with scrutiny. She could always tell when he had news.

"Have you ventured next door today, George? Done a little reconnoitering, by chance?" She paused to dab the corners of her mouth with a spotless square of linen. George really was a jack of all trades – no, indeed a master of all trades. He could always buoy her spirits, and they needed a lot of elevating these days.

George tossed that lock of hair that was always flopping across his eyes and responded with a cat and cream smile.

"Tell, George, tell," laughed Alice, enjoying the boy's teasing.

"They caught 'er, missus," George said. "The lady from the lunatic place."

"What?" said Alice, leaning forward across her scones and unwittingly pressing her overlarge bosom into the whipped cream topping.

"They've had a man in London lookin' for 'er. You know, the morgue, p'lice stations, places she might end up, and the other day they got a telegram from 'im. Coppers found some woman lyin' in a street somewheres, Whitechapel, I think, nits crawlin' on 'er and in an awful state. She were wearin' men's trousers and old boots what stained her feet blue. They took 'er off to the Cloak Lane P'lice Station and filled out one o' them papers – Lunatic Wandering at Large."

"All that was in the telegram?" Alice asked skeptically.

George, consummate embellisher, shrugged, and continued. "Lieutenant-Colonel Barks has gone to London to confirm 'er identity, but Cap'n Plucky says they're sure it's her, and it's just a matter of signing the papers and arranging her return to where she come from. Cane Hill, 'e said. I heard of that place. They send all sorts there; yer woefuls, yer wild-eyes, yer bellowers, an' sometimes jus' yer old auntie what don't recall 'er name anymore." He shook his head sadly, commiserating with the anonymous inmates.

"Indeed," said Alice, barely listening. So, Woody had gone off to London to re-commit his wife. That was satisfactory. But once done, then what? She leaned back in her chair and noticed the whipped cream on her bosom, and because it was only she and George to dinner, and George made allowances for these kinds of mishaps, she used her finger to scrape off the excess and pop it in her mouth. "I'd like to know when he returns, George, if you'd be so kind," she said, and deciding the news was something to celebrate, reached for a fourth scone.

*

Woody didn't return. In fact, he had disappeared. After hearing from George at dinner several days after Woody's departure that he had not yet returned from London and no-one was quite sure where he was, Alice decided to seek out Serhan and hear the details firsthand. She told herself not to panic, that there was likely a good explanation, but her concern was such that she left dinner half-eaten and tromped through the Whortleberry Woods in wellingtons and a long dinner dress, George in the rear. After all, how long could it possibly take to sign a committal paper and speak with a doctor? Surely that's all that was required for a gentleman to send his lunatic wife back to an asylum?

Happily, Eglantine was not present for Alice's visit. As George and Alice emerged from the woods, the young lady exited Natterjack Hall wearing a fur collar and a rhinestone headband and escorted by a rather dashing looking Captain Plucky in a dove grey homburg. The captain guided her towards his automobile – a red Morris, Alice saw, that looked suspiciously like the one in which she and Woody had absconded to Nookey Hollow – and opened the door for her, then hopped into the driver's seat and sped away, the Morris roaring down the driveway spitting gravel. Eglantine's laughter merged into the throaty growl of the exhaust and the car rounded the bend. This played out rather well, Alice thought, for Serhan was more likely than Eglantine to share what news they had – or did not have – of their father.

And indeed, he knew little. Serhan ushered them into the drawing room, and confirmed what Captain Plucky had shared with George, that Woody seemed to have disappeared. He'd been staying at his club in Upper Berkeley while concluding the business of identifying his wife – yes, it was her, captured – and returning her to Cane Hill, all but done, when he simply vanished.

"But – how can that be?" Alice asked, distraught. Darling Woody, gone like some kind of mote up a chimney? A man of his impressive girth and demeanour couldn't simply slip down a crack, the way someone like Mr, for example, might do. Had done, really. The reminder of Mr's desertion made her bristle, but she reigned in her acrimony, and drew her attention back to Serhan, who was speaking.

"The club sent a telegram when they realised something was amiss. There isn't much to go on, I'm afraid. Egg has gone into Lesser Plumpton to find a telephone to call the club and ascertain what, exactly, they do know. Blasted inconvenient, not having a telly. As far as we can tell, he'd requested a taxi to the train station to return home, then just vanished." Serhan's eyes were limpid and dark, and Alice supposed they were his mother's. She thought of Woody swooning to that mesmeric gaze, the depths of which one could lose oneself in.

"Well," she said. "Well, well." Panic struggled to burst from her breast, and she thought she might cry. She could think of nothing coherent to say, so she repeated "well, well," again, and George, ever intuitive, sprang to the rescue.

"Nothin' for it, then, eh missus? We'll go find 'im. You'n' me. Straight on to London first thing." He patted her shoulder and took her elbow, hoisting her to her feet. Her knees wobbled, but she remained upright. George was such a rock.

"I'll come with you," Serhan said, seemingly relieved that someone had taken charge. "I know the name of the club, and how to get there from the station. We can take the nine o'clock to Paddington."

Alice felt her strength return, and her earlier panic subside. Yes, doing was the thing. Alice had never been a wet rag sort of person. When something needed righting, one got on with it, and no fiddle-faddle. She smiled bravely, and said to Serhan, "Thank you, young man, I feel better already having a plan. It'll all come right in the end, I'm sure." She paused, and added, "Might we take a later train? Nine o'clock is such an uncivilized hour." Then, assuming it agreed, she turned and strode from the room, elegant despite the clump of her wellingtons, and George followed, flashing a grin and a shrug at Serhan, whose mouth hung agape.

Despite her brave words, Alice wasn't at all sure that things would come right, but if she'd learned one thing from George, it was the value of optimism.

Chapter 29
THE PROMISE OF A TREACLE TART

The train deposited the unlikely group of Alice, George, Serhan and Eglantine at Paddington Station in London at 12:45 the next afternoon. Eglantine hadn't been part of the original plan, but she'd appeared at the station in Watton Hoo with her brother, muttering about having to be up and about in the morning "like a milkmaid," and protesting the presence of Alice and George on what was a family matter. Alice and George took their cue from Serhan, who ignored his sister, and the four endured the trip together with only minimal conversation, Serhan sharing the outcome of Eglantine's telephone call to the club. Woody, apparently, had requested a taxicab to Paddington, so they assumed he'd been on his way home, however when summoned for his ride, the club's staff found his room empty, his overnight bag packed but left behind, his overdue membership, regrettably, unpaid. At this last tidbit, Alice felt a disloyal squirm of familiarity, and wondered what Woody's excuse would be when they found him.

Once the group had disembarked, George and Serhan took charge, navigating the bustle of Paddington Station and out into the crowded city streets. With a deft flick of the wrist Serhan hailed a taxicab – a black automobile much larger than the zippy little Morris that had spirited Alice and Woody to Nookey Hollow – and they were transported to Woody's gentlemen's club in Upper Berkeley. It was such a short jaunt that Alice almost wondered why they'd hired a conveyance at all, although she did not enjoy walking, and was fairly certain she'd like it even less on busy city streets.

Citing the obvious, that Serhan, as a gently-reared male, was the only one among them who would be allowed in (club rules: no ladies, no children, no waifs, no strays), that one exited the vehicle and lifted the lion's head knocker. When the lacquered black door opened, Serhan was ushered through, and Alice caught a glimpse of thick Turkish carpets and heavy polished wood. The door closed, barring ladies and other problems, and Alice, George, and Eglantine sat blinking in the uncomfortable silence. Mere moments later, Serhan reappeared, carrying Woody's overnight bag and looking somewhat disgruntled, and said the club had been rather grudging in their assistance, preferring to discuss Woody's outstanding membership dues over the circumstances of his disappearance.

"How tedious," said Eglantine with a sniff.

"I gave them what money I had with me to keep Father in good standing. Not the full amount, but enough that they at least answered my questions," Serhan said, a pout tugging the edges of his usually smiling mouth.

"And?" Eglantine asked.

"And nothing," Serhan replied. "They knew no more than they told you on the telephone yesterday." He nodded toward the bag on his lap. "Obviously, he hasn't come back."

"I knew this would be a waste of time," Eglantine said petulantly. "What do we do now?"

Disagreement ensued. Alice suggested stopping off somewhere for lunch, while Serhan pressed the idea of checking infirmaries one by one, a sort of hospital tour of the great metropolis. Eglantine thought that notion ridiculous, and Alice agreed but didn't want to approve anything Eglantine said, so kept championing a lunch break. The driver, growing impatient in the front of the automobile, called out "where to, gov?" and above the whining and insistent voices, George shouted, "Cloak Lane P'lice Station, yer honour," and the driver, relieved to find someone with good sense among his fares, pulled the taxicab out into the rolling traffic.

Cloak Lane *was* the last place the twins' mother had been reported, George reasoned, explaining his direction, and since their father had been here to sort her out, as he put it, the station where she'd been picked up seemed a good place to start. Alice thought it made sense, to get onto Woody's trail by determining where his wife was, and she settled back on the button-tufted seat of the taxicab as they travelled towards Whitechapel, agog at the seeming vastness of the great city of London. Truth be told, Alice was a country girl whose cosmopolitan reach had extended no further than tepid Bristol, and London – teeming with people, reeking of unfathomable smells, roaring with shouts, screams, chatter, laughter, barks, whinnies, clip-clops, clangs, bangs, whistles and the thrum of automobiles – was an assault on the senses that was both fascinating and terrifying. Had she not been on a mission to find Woody, she'd have hopped the first train back to Watton Hoo and breathed much easier once home.

At the police station they disembarked, George in the lead. Eglantine, last out, was left to pay the fare. Alice noted her scowl of displeasure as she joined the others inside the precinct walls, but there was no time for Eglantine's petulance. George was at the counter, just barely able to see over the height of it, and he knocked to draw the attention of the desk sergeant, a slick-haired fellow with a rash of red pimples and the sketching of a moustache above a thin lip.

"'Allo, sarg," George said, the appearance of a broad London accent raising brows all around. "This 'ere party's come askin' after a lady wot you lot 'rested a few days back. Nutter, she was. Come right off 'er trolley." Eglantine glowered and made a noise of disapproval from the shadow of her fashionable hat. Distracted from his story, George glanced around at her and said, "What? She did," then turned back to the sergeant whose eyes were making the rounds of the group as if trying to determine why a boy, albeit bold as brass, was their spokesman. "Jumped the fence at the Cane 'ill Lunatic Asylum," George continued, "and who knows what she did 'twixt then and when you coppers picked 'er up in a street near here."

"Name?" asked the sergeant, turning to a large ledger and tapping his pimpled chin with the stub of a pencil.

"What y'need to know me name for?" George asked suspiciously, giving the sergeant his best tough guy snurl. Alice, watching admiringly from the sidelines, found herself again applauding George's seemingly bottomless trunk of talents.

"The lady's name, o' course," replied the sergeant with a roll of his eyes.

"Defne," said Serhan, pronouncing the name with a curl of a foreign accent presumably the way his mother would say it, at the same time that Eglantine retorted in her cut-glass English, "Daphne," and Alice responded "Barks."

The young sergeant blinked several times, and George again leaned through the confusion and said, "Daphne Barks, I'd wager. Mrs."

The sergeant consulted his black spined ledger, running his finger down column after column and flipping dog-eared pages. Serhan, impatient, drummed his fingers on the counter which only served to make the sergeant scroll more slowly and with a sheen of oily contempt on his unfortunate countenance.

"Get a lot of lunatics through the station, do yer?" George asked, standing on tiptoe to peer at the upside-down ledger. The sergeant drew it away, as if protecting a ham sandwich.

"We get enough," he replied, and just then his finger stopped its relentless downward pull and fastened on an entry. "Unknown female, drunk, disorderly, called 'erself Dippers. Might that be the lady in question?" Without pausing for a reply, he pulled forth a second ledger, this one thicker than the first and cross-referenced, finding the entry he sought. He continued, matter-of-factly, "Found in state o' dishabille, trousers but no top, beggin' yer pardon, ladies. Filthy and lousy. Feet turned blue from old boots."

"That sounds about right," George said. "Can we see 'er?"

"Well, she's not here anymore, is she?" answered the sergeant. "We don't keep 'em, do we? What d'we look like? Bloody nannies?"

"See here, there's no cause for such talk in front of ladies," Serhan interjected, leaning forward past George.

"Yeah," said George, angling his elbow and jostling Serhan. He was enjoying the limelight and was not about to relinquish it. "Them're ladies. And there won't be no such bloody talk." Reclaiming the role of leader, he added, "What does yer book say 'bout where they sent the Dippers person?"

"Bow Road Infirmary," the desk sergeant confirmed, his finger on the entry. "Escorted there by one Constable Crumb and Nurse Fettle." As he spoke the last name he leaned towards George and split his moustache-lined lip into a wing-backed grin. "An' let me tell you, young master, you don't wanna be giving *that* nightingale any guff should you cross her path, or you'll be findin' yerself in a fine fettle o' fish!"

He and George shared a chortle, but it was perfunctory, and moments later, after determining that the desk sargeant didn't recall a husband coming asking for the prisoner, the foursome was hailing their second taxicab of the day and threading the narrow streets of London. George kept up a banter with the driver, that strange sounding accent full of y'aroights and wotchers and eh mates rolling out of his mouth like he was born to it. Alice stared through the taxicab window at the maze of shops and buildings lining the streets, and the throngs of humanity populating the sidewalks – street urchins and old women, girls selling flowers, men in dun-coloured work clothes pushing barrows, others in aprons tidying shopfronts and still more carting buckets or ladders or crates, or simply lounging against a wall with a twist of a cigarette hanging from a lip. Vehicles of all sorts careened through the streets – carts and wagons and lorries, bicycles and taxicabs like the one they rode in, but also double-decker buses both horse-drawn and motorized and polished automobiles that were free with the horn. There was a yellowish fog in the air that Alice supposed was that soupy phenom London was known for, an offensive combination of weather, coal smoke and the spew of motorized traffic. She rifled in her reticule for a handkerchief, one of the lemon-scented ones that George usually tucked away for her, and covered her nose. The smell in this city was abominable.

Bow Road Infirmary was housed in a rather elegant looking yellow stone building with a tall clock tower and a set of heavy doors. As the group climbed down from the taxicab, the driver, perhaps on account of his newfound friendship with George, and surmising that they didn't know what they were in for, said by way of caution, "They bring the crazy ones here, y'see. All sorts head through them doors – yer criers and yer screamers, yer sobbers and yer melancholy starers. And then there's yer vicious type. You want to watch out for them ones especially." Alice, last to disembark and stuck with settling the fare and giving the tip, thanked him for the information and avoided his pitying stare.

Beyond the big doors was a lobby of sorts, with black and white tiles patterning the floor, high walls painted a sterile pale green and a tall counter not unlike the one over which they'd conferred at the Cloak Lane Police Station. It was a small reception room with no way out but the way you came in, unless you passed through a narrow door to the right which would be hard to do given that it was barred with curling wrought iron grillwork, its hasp closed with a padlock. A corridor stretched beyond, and from those inaccessible reaches came faint sounds that seemed almost animal-like: grunts and shrieks and yells and, oddly, laughter. Alice was not alone, she noted, in the expression of alarm she directed at that gloomy hallway, and she jumped when George hit the bell that sat upon the counter.

From somewhere behind that polished surface came a scuffling sound, and then silence. The group waited politely, but when no one came George rang the bell a second time. There was a scrape and a small thump, and then a disembodied voice, somewhat muffled, called, "Dropping off or picking up?" The foursome glanced around, seeing no-one. "Dropping off or picking up?" the voice called again, this time with a grate of irritation. George craned his neck, trying to peer over the counter, and retorted, "Does it have to be one or t'other?" Alice felt something resembling a wiggle of maternal pride, and leaned forward to pat George's arm encouragingly. Not many would slip much past that boy, she felt sure.

A head popped up then, appearing right in front of George and startling the foursome. The head belonged to a fellow only a little taller than George, with receding black hair and a widow's peak. His brows were pitched like tents over each eye, which were themselves hidden behind the thick lenses of spectacles so smeary with fingerprints Alice thought it a wonder the man could see at all.

"What were you doing on the floor?" George asked bluntly.

"Lost me pencil," the man replied. He held up a nub stuck with dustballs. "And whilst I were down there, I lost me specs." He tapped a grimy lens with his index finger. "Can't see without me specs, and can't afford to lose me pencil. I'm only allowed one a month." He picked off the dust and flicked it back onto the floor. "State your business," he said curtly, giving the pencil end a lick of his tongue.

"We're looking for a lady goes by the name o' Dippers. Brought here from Cloak Lane P'lice Station a few days back," George replied, still in charge. Serhan stood behind him, nodding. Eglantine glowered from beneath her hat and added, "Mrs Daphne Barks."

"Barks, eh?" said the man. He pressed fingers again to the lenses of his spectacles, and Alice wondered why he did that when it was so obviously not conducive to his seeing much of anything. At the same time, she noticed what she hadn't before: the shapeless smock he wore, grey with a light pinstripe. Rather less clerical than one might expect. She frowned and took a step back from the counter as the man continued, "Did something bad, did she? Run amok? Spoke to people what weren't there? Abandoned her children? Drowned kittens?"

"I beg your pardon —" interjected Serhan, offended, while Eglantine spat, "How dare you!" and George said, "Say what?" Alice retreated another foot from the counter. Just then footsteps came at sharp clip down the barred hallway, and a matron appeared, a scowl creasing her wide face. When she reached the padlocked door she rattled its metal ribs, peering through the bars.

"Mr Crumpet, you've stolen my keys again," she said in a sing-song voice that did not match the thunder of her expression. "Doctor Hamilton will be most displeased. Be a good fellow and undo the padlock and we'll see to it he's none the wiser, shall we?"

Mr Crumpet, if that was his name, cowered at the sound of the matron's voice, and his eyes behind the spectacles darted from her to Alice's party gathered on the other side of the counter and back to the matron. He reached up and smoothed his oily locks in a nervous gesture, then pressed again at the lenses of his glasses.

"You're going to strap me," he said in a plaintive voice. "I don't want to be strapped. It hurts."

The matron gave a loud hee-hee-hee that was anything but humourous and said, more to Alice's party than to Mr Crumpet, "Nonsense, we don't strap people here. We are a modern establishment with thoroughly humane and decent practices." Hee-hee-hee, again. She rattled the bars once more. "Come now, Mr Crumpet. Show these people what a good fellow you are and bring me the keys."

Mr Crumpet hesitated, his hair on the receiving end of a thorough and vigorous comb-through. His stub of a pencil tap-tapped on the counter, and he began to wheeze with indecision. Alice stared at him in alarm. Good heavens, the man was a lunatic, and here he was, no more than a yard away. Muddy would've been apoplectic. Alice took another step backwards, wondering if she could make it to the exit before the Crumpet fellow vaulted the counter and overtook her.

George, as was becoming his habit, stepped up to save the day. "I say, Crump me lad, never mind what *she* says." He jerked his head in the matron's direction and leaned a shoulder towards the man conspiratorially. He held out his hand, palm up. "You give *me* the keys, and I'll see there's no strapping done. You hand *me* the keys, and I'll see that matron here gives you a nice bit o' treacle tart at tea time, yes matron?"

"I can't promise that," matron said indignantly, but under George's withering stare, she retreated. "Alright, yes. It might not be treacle tart, mind, that depends on Cook, but I'll see you get something special for co-operating, Crumpet, there's a good fellow."

Inmate Crumpet, lunatic though he might be, had the sense to weigh his options, and he glanced from the glowering, tittering matron, still safely behind the barred door, to the foursome across the counter from him, all wearing a variety of expressions. Alice wondered if the man might indeed have been a clerk in his rational days, hence his desire to act out the scene, and if he knew, in some part of his erratic brain, that the matron might not honour her part of the bargain. She also wondered how co-operative the matron might be once released from the corridor, and thought it might behoove the group to take advantage of the situation as it currently presented itself. She swallowed her unease and stepped up to the counter, knowing that her sheer size was a wonderful intimidator.

"Mr Crumpet, you look like a man who has served the office of clerk in some capacity in the past, no doubt with much success," Alice began, her voice firm and authoritative. Mr Crumpet stood a little straighter, and gripped his pencil. "Most likely when you – er – borrowed the matron's keys you were hoping to assist the infirmary in that regard by employing your plainly enviable talents here in the area of admissions and departures." She held the room, and gathering confidence as she spoke, Alice leaned towards the shriveled Mr Crumpet and said "Keys aside, my companions and I would be most grateful, Mr Crumpet, if you would consult the ledger for the admission record and current location of a Mrs Daphne Barks, aka Dippers, who would have been brought here from the Cloak Lane Police Station several days ago."

Mr Crumpet succumbed, as Alice had hoped he would, and looked ever so pleased, the matron temporarily forgotten. He licked the end of his pencil with gusto. This was his forté, and his felicity. He squared his shoulders, stepped up to the ledger and said, "I do recall an admission on Tuesday last of a foreign-looking lady, had to be carried in, though, kicking and screaming the walls down –"

"Mr Crumpet!" cried the matron. "You will not discuss patients with these people! *I* will not discuss patients with these people until their credentials have been thoroughly checked and Doctor Hamilton has agreed to see them! Bring me my keys this instant!"

Mr Crumpet hesitated and his shoulders drooped, his eyes darting from Alice to the matron and back again.

"Don't mind the matron, Mr Crumpet," said Alice firmly. "She has promised you a treacle tart or its equivalent, has she not? Matron, you will hold your tongue unless you would prefer the good Doctor Hamilton to be apprised of your negligence in losing track of your keys. Mr Crumpet, continue."

The matron was visibly furious – fit to be tied, George might say – but she made no other noise than a hiss of frustration. Mr Crumpet dutifully consulted the ledger, seeming to enjoy the scan of its many pages, and with a lift of his tented brows cried, "Aha!"

The foursome surged to the counter, craning to see what the fellow had found, but he shielded the book possessively, and Alice was reminded of the police sergeant at the Cloak Lane precinct. Were all clerks such indignant stewards?

"It's wrote Dappers, and no last name, but I'd say this might be your lady," Mr Crumpet said, blinking over the top of his specs. "Brought in Tuesday last, as I said, spitting like a cat and claws out. Does she speak a foreign language? This lady did. Babbled all sorts of nonsense."

"Is she here?" Eglantine asked, ignoring the clerk's question.

"Was her husband here? A Woodward Barks," Alice said, interrupting. "He might have come to arrange a move to Cane Hill."

"First things first, Mrs Isbister, if you don't mind," Eglantine said. "This is a family matter."

"Woody's whereabouts is paramount," Alice retorted, and Eglantine snorted.

"Woody, indeed," the younger woman said with disdain.

Mr Crumpet was thumbing happily through the ledger, ignoring the argument between the ladies, when he paused on a second entry, and repeated, "Aha!" The smeared spectacles lifted. "Another entry, this one referencing a Daphne Barks, question mark, and in pencil, Major W. Barks, Watton Hoo."

"Yes, yes!" cried Eglantine and Serhan together. "That's her! Major Barks is our father."

Alice was about to interject that it wasn't *Major* Barks, in fact, but the much higher and more prestigious rank of *Lieutenant-Colonel* Barks, thank you very much, when Mr Crumpet spoke further, and her correction seemed immaterial.

"Then I'm sorry to be the bearer of sad tidings," he said, "This patient's dead." He closed the ledger, and pushed his sliding spectacles up his nose.

Everyone stood in stunned silence except Matron, who could be quiet no longer. She rattled her cage and shouted, "Mr Crumpet! Unlock this door immediately! You have no authority to issue statements regarding a patient's status! Dr Hamilton will hear about this! I demand to be released!"

Mr Crumpet leaned across the high counter to the gaping foursome and said conspiratorially, "That's what *she* said too. The Dippers lady. I heard her. Release me at once, she shouted. I have a cake in the oven. Victoria sponge! You'd think she was the Queen of Sheba, way she talked."

"So the lady was well – at least well enough to shout – when she was brought in?" Alice asked. "How did she die, Mr Crumpet? Do you know?"

Mr Crumpet reopened the ledger and flipped pages until he found the entry again, then peered at it through his smeared spectacles. "TRF it says, under discharge. TRF." He shook his head and looked apologetically at Alice and her companions. "It's what most of 'em in here die of. Bad disease, that one. TRF. I've checked this ledger before. They come in, and before you know it, they're gone. TRF."

"TRF?" repeated Alice, frowning. A thought occurred, and she smiled. TRF was not a disease at all, but an abbreviation of the word transfer. She glanced over at the matron, livid but silent behind the bars. "Where did they send Mrs Barks, Matron? These are her children. They have a right to know what happened to their mother." And when the matron's lips remained stubbornly pinched, Alice added, "Mr Crumpet has generously agreed to hand me the keys, haven't you, Mr Crumpet? And when he does, I will let you out, but you must first tell me where they took Mrs Barks, and you must further promise, in front of four witnesses, mind, and who will return to check, that Mr Crumpet will not suffer for his actions this day. Will you agree? Or will we depart now, and take with us Mr Crumpet and this ledger, leaving you locked behind your bars?" From the corner of her eye Alice saw George blanch and then grin. Serhan squared his shoulders, and even Eglantine managed a nod of approval. Alice felt vindicated in her decision to lay down the ultimatum, and although the matron hissed her frustration yet again, the woman reluctantly acquiesced.

"Mr Crumpet, do you understand?" Alice asked, and held out her palm for the keys.

"What about my treacle tart?" he asked, hesitating.

Everyone turned to the matron.

"I already made that promise," she said stiffly. "And I will keep it."

Mr Crumpet then happily handed over the keys, and Alice gave them to George, who strode to the padlock and inserted the key. Before he turned it, everyone waited for the answer to the question of where Mrs Barks had been taken.

"Stone Asylum in Dartford," came the grudging reply. "Her husband authorized the transfer. They will not be so lackadaisical, if you are hoping to break her out."

"In fact," said Serhan, "We are hoping to ensure she stays in. Most decidedly in."

Chapter 30
A SLICE OF VICTORIA SPONGE

Getting to Stone Asylum in Dartford where the elusive Mrs Barks had been transferred would require a train journey, Alice's group discovered when they made further inquiries of the fuming but grudgingly co-operative matron at the Bow Road Infirmary. Not a long one, mind, in comparison to the trip from Watton Hoo, but the hour had grown late and there was some uncertainty about a return train in the evening hours. On the sidewalk outside the infirmary the group fell to arguing about taking a chance on getting stuck in Dartford, and then what, or checking into a hotel for the night and starting fresh in the morning. It was George who made the novel suggestion of using a telephone to make their inquiry, and perhaps save themselves both a trek to Dartford and the expense of a hotel.

"If yer mum's there, at the whatsit asylum, you can tell 'em to keep 'er," said George with a shrug. "If she's not, well, that's a different breed o' cat, as they say."

"And they can tell us if Father has been there. A clever idea, George!" Serhan crowed. Eglantine did not disagree, but stated with her customary pessimism, "Why would a lunatic asylum need a telephone?" Alice, for her part, found yet another reason to admire her young charge. Leave it to the youthful to think of a modern idea like a telephone. She, of course, had no idea how to use one – she had no need of such a contraption at Sowerby Grange – or, indeed, where one might be found on a city street, but George obviously knew, for he charged off and she, Eglantine and Serhan followed, weaving through the odourous stream of people that cluttered every available inch of sidewalk in this metropolis. One or two urchins bumped up against Alice – pickpockets, she suspected – and she shot them a withering glare and clutched her reticule close. She was by far the slowest of the group, but she was careful to keep George's dark head in sight, and she saw him finally pause alongside what appeared to be a little hut, big enough for one person to stand inside. As she puffed to a stop alongside George she saw stencilled on the windows 'Public Telephone. Open Always.'

"Is that it?" she asked, nodding to the kiosk. It seemed rather unassuming for such a marvel of technology, tucked up as it was against a grimy, soot-stained building. Winded from her brisk steps she reached out to steady herself against the wall, and her hand came away black. George, ever the gentleman, wordlessly handed her a handkerchief.

"This is it," he said. He pulled wide the door, and over his shoulder Alice could see the contraption itself – the plain black box, the earpiece hanging on its long cord, a small crank handle and a slot for coins.

"It costs," George said, hesitating. He glanced back at Serhan, Eglantine and Alice.

"I'll ring," Eglantine said, pushing past him into the kiosk.

"We'll both ring," Serhan said, and pressed in beside her, though there was scant space. Nevertheless, they seemed to agree on sharing the call, and pulled the door closed to shut out the noise from the street.

Alice and George stood outside, and it occurred to Alice that it was a curious thing indeed that she should be standing here on a busy London thoroughfare with her dustbin boy whilst her lover's two grown children tried to ring a lunatic asylum on a telephone. She shook her head. What would Mr Isbister think of her now, she wondered, infidelity aside? No doubt his mouth would hang open and his chin would disappear as it did when anything at all surprised him. Just the idea of she having such an unconventional adventure would have him tugging on his wellingtons and heading for the woods, the one place, Alice felt sure, where he imagined himself superior to her. That life had conspired to burden her with such a mouse of a husband she could not credit, and she pushed him from her thoughts.

Inside the phone box Eglantine was speaking into the instrument, the earpiece held loosely that Serhan might hear the conversation. She appeared cross, although irritability, Alice reminded herself, was Eglantine's perpetual state. The girl's black, winged brows arrowed in a downward dive, and her full mouth scowled. But Serhan too was frowning, and Alice exchanged a worried glance with George.

"Comes to it, missus," George said in a low tone, his eyeball trained on the siblings in the booth, "Whatever you decide I'll be stickin' wiff you. We can head back to Watton Hoo anytime you like and it'd suit me just fine. Chasin' after men on the game – beggin' yer pardon, missus – and nutters what gives coppers and the like the slip ain't no lark. If the lady's mad as a hatter, things could get dangerous. And if the lieutenant-colonel don't want to be found, well…"

Alice felt a sinking in her stomach at his words and swallowed down the nervous lump in her throat. She acknowledged his words with an almost imperceptible nod of her head as the door to the telephone box opened and the siblings stepped out, ashen-faced.

"She's not there," Serhan said in a strangled voice. He glanced wildly around the street, as if expecting the lady to suddenly appear, knife brandished.

"Where is she then?" George asked boldly. He stepped in front of Alice, as if to shield her from harm.

"She gave them the slip," Eglantine spat, but there was no mistaking the sharpness of fear in her eyes. "She always was a clever one, despite her madness." Her lips twisted into a grimace, and she stared down at the dirty pavement.

"Well, isn't anyone looking for her?" asked Alice shrilly. "Surely they don't just let lunatics go running around the city. And where's Woody? Had they seen him?"

George muttered something under his breath that Alice couldn't make out, and Eglantine gave a short barking laugh and said, "Father had telephoned, apparently, but that was before she'd gone missing. The asylum has notified the precincts in the area, but there really isn't much more they can do."

"If they sent a copper after every nutter loose in the city there'd be no one to man the stations," said George confidently. "'Sides, she'll blend right in if she heads down to the taverns near the docks, or finds her way over the river to the Borough."

"Has she friends or acquaintances she might seek out?" Alice asked, trying to be helpful.

"Friends?" Eglantine repeated incredulously. "She's been locked in an institution for twelve years. I doubt she'd be dropping in on anyone for tea."

"Then she could be anywhere," said Alice, for London was surely the busiest place she had ever seen. The constant movement of people and things was a barrage, and even things that didn't move distracted: bills and notices were pasted upon every surface, prodding the viewer to a purchase of goods or services. Within the immediate vicinity Alice could see whole walls of soot-stained buildings painted or hung with signs that cried 'Money Lent' and 'High Class Artificial Teeth' and 'Buy Our Lucky Wedding Rings,' not to mention the constant push of wares – Lyon's Tea, Colman's Mustard, White's Ginger Beer, Fry's Chocolate, Nestle's Milk. The mind boggled.

"She could indeed have returned to the squalid back alleys," Serhan was saying, a pensive look upon his face, "But if I were a betting man, which I am, I'd put my money on an exit from the charms of the metropolis. I'd wager she's on her way to Natterjack Hall, hotfoot, or is at least trying to figure out how to get there."

"Natterjack Hall?" said Alice, aghast. She felt the sudden need to sit down but there was no bench. "How on earth would she know about Natterjack Hall?"

"Egg wrote to her, didn't she? When our father first let the place," Serhan replied, his tone accusing. "Sent a nice little daughterly card to keep her apprised of where she could find us, should she wish to write. Never could stop believing she'd get better, would stop trying to murder us in our beds."

Alice looked from one twin to the other, fear mounting. Murder them in their beds? That was a far cry from leaving them unsupervised, or frightening them, or whatever she'd understood Woody to imply. There must have been a barb of truth to Serhan's accusation, for the usually spitfire Eglantine said nothing, and her gaze remained turned away.

"Surely murder is an exaggeration," Alice said doubtfully, but her inflection made it clear the statement was more a question.

"She set fire to my bedclothes while I was sleeping," Serhan said flatly. "I awoke, but realised she'd tethered my ankle to the bedpost."

"Dear heaven," said Alice, shocked. She put a hand out and George stepped into her reach. Though his shoulder was thin it steadied her, much the way a weight anchored a wobbling balloon.

"I doused the flame before it did any damage," Eglantine snapped, but there was obvious strain on her elegant features, and no bite in her bark. "She never would have let you burn."

"Forgive me if I doubt," Serhan retorted. "I think, dear sister, of the time she locked us in the armoire and disappeared. Two days we were in there. What would have become of us if the woman in the next flat hadn't heard our shouts?"

Eglantine made no reply. Alice looked in horror from one twin to the other, and then to George, pillar of pragmatism, who said, "Right, then, what's the plan?"

Eglantine turned to Serhan, and Serhan to Alice. It seemed her decision to make, and so she chose what was of greatest importance to her – Woody. "We go back to Watton Hoo," she said firmly. "Your father has most likely gone home, believing your mother to be admitted at Stone, and first and foremost we must assure ourselves of his safety. There's no point chasing about these streets; we may never find your mother even if she's here. If she does intend to go to Natterjack Hall, as Serhan suspects, then such a plan will take some effort. One cannot simply hop a train wearing a skirt stamped 'Stone Asylum,' presumably. And how would she pay the fare?"

No one retorted that a wily person could find a way to do just about anything, regardless of their garb, and a lack of money, though Alice suspected she was not the only one with little faith in her own words. George, with a direction decided, hailed a taxicab.

"Paddington Station, milord," he cried when the automobile pulled to the curb. This time there was no argument. Indeed, there was no talk at all.

*

Alice, George, Serhan and Eglantine were the only passengers to disembark at Watton Hoo. It was late, and dark, and the ticket office was shuttered; in fact, the station was deserted. Despite the lack of travellers, the platform lights burned brightly, and once the train departed in a chuff of smoke the hum of the electric bulbs was audible in the still night. It occurred to Alice that she had never been in the village at such an hour. In fact, she'd only rarely been out of doors at all after dinnertime. The solitude felt a bit ghoulish, although she conceded that such a feeling was likely heightened by the knowledge that there could be a murderous lunatic in the vicinity.

George led her to a bench next to the closed station office, and Alice sat gratefully, wondering how they would get from here to Sowerby Grange and Natterjack Hall. Outward bound, George had arranged a ride in the baker's delivery wagon which Alice had accepted with good grace, though she'd have preferred something less plebeian, and had had to dust a bit of flour from her clothes upon disembarking. How Eglantine and Serhan had travelled to the station in the morning she had no idea. Those two now sat on the next bench along the platform, while George scurried off to try to find transportation. Alice, Eglantine and Serhan sat unspeaking, watching a leaf skitter, blown by the light evening breeze. Alice found the buzz of the electric lights grating, and wondered why anyone would want such contrivances in their home, and yet everyone did. Times surely were changing.

After what seemed an age George was back to say there was no conveyance to be found, and Alice concealed her annoyance, in part because Serhan and Eglantine expressed theirs so openly. George, ever eager, told Alice that if she would stay put upon the station bench, he would himself walk to Sowerby Grange and fetch the cart. Alice, weighing the darkness of the shadows beyond the station platform against the irritating light bulbs overhead, tsked over the great burden that would be on poor George, but settled back, content to wait. After all, she had Serhan and Eglantine for company. The possibility occurred that although the crazed Mrs Barks could be in the vicinity, surely no murderer, lunatic or otherwise, would attack all three of them, and in a lighted venue.

But Serhan jumped to his feet. "I'll go with you, George," he said, and then Eglantine rose, brushing at her skirt as if it had cobwebs on it. "Well, I'm not sitting here alone," she said, discounting Alice.

Alice, instantly alarmed at the idea of being left, sat forward on the bench and expelled a noise that sounded embarrassingly like the bleat of a sheep. Surely they would not simply abandon her? But George, dear

George, was hesitating, and Alice saw that he was waiting for her to give some sort of order, and so she stood, doing her best to be dignified in spite of her breast pounding with fright at the idea of remaining behind in the deserted train station, and said, "If we are walking, we walk together. Of course, it's the simplest solution."

And, though her feet were already pinching in tight shoes and her corset desperately wanted loosening, Alice raised a hand in a sergeant-major-like gesture and led the way out of the overly lit station into the dark and possibly lunatic-infested night.

*

It was a long walk. Huffing and puffing and near dead on her feet, Alice, with George and the twins, reached the laneway to Sowerby Grange beneath a sliver of moon that hung overhead like a mottled bone. If there was a chill in the air on this summer night Alice certainly could not feel it; instead, there was a clinging dampness in the crescents beneath her armpits and bosom, and in other places even more unmentionable. Despite her initial leadership, she'd quickly fallen to the back of the pack, and George had been ever so considerate, insisting on pauses along the way where a wall was low enough for her to perch and catch her breath. Everyone was as skittery as mice, and no one, she included, wanted to stop for long, so they'd trudged on beneath the thin light of the moon.

There'd been no discussion of what they would do once they reached their destination, but now that they stood at the intersection of laneway and road, Alice was loathe to part from the twins. It wasn't that she enjoyed their company particularly, but there was safety in numbers, after all. Selfishly she considered suggesting that they remain with her at Sowerby Grange until morning, and turned several approaches over in her mind – after all, the dark of night seemed the worst possible time to tangle with a crazed person, should there be one in the vicinity. But the right words were hard to find, for surely 'For your own safety,' and 'For my own safety,' and 'Lest your lunatic mother be already there,' all sounded rather dismissive of any peril Woody might be in. Alice told herself it was not certain that the lamentable Mrs Barks had in fact travelled to Watton Hoo, and in the end she simply bid Serhan and Eglantine goodnight, taking comfort in the fact that if indeed Woody was at Natterjack Hall, he was not alone. There were servants present, and possibly Captain Plucky, and certainly Woody, great big man that he was, should be more than a match for one unhinged woman. She and George trudged in silence up the moonlit lane towards Sowerby Grange, and despite the tensions of the day, Alice began to look forward to her big wide bed and one of George's midnight snacks, and ultimately, the bliss of her head upon the pressed linen of her pillow.

*

George brought hot water and turned down the coverlet on the bed. As always, he helped with Alice's corset and knelt to tug her shoes from her swollen feet. While she washed the dust and dirt of London and the train from her various surfaces, pulled on her voluminous nightgown and climbed into bed, George went to fetch cocoa and a slice of Victoria sponge.

She closed her eyes as she waited, revelling in the feel of the clean, cool sheets and the cushion of the feather pillow beneath her head. Her feet still throbbed and despite her ablutions she could smell something oddly grimy and sour. Perhaps she should have asked George to draw her a bath, although a sniff of her armpits returned only the scent of pleasant rosewater. But the hour was late, and she suspected George was as tired as she. Alice wanted nothing more than food, followed by sleep. Tomorrow would be time enough for complete cleanliness. Her body felt blissfully heavy, and she thought she heard George's footfall on the stairs. He'd be bringing her cake. Expecting to rouse when he set the tray by her side, she allowed herself to doze.

*

A slight creak sounded in the stillness of the room, and Alice's eyes popped open. She had indeed fallen deeply asleep, she realised, and she sat up in bed, disoriented. The Victoria sponge and cocoa were on a silver tray next to her, the cake half eaten and the cocoa all gone. She didn't recall partaking, or indeed, George bringing the food and drink. Another noise sounded, a slight thump, and her heart gave a mirroring jump.

"George?" she called, her voice shrill with tension. The door to her armoire was slightly ajar. Had she left it open? It was unlike her; she was usually fastidious. Well, George was. The drapery next to the cupboard – had it just stirred?

"George!" she cried a second time.

The bedroom door swung slowly inward and Alice gave an involuntary cry of fear. George would not enter so hesitantly. What if it was the murderous Dippers – Daphne –Defne!? She grabbed the little brass clock from her bedside table and threw it at the door. It struck with a thud, denting the wood, and landed on the carpet. The alarm sounded with a frenzied peal, shattering the silence. The door continued to open, and George's face peered guardedly around it.

"Missus?" he said, his voice a question. He came hesitantly into the room carrying a brass warming pan at arm's length – the reason, Alice saw now, for his cautious entry.

"George," she said again, stoutly relieved. "Gracious, you frightened me. Why didn't you wake me for my cake?"

George eyed the partly eaten morsel and frowned. "Looks like you did wake, missus," he said.

"I didn't," Alice said. She frowned at the tray. "I don't think I did." She pointed to the armoire, then, a fresh quiver in her voice. "That door opened, George. At least I think I heard it squeak. And the drapes moved…" Her own words sounded ridiculous, and she watched George for a hint of a smile, for surely he'd think these the imaginings of a silly woman. Instead, he avoided her eye and busied himself sliding the warming pan between the sheets. She stretched her cold feet towards the warmth. It should have had a calming effect, but tonight she could not shake the feeling that all was not well.

"George?" she asked again, hearing a plaintiveness in her voice that further alarmed her. Where was her nerve?

"Missus," he answered, but with none of his usual swagger and teasing good humour. He took a deep breath and went to the armoire, throwing wide the door. He rummaged inside and came out with a silk stocking. "Wondered where that got to," he said, and Alice understood that he was attempting humour, even if it fell flat. She smiled tremulously. She wanted to cry because George, her stalwart knight in shining armour, appeared as frightened as she was, and how would she find courage if he was afraid? Shoulders squared, he approached the drapery and tugged it back, revealing nothing but the long dark window shrouded by its lace curtain. George looked at Alice and she nodded, feeling foolish. He gestured to the tray with the cake and cocoa. "Will you eat that, missus, or will I take it?"

"You can take it, George," she said. Her appetite had departed.

He left the oil lamp on her bedside table burning but turned the wick down low, and before he exited the room he paused by the door, tray in hand. "All will be well, missus. Ain't nothing to be afeared of," he said, but his effort was obvious, and Alice suspected he said it as much to himself as to her. Nevertheless, she closed her eyes, took a shuddering breath and rolled onto her side, burrowed in the bedding.

*

Sleep was immediate, though fitful and restless. Alice tossed and turned and woke periodically only to doze off again, too tired to come fully to her senses. Each time she surfaced she noted the still-burning lamp, and was grateful for the small bit of light glowing like a beacon. She dreamt of the dark cave at Nookey Hollow, she and Woody and their wordless guide Coddle creeping along underground, she worrying about bats and other lurking beasties. In her dream the lantern extinguished as it had in the real-life adventure, but in this incarnation, she was the sole spelunker, and there was no one to re-light the lamp. She was alone in the cavern and something touched her.

Alice startled awake. She was damp with the perspiration of fear and she pulled herself up on one elbow, her breath coming heavily, and used her nightgown to mop the sheen of sweat from her bosom. Then she noticed that although her room was lit by a dim glow, her lamp was not in its place on the bedside table. She swallowed, the blood whooshing in her ears, but forced herself to be very still. She smelled that awful grimy odour she had noticed earlier, and sensed she was not alone in the room. Ever so slowly, she twisted to look behind her, and saw a woman sitting in a chair at her bedside, holding the burning lamp. The low light cast her face in stretched shadows, but Alice could see black eyes that glittered like jet, and black hair that was wiry and liberally streaked with white. She'd been living rough, that much was clear, for her skin was filthy, her nails broken and dirty, and her face bore scratches as if she'd been crawling through bramble bushes. She was so thin she was almost skeletal. Strangely she had donned one of Alice's dresses, the black moiré silk, Alice saw, and the garment, far too large for her scrawny frame, hung from her shoulders. It was her; Alice knew it with horrified certainty. The escaped lunatic. Woody's wife, Defne, who'd tried to murder her own children.

"Hello," said Alice tentatively, her voice a-quiver.

"Hello," the woman answered, equally hesitant.

"Are you alright?" Alice asked. What did one say to a lunatic, after all?

"Probably not," the woman answered. "At least, that's usually what people think."

"Oh," said Alice. Dear God, should she shout for George? She eyed the lamp the woman held. Surely flame in a crazy person's hands was never a good idea, especially one who had previously attempted to set her son on fire.

"Do you have any more cake?" the woman asked. She smiled timidly at Alice, as if embarrassed to ask such a question.

"Oh," said Alice, remembering her partially eaten Victoria sponge, and thinking this a perfect way to summon help. "I'm sure there's more in the kitchen. I'll call George, shall I?"

It was the wrong thing to say. The woman grew immediately agitated, rising from her chair and backing away from Alice's bed. She held the lamp high, lighting the room, and Alice saw with horror that the covers at the foot of her bed were peeled back and her own thick ankle was tied to the bedpost with one of the drapery cords. The woman began to moan just as Alice started to shout, and in the cacophony of noise the woman tossed the lamp, lighting the bedclothes on fire. Alice bellowed louder yet and the woman ran.

Never a hysterical sort, Alice did what she could. She tossed the heavy coverlet upon the flames and began to beat on it – effectively, if she did later say so herself repeatedly – extinguishing what might have been a disaster. Not only did she save herself from death by immolation, but she rescued Sowerby Grange from a madwoman's pyromaniacal intent. Once the flames were out, she worked the knot in the drapery cord free, loosing her ankle, and stumbled out of the bedroom and down the stairs. This night's work was not over.

"George!" she cried, running through the lower levels of the house, nightgown a-billow. Gracious, where did the boy sleep, anyway? More than once she barked her shins when she encountered furniture she couldn't see in the dark, and she wished for a brighter moon to shine through the curtains to light her way. She stumbled from room to room, shouting George's name, fearing for his life and fearing too that the deranged Mrs Barks might jump out at any moment, knife, perhaps, in hand. She paused to catch her breath in the parlour where the moon angled just so through the long lace-hung windows, casting a shred of light. She pressed a hand to her bosom, and when she'd calmed, she went with purpose to the bureau and fumbled in the drawer for the matches she knew were kept there. Just as she was about to light a lamp, she noticed through the curtain a movement outside by the greenhouse. She put down the matches and the lamp and drew back the lace. Someone was skulking furtively near the greenhouse door, though whether it was George or the elusive Mrs Barks or someone else she couldn't be sure.

Alice took up the fireplace poker. The weight of it in her hand was alarming, but she told herself it was for self defence only, or to protect George. The woman might be mad, and frightening, but Alice had seen a glimmer of rationality in her face when she'd calmly said hello and admitted that most people thought she was not alright. Alice was surprised to realise she felt sorry for Defne Barks, no longer herself and alone in the world, but shrugged it off. One simply couldn't go through life feeling badly for every waif and stray and lunatic one encountered. Compassion was a fool's tool, after all, and no one ever got ahead in life by being tender-hearted. Alice squared her shoulders and crept toward the door that led to the gardens nearest the greenhouse, brandishing the brass poker.

Out in the quiet yard, clouds scudded overhead. A breeze stirred, and there was the smell of rain in the air. The windchimes Mr Isbister had fashioned from old silverware and hung by the greenhouse door tinkled. Alice had forgotten about them, and made a mental note to throw them away when things returned to normal. She had never liked their insipid little noise, and thought it silly to hang forks and spoons on a string.

Someone was definitely in the greenhouse. She could see a shape, and, as she moved closer, glancing nervously to her left and right and behind her lest her quarry be not the person inside, she could hear the low mutter of a voice. She hunkered down by the door, trying to find a break in the whitewash of the glass to see who lurked beyond.

A slight sound behind her put her heart in her mouth, but when she spun around, brandishing the poker, she saw Captain Plucky hurrying across the lawn, bent low to avoid detection. Alice was overjoyed to see him; had there not been a need for stealth she'd have happily flung her arms around him or jumped up and down, both things completely out of character for her, but a testament, she felt sure, to the strangeness of recent events. Captain Plucky crouched next to her, the only indication that he'd noticed her inappropriate attire – nightgown and cap – the quick sweep of his gaze and ever so slight lift of one slender brow.

"Is she in there? The renegade Mrs Barks?" he asked in hushed tones.

"Someone is," Alice whispered back. "Though I'm not sure who. I can't find George."

"George is unlikely to be lurking in the greenhouse in the dead of night, though, is he?" Captain Plucky said dismissively. "Give me the poker," he added, and Alice obliged, though she wondered as she did if she ought to admonish Captain Plucky not to hurt the woman. She was, surely, not responsible for her actions, and Captain Plucky, after all, was a military man. But Captain Plucky had moved away, crab-walking through the long grass next to the greenhouse, looking for a sightline. He appeared to find one, for he paused, peered, and then leapt to his feet, crying in an anguished voice "George!" and rushing back towards the door where Alice crouched.

Alice, being right there, was quicker. The moment she heard Captain Plucky shout George's name she knew he was inside and all was not well. She leapt forward and flung open the door, and what happened next was a horror that Alice would re-live in her nightmares. Mrs Barks stood in the middle of the greenhouse, the hooked blade of one of Mr Isbister's pruning knives in one hand, and the branch of one of his awful plants – the one with the razor-sharp spines and prickly leaves – in the other. George was opposite her, his arms extended in a pleading gesture as if he'd been reasoning with her, perhaps trying to talk her into putting down her weapons. Instead, spurred by either Captain Plucky's yell or the crash of the door as Alice tore it open, Mrs Barks lunged toward George. Alice bellowed and then everything seemed to happen in slow motion: George stumbling backwards, Defne Barks shrieking, the loose pane of glass Alice had admonished Mr to fix time and again falling from the ceiling and shattering onto the madwoman's head, one long broken spear piercing her body like a knife into butter. Alice pulled George to her in an embrace that all but buried his body in the massive folds of her nightdress, and Captain Plucky ran to check the woman's vital signs, but there was little need. It was quite plain she was dead. Captain Plucky turned back to Alice and George, obviously shaken, his face white as a sheet, but, recovering some of his signature bravado, he located George's head poking from the pillow of Alice's bosom and gave him a tousle. "Well done, soldier," he said, and then fainted onto the greenhouse floor.

*

Much later, when the police had come and the body had been removed, the whole picture emerged. Long before visiting Alice in her bedroom, Mrs Barks had indeed been at Natterjack Hall, presumably searching for her husband, though with what intent the police could not determine. Woody had indeed been at home, returned from London on an earlier train, and upon realising there was an intruder, had hidden in a closet, the image of which Alice admittedly found rather disconcerting, but there it was.

Captain Plucky too had been at home, but had been blissfully unaware of the visitor, asleep as he was in his bed, although when he eventually awoke it was to find his ankle inexplicably tied to the bedpost.

Around this time, Eglantine and Serhan had arrived after their walk from Watton Hoo, but their mother had gone, perhaps finding her way through the Whortleberry Wood to Sowerby Grange, and Alice's Victoria sponge. The twins had flushed their father from his hiding place, and Captain Plucky, upon hearing the tale of their adventure in London and their pursuit of the elusive Dippers, had volunteered to have a look around outside, perhaps go next door and make sure all was well. Which, of course, it was not. Alice shuddered to think what could have happened, and indeed what *had* happened. Perhaps, she thought, she would reconsider electric lights.

George, less rattled, set up a trundle bed for himself outside Alice's door and at her request, threw out the remains of the Victoria sponge.

Chapter 31
DR SYNTAX'S HEAD

Penzance was a town of a few thousand souls, with a beautiful promenade that wound along its seawall and romanced visitors with decorated pavilions and gracious hotels and sub-tropical palm trees. Out in the harbour, with the tide in, fishing boats bobbed in the water as in every Cornish village they'd passed, but here two grey-hulled destroyers sprawled inertly, rust oozing from their seams, a war's discarded machines. They were the only blight on an otherwise pristine panorama of surf, sky and wheeling terns, and as Throck, Eliza and Mungo arrived, the sun found a way through the overcast, sharing its warmth.

Since their disagreement, there'd been no further stops, and no further discussion of destinations, or endings. Throck felt badly for having been the cause of such awkwardness between the three of them, and wondered if Mungo wished to retract his declaration of them as a proper good triumvirate. But there was no sign, on his part, of ill feeling, and as first the Trusty, and then Mungo on his bicycle pulled to a stop at the ferry terminal on the South Pier, they all three ignored the proverbial pachyderm squatted on the quay and acted as if there was no discord amongst them. Docked nearby was RMS Peninnis, the ferry to the Scillies, a capable-looking mail steamer flying His Majesty's pennant, already being loaded with sacks of mail and other cargo, and boarding some passengers. A passing navvy, balancing a crate on one shoulder, replied to a query from Mungo that she was due to depart in half an hour, and tickets could be purchased at the office, housed in a lopsided building upon which a line of seagulls perched, raucously declaring their presence. Mungo lumbered off towards the office.

Eliza and Throck stood awkwardly, awaiting Mungo's return. After a moment Eliza said, "I'm sorry I got angry. It were never bypassing Land's End that upset me. Well, not entirely. It were that you seemed to still see me as your servant, that you could just make a decision

302

and I'd go along. That what I think isn't important. I thought we were a team, not a triumvirate, proper good or not." She smiled sadly as she quoted Mungo. "It's not even being a threesome. I like Mungo. I like him a lot. But it's not practical to be three right now. If we travel at bicycle speed, we'll be a day just getting to Land's End. Do you see? And despite what I said, I never saw Land's End as an ending."

There was no time for Throck to answer, for Mungo lumbered up, his shaven face woeful.

"I know your feelings, Eliza, about not coming to the Scillies – no, no apology necessary." He held up his hands as Eliza started to speak. "As it turns out, 'tis just as well." He turned to Throck. "Throck, they won't allow the Trusty on board. I asked, just in case the two of ye had a change o' heart, but there be'nt no way they're havin' the motorcycle. They've a few sheep goin' across, y'see, and they think the bike'll scare the sheep, and, well, chaos be what they're afeared of. Saw it once in Morocco on a little flat-bottom ferry. Me and another feller, Boyle were his name, went aboard with the locals – 'cept Boyle had a Norton motorcycle. Snappy thing, that bike, and didn't he just decide to rev her up for the gents sat there in their djellabas." He shook his head and smiled at the memory. "Now the thing about djellabas, see, is that they be a fine garment for both yer hot weather and yer cold on account of their bein' long and loose, and they be great protection when the wind blows the sand off the desert, which it does aplenty. But they be not so great when a body's hunkered down in a leaky ferry with ten other djellaba-wearing fellas and two sun-burned Englishmen, one pushin' a Norton and thinkin' to show off by revving her engine, and one of those djellaba-wearing fellas has a goat on a rope. Well, see, the goat's eyeballs were already rollin' at the smell of the machine, and when Boyle gunned the motor didn't that animal try to climb right up and over everyone. The locals were scrambling to catch the goat's rope or get out of the way of its hooves, I'm not sure which, but djellabas were getting snagged on this or that protrusion and feet were caught by the length of the garments and it were just general chaos all round. The goat, in the end, went overboard, and his owner leaped in after him. It were a lucky thing we hadn't left the dock and we were only in three feet of water, or it might have been a worse disaster than it was." Mungo shook his head, and scratched his stubble. Throck, still picturing the flailing goat and a motorcycle on a rickety ferry in Morocco, and thinking, suddenly, of Angus, and Alice's yellow dress, had no chance to comment before Mungo continued. "So there's that, and then there be the fact that no one owns a car over there on the Scillies, so the ticketmaster says. Who knows what the roads'll be like, and he says there be a scarcity of petrol too. Mostly it be a bicycle, horse and wagon kind of place. So, sad as it be, per'aps it be best if ye don't come along to the Scilly Isles after all...." He trailed off, looking guilty, and Throck, fleetingly, wondered if any of this was true. He suspected Mungo was trying to be the resolution to his conflict with Eliza, instead of the cause. If the ferry wouldn't take the bike, then of course he and Eliza could simply resume their original plan. Throck smiled. He was a generous soul, was Mungo Large. Had a man ever had a friend with a bigger heart?

A bell clanged loudly to announce the ferry's imminent departure, and Mungo stuck out his hand, crushing Throck's in a fierce grip. "That's me, then," Mungo said briskly. Throck hoped his watery smile conveyed how thoroughly he would miss this fellow. Words were impossible as something had gathered in his throat. Mungo, perhaps experiencing the same wobble of emotion, turned quickly away to scoop Eliza into an enthusiastic hug. Throck saw him mutter something in her ear that Throck could not hear, and she nodded and squeezed shut her eyes, pressing her cheek to his stubble. Mungo stood there a moment, looking uncertain, then dug into his pack and withdrew a knife – the one he and Eliza had used when they'd shared cooking duties in the Blackdown Hills. The metal of the blade, Throck saw, was smooth and well-oiled and very sharp, and its handle was wrapped in thin strips of leather darkened with age and much use. The blade itself was tucked into a sturdy sheath that Mungo had said was sewn from Canadian buffalo hide. He'd made a trade for the knife with a fellow traveller somewhere, sometime, but he hadn't said for what, and Throck remembered joking that Mungo had perhaps swapped a bottle of Portuguese firewater.

Setting the knife aside, Mungo worked the buckle of the belt he wore, and Throck glanced at Eliza, who looked as puzzled as he felt. What was Mungo doing with the belt and the knife? The ferry bell clanged again, and Mungo pulled the thick piece of leather free of his belt loops and held it up, but not before glancing over his shoulder and reassuring himself that the lineup of passengers to board was quite long, and the ferry would not depart without him.

"See here?" he said, turning the belt over in his palms. "This were given me by a lovely I met in Cordoba. Isabella of Spain...." His face softened for a moment as it always did when he spoke of the women he'd known, and he stroked the decorated leather, recalling things he did not share. "There be a story or two there, but they'll have to wait for another time. Suffice to say that if ye know anything at all of Cordoba, ye'll know the skill of the leatherworkers there be unmatched, and they be famous for their intricate embossing technique. *Guadameci*, they call it." The word rolled off Mungo's tongue as if he were Spanish born, and Throck smiled admiringly. "Isabella wanted to make a belt for me, but as ye can see she did not complete the work before I had to depart Cordoba on a fast horse." He winked and added as an aside, "Jealous husband. Seems to be a pattern."

"But there *are* designs," Eliza pointed out, and Throck peered to see crudely fashioned motifs, pictures, symbols and sometimes words alongside the more obviously proficient workmanship.

Mungo nodded. "Those I've done meself, though not with any hint of the skill of the Cordoban leatherworkers, or *mi querida* Isabella. No, these patterns I carved into the leather as a record of me travels, a pastime when it's been lonely by a campfire, but also a means of enjoyin' me memories. And now I'd like it, Throck, if ye'd take me belt as a token, and continue its decoration. And when we meet again, ye'll have your own stories to share." He placed the belt into Throck's hands, and then turned to Eliza and passed her the knife in its sheath. "Ye're a capable lass, me lovely, and I want ye to have this knife. It's served me well on me travels, and I know ye'll make good use of it. Butcherin' chickens, mayhap, or makin' extra holes in a belt leather to help out a friend." He winked. "Whatever ye do with it, it be me hope ye'll think of old Mungo when ye wield it."

The ferry's bell clanged with an urgency, and Mungo hoisted his pack onto his back. "Celestine, I hope ye're waitin'," he said with a grin, then he gripped the handlebars of the BSA and hopped on, pedaling the bike the short distance to the ferry. As he pushed her up the gangplank he turned back, lifted his hand in a wave and shouted, "Until we meet again!"

Throck and Eliza stood together and watched the RMS *Peninnis* cast her lines and chug away into the harbour. A sob caught in Throck's throat, and he made a noise like he had something stuck there, hoping to disguise it. He was surprised by his mix of feelings: joyed to have met someone like Mungo, disappointed to see the back of him, and overwhelmingly sad because he did not believe for one moment that they would, in fact, meet again.

*

Land's End was anti-climactic, but Throck did not say so to Eliza. It wasn't that the scenery wasn't spectacular; indeed, the vista from the clifftops was raw and beautiful: granite crags and islets and pillars shot through with glittering quartz pressing up through a sea that, on the day Throck and Eliza saw it, was turquoise and moved as if breathing. The rock arch of Enys Dodnan, through which could be seen the islet known as the Armed Knight of Arthurian fame, and beyond that the Longships lighthouse perched on its rocky outcrop, left Throck marveling at both nature's artistry and man's determination to make a bob from it. For only a short distance out of Penzance they'd gotten stuck behind a charabanc that filled the narrow road, and that was itself filled with holiday-makers, four or five to a seat, gloved hands clutching fashionable hats or snatching at scarves that threatened to take flight in the snapping wind, arms slung round shoulders, fingers pointing. On the back and sides of the long maroon-coloured vehicle was painted in block letters 'Land's End Tours'. Throck counted thirty or more passengers, their laughing faces peering cliffside, and at the rear, a few people glanced over the retracted canvas roof, and waved when they spotted Throck and Eliza on the Trusty.

They dogged the charabanc, traversing a stark landscape of boulders and wind-flattened grasses, down one side of a ravine and up the other, the climbs so steep that on occasion Throck worried he might have to push the Trusty, not a happy prospect with Eliza in the sidecar, still unable to hobble very far. The tourists in the bus ahead cheered them on, and if Throck believed in that sort of thing he'd have thought their shouts of encouragement actually helped propel the motorcycle onward and upward, until at last the road ended near a whitewashed stone building alone on a promontory overlooking the sea, hung with a large sign that read 'First and Last Inn.' He sat for a moment looking at the sign, and considering its message, that so much in life was really about perspective.

The charabanc passengers had exited their transport like a swarm of bees, and there was no escaping the group who gathered Throck and Eliza into their midst like children might a couple of lost puppies. "Ooo, you're so cute!" squealed one woman in a fashionable dress and impractical shoes, though whether she meant Throck or Eliza, both dusty and be-goggled, Throck couldn't be sure. "Where ya from?" a gent with the angular accent of an American asked. He grasped Throck's hand and shook it, pressing a business card into his palm, but didn't pause to hear the answer.

The inn was expecting the tour group, it appeared, and inside the First and Last Inn a dinner had been prepared, laid out rather casually on tables so the guests helped themselves and then stood about eating. Two more guests seemed neither here nor there, Throck saw, and so he and Eliza gladly partook of the fare: blue and Yarg cheeses, pasties filled with shredded beef, potato, onion and swede, and something someone said with a giggle was stargazy pie, a whimsical custardy concoction of egg, bacon, potatoes and whole sardines with their heads poking up through the crust. Hot tea followed, but by then most of the chattering mass had moved outside to explore the rocky terrain of Land's End, with the charabanc driver as their tour guide. Throck and Eliza followed, Throck holding fast to Eliza's elbow. They listened as the uniformed driver spoke his piece to the assembled group, droningly informing them that Land's End was the most westerly point of mainland Cornwall and England, mentioning the sorts of granite present in the area, and sharing something of Land's End's smuggling past. Throck found the lesson mildly interesting, and he listened politely, but he noted that most of the crowd wandered away to explore the cliffs on their own, ignoring their guide's dry monologue. The man seemed used to this, for he remained in position and continued to make his speech, and perhaps because his audience had thinned to only Throck and Eliza, captive listeners on account of Eliza's lack of mobility, he grew slightly more poetic. The westernmost promontory, he told them, was known as Dr Syntax's Head, named, incredibly, after a character invented in 1809 by the writer William Combe in his comic verse, *The Tour of Dr Syntax in Search of the Picturesque*. The fictional Reverend Dr Syntax, explained the driver, was a cleric, an artist and a schoolmaster, who thought to make his fortune sketching and writing about the countryside where he travelled in search of the perfect scenery. Along the way he found both adventure and mishap when he fell in a lake, was chased by a bull, and had his purse stolen by highwaymen. He was a bit of a fool, the driver said, but well-intentioned, and easily loved. The charabanc driver then squared his shoulders and quoted a verse with volume and dramatic flair fit for the stage. *"Nature, dear nature, is my goddess/ Whether arrayed in rustic bodice/ Or, when the nicest touch of Art/ Doth to her charms new charms impart."*

"Yes, yes, I know this!" cried Throck, suddenly recalling a slim volume he'd found on a shelf at Sowerby Grange. Presumably the book had belonged to Alice's father, for he'd never seen Alice read much of anything that wasn't romantic. He, though, had spirited the book to his room, chuckling over the clever poeticism of the verse, and the comical illustrations of the earnest but quixotic Dr Syntax on his horse Grizzle, the good doctor distinctive with his powdered wig, black garments, long nose and conspicuous chin. Grinning at the charabanc driver, Throck picked up where the fellow had left off. *"But still I, somehow, love her best/ When she's in ruder mantle drest/ I do not mean in shape grotesque/ but when she's truly picturesque!"*

Eliza clapped, the driver bowed, accepting accolades and acknowledging his fellow thespian. Throck, never a performer, blushed, and said "Goodness." Turning away, he searched through the dimming evening light for the rock known as Dr Syntax's Head, and spied, in the distance, that unmistakeable chin jutting eternally forward.

*

The coolness of evening was drawing down, and with the help of a few of the more stalwart passengers the driver unfolded the accordioned roof and the charabanc revellers piled back into the transport for the return journey to Penzance. Not as exuberant as they'd been on the outward leg, they nonetheless called farewells to Throck and Eliza, wishing them godspeed, though no one among them had actually asked where they were headed. Nor had Throck and Eliza discussed what came next after the milestone of Land's End, either in the wider future or immediately. As the lights of the charabanc disappeared down the road, they stood by the Trusty, the hush of a relatively calm searoll moving among the rocks below the cliff. Stars were making pinpricks in a purpling sky, and the inn's white walls greyed in the dusk. Eliza reached for Throck's hand and held it, and Throck was reminded of the day in the Blackdown Hills when she'd done the same. An innocent gesture, was it not?

"What now?" she asked.

Throck thought of what Mungo had said about Land's End being a grand spit at the end of the civilized world. A jumping off point, he'd called it. But if this was that, what was one jumping in to? He stole a sideways glance at Eliza, red hair a-tumble, a smudge of oil from the Trusty on her cheek and the smell of sardines on her breath. She was a warmth next to him, her hand in his comforting, and something glowed inside him when he looked at her. He wondered, if one were to name that something, what it would be called.

They decided, after some discussion, that since they weren't tired they would drive on, so they lit the Trusty's headlamp, used her light to consult their map, then climbed aboard and followed a road that swung inland and up Cornwall's north shore. Land's End faded into the gloaming behind them, just another stop on a journey that wasn't over.

Chapter 32
JUG O' RUM

They were tootling along on what was a relatively good road through the picturesque Malvern Hills, Eliza at the controls of the Trusty. Her wrist and ankle were much improved now, days on from Land's End and with Pascoe Bonny and Loveday Quick a fading memory, and she seemed to be enjoying again piloting the motorcycle. Throck, on the other hand, was feeling rather under the weather since they'd crossed the Bristol Channel on a fishing trawler. Embarrassingly, he'd turned green almost the minute they'd left shore, and had been unable to contain himself, vomiting nigh on ceaselessly as he draped the vessel's side. He blamed the overwhelming stench of fishy things for tipping him over the razor thin edge of self control, and swore in his misery never to slurp another oyster, with or without lemon. Eliza and the boat's crew made murmuring noises of sympathy, but nonetheless stayed as far from him as possible. He was not so far gone that he couldn't smell what they did, or see what they saw: the contents of his stomach churned up and spewed with a horrid miasma, bits floating as blatant as an accusation upon the water before sinking beneath the waves. Why he was so cursed he could not fathom, but he thought for sure it was a judgment of sorts, and he vowed that whatever it was he had not done well in his life, he would improve.

Eliza was kind enough not to make mention of his seasickness upon docking, but the sailors did have to help her unload the motorcycle, and then they carried him, knees a-quiver, to the sidecar. He was embarrassed, but not so much that he did not sag gratefully in their tattooed and whippet-strong arms, nor refuse the cushion Eliza made of a lap rug, the better to rest his head on the wall of the sidecar. He was aware of the Trusty firing up and of the bike's movement, but it was good, solid road beneath her tyres, not undulating seas, and in his mind's eye, if not upon his lips, he smiled.

That was a day or so ago, and he was now much better. He no longer felt like a wrung rag, but more like a man who'd overindulged at his local, chasing stout with bitters. He was well enough to enjoy the scenery: farmland laid out like a patchwork quilt and gentle hills threaded through with cool forests and pebbled streams, but he'd not felt well enough to appreciate the bit of south Wales they'd travelled through, nor had he been much use when they'd made camp along the River Usk under the arch of a long red sandstone bridge. Eliza, as ever, had carried the load uncomplaining, and after they'd settled, pointed out the strange round holes built into the bridge's spans, knowing he would find the feature interesting. In the morning before they set off again, she presented him with a lovely blue blossom – a Spreading Bellflower, or *campanula patula* – which she could not have known was rather rare, and therefore not to be picked. He did not embarrass her by pointing that out, and instead thanked her, tucking the petals between the covers of his copy of *The Illustrated Handbook of English Botany*. It occurred to him that one day he would open the book and find the faded blue of it, and this time would be recalled.

No further mention had been made of Eliza's accusation that he still looked at her like a servant, but Throck had given it some thought, weighed his own inadequacies, and decided that he would make every effort to demonstrate by action and deed that that was not true. And while he felt they were on better footing, one small incident left a worm of unease wriggling in his belly. Perhaps he should have addressed it forthwith, but in his efforts to prove himself a friend rather than a master, he could not bring himself to broach a rather awkward subject, and perhaps ruin what was becoming, in Throck's view, a treasured companionship.

Eliza had disappeared on a hunt for fuel for a cooking fire, after presenting him with the flower, and Throck, glancing about for a place to keep the blossom, spied the corner of the handbook poking out of her voluminous carpet bag. He never went into Eliza's bag, indeed had never had cause to, just as he assumed she did not rifle through his, but it was sat there next to him, and he thought she wouldn't mind if he plucked it free. As he did so, the bag flopped open and there, oddly, amongst all the paraphernalia and stowed odds and sods, he saw a familiar brown leather billfold. It looked out of sorts, a-jumble with Eliza's things, but he recognised it nonetheless. It was the one containing Mrs Isbister's household fund, the one she kept locked away in her strongbox, the one he'd congratulated himself on not taking on the day of his departure. He was certain it was that very wallet because it bore the ostentatious Sowerby family crest.

Eliza had stolen it, that much seemed obvious. But in fairness, they had both been scouting the house for useful items to tuck into their bags – Throck had brought the Trusty's manual, for example, and the extra-large handkerchiefs, and sock braces. Eliza had simply been more resourceful, he told himself, trying to shed the squirm of disquiet he felt as he stared at the billfold. She'd brought all sorts of clever things, pulling items out of her seemingly bottomless bag and saving the day on several occasions. She'd had skin plasters and a tin of Holloway's ointment, headache powder, tea leaves, mint candies, all of which Throck had partaken of gratefully, and she'd had the foresight to bring the extra petrol can, and a tube of grease for the Trusty. Why should she not also have considered their need for funds, and addressed that as she'd done the rest? Perhaps stolen was a poor choice of words, he thought. Yet he frowned.

Eliza had reappeared then, carrying an armload of sticks for their fire, and Throck had quickly flipped closed the carpet bag. Eliza, as usual, had lit the fire and prepared a fine repast from the stores brought forth from her bag, and afterwards Throck curled into his rug, telling himself the knot in his belly was a result of overeating.

*

A day or so later, the billfold shoved to the back of his mind and feeling himself again, Throck was at the controls of the Trusty and enjoying the undulating curve of the road to a village called Little Malvern. They'd fallen back on selecting their route by whimsy, but now when they paused at road signs they also consulted their map. Whimsy was all fine and well, they agreed, but a day of going in circles accomplished little more than wasting time. Although the ultimate *Where* was never discussed, the topic of destination sat like a baby elephant squeezed into the sidecar. Throck, for his part, avoided mention of London or the question of a heading on account of previous unpleasantness, and presumably Eliza too was loathe to begin a like discussion, perhaps for the same reasons. Instead, they meandered, keeping the conversation light and comic, referring frequently to Dr Syntax and his search for the perfect scenery, and with Throck throwing out appropriate witty quotes when he could recall them. They'd steered the Trusty on a long, luxurious coast down a pebbled hill, hemmed by low stone walls overgrown with flowering vegetation, and Throck, inspired, flung out one arm and cried, reciting butchered Syntax, "Along the ground the brambles crawl, and something something tops the wall; the bulrush rises from the sedge, the wild-rose blossoms in the hedge; while flowers of every colour shed a fragrance from their native bed!"

His last words were nearly drowned out by the thrum of a motorcycle overtaking them – a Norton, Throck saw as it flew past, spinning dust and gravel in its wake. Throck, in full theatric pose, nearly lost control of the Trusty. Quickly he returned his flailing hand to the bar, and glanced at Eliza, raising his brows beneath his goggles. What on earth was that fellow thinking, he wondered, but as he thought it, a second motorcycle, a Triumph this time, although not a Trusty, shot by them, a dangerous manoeuvre, Throck felt, given that the fellow passed them on a blind curve in the road. He leaned towards Eliza, snug in the sidecar, and called over the putt-putt of his engine, "Am I driving too slow?" She shrugged in reply, and as she did so yet a third bike blew by them, and now the way was so dusty Throck could hardly see where he was going. Eliza tapped his arm and gestured over her shoulder, and glancing back, he saw at least four more motorcycles on their tail, and noticed what he'd missed before: the bikes had numbers affixed to their handlebars, and the drivers wore identical plaquards on their chests.

"It's a race!" cried Eliza, and he heard the excitement in her voice. They exchanged a grin and Throck bent low over the handlebar, pressing hard on the throttle. The Trusty leaped forward, game for a go, and Eliza ducked low in the sidecar and held onto her hat, even though it was well pinned to her head by her goggles. The bikes behind them stayed in the rear. Over hill and dale they sped, the trees and stone walls that lined the road rushing past in a blur. Despite the added weight of the sidecar the Trusty kept pace and held her spot in the pack, thanks in part, if Throck did say so himself, to his own skilful manoeuvring, giving the drivers in back of him no chance to get by. The thrill of the race was exquisite! The speed, the competition, the noise of the Trusty positively singing her joy, even the occasional bug in his teeth had Throck in high form, and he found himself thinking in the one corner of his brain not completely enthralled with the race that the last time he'd felt such joy was in the balloon gliding over the treetops of Watton Hoo.

All too quickly the winding, hilly road flattened out and crowds appeared, lining the roadway and waving scarves or handkerchiefs and cheering the men on their machines. The village, presumably Little Malvern, lay ahead, and ladies in lawn dresses and men in straw boaters sat upon the top of the wall, and a policeman patrolled, lest some over-exuberant fan jump into the path of the motorcyclists. Throck would have waved, but the race was still on and coming to a close, and it wouldn't do to compromise what would surely be a respectable fourth place showing. And indeed, the end hove in sight with a banner declaring FINISH strung between two poles, and men in tweed coats with pencils in hand jotted numbers as the motorcycles whooshed across the line one by one. Throck, as he'd expected, placed fourth, and, exuberant, he brought the triumphant Trusty to a halt amongst the other race drivers and leapt off to mingle with his fellow sportsmen. Eliza gave him an encouraging wave.

"You there!" came a voice, and Throck turned, wondering at the unfriendly tone. A driver with the number 7 pinned to his jumper was stalking towards him, pulling a leather helmet from a head of sweaty blond hair. From his number Throck recognised him as the driver who'd been right behind him during the race, and whom Throck had out-manoeuvred. The man stopped in front of Throck and poked him in the chest with an aggressive finger. Throck stumbled.

"I say, what do you think you're playing at, you scoundrel?" the fellow said, his thin lips pulled into a snarl. His nostrils were ringed in dust and flared angrily. "This is an official race, and you and your sidecar are an infraction. You might think you beat me, but I'll see you're disqualified, so there. I'll be filing an official complaint with the race officials. Officially."

"Now see here —" Throck began with indignation, but he was interrupted by one of the race organisers who'd stepped onto a platform set up in front of a large white pavilion over which hung a banner that advertised petrol. 'National Benzole' it screamed in blue and gold, and below it a second sign read '1ˢᵗ Annual Malvern Hills Time Trial.'

"Gentlemen!" cried the man, his voice booming through a megaphone. "The 1ˢᵗ Annual Malvern Hills Time Trial organisers would like to thank our sponsor, National Benzole, without whose support this race likely would not have gotten out of the starting gate." The man's cream linen coat flapped in the wind, and he seemed to peacock for a moment, angling towards a brown-suited fellow in front who was peering into a wooden box on a tripod, and cranking a handle that protruded from its side. The man with the megaphone pulled a sheet of paper from his pocket with a flourish, cleared his throat with a hem-hem-hem, and read, again seemingly to the man with the box, "In these days of necessary frugality, every motorcyclist keeps an eye on running costs. National Benzole motor spirits will save you money. Cheaper to buy per gallon, National Benzole gives 20 per cent more mileage, yields greater pulling power on hills, and makes for sweeter running. National Benzole, the home-produced motor spirit."

Eliza sidled up to Throck's side, and said in his ear, "Advertising at a motorcycle race. What will they think of next? And filming it, no less, as if 'twere a moving picture." She gestured towards the brown-suited man, and Throck understood that the box he peered into was in fact a camera for filming moving pictures. Goodness. He looked around at the cluster of motorcycles and the sweaty men who'd piloted them, and saw now that the cameraman had swung his contraption about and was panning slowly across the group that included him and Eliza, and he flushed. Ought he do something? Wave? Tip his hat? Bow? No one else seemed to be reacting in such a way, so he curbed his inclination, although Number 7 who'd been so thunderously angry moments ago now leaned with studied nonchalance against his bike, and lit a pipe. Another driver found something to fiddle with on his machine whilst casting self-conscious glances at the camera, and a third wore a toothy grin, and shuffled sideways, attempting to stay in the camera's eye.

The camera, though, had come to rest on Eliza, and Throck, standing beside her, could see the hostility of the drivers as the photographer and his lens focused on her over them. She played her part, favouring the box with a coy smile and a toss of her tangled hair and dangling her dusty goggles from a finger held aloft, and Throck found himself surprised by her flirtatiousness. Was it the effect of the camera, he wondered, drawing out the performer in her – she had, after all been raised by a music hall singer, and was delightful on the stage. Or was it the presence of so many envious men, and the irresistible urge to thumb her nose at them?

The race organiser in his cream coat was speaking again, his tone somewhat giddy. "Ladies and gentlemen, I believe we have a special treat today in addition to this fine race – Lillian Gish graces our driver's pit!"

Throck glanced around, searching out this Lillian Gish person who was apparently a treat, but instead saw that all eyes, in addition to the lens of the film camera, were turned to Eliza, who was blushing and shaking her head and holding up her hands in protest. Several people came forward with pens and notepads, asking for her autograph, and others seemed to want to touch her coat sleeve. Throck frowned in confusion. Who on earth was Lillian Gish that everyone made such a fuss, and why did they think Eliza was she? He found himself shunted to the back of the crowd until all he could see of Eliza was her hat, and realised with alarm that Number 7 was again at his elbow. This time, though, the fellow's expression was more congenial, and he pulled the pipe from his mouth and stuck out his free hand, presumably for Throck to shake.

"You should've said you were bringing Lillian Gish, old chap. I never would've gotten testy. Crikey, but she looks just as good in person as she does in those films. Never imagined she had red hair, but then film stars are always changing it up, aren't they?" He stuck the pipe back in his mouth and puffed, his eyes trained on Eliza's hat, still bobbing in the midst of her admirers. "Saw her just a couple of months back in *Broken Blossoms* when she played that poor little Lucy Burrows. I don't mind saying it was a tough picture to watch, emotionally speaking – I could've happily thumped the actor that played her abusive father, he made such a convincing job of it. But it was Lucy – Lillian – *her* – that had me near to tears." He nodded in Eliza's direction. "Fine, fine acting, in my opinion, and I see a lot of films."

"Oh?" said Throck, interested only in the information that Lillian Gish was a silent film star, and that Eliza, presumably, looked like her. The crowd certainly seemed to think Lillian and Eliza were one and the same person, for they clamoured about her like bees on honey, and as Throck watched he saw her hat begin to move through the crowd, but away from him, towards the dais where the cream-coated man was beckoning her forward. The man reached out a hand and Eliza must have taken it, for suddenly she popped up on the stage alongside him, and beamed at the admiring crowd. She waved, and they cheered, and Throck thought it odd indeed that rational people, who just moments before had been enjoying a motorcycle race – something worthy of a cheer or two – now seemed to have forgotten all about its winners and losers and were mindlessly exclaiming over a thin red-haired girl they thought was an actress named Lillian Gish. Throck shook his head at the irrationality of it.

"Well, hullo there, England!" Eliza/Lillian called out to the crowd, and Throck was startled to hear a voice that did not belong to Eliza come out of her mouth. This voice had the flat tones of an American accent in a kitten-soft purr, and he was reminded of her performance at the Lesser Plumpton School of the Arts fundraiser when she'd sang Ta-ra-ra-boom-de-ay and showed off red stockings and a black garter. Eliza/Lillian quieted the cheers of the crowd with a deft wave of her hand, and said, "I'm thrilled to have joined in your little race today, although I must say it was not our intent to disrupt anything. I hope you'll excuse my friend and me for our mischief and for jumping in the way we did." The crowd forgave her that transgression, it was obvious, and Throck watched the way she smiled and gestured and spoke, and he realised that she was entertaining them, drawing their attention and holding it, encouraging their adoration. She might not be a film star, he thought, but she most definitely could act the part.

She was coaxed into handing out the trophies to the first, second and third place racers, and the man with the camera filmed her on the podium with those sweaty men, Numbers 2, 5 and 11, her pale face under its paler cloche hat pressed rather intimately between theirs. To close the ceremony the cream-coated man climbed back onstage, thanked everyone for coming, and audaciously, Throck thought, asked Miss Gish if she'd read a final word from the race's sponsor, National Benzole, which, graciously, she did. That should have been the finish, but Throck could see that the cream-coated man and the sweaty winners were loathe to part with their bit of fame in the flesh, and Eliza was having a hard time getting off the stage. Number 2 had become emboldened, and made the forward move of slinging his arm around her shoulders and mugging for the camera that had continued filming, and although Eliza shrugged him off and appeared to reproach him, Number 5 then ducked in and pecked her on the cheek. The still milling crowd seemed to like that, and someone shouted, "Give *us* a kiss, Lil!"

"Now see here," said Throck indignantly from the back of the crowd, though of course no one but Number 7 could hear him. He plunged into the throng, using his elbows to press his way forward, but when he reached the steps and tried to climb onto the dais someone from the pack grasped the seat of his trousers and pulled him back. Everyone laughed and a man stepped on his toe. That humiliation went too far, and Throck lost his temper. He turned and swung blindly, hitting someone in the jaw, and though the strength of his delivery was not great, it was enough to set the fellow off balance, and he reeled into the press of bodies, sparking a bit of a skirmish. Racers, spectators and organisers alike jumped into the fray, with punches thrown at chins, elbows shoved into stomachs, slaps delivered to cheeks, and insults flung with abandon. Throck stood stupidly in its midst, startled by the violence he'd ignited, but then Eliza appeared, grabbing his hand and pulling him through the melee to the Trusty. Number 7, it seemed, had started the bike and turned the machine back towards the road so they might make a quick escape, and he stood alongside it, grinning as Eliza clamoured into the sidecar.

"Miss Gish," he said, extending his hand for Eliza to shake. "I just wanted to say I love your work, and I can't believe I've had the opportunity to meet you!" Throck pressed on the throttle and the bike started to move. He called out a thank you to Number 7, but really, could the fellow not see there was no time for niceties? The rabid crowd had noticed that Lillian Gish had left the winners' circle, and several people had begun to shout and point. Throck feared they might give chase, and then what? Would they run them down? Number 7 was jogging alongside the bike as the Trusty picked up speed, and though Throck wanted to press hard on the throttle and give the Trusty her head Eliza, incredibly, continued with her charade of being Lillian Gish.

"Thank you, Number 7!" she cried, film queen to knave. "I won't forget your help!" Then she pulled a white silk scarf from her carpet bag and tossed it to the running Number 7. It fluttered in the air before the man caught it, and Throck recognised it as *his* scarf, the one he'd worn on that night ride to Lesser Plumpton in what felt ages ago. He wondered how it had come to be in Eliza's bag, for he had certainly not brought it, having deemed it too chilly a garment for motorcycle excursions. There was no mistaking it, for his initials, RTI, were embroidered on one corner, and he saw the dark red of the thread as the fabric blew aloft. Number 7 had stopped running and appeared in Throck's rearview mirror, waving the scarf like a damsel. What would he make of those initials, Throck mused, once he'd done sniffing the silk and dreaming of Lillian Gish? Not for the first time that day Throck marveled at the absurdity fame begot, and was glad to leave its craziness in his dust. He gunned the Trusty and sped off down the road leading out of Little Malvern, heading goodness knew where.

*

They drove too far and waited too long to decide on a place to stop for the night. Throck's fault, for Eliza had dozed off in the sidecar. The day's light was fading when he pulled the Trusty to the side of a wooded road. He had no idea where they were, but the last road sign had said Cookley. They'd seen no other vehicles since leaving the Malvern Hills, and he turned off the Trusty's engine, sitting for a moment in the gloaming and listening to a throaty chorus of frogs. There must be water nearby. Their song made him think of the Whortleberry Wood and its magic at this time of day: the sun gilding spider webs and turning insects silvery, and shadows thrown long and deep, darkening the trail where the sun could not reach. And he and Harold picking their way through it after a day of watching and observing and seeking, the seats of their trousers as wet as their wellingtons. Harold was usually the one to do the talking; Throck didn't mind, Harold after all was the academic, the man with the knowledge and a fellowship at Oxford. Throck considered himself a student, in a way, and grateful for such a learned friend, even if it would have been nice if once in a while Harold had been the one to listen.

Throck climbed off the bike and stretched. As he did so, a frog call he'd not heard before came through the trees – a deep, bass thrum that said to Throck distinctively, "jug-o-rum, jug-o-rum." A thrill skittered through Throck's chest. What sort of frog made a noise like *that*? Throck glanced at Eliza, sleeping on, her goggles riding crooked on her face and her cheek pressed against the padding of the sidecar's seat. Her mouth hung open and she snored, and Throck decided 'twould be neither here nor there if he went and explored for a few minutes, maybe sought out those bellowing amphibians before the sun sank completely. That it would be more practical to set up tarps in the light of day he did not consider. The frogs had his attention. He spied a narrow path leading through the trees and set off, the unmistakeably pungent smells of bracken and moss and all things bog filling his nostrils. He plunged through the foliage, the woods wet with evening's falling dew, slipping on the damp pack of the trail and stumbling now and again over a boulder. The trail seemed to go on a way. Just as he wondered if he ought to give up and turn back, the frog's baritone came again, and Throck had a sudden thought: what if he were to discover a new species?! He pictured Harold's face suffused with admiration and yes, even envy, and imagined his learned friend's compliments. "Well done," Harold might say as he shook Throck's hand. And then, "Impressive discovery, I don't mind saying." And finally, beaming with pride, "I've submitted a proposal to call this one the Throckmorton Frog." Throck could see the ceremony at Oxford, or perhaps the Royal Geographical Society, with a formal dinner afterwards. The Society's fellows in white tie and ladies in ball gowns. Eliza would charm them all, he was sure, and he, R. Throckmorton Isbister, would make a speech and accept accolades with dignified humility.

"Jug-o-rum," called his new friend, and Throck spotted the shimmer of water ahead through the thinning trees. The path opened onto a long pond, thick with grasses and water lilies and bogbean and perky marsh marigolds. It was a bogger's paradise, complete with a thin layer of mist hovering a foot or so off the water and adding to the mysticism Throck always found so enthralling about such places. He nearly skipped as he hurried forward, following the trail to the water's edge, but once there he saw that the path turned neither left nor right as he'd expected, but instead abruptly ended. What was the purpose of a trail that went nowhere? If it was simply a means for some bog-lover such as himself to reach the verge and observe, then where was the perch such a one would wish for, for there was neither bench nor boulder in the vicinity.

The long grasses at the water's edge were well trampled, Throck now saw, and there were grooves in the mud as if someone had dragged a boat into and out of the water here, and did so frequently. Perhaps a fisherman? And yet, what did one fish for in shallow bog water? As he puzzled over this, a crane lifted off from a hidden nest nearby, the flap of its massive wings startling Throck and drawing his attention from the mud and flattened vegetation at his feet, and as he looked up, he saw a small boat moving silently through the mist. It drifted nearer, and Throck, watching silently, remained unnoticed by the person who rode it. The hatted figure stood, feet braced, holding what looked to Throck to be a multi-pronged spear, his gaze intent on the bog water, hunting, it seemed to Throck, though for what he couldn't guess. An ember burned through the clinging fog – the tip of a cigarette, Throck surmised, hanging from the fellow's lip. But its faint glow was eclipsed by the sudden blaze of yellow torchlight, the beam aimed at something in the water. The man in the boat struck with his spear, sending the prongs into the water with a swift jab. Throck cried out as the hunter raised his kill aloft - an enormous frog, bigger than any Throck had seen before, legs kicking fiercely as it jerked on the end of the lance. Throck's only thought was of murder. How could anyone kill so majestic and beautiful a creature, and in such a manner? He felt as if he were witnessing Harold Guppletwill himself being slain, and he was stunned.

The hunter's head swiveled at the noise Throck made and the torch's beam sought him out, but Throck didn't pause for conversation. He turned and began to run back along the path through the woods, tripping over boulders and slipping in mud slime, his heart in his mouth and his breath coming in great gulps. He wanted nothing more than to climb onto the Trusty, start her engine and drive until he could no longer see the poor magnificent frog dancing his last on the end of that lethal pole. But when he staggered out of the wood there were several people standing next to the motorcycle, one with a long spear like the one the man at the pond had wielded, and his heart jumped into his mouth. Why had he thought it alright to leave Eliza alone?

He shouted her name and ran towards the bike, pausing to scoop up a rock lest he need a weapon against these scoundrels. There were four of them, he saw as he approached, two old men – well, Throck's age or thereabouts, if he were honest – a woman, and a boy perhaps a little older than Eliza's George. They regarded Throck with amusement as he drew up short by the bike, his rock raised over his head.

"Hey, now, old fella," one of the men said, holding up a hand as if by his very command he could stop Throck's assault. Throck took exception to being called 'old fella' by a contemporary, but ignored the insult in light of the bigger picture. What on earth was going on here, anyway? He stole a glance at the sidecar and saw Eliza, alive, awake and smiling, her goggles resting in her lap. He lowered his arm, but held onto the rock.

"Throck, these're the Kings. They live hereabouts." She set aside her goggles and moved to climb out of the sidecar. One of the King men offered a hand. "This is Aberfoyle," she said by way of introduction when she had alighted, indicating the man who'd helped her. "And Esau, his brother. And this is Isadora, their sister-in-law. And this young man is…." She paused uncertainly, trying to recall.

"Dangerfield!" the boy declared. He stuck out his hand for Throck to shake. "You can call me Danger."

"Well, well," said Throck. He let the rock drop from his hand, hoping no one noticed as it thudded to the ground. He exchanged handshakes first with the boy, since his hand was inserted there in the space between them, and then with the two men. He nodded to the woman named Isadora but she seemed either shy or unfriendly, and barely glanced at him. She was smoking a pipe, he noticed with a start, and he thought of Mungo. "Delighted, I'm sure," he offered.

"The young miss says you're travellers," said the man named Aberfoyle. He seemed to be the oldest; he had thick dark hair liberally laced with grey, and Throck could see a gold tooth when he spoke. "That makes us brethren, in a sense. We're travellers too, although I imagine ours is a more permanent way of life than yours." He glanced at the motorcycle and its sidecar stuffed with Throck's haversack, Eliza's carpet bag and their other paraphernalia.

"Well, you know," Throck replied noncommittally, not wanting to comment on how permanent their current state of affairs might be. The subject had yet to be broached between them, after all. Were they going to London? Weren't they? If they were, why, and for how long? And what would happen when they got there? Those questions left a sense of unease in Throck's belly, as if he had gas that rumbled but would not expel.

"They've invited us to their camp," Eliza said, smiling.

"Oh-ho," Throck said, the sound a cross between a chuckle and a protest. He tried to catch Eliza's eye but she seemed intent on charming the Kings, her toothy gap on full display.

"I've said we'd be delighted," she continued, still glowing at the foursome as if they were actually royalty, and not merely Kings.

"Oh-ho," Throck repeated. And seeing no choice, needing to point out the danger of strangers, he indicated the spear the man called Esau held. "Forgive my boldness, Mr – er – King, but what is this lethal weapon for?" He drew himself up. "Only…I believe I just witnessed a man commit a murder with exactly such an implement."

Eliza gave a short laugh as if she doubted, yet she moved ever so slightly towards Throck. "Murder?" she repeated.

"Indeed," cried Throck, emboldened. In his mind's eye he watched the man in the flat-bottomed boat stab the enormous frog with his lance, and hold it aloft like a prize. He shuddered, and pointed behind him. "Through those woods I saw it! At the pond! A man in a boat with a spear just like that one."

The words were no sooner out of his mouth than the woman, Isadora, plucked her pipe from her mouth and lurched towards him, her face mere inches from his. "Kek!" she spat, and pressed against his chest with the bowl of her pipe. "You know nothing. You are a silly man." She turned her aggression to Eliza then, stabbing her finger into the hollow of her shoulder. "And you are a stupid girl, to be with such a one! A curse on –"

"Mother!" came a voice, shouting, interrupting, and everyone turned together towards the now dark path through the woods from which Throck had so recently emerged. In the dim light Throck could see a figure, and as the fellow approached Throck recognised him as the man he'd seen in the boat on the waters of the bog. He wore wire spectacles and a battered felt hat that somehow appeared dapper despite its holes, and wellingtons that on any other day Throck would have noted with envy. He held the spear in one hand and several enormous, long-legged beasties of frogs dangled from the other.

"There, d'you see?" cried Throck indignantly, pointing at the fellow's amphibian bounty.

There was a pause, and then everyone except Throck was laughing. Even Isadora King gave a sort of snort that Throck supposed was mirth, though she looked as grim as before. Throck glared at each face in turn, his gaze settling on Eliza.

"Oh Throck," she said, the laughter still in her voice. "They're only frogs."

"Only frogs?" he repeated incredulously. He gaped at her, shocked by her dismissiveness. Surely she of all people understood why he would protest this young man's heinous deed. "Only frogs? No frog is *only* a frog. And these are also giant frogs, Eliza, and unusual. Surely even you can see that!"

She looked so hurt he immediately wished he could take back those last words, but there was no chance, for the frog killer held up a hand as if assuming the role of would-be peacemaker.

"Please, this is a misunderstanding," he said reassuringly. He smiled at Eliza, but to Throck pointedly he said, "We don't want any trouble over these giant frogs. They're unusual, that's a truth, but they're also a problem."

"A tasty problem though," muttered the man named Esau, grinning and looking out from beneath enormous black brows that hung like a shelf over deep-set eyes.

Throck frowned and the younger man sighed.

"Please, Uncle Esau, that's not helping." To Throck he said, "Come to our camp. We'd be honoured to give you some dinner. I'll explain, and perhaps set your mind at ease."

Throck eyed the fellow. It was difficult to see him well in the descending dusk and under the hat, but he appeared to be Eliza's age, or thereabouts, with a slender build and a warmth to his voice that Throck supposed could charm less discerning people. Throck wanted to decline the offer, but Eliza was already accepting on their behalf, and so he instead harrumphed with what sounded even to his own ears like the churlishness of an old grump. The Kings then set off down the rutted road with Eliza in their midst, and Throck climbed onto the Trusty. No one looked back to see if he followed, and he sat a moment, watching them disappear into the darkness. He conceded that it surely felt good to a young woman like Eliza to be on foot for a change after so much sitting and driving, but her choice to walk away instead of riding along with him felt like an admonishment, as if she had taken a side and it was not his.

*

Throck had seen gypsy caravans before on the heath outside Watton Hoo, and these were very similar. Round-topped conveyances with curtained windows and bright paint, there were perhaps eight in a loose formation, and Throck spotted tents of a similar design to the one he and Eliza had built in the Blackdown Hills, only these were larger, and had rough chimneys fashioned to poke through their roofs. Although night had fallen fully by the time Throck followed the Kings and Eliza into camp, children ran and played, shouting and laughing amongst the caravans. Rather than one communal fire, several smaller ones blazed, illuminating this common area. Throck's immediate impression was of a haphazard outdoor parlour: scissor chairs sat with a welcome next to one fire, potted herbs used space on the steps of several caravans, and a plank of wood balanced on stumps made a makeshift table that was stacked with battered tin bowls. Iron tripods straddled a couple of fires, and blackened kettles hung over the flames, emitting steam and good smells. Throck's belly rumbled, but he didn't think long about his stomach, for everyone in the camp – old men and young, girls and women, children of all ages – stopped and stared as the Trusty putted into their midst. No one was smiling.

Several of the older men stood, setting aside whatever task they'd been about, and approached Aberfoyle's group, still with Eliza in their midst, and there was some conversation in low tones, with frequent glances at Throck and the motorcycle. Despite the seemingly solemn discussion, Eliza smiled and nodded and shook hands all around, and Throck wondered if he should dismount and walk over and attempt to introduce himself. They'd gotten off on the wrong foot, of course, on account of the frogs, but Throck still felt an explanation was required on the young man's part, and until he got one that excused such callous behaviour he did not feel overly friendly. So he sat, aloof, and waited.

At length, Aberfoyle and Esau and the rest of the gathered group dispersed, leaving Eliza and the young man conversing alone. He still held the spear, and he still held the frogs. In spite of his disapproval at their slaughter Throck watched the dangle of their long legs with a giddiness that he knew Harold would share, and he longed to inspect the giant amphibians up close – make a loose sketch, scribe a description. His gaze was riveted on those dead but dancing limbs when a woman approached the young man and Eliza and held out a pot, and the fellow, laughingly apologetic, dropped the frogs into the cooking vessel. Throck was instantly galvanized to action.

"No!!" he cried, scrambling to dismount the Trusty. "Wait!" And for the second time that night a silence descended and all eyes in the camp turned towards him. Throck, his face infused with both anger and embarrassment, stumbled across the divide and planted himself, a-tremble, before the frog killer and the woman with pot.

"Throck," said Eliza in a cautioning tone, but Throck brushed off the hand she put on his arm.

"No!" he repeated sternly. His gaze swept the three of them and stopped on the young man. "You said these frogs are a problem. You said I did not understand, and that you would explain. Then do so, if you would be so kind, before you boil them in a pot." He spat the last words out with venom, glaring. At this point he didn't care that people were staring, or that they thought him a fool.

The young man took the pot from the woman, nodding to her to demonstrate, Throck supposed, that he had this crazy oldster in hand. He motioned to Throck to follow him, and led the way between two large caravans to a smaller encampment, this one almost entirely of low, chimneyless bender tents, smaller than those in the main camp. The familiar sight of them softened Throck's opinion of the young man and his ilk not at all. Instead, it reminded him that he'd never asked Eliza how it was she knew the design and build of such a structure, home as they were to gypsy people, and the confirmation of how little he still knew about her only added irascibility to his anger. So too did the fact that Eliza had not come along to hear what the young man had to say in defense of his crime. Whether or not she cared about the frogs she should at least have come as his friend. Throck felt betrayed.

A small fire, no more than a bed of coals really, smouldered next to a low bench, and the frog killer gestured to Throck to sit. He stirred the embers and tossed some wood on the fire, then sat next to Throck, too close, really, for Throck's comfort and, Throck suspected, a tactic, for how did one pin one's opponent with a steely gaze of anger and mistrust when one had to twist one's head at a sharp right angle to see him?

"We've not properly met," the young man said, and held out his hand. "Goliath King."

Throck snorted. Goliath indeed. He sized the fellow up, taking in his slender build and the earnest, astute look in his eye behind wire spectacles, the smooth angle of his jaw that women, admittedly, might find attractive, but which all together were decidedly un-Goliathlike. He'd been misnamed, Throck thought, for he was not overly tall, nor muscular, nor even remotely frightening as one might expect for a man named after a biblical giant. Nevertheless, Throck did the gentlemanly thing and shook his hand.

"Roderick Throckmorton Isbister," he replied, purposely using all three of his names, and stiffening his lip as he threw them out like a challenge. Beat that. He was impatient with niceties. "So what of the frogs?"

Goliath King reached into the bucket and drew forth one of the creatures. He lay the amphibian in the palm of his hand, and Throck noted that the ridiculously long and plump legs banded with grey hung almost to his elbow. The creature had a mottled yellow underbelly and an olive-green dorsal side, and Throck particularly noted the prominent, buggy eyes flecked with gold, and the wide mouth, and he itched to ask for paper and pencil that he might take some notes, perhaps make a quick sketch. Harold would be thrilled, Throck thought, for this, he was sure, was no ordinary specimen. He thought of Harold travelling all the way to the Amazon rain forest to search out a giant toad when a giant frog was right here, near enough to his own back yard.

"It's lovely, really," Goliath said, turning the frog over. "Look at the pattern on its belly. And the brilliant colouring round its mouth. This is a small one. The females are often larger." He held it out to Throck. "Would you like to inspect it?"

It was a tactic to win him over, Throck knew, but he couldn't help his scientific curiosity. Trying to hide his eagerness, he held out his hands and felt the heft of the thing as Goliath placed the frog in his palms. He figured it weighed around a pound. "What do you call it?" he asked, peering in wonder at the thing.

"It's an American Bullfrog," replied Goliath. "A true ogre of the frog world."

"Oh, indeed," said Throck admiringly, turning the dead frog around in his hands, examining all its various surfaces. He noted the exceptionally large eardrum, bigger than its eye, even, and the lack of dorsolateral ridges typically found on a frog's back. One simply couldn't overlook the stab wounds, though, and the bits of innard protruding therefrom, and Throck was reminded that he was angry with this young man. He frowned up at him. "Why on earth would you harm such an incredible specimen of amphibian?"

"Well, some years back I chanced to meet a man of learning at the very bog where you and I – er – came upon one another. He knew everything there was to know about frogs, or so it seemed to me. A right interesting fellow."

Throck peered at Goliath. A man of learning? His curiosity was piqued, and he thought of Harold, vanished all these years. Surely it could not have been him?

Goliath continued. "He told me that these American Bullfrogs had appeared in our English bogs by happenstance – a wealthy man, for instance, thinks it a lark to purchase a few curiosities from America as pets for his goldfish pond. But frogs, as you can imagine, don't stay where you put them, especially champion jumpers like these fellows. Before long they've moved into the local bog. A frog as mighty as this one will soon take over, the man from Oxford said –"

Throck couldn't help but interject. "From Oxford you say?"

"– and so I watched and saw that what he said was true. These frogs eat almost anything – toads, crayfish, snails, small lizards and snakes, but other frogs too until they're pretty much king of the bog, and then they even eat each other," Goliath continued, ignoring Throck's excited interruption.

"Goodness," said Throck, mesmerized.

"The Oxford man said we couldn't get rid of them completely, but we could help the smaller frogs survive by killing as many of the giants as we could before they ruined the bog entirely, and so…." Goliath wagged his spear. "They're not easy hunting, but we do our part for the bog and the little English frogs. Turns out the legs of these great beasties taste good fried in a bit of butter."

"Goodness," Throck repeated. A giant, cannibalistic killer frog. What a find. He was tempted to ask if he might keep the thing, at least until he'd had a chance to make notes and a sketch, but from the corner of his eye he saw the woman with the pot hovering near one of the caravans, wanting to cook the thing, no doubt, before it turned. He reluctantly handed it over to Goliath and asked, "The Oxford researcher. Do you know his name?"

Goliath thought a moment. "Harold something," he said, and Throck's heart gave an excited tha-rump.

"Guppletwill?" he asked eagerly.

Goliath laughed. "Nothing so unusual. Smith-Dubbins, I think, or Dubbins-Smith. Hyphenated, I remember. Smith for sure."

Throck laughed too, disguising his disappointment. Smith for sure.

Chapter 33
A FROG HE WOULD A-WOOING GO

Throck and Eliza had been with the gypsies more than a week. They hadn't discussed staying so long, or staying at all, but somehow it had happened, and in spite of the sour note of his initial introduction to the group, Throck found he was enjoying himself. His only complaint, if he had one, was that Eliza and he had exchanged no more than a few words in all that time, and were never alone. They didn't share a tent, as they'd done on the road, however platonically; Eliza was given a place in one of the caravans – vardos, as they called them – and Throck bunked in a small bender set up just for him. No one, it seemed, thought it even possible they were a couple – which of course they weren't, not in *that* way – but Throck felt slightly put out that the idea hadn't occurred. He was put in mind of their experiences in Portluce, but certainly no one here drew the conclusions Pascoe Bonny and Loveday Quick had, or were remotely reminiscent of those two. In fact everyone, except perhaps the intimidating Isadora King, Goliath's mother, was friendly and welcoming. Isadora, Throck saw as the days passed, was treated with unusual deference by the others, and kept very much to herself, smoking her pipe.

Throck, on the other hand, had a constant companion in young Dangerfield King. Brash, capable, clever beyond his years, the boy put him in mind of George, and Throck rarely stirred but Dangerfield was at his elbow, his chatter incessant. Some might have found such attention annoying, but Throck, being a rather quiet sort himself, appreciated it when others made up for his own poor conversation skills. Dangerfield, or Danger, as the boy insisted on being called, was also a buffer of sorts. Any tension that might have remained from Throck's first encounter with the camp dissipated when Danger was around, and it wasn't long before sidelong glances became open smiles. Danger tugged Throck this way and that, showing off the wooden pipes one woman carved, and the baskets someone else had woven, and which Throck saw were truly fine workmanship. Danger's Uncle Esau, whom Throck had met that first night on the road, was a silversmith and made exquisite, lacelike jewellery. Throck eyed a necklace admiringly, and thought that, were his funds not already running low, he'd have liked to have purchased the piece for Eliza.

Everyone, it appeared, was a craftsman or had a skill, and from Danger Throck learned that the artisans had regular customers who bought their wares, or bartered for things they needed but didn't have. Aberfoyle was good with horses, although after watching the fellow work with the sturdy animals, Throck thought that was most likely an understatement. Danger referred to Aberfoyle's horses as vanners, on account of their ability to pull the heavy caravans, and when Throck worked up the courage to ask Aberfoyle about the beasts he seemed so at ease with, Aberfoyle talked glowingly about the horses' strong necks, powerful hips, and well-muscled hind quarters. Teeth were important, Aberfoyle said, when judging a horse. You could tell from his mouth where he'd been, how he'd been treated. These horses were smaller than a draft horse, he pointed out to Throck's novice gaze, and had an abundance of feathering on their lower legs that Throck thought made them look as if they wore fluffy gaiters, fastened at each knee. Without anyone directing his view Throck admired their full, flowing manes and silky tails, saying as much to Aberfoyle, who puffed up and seemed to take the comment as a personal compliment.

"They're gentle and smart, too, and they'll never quit on you," Aberfoyle told Throck proudly, running his big hand lovingly over the horse's nose. "You'll never find a high-strung vanner." Throck, not overly comfortable with animals of any kind, save frogs and toads and such, thought that a good thing. Aberfoyle, he suspected, was a good salesman, although Danger said he didn't often sell an animal. The horses they had, they used. Instead, his services were sought after as a trainer, a horse medic, and for general equine advice.

Before long, Danger had coaxed Throck into a saddle, with Aberfoyle leading him around the paddock on a tall piebald beauty. Throck was terrified, but after a few circuits decided that riding such a magnificent beast was easily as thrilling as his soar in the hot air balloon all those years ago in Watton Hoo. It wasn't the ride itself that was spectacular, although it was a regal feeling to be so high and still be on the ground. Rather it was the sensation of the horse below him. The warmth, the smooth rocking movement as the animal walked, the sensation of gentle strength that seemed to move from the horse to him, perched in the saddle. He could almost believe they were one, he and this quiet, powerful, beautiful creature. Throck reached out and patted his neck – Cimbalom, Aberfoyle called him –then let out a small, happy whoop and shared a grin with Danger, watching from the fence.

*

Nights were spent around the communal fire. There were other, smaller cooking fires, but this was an obvious gathering place, and after pots and pans were washed and put away and the sun had sunk behind the trees, the bigger fire drew the men with their pipes, the women with theirs, and those with a musical bent brought out fiddles and flutes and a drum that Danger told Throck, when he asked, was an Irish bodhran, made of stretched goat skin and played with a stick. Those nights were exhilarating. Throck, cheeks bright with the heat of the flames and maybe a little Irish whiskey, watched the men, women and children around the fire, toes tapping, hands clapping, some dancing, others singing, and was aware with every fibre of his being that these were happy times. He thought of Mungo, and missed him.

One night, while thinking of his friend and by happenstance sitting next to a leatherworker named Carlotta, Throck showed her his belt, sized to fit with help from Eliza and the knife Mungo had gifted her. He held it to the firelight and pointed out the Spanish embossings, but she recognised the workmanship immediately, exclaiming over the designs and looping patterns.

"Cordovan," she said with admiration, holding the leather in the palm of her hands almost reverently. Throck nodded, pleased that she knew, and couldn't help but notice her big knuckles and blunt nails, the strong fingers of a working woman.

Puzzling, frowning, Carlotta indicated the crude markings on the belt that were Mungo's. "What happened?" she asked Throck sadly.

"It's a record, you see," Throck said, taking the piece back and thumbing it thoughtfully. "The Cordovan part, beautiful as it is, well, that's only part of the story. What came after is told in the rest of the workings, crude though they are."

"Your story?" Carlotta asked, peering at him curiously. She had a mass of wiry grey hair tamed with a braided red leather band, and a frank way about her that Throck liked.

"No, no," Throck said with a self-deprecating laugh. "Goodness, *I* have no story."

"That is not possible," Carlotta replied dismissively. "Everyone has a story." And Throck, if he was honest, knew Mungo would agree with her; would, if he were here, be disappointed that Throck would say such a thing, and had yet to add a decoration to the belt.

Carlotta rummaged in the pocket of her jacket and pulled out a wooden-handled awl. "Here," she said to Throck, passing him the tool. "You can start tonight. Wet the leather first, there in that bucket. Scribe your design, then come and see me. I'll give you a lesson." She patted his shoulder and left him, and Throck stared at the belt for a moment, considering. He got up, soaked the belt in the water Carlotta had indicated, then sat back down and by the light of the fire began, very carefully, to scratch the shape of his Trusty Triumph, sidecar and all, in the leather.

*

Goliath, Throck learned, worked in a steel mill in Birmingham. He and another man who was employed at a dockyard rose early each morning and rode into the city on a cart pulled by one of Aberfoyle's horses. Aberfoyle usually went along, either needing feed for his animals or having to call in at this breeder's stable or at that farm, his services being in high demand. Throck would have liked to have gone along even if just to watch Aberfoyle work, but he wasn't terribly good with early rising, at least not when it was still pitch dark outside, and anyway, Danger had plans for him almost everyday. They repaired a section of Aberfoyle's paddock fence and they built a shelf in one of the caravans (Throck's first chance to see inside, and he noted with interest the compact living quarters strewn with tapestry carpets and woven blankets). When there wasn't a specific job to do or Danger disappeared on an errand Throck tinkered with the Trusty, following the recommendations in the manual penned by the intrepid Phoenix and oiling this or tightening that or checking the other thing. Now and again, he started her up and gave some of the children rides in the sidecar.

He didn't see much of Eliza; she was usually occupied in one way or another just as Throck was. He'd noticed her learning to polish Esau's silverwork, and laughing with some of the women as she helped chop vegetables for a soup, or hack up a rabbit for stewing, showing off Mungo's knife. She looked as happy as Throck felt, and although Throck knew that was a good thing for both of them, there was something melancholy lurking in the back of his mind. He couldn't put a finger on a reason, but he thought it had something to do with their open-ended plans, and that undiscussed topic of endings. One day soon, after all, it would be time to move on, but perhaps because the camp was such a busy, industrious and communal place, Throck found it easy to stay. He wondered, too, if the reason for his unease was the knowledge that broaching the idea of their departure meant talking, again, about what came next, and he couldn't stop thinking of Eliza's words on the Cornish moor about all things coming to an end. They'd been spoken in anger, granted, but sometimes the truth was buried in the strongest emotion.

*

This morning, well before sunrise, Eliza had taken the Trusty. Throck, burrowed like a mole in the blankets inside his bender tent, woke when he heard it start, and recalled that she'd asked if she could borrow it to drive Goliath to work one day. He'd never ridden on a motorcycle, she'd said. Golly, she'd called him, and smiled. Throck had felt a little pang of something unpleasant, and wondered if his chuckle was too hearty, or if she'd noticed that he'd busied himself with his belt etchings as he gave his permission.

All that day he kept an eye on the track that led through the woods to the road that led to the city, and listened for the pop-pop of his machine. He recalled the last time Eliza had borrowed the Trusty, when he thought she'd deserted him. She hadn't been honest then, but she had come back. And though it did occur to him, he doubted she and Goliath would run away, steal the Trusty, leave this large family – leave him. He worked on his belt, tap-tapping with Carlotta's tools on the little bench set up in front of her caravan, pleased to see his designs come to fruition with her tutelage. So far, he'd crafted a respectable likeness of the Trusty and her sidecar, and another less impressive rendering of Mungo that Carlotta, usually so encouraging, had guffawed over, though she'd immediately apologized. "Faces are difficult," she acknowledged, straightening her mouth. "Best you stick to other things." And so he'd followed up with something roughly resembling a charabanc, and the lighthouse at Land's End, and Carlotta nodded approvingly, suggesting which tools could give the best effect.

Goliath's work days were always long, Throck knew, so he didn't expect him to turn up at anything but the usual hour. Eliza, he'd assumed, would simply deliver Goliath to the steel mill in Birmingham and come back forthwith. Goliath would ride home in the cart with Corky, the dock worker, as he usually did. But as the day wore on and Eliza did not return, Throck grew both concerned and not a little miffed. He hoped nothing had gone wrong, or that she hadn't become lost. And if neither of those things had happened, then he wondered crossly why she hadn't made it clear, yet again, that she intended to be away the entire day. He hit one of the stamping tools a little too hard with the mallet and the fishing boat he'd been perfecting suddenly looked more like a tug. He sighed and put down the tools, and Carlotta twisted to look at him, pausing over the saddlebag she was crafting.

"Take a break," she said, sizing him up. She blew at a lock of frizzy grey hair that had escaped the red band and hung across her face. "Danger's gone frog hunting. Why don't you go find him?"

And Throck, feeling rather like a little boy shooed off by his mother, though he and Carlotta were of an age, tidied the bench where he'd been working and headed out of camp. He wasn't sure he wanted to take part in frog hunting. Even though he understood the reason for it, and the threat an invasive species posed, he struggled with the idea of killing at all, and frogs especially. But he did relish the idea of seeing another of the magnificent bullfrogs up close, and considered that he might even have a chance to witness one of them in action – leaping with those splendid legs, or hunting prey. What a thrill that would be! He should have brought note paper, he thought belatedly as he hurried along the road, looking for the path that led through the woods.

Danger was a less stealthy hunter than Goliath had been. Throck heard him before he saw him, singing as he stood in the boat on the water, poling his way among the reeds. Throck grinned to hear the words.

"A frog he would a-wooing go, m-hmm, a frog he would a-wooing go, m-hmm, a frog he would a-wooing go, whether his mother would let him or no, m-hmm!" Danger's voice warbled and cracked as he sang, and just as Throck called out a halloo, Danger tensed, raised the spear he'd held at his side, and thrust it into the water.

"Did you get him?" Throck cried, making an effort to sound enthusiastic.

"Missed him!" Danger called back.

"I hope it wasn't my fault," Throck returned.

"Naw, they're fast. It's pretty hard to get them," Danger replied. He poled the boat across the expanse of water and when he reached the muddy edge, Throck helped steady the boat so Danger could climb out. They hauled the little craft out of the water and tipped it over so they could perch on its bottom.

"Want a sandwich?" Danger asked. He had a leather bag strapped across his torso, and he lifted the flap and pulled out a checkered cloth, spreading it open on his knee.

"I wouldn't eat your lunch," Throck said in protest, but he was a bit peckish, and he could see several slices of dark bread thick with tart pickle and sliced chicken.

"I got more'n I can eat," Danger said, gesturing that Throck should help himself. "I don't have a mum, see, only I've got ten of 'em, and they all feed me like I was theirs alone." He chuckled and took a bite of one of the sandwiches.

"I'm sorry," said Throck. "You and Goliath aren't brothers then?"

"Cousins, I think," replied Danger. "Isadora is Golly's mum. She's our leader. I never knew me mum, but I think maybe she was Isadora's sister. She died when I was very young. It doesn't make me sad, or anything. I mean, I don't even remember her."

Throck and Danger chewed their food in silence, and then Danger said, "I think our Golly's taken with your 'Liza."

Throck choked on the bit of chicken he'd been swallowing, and Danger thumped his back and offered his thermos of tea. When Throck quieted, Danger asked, sympathetically, misunderstanding, "She your daughter?" He didn't wait for an answer, and continued, "She could do worse, you know. Golly's a good sort. He's just a bit troubled after the war, is all. His demons, Isadora calls 'em, though she's sure to spit after. Every now and then a mood comes on him. He gets all broody and dark, he can't sleep or he lashes out at people, but he doesn't mean any harm. He usually disappears for a day or two and comes back right as rain. He'd really never hurt a fly." He slurped his tea and grinned at Throck, who sat, blinking. "That's not exactly true, though, you're thinking, having seen him spear that monster frog. He is damn good at that. You want to give it a try? Maybe you'll get one as big as he got!"

Without waiting for an answer Danger jumped off the boat and stuffed the remaining food and his thermos into his leather sack. Throck, all a-jumble over the information Danger had just shared, followed dumbly along, helping to right the boat and shove it through the mud into the lapping water. Goliath and Eliza. What was he to make of that? And what did it mean for their travels, if indeed Danger was correct? Was Eliza equally enamoured of Golly – Goliath?

"You climb in," directed Danger, "and I'll shove us off. Watch the spear, the prongs are sharp."

They poled about the pond for the better part of the afternoon, but saw no bullfrogs. Nor heard their jug-o-rum call. Throck chalked up their lack of success to Danger's incessant chatter and boisterous song, or, more kindly, the mere luck of the draw, and was secretly glad he wouldn't have to spear one of the devils, and have everyone inspect it to see if it measured up to Goliath's.

*

There were visitors to the camp that evening. Another band of travellers trundled up in vardos, and there were happy greetings all around. Some members of the two groups obviously knew one another, were maybe even relatives, Throck wasn't sure. The newcomers seemed to be a troupe of actors, for Throck saw bold lettering on the side of one caravan that proclaimed them The Quintupple Players, though Throck heard someone call them the Ingram Players. Several of the actors among them wore costumes – the women flowy fairy garb with fake leaves, the men embarrassingly tight hose, and Throck, watching from the sidelines, wondered why actors would travel about in costume. Surely even those thoroughly immersed in their characters put the elaborate dress and skimpy stockings into a trunk between shows, if only to avoid dirt and snags. As he sat idly whittling, distracted by the fact that Eliza and Goliath had still not returned with the Trusty, he overheard the reason for the company's odd attire. Apparently, they'd set up outside a nearby town, intending a three-night stand, the most the troupe could get without purchasing a license to perform. But someone must have lodged a complaint, for on their very first evening, just as the actors had paused for intermission, the local constabulary arrived, whistles blowing and voices raised. The troupe had tried to convince the authorities to let them finish the show, not wishing to disappoint a paid audience, but the police ordered them to move on, and threatened a fine, so they'd had little choice but to pack up to the jeers and catcalls of their jilted audience, and slink away into the night.

That audience's loss was this one's gain, and egged on by their hosts the little band of thespians set up their stage and performed something Throck thought was likely a very condensed and loosely interpreted version of *A Midsummer Night's Dream*, for there was a rather short fellow sporting the head of an ass, and a fairy queen named Titania, who stroked the donkey's snout and asked, "What angel wakes me from my flow'ry bed?" Throck gave a short snort of laughter, not truly paying the act any heed. He'd set aside his aimless whittling and instead was working studiously, with head bent, upon the next scratchings on his belt. This pictograph was to be a frog – the American Bullfrog, specifically, or at least that was his intent. Admittedly, he wasn't making a very good job of it. If he could just see another example of the amphibian; inspect it, make notes, sketch and label a diagram. He sighed, uncertain, Carlotta's awl poised over his rendering, when, through the noise of the actors' final scene and the cheers of the audience, he heard the unmistakeable pop-pop of the Trusty. He stood, belt and awl forgotten, searching the darkness beyond the vardos for the prick of light that would be his bike and her passengers. The circled caravans must have bent the sound, or the bike came on a different track, for he was still peering into the night when the engine shut off and he heard Eliza's voice ring out.

"Julio!"

Throck turned and saw Eliza scrambling from the sidecar that had indeed pulled up on the opposite side of the camp. Her smile was wide, and her cloche hat crushed her hair. Throck took in the less than appealing fact that she'd allowed Goliath to pilot *his* Trusty, and at the same time realised that the little man on stage who'd just pulled free of the donkey's head was none other than Julio Quint, once of the Lesser Plumpton School of the Arts, fellow charadist and purveyor of far too much absinthe. Throck's mouth popped open at the sight of him.

"Eliza Vanson, as I live and breathe!" Julio cried, setting aside the head and embracing her as she reached the elevated stage. "How is it you're here? By God, you're a sight for sore eyes! We thought maybe the elephants got to you, but then we heard you'd run off with Isbister, the Lord of the Grange!"

Throck heard the moniker, and heard Eliza laugh. Was that what they called him? It didn't sound complimentary. And what did Julio mean about elephants? Throck's mood was soured by the lateness of her arrival and by the fact she'd allowed Goliath at the controls of the Trusty, but he also recognised that his ill temper was a common theme of late, and he had vowed to do better. So he stretched his mouth into something he hoped resembled a happy smile and stalked towards the dais where Eliza and Julio were exclaiming over one another as if it had been decades since they'd last crossed paths. To his further annoyance, Goliath King approached at the same moment from the other direction, and Eliza, her back already to Throck, hooked her arm through "Golly's" and made introductions. Throck stood awkwardly behind her, waiting to be acknowledged.

Julio noticed him first, and proof of his skill as an actor was apparent as he batted not so much as an eyelash, despite his earlier derogatory reference, and cried, "Roddy! Delighted to see you, gov. Look at you, living amongst the Roma." He curled his lips, and Throck wondered how it was he hadn't previously thought Julio's smile reptilian. "I say, life on the road appears to agree with you. You *are* on the road, I take it?" He glanced towards the Trusty, parked somewhat haphazardly and rather too near, Throck felt with a spurt of annoyance, one of the smouldering cooking fires.

"I am," Throck replied. "That is, *we* are. Eliza and I. Having a dashing adventure, hither and thither like two madcaps. Time of our lives, you see. Someone ought to write an ode." These words were spoken rather less casually than Throck had intended, and he noticed Eliza cast a puzzled glance his way. Still, he congratulated himself on his restraint, for he'd been about to fasten a title to that non-existent ballad: The Lord of the Grange and the Maid.

Julio, though, went happily along with Throck's boastful claim. "And why not, eh gov? There should be a bit of the wanderer in all of us, and we'd be better off. Myself, I prefer not to stay in one place overlong. Makes for a dull and sometimes perilous existence. Eliza would agree, I'm sure."

But whether Eliza did or didn't was never determined, for Goliath, standing overly close to Eliza in Throck's opinion, posed the next question, and one Throck also wanted an answer to. "How do you come to be here, and as one of the Ingram Players? We know them well here; they come by these parts often, but I'm sure you and I have never met."

"We have not, young man," Julio replied, acknowledging him with a quickly executed bow. "The Ingram Players, I'm sorry to say, are defunct. Arthur Ingram, leader of that esteemed group, has retired to Lancashire. Blackpool. Don't ask me why. Anyway, the Ingrams were looking for someone to fill his admittedly large shoes, and, well, right place, right time and all that."

A man approached just then, sporting shaggy lambswool breeches, elfin ears, and with horns sprouting through his unruly brown curls. Throck, peering, realised the horns were in fact cleverly attached to a sort of headband, and the pointed ears were fashioned from wax. In spite of himself he admired the ingenuity. The fellow's exceedingly hairy chest – in competition, Throck felt, with his breeches – was bare, and Throck knew without asking that this actor's role was that of Puck, mischievous trickster and quick-witted sprite of renown, a principal character in *A Midsummer Night's Dream*.

Julio introduced this Puck as Fred Tupple, and Fred said hello in an oiled baritone. "Old friend, is Fred," said Julio. "My partner in the venture." He indicated one of the vardos, its lettering glittering in the light from the fire. "Hence the name – Quintupple. Rather clever, we do say so ourselves. You know, Quint? Tupple? We've both had fingers in the entertainment business – music halls and, er, whatnot – so between us we figured we could make a go of Arthur's operation. They're a talented bunch, his Ingrams, when it comes to theatre, but there's not a business head among them." He tsk-tsked sadly.

"But what of Lesser Plumpton?" asked Throck, curious. He thought of the fundraiser at the School of the Arts; Puss-in-Boots, and the juggler, and Eliza's grand finale. Julio had seemed invested there.

"And Magnus?" added Eliza, her concern apparent. Throck recalled Julio's willowy companion, sometimes Maggie, sometimes Magnus. Maggie in a long red skirt. Magnus in a turban-style headdress. Or did he have that backwards?

"All good things come to an end," Julio replied flippantly, and with a sniff. "As you know I was never one to put down roots."

Throck pinched his lips, resisting a glance at Eliza. He'd heard that before. If Eliza marked it, she gave no sign, and persisted questioning Julio.

"Magnus stayed in Lesser Plumpton then? I always thought Magnus were there on account of you."

Julio sighed, as if reluctant to discuss Magnus further but pushed to it. "They wanted to go back to London," he said with a shrug. "They never were entirely happy in the Cotswolds, despite its obvious charms. Myself, I rather enjoyed the provincial charms of the rural life, but they did go on so. London, London, Soho. It became rather *ennui*." He rolled his eyes in apparent irritation.

Throck frowned in confusion. They? Wasn't this conversation about Magnus/Maggie? He tried to follow as Julio continued.

"So I took them back to London. And we parted ways. Amicably, in case you're worried for dear Maggie. I'm sure they are deliriously happy to be back in Walworth Road." He turned to Fred in his horns, who stood patiently, his long face remarkably expressionless, Throck thought, for a thespian. "I ran into Fred whilst sowing a few reminiscent oats in Soho, and Fred here knew someone who knew someone who knew Arthur Ingram, and, well, there you have it, the Quintupple Players!"

Eliza waved a hand as if to dismiss Julio's recounting. Her blue eyes glinted in the firelight, pinned as they were to the dwarf, who, it seemed to Throck, was trying to steer the conversation to the here and now rather than the there and then.

"Did you go to Lant Street?" she asked. Her chin tilted slightly upwards, as if she had to brace herself for the answer.

"No point," Julio replied with a shake of his head. He frowned, and his expression, defensive before, softened. "She died, my dear. Several months ago. Keeled over on her way home from the music hall. Not a little intoxicated, which news I know will come as no great surprise. But her imbibing hadn't affected her performance, or at least that's how the story was told to me. She sang her heart out that last night, like she knew it was her dénouement. The world has lost another legend, but rest assured, my dear, she had a capital send-off. They buried her at Nunhead, with a winged angel overlooking her grave."

Eliza's shoulders slumped and Throck, seeing her hurt, wanted to hug her. This was surely about Gin-Gin Geneva, the music hall performer who had been all but a mother to her. He gathered his courage and stepped forward, but Goliath King got there first, seeming not to notice Throck's movement, and took Eliza's hand.

"I should have gone back," Eliza said miserably. "There were things that needed saying. Important things." She gave an angry shake of her head. "And there was me, havin' a lark, traipsing about the countryside." Her eyes flicked over Throck but did not appear to see him, and she shook off Goliath's hand. To Julio she said, her voice strained, "I were going back. I were. Despite – everything. But I waited too long, and now it's too late."

"Never mind, love," Julio said, consoling.

"Who paid for the angel?" she persisted. "For the funeral? She had no-one. She had no money. If it were the elephants, I'll pay back every penny." She spat out the words, and Throck, despite himself, shared a puzzled glance with Goliath. Elephants? Fleetingly, he recalled another odd mention of elephants – at the Cock and Bull pub in Lesser

Plumpton when that Poppy Kellow of the bottle brush hair had threatened Stephen over the Trusty. She'd tossed a calling card onto the table – Throck remembered the stark contrast of the gold elephant against the black background – and then she had reminded Stephen that elephants never forget. A cryptic reference to – what?

"All in good time, my dear," replied Julio. Ignoring both Goliath and Throck standing dumbly by, he drew the distraught Eliza away, past the snap of the campfire and the talk and laughter round its ring and into the shadows of the vardos.

Throck and Goliath looked at one another, and Goliath said, bewildered, "What was that about?"

Throck, who knew only some of the tale but was not feeling inclined to share, replied, "If she wants you to know, she'll tell you." Then he too walked away, feeling a kind of grumpy satisfaction in doing so. The young man, after all, had been driving his Trusty without permission, and seemed to think he had a right to more than he did. But sitting down by the fire, taking up his belt and awl, Throck frowned. There had always been more to Eliza Vanson than met the eye, and it was a sad testament to his own character, he felt sure, that she had not chosen to confide in him her whole story.

Chapter 34
FORTY ELEPHANTS AND A PLUCKED PARROT

Eliza was subdued in the days that followed Julio's news about Gin-Gin. Throck tried to find a moment to speak to her alone but the camp was a busy place, and with the Quintupple Players not inclined, it seemed, to leave anytime soon, it was even more so. There was an upturn in activity by day with the usual quotidian tasks requiring more effort and energy to accommodate the increased population of the camp, and nights around the fire were boisterous, with singing, dancing and a general hub-bub that Throck began to find a bit grating, if he was honest. Children ran hither and thither and there seemed more dogs underfoot than before, and Throck had several close calls with what he would have deemed rowdy behaviour, both animal and child, and being almost knocked off his feet. It further irked him that Eliza was alongside Goliath when that young man wasn't at work at the Birmingham steel mills, and when Goliath was not around, she was in the midst of a gaggle of women, or deep in what appeared to be private conversations with Julio, though he seemed to be doing most of the talking. Throck took his company to Carlotta, who was content to scrape and hammer and tool her leather and keep speech to a minimum. Throck, partly diverted, produced some work that made him think he might even have a bit of a knack for leatherwork, if he did say so himself, though admittedly he had a long way to go before he could be considered a true craftsman in Carlotta's vein.

Leatherwork required bent-over concentration, and when Throck felt the need to stretch his legs he hiked off to the swamp where the bullfrogs lived. He found a cluster of *marasmius rotula*, those delicate little fungi that looked like tiny parachutes, and felt a pang of homesickness. He wished for his wellingtons that he might better poke amongst the reeds and rotten stumps and sedge grass. The regrettable lack of gumboots did not stop him exploring, but the cost was squelching shoes and wet socks and mud-stained trousers, and the need to spend time after each trek scraping the thick mud from his shoes. It would never do as a guest, after all, to track mud into someone's vardo. Not that he expected such an invitation. He had his own little tent, and was quite content with its privacy, but he did note that Eliza was frequently in and out of various caravans with the women, which would indicate that his exclusion was nothing to do with the fact he was an outsider.

If Carlotta noticed the different treatment, she didn't say, but she did one day allow him into her inner sanctum soon after the acting troupe arrived. Throck had been to the frog pond, and upon his return Carlotta wrinkled her nose, set down her tools, put her hands on her hips and told him he smelled bad.

"You're a man in need of a good scrub," she said plainly, and shooed him into her vardo to remove his clothes. Feeling rather awkward, Throck crept inside, stripped to his smalls as ordered, and hid behind the door as he passed the soiled garments to Carlotta who waited on the other side. She washed his clothes and brought him hot water and a bar of soap for his own ablutions, and perhaps owing to his tendency towards naps when a bed was nearby, he promptly fell asleep on the bright weave of her blankets. Much later, he woke with a start, disoriented, and was aghast to see Carlotta's grey locks on the pillow next to him, the woman herself in full slumber and snoring slightly. Appalled, wondering that she had not woken him and sent him off to his own bed, he gathered his washed things (left folded nearby), and crept out of her vardo, the groan of the steps as he descended in his bare feet sounding loud in the quiet. It was near to dawn, he figured, for the sky was a milky grey and a waking thrush chirped, and there was a chill in the air that was a residue of stillness and the moon's bald eye. He slunk between the caravans and was almost to his tent when he noticed a figure some way away, slumped on a bench next to a cold fire. It was Goliath, he saw, his head in his hands, softly moaning. He was rocking slightly, and the moaning was growing in volume, and Throck, alarmed, wondered if he should approach and attempt to comfort the fellow. But the dawn was cool and Throck's naked feet were wet with dew and he shivered, reminded of his embarrassing state of dishabille, clad as he was in nothing but his smalls and clutching the remainder of his wardrobe. He looked as one retreating from a clandestine union, and, considerate of his own and Carlotta's reputation, he paused to tug on his clothes and shoes, deciding that the thing to do was offer some companionship to the distraught Goliath.

It occurred to Throck that this moaning, this obvious turmoil, must be what Danger had referred to when he'd spoken of Goliath's demons. What horrors had this young man experienced, Throck wondered, that they would manifest with such agitation, reducing an otherwise seemingly capable, pleasant and steady young man to a trembling fig. He felt an honest sorrow for the fellow, and not a little ashamed of his own past envy and unfriendliness. His intent benevolent, he tiptoed forward so as not to startle Goliath, but upon reaching his side, he hesitated, for Goliath remained wrapped in his misery and had not noticed him. Throck gave a little hem-hem-hem to no effect, so he leaned forward and said, a little louder, but tentatively, "Hello?"

Goliath's reaction was immediate, and he reared up, bellowing as if prodded by a hot poker. Throck stumbled backwards. Goliath's eyes, Throck saw with alarm, were wild and unfocused, his face twisted into lines, old beyond its years, and before Throck could speak, Goliath ran from the camp, disappearing into the woods.

Throck stood frozen to the spot. What had he done? Should he pursue? Call for help? His throat was tight and his heart was a-thunder in his chest. Goliath's shout had been the desperate scream of an animal defending itself, and had unnerved Throck thoroughly, but feeling responsible, he took a few hesitant steps to follow him. He was stopped by a voice, and Throck turned to see Aberfoyle behind him, a cup of steaming coffee in his hand.

"No sense going after him," Aberfoyle said calmly. He squinted in the direction Goliath had gone and shook his head. "He'll come around. He always does. There's a lot pent up inside that boy since the war. Just got to leave him be." He took a sip from his mug, nodded to Throck, and began walking towards his paddock, but after a several steps, turned back.

"I saw you coming out of Carlotta's caravan," he said.

Throck blanched. Faltering over his words, he hastened to deny anything inappropriate, but Aberfoyle cut off his protests.

"I don't know how things are done where you come from," he said in a measured tone, "but Carlotta's a good woman. And while I don't claim to know what sort of understanding you two have arranged, I'd be remiss if I didn't let you know that among the Kings, an insult to one is an insult to us all."

Throck attempted another protest, certain his face was tomato red, but Aberfoyle tipped his hat with calm politeness, and walked off to tend to his horses.

Discombobulated, Throck stood uncertainly, trying to ascertain if Aberfoyle had meant his words as a threat. Did he truly think Throck had wooed Carlotta like some shameless Lothario, charming her with his rakish good looks and unscrupulous behaviour? He scratched his balding pate and rubbed the growth of hair on his chin and repeated his denial in a mutter, and decided that it was beyond time he and Eliza moved on; this stopover was becoming rather unpleasant, and seemed to be fast growing roots and tethers he'd rather did not take hold. For himself, he'd jump on the Trusty today with a happy toodle-oo, but of Eliza's choice he was not so sure.

*

By the time the rest of the camp stirred, Throck had resolved to approach Eliza with a proposal that they be on their way, and resume their travels. He sat by the cooking fire which Aberfoyle had stoked, a pan of coffee hanging above it, gently bubbling. Throck had partaken of several cups while he waited for the camp to rouse, and, not usually an imbiber of the muddy brew, felt rather like a bowstring drawn overtight. His upper lip quivered. He was aware that, were he pluckable, and should he be plucked, he might very well snap. He waited, watching for Eliza, but she did not appear. Instead, Carlotta came and sat alongside him, a pair of well-worn but still serviceable wellingtons in her hand. Throck looked nervously towards Aberfoyle's paddock, but the fellow was not in evidence.

"These were my son's," Carlotta said without preamble, and with no mention of the night just past, or the fact that he had snuck out of her vardo like a guilty lover before she woke. "He was in the war with Goliath, but he didn't come back. Don't know why I kept 'em, but you might as well have the use of them. Save your shoes. And save me cleaning them."

Throck was touched, although he wanted to protest that she needn't feel she must clean his shoes or anything else of his. But he sensed that if he did, he would insult her, and Aberfoyle's warning rattled. Besides, he liked Carlotta, if he was honest. She was plain-spoken and undemanding, and took things in hand. She was bossy, but not the way Mrs had been. Carlotta's forcefulness felt more like efficiency, where Mrs' had seemed like judgement. Now in the light of day he supposed Carlotta leaving him to sleep in her bed was no more than a kindness. She hadn't wanted to wake him, perhaps, and disturb his slumber. It was his fault he'd fallen asleep there, an intrusion and a liberty he should not have taken. He opened his mouth to say as much, but she was already rising to go about her day, and Throck considered the wellingtons, the presence of which stirred a yearning to visit the frog pond. He knew he ought to find Eliza and broach the subject of their departure, but the boots – and perhaps the coffee – distracted him from his purpose. It was possible, he told himself, if not probable, that were he to suggest they leave, she might hop in the sidecar there and then and say let's go, the way she had on their departure from Sowerby Grange, and what opportunity then for a last pond visit? He wanted to be gone from here, but he also wanted another poke around that fascinating frog habitat and have one more chance at a sighting of the renegade bullfrog, or at the very least to hear again its throaty jug-o-rum call. Of course, it seemed equally possible, and perhaps even probable, that Eliza would choose to stay here, and this would be goodbye. So, opting for avoidance, Throck pulled on Carlotta's son's well-worn wellingtons and tromped out of the camp, the noise of its industry quickly fading, replaced by the thump of the overlarge boots on the track. He noticed a cool dampness in the air and saw that the sky was a flat grey. He could smell rain in the air, a tinny odour he'd never have recognised before this trip, and he thought of his days traipsing about the Whortleberry Woods, and how he'd considered himself a bold soul for those small forays, and well versed in the ways of nature. Natterjack toad aside, those adventures seemed trivial compared to the past weeks spent for the most part on the open road and asleep beneath the stars – well, beneath the flap of a tent actually, but it was undeniably more intrepid than his comfortable bed, overwarm room, and with a jam tart for a bedtime snack. Comparing one to the other, there really was no contest. He hadn't thought about the future in any concrete terms until now, but he knew he could not return to his life as it had been. And if he couldn't go back, where would he go?

Throck turned onto the path that led to the pond, plunging quickly into the forested stillness. Birdsong was audible – a happy trill that soothed the coffee jangle of his nerves. Here was peace. Here was serenity. Perhaps he'd take up the life of a hermit, find a pleasant spot near a pond or stream and build a little cabin. He pictured himself, bearded and grizzled, making welcome the odd visitor that happened upon his abode. He might borrow Mungo's expression, and call them young'un, and if they were curious, and seemed trustworthy, he might show them the Trusty, snug beneath a tarp. They'd ask about his adventures, and he'd show them his belt and regale them with his stories, tell them about a red-haired girl who'd shared them, once upon a time.

Throck stopped. Around him, the birds flitted and tweeted and a damp-smelling breeze lifted the leaves on the trees, but he stood stock still on the path, realizing that he'd just imagined a life for himself without Eliza. Was it a portent? A premonition? Or a sign, maybe, that subconsciously he did not expect this time they were sharing to continue, that he understood the inevitability that at some point their lives would diverge, and they would go in different directions. Throck looked down at his boots, ridiculously large, and pictured himself as that imaginary traveller might see him: a bald-pated oldster of unimpressive stature and with skin that hung slack on his bones. And yet, Throck told himself, drawing up his chin, that same traveller might note the glint of good humour in his somewhat faded gaze, and see that the lines on his face were not drawn by disappointment and disillusion but by sun and laughter, and that when he talked about the red-haired girl, or indeed others he'd met on his travels, his expression grew tender, and he smiled.

Throck chuckled, drawing himself from his reverie. What fancies were these, anyway? Today was today, Eliza was still his travel partner, as far as he knew, and there were giant frogs awaiting. On to the pond, he told himself with a wordless tally ho cry, and stumbled over a rock.

*

Throck pushed through the reeds and rushes to the far end of the pond where he'd seen Goliath going about his lethal work that first day. The overlarge wellingtons sucked the mud and his heels pulled out of them at every step, making the going difficult, but he pressed on, spying at the pond's edge a toppled tree, its long dead crown submerged in the water. It seemed the perfect spot to spy a monster, and he shinnied out on its length, snagging his trousers once or twice on naked branches, until he was perched almost comfortably above the pond. Close below him, fat lily pads and bits of slimy pond scum and lovely swathes of brilliant green duckweed filled the still water. He hunkered there, watching insects come and go on the verdant surface, and so determined was he for the appearance of a bullfrog he did not move even when it began to rain, and the droplets soaked through his clothing. Frogs, like their toady cousins, loved the wet and the rain, he well knew, and though he was developing a cramp in his leg, and his shoulder, wedged against a bare limb, was beginning to ache, he remained poised, thinking of Harold Guppletwill, knowing that a dedicated researcher endures what he must to make a worthwhile discovery. The barrel-throated noise, when it came, was so loud he almost fell from his perch.

But the call – and there were several now, melding into a glorious bullfrog symphony – came from the far end of the pond, well away from his roosting spot, and almost gratefully Throck unbent, shinnying his way back down the trunk of the fallen tree. His excitement was palpable, and though he wanted to run in his clumsy boots towards the sound he willed himself to move stealthily through the long, waving grasses at the pond's edge, for it would never do to be so close and scare the creatures to silence, or worse, into hiding. As he neared their location and the bugling grew louder, he crouched, peering through the foliage, scanning the water for the telltale bulge of their eyes above the surface. His heart lurched as he spied one, then another, then counted a half dozen or more giant frogs hunkered amongst the duckweed. Throck clapped a hand over his mouth to stifle a giggle of delight. Then, like a gift, one of the beasts leapt, its powerful body surely as long as Throck's forearm, and Throck, elated, decided he must get closer. He spied a rocky ledge overhanging the little gathering, but in his floppy wellingtons he doubted he could reach it without sending the whole flotilla of frogs diving for cover, so he sat down, heedless of the wet mud soaking his bottom, and pulled off the boots, abandoning them on the ground. The muck was cold and squelched through his toes as Throck crept forward, but so focused was he on the frogs bobbing in the water, enjoying the rain, that he took no notice.

Up onto the wet ledge he skuttled, wiggling on his belly and inching forward that he might surreptitiously peer over the edge, a veritable voyeur. And there, just below him, one big fellow sat, its golden iridescent eyes peering out over the rain dappled pond, never suspecting that Throck prostrated mere inches above, enthralled. A few feet away one of the creatures let out its jug-o-rum call, and Throck thrilled anew. If only Harold could see this, he thought, and he vowed to write a full accounting that he might at least share his impressions should he and Harold ever meet again. He wished for a net, not to hurt one of the grand beasties, despite what Goliath said about them being invasive, but so he might capture one to feel the weight of it in his palm, see up close the blink of its eye and the circular whorl of its tympanum. The big boy below him shifted slightly in the water, and it occurred to Throck that he might glide away, out of reach. Without a second thought Throck's hand shot forward, closing on the frog's solid body and plucking him out of his watery hidey hole and into the cup of his hand. He'd handled many a frog in his day, and though this one was ridiculously large, the technique, he expected, was the same, and he held the frog's powerful legs just below its body, taking care to squeeze only hard enough to hold onto the creature without inflicting any damage, and it sat there, docile, its huge eyes unblinking, while Throck took careful note of its extraordinarily wide mouth, its long, webbed toes and its white throat. He hefted the frog, guessing its weight at round about a pound, and noted that this fellow had dark bands on its long legs, and its colour was brown rather than the olive green of the one Goliath had let him hold, gutted. The frog in his hand squirmed slightly, and Throck was reminded that this was a living specimen, and though he could poke and prod it indefinitely in pursuit of knowledge it could never withstand such treatment for long, for a frog needed water upon its skin. Reluctantly, resisting the urge to kiss the beast farewell, he loosed his grip, and the frog leapt back into the water, diving away with speed. His frog friends had long disappeared, in fact had abandoned their brother as soon as Throck had snatched him from the water, and the pond was now quiet, frogs no longer in evidence. Throck sighed, and rested his chin upon his clasped hands, the smell of the duckweed and the frog he'd so recently held pungent on his skin. He smiled, and realised that the rain had begun to pelt down, and his clothes were soaked through. He should move, he knew. Rise up, retrieve Carlotta's boots, and make his way back to the camp, but instead he remained prostrate upon the rock, content and happy. The rain plunged into the pond with enough force to dimple the surface, the noise of it so loud Throck doubted he'd hear even the loud call of the bullfrogs had they not deserted him. So heavy was the downpour he could no longer make out the other end of the pond, but through the grey veil of precipitation he saw something – a vague shape floating on the surface of the water, drawing nearer. He scrambled up off his belly and, shielding his eyes against the drip of the rain that ran down his head, made out the same crude little boat he'd first seen Goliath in, hunting frogs, and usually stored overturned at the water's edge. As the craft floated nearer, Throck saw Goliath's hunched figure seated in the bottom of the boat. Throck raised a hand in greeting, but the little vessel slipped past, propelled by the nothing more than the rain on the water, and Throck saw that Goliath's eyes were closed. The boat turned slowly, Goliath its single, unmoving passenger, and began to float towards the other end of the pond, and Throck, watching the placid progress, supposed such a ride was cathartic, and as effective a cure as any for the young man's troubles.

*

The rain let up as Throck trudged back to the camp, but he was embarrassingly wet, and his feet so coated with muck he could never have gotten Carlotta's boots back onto his feet had he tried, so he was not only soaked to the skin but barefoot. Attempting to enter the camp undetected, he avoided the cart track and came through the woods, an unpleasant trek unshod, and with all manner of forest detriment stabbing and sticking to his mud-caked feet, and as it turned out, he need not have bothered. Most people were indoors on account of the rain, and though a dog barked at him as he scurried the last few yards to his tent, he plunged beneath its cover otherwise unnoticed. He peeled off his wet things and reached for his haversack and a change of clothes, but tucked into the buckle of the kitbag was a folded piece of paper, obviously placed there that it should not be easily dislodged. Curious, he pulled it free. It was a scrap torn from a playbill, he saw, advertising *A Midsummer Night's Dream*. On the back there was writing done in a crude hand.

'*I no yor frend. She's an elifant. You otter keep an ey on her.*'

Throck frowned. Was this some kind of joke? The note was obviously about Eliza, but why? And there was that obscure reference to elephants again. He re-read the message, noting the ill-formed handwriting, the atrocious spelling. Who would have come into his tent to leave such a thing? It seemed likely that it was a member of the Quintupple Players, unless one of the Kings had used the troupe's playbill as a red herring, but who among the Kings might have known Eliza before she came here? No one had given any indication of familiarity. Throck shook his head, tucked the paper into his haversack for later reference, and got dressed, wiping the mud from his feet with a handkerchief, all the while mulling over his course of action.

*

Throck considered approaching Eliza and asking her flat out about the accusation on the playbill, but he feared such an approach would seem like an accusation, as if he didn't trust her. He did look for her in the camp once the rain let up, but she was nowhere in evidence; busy in a caravan with some of the other women, no doubt. He returned to Carlotta's vardo, and distracted himself making a sketch of the bullfrog he'd inspected earlier, pencilling its likeness inside the front cover of his botany book where a blank page cried out for decoration. He did a capital job, if he did say so himself, and Carlotta, looking over his shoulder, complimented his effort. Encouraged, he took up his belt again, and worked for the rest of the day on improving the earlier image of the bullfrog he'd chiseled into the leather. Usually, such work was rewarding and soothing, but today he could not get the mysterious note out of his head, and by the time dinner came – a delicious rabbit stew that Throck hardly tasted – he had a headache, and was in rather a foul mood, and had come up with no ideas. He ate the stew, barked at Danger with his incessant chatter, and ignored Carlotta's frown of disapproval. He sat alone, chin in hand and with a scowl on his face.

True to Aberfoyle's prediction, Goliath had returned to camp, apparently unscathed by his tremors, perhaps even unaware of them. Throck didn't see the young man come back, but he was there, across the compound, sitting next to Eliza and engaging her in conversation, at ease and seemingly in good spirits. Throck, intent upon the crowd around the fire, looked for a suspicious person, someone whose gaze, perhaps, met his own with a narrowing, or who watched Eliza with a less than friendly stare.

The hour grew late. Fiddles and bodhrans and pipes came out, and Throck watched without admiration the fleet feet and spinning forms of the dancers. He paid no attention to the words of the songs being sung, though he did make perfunctory note that it was Esau, the silversmith, who owned the rich voice. Danger, annoyingly optimistic, returned and plunked himself down next to Throck, but not even his chatter could draw Throck out of his dark mood, and before long he was again by himself. He studied the faces around the fire, most of whom he did not know from Adam, and was filled with apprehension.

"Penny for your thoughts, gov," said Julio, appearing suddenly and taking a seat on the bench next to him. "You've the look of a plucked parrot."

The remark annoyed Throck further. He turned to Julio and snapped, "If I appear distressed that's because I am." Impulsively, he pulled the torn playbill from his pocket and thrust it at the other man. "Read that – no, not the advertising, the hen scratch on the back."

Julio turned the paper over and peered at the nearly illegible scrawl, and Throck watched his brows lift and his full lips pinch as if tasting something unpleasant. He folded the note and handed it back to Throck, and like the thespian he was, his expression smoothed as though a curtain had been drawn across a stage. "What do you make of it, gov?" he asked, cocking one reddish brow.

Throck was in no mood for games. He scowled at Julio, and said, "What do I make of it? What *am* I to make of it? It's clearly about Eliza, but it's a damned vindictive thing to do. The fact they've used one of your playbills makes me think it must have been written – if you can call it that – by one of your actors. Can you think who?"

Julio scanned the laughing, dancing, drinking crowd with mock seriousness, stroking his tidy pointed beard like a wise man mulling a philosophical conundrum. He did this for several long minutes, causing Throck to steam at the lightness with which he was treating this serious matter. Throck hissed with exasperation, and made to move away from the dwarf but Julio stayed him with a hand on his arm.

"Settle down, gov, and let's have a chat," he said. He patted Throck's forearm as one might a puppy, but Throck chose to ignore the patronizing gesture in anticipation of what Julio might share. He waited, unsmiling.

"How well do you know our young lady?" Julio asked, nodding across the firelit expanse to where Eliza sat, her face animated as she talked with Goliath, and Aberfoyle next to him. She had silver bangles on her arm he'd not seen before. She was popular here; with Goliath, but also with most everyone else, or so it seemed. Aberfoyle treated her with a fatherly fondness, and Esau, though more reserved, had an obvious soft spot for her, and had probably gifted her with the bangles. Throck had even noticed Isadora, who was otherwise so aloof, sitting beside her on the steps of her vardo while Eliza showed her Mungo's knife.

"I know her well enough," Throck said, but heard the defensiveness in his response.

"Do you know where she came from? Before she was your maid, I mean?" Julio persisted. "If she hasn't shared her story, it's not mine to repeat."

"She shared," Throck said, insisting, though he squirmed as he said it. His statement was, after all, only partially factual.

Julio eyed him skeptically. "What has she told you?"

Not to be outdone, Throck eyeballed the dwarf, and countered, "What has she told *you*?"

But his bluff did not work, and Julio sighed. "We'll get nowhere this way, Roddy. Let me just say that *I* have been a part of Eliza's past as you have not. She and I share some history. There are things I know without having to be told, unlike you. If you'd like to benefit from my knowledge, I can – might – oblige, but only if I think it's in the girl's interests. I won't tell tales simply to satisfy a prying mind."

Throck took offense at that, and spluttered indignantly. But the set of Julio's jaw gave him pause, and he considered that, despite the insult such a statement was to Throck himself, it suggested loyalty to Eliza, and was indicative of a friend. He drew a breath and nodded. "I can appreciate that," he conceded. "Eliza has told me that she lived in a part of London known as The Borough – Southwark, I believe, although I don't know the city well myself – and that a music hall performer named Gin-Gin raised her after her mother died. That woman, I believe, is the one you spoke of when you arrived here. She died recently."

"That is correct," Julio confirmed. "The news was upsetting to Eliza; she apparently felt there were things left unsaid between them."

Throck nodded slowly. That much he'd gleaned already. "Eliza said she worked in a munitions factory during the war. And before that, here and there as a maid, or in shops and whatnot. Wherever she could find work. She was responsible for George, she said. Her friend's child."

Other than a single raised brow that gave no indication of the veracity of this information, Julio did not respond. He looked at Throck with a decidedly impassive gaze, waiting for him to go on. Throck considered how best to pose his next questions, and what Julio might feel he could safely answer without betraying Eliza's trust. He thought of the note, and of earlier cryptic references to elephants, but skirting the direct question of what such animals had to do with Eliza, he instead asked, "Why do you think the author of that note suggested that I watch Eliza? Watch her for what? They're inferring that she is untrustworthy, of course, but I do not give such a caution credence unless you, who know Eliza's past, tell me I ought to."

"I would never presume to tell you what you ought, or ought not, to do where Eliza is concerned," Julio replied, maddeningly deadpan, "but I will say emphatically that I, personally, consider her completely trustworthy, most of the time."

"Most of the time?" Throck repeated, puzzled. "What am I to make of that caveat?"

But Julio stood, and gave Throck a slight bow. "You'll excuse me, Roddy. I must find Fred." He tapped Throck's shoulder as if to placate him. "A word of advice, my friend. That note you've got was most likely scribed by one of the Ingram Players – now my own

Quintupples. I admit I do not know them all, some, in fact, not at all. It would appear that someone among them thinks they have something on our Eliza; I will not speculate what, although I can make a pretty good guess. Suffice to say that it might be best if you convince your travel companion that time is nigh to go on your merry way. I'll have a word myself, but Eliza can be a bit headstrong, and sometimes unpredictable. A suggestion to move along may prove more impactful coming from you. True, we Quintupple Players will be departing for other pastures soon, but it might be best for Eliza to make haste while in possession of the whip hand."

Julio started to move off, but Throck caught his sleeve. Julio's warning had alarmed him, and he threw caution to the wind and asked, "What is an elephant?" But Julio merely gave him a wan smile and strode away.

"What kind of elephants you talkin' about?" It was Danger, plunking himself down in Julio's vacated seat. The boy was munching on a sausage, and he had remnants of rabbit stew on his chin. His face appeared orange in the firelight. "There's Asian elephants and then there's African elephants. Asians are the ones you see in the circus on account of them being easier to manage, and smaller…"

Throck ignored him. He frowned into the blur of heat above the fire, and through it, on the other side of the circle, he saw Eliza throw her head back and laugh at something Goliath said. The two of them certainly seemed to enjoy one another's company, he thought. He himself had hardly spent any time at all with her since coming here, though she seemed not to mind, or even to notice. The Kings had all but adopted her. A feeling he did not like but recognised as jealousy gave him a sour taste in his mouth, and he decided to go and look for some water, but just as he started to rise, Danger, who'd continued to talk despite Throck's inattention, said something that gave him pause. He didn't hear the beginning of the sentence, but he distinctly heard Danger say "Elephant and Castle, in The Borough." Throck sat back down and turned to the boy.

"What did you just say about elephants?" he asked, his tone urgent.

"What, African, or Asian?" said Danger. "African're bigger –"

"No, something about The Borough," Throck said, interrupting.

"Oh, yeah, the Forty Elephants," Danger said, nodding sagely. "They're a gang of thieves. They run out of the Elephant and Castle area in Southwark. I heard about 'em from Corky. He works in the dockyard, goes into Birmingham with Golly every morning –"

"I know who Corky is," Throck said impatiently. His heart was a-thunder. He felt he'd stumbled onto something that he wasn't sure he wanted to know, but he could not help asking. "What about this gang?"

Danger continued, nonplussed by Throck's rudeness. "Corky hears all the news on account o' the barges comin' up the canal from London. He knows all sorts. Once he unloaded these big crates marked bicycle parts, but Corky said they were full of contraband liquor and guns. Gang stuff. That's hush-hush, though. Corky could get in big trouble." He stuffed the last of his sausage into his mouth and chewed, continuing his narrative while he macerated the meat. "He told me about the Sabini gang too. Italians. Racecourse rackets, knives and razors, stuff like that."

Throck blanched. Despite his curiosity he could not help but be shocked that a nice boy like Danger could know so much about such, well, dangerous things. It was disconcerting, too, to see Danger's eyes sparkle with excitement, and to hear the obvious thrill in his voice as if he yearned to live up to his name.

"And the Forty Elephants?" he prompted, fearing the answer.

"Yeah, nothing as fearsome as the Sabinis. Ace at stealing from shops and department stores, but no razors or knives, least that's what Corky says. The Elephants are all women, see, and go about in twos and threes, and while one of 'em distracts the sales clerks the others pinch the goods. When things get too hot for 'em in the city they get jobs as maids in country houses and steal stuff – jewelry, money, silverware – first chance they get. It's a pretty good racket. Lucrative, is what Corky called it."

Throck sat, benumbed. He knew he shouldn't believe that Eliza was capable of such behaviour. He knew he should give her the benefit of his doubts – no, he told himself, he *did* give her that. And yet, an ugly worm of suspicion was a-slither in his belly, and he thought of Mrs' unmentioned billfold tucked into Eliza's bag, and his silk scarf, even, fluttering through the air as she'd tossed it to Number 7. He'd been startled that day at the motorcycle race by what a consummate actress she was. Perhaps he himself was nothing but an old fool taken in by a clever girl.

Danger chattered on, warmed to his topic of contraband goods on the canal barges and big city gangs, although it was obvious that he was more enthralled with the cut-throat Sabinis than the Forty Elephants. Throck tuned out the details of razors hidden in boots and criminals that looked at home at Ascot, sporting fur-collared Ulsters and wingtip Oxfords, and kid gloves concealing blood-stained hands. On the other side of the campfire, Eliza and Goliath rose to dance. Sparks impeded his view, and the blur from the heat of the flames warped it, but Throck watched their whirling shapes nonetheless, one possessed of demons, the other perhaps a thief.

Chapter 35
STABBING THE FINGER

In a roundabout way, what happened was Danger's fault, although Throck later surmised he wouldn't have let the night get so carried away if he hadn't already been in a bit of a mood. Throck had taken himself off to tinker with the Trusty, not wanting to stay and participate in the evening's social nature after learning about the Forty Elephants gang from Danger, but that lad being the way he was he sought Throck out, indifferent to his silence, and brought along Corky, the dockworker, who was curious about the motorcycle. Questions about the bike improved Throck's mood, and before long Corky had pulled out a bottle of rather excellent Scottish whisky, confirming what Danger had said about his knack for light-fingering a sample or two of the contraband that arrived on the docks from London. One thing led to another and Throck found himself agreeing to a trip into Birmingham on the bike to visit the pubs in an area of the city called Small Heath, where Corky worked. It wasn't wise, of course, to pilot the Trusty after imbibing, as Throck had learned the night he'd killed Angus the goat, but Danger was game to drive, and Throck, influenced by his fair share of Corky's whisky, thought that a capital idea. So Danger had driven, and Throck had ridden in the sidecar, and Corky had clung somehow to the back of the bike, which, due to Danger's inexperience at operating a motor vehicle of any size or shape, not to mention Throck's inebriated inability to light the headlamp so they might see where they were going, weaved slowly down the road, transporting its unruly cargo. Corky fell off several times, but quickly caught up and jumped back on the Trusty, crying "Wa-roo!"

Corky was a ropey fellow, with a permanently bowed back and limbs, perhaps owing to his occupation as a lifter and carrier. When he walked, he raised each foot high in the air, as if so used to stepping over ropes and other tripping hazards that might lay about a wharf that he could no longer tame his gait. He had a loud laugh that sounded to Throck something like gar-gar-gar, but after a few whiskys Throck didn't hold that against him, or the fact that, owing to several missing teeth, Corky had trouble with the first three consonants of Throck's name, and called him Trock, speaking out of the corner of his mouth. Corky seemed to be pals with the bartender at every establishment in Small Heath and most of the patrons therein, and everyone wanted to buy Corky and his new pal Trock a drink. Admittedly Throck went a little loopy that night, and drank far too much in addition to the whisky he and Corky had already consumed even before leaving camp. Throck was reminded of Mungo and the Portuguese firewater, but that had been a less raucous affair – more a meeting of less than sharp minds than a melee. Danger, despite being too young for pubs, managed to stay within shouting distance, and must have kept an eye out for Throck throughout his night with Corky, although not enough to discourage every bad idea that was proposed. The next day, waking beneath the artificial dawn of a pink silk lampshade in an unfamiliar room, Throck discovered he'd gotten a tattoo on his forearm, and vaguely recalled bellowing for the tattooist to give him a Chimera, that intrepid beast of legend, part lion, part goat, part snake. But the poor fellow hadn't the first clue what a Chimera was, so Throck had settled for a frog. Unfortunately, even on that count his idea and the tattooist's differed, and rather than the impressive, cannibalistic bullfrog Throck had envisioned, he got something that looked more like a squat and lumpy toad. Worse, it throbbed like the dickens.

The flat in which Throck awoke belonged to Corky's sister, Maisy, who worked for a bookie and introduced herself as if it were the most normal thing in the world for her brother to deposit a drunk on her doorstep in the middle of the night. Corky had slept in the spare room, she explained to Throck as she bustled about preparing toast and tea, but he had to work at cock's crow, as she put it, so had been gone these last several hours. Where one might find a cock to crow in the midst of the soot-stained bricks and cobbles of Small Heath with nary a square foot of dirt for a fowl to scratch, Throck only dimly thought to wonder. More pressing was the embarrassment of his presence in this good lady's home, and he slumped in mortified misery on the edge of the sofa where he'd slept, painfully aware of his rumpled clothes and fetid breath and the general sour state of himself. Maisy, though, seemed to take it all in stride. Her flat was as tidy as she was herself, dressed, it seemed, for her own work day, which did in fact turn out to be the case. As she set a cup of piping hot tea and a plate of toast on the table, inviting him to eat, she told him he'd have to let himself out, as she was leaving momentarily for work. There was water in the basin and a towel, she said, and he was welcome to freshen up before he faced the world. Throck mumbled an apology and his appreciation for – well, everything, and as Maisy pinned her hat onto her hair, he had the presence of mind to ask if she knew what had happened to Danger, and to his motorcycle.

"Ah," said Maisy, as if recalling something she'd forgotten, "Dangerfield took hisself home. He's a good lad, is Dangerfield, looks out for our Corky when needs must, if you know what I mean." Throck thought that, yes, he was pretty certain he did. "Corky said to let you know the motorcycle will be at the docks. He put it in a shed there, to keep it safe." And before she left, she explained to Throck how to make his way over to what she called the cut, which Throck surmised was the dock area where Corky worked.

After Maisy departed, Throck ate the breakfast she'd kindly left him and washed his face and felt much improved. Then he let himself out of Maisy's flat, avoiding the curious stares of the people in other flats who opened their doors to peer out as he passed on his way down the hallway and the four flights of stairs. He stood in line for the privy, a dilapidated shed in the building's rear yard, and was told by one of the men waiting that it was residents only, and unless he had "serious business" he should find an alley. Throck mumbled that he was a guest of Maisy on the fourth floor, and when it was his turn over the hole, he made appropriate grunting noises and exited as quickly as he could. Out in the street, the scene did not impress. Tattered bits of laundry hung overhead between the grubby walls of the tenement buildings, while tired-looking women stood about gossiping and old men leaned in doorways and smoked. The odd delivery wagon trundled past, and some children kicked a ball in a rough sort of game that used as a goalpost the dented side of the lone automobile parked outside a closed door. Throck wondered that the owner of the vehicle didn't burst into the street and chase them off, and was thankful that his own Trusty was, hopefully, safely stored out of the reach of these young ruffians. He started up the street, passing the group of gossiping women who stopped their chatter and gave him a bland stare. He nodded politely, but the gesture brought loud, and rather rude, laughter, and Throck put his head down and hurried past. Turn right onto Canal Street, Maisy had said, and he'd find the dockyard in no time.

He could smell the water well before he arrived at the dockyard, and with it, the odour of petrol fumes and rotten fish, and the acrid creosote that coated the timber pilings. It was a busy place; long barges were tied up at the edge of the narrow wharf and a steady stream of men loaded and unloaded cargo, carrying sacks and crates up and down rickety steps into clapboard warehouses. Horse-drawn drays stood nearby, their flatbeds laden with barrels or crates, and a fellow checked the loads and snugged the horses' harnesses. A fire burned in an old barrel, and though several men stood around it, talking and sipping steaming drinks from tin mugs, Throck didn't see the point of it on a summer day, other than to make the air more noxious than it already was. He scanned the bustle for Corky, but he seemed to be nowhere in sight. He wondered where the Trusty might be, and noticed several padlocked sheds, although truth be told it didn't appear that the padlock would do much good given the gaps between the boards on the doors they were intended to secure. He wandered towards one and peered through the crevice only to have a rather vicious-sounding dog attack the other side of the door, all snarls and bark and spit. Throck jumped back, his heart in his throat.

"That's Larry," said a voice, and Throck turned to see Corky grinning behind him. "Larry don't like to be disturbed during the day on account of he works nights. Patrols the yard, see, so's nobody gets any fancy ideas about stealin' from the warehouses." He jerked his head to indicate the building that was rapidly filling with the goods from the barges. "Valuable stuff that." He winked, and Throck supposed he referred to the whisky Throck was unhappily familiar with, and perhaps other things.

"Well, yes, I can see how – er – Larry might be put to good use hereabouts," Throck said weakly, keeping his eye on the flimsy door lest it suddenly give way.

"Yeah, this here's a busy wharf. Connects right up to the Birmingham and Warwick Canal. You can go all the way to London on this here water. Four days to Heat'row. Five if you go further on into Camden Town," Corky told him. "If you've a mind, you can go pretty much in any direction from here. Stafford, if you've an itch to go nort'. Oxford, maybe, if you'd rather go sout'."

"Really," said Throck politely. This was all fine and well, of course, and it was remotely interesting should he ever find himself wishing to take a canal barge somewhere, but for now, he wanted his motorcycle. Corky seemed to catch on.

"You're wantin' your Twisty," he said, and when Throck hesitated, puzzled, Corky added, "Your motorcycle. You *did* have a name for it last night, as I recall. Kept patting her petrol tank and sayin' she was your best friend." Corky waggled his brows as if to imply that such behaviour was a little barmy, but who was he to question where a man might place his loyalties.

"Actually," said Throck instructively, "she's called a Trusty. A Trusty Triumph. The Triumph Motor Company itself bestowed that moniker on account of the machine's reliability." Throck's smile was indulgent, for how would a bloke like Corky be expected to know such a thing, after all? "It's in all the advertisements."

"Right," said Corky, but Throck could hear the disinterest in his voice. He tried again. It seemed important that the Trusty get her due, after all they'd been through together.

"She was in the war, the old girl," Throck said proudly. But then, not wishing to spread misinformation, added, "Well, perhaps not my Trusty, precisely. That is to say, I'm not entirely sure if mine was over there, but it's a fact that many, many others just like her did their part. And mine may have too."

"That's great," Corky said noncommittally. He glanced over his shoulder at a foreman, who had taken note of Corky's chit-chat, and began to walk towards them, scowling. Corky's next words came in a hurry. "I've gotta get back to work, but listen, Trock, about the damage, I know a welder who can fix that little problem with the sidecar, no trouble at all. He'll not charge much, either, leastways not if I sweeten the pot with a bit o' –" Corky paused, glanced again at the foreman, and lowered his voice before finishing his sentence "whisky."

But Throck was still back on the first part about damage. He frowned and took a step towards Corky. From behind the shed door, Larry growled. "What damage?" Throck asked, ignoring the dog. He could hear the shrillness in his voice, and Corky took a step back.

"Gotta go, Trock," Corky said, turning away.

Just then a shrill whistle sounded three sharp, piping blasts, and someone shouted "Strike!" and suddenly the wharf was a flurry of activity as the dock workers dropped the cargo they'd been shunting and began to run from the yard. The foreman yelled, but no one paid the least heed, and Throck, stunned, was buffeted by men sprinting past him toward the street. Corky grabbed his arm and tugged him along, and so Throck ran too, startled and bewildered and disoriented. What about his bike?! His *damaged* bike!

Out in the street it appeared that others, too, had joined in the strike action, and workers were flooding out of factories and yards. Whistles blasted and people yelled, and there was a general fracas that only got worse as uniformed police arrived, plunging into the crowds and lashing out with truncheons. Canal Street was in riot mode, with even women getting in on the action, throwing rocks and bricks and whatever they could get their hands on in support of their menfolk. Corky and Throck hid behind a lorry, but its engine roared to life and it sped away. They ran a bit further and took cover behind an overturned wagon only to be quickly seen by baton-wielding police who shouted and ran towards them. Corky sprinted, and Throck, not knowing what else to do, followed. There were fist fights breaking out here and there, and Throck saw noses crack and spittle fly before Corky ducked into an alley and pulled Throck with him. They paused there, crouched behind a stack of crates. Throck was breathing so hard he could barely speak, and when he reached up to touch the spot where a rock had bounced off his head, his fingers came away bloody.

"Bit o' what for, eh, Trock?" Corky said, grinning. He took off his flat cap and wiped sweat from his forehead. "You never know when these wildcat strikes are gonna happen, but they do seem to happen more and more these days. People're angry, Trock. No doubt about it."

"Angry? About what?" Throck asked between heaving breaths. He wasn't recovering from the exertion as quickly as Corky, who had straightened and now lounged against the sooty wall. Throck remained stooped, his hands on his knees, and it was painfully obvious that all the riding about on the Trusty these last weeks hadn't helped his fitness any. Not that it had been stellar in the first place. And a night of leaping about Small Heath's pubs hadn't done him much good either.

"About what?" Corky repeated incredulously. "Where you been, man, under a rock? Low wages. Long hours. Poor workin' conditions. Unfair layoffs. Safety. Hirin' children instead o' men. Blokes're not going to stand for the way things were before the war."

"Ah," said Throck, and, embarrassed by his ignorance of the working man's difficulties, added, "Those seem like valid grievances, most certainly." He nodded sagely. "Is there no negotiating these issues?"

"Maybe," Corky conceded. "But you gotta show 'em you mean business, too, or they don't take you seriously." Out in the street beyond the shelter of their hiding spot the riot seemed to be settling down. The police whistles no longer sounded, there were fewer shouts and running feet, and the general din was quieting. "Lunchtime," Corky said, grinning. "The strikes usually peter out pretty quick. Men'll be gone home for a bite, and afterwards will likely head to the pub. You and me should get back to camp. If Golly came into work this morning – and he rarely misses – he's out there in the t'rum somewhere. If we start walkin' he'll pick us up with the cart on his way home."

"But – my motorcycle," Throck protested.

"Well, we can't get it now, Trock," Corky said. "Boss'll need the rest o' the day to cool down before anyone ventures back to the yard. And he's got the key." He walked out into the street with his tromping step, and Throck had no alternative but to follow.

*

In fact, it didn't take long for Corky and Throck to get out of the city and back on the road to the camp. Corky hitched a ride with a horse-drawn delivery wagon that took them clopping through Birmingham's streets, and as they rode, Throck asked again about the damage to the Trusty, and hoped it was, as Corky described, a simple enough repair if one knew a welder. To his shame, Throck could only vaguely recall a rather narrow alleyway, and as Corky explained, the motorcycle had attempted a manoeuvre and gotten wedged between two buildings, busting one of the brackets that attached the sidecar. Just who was piloting the machine at the time of the incident was unclear, and even when Throck inquired pointedly, Corky managed an evasive reply.

"Aw, Trock, there's no sense in stabbin' the finger," he said appeasingly. "We was all havin' a little too much fun for our own good, and you did let some o' the lads from the pub have a go on the thing. After all, you had to pay for that tattoo somehow." He chuckled, and the inked amphibian on Throck's arm throbbed. Throck supposed, miserably, that it didn't really matter who had affected the damage to the Trusty. It was done, and would have to be fixed before he and Eliza could carry on. His tattoo, on the other hand, was going to be a scar of a more permanent nature.

*

The city was falling away, the buildings less densely constructed, the streets not quite so narrow, the traffic thinner. On Corky's signal, they hopped off the wagon and Corky called out a ta-ra to the driver who trundled on, waving a hand without even glancing over his shoulder. On foot, Throck and Corky left the dreary city behind, trudging under a grey sky that threatened rain, and Throck realised that he hadn't actually noticed the weather at all whilst travelling the city streets. He supposed there were other things to draw the attention in a metropolis of so many people, even in spite of its drabness: soot-stained buildings, grimy roads, bridges spanning stagnant water, shops advertising wares for every conceived need, to say nothing of the crowds of citizens about their daily bustle. He mentioned his musings to Corky, but that fellow simply shrugged and gave him a look that indicated he didn't think about such things, and why would he? Throck then broached a subject closer to his companion's heart: the gangs of London and what he might know about one called the Forty Elephants.

"Women gangsters, eh, Trock? Who ever thought to hear o' such a thing?" He brought out a cigarette from a pocket, offered it first to Throck who declined, and lit it, puffing determinedly as he walked. "They work mostly in London, o' course. Elephant and Castle area o' Southwark, which way is how they came up with their name, more'n like. And I suppose there must be forty of 'em, give or take." He considered that statement for a moment, as if it was rather an epiphany for him, then went on. "Every now and again, things get a bit hot for 'em on their home turf, and they need to find somewheres else to run their rackets, so a horde of 'em come on the train north fast as you can say Jack Robinson, all dressed up like respectable ladies. Birmingham, Liverpool, Manchester, anyplace big enough to have them fancy department stores, which is their quarry o' choice, so to speak." Corky fell silent for a moment, trudging and puffing on the cigarette that seemed attached to his lower lip, dangling, yet never letting go. He was able to talk from one side of his mouth and smoke from the other, an interesting talent, though not one Throck himself could see desiring to learn. After a while, Corky continued with his narrative. "Once they arrive here and pull a few jobs and the local constabulary gets wind of their presence, well, then I guess that means it's time to go home to London, so to t'row the p'lice off the scent a few girls go to the train station with empty suitcases. When the p'lice nab the ladies at the station they got nothin' on 'em, see, and in the meantime, the actual goods are in a boyfriend's car, speedin' back to London." He shook his head and chuckled. "Clever, y'ask me. And they say it's all the doings of them ladies, meaning they don't work for no men. How's that for modern?"

"What about country houses? I heard they sometimes pose as maids and target the affluent outside the cities," Throck said, despising himself for his suspicions, but asking anyway.

"I heard that too," Corky said, nodding. "It's a pretty successful racket they got going on. Sure, they get caught now and again, but there's forty of 'em. They can't all be in jail at the same time, so on it goes."

"On it goes, indeed," Throck said, his eyes on the ground in front of him. His head was a-muddle, though whether because of last night's drink or the unpleasantness of Corky's information, Throck wasn't sure. Was it really possible that Eliza was a member of this Elephant gang? Had she come to Sowerby Grange as nothing but a fraud, waiting for her chance to rob the place and flee? But what of young George? What of Stephen, her brother? Surely she wouldn't have brought her entire family along if she meant to steal and be gone?

Corky paused to take a last haul on his cigarette and ground it out under his boot, then turned and shaded his eyes. "Heyup, here comes Golly, like I told you." He waved his arm at an approaching dray. Sure enough, when the wagon drew up alongside them, it was Golly under his battered felt hat, and he greeted them as they hopped on, Corky alongside him on the bench, Throck in the back. Corky and Golly talked with enthusiasm about the strike and the events of the day, and Throck, all but forgotten, rode in contemplative silence, worrying over what to do about Eliza and the Forty Elephants.

*

Eliza, as it turned out, had gone with Aberfoyle for the day, and wasn't in camp. Aberfoyle was paying one of his regular visits to a wealthy customer who had an aggressive horse with which Aberfoyle had been working, trying to bring the animal under control.

"Gone whispering," was how Danger described it, attaching himself to Throck as soon as he hopped off the back of Golly's wagon. "Aberfoyle doesn't call it that, but I've seen him do it. It's like magic, it is, the way he talks real quiet to the horse and strokes him just so, once the beast lets him near, o' course. Aberfoyle says there's no magic in it, that it's just a gentleness the horse can sense, but no one else hereabouts seems able to do it, so if that's not magical then I don't know what is."

"Indeed," said Throck, only mildly curious. His own interest ran to a rather different branch of the animal kingdom, the truly fascinating amphibians. There was no whispering to a frog, at least not with any expected alteration of their behaviour.

Despite Danger's late night out in Birmingham playing, if Throck was honest, nursemaid to a couple of men who should have known better, Danger was full of his usual vim and vigour. The joys of youth, Throck thought with a touch of melancholy, although admittedly his mood may have been tempered by the regrettable after-effects of the past night. His disposition was sour, he had a headache, his feet hurt, and he suspected there was a lump on his skull where he'd been pinged by the rock during the strike. Danger pestered him to go to the pond but Throck declined, firmly. In truth he wanted nothing more than to crawl into his bender tent and take a nap, but he had to consider what to do about travelling on, and, though the thought made him squirm, confronting Eliza about the Forty Elephants. He hunkered down on a bench and put his chin in his hand.

"I see you met Picky." It was Carlotta, settling herself beside him and nodding at his tattooed forearm.

"Was that his name?" Throck asked miserably. He regarded his arm. In the sober light of day, the inflamed pictograph was, at best, unimpressive. At a good angle, it was a lumpy toad. Arguably, he admitted to himself, it was a more like a potato with long toes. He sighed, and made a silent promise to swear off tattoo artists after indulging in whisky.

"Friend of Corky's," said Carlotta, as if that explained everything. She rolled up her own sleeve and showed him an impressive rendition of a leatherworking awl, entwined with a briar rose and with her name, Carlotta, in swirling letters beneath. It was obviously the work of a tattooist with skill.

"Did this, er – Picky – do yours?" Throck asked, thinking that surely, between creating the piece of art that Carlotta bore upon her arm and the thing Throck sported, the fellow had suffered some awful calamity that had affected his abilities.

"No," Carlotta replied flatly. "My tattoo was done by an acquaintance of mine, name of George Burchett. Nice gent. Tattooed the king, George did. Or so they say. I knew his wife, Edith, once upon a time in London. George keeps a studio in Waterloo Road not far from Elephant and Castle."

At the mention of London and Elephant and Castle Throck glanced at Carlotta. What did she know, he wondered? But Carlotta was rolling her sleeve down, no apparent concern or motive upon her face. They sat in silence for a few minutes. Then Carlotta said, "You're ready to move on, I think," and Throck looked at her with surprise. How had she gleaned that? Was he so transparent?

"I envy you," she said. She didn't look at him. Instead, she focussed intently on buttoning the sleeve of her shirt. A lock of her grey hair obscured her face, but Throck thought there was sadness there. Was he the cause of her melancholy? He frowned, conflicted over the idea. He liked her, certainly, and assumed she liked him, but in what context?

"We're travellers, you and me. All of us, in fact." She gestured around at the caravans, the bender tents, everything in the camp that was portable, movable, packable. There was nothing that signified permanence. "And yet," she continued, her tone indicating regret, "the Kings have lived on these commons for nigh on a decade. Feels damn near permanent to me. I recall a time when we moved with the seasons; hay harvesting here, fruit picking there, and in the winter months, trundling the sharpening stone through villages. I miss that life…" She trailed off, and Throck glanced at her surreptitiously. Was she implying something?

As if in response, Carlotta shrugged, though she didn't meet his eye. "I recognise the wanderlust, is all. I know it when I see it, and I see it in you." She looked up suddenly, her wrinkled gaze meeting his with candour. "You're leaving. I'll be sorry to see you go." She put out her hand, and he shook it, feeling its arthritic knobs and bumps. "It has been good to know you, Throck Isbister." She nodded across the camp, and Throck, following her gaze, saw Eliza in earnest conversation with Julio. She and Aberfoyle obviously had returned, though he'd not noticed their arrival. "Whether or not the young miss goes with you remains in question, I think. I've seen the way she and Golly look at one another. But you, you are not ready to give up the life of a nomad. Your travels are not done, my friend." She smiled, and leaned in close for a brief moment, and Throck had to restrain himself from reaching to trace the deep lines of her face. That he even considered such an action both shocked and thrilled him, and he wondered when he had become so intrepid? He forced himself to focus on what Carlotta was saying, and heard what he thought was regret in her voice. "You know, last night I touched a spider's web in my caravan. That's a sign that someone you like is moving on. A traveller at heart." She squeezed his hand, which she had not let go of, then stood and walked away.

Throck watched her depart with a lump in his throat. He was surprised to realise that she was right. Not about moving on; that was a given. But about him being a nomad. A traveller at heart. And even if he eventually ended up back at Sowerby Grange, he'd never be the R. Throckmorton Isbister who'd lived there before, shuffling about in old bedroom slippers and envying others' accomplishments. Mungo's face surfaced in his mind, and Throck could hear the deep timbre of his voice as clearly as if he sat here beside him. "I've seen and done things most people could only imagine, and I've learned things that I do believe have made me a better man." Throck's own adventures hadn't been as far-reaching as Mungo's, yet he hoped that in some regard the same was true of him, that, for all his faults and foibles, and no matter where he ended up, he too could feel that his experiences had changed him for the better.

It had been a long day, with a night before longer still. The dinner hour arrived, and Throck accepted a bowl of stew, stifling a large yawn as he took it. The little girl who gave it to him giggled as she darted off. Throck spooned the food into his mouth, barely tasting it, and thought it likely his eyes were great sagging bags. Night fell while he ate, and though there was an unusually lovely sunset Throck hadn't the energy to appreciate it. He finished his stew, glanced without much effort around the busy common area of the camp, but not seeing Eliza anywhere, stumbled gladly to his tent. Tomorrow would be time enough to decide what to do, what to ask, where to go, how to handle her deceit, if that's what it was.

*

Throck woke in the night to find Carlotta's long grey locks fanned across his own surprisingly muscular and bare torso. Despite the darkness he could see her hair quite clearly, a stream that seemed to ripple as his Adonis-like chest rose and fell in calm, even breaths. Two additional things he noted: first, that he was naked, a starkers state of things that he never indulged in outside of a bath, and second, that he was not embarrassed. Rather, he simply acknowledged it along with the fact that the night air was as warm and soft as a caress, and he considered reaching to touch Carlotta's tresses – so lovely – but his limbs felt too wonderfully heavy and immovable. Oddly, his inability to move was not frightening; in fact, it was rather blissful, and he watched with decided unconcern as the strands of grey hair silvered and transformed into an intricately woven spider's web, then darkened and became a thick piece of brown leather, tooled with Cordovan designs.

"Throck," came a voice, whispering urgently, and he surfaced from what he realised with disappointment was a dream. He saw Eliza crouched at the door of his tent, silhouetted in the murky half-light of pre-dawn, and glanced about in embarrassed confusion. Where was Carlotta?

"Throck," Eliza said again, reaching to shake his leg. "We have to go."

"Go?" he mumbled. He sat up and rubbed sleep from his eyes. He fumbled for a blanket to cover his nakedness only to realise he was fully clothed. He frowned in confusion and ran a hand over the stubble on his chin– it had been a while since he'd shaved and his chops felt a bit like the spiny end of a hedgehog – and said again, "Go?"

"Please, Throck," Eliza whispered impatiently. "Bring everything. I'll explain on the way." And she backed out of his tent.

Throck sat for a moment, struggling out of his muddle. Part of him wished to lay down again and sink back into the rather pleasant fiction of that dream, see where it might lead, but as he came more fully awake, he realised that this, of course, was what he'd hoped for: a departure. The fact that it would now include Eliza he could not deny made him happy, in spite of the questions that remained. He began to gather his things which had become strewn around the little space he'd called his own for these last few weeks, folding his rug and finding socks both smelly and clean, and as he opened his haversack to stuff things inside, he stopped short. There, lying in the bottom of the bag, was the braided red leather band that Carlotta always wore to harness her unkempt hair. He drew it out, and slid it slowly, like a caress, across his palm. A single, long strand of grey was caught in the weaving. How had it come to be in his bag unless Carlotta had indeed been here in the night, though she must have been incredibly stealthy in her delivery of this gift, for he thought himself a light sleeper. He recalled her words about touching a spider's web, and how that meant someone you cared about was moving on. Of course, she would believe those sorts of fancies, and who was he to say there wasn't some truth in them, since here he was, as she'd predicted, preparing to leave. He wound the leather around his wrist and tied it snugly. He blinked back a tear, thinking suddenly of Mungo, and how he must have experienced this same feeling of melancholy time and again as friends were met and left. It was the bane, and the beauty, of being a traveller, he supposed. To meet, to love, and to leave.

*

Goliath and Corky sat up on the wagon's bench, Goliath with the reins loose in his hand. A lighted lamp swung from the lantern post, casting long shadows. Goliath wore his battered felt hat pulled low and the lenses of his spectacles glinted. If he and Eliza had discussed what this sudden departure was, or what it meant, neither gave any indication. Eliza was sitting in the back of wagon, her feet dangling over the side, and Throck glanced at her, as wan as the pale cockcrow, and tossed his haversack next to her sturdy carpetbag. He stood for a moment, feeling that he should say something, object, perhaps, to their sneaking off like bandits, like people with something to hide, though one of them, perhaps, did. At the very least they owed the Kings – Carlotta, yes, but young Dangerfield, Aberfoyle, Esau and the rest – a farewell. An expression of gratitude for their hospitality. But Eliza was stony, and would not meet his eye, and, well, they did have two Kings as accomplices in their disappearance. He climbed up onto the hard planked bed of the dray and perched alongside her, and Goliath flicked the reins.

Throck waited for Eliza to share her reason for this sudden, secretive departure, but she remained silent, which was for the best, Throck supposed, for whatever must be said between them must be discussed alone, without Corky or Goliath or anyone else to hear. For miles they bumped along the cart track, and Throck began to consider their destination. They were headed towards Birmingham, that much he could tell. He recognised the track as the one he and Corky had walked, heading home after the dockworkers' strike. Birmingham was where he had to go, of course, since the Trusty was there, and Eliza surely knew he wouldn't go anywhere without the motorcycle. With a start, he recalled the broken sidecar. Corky was supposed to arrange a repair, but that hadn't happened yet. He tapped Corky's back, drawing his attention.

"My motorcycle," he said with concern. "I can't leave without my motorcycle, and the sidecar needs welding. There's no taking a passenger with a broken mount. It simply isn't safe."

"And if you had a day or two to twiddle your thumbs, we'd have her fixed up, as promised," Corky replied, then cocked his head at Eliza. "Eliza here says you've got to go straightaway, though, so it looks like you'll have to make your departure on a different sort of conveyance." He grinned, nodded again towards Eliza as if to indicate that Throck should look to her for explanations, and turned his attention forward. Goliath, Throck noticed, watched this exchange in silence, though Throck thought he seemed grim. Then Goliath, too, presented his back.

"Well?" Throck said sharply to Eliza, alarmed now in case she expected him to abandon his motorcycle.

"Don't worry," she said, her tone equally clipped. "We're not leaving the Trusty behind. We're taking a canal barge to Oxford, if Corky can arrange it, which he says he can, and there's plenty o' room for us and the motorcycle."

Throck had been about to protest the idea of his wounded bike shoved onto a canal barge, for how was he to arrange a repair without the help of Corky, or someone equally knowledgeable in these things? But the mention of Oxford stayed his tongue. He'd always wanted to visit Oxford, Harold Guppletwill's alma mater. Perhaps there'd be a chance for him to poke around in the university's archives, peruse their library? Possibly he could mention the American Bullfrog to someone. Or the natterjack toad. He remained silent, considering. He wished he'd done more drawings.

Eliza laid a hand on his arm, drawing him from his reverie. Her earlier terseness was gone, and she'd seemed to have decided to take a different approach. She had obviously not intuited his receptiveness to the idea of Oxford.

"I want to thank you, Throck," she said, "for trusting me." Her eyes were wide, her expression suppliant. Throck noted the gap between her front teeth that always charmed him. It crossed his mind fleetingly that she might be manipulating him, perhaps had done so from the very beginning.

"You've been more than kind to me," she went on, "and there are things you deserve to know."

Throck harrumphed, but didn't disagree. He *had* been kind, he thought, and indeed she *did* owe him some answers. If she'd been hoping he might let her off the proverbial hook, she was mistaken.

She continued, lowering her voice slightly and glancing over her shoulder at Corky and Goliath, who, Throck thought, appeared intent upon the road. "I promise to explain everything when we're on the boat.

There'll be time aplenty then for us to say what must be said, and to make decisions."

Throck nodded, but his heart gave a nervous jump. Would they part ways? Did he want that, even if she proved to be a thief and a liar? He stole a sideways glance at her, but if she knew he studied her, she did not let on, and after a while she shifted to lean against the slatted wall of the wagon, closing her eyes and appearing to sleep.

Chapter 36
DASHING AWAY WITH THE SMOOTHING IRON

The dockyard in Small Heath was just coming to life as the cart bearing Throck, Eliza, Goliath and Corky trundled up. There was nothing yet of the bustle Throck had noticed on his previous visit, but one similarity was the cluster of workers around the fire barrel, sipping their morning beverage. The warehouses were still shuttered, and the only dray present was theirs. The air smelled like old muck, and a low mist hung over the still water of the canal. Throck glanced around for Larry, but the guard dog was probably already off duty.

Corky leaped down from the cart and called out a greeting, and one of the men in a patch-pocket jacket and tweed flat cap detached himself from the group round the barrel. He and Corky exchanged mumbled words, and the man's eyes flicked over Throck and Eliza. With a shrug of his shoulders the fellow left the yard, and Corky went over to a long, narrow canal boat roped to the wharf. He stepped aboard, and Throck saw him knock on the closed cabin hatch and duck inside. A short time later Corky reappeared, and catching Throck's inquisitive look, lifted a thumb in the air, indicating he'd been successful, Throck presumed, in securing them a berth on this vessel.

Just then, the Trusty appeared, pushed by the same man who'd left earlier. To his consternation, Throck saw that there was more damage than Corky had reported, for the front wheel skidded along the ground without turning, and appeared to be bent. Scowling, Throck watched as the man and Corky again spoke, and the fellow glanced at Throck from beneath his hat's shadow. Corky then loped over with his ranging gait and told Throck that the man wanted payment for storing the bike. He named a sum which Throck thought excessive, but deciding against a protest which might spur unpleasantness, Throck dug into his haversack and handed over the money. His funds were low, but, as he reminded himself with a grimace, there was more in the Sowerby purse, assuming either Eliza admitted possession of it, or Throck challenged her to hand it over. It was a conversation Throck was not anticipating with any joy.

While the transaction over the storage of the Trusty took place, Eliza and Goliath said goodbye. Throck did not openly watch, but from the corner of his eye he saw Goliath take her hand, and Eliza look at the ground. Throck couldn't hear what was said, and neither looked happy as they parted, each with an identical frozen smile. Throck took the opportunity make his own farewells, and shook Corky's hand first.

"Front wheel's bent," Throck said, unable to resist mentioning the additional damage.

"Don't know nothin' about that, Trock," Corky replied with a shrug. He nodded in the direction the patch-pocketed man had gone, and said, "You might try takin' it up with Donald, but can't say for sure what his reaction'd be."

Throck pressed his lips together and nodded. Some things you had to let lie. He pressed Corky's hand and moved on to Goliath.

"Please convey our thanks to everyone," he said, surprised to feel a lump of something akin to sadness in his throat. Goliath nodded solemnly. "Tell young Danger that I would have liked to have said a proper goodbye, but, well," he shrugged and smiled, but suspected it appeared more like a grimace.

"And – and thank Carlotta, if you don't mind," he continued, suffering through an obvious blush, "for her generosity in teaching me about – er – leatherwork and whatnot. And Aberfoyle. A pleasure to have met him, really. Such a surprising fellow. His gift with horses is a true talent. Unlike anything I've ever seen, or even heard of. Horse whispering, my goodness. And Esau, of course. His silversmithing – silversmithery? – is quite exquisite. I had hoped to make a purchase –"

Eliza tugged his sleeve. "Throck, you're babbling," she said gently.

Throck looked around with embarrassment. He had been, he supposed, but his words had sufficed to add some levity to an otherwise morose leave-taking, and now everyone was smiling. More labourers were arriving and the yard was beginning to bustle, and Corky moved off toward his crew, raising a hand in farewell. Goliath mumbled something about being late for work, and climbed onto the cart's bench. With a single backward glance at Eliza, he flicked the reins and set off. Eliza made a small hiccupping sound that might have been a sob, but Throck, in what he considered gentlemanly fashion, pretended not to hear. He hefted his bag and she hers, and together they turned toward the wooden craft waiting at the wharf.

*

The narrowboat, as it was called, was, in Throck's estimation, some sixty feet long, and almost incredibly slender, surely no more than seven feet wide. She was painted a non-descript brown, and her heavy canvas, which Throck heard referred to as the cratch cover, kept her cargo dry. She was a working vessel, not built for comfort or leisure, a fact apparent in every oily, plain plank of her, but it also meant that no one blinked an eye when Corky and one of the other dockworkers pushed the Trusty up the loading ramp and manoeuvred her into the cargo area of the boat along with the various crates, barrels and boxes tucked in on every side. Throck had no chance to inspect the bike, but the bent wheel was obvious and he could see how the sidecar listed. He frowned and rubbed the worry lines between his eyebrows that Eliza called his crows' feet. A repair was definitely in order.

As Throck and Eliza climbed aboard, the pilot of the vessel met them on the aft deck, a small platform made even smaller by the intrusion of a long tiller handle. The three stood almost shoulder to shoulder in the tiny space, and Throck took the measure of the fellow who would be their companion for the next several days. He was tall and thick-boned, with a glass eye and one empty jacket sleeve where his right arm should have been. Throck tried not to gawp when the man stuck out his left hand for a shake.

"Boudewijn Kemp, at your service," the man said, lifting his cap off a shiningly bald head. Throck was suddenly proud of his own few remaining tufts. Without missing a beat, the fellow added, "Yep, I know," and he repeated the name, enunciating carefully so that Throck heard Bow-Divine, or near enough. "It's Dutch," said the pilot, and in a distinctly not-Dutch accent, continued, "but me mother was apparently a Lancashire lass. She run off with an Irishman soon as I was born, so they tell me, and me father, who was a sea captain from Rotterdam, raised me up. Took me with him all over the world, he did. A fine sailor. I never wanted much for a mother, seeing as the old man had a sweetheart in every port." He grinned. "Any which ways, a learned passenger on one of our voyages told us that the English equivalent of Boudewijn is Baldwin, which me old man thought was roaringly funny. Must've been a language thing, his first being Dutch. For some reason, he wanted to make sure I spoke English, was taken for English – God knows why – and he insisted on using the English name. I insisted on the original, so here I am, Boudewijn Kemp, a Dutchman in name only, although people call me Baldy on account of my lack of hair. I sometimes wonder if my hair fell out just to make sure the name stuck."

"Well, how do you do, Captain Kemp," Throck said, exchanging a raised brow with Eliza. The upcoming journey might prove interesting with this chatty fellow around. At the very least, Throck's vocal chords would get a rest as he wouldn't be expected to say much.

"Nay, don't call me cap'n. That's a bit ta-ra for us canal boaters. Technically, I *am* a cap'n, as I've been a sailing man in command of me own boat most of me life, or was, until I had a mishap that shaved me arm off nice and neat. Not that that little inconvenience would've stopped me, but while I was recuperating in Shanghai my boat got stolen and I never got her back. Hard to get justice in some of those places, especially when you're a transient English-speaking Dutchman whose papers've been filched along with his boat."

"That's awful," said Eliza. "How did you get home?"

"Well, the beauty of my sort of life – my life then, anyway – was knowing someone everywhere. Recall the mother in every port? I used a connection here and sent a letter there and found a berth on one ship or another, didn't matter the destination, and, oh, ten or so years later arrived back home." He lifted his cap again and scratched his dome. "I use the word loosely, of course, since home is in fact this here vessel. She isn't pretty but she's mine, and she's a damn sight more reliable than most people I know. Beggin' your pardon, miss." He smiled at Eliza, showing long teeth that appeared extraordinarily white against his well-bronzed face.

"Er – Mr Kemp –" Throck began.

"Don't know that I've ever been called Mr Kemp by anyone," said the pilot, interrupting. "You needn't be so formal."

Throck hesitated. If not Captain or Mr Kemp, what, then? Baldy? Boudewijn? The fellow had put forward both options in a roundabout sort of way, and while Throck himself felt somewhat uncomfortable with the sobriquet, he was equally unsure of his ability to correctly pronounce the given. Weighing the choices, he opted for the easier nickname. An abnegation, granted, but there you have it.

"Baldy, then?" he revised, making it a question, and when the man didn't object, Throck plunged on with his original query, thinking better of inquiring about the fellow's absent eyeball. That he'd been forthright about his missing arm, Throck told himself, did not necessarily mean he'd be equally effuse about his glass orb. "Is there a spot we might stow our bags?"

Eliza had been shifting the weight of her substantial Brussels carpet bag, and his own haversack had grown heavy on his shoulder. They'd stood, throughout this exchange, on the small aft deck, and there didn't seem to be anywhere to go but through the hatchway out of which the pilot had come. Throck supposed a nimble person could sneak alongside the canvas cover, but he doubted he was lissom enough to navigate the footing without falling into the water. And, should one manage to pussyfoot one's way to the front of the boat, there did not seem to be much up there, although to avoid displaying his ignorance of all things boat, he did not ask. He thought of Pascoe Bonny, and shuddered, but Baldy Kemp, he noticed with some relief, did not wear wellingtons or a knitted jumper, and this vessel did not smell of fish.

"Well, damn me for a clodpoll. Not used to passengers, especially ladies." Baldy Kemp's grin flashed again. "Right through that hatchway there," he said, indicating the louvered door behind them, "is the living quarters. Sleeps crew if you've got 'em, but on this special occasion it'll be the domain of ladies only. No, don't protest. Pilot's word goes." Eliza had opened her mouth to object, but closed it again at Baldy Kemp's firm insistence. "We men'll kip with the load. Not that I sleep much anyway if I'm single-handing." He paused and grinned, because of course, in one respect, he was always single-handed. Throck smiled back, appreciating the fellow's humour. "Any which ways," Baldy Kemp continued, "sleeping means mooring somewhere, and the longer I'm snoring, the longer it takes to deliver a load, and the longer it takes the less money I make. Not that I'm looking to hoard away great stacks of money; after all, it's a simple life I've got, and it suits me. I don't need much to live on here on me boat, I don't have a family – by choice – and I'm generally a happy man. But I like efficiencies and I'm not a lazy sort. Deliver the load on time, collect the pay, then enjoy a fine meal and a bottle of French wine. Next job." He nodded to indicate that they should go on in, and his admonishment of "watch your step" came a second too late as Throck banged his head on the lintel. Pretending it didn't smart, he proceeded through the hatchway and down a few steps, then held out a hand to assist Eliza.

The canal boat's living quarters were spare but neat, consisting of a coal-burning stove for heat and cooking, and plenty of cupboards that stowed everything from pots and pans and utensils to thin mattresses and blankets. One of the doors opened horizontally, creating a flat surface for a bed, and Eliza exclaimed over it, calling the idea of a cupboard-bed brilliant. Throck thought it more dangerous than clever, wondering how one did not roll off the thing in the night and smack oneself onto the hard planks of the floor.

Behind the back wall of the cabin was another door, and behind that, Baldy explained, was the heart of this old boat, a workhorse Bolinder semi-diesel engine.

"That's the music you can hear," Baldy told them with obvious pride and affection, and although Throck would not have called it music, exactly, he had noticed the loud pup-pup-pup noise of the thing and smelled its exhaust. The sound was something he thought he and Baldy could potentially build a friendship over, for the Bolinder's throb was not unlike the sound the Trusty made, though in a grandfatherly sort of way.

"It's got a fine rhythm," Throck commented with a nod, and Baldy, encouraged, scraped the door open to reveal the machinery beyond. Unmuffled, the Bolinder's chug had volume, and Baldy had to speak loudly and bend toward his guests as he explained, with glowing fondness, the workings of the big engine. Throck didn't understand much of what Baldy said, but he did learn that the pup-pup-pup sound seemed to come, for the most part, from something called the pecker injector, and indeed the thing resembled a woodpecker of sorts, pecking urgently with its mechanical beak as it fed the engine fuel.

"Lubrication's important too," called Baldy over the din, taking up a little oiling can and pumping its lever with his thumb as he dribbled lubricant over various nuts and widgets. "The old girl's got an automatic oiling system for the main bearing, but she's a thirsty wench, and likes her other moving parts to stay slick too." Throck nodded sagely. That was something he could understand, for the Trusty similarly begged a squirt of the oil tin on a regular basis. He said as much to Baldy, and was gratified when the pilot reciprocated a genuine interest in the motorcycle, and for a few minutes they conversed on the joys and sorrows of engines large and small. Throck promised to show him the Trusty and let him listen to her run, and said it was too bad she had a bent wheel and a broken mount on her sidecar, else he'd happily take him for a spin.

All this was said over the noise of the working Bolinder, and Throck felt badly when it was Baldy who noticed Eliza wilting with boredom. The pilot ushered both of them back through the engine room door and shoved it closed, apologizing for what he called his unbridled enthusiasm.

"Not often I have guests, you see, leastways not one with a kindred interest in things mechanical. It's also rare that I have a lady on board, as I mentioned, so you'll forgive an old salt if he's not up to snuff in polite behaviour."

Eliza tried to protest, but Baldy held up his hand and gestured Throck towards the hatchway through which they'd entered a few minutes before. Throck climbed up the steps and went through, remembering to duck, and glanced back as Baldy joined Throck on the narrow aft deck.

"You settle yourself there, young miss," he said to Eliza through the opening. "Stow your bag where you best like it, then just relax. Put your feet up. Have a poke around if you like, I've a few trinkets from me travels in me younger days that might interest you. Throck and I'll manage things out here." He closed the louvered hatchway door. Throck couldn't see beyond Baldy's bulk, but he suspected Eliza neither appreciated being tagged a young miss nor enjoyed being told to relax while he and Baldy got the narrowboat underway. How could he protest, though, without insulting their host? And, if he was completely honest, he was a little nervous about the idea of Eliza left alone with Baldy's trinkets. What if she pinched something, and stowed it in her big carpet bag? The Sowerby wallet, after all, had still not been mentioned. But he chastised himself for the disloyal thought and told himself Eliza was at least due the benefit of the doubt until matters could be clarified, and so, as if to make amends, he said politely, "Eliza's darn capable – er – Baldy –" the name sounded odd on his tongue. "She can drive my motorcycle as well as I can, maybe better, and she's not afraid to get her hands dirty." He smiled, and continued, "She'd like to learn the workings of a canal boat like this one, I'm sure. In fact, she'd likely be a more useful boat's mate than I."

Baldy eyed him skeptically. "That's as may be on a good day, my friend, but have you seen the look on the lass's face? She appears about to crumble, you ask me." He tugged on his chin, and his glass eye glinted in the morning sun. "Something bothering that miss, and no mistake."

Throck frowned. How had he not noticed? Was it their impending conversation, the things she'd promised to tell him? Or was she regretting her decision to leave the Kings – Goliath, more to the point. And yet she'd been the one to come to his tent and wake him in an urgent manner, tell him they had to go.

"Help me snug the cratch cover, Throck, there's a fellow," Baldy said, and, nimble as a goat despite his bigness, scrambled out onto the narrow gunwale that Throck had earlier decided was a spot he could surely never manoeuvre.

"Er – I'm not sure I have the correct footwear…" Throck called lamely. He eyed the murky water, slick with a rainbow of fuel and with a dead fish floating on its side, and felt fairly certain he would fall in.

"You don't need footwear, Throck," Baldy called back. He was out of sight behind the pilothouse, but his voice carried well enough. "Barefoot'll do. C'mon, mate. I really could use a hand. Climb up and over if you don't trust your landlubber feet on the gunwales."

Up and over? Throck wondered what he meant, but then he spied a narrow rung fastened into the wall of the cabin, and he supposed it was a ladder of sorts, providing access to the roof. He stripped off his shoes and socks and rolled up his pant legs and stepped up, and once onto the flat roof of the cabin spied Baldy on the other side, nimbly working to secure the thick canvas cover. Its hem was punched through with brass grommets into which a rope was threaded, and Baldy was hooking each loop of the rope onto a cleat, then moving on to the next one. Beyond him, in the cargo area, sat the Trusty with her bent wheel and limp sidecar, surrounded by wooden crates, sack-cloth bags and iron-hooped barrels.

"Well done, mate," Baldy said, seeing him up on the roof. "Now shinny down to the hold and help me tug this cover forward. It's heavy. I can do it myself if I have to, but I don't have to today, do I?" He flashed Throck his toothy smile and Throck did as he was told, cautiously lowering himself down to the cargo area of the narrowboat, though his shirt slid up and he scraped his belly on a rivet.

"Not really a physical sort, then?" Baldy said, noting his ungainly slither down the side of the cabin. "Not on a rowing team in your salad days, I'm guessing? More a reader than a runner?" He didn't wait for an answer, but indicated the slumped canvas and Throck grasped it, surprised by its weight. How anyone managed the thing on his own Throck couldn't comprehend. But he did his best to heft it, and with Baldy on the other side they slid the tarpaulin along the overhead beam, Baldy pausing to snug its rope onto a cleat. When they were finished, the cratch cover formed a long tent over the cargo, and closed with flaps that kept out the wind and rain, and with space at one end where the two of them, presumably, could sleep when the need arose. Throck looked around with a satisfied smile, and thought he could be comfortable in this nest-like space. It was dim, and warm, and smelled of old canvas and oil. Briefly, he considered trying life as a narrowboat hand.

"Right," said Baldy, holding the flap, and Throck joined him on the foredeck. He blinked in the watery morning light. Behind him, rising just above the long, inverted V of the cratch cover, was the roof of the cabin that housed Eliza and the Bolinder, albeit in separate compartments. The engine's exhaust stack poked through the roof and glinted in the pale sun, and puffed a bit of smoke. Ahead, the morning mist was lifting off the water.

"Time's a-wasting, mate," Baldy said, and stepped deftly off the narrowboat and onto the wharf, then proceeded to unwind the mooring rope from the closest bollard. Throck, despite watching, was unprepared when Baldy tossed the rope, and though Throck caught it in a clumsy fashion, the weight of the thick line nearly knocked him onto his backside. Recovering, he made a neat coil of the rope and placed it on the deck, congratulating himself for having retained at least something of what Pascoe Bonny had told him about tidy ships and obeying one's captain. When he looked up from the task, he realised the wharf had moved – or more correctly, they had moved away from the wharf. Baldy had released the aft mooring line, stepped back aboard, and the narrowboat, with Throck, Eliza and the Trusty passengers all, was underway, heading, presumably, for the Birmingham and Warwick Canal.

*

It was a slow chug. Throck was surprised at just how slowly and, yes, gracefully the narrowboat slipped through the placid water of the cut, as Baldy called the canal. Despite the boat's great length – she was some seventy feet long, according to her captain – he was adept at handling her, guiding her with ease beneath old stone bridges and through a long tunnel, the factories and warehouses of Birmingham proper fading gradually behind them. Baldy stood at the helm, his feet planted well apart, although no raucous waves stirred these waters, threatening the seasickness Throck had experienced on the fishing boat crossing the Bristol Channel. On the narrowboat, floating with a dignified precision, there was hardly a breeze, hardly a wake, and the water was a-dot with swans, geese and ducks that could have given the craft a hard contest. This, in Throck's mind, was water travel at its best.

At Baldy's invitation, he was sitting cross-legged upon the roof of the cabin, feeling rather like a roosting hen, or perhaps a maharajah, minus the elegant robes and sumptuous carpets. The reference brought Mrs Isbister to mind, and he recalled the day he'd so flippantly trotted out his imagined escape to some exotic locale. He chuckled. She'd been quite angry, as he remembered. She never had understood his humour, or much of anything, really, about him. And, he supposed, neither had he her. He wondered what she'd made of his disappearance, and felt a momentary pang of remorse. He ought to have written. But it was tit for tat, surely, for she had snuck away on a holiday of her own, secretively. Not that he liked to play such games. Nor even felt the need for dishing out a comeuppance, or delivering punishment or retaliation. At the bottom of it all, Mrs didn't want his company; he didn't want hers. There really was no blame to be laid. There was only, perhaps, amends to be made. Or if not amends, then an agreement that life as they'd known it as the venerable Mr and Mrs Isbister of Sowerby Grange was now irrevocably changed. If he went back to Sowerby Grange, he would say as much to her, just to be clear. Throck nodded to himself, looking out at the placid scenery, and felt a contentment settle into his bones that had not been there before.

Eliza had not put her head through the hatchway, and Throck wondered if she'd fallen asleep upon the cupboard bed. They'd had a very early start, granted; perhaps she had not slept at all the previous night. Perhaps she had been tête à tête, as it were, with Julio, plotting her escape from the person with the poison pen. Although a narrowboat that floated at a snail's pace along a canal with banks so close that the breach could be closed with little more than a long leap seemed an odd method of getaway. Of course, beggars could not be choosers, as the saying went. And Throck had decided to enjoy himself, despite Eliza's apparently urgent need to disappear. Until she told him exactly what was going on, he would make the best of the situation. He glanced over his shoulder at Baldy, calmly steering this long tube of a boat, and waved.

*

Before long, Throck was rethinking his opinion of narrowboat cruising as an idyllic mode of water travel. As they'd chugged up to the first of what was apparently many locks on the canal, he'd been handed a spanner-like object that Baldy called a windlass, although Throck could see nothing either remotely wind-related or lass-like about the thing. At Baldy's barked directions, Throck had leapt from the boat onto the towpath that ran alongside the canal and hurried back to the open gates through which the narrowboat had slid, and proceeded to "put his back into it," as Baldy commanded (repeatedly, and not a little gustily), pressing his weight against the heavy oak beams and swinging the great doors closed. Quickly, he realised the raised bricks embedded in the ground were meant as a brace for one's feet while one pushed upon the heavy beam, and with a more solid purchase the task was less strenuous. He wiped his brow, congratulating himself on a tough job well done, and wished Eliza had been about to see his accomplishment. Then Baldy bellowed again, shouting something about standing around like a gongoozler, and Throck had only time to make a mental note to ask Baldy what on earth the term meant before he was sent double-quick to the front end of the lock, there to fit windlass to pinion and crank hard, ratcheting the sluice slowly open to empty the water from the lock where the narrowboat floated, to the waterway beyond. Throck's hands were red and not a little sore when he'd finished, and at Baldy's next shouted command, he retrieved the windlass and pried open the forward gate. The narrowboat glided free of its bathtub, and Throck watched from the towpath with exhaustion but not a little admiration for the craft's gracefulness, not to mention the heart-melting pup-pup-pup of its sturdy Bolinder engine.

"Hop to it, Throck, there's a lad!" shouted Baldy, grinning, as the boat swung past him and beyond, and for a heart-pounding moment Throck thought he wasn't going to stop. Waving the windlass and crying out, he rushed along the towpath, fearing that Baldy intended to abandon him there, alone and without transportation or provisions. Then he realised that he was, in fact, running rather faster than the boat was travelling, and he saw that Baldy had brought her alongside the concrete lip of the canal. With a heroic effort, he leaped, and though Baldy had to grab his arm to save him falling into the water between the boat and the canal edge, he did land successfully aboard.

"Well done," Baldy said, and slapped him on the back. "I can see you're a natural. You'll have your canal legs in no time!"

Throck was not feeling congenial. He shrugged off Baldy's hand and thrust the windlass at him, his chest heaving with both his fright at the thought of being left behind and the over-exertion of running to catch the boat, not to mention the rather enthusiastic effort it had taken to crank the damn windlass. He was not a little angry.

"You – you weren't going to stop," he panted accusingly. "You – you made me run. Did you think it was funny? Did you think to make a joke of a fellow so obviously out of his element?"

Baldy gawped. He appeared truly stunned by Throck's sputterings, and his mouth opened and closed. Then he shook his head, and gestured over his shoulder to a second narrowboat, whose crew was just now repeating the very actions Throck had felt he'd stumbled over. Throck watched as the fellow on the towpath cranked like a fiend on the pinion, and once the sequence of raising and lowering the water was complete, pushed on the balance beam to open the gate, then trotted to catch up as the narrowboat slipped by him and out of the open lock.

"Y'see you can't hang around once you're through the lock, Throck," Baldy explained patiently. "It's a poor narrowboat pilot what holds up the boat behind him, or the one in front of him waiting to come through the other way. You have to move along aways before you pick up your crew if there's a boat on your stern. D'you see?"

And, of course, Throck did. He hung his head sheepishly and mumbled an apology, but Baldy had already forgiven him and was barking at him to stow the mooring line he'd been about to throw when Throck made his not so tidy leap aboard.

*

That was hours ago. Now, several sluice gates and balance beams beyond that first lesson, Throck had become a dab hand with a windlass, though his blisters, bruises and scrapes were those of a novice. As Baldy had promised, there were more than a few locks to traverse, and despite Baldy's encouragements, Throck was wilting from a level of exertion he was most definitely not used to. He recalled with fondness the sore bottom he used to get from the Trusty's unforgiving seat, and the need, whilst driving, to remember to keep one's mouth closed when evening drew down and the insects were out. He was sorely in need of a rest, and suspected his droop had been duly noted by Baldy. Asking and receiving permission, Throck climbed over the boathouse and lowered himself into the cargo area, pulling back a flap of the cratch cover to give some light, and hunkering down alongside the motorcycle. He'd had no chance until now to inspect her since learning from Corky of her damage, and the old girl looked dusty and unloved, her sidecar listing like a sorry afterthought. There were some new scratches on the body of the sidecar, and a small tear in her leather seat, and up front one of the fender brackets had a bit of a bend in it, although Throck felt fairly confident he could hammer that back into shape himself given a tool with some weight behind it. He checked the steering and decided it would be sound once he replaced the front wheel, then inspected the chain – not too loose despite her night on the town with who knew how many inexperienced drivers – and doused it with a squirt of oil from the tin in the rear satchel. He checked her sparkplug and magneto, then he pulled a handkerchief from his pocket and began to give the Trusty a bit of a cleaning. It was long overdue. He'd neglected the old girl, no doubt about it, and he tsk-tsked as he rubbed. There was no excuse, really, for his scrimshank ways of late. He vowed to do better.

As he polished, he considered his host, Boudewijn Kemp. What made a man raised on adventure, as he'd seemingly been, settle for the back-and-forth plying of placid English canals? Hauling cargo from one place to another, moving so slowly that the water voles could win in a head-to-head race. A life dull as ditch water, Throck would have thought, for a fellow like Baldy. Baldy. The man's very name gave Throck pause. It felt somehow wrong, or mean, and Throck was reminded of a boy at grammar school the others had called Fatso. And yet, that same boy, as Throck recalled, was adept at his own pettiness. One of many memories of unwanted attention surfaced: "Isbister!" the headmaster had called out, directing him to the blackboard. And as Throck had moved reluctantly to the front of the room to demonstrate yet again his lack of arithmetical competence, the boy called Fatso remarked snidely, "Is Bister what, sir?" Everyone had laughed, and the teacher had smirked too.

Once he'd cleaned the motorcycle as best he could without the full soap and water treatment, Throck hunkered down alongside her, his back against a crate. A doze'd be a fine thing, he thought, but he rather suspected Baldy would be hailing him in due course to give a hand at the next set of locks. He marveled at the engineering feat that locks surely were, and though a simple enough concept, there was a bit of genius behind the inception of such an idea. Someone, after all, had to come up with the notion of what was, in effect, a water staircase, figure out how to design it, convince others, presumably, that it was a sound theory, and then build it so it worked. Throck gave an admiring shake of his head at such inventive brilliance as was, indeed, beyond his capabilities. Although perhaps there was room for improvement, he thought, glancing at the blisters on his hand from the windlass. Automation, perhaps. Some kind of engine application.

As if stirred by his thoughts, the pitch of the Bolinder eased, and Throck roused himself to peer out of the cratch cover where he'd loosened it for light. The change in speed was almost imperceptible, but he was fairly certain the pace of the narrowboat had slowed, and he watched as she proceeded regally past banks choked with purple loosestrife, bulrushes, and nodding forget-me-nots. Drooping willows dipped the slender tips of their branches into the water, and ducks paddled. It made a pretty picture. Despite what he'd thought earlier about such a life being mundane, he admitted to finding this canal boat journey rather interesting, and decided he should wake Eliza, who was missing out on the scenery. He stood on a crate and hoisted himself onto the roof to wriggle his way to the deck where Baldy had the helm, but as he did so the narrowboat's horn sounded, and Baldy called out a warning. Throck flattened himself onto the cabin roof just as the underbelly of a wooden bridge slipped by overhead. Baldy grinned and motioned him onto the aft deck.

"Thought you were going to sleep the day away down there," he said. With his good eye he winked at Throck, adding levity to his comment. His glass eye, Throck noticed, stared straight ahead, fixated on the boat's course. A handy feature, eyes that looked in different directions, if both were functional. He was reminded of Minnie Small.

"I wasn't sleeping," Throck said for the record. His tone sound more defensive than he'd intended, but he felt it important to clarify. He was not, at least not intentionally, a lay-about, even if he had been in need of a rest.

"Nay? What were you doing, then? Reading a newspaper?" Baldy asked, grinning. "There is a big stack down there. I use 'em when a load needs a bit of extra packing, but I also admit to being a bit of a news nut. Passes the time when there's no crew."

"Hmm," replied Throck, only mildly interested. He was about to ask if Eliza was still sleeping – surely not – when Baldy reached for the horn again and gave a blast, then shouted past Throck's shoulder, "Get ready with the lamp, lass!" Throck turned to peer over the cabin roof and saw Eliza scramble up from the bow of the boat where she'd been sitting. She held a lit lantern. Ahead of her, spills of greenery decorated the arched mouth of a brick tunnel that yawned blackly, and

Throck saw that the narrowboat was about to slide into it, like a finger into a glove.

"How did she get up there?" he puzzled aloud. She certainly hadn't come down into the cargo area. He scratched at his wiry growth of beard. "I thought she was sleeping."

Baldy chuckled. "She popped her head out as soon as you disappeared for your nap. We had a little chat, and, well, 'twas you said she'd make a better ship's mate than you, so I gave her a job. Lantern girl through the tunnel. She's a plucky thing. Scampered her way up there, dancing along the gunnels like she was born on a boat. Fleet of foot, that one. Seems clever, too."

"She is," said Throck, proudly, as if he had anything at all to do with it. He chose to let the comment about the nap go. He watched her, likening her pose to that of a nautical figurehead from a centuries old sailing ship. Then the tunnel swallowed her. For a second, he could see nothing at all of her, but as she held the lantern aloft, she became a beacon, red hair glowing. Seventy feet later, the tunnel swallowed him and Baldy, too, and by the light of a second lantern that swung from the back of the boat, Throck could make out the curve of the damp brick that arched overhead sprouting tufts of green moss, and further on, the stunning sheen of something Baldy said was called flowstone. It looked like rivulets of alabaster, Throck thought, but Baldy said it was caused by the constant trickle of water down the tunnel's walls. And certainly, it was a damp ride, with water dripping from the ceiling as if from a leaky faucet. Throck would have thought rain gear would have been appropriate, but Baldy seemed impervious, and let the water drip off his nose.

"How long is the tunnel?" Throck asked, trying to peer beyond the glare of Eliza's lantern where he thought he could see an exit, a dim keyhole of daylight beckoning them on.

"Four hundred and thirty-three yards," Baldy replied. "Long enough for a lay of eighteen narrowboats like this one, end to end." He grinned, and in the lantern light that reflected eerily in the black water and ghosted the tunnel walls, Baldy's good eye glittered like his glass one. "Good for singing," he added. And then he opened his mouth and sang in a beautiful, rich baritone, "*Twas on a Monday morning, when I beheld my darling. She looked so neat and charming, in every high degree. She looked so neat and nimble-o, a-washing of her linen-o, dashing away with the smoothing iron, she stole my heart away."*

Throck tried not to gape, for Baldy's singing voice was superb, and was made more so by the pleasant echo of the tunnel. When, up ahead, Eliza joined in on the chorus of *"Dashing away with the smoothing iron,"* Throck clapped his hands to his cheeks and laughed in delight. The pair could have made a music hall spectacle, such was their talent.

"That was fantastic!" he cried, his voice reverberating off the dripping walls, but neither Baldy nor Eliza was paying his compliment heed. Baldy was peering into the distance, trying to see through the lamplight at the front of the boat, just as Eliza called out, "Boat approaching!" And Throck heard a horn sound from the far end of the tunnel, which Baldy answered with a toot of his own.

"Not to worry," Baldy said to Throck. "Plenty of room for two to pass, and a foot or so to spare."

A foot or so? In the dark? With a slimy brick wall to crash into on either side? Throck was glad of Baldy's confidence but just in case, gripped the iron railing that surrounded the aft deck. To Eliza, holding the lantern aloft at the bow of the boat where there was no railing to hang onto, he called, "Be careful," though he wasn't sure she heard him. What would happen if the two boats collided, and Eliza were to topple into the inky water? Would he jump in after her? Risk drowning in the still, black water? What if he floundered? Got a cramp? Couldn't find her in the dark with the lantern extinguished? He wasn't an excellent swimmer, although he'd always gotten by. He *would* attempt a rescue – of course he would – but he recalled his near-drowning in Cornwall, the doc's hesitation at rescue, and hoped, should it come to it, that Baldy would be quicker to the mark.

In the end, there was no need of heroics, successful or otherwise. The other narrowboat appeared out of the darkness, its pinprick lantern brightening as it neared, and the two pilots guided their vessels past one another with ease, calling echoey greetings and tooting horns. Throck did his part and waved.

Moments later they were blinking in bright daylight, sliding beneath the tunnel opening into the open air. Birds flitted and the sun shone, and the high banks of the canal passed by on either side. The entire traverse of the tunnel had taken about ten minutes, but Throck felt it had truly been an adventure. He babbled to Baldy about the flowstone, and to Eliza, when she rejoined them, about the luminescent green of the mold on the brick walls when they'd first entered the tunnel, and then about the blackness of the water – had they ever seen such a thing, glinting like jet in the lamplight? And then, almost shyly, he asked them both if they'd sing again, and this time, when they obliged, Throck sang along in his less than stellar pitch, feeling inexplicably happy: "*Dashing away with the smoothing iron, she stole my heart away!*"

Chapter 37
QUEEN OF THIEVES

The narrowboat had a name, Throck discovered, though it wasn't painted in cheery-coloured, fairground script on the cabin side as with other boats. The placard on Baldy's boat advertised – rather glumly, Throck thought – B. Kemp, Canal Haulage, Oxford, in faded red letters on a dark green background. The whole thing did little, in Throck's opinion, to inspire customers to entrust their cargo to so lacklustre a vessel. Throck wondered if Baldy would take kindly to a suggestion of perking up the signboard a bit, perhaps fluttering a happy little pennant, but decided against offering his layman's advice. What did he know, after all, about narrowboat signage and the greater topic of advertising in the world of canal transport?

Baldy's boat was called *Katherine*, and this Throck discovered after securing his end of the vessel to a mooring ring at the top of the Hatton Flight locks. They'd stopped here for the night, outside the small village of Hatton, and in the morning, they'd be tackling the conduit, a harrying affair of some twenty-one locks in succession, a process that would apparently take a good four hours or more to complete. It'd be a bit of a workout, Throck thought without relish, picturing the manoeuvre of a seventy-foot boat down what was essentially a staircase, and opening and closing doors upon every tread. His hand throbbed at the idea of cranking the windlass and pressing those balance beams twenty-one times in a row, no less.

But in the meantime, the damselflies had begun to flit low over the water, the noisy Bolinder was silent, and without the clack of the engine Throck could hear cows lowing in a field, and birdsong in the willows. A bell rang in a church tower somewhere beyond the treeline, and there was a wonderful quenching smell all around: sweet grass and wildflowers and always, always the muddy, fishy damp of the water. Throck sat back on his haunches, resting his hands upon his knees, and saw before him on the boat's hull the name *Katherine* painted in an almost childish hand. Not a professional job this, as was the placard on the cabin side. There was something almost tender about the way the name had been lettered, the K with a bit of a wobble on the stem, yet redeemed by a flourish on the downward stroke. He glanced the length of the boat, snug now against the Hatton wharf, and eyed Baldy, laughing at something Eliza said, his white teeth a-glint. Who was this *Katherine* to him, lone wolf of a man who professed contentment with his solitary boatman's life? A girl who'd once made his heart tender, perhaps? Whom he'd loved and lost, or whom he'd never had, even, but had yearned for? Throck thought of Mungo in that moment, with his various sweethearts, and the way his eyes went soft when he talked of them. Was Baldy a romantic, as Mungo had been? A drifter, albeit one who floated rather than trekked? Another kindred soul, as he felt Mungo surely had been?

Throck sighed, and glanced along the pencil-straight line of the canal. Despite the appearance of stillness, the water flowed, and he pictured its beginning – a spring in a hillside grotto, perhaps, or bubbling up from a moist woodland. There was joy in that kind of movement, it seemed to Throck. An unfettered-ness that he could identify with. No matter its beginning, it moved. It travelled. It started in one place and continued on to another, and then another, and then another. Changing size and shape, perhaps, constrained, even, in canal or creek form, but forever going. By the time this water joined with that of another canal and then another until finally it reached some river that eventually reached the sea, it was no longer the bubbling spring it had been, nor the placid canal it had become, nor the mightier river, nor even the grand, wild ocean, because that in itself was ever changing. And yet, that little stream was still there, just different, and part of something bigger. Perhaps travellers such as Mungo – or himself, even, in his smaller way – were akin to water. Altered by their journey. Unrecognizable, he might argue, in some ways. The same as when they'd started out, but not.

Out on the smooth surface of the canal a fish stirred the surface, causing a ripple, and Throck gave a small huff of a half chuckle. What fancies he could get up to when his mind was left to wander where it would. He tossed a pebble, causing a second ripple next to the first, and got to his feet. Baldy and Eliza had gone inside and were cooking something in the little cabin; he could hear their voices and smell the food. He should offer to help, he thought, instead of mooning about out here like a dreamer. He walked back to the aft deck and stepped aboard, but before he poked his head through the cabin door, he paused. He wasn't sure why he hesitated, but Eliza was speaking and he heard his name, and, chalk it up to his newly acquired suspicious nature, he decided to eavesdrop.

"Throck's been a good friend," she was saying. "The best, in fact. Maybe the best I ever had. I never thought when we started out on this adventure together that he'd become that. I thought he were just a bit of a codger and we'd get on for awhile. Have a lark, maybe. But it didn't turn out that way. He's a fine man, is Throck. Straight as an arrow. He looks out for me; rescued me more than once." She paused, and gave a little laugh. "In fact," she continued, "he's rescuing me now."

"Oh?" Baldy said, his tone curious. "From what, if you don't mind me asking?"

"Meself, in a way," Eliza answered.

If Throck hoped to hear more, he himself thwarted it. His heart full with Eliza's praise, he tried to sneak a peak round the cabin door, eager to see both her expression as she spoke her feelings, and Baldy's as he heard them, but his shoulder brushed the brass bell next to the doorway as he leaned forward, and its clang announced his presence. Eliza and Baldy glanced up with a start, and he smiled sheepishly.

"I – er – wondered if any assistance was needed in here?" he asked. Then, in a torrent of verbiage he hoped would disguise his guilt, he added, without pause, "I secured the mooring line, Baldy, as you asked. Just climbed aboard now. All snug, though. Made sure of it. Extra knots and so forth. Hefty line, that. Can't see it slipping off anytime soon." He smiled again apologetically, and cast extra warmth in Eliza's direction – she, who thought him perhaps her best friend ever. Something happy skittered in his stomach.

"Don't need help right now, Throck," Baldy said, turning his attention back to the pot. "Any which ways, not a lot of room in here, so if you've a mind to take a little walk or just relax for awhile, Eliza and I'll be sure you know when dinner's ready."

"Oh," said Throck. "Right." And before he backed out of the companionway, he flashed Eliza another smile. See you later, best friend, he added silently.

*

A stone wall separated the canal and its towpath from the fields beyond, but Throck hopped it easily enough, feeling almost as light as air. He stuck his hands in his pocket and whistled as he walked, not minding when his trousers picked up burrs and he stepped in a bit of sheep dung. He considered how nice it was to feel happy, and thought of all the times in his life when he'd experienced this sensation of gladness, and came to the conclusion that while they were few and far between, they were at least easy to count. He grinned at what might on another occasion be a rather morose thought – that he had rarely been happy in his life and hence he could easily recall when he had been. In recent memory, at least, he would count among them moments spent in the company of friends – Eliza and Mungo, certainly, Harold Guppletwill, definitely – and moments of adventure – the balloon ride over Watton Hoo and racing the Trusty through the Malvern Hills came immediately to mind. Good times.

He walked through the field, noting the way the setting sun burnished the tree tops a rosy gold, and gave the scattered sheep a mellow tone, as if they weren't real at all but painted with the soft, dappling daubs of an Impressionist. Monet, perhaps, or Pissarro. It had been a while since he'd thumbed through his art book, or looked with any seriousness at *The Illustrated Handbook of English Botany*, and he decided he'd do that tomorrow, time permitting, and once they'd gotten through the twenty-one locks, of course. He chuckled to realise that even the idea of that gruelling feat could not deflate his mood, and he wondered if he and Eliza might work the locks together whilst Baldy shouted his commands. He imagined their shared grins as they heaved in unison on the balance beam, and took turns with the windlass. Best friends, sharing a grand caper.

The church bell clanged, and Throck saw he'd come quite a distance and had almost reached the village proper. He decided it was time to turn back, but the sun, sunk nearly to the horizon, was a brilliant orb that blinded him, and he almost tripped over a fat sheep that must have been following close in his track. He shooed the woolly beast away and retraced his steps, keeping his gaze downcast to avoid the glare, and managing to hop over the dung piles at the same time. He reached the fence as the sun settled beyond the horizon, and peering down on the scene below, saw Aberfoyle King, of all people, standing alongside a tall horse and speaking to Eliza and Baldy. Throck would recognise Aberfoyle anywhere even though he was a distance away. What on earth could he want that he'd pursued them all this way – although in truth, Throck supposed, they had not really come that far. The narrowboat's speed was not bracing, by any stretch of the imagination, and a man on a horse could easily catch them up. Which, obviously, he had.

It did not occur to Throck to call out a hello; this visit was likely not about him. He watched as the three conversed, then Baldy stepped away and busied himself with a table set up for dinner at the edge of the canal, complete with tablecloth and folding chairs and a lantern. If Throck hadn't been disturbed by Aberfoyle's appearance, he'd have admired the effort. Instead, he frowned as he watched Aberfoyle lean in towards Eliza and say something obviously intended for her ears only, then tip his hat, nod to Baldy, and climb onto the horse, riding slowly back along the towpath. Throck remained unnoticed at the top of the small hill, partly hidden by the stone fence and some brambles.

*

Eliza was quiet throughout dinner. Throck waited for someone to mention Aberfoyle's appearance, but Baldy supplied the majority of conversation, and said nothing about a visitor. He seemed to Throck uncharacteristically shifty, and Throck suspected he'd been asked to say nothing of the visit but was uncomfortable with the duplicity. No one ate much, although the soup was hearty and the bread butter-slathered. Throck remembered his manners in time to comment on his appreciation for the lovely table and tasty fare as Eliza rose to clear away the bowls. The smile she gave him was genuine, perhaps even apologetic, he thought, analysing. But he didn't want a smile or an apology. He wanted an explanation, and he wanted it freely given. Here was another secret to add to the bundle Eliza seemed intent on collecting. Throck's earlier high spirits had drained away like water through a sluice gate.

Baldy lit a twist of a cigarette, and offered one to Throck, who at first thought to decline – he was not given to the vice of tobacco – but instead accepted, deciding that partaking of a pungent smoke suited his melancholy mood. He choked with the first draw, attempting to suck the smoke into his lungs the way Baldy did, seemingly with pleasure, but once he recovered from the coughing and wiped the weep from his eyes, he figured out a method of clamping the thing between his lips and puffing energetically without inhaling, creating a nice fug around his head. He and Baldy smoked in silence, sharing contemplation of the black water, lit now by the lantern that burned on the tabletop and a low-hanging moon, and Throck, momentarily distracted from his troubles, asked Baldy about *Katherine*.

"*Katherine?*" Baldy responded, puzzled. One eye swivelled in Throck's direction, and Throck could only assume it was the one out of which he could see.

"Your boat," Throck persisted. "She has the name *Katherine* painted on her hull. I sensed a tenderness in the sketching of the letters. Was she – someone special?"

Baldy laughed. Guffawed, actually, though Throck chose to ignore the discourtesy. "A tenderness in the letters? I fear you're a bit of a romantic, Throck. Next, you'll be sporting a rose in your teeth and writing sonnets." He chuckled. "In all seriousness, though, she was no one. Is no one. Well, no one *I* knew, anyway."

"But – then, why is your boat named *Katherine?*" Throck asked, confused.

"I don't know," Baldy replied. "She had that name painted on her side when I bought her, and I didn't see the point in changing it. It's bad luck to change your boat's name, Throck, didn't you know that? You upset Neptune, or so every good river-plying, sea-faring, boat-sailing man'll tell you." He shrugged. "Any which ways, I don't much care what me boat's called; *Katherine* or Misty Moon or Dog's Hackles, it's all the same to me. The fact she's called after some woman who's probably long dead is neither here nor there, as long as she don't haunt me."

"Oh," said Throck. He'd imagined a romantic story, or a tragedy, even, but instead, there was no story at all. He must have looked somewhat crestfallen, for Baldy reached over and patted his shoulder.

"Throck, my friend, don't get attached to boats or women," he said, his eyeball fixed on Throck with sympathetic earnestness. "It's been my practice never to give my heart to either, if you don't mind my saying. Boats sink, or they get dry rot, or their engine fails and they leave you high and dry at the worst possible moment. Women do much of the same, in my observation. I'm a happier man, I believe, for following that credo."

Throck, still puffing, looked at him through the fog of his cigarette smoke, trying to determine if his words were cryptic, and referred specifically to Eliza. If they were meant as advice. But Eliza rejoined them just then, waving a hand to disperse the smoke, and Baldy pulled a small pipe from his coat pocket and began to play a simple tune. Eliza knew the words – Throck thought she must know the words to every song ever written – and she sang along quietly, her voice clear in the still night. It was a melancholy number – something about sailing a balloon to the silvery moon – and Throck wondered if Baldy had chosen the song with a purpose. "*There's something I want up there,*" Eliza crooned. Throck kept his eye on the black mirror of the canal, and saw how it reflected a sky spangled with stars.

Before long, Baldy put down his pipe and lit another cigarette. Throck declined; one was more than enough for at least a year, although he didn't say as much to his host who seemed to savour the pungent tobacco, sending the smoke out of his mouth and back up his nose in a resplendent curl. Throck was glad to see that Eliza, too, begged off Baldy's offer. It was fashionable, he understood, for ladies to smoke in this modern age, but he felt it was unbecoming, and rather coarse. Not for men, granted, but there you have it. Eliza yawned. She asked Baldy if she could help dismantle the table and stow it before she turned in, but Baldy waved her off, saying Throck would assist, so she bid the men goodnight and climbed aboard the narrowboat, disappearing inside the cabin to her berth on the cupboard door.

Throck and Baldy sat in silence, but it was a pregnant silence, as if both men sensed the spectre of a man upon a horse. Across the canal, fireflies lit the shrubs at the water's edge, and a night bird trilled. Baldy said "a-hem," and pulled a flask from his pocket. Throck gave a small cough – the tickle from the cigarette smoke was still with him – and accepted the flask when Baldy held it out. He sniffed it first, happy not to detect Scotch whisky or Portuguese firewater or French absinthe.

"Jamaican rum," Baldy said, seeing Throck hesitate. "Yep, it'll put hair on your chest, but only if you're greedy with the stuff." Throck was of no opinion about acquiring hair for his admittedly narrow chest, but he took a thin drink anyway, and passed it back to Baldy.

"Had a visitor while you were out strolling," Baldy said at last, his voice low. He glanced toward the narrowboat, and Throck detected a guilty wince as he spoke.

"Oh?" said Throck, feigning only mild interest.

"Maybe I shouldn't be telling you this, seein' as the miss didn't mention it, and if it's a secret it's not mine to share. But she didn't exactly say I shouldn't tell, either." Baldy seemed to be convincing himself he was doing the right thing, and Throck sat in silence. Baldy took a long swig from the rum flask and passed it over to Throck. To be courteous, and to encourage Baldy to continue, for he did want to hear about Aberfoyle's visit, Throck took a small sip.

"Fellow wearing a big hat rides up on a horse. Looked like one of those travellers. Roma, they call them. Gypsy. Gold tooth in his mouth. Handsome fellow, I'd wager the ladies would say, but old enough to be the miss's father." He eyeballed Throck appraisingly, and added, "About your age, I'd guess."

Throck shifted on his chair, uncomfortably aware of his skinny backside. "A-hem-hem," he said, by way of no comment.

"After I determined he didn't mean us no harm and I could see the miss wanted to talk to him, I shuffled off a way, but I could still overhear quite a bit of their conversation. Not that I was trying to eavesdrop," he hastened to add, and Throck nodded and murmured "no, no," and "of course not."

"Well, didn't the fellow profess to love her, and didn't he ask her to climb up on his horse and go back with him, though whereto I don't know," Baldy had warmed to sharing this information, and was leaning across the table, his good eye bulging. "Said she must know her place were with him, that since she'd gone, he'd been miserable." He lifted his eyebrows at his own salacious gossip, and didn't notice that Throck frowned. Aberfoyle? In love with Eliza?

Baldy continued. "But, Throck, here's the thing – the miss stood her ground, she did. Said she and you were a team, and she couldn't just up and leave." He poked Throck's arm, as if to reinforce the happy point. "Said it would be fatal…although now I think about it, she probably said ungrateful." He paused, frowned, thought, and then amended yet again. "Betrayal, actually. Said betrayal, pretty sure. Said she'd done that before and wouldn't do it again. The betraying, I guess, rather than the running off with a man on horseback." He took a fast swig from the flask and handed it to Throck with a grin. "How's that for devotion, I ask you? You're a lucky fellow, if a woman feels that way about you, although I stand by what I said earlier about not getting attached." He nodded, though more to himself, it seemed, than to Throck. "Any which ways, it does a bit to plump a fellow's cushions, eh?" He drummed his fingers on the table in a gesture that signalled impatience, and Throck passed the rum back without partaking. Baldy didn't seem to notice that his companion wasn't drinking, and took a long pull of the liquor, smacking his lips. Throck thought the captain liked the rum better than he ought, and, himself the recent victim of over-imbibing, supposed the man would have a sore head in the morning if he didn't soon cap the flask and tuck it back into his pocket and retire to his bed. He tried to consider what Baldy had reported, Aberfoyle in love with Eliza, Eliza declining to go with him, not because she didn't love him back but because she felt beholden to Throck, but Baldy had moved beyond the topic of Eliza's visitor and filled the space with rambling talk, and Throck couldn't let his thoughts settle enough to sort through them. He tuned his ear to Baldy's diatribe in time to hear him quote poetry, his voice tinged with a wistfulness fed, no doubt, by inebriation.

"Go forth into the country | from a world of care and guile | go forth to the untainted air | and the sunshine's open smile | It shall clear thy brow | it shall loose the worldly coil that binds thy heart too closely up | thou man of care and toil!"

Despite his confusion over the context of Baldy recital, Throck considered the poet's words. He, himself, had taken that very advice, had he not? Gone forth into the country? And indeed, the act had cleared his brow – for a time. But a man could never be entirely carefree. That, surely, was a utopian ideal and completely impractical and unrealistic. Everyone – even the wealthy, the happy, the healthy – eventually found that within their daily existence to fret over. And while one might scoff at what ailed another as a trivial concern, that did not make it less so in the eyes of the worrier. His was a case in point: a relatively healthy man, not overly aged although certainly no cockerel, travelling by whatever means took his fancy – currently a narrowboat – throughout the glorious English countryside, nothing to do but enjoy the scenery, breathe the fresh air, and engage his fellow man when the whim dictated. Shades of Dr Syntax. And yet....

"Have you ever heard of the Forty Elephants gang?" Throck blurted, his musings coming to an abrupt head.

Baldy paused in mid-swill and lowered his rum flask. He narrowed his somewhat bleary eyes at Throck. "Eh, bad lot. Ladies, if you can call 'em that. Steal the pap from a babe's mouth, they would, and not a ring o' remorse. Crafty bunch. I read about 'em in one of me papers. So far, they haven't targeted narrowboats that I know of, so I figure we're safe here."

Throck returned a weak smile, and the fact that his thoughts went immediately to Eliza asleep on board the *Katharine* felt like fear, betrayal, suspicion and deceit all rolled into one.

*

Later, in the cargo area of the narrowboat, with Baldy snoring in his makeshift bed, Throck used the low light of the lantern to thumb through the stack of newspapers Baldy had referred to earlier, tempted by the further mention of an article about the gang. He felt horribly guilty as he did it, but couldn't help himself. Sure enough, near the top of the stack he found an issue of the London Illustrated Police News dated several years past, and on the second page an article caught his eye: '*The Forty Elephants – Woman's Courageous Conduct Helps Police*'.

The story lauded a woman who came forward when no one else would at the scene of a break-in in Union Street, Borough. An old man, a clockmaker, was bludgeoned almost to death in a robbery gone wrong, and the woman, who lived above the shop with her young son, identified the men involved: three fellows known to police for their association with the Forty Elephants, a gang of females notorious for their successes as shoplifters, connivers and thieves. The woman named in the article was one Ellie Geneva, and Throck gaped. Geneva? Could this be a mere co-incidence? Eliza, after all, had been raised by the music hall singer Gin-Gin Geneva, and had charge of Stephen's young son, George. Was this Ellie, perhaps, Eliza?

The article went on to detail the crimes of the infamous female gang and their male counterparts, the Elephant and Castle Mob, and the ruthless leadership of the Forty Elephants by a woman named Polly Carr, who ruled the ring with an iron fist even while serving prison sentences. Throck frowned over the story and realised he was holding his breath. Perhaps Eliza had told him only part of her tale. Perhaps the real reason she'd come to the countryside – to Sowerby Grange – was to escape this gang of criminals who surely would have been after her if she'd fingered them at this robbery. It made complete sense. He closed the paper and picked up another, thumbing through it until he found a second article mentioning the Elephants, and read on. They were a bad lot, to be sure, and if Eliza had taken George and given them the slip it seemed it was to her credit. The newspapers reported that the band of thieves' web was far-reaching, its sticky threads difficult to disentangle oneself from, and that the gang was ruthless when they caught up with anyone trying to escape. Throck felt a sense of pride. Plucky Eliza. If anyone could do it, she could. Perhaps had.

Across the boat's hold, Baldy snorted and rolled over, smacking his lips. Throck was glad enough for the privacy Baldy's slumber afforded him to continue probing without having to explain himself: there was yet another paper from the war years in Baldy's stack, and Throck supposed he'd find an Elephant article within its pages. It seemed stories about lady criminals were popular, and who could blame readers? Throck certainly felt like he was reading one of those working man's serials, all shock and bluster and romance, and in spite of the sordid details he couldn't put it down. He thumbed through the last newspaper, this one dated July, 1918, and there it was, a piece about the leading lady herself, Polly Carr, including a grainy photograph of the Elephants' mastermind. Throck drew the lantern for a closer look – and saw Eliza's face above the caption *Queen of Thieves*.

Chapter 38
SWAN SONG

It wasn't possible, was it, that Eliza Vanson was in fact Polly Carr, notorious gang leader? Throck asked himself if he could really be such a pathetic judge of a person's character that he hadn't seen clues – although perhaps he had: the purse with the Sowerby crest tucked into her carpetbag, his monogrammed scarf fluttering through the air at the Malvern races. He chastised himself for having been duped by her so completely, and for so long, but then apportioned some of the blame to Mrs, who'd hired her in the first place. Had she not checked her references? Investigated her background? For while Mrs Isbister had never been the most attentive or interested person when it came to the staff at Sowerby Grange, she'd always been rather good at suspicion.

For the remainder of the narrowboat's journey through Hatton Flight and its twenty-one locks and on to Napton for another seven, Throck worked like an automaton, albeit one whose gears needed lubricating. His mind was clearly elsewhere, as Baldy pointed out with annoyance when Throck was slow with the windlass and had to be reminded to tend to the sluice gates, and, once through the locks, stood like a dunce on the towpath, forgetting to climb aboard. Eliza – or Polly – was subdued as well, although it took Baldy's pointing it out for Throck to take notice. Throck supposed she was troubled over Aberfoyle's visit, and he professed himself completely at odds over what to make of that, since it really seemed he knew nothing at all of this young woman with whom he'd shared what, until now, he'd thought of as a grand adventure.

At Napton, Baldy steered the boat south into the Oxford Canal, and before long they'd encountered a lift bridge. Baldy sent both Throck and Eliza out to haul the chain and raise the bridge, commenting wryly that between the two of them, distracted as they were, they might manage the task. Thanks, Throck supposed, to its gearing, the bridge lifted rather smoothly, and the *Katherine* slipped between its abutments, slowing on the far side to let Throck and Eliza catch up and re-board. Before they did, though, Eliza put her hand on Throck's forearm, staying him.

"We're all right, aren't we, Throck?" she asked, her brow furrowed. Her eyes, he noticed, were the incredible blue of sapphires, an association he once would have thought of fancifully, but which now only conjured her title: Queen of Thieves. He paused, matching her frown. All right? How could they be all right, he wanted to ask. But this was not the time for all that needed to be said, and so he responded with a forced smile, and hurried to the waiting narrowboat.

*

They spent a night at Marston Doles where Throck was kept awake not only by Baldy's snoring but by a forlorn sheep bleating in the pasture next to the towpath. Eliza, presumably, slept the sleep of the charmed in the cabin she had all to herself. Throughout the day the narrowboat slid over the Oxford Canal's pea-green water accompanied by gliding swans and paddling ducks and twitching moorhens, and while the countryside they passed through was surely idyllic and lovely, Throck hardly noticed, and found ways to be busy or alone when he wasn't obeying Baldy's barked commands.

Part of the *Katherine*'s cargo was destined for Banbury, and towards the end of the third day the narrowboat chugged up to that town's wharf. Throck, who felt the need to prove that he was, in fact, paying attention, stepped nimbly ashore and lashed the heavy mooring lines to the bollards. Baldy nodded his approval and went off to find the dockmaster. Throck, avoiding Eliza who seemed bent on batting sad eyes at him at every opportunity, wandered through the dockyard, hands thrust casually into his pockets, whistling a tuneless melody. He didn't want to talk to Eliza yet; he certainly didn't want to assure her that things were "all right," when clearly there was much that was wrong.

There weren't many people about, but Banbury's was a small operation, not a bustling concern like the dockyard at Small Heath. There was a small stone dockmaster's house, a few sheds, and a warehouse into which Baldy had disappeared, and an open stable where an old fellow in a worn flat cap was pitching hay. Throck wandered over for a chat, thinking to pass a few minutes while Baldy took care of his business. As he approached, he saw that the stable had two stalls, one that housed a slump-backed horse, and the other a Trusty Triumph very similar to his own, albeit a bit rusty, and missing its rear wheel. The motorcycle's chain hung limply from its sprocket, and the hay beneath the bike was an oily mess. Still, Throck's heart sped up. He'd been too long on a boat and missed the sound of his old girl's happy putt-putt, and the chance to talk about motorcycles with someone in the know buoyed his spirits.

"Ahoy," Throck called in a friendly tone. The old man looked up from his pitching, and leaned on the fork. A wad of what was presumably tobacco bulged in his lower lip. He regarded Throck with a steady stare of bloodshot eyes.

"That's a Trusty you've got there," Throck said, stopping just outside the stable and pointing to the motorcycle.

"Yep," responded the fellow. The word sounded rather like a burp, and Throck suppressed a giddy giggle.

"She's missing a wheel, I see," Throck said by way of conversation, hoping to draw the fellow out. But the man only shrugged, and responded with another burp. Throck tried again. "Yours, is she?"

"Yep," said the man.

"It doesn't appear you've ridden her in a while," Throck said, and when the man glanced over at the bike as if to ascertain why Throck might draw such a conclusion, Throck added, "the rust, you see. Left outside, was she?"

"Guess so," replied the man. The lump beneath his lip wobbled, and the man spat a great gob of brown mush into the hay. He coughed, hawked again for good measure, all of which seemed to free up his tongue. "Ain't never rid her. Beast of a thing. All that noise. Cold steel and grease and all sorts. Ain't bloody natural, ask me, ride on somethin' like that. Horses, now that's how a man ought to get around. As God made it."

"Ah," said Throck, noncommittally. "How do you come to own her, if you don't mind my asking? If you don't ride, I mean."

The fellow shifted to rest his other arm on the pitchfork and levelled a frown at Throck. "How come you ask so many questions?" he countered.

Throck laughed uneasily, seeing the man's sudden hostility. He took a step back, and held up his hands, saying hurriedly, "Just interested, is all. Didn't mean to bother you. I'll leave you to it, shall I?"

"You want to buy her?" the man asked bluntly. "Price won't be cheap, but it'll be fair."

Throck paused. Buy her? No, of course not. She was surely destined for the scrap heap. However, …

"I might buy her wheel," Throck suggested, stepping forward again. "What would you take to part with that wheel?" He nodded toward the perfectly straight, unbent front wheel, and felt a small thrill rush through him. Repairs half done, if he could get that wheel.

"You want the wheel?" the man asked, eyeing Throck skeptically. Throck supposed he thought him unhinged, but never mind.

"I do," replied Throck. "Wheel only. Give you your price."

"Well," said the man, and he tapped a filthy finger against his chin, and Throck knew the wheel was his. He returned to the narrowboat with his happy purchase just as Baldy too arrived back, his business complete, and it was decided that dinner, by way of celebration, would be pints and kidney pie at a pub Baldy knew of over the way. Throck put his troubles to the back of his mind, and on their way back to the narrowboat late that night, stumbling along the towpath, the three hooked arms and Throck warbled a solo version of *Dashing Away with the Smoothing Iron*, to Baldy and Eliza's laughter.

*

Throck woke in the night to a scratching noise on the cratch cover beneath which he and Baldy slept. At first he thought it must be a mouse, or a frightful river rat – he recalled with a shudder Minnie Small and her otters, and his night spent in the outdoor privy. The scratching came again, and he thought he heard a whisper, and so, reluctantly, he climbed out from under his rug and crept past a roundly snoring Baldy to push back the cover at the bow of the boat. Eliza was there, her face white in the ghostly light of a full moon.

"We need to talk," she said, and Throck, with a sigh, knowing this was a conversation that must be had but reluctant to have it in the middle of the night after too many pints and over water, stepped through onto the boat's painted deck. The air was chill. Throck shivered. He wished he'd brought his rug. Eliza, he saw, was wrapped in hers. Fleetingly, he wondered how she manoeuvred the narrow gunwales whilst holding a rug about her, but there seemed much she was able to do that Throck wasn't. Stealing came to mind.

"Are you Polly Carr?" he blurted, deciding to get right to it, and was gratified to see her mouth gape.

"What?" she responded, and then, belatedly, "Who?" She was clearly taken aback by his challenge. He tried to read her in the bone-white light, but her eyes were in shadow, her face strangely monochrome as if drawn in pen and ink.

"I saw a photograph of you in a newspaper. It was undeniably you. Only the paper identified you as Polly Carr, Queen of Thieves. Notorious criminal. Does the name Forty Elephants mean anything to you?" He was rising to this final showdown, if that's what this was to be, and his tone was clipped, his words sharp and staccato.

"Yes, it does," she replied. To his surprise, she laughed, although bitterly. "In fact, both those names mean some'at to me, but not the way you think. Polly Carr *is* the so-called Queen of Thieves, although from what I heard she may have lost that title to another that I knew as Anna Diamond. Sayin' both those names right now could get me a knife between me ribs." She paused, as if to give her words weight, then continued. "Either way, I'm not Polly, and never have been. The newspapers have that wrong, or perhaps they were given bad information on purpose." She shrugged, and tossed her head. He sensed a hardness in her he'd not seen before. "Polly Carr's about fifty, older even, I guess, if she's still alive. Say what you like, but I don't believe I've the look of a woman that old."

"But you knew her? How? And why would someone intentionally mis-identify you as a notorious gang leader?" Throck persisted. "Who *are* you?"

"Me real name's Ellie Vanson, although I always liked the name Eliza. When I had a chance to start over, I changed it."

"Start over," Throck repeated. "What about the story you told me in the Blackdown Hills? About you and George and that Nancy woman. And later, what you said to the otter lady – Minnie Small – about this Gin-Gin Geneva person having raised you. Fish and chips and music halls. All lies?"

"No," Eliza said with a quick shake of her head. "All true. Except for the factory work during the war. That part I made up. It sounds more respectable than saying you were a thief. That at some low point in your life you'd got messed up with the wrong sort and couldn't get out of it, even though it soon felt bad and you knew what you were doing were wrong and awful. Gin-Gin knew I were in with a bad bunch, tried to warn me off of the Polly Carrs and the Anna Diamonds of the world. The Forty Thieves were a gang to be reckoned with long before I were born; everyone knew about 'em, but I were young and headstrong and I liked the idea of silk stockings and crepe de chine lingerie and diamond bracelets, there for the taking if you were clever enough and didn't get caught."

Throck thought again of the woman with the bottle brush hair who'd approached Stephen Vanson in the pub that day in Lesser Plumpton. Poppy Kellow, she'd called herself. Elephants don't forget, she'd told him. Throck had been puzzled by the reference to elephants at the time, but now supposed she'd meant the gang, had perhaps been threatening Stephen, or Eliza, even, through him. What an awful, sordid world to get tangled up in. He shook his head.

"And did you? Get caught?" he asked. He was incredulous, and yet not, for he had indeed suspected as much, that Eliza had been a member of this notorious Forty Thieves gang, shoplifting, stealing, masquerading, even, as a maid to set up thefts from country houses. Had Sowerby Grange been a target?

"I were never caught, but I found meself on the wrong side of the pack when I fingered a few of the toughs what worked with us. They went too far, beating up an old man, a clockmaker, who lived in the flat below me on Union Street in the Borough. Almost killed 'im, they did. No excuse for that. He were just old and stubborn, and wouldn't give 'em what they wanted out of his shop, so they set to with bats and bricks and boots. I'd wanted out long before that happened, but it were hard. You couldn't get away; they'd threaten, bully, leave warnings if they thought you were going soft. But that old man, I still remember his name,

Jedediah Skinner, what they did to him – it was me straw, know what I mean? I went to the police."

"And the Thieves couldn't allow that, could they?" Throck said, nodding. Eliza shook her head. Throck couldn't see her face; she was staring down at her feet, and her hair made a curtain. "How did you get away?"

"Julio helped me. He'd been a friend of Gin-Gin's for a long time, were like an old uncle to me and Stephen, but had never had nothin' to do wi' the gang life. After I fingered those boys, he took me in, knew they'd be looking for me. Knew it were best if Gin-Gin had no idea where I were or who I were with. He found the ad your missus placed looking for a maid, and he knew someone at the art school, and so we scuppered, me, him and George, in the dead o' night. Watton Hoo and Lesser Plumpton, here we come." She raised her head and smiled, but the effect in the cold light of the full moon was not pretty. Throck shivered in spite of himself.

"You're cold," Eliza said. She allowed her rug to slip from her shoulders and held it out to him, but he laughed, a weak, shivery sound, and shook his head.

"Nonsense, I'm fine," he said, lying. He flapped his arms and made a gruff noise that he thought might be reminiscent of the sound an athlete makes in preparation for activity. Jumping jacks, perhaps, or jogging on the spot. Why he did that, he wasn't sure. He was cold, but a man would not take a rug from a lady. And she did deserve that epithet, he felt, even if she'd once been – was still? – a thief. He stared across the dark water of the canal, knowing that she was waiting for more from him. A judgement, perhaps. Forgiveness even, and so he said, carefully, "All this is a lot to consider, you understand. You are not, after all, whom you professed to be. Who I thought you were. To be quite honest, I don't know what to think just now. I don't know why you didn't tell me, if, as you say, this is all behind you."

"I'm telling you now," she replied. Throck said nothing and the silence hung. In the field on the other side of the canal a frog chirred, then more joined in. In spite of himself, Throck smiled. Not the jug-o-rum call of the mighty bullfrog, but lovely just the same. *Rana temporaria*,

Throck thought. A plain little English frog. Apropos. He thought of Goliath, and not unkindly.

"I didn't tell you," Eliza went on, "because I'm ashamed, and because I thought you'd as quick leave me on side of the road if you knew. Who wants a thief – never mind an Elephant – for a travel companion? I liked you, Throck. And we *were* having a grand adventure."

"We were," Throck agreed. "But as you once said to me, in Cornwall, I think it was, all things come to end sooner or later. And here we are, on the cusp, I believe, of a decision."

"A cusp?" Eliza echoed.

"Indeed," said Throck. He paused. "There's still something you haven't told me."

"There is?" Eliza asked, seemingly perplexed. The frog chorus was loud now, a veritable choir.

"Aberfoyle visited. Two days ago."

"Oh, that," she said, flatly. "How did you know?"

"I saw him on the way back from my walk. And Baldy told me, later on. He said he couldn't help overhearing that Aberfoyle had professed love for you. Wanted you to go back with him."

"What?" She shook her head incredulously, and laughed. "That weren't at all what Aberfoyle said. Baldy's hearing is none so good."

"No?" Throck asked.

"No," Eliza replied. She tilted her chin, and there was a bit of defiance in the gesture that Throck couldn't help but admire. "Aberfoyle came on Golly's behalf. It's Golly who loves me – who wants me to return." Even in the moonlight, Throck could see her intense blush, and he knew with certainty how it was with her. She'd be going, then. He was not surprised, despite his earlier claim that he needed time to think about her lies and her admission to being a thief, that his heart sank at that realization, and that he'd miss her terribly when she left.

"I sent him on his way, though, didn't I?" Eliza continued, her tone defensive. "I said I'd take me chances with you, Throck. You been good to me, and kind, and despite what you might think of me after what I just told you about the Elephants, I am a loyal person. Friends are all a body's got in this world, and I'd feel I were betraying that if I went back."

Throck knew what he should say in response. That he didn't want to be chosen out of a sense of duty. That she should follow her heart. He willed the words to come, but his throat seemed closed up tight, stoppered by selfishness. In his mind, he said, bravely and with heartfelt magnanimity, "I appreciate that, Eliza, I do. And I believe you about the Elephants, and admire your bravery in standing up to them and escaping that world. But love – not just that between friends, such as we share – is a rare, fine thing, and if you feel it for Golly, you should go." But the chorus of frogs filled the space his words should have taken, and his chance to say anything at all evaporated when a rooster crowed from somewhere distant. Eliza pointed to the faint lightness in the east, and said, "It's going to be morning soon. Baldy says we'll be in Oxford late tomorrow – today, now. I suppose we can get the Trusty welded at the dockyard there?"

"I expect so," Throck replied.

"We'll need supplies. Cheese and bread and sausage. The staples of travellers, eh, Throck?" She spoke brightly, but to Throck's ears there was a falsity to her cheerfulness. "It'll be good to be back on the road," she added, and Throck wondered with a sinking feeling if she was trying to convince herself she'd made the right choice, and that he had none to make.

*

There was no opportunity for further discussion, even had Throck wanted more. If he was honest with himself, he'd admit that he would have liked an apology, or some hint of remorse on Eliza's part for her deceit, but it was also true that he shied away from conflict, and feared that she would change her mind and go back to Golly and the Kings if he pressed her. Instead, he stuck his head in the proverbial sand, and told himself all was well between them, two intrepid travellers about to embark on yet another leg of this grand adventure. Between helping to operate locks and bridges, he huddled beneath the cratch cover, worked on the Trusty, removing the bent wheel and replacing it with the newly purchased one, oiling the old girl's chain and cleaning her spark plug. He polished her, too, and in the little handlebar mirror he caught sight of himself, an old fellow with a cross-hatch of wrinkles and rheumy eyes, and wished he was brave enough to tell her to go.

The trees seemed to grow bigger as the *Katherine* slid further south, the farms fewer. Tall willows shrouded the water, their graceful branches trailing languidly over the narrowboat and shading the canal, creating what might have been a mystical feel had it not been for the increase in both water and pedestrian traffic as they motored through Thrupp and approached Oxford. Baldy exchanged greetings, "Y'aright," with passing boaters, and nodded to people who waved from the towpath, but Throck sensed his growing frustration when there were queues to get through the locks.

Throck was tidying up below, folding the rug he'd used as a blanket, stuffing belongings into his haversack – a shirt and socks he'd rinsed out in the canal and which were now dry, his botany book, unread, though he'd had good intentions – when he heard a cacophony of splashing and honking. The *Katherine* was tied to mooring rings outside a lock; they'd been waiting their turn in what was a long line to go through, and there were other boats similarly tethered. Alongside the watery disturbance he heard shouts and laughter, and he climbed through to the bow of the boat to see what was going on.

Two great, beautiful swans – males, presumably – were engaged in what seemed to be a battle to the death. Viciously, they bit one another and slapped with their massive wings, twining their strong necks as they wrestled and fought. The usually placid canal churned with their thrashing, and bits of vegetation floated up in a stir of muddy water. It was a horrible sight, these two birds, the epitome of grace and elegance, desperate to kill one another, while the female and her cygnets, perhaps the focus of the dispute, circled in agitation. Aboard the waiting narrowboats and on the towpath behind them, people watched, and Throck was shocked to see many laughing and egging on the struggle. One man, luckily too far away on his moored narrowboat, was shouting like a spectator at a cock fight, and trying to reach the pair with his grappling hook, seemingly to agitate the combatants further.

One of the swans was clearly weakening, and the dominant bird took advantage. Through the desperate flapping of the other's wings, he climbed onto the sinking bird's back and bit down hard on his foe's neck, with the obvious intent of drowning him. They were birds, but it felt like murder nonetheless, and Throck shouted. "Stop!"

Tracy Kasaboski

No one heard, or paid attention, certainly not the almost-victorious swan. But the avian pair had drifted close to the *Katherine* where Eliza and Baldy stood on the stern deck, and the swans were bumping against the side of the narrowboat in the final throes of the tragedy when Eliza knelt and reached out, grabbing the topmost swan by its neck with both hands. It was strong, and fought against her grip but Baldy too had come to the rescue and held Eliza, ensuring she wouldn't be tugged into the water by the large bird. Her actions forced the swan to let go of his enemy, and the battered, bloodied adversary swam away, presumably to nurse his wounds. When he'd disappeared, Eliza released the bigger male who swam in the opposite direction, perhaps to nurse his pride. The spectators, despite their earlier bloodlust, applauded her, and Throck stood, agape, hardly believing what he'd just witnessed. It wasn't just the battle of the swans that had enthralled, but Eliza's bravery, and her instinct to act when others were content to be merely bystanders. It brought home to him how courageous she'd been to go to the police when those thugs had beaten that clockmaker, and she'd now demonstrated that same sort of pluck before his very eyes. She might have once been a thief, but everyone deserved a chance to move on from their mistakes. She was making another one now, choosing to come with him. And he was making one by letting her. When he had a moment alone with her, he would tell her so, and send her back to Golly. He promised.

*

The wharf where the *Katherine* docked in Oxford was a hive of activity, and it took Baldy a while to locate the warehouse where he was to unload his cargo, and then longer still to square away the paperwork. Eventually, things were sorted to his and his customer's satisfaction, and dockhands swarmed the narrowboat to empty her of her barrels and crates, and the *Katherine* rode a little higher in the water. Throck had hoped to find a chance to talk to Eliza about returning with Baldy to Birmingham and finding Golly, but the opportunity did not present. He wanted to choose his words carefully, explain that he did not judge her harshly for her past but only wanted her to go back to Golly so she could find the happiness she deserved. The last thing he wished was for her to think he did not care, did not still consider her his best friend, and such

416

a conversation, he felt, could not be had in the midst of a dockyard overrun with flat-capped dockers and draymen who, when they didn't have a crate on their shoulder, had no compunction at all over sending a whistle or a wink Eliza's way. Throck was a little put out, but as always, Eliza handled the fellows with practiced ease just as she had the racing crowd at the Malvern Hills track, and Throck was reminded of her music hall past, not to mention her life as a thief when a brash boldness must have stood her in good stead.

Of immediate concern was the repair of the Trusty, and after his cargo was unloaded, Baldy helped Throck make arrangements with a narrow-nosed fellow who had a small shop in a lane just behind the wharf warehouses. Throck was instructed to return the following day, mid-morning, and the job would be complete. He was disappointed that there'd be yet further delay, but Baldy shrugged, clapped him on the shoulder and said, "These lads can't work round the clock, y'know, Throck. Fellow's gotta have time for a bit o' grub and a bevvy and maybe a few hours sleep at night before he starts pounding away on the metal again." And of course, Throck knew that was true – he'd been in a strike, after all, had heard the working man's complaints and had seen the bricks thrown – but it didn't stop him wanting the work done yesterday. Reluctantly he resolved for yet another night on the *Katherine*, but there, too, he was to be disappointed. Back at the wharf, Baldy paused next to the narrowboat and stuck out his hand for a shake. "It's been a pleasure knowin' the pair of you. Never had such a pretty hand on board, nor one so quick to learn." That last he directed to Eliza, but with a wink, nodded to Throck and added, "You weren't so bad yourself, old timer, even if you weren't much to look at." He guffawed at his own joke.

"You're leaving?" Throck said dumbly while Baldy pumped his hand. He'd expected a berth for the night, and Baldy's company, at least, until the Trusty was fixed. He was surprised to feel somewhat disheartened. He'd grown to like the narrowboat captain, despite his gruff demeanour and his sternness as a skipper. The blisters on his windlass hand throbbed.

"A man can't make a living tied up to a wharf, empty and going nowhere," Baldy replied. "I got a load to collect up north in Braunceston, and I'll lose the job if I don't get the boat there on time. It's easy for you two, not a care in the world, free as a lark, but in my world, people have to make a living." He smiled, softening the reproving tone of his words.

"Of course," Throck said apologetically. "I must say I have a new appreciation for our English canals, and for the fine fellows who ply them. When I stand at a lift bridge waiting for one of these workhorses –" he gestured to the *Katherine*, "to manoeuvre through at a snail's pace, I shall do so with admiration rather than impatience in my gaze, and cheer her on. You may count on it."

"And a fine gongoozler you'll make, Throck, of that I've no doubt," Baldy said with a grin, swinging aboard with practiced ease. Throck cast off the mooring lines while Eliza collected his haversack and her carpetbag, and then they were waving Baldy and the *Katherine* off as a wisp of smoke puffed from the exhaust of her Bolinder engine. A fine craft, Throck thought, watching her go.

"What's a gongoozler?" Eliza said to Throck.

"A bloke with nothin' better to do than stand around watchin' boats go by," one of the dock workers said, overhearing Eliza's query as he passed by with a sack on his shoulder. He paused and gave them a toothless grin. "Sort of like you two're doin' right now."

"Actually, we're travellers, and if you were at all observant, you'd have seen that we weren't mere onlookers, we were, in fact, bidding a farewell to our friend," Throck said, affronted. He hoisted his haversack with a huff. He didn't know what annoyed him more, the dockworker's assumption that they were idly gawking at the boat traffic, or Baldy's insinuation that Throck was someone who was content to merely watch and not participate.

"Is that so," replied the worker. He set down his sack and wiped his big-knuckled hands on his pants. His grin of moments before had slid into something that more closely resembled a sneer. A couple of his fellow dockworkers stopped too, and Throck saw with trepidation that he might have gotten himself into a bit of hot water with his testy remark. Eliza, as ever, it seemed, came to the rescue.

"Now lads, don't mind me old uncle," she said, her tone a mix of sassiness and sweet cajole. "He blurts things out he don't mean. He's harmless enough, really. I mean, look at him." She hooked her arm through Throck's and rolled her eyes, and although Throck wanted to protest not only the implication that he was unhinged but that she called him uncle, he saw the effect her words had to diffuse the situation. There was a bit of grumbling, and one or two invitations for Eliza to accompany them, but the tension of a moment ago had dissipated, and the dockworkers shouldered their loads and continued on their way.

"Uncle?" he said to her when they'd gone.

"Well, it worked," she answered with a shrug. "Let's go find us some lodgings."

He should have said, then and there. He should have told her to go back to Golly. He could have even helped her find passage. But he didn't. Yet again he kept quiet, and together they walked into Oxford to look for a lodging house and a bed for the night.

Chapter 39
GONE AND GONE

The University at Oxford. Renowned place of learning for hundreds of years. One of the oldest and most highly regarded of such institutions in the world, Harold Guppletwill used to say. And Harold's alma mater. Throck stood on the polished wood floor of the magnificent Bodleian Library and breathed the scent of carnauba wax, oiled leather, old paper, and dust, and could hardly believe he was in the very spot Harold used to speak of when telling Throck about his studies.

"A treasure trove, Throck old boy, you've no idea. But the librarian, Mr Diggory, is rather a rum sort. I think his life's work is trying to ensure no-one actually accesses the collections. And if you're wanting something from the restricted sections, well, you might as well have asked the fellow for his first-born child."

Throck had begun his search for Harold, or news of Harold, at least, at the University's Museum of Natural History, which he thought he remembered as having a connection to Harold's research trip to the Amazon jungle. No one there was particularly helpful, or even seemed to have heard of an alumnus by the name of Harold Guppletwill or indeed an Amazonian expedition from 1914, but they'd been pleasant enough, and had suggested he try a Dr Smythe-Leslie, whom he might find in his office at Merton College. So Throck had trekked there, his feet growing rather hot and sore on this cobblestone trudge, not used to walking anywhere, really, after days aboard the narrowboat. Who'd supposed that Oxford University was such a sprawling place, and with so many elegant yet similar buildings seemingly spread throughout the town?

Merton College was lovely, all pale stone and carved archways and with climbing ivy on its walls and lengths of green lawn on its perimeter, but Throck had no luck there either. Dr Smythe-Leslie had gone out earlier, briefcase in hand, the porter at the arched gateway told him, and although the porter claimed that he did not stick his nose in, as he put it, the business of the college's esteemed members, he did share in a gossipy sort of way that the good doctor had of late been spending time at the old Bodleian Library researching an important project. The porter tapped his nose and winked. "And if you don't find 'im there, gov, you might try his club. Whisky sours. Never mind that it's before tea time."

Throck had thanked the fellow and gotten directions to the library. He decided that this would be his last port of call on his quest – long shot though it was – to find some news of Harold, for he'd already been gone for several hours from the boarding house where he and Eliza had shared a room (he on the floor, she on the narrow bed). He'd not slept well on account of some unsavoury noises from the other side of the thin wall, and he'd crept out in the early morning, leaving a note by Eliza's pillow to assure her of his return, but he'd not expected to be gone so long, and it was surely time for them to collect the Trusty from the repair shop. It was unlikely he'd find news of Harold anyway, but he felt, given the opportunity of location, he had to try.

And now here he was, acutely aware of the long glances he was drawing from the studious types seated at the heavy oak tables who sensed an imposter, perhaps, in their midst. Certainly, he did not look the part of the academic with his rumpled clothing, scruff of beard and longish hair. But never mind. He put a brave face on it and walked towards the desk at the head of the library's reading room, where a man, Mr Diggory, presumably, scratched in a ledger with a shiny fountain pen. Throck waited politely for the librarian to look up, and when that did not seem to be going to happen, he cleared his throat, the noise echoing loudly around the vault-ceilinged room. Mr Diggory looked up very slowly, and Throck saw a man of almost cadaverous demeanour – long, stretched neck, hollow-thin cheeks, dark-circled eyes beneath reptilian lids, and oiled hair parted with razor-like precision down the middle of his head.

"Yes?" he asked, after a thorough scrutinize of Throck's unkempt and un-Oxfordian appearance. Someone behind Throck sniggered, and the librarian's gaze darted past Throck to the offender, who must have found a way to suppress their mirth.

"Thank you, sir, yes," Throck said, nerves getting the better of him. What, in fact, was he thanking the fellow for, when he hadn't yet asked his question? He cleared his throat and began again. "I wondered – Mr Diggory, is it?"

The eyes raked him again, but the man nodded. Throck continued.

"I wondered, sir – that is, I'm looking for Dr Smythe-Leslie –"

"Not here," Mr Diggory interrupted, rudely, Throck thought. He stood his ground in front of the librarian who had turned away dismissively.

"I wonder if you might direct me to his club?" Throck persisted.

"No," answered Mr Diggory. His long fingers had begun leafing the pages of his ledger, but Throck could see the columns were blank, and the man was merely trying to be rid of Throck. Throck pinched his lips together determinedly. He hadn't much time, and this was likely to be his only chance to find out what might have happened to Harold. He leaned on the librarian's desk, and stuck out his neck.

"See here, you've no call to be rude. I'm a friend of Dr Harold Guppletwill – you might have heard of him – he was on a research trip to the Amazon in 1914 and –"

"Stop right there," the librarian hissed, leaning on the desk in a mirror of Throck's stance, his nose mere inches from Throck's. Throck could smell the faint odor of tooth rot beneath the peppermint on the man's breath. "Where Dr Smythe-Leslie is at this moment is not my place to divulge, even should I be aware of his location. I am not a directory. Now please leave my library. This is a place of study for Oxford students and faculty, neither of which, I would wager a guess, you are. Go." He drew back, closed the ledger in front of him and walked away, and Throck stood for a moment, flabbergasted at having been so summarily dismissed.

Reluctantly, he left the reading room and walked through the halls, in spite of his disappointment enjoying the echo footsteps made on the centuries-old flagstones, and the way the light slanted through the beveled, leaded glass windows. It was not hard to picture Harold here, one in a cluster of emeritus professors pausing to exchange pleasantries in an absent-minded sort of way. He was sorry to have failed to glean any news of Harold, but in truth there was only so much one could do when one's great friend had sent no word in all this time. Not a single letter. Not a message even, passed to him through other channels. Throck feared for Harold, for what awful fate might have befallen him, missing all these years in the Amazonian jungle, but a small piece of him worried over something worse: that Harold had not written by oversight. That in Harold's heart, Throck was a friendly neighbour who liked toads, and nothing more.

Outside in the courtyard, students hurried past laden with books, and black-robed dons stalked by with a purpose, their gowns flapping like the wings of some great bird. A bell rang in a clock tower somewhere, and Throck was reminded that Eliza would be waiting for him in their rented room, and the Trusty was most likely ready for pickup. He was almost to the archway that led to the street when he heard running footsteps behind him, and someone called out, "Sir!" and he turned to see a young man, his Oxford tie flapping, hurrying towards him. The fellow stopped, panting from his run, and Throck took in a plethora of pimples on a round face beneath a shock of hair the colour of persimmons.

"Guy Bletherington, sir," the young man said, and shook Throck's hand. "I beg your pardon, sir, and the intrusion, but I couldn't help overhearing what you said in the library. You're looking for information about the lost expedition. Amazonia 1914."

"Yes," said Throck. "Do you know it?"

"Oh, yes, sir, we all know it," Guy replied. "We study it, sir. In Bumpy's class."

"Bumpy?" Throck repeated.

Guy's pimples reddened. "Sorry, sir. Oxford humour. Forgot myself for a moment. Dr Ernest Deverill's class, I should have said."

"Oh," said Throck. He'd been a schoolboy once, and nicknamed his teachers. He smiled congenially. He wondered why they called the fellow Bumpy, but didn't ask. If the fellow knew something of Harold, he didn't much care what he was called. "Is Dr Deverill available, would you know?"

"Available, yes, I shouldn't wonder. He'll be in his office, sir, if he's not in the lecture hall. We all think he sleeps in that office on account of he's there all the time. It's right through there, sir," he pointed to an arched portico. "Turn right, go through the doors at the end, and you'll find old Bumpy – sorry, Dr Deverill – in the office with his name on it. I'd take you myself but I'm late for class as it is."

"No, this is fine, you've been more than helpful," Throck said. He shook the young man's hand and watched him dash off, thankful that the world held its share of Guy Bletheringtons to compensate for the Mr Diggorys, then went in search of Dr. Ernest "Bumpy" Deverill.

*

He saw right away why the professor might have been nicknamed Bumpy, for he had a rather pronounced line of puckered skin across his forehead, and each bump was coloured with a bright yellow dye. Throck supposed it was some sort of strange tattoo, and thought of his own lacklustre example. Dr Deverill – Ernie, as the fellow bade him say – seemed a kindly fellow, small of stature not unlike Throck himself, so the two men stood eye to eye, something that rarely happened to Throck. He liked the fellow almost right away for that single reason, even without his kindly smile and engaging manner, and Throck suspected the nickname Bumpy had been bestowed affectionately rather than with any malice. Throck accepted the offer of tea, for it would seem rude to refuse, and while Dr Deverill – Ernie – steeped and poured and stirred, Throck wandered about the carpeted, oak-panelled room, peering at framed photographs of the doctor in what appeared to be various wild locales – there he was in a canoe with a rushing river in the background, there next to a grass-skirted fellow with an enormous plate-like object embedded in his lower lip, there clad head to toe in fur and standing in some ice-encased landscape. Throck gaped further at the exotic treasures on display round the room: an animal skin on one wall, leopard, Throck thought, but supposed it could be jaguar. A rudely crafted spear with an ivory blade. Some sort of head-dress decorated with feathers and bones and claws. A cabinet held several shelves of glazed pots and vessels, while in a glass case Throck saw examples of jewelry: earrings and circlets of hammered metal, though none quite so finely made as Esau King's silverwork. One necklace was rather more unusual than the rest, and Throck, bending closely, saw it was strung with teeth, blunt and rather human-like.

424

"A few souvenirs of my travels," the good doctor said modestly, noting Throck's interest. "Gifts, all, you understand. Nothing taken without permission. I have quite strong views on that, I'm afraid, and it puts me at odds with many of my colleagues. The monkey-tooth necklace gives many people a start, but I can assure you the monkeys were quite expired from natural causes before any extractions occurred." He handed Throck a porcelain teacup on a saucer and gestured to two armchairs tucked cosily by an unlit fireplace, separated by a small table inlaid with what Throck suspected was ivory. "Now, what can I do for you, Mr Isbister?" he asked when they settled.

"Throck, please," said Throck, and Ernie acknowledged the request with a nod. "I've come to ask about a 1914 expedition to the Amazon –"

"Ah," said Ernie. "The so-called Lost Expedition. Yes, that's a popular one with the students. They do enjoy my Amazonian stories."

"Your stories?" Throck repeated. "Were you there? Were you part of it, I mean?"

"No, no. I suppose if I had been it wouldn't be called Lost, would it?" Ernie chuckled. "I have been to the Amazon myself, though, several times. That's how I acquired these markings on my forehead. I lived for quite awhile with a tribe on the Putumayo River, and this sort of thing is a part of one of their rituals. Lovely people. Wonderfully self-sufficient. Minimal contact with the wider world, and it would have been much better for them if things had remained thus, but along came the rubber trade and, well, it all went rather hard on them. Suffered, they did. Some unscrupulous people, working on behalf of the rubber companies, tried to press-gang them into hard labour. Nasty stuff. Anyway, the whole tribe eventually upped sticks and as many as could escaped further into the jungle. I was lucky not to be enslaved myself but I was able to convince the recruiters, if you can call them that, that I was English, and the British government wouldn't take too kindly to one of its own being shackled and forced onto a jungle labour gang." Ernie sipped his tea. "But you didn't come to ask about all that. What's your interest in the 1914 expedition?"

"A friend of mine, Harold Guppletwill, was one of the members," Throck said. "But after he left, I didn't hear from him again.

I wondered if – hoped – the university might have had word where I did not. He was a good friend. We shared an interest in amphibians."

"Guppy," said Ernie affectionately, nodding and smiling. He sipped from his tea and nodded again. "Yes, Guppy was a good sort. Did love his frogs. That was his interest in the expedition, I believe. Some kind of giant frog if I recall correctly."

"Toad, actually," said Throck, sitting forward eagerly. It was wonderful to talk to someone else who knew Harold. Someone who knew about his research. "He went to find a giant toad. Or hoped to."

"And he did, Throck, he did," Ernie said. He set down his teacup and went to a wooden filing cabinet, pulling open the top drawer. "There are reports here somewhere…ah! Here we are. Letters, too, I believe."

Throck's heart was tip-tapping in his chest. Reports? Letters, even? He gulped his tea and set the cup down, not trusting it to his trembling hand.

"Was the expedition lost, then, or not?" Throck asked.

"Well, it was thought to be lost. There was no word for the longest time, you see. But they *were* in the Amazon, so minimal communication was at least somewhat to be expected. There isn't a post office box on every corner, needless to say," Ernie chuckled. "In this case, there was absolutely nothing for several years, and that is not usual with expeditions of this nature. Most of the time, reports come back with somewhat reliable regularity. However, no one had banked on a war upsetting the state of things, and by the time the expedition members got a report off to Rio de Janeiro, their contact people had upped sticks. Later, when they finished up their research, ships in and out of Brazil were irregular, and the members of the expedition, some of whom were German, went their own separate ways." He sat down opposite Throck again, this time with a sheaf of papers – reports, presumably – and a small packet of letters tied up with twine. He handed them to Throck. "Have a riffle, if you like. They were sent from various members of the expedition to the university, but there are a few that were meant to be forwarded on. If they're still there it's because the addresses were illegible. Looks like the rain blurred the ink. If they couldn't be deciphered, well, we just tucked them away."

Throck untied the twine. As Ernie had said, most of the letters were addressed to the university, but midway through the stack there was one, its ink well smeared, addressed to Mr R.T. Is…, Sowerby G…, Wat…Glouce…

"This is me! This is mine!" cried Throck. He looked over at Ernest Deverill, and was embarrassed to feel tears prick his eyes. Harold had written him. He hadn't forgotten. The letter was sealed, the stamp Brazilian, the postmark a date in 1919. He flipped through the rest of the stack, but there was nothing else addressed to him. To Ernie he said, "This letter was written more than two years ago. Is there any chance you know where Harold is now?"

"Africa, last I heard," Ernie Deverill replied, then elaborated, "Cape Town, I think, though whether he's still there is anyone's guess. It's rather a long way away, I'm afraid, but Harold never was one to do things in half measures." He smiled encouragingly. "There's a postcard in there; a city scene with flower sellers and a clock tower."

Throck found the card near the bottom of the pile, a lovely coloured photograph that could have been taken in any English city, except for the mountain in the far background, and the fact the vendors, standing before enormous baskets of flowers, were all dark-skinned. Adderley Street, Cape Town, read the caption, and Throck turned the card over to see Harold's handwriting, and a date from nearly two years ago, October 10, 1920. Eagerly, Throck read his friend's familiar scrawl. *Dear Ernie, I've jumped continents. Going in search of a ghost frog that only comes out on a full moon! Give my best to old Oxford. Harold.*

Throck looked up at Dr Deverill, his eyes shining. "Goodness, a ghost frog." He chuckled, shaking his head. "If anyone can find it, Harold will. He and I spent more hours than was probably good for us poking about the woods between our two houses in search of the elusive natterjack toad. It's not an incredibly unusual amphibian, but rather difficult to spot, you see, and Harold and I quite liked the game of it. My goodness, what great times we had." He stared down at the postcard, and felt his eyes go misty. He blinked, afraid for a moment that he might cry, and cleared his throat.

"And did you?" prompted Ernie Deverill.

"Did we what?"

"Find the natterjack?"

"Oh," Throck laughed, embarrassed to appear so scatterbrained. The finding of Harold, in a manner of speaking, had him feeling quite nostalgic. "Unfortunately, not," he said, "although Harold was sure of its presence and had heard it several times. I myself heard it once, but only after Harold had gone on his research trip for many years. I can't tell you what a bittersweet moment that was. It was as if Harold was reaching out to say hello."

"It sounds like a most transcendent experience. We should never discount those, I believe." The professor smiled at Throck, his eyes crinkling into little crescents and the yellow bumps on his forehead puckering. "You know, I think you should have been Harold's research assistant on that Amazonian expedition. I don't believe he ever did have a partner with quite your enthusiasm."

Throck glanced at him, flattered by the comment. Could he mean it?

Just then the cuckoo clock on the wall squawked, and Throck jumped. "Good gracious, look at the time. I really must go." He stood, suddenly picturing Eliza impatiently pacing the floor of the rooming house, and placed Ernie Deverill's postcard and the stack of correspondence on the small table next to his empty teacup. The unopened letter addressed to him he held back, unsure of the protocol for such an item. Would the university feel that the letter, as part of a collection, did not, in fact, belong to him?

"Might I keep this one?" he asked.

But Ernest Deverill was nodding and smiling. "Of course, Throck. It is entirely yours. I'm delighted it has found its way to its intended recipient. Please don't feel you must hurry off. I have a lecture I must get to, but my office is at your disposal. You are, of course, free to remain and read the rest of Harold's communiqué, if you're so inclined." He gestured to the untouched stack.

"I would dearly love to," Throck said, earnestly. "But someone is waiting for me, and I fear I am rather late. I really should not tarry a moment longer." He tucked the letter into his pocket, feeling immensely pleased. Dr Deverill put out his hand and Throck clasped it, pumping it vigorously. "I can't say how happy you've made me, doctor – Ernie.

You've given me great hope for the well-being of my old friend, and news I honestly never expected to hear, so thank you."

Ernest Deverill walked him to the courtyard, and Throck went on his way with a spring in his step.

*

The landlady of the lodging house stopped Throck at the bottom of the stairs.

"You can't go up there, room's let to someone else," she said, hands on her hips and a frown pulling her eyebrows down to her nose.

"But – my companion," protested Throck. "My bag –"

"Gone and gone," snapped the woman. "Like I told the miss, if you wants the room another night, pay up. If you don't, out you go. So out she went." She gestured with her thumb over her shoulder, and so Throck turned and went back out into the street.

She'd have gone to collect the Trusty, he supposed. He was terribly late, of course, but with the treasure of Harold's letter snug in his pocket he simply couldn't feel overly concerned. Eliza would understand once he explained, and she'd certainly be happy, too, for the news. The very thought of word from Harold after all this time buoyed his spirits – but for Eliza's sake he hurried, his footsteps light and a whistle on his lips. He walked in what he thought was the direction of the repair shop, through narrow, cobbled streets, the water smell of the canal pulling him onward, but took several wrong turns and had to ask directions. His stomach was rumbling, and so he paused at a cake shop where he bought two lovely little fingers with strawberry filling, one for him and one for Eliza. The shop girl put them in a dainty box and tied it with a string. His money was running a bit shy, but in his euphoric state he told himself Eliza would offer up the Sowerby wallet soon, surprising him with it just at the right moment. Most likely that had been her intent all along, and he'd been silly to consider it a theft. She'd been resourceful, is all.

"Look what I've had set by," she might say, pulling it out and dangling it before him like a treat.

And of course, he'd feign great surprise and express admiration for her ingenuity, and say something like, "You are a clever girl," and they'd laugh together, and she'd hang on his words as he talked of Harold and read aloud his letter – sent all the way from Brazil, no less. She might even suggest they travel to find Harold – a true adventure of epic proportions that one would surely only undertake with the best of friends. Yes, he could picture it. To the back of his mind, he shoved his earlier resolve to tell Eliza to follow her heart, for this, surely – the continuation of their travels together – was what they both really wanted.

When he finally turned into the right street, there was Eliza, leaning against his motorcycle parked outside the repair shop. He felt another surge of happiness.

"I'm sorry!" he called when he spotted her. "You won't believe what's happened!" He pulled forth the letter, and waved it, hurrying towards her. "My friend, Harold Guppletwill, I've found him! He's written! I've got the letter!"

People paused to stare, and he supposed he must seem like some kind of imbecile, albeit a happy one. He laughed, uncaring. He reached Eliza's side, and impetuously, hugged her. As he did, she hugged him back, but he realised hers was a different sort of embrace, and she was quietly sobbing. All was not well here. He drew back, concerned, and tucked Harold's letter away. Time enough for that later. He offered her a handkerchief, belatedly realizing he'd used it to polish the Trusty and it wasn't as clean as it ought to be. Eliza did not notice, and dried her eyes, coming away with a smudge of grease on her face.

"Whatever is the matter, dear girl?" Throck asked. "Did you fear I'd gone and left you? I put a note on your pillow…."

"I got the note, Throck," Eliza replied. "I knew you wouldn't just leave me. I've never had so reliable and wonderful a friend as you." She started to sniffle again, and Throck patted her shoulder tentatively.

"There, there," he said, awkwardly. What did one say in these sorts of situations, when one did not fully comprehend what the problem was? And when one's own self was ebulliently happy for other reasons. He felt very much out of his element.

"I-I'm leaving, Throck," Eliza said, after she'd blown her nose into Throck's handkerchief and smeared some grease onto her lip.

"Leaving?" he repeated. His happiness deflated ever so slightly. Leaving?

"I'm sorry," she said, her voice quavering. She drew a shaky breath and plunged on. "I miss Golly terribly. I can't help it. I've tried,

Throck, but I love 'im, and Aberfoyle says Golly wants to marry me." She smiled tremulously. "Me, married. Never thought to see the day. Mrs Eliza King, fancy that," and Throck, for all his desire not to, saw her face light up as if the sun had just shone upon it.

"I don't understand," he said limply, but of course he did.

"I know this isn't fair to you, Throck," Eliza continued, "you've been my best friend, you trusted me, you looked out for me, and I've always set great store by loyalty, I have, but...I'm going." She reached out and squeezed his hand. "I hope you won't be too sad."

Throck saw then that her carpetbag sat alone on the cobbles. His belongings were stowed in the newly repaired sidecar – his haversack, his rug, the petrol cans and the last of Minnie Small's cider. Atop it all she had placed his books, and – his heart gave a little lurch – the Sowerby purse. His last shred of doubt about her character evaporated. In the end, she'd been honest.

"It's too bad Baldy's gone," she said. "I'm sure he'd have taken me as far as he could. But I'm not worried. I'm sure I can get passage on another narrowboat. Maybe they'll let me work the locks in exchange for fare." She paused and looked at him, her eyes wide and so incredibly blue. "Of course, it won't be the same as crewin' with you, Throck. We were a team, an' no mistake." She smiled tremulously. "This is our ending, Throck. A long way from Land's End, and all. I wouldn't have traded away a day."

She could beguile, of that there was no doubt. And yet, Throck found he didn't care. This was it. She was really going. He knew he should say something, but his tongue felt twisted and numb. He needed a gesture, something to show her how important she'd been to him, and in that moment, he made a decision. This was one of those forks in the road, so to speak, where one had an epiphany, as if one's course was predestined, and as soon as the idea occurred to him, he knew without doubt that this was what he wanted to do. He'd miss the old girl. He might even cry. But it was right. He reached into the sidecar and removed his haversack and his books and the Sowerby wallet. He picked up Eliza's carpetbag and plunked it on the seat.

"Take the Trusty," he said. His voice warbled dangerously, and his heart hammered. He'd really hoped this wouldn't be hard. "She's my gift to you. I have no further need of her, as this trip has come to an end." He held up his hand as she started to protest, her eyes round and filling with water again. "No – you may not argue." He pulled Harold's letter from his pocket and held it up. "I've found my friend Harold. Can you believe it? He's waiting at Natterjack Hall for me, and I'm looking forward to getting home and hearing all about his expedition. He's invited me on a research trip. Africa – imagine that! He and I shall hunt toads together again, although perhaps not the way Golly hunts them." He managed what he thought was a believable chuckle. "I really didn't know how I was going to break it to you, but now I don't have to. You and I shall go our separate ways with the proverbial spring in our respective steps." He did his best to smile eagerly, genuinely, as Eliza searched his face for the truth. He must have done a passable job, for after a moment she kissed his cheek.

"Are you sure?" she asked. There was worry in her voice, but thrill too, and Throck nodded vigorously.

"What will I do with the old girl, once I'm off on my African research trip? Leave her to rust in the shed?" And he gestured towards the bike, "Go, I say."

"I couldn't," she said, but Throck could hear in her words that she could, and she would. Any lingering hope that she would choose him evaporated as she climbed onto the machine.

"That's wonderful, Throck, the research trip. I guess I'm as happy for you as you are for me." She turned the lever for the petrol and kicked the pedal. The engine started with only the merest hesitation, and at the sound of her pert pup-pup-pup, Throck swallowed the huge lump that had grown in his throat. Could he change his mind? What was he thinking, letting go of the two things most dear to his heart: his motorcycle and his friend?

Eliza reached out and squeezed his arm. "Are you sure – about the Trusty, I mean?" she asked. And when he didn't – couldn't – reply, she nodded, presuming a yes, and said, "This is goodbye, then. I'll think of you when I look up at the wide sky, Throck. Thank you for everything. And tell George I'll write." She gunned the motorcycle, driving off with a backward wave, and calling, "I'm glad about Harold!"

Throck watched the Trusty disappear around a corner, and he stood for awhile in the street until the smell of her exhaust dissipated. He put the Sowerby purse into his jacket pocket alongside the letter from Harold and was stuffing his books into his haversack when the shop door opened and the narrow-nosed repairman stood there.

"Oi, where d'you think you're goin' without payin'," he said to Throck, stepping into the street.

"I beg your pardon?" said Throck, taken aback. It never occurred to him that Eliza hadn't paid the man. Why hadn't she mentioned it?

"The miss said you'd pay when you got back, said it were your motorcycle," his tone was gruff, and Throck supposed the man was confused by the fact that Eliza had just driven off with the motorcycle.

"Yes, yes of course," said Throck, hastening to reassure the fellow. He didn't want to escalate any trouble; he was on his own, now, and there'd be no relying on Eliza to get him out a scrape. He pulled out the Sowerby wallet and undid the clasp, expecting to see a goodly sum of money, for he had, after all, paid most of the expenses on this trip. But the purse was empty. Not so much as a coin had she left him. He shook his head in disbelief.

The repair shop owner said, suspiciously, "Something wrong?"

"No," replied Throck. He dug for his own purse which, thankfully, still contained enough money to pay for the repair of the Trusty and perhaps a third-class ticket for the train to Watton Hoo. He was glad he had the two cakes purchased on the way from the university, and which, in the moment, he'd forgotten to share with Eliza. At least he wouldn't go hungry on the train ride home. He paid the frowning repairman, and after the fellow had gone back inside his shop, Throck hoisted his haversack. He asked a passerby for directions to the train station. As he trudged there, agog over the fact of the empty wallet, feeling horribly betrayed, he realised what he'd seen on Eliza's wrist as she'd grasped his arm in farewell: a black pearl bracelet that belonged to Loveday Quick.

Chapter 40
JUICY REVELATIONS

Throck alighted from the third-class carriage at the Watton Hoo train station, exhausted by what had been a tedious journey made worse by a talkative fellow seatmate, a woman across the aisle with too many children she couldn't – or wouldn't – keep track of, and a couple behind her, newlyweds perhaps, who giggled and kissed and drowned in one another's stares until Throck had thought he should protest the very indecency of it. But of course, it wasn't indecent, it was just love, and Throck chided himself for his irritation, knowing the root cause of it.

Eliza was gone. Eliza had chosen Golly, and so she should. She was a young lady whose young man loved her. Not once in his life had Throck been a contender for that kind of affection, and he recognised his feelings as envy. He'd never expected a romantic attachment from Eliza, she was young and he was old, but they'd been friends, he thought, and he had admired her. What bothered him was not some unrequited love, but the fact that, in the end, and after all they'd been through together, he'd misjudged her, and had been made to look a fool.

Throck hoisted his grubby haversack and began to walk down the platform. Watton Hoo was a small station, and it seemed to Throck to be busier than he remembered; around him people pushed and jostled, and porters rushed by with trolleys. In the midst of the melee, he heard his name being called, and he turned to see the Mrses Mellows and Meake bearing down on him. They must have exited the first-class carriage, for he hadn't seen them in third. He recalled that the sisters were members of one of Mrs Isbister's clubs, and that she'd never spoken of them over fondly.

"Why, Mr Isbister, as I live and breathe," said one of the ladies. Mrs Meake, he thought. He nodded, and would have carried on but Mrs Mellows, slightly bolder than her sister, put a hand on his arm.

"Gracious, Mr Isbister, you do look a little – worn," she said, and her eyes raked him appraisingly.

"Indeed, Ada," agreed her sister. "If I hadn't just seen you step off the train, Mr Isbister, I'd have thought you must have walked all the way from Scotland."

"I'd have thought the same, Ida," concurred Mrs Mellows, smirking. The ladies seemed to be sharing some sort of humourous innuendo that only they understood. Throck felt impatient, and nodded a second time, trying yet again to be on his way.

"How was Scotland, then, Mr Isbister?" Mrs Meake asked, moving to bar his way. "A sick relative, wasn't it?"

"Or two," added Mrs Mellows, and tittered behind her hand. She didn't pause for an answer, but grasped her sister's arm as if she couldn't bear to suppress her excitement a moment longer, and blurted, "I suppose Mrs Isbister will have written to tell you about the strange turn of events at Sowerby Grange since your departure? The long-lost cousin, and whatnot. Imagine him living right next door at Natterjack Hall all this time and never saying."

"Imagine," repeated Mrs Meake, and raised her eyebrows. "Everyone remarked on how odd it was that this army fellow – the cousin – only discovered his relationship *after* you'd already left for Scotland."

"Indeed," said Mrs Mellows, leaning forward in a conspiratorial manner. "We all thought it a dreadfully difficult position for Mrs Isbister to be in. She there, alone, and without her husband to confirm the fellow's claim. Well, anyone can see how it looks."

Throck's lips were pinched together so tightly he thought they must be white.

Lieutenant-Colonel Barks, then, had moved into Sowerby Grange. His home. Well, Mrs Isbister's family home, but his by address for the last twenty-five years. And if the sisters Meake and Mellows' innuendo were correct, she and Lieutenant-Colonel Barks were, more than likely, romantically involved. He found he wasn't particularly upset, or even very surprised, other than that his usually scandal-averse wife would have taken such a risk. That this was all news to him he was sure the sisters must be dying to confirm, and so he kept his expression neutral and said, "I'm sure I don't know what you mean to imply, ladies. Cousin Barks is a respected military officer, retired. He is a most welcome guest at Sowerby Grange, for however long he chooses to remain." Throck would have tipped his hat and moved on, but he had no hat, so he nodded and started off down the platform.

The sisters were not so easily put off, and hastened after him, catching up and stalking along with him, one on each side. "The – er – relative you went to tend in Scotland," said Mrs Meake. "Much improved, are they?" To which Mrs Mellows added, "It would be impolite of us not to inquire. As friends, we are naturally concerned. Who did you say was ill?"

Throck came to a full stop. He felt entirely ambushed by their pressing, and it got his dander up. "I didn't go to tend a sick relative, if you must know. I wasn't even in Scotland." And here he paused, for angry though he was at the ladies' audacity, he knew he couldn't jeopardize Mrs Isbister's reputation. He sucked in a noseful of air as the sisters hovered, all but rubbing their hands over the expected juicy revelation, and said, "I was despatched by the university at Oxford on a research trip. Very important stuff, new discoveries and whatnot. In collaboration with the esteemed Harold Guppletwill, late of Natterjack Hall. You'll recall him, ladies?"

The sisters, to Throck's pleasure, blinked, for a moment at a loss for words. Obviously, they'd been expecting a rather different confession, and did not know what to make of this information. Throck, taking advantage of their momentary confusion, turned and walked away, but couldn't resist one last fib. Over his shoulder he called importantly, "I'll soon be going on another trip. Cape Town, South Africa. Ghost frogs that only come out on a full moon!"

*

He walked much of the way from the station, although a farmer, the owner of the deranged and now deceased goat, Angus, offered him a lift in the back of his wagon for the last leg. Oddly, the farmer seemed not to recognise him, but Throck supposed he must look rather different, with a scruffy growth of beard and wind-burned skin. More like a tramp than a squire. He jumped off at Sowerby Grange and the farmer gave him a puzzled wave but continued on his way.

There were new black gates at the end of the lane. Dusty, but they swung on well-oiled hinges when Throck pushed them open and walked through. Mrs' garish zinnias, a rather jarring mix of hard pinks and sharp oranges and explosive yellows, stood like soldiers in tidy formation in their beds along the lane. They'd not been in bloom when Throck had left. He rounded the bend in the lane and the house came into view, its stolid, ivy-clad gray walls unchanged, the same lace curtains in the windows, the same heavy polished knocker on the door. He felt a sudden reluctance, as if he didn't belong, and wouldn't be welcomed with open arms. But what had he expected, he asked himself? Even without the complication of Woody Barks.

Trusting no one had spotted him coming up the lane, he veered away from the front of the house, deciding to first pay a visit to his greenhouse. He had no illusions that his ocotillo or his bromeliads or indeed any of his other interesting specimens might have survived his absence, but one could hope. He ducked through the trellised opening in the privet hedge and stopped. The greenhouse was gone. Razed. In its place, a folly – one of those ornamental structures with no actual purpose, often seen on the grounds of some wealthy baron's estate. This one was circular, with Grecian-style pillars and large urns holding nothing. A rather uninviting stone bench was placed to the right of the structure, as if whomever had placed it there expected it to be used to sit and admire – what? The folly's shape? It's audaciousness? It's aspiration to grandeur? Throck shook his head. What on earth had happened to his greenhouse?

Beyond the folly the little shed where he'd hidden the Trusty remained, as dilapidated as ever and with brambles grown up on three sides, but with a small greenhouse-like addition tacked onto its front. Curious, Throck went to investigate. The shed itself smelled faintly of the Trusty, oil and petrol and a remnant of old exhaust, and Throck experienced a sharp pang of nostalgia. In the motorcycle's place were a few of his greenhouse tools: pruners and shears, sieves and hand spades, stacks of pots and seedling trays and even his rubberized apron. Someone, at least, was valiantly continuing his greenhouse efforts, if on a much smaller scale, and when he entered the glass structure itself, he decided it must be George, for there was his ocotillo and a bromeliad and several orchids, duly labelled, chalk on slate, in a childish hand. *Spiky bugr*, read the one sign, stuck into the ocotillo.

It was growing dark, and Throck sighed. There was nothing for it but to show himself at the house, and face whatever he must. He was fully aware that his appearance would cause a bit of a shockwave, and also that he might not be entirely welcomed. If Mrs refused him admittance, he wouldn't blame her, but then what? He hoisted his haversack and went to the house, deciding to simply take things one step at a time.

Chapter 41
FAST FOOTWORK

There'd been no shortage of workmen for the job of dismantling the greenhouse at Sowerby Grange. It seemed everyone in the area, from Watton Hoo to Lesser Plumpton, had not only heard about the gruesome event that had taken place within its glass walls, but had, themselves, a morbid bent, and wanted to be able to claim some small part of it for their own. Alice hired the few men who actually had references and experience with greenhouses, and the job was carried out expeditiously – or chop, chop, as George liked to say, barking at the workmen, until Alice drew him aside and said it was in poor taste, given the outcome for the late Mrs Barks.

For her part, Alice was sorry to let go the potting space for her roses, but not bothered at all to be rid of the memory of the woman she'd begun to refer to as the poor dear, impaled by the pane of glass. Now that Woody's wife was undeniably dead, Alice felt she could be magnanimous. Nor was she unhappy to have Mr's awful, spikey excuses for plants gone, although George had requested, and been granted, a bit of a salvage of some of the glass and several of Mr's botanical specimens. Alice enjoyed indulging George, and assigned one of the workmen to help him erect a smaller, quasi-greenhouse attached to an old shed and with a good, solid, shingled roof, and there George pottered. He looked like a little old man, she thought affectionately, watching him clump about the place in Mr's discarded wellingtons, wearing a pair of his braces to hold up his trousers and whistling jaunty tunes.

In place of the large greenhouse, Alice had had erected a bower, complete with Grecian statues and stone benches, and was fully confident that eventually a respectable garden would be cultivated in the space to enhance its charm. Serhan's friends – artists, no less, though she'd learned not to hold that against them – professed not to mind the lack of privet hedges and climbing roses and topiary shrubbery, but Alice had assured them all that such necessities were indeed forthcoming, given time.

That she would not have entertained, mere months ago, such friends as Serhan kept, Alice was quite aware. She supposed Mr Isbister, were he ever to know, would say she'd grown as a person, widened her horizons, become more accepting. And while that was probably true (though she'd never admit it to him, of all people), the reality was that she'd felt less constricted, less pinched, more able to breathe, as silly as that sounded, after he'd disappeared. But it was a fact. The Alice of old was, if not gone, certainly transformed, as the way the whorls and swoops and daubs of Serhan's paintings came of single blobs of oiled colour on a pallet. Alice professed quite honestly that she did not understand Serhan's work at all – he called it Abstractionism – but she could appreciate his ability to create something from nothing and the satisfaction it gave him to do it. She likened her talent at designing a new garden, or redecorating a room, to his with a brush, and commended herself that she and Serhan – an artist – had a common bond.

Eglantine was another matter, but Alice did not feel the need to curry any favour in that quarter. She had resigned herself to the fact that she and Eglantine would never form any attachments, or develop any bonds. They disliked one another, and that was the plain truth of it. It irked Alice no end that Eglantine was included in the arrangements that had been made regarding Natterjack Hall next door, but what could Alice say? It was not her business and she knew it, and she also knew better than to say too much at all where Eglantine was concerned, for the woman would be defended, albeit gently, by both Woody and Serhan. Alice had learned, when Eglantine was mentioned, to pinch her lips as tightly as possible lest anything escape – a snort, a sniff, a pfft, a pshaw, a sneer – and earn her a look of disappointment from her beloved. That, she could not bear. So, she put up with Eglantine residing next door, parading about like the mistress of Natterjack Hall, and whilst in fact the arrangement was that Woody had given up his interest in the residence and Captain Plucky held the lease, Eglantine and Serhan lived there, and Serhan had turned the place into a retreat of sorts for his artist friends. That Serhan and his fellow painters chose to spend so much time at Sowerby Grange instead of Natterjack Hall reinforced Alice's opinion that Eglantine was simply too unpleasant to tolerate for very long. Alice, in contrast, made an effort for Serhan's sake to be welcoming, and even tried to remember the names of his friends. Alice was also aware that Captain Plucky continued to visit Natterjack Hall, though what the man saw in such a harridan Alice could not credit. George, her font of information, relayed the gossip that they were engaged to be married, but neither Serhan nor Woody had mentioned such an event, and Alice chalked the idea up to George's fancies. She knew, of course, that Woody and Serhan tiptoed around the topic of Eglantine in Alice's presence, so it was possible that there were impending nuptials of which Alice was blissfully ignorant. She told herself that if the two did wed, perhaps Woody would gift them with an extended honeymoon somewhere far away – Canada, mayhap, or Australia – and they'd love it so much they'd stay there. She made a mental note to suggest such a trip, should the opportunity arise. In the meantime, Captain Plucky was often at Natterjack Hall for indecent periods of time, likely setting chins wagging in Watton Hoo.

That Alice herself was the subject of malicious tongues she chose to ignore, and by only occasionally associating with anyone from the villages – she continued with her Horticultural Society, of course, and felt it her duty to attend the local Women's Institute – she was able to do so rather successfully. George was her fetcher and carrier, her maid and cook, her delivery boy and staunch supporter. If he defended her honour in the village shops, Alice appreciated it, but took it as her due. George's loyalty was unparalleled, and for that she treated him like the son she'd never had, once removed. Since the incident in the greenhouse with the late Mrs Barks, she'd expanded her generosity where he was concerned, providing him his own rooms (Mr's old ones) and the contents therein, leaving him to his own devices, and giving him use of the cart and pony whenever he wanted it. She cared about him mightily, and indulged him with pocket money and bosomy hugs that he endured with a roll of his eyes. In return, meals were never late and were always delicious; her clothes were always freshly laundered and tidied away in armoire and bureau; the furniture smelled pleasantly of lemon oil, and the carpets were never dusty. He took care of Sowerby Grange as skilfully and with as much dedication as he took care of her, and she was currently considering including him in her will.

For the most part, if one disregarded the circumstance of the demise of the late Mrs Barks, Alice's life since Mr had disappeared had been rather pleasant. The idea that one could be abandoned by one's husband of many years – not even a horrible fellow, mind, just a rather ordinary man – and be happier for it was something that ought to be blamed on someone, she felt sure. She supposed there were any number of candidates for the target of her recrimination, herself among them, but Alice was not one to plumb feelings in any depth, and so the most she would allow herself was the recognition that her current happiness was rather less the result of the absence of Mr and rather more the fact of the presence of Woody. For Woody had moved into Sowerby Grange, and behind closed doors, at least, he and she were man and wife.

As scandalous as the old Alice would have found that state of affairs, the new Alice told herself it was the least she deserved after a life spent apart from her beloved. With the help of George, she put it about in the villages that Woody was a long-lost cousin, that his residence at Natterjack Hall had been pure coincidence and that one day, in conversation, they'd realised they were related! Of course, once she'd written to Mr – in Scotland, remember, tending the still-sick relative – he'd insisted that Woody stay with them at Sowerby Grange. Given the confusion of the tenancies at Natterjack Hall which had yet to be resolved, it seemed only prudent that Woody graciously concede to Captain Plucky, with whom he'd been sharing the house, and move his bags to Sowerby Grange. George, telling the various big-eared shopkeepers the story, worded it differently, "it were only fittin', then, weren't it, that the honourable Barks give over to Cap'n Plucky, an' thanks be to his cousin, Mrs Isbister, he ain't havin' to live in the gutter. She put him in the finest guest room, and I unpacked his bags. Cor', you should see his uniform! Smart as you like red wool, brass buttons all polished. Gots a medal tucked in a fancy box, too, on account of he's an 'ero." These partial truths – there *was* a grand uniform, there *were* a couple of medals – George trotted out to distract his listeners from considering too closely the fact that Woody had moved in with Alice.

In truth, the village wags were much more interested in the goings-on at Natterjack Hall. Captain Plucky was often seen about the countryside in the company of Eglantine, and they did make a dashing couple, even Alice could admit. Captain Plucky wore slim-fitting cream suits, bow ties and a Panama hat, whilst Eglantine sashayed in fluttery frocks that left little to the imagination – no sleeves, low necklines, high hemlines, sheer fabrics – it was enough to shock a frog. The two entertained rather more than was decent; dashing city people, Alice suspected, seeing several jaunty automobiles flash by, one after another, when she was inspecting the zinnia beds near the road. She could hear the cars gear down, and knew without being able to see them that they were turning into the lane at Natterjack Hall. From George, she knew that Eglantine ran with a modern crowd, and had "weekends," whatever that was, and that "posh" types, to use George's expression, frequented the house for her parties. Alice complained to Woody about the traffic on the road – the dust was playing havoc with her zinnias, and the black iron gate she'd had installed at the end of the driveway seemed always in need of cleaning – but Woody haha'd nervously and tugged at his whiskers, indication, Alice knew, that he didn't want to discuss it.

In addition to the guests that arrived for Captain Plucky and Eglantine's weekends, a steady stream of artists, friends of Serhan's, came and went from Natterjack Hall. George said they were Bohemian, but Alice couldn't detect any sort of foreign accent. They were young and, in Alice's opinion, exceedingly odd; the women wore their hair short, the men long, they strode about barefoot, and had not a care for their clothing, which might be velvet short pants or old-fashioned cloaks or paint-smeared tunics. George said Natterjack Hall had become an artists' colony, which made Alice think of something Mr had once said about ants, and it was true that these odd young people did run about hither and thither like insects, their purpose in question, at a loss as to where they'd left their artists' accoutrements, or indeed, Alice thought not unkindly, their good sense. They seemed the very opposite of the people that visited Captain Plucky and Eglantine, they with their foot-long cigarette holders and their silver-headed walking sticks and their carefully cultivated accents (so George reported), and it was for this reason, Alice suspected, that on those weekends when Eglantine's crowd came,

Serhan's friends gravitated to Sowerby Grange, traipsing through Whortleberry Wood at all hours, setting up easels in the back garden and eating in her kitchen. At first, Alice had felt rather affronted by the audacity, but Serhan could always win her over, and when the young people smiled so charmingly and called her Mrs B, well, how could she resist? Before long, she was not startled to walk into her kitchen, or her parlour, or her garden at any given hour of the day and find pixie-like Seraphine there, or moustachioed Claude, who drank more coffee than was healthy, surely, or Lionel who wore a Scottish tam morning, noon and night. If it was early, she wouldn't see Tupper or Philo, who always slept until noon, nor likely Flower – was that really the girl's name? – for when she wasn't painting, she seemed to enjoy flitting about the woods, which she'd deemed "ethereal." Serhan, if he was present, never failed to jump up and offer Alice his chair, and once in a while, she accepted. Invariably, she'd interrupted a conversation about something in the art world, but the chatter resumed as casually as if she was one of them, and she listened to the group of friends talk about everything painterly, from the quality of canvas to Lionel's choice of crimson or vermillion for the focal point of his latest work, to the rise and perhaps fall of Fauvism, whatever that was. If, occasionally, she felt a mild twinge of guilt that had to do with a vague recollection of objecting to Mr's interest in art, if that's what he'd had, she batted it away. This, she told herself, was quite a different thing. These young people, these eager, pleasant and polite friends of Serhan's, working so diligently over their easels, sipping her coffee and including her, were not at all the same kettle of fish, she was quite sure.

*

It was a Saturday evening, and the drawing room at Sowerby Grange was full, the air a fug of cigarette and pipe smoke, another thing Alice had learned not to mind in this new modern age. Claude, who loved to cook almost as much as he loved to paint, had, with George, put together a lovely dinner of stuffed quail, tomato aspic and iced curry in cucumber cases, and now the whole gang, Alice, Woody, George, Serhan and his six painter friends, well fed and with cocktails in hand (except for George, who had chocolate milk, his favourite), had retired for a bit of leisure. Serhan asked Alice about the old square piano in the corner of the room, covered with a heavy brocade cloth, and when she admitted she could play, although not very well, he and his friends egged her on until she agreed to perform a piece. George helped her removed the bric-a-brac and the brocaded cover, and Alice opened the keyboard lid and plunked hesitantly at the ivory keys.

"What shall I play?" she asked shyly. Her repertoire was not large or modern, she told them, and when she did play, it was Mozart, or Bach, or Beethoven, and all rather poorly. George had taught her a few songs on the little upright piano in her sitting room, but for the life of her she couldn't recall them now. She tinkled the keys hesitantly, sounding out the somewhat morose first few bars of Beethoven's *Moonlight Sonata*, made worse when she hit several wrong notes. The company glanced at one another, and Alice felt a moment of acute embarrassment.

"Perhaps this was a bad idea," she said, twisting towards Woody, hoping for deliverance. He looked sheepish, and said with a shrug, "I don't know, old girl, maybe give it a go?"

"I'll play," George said, jumping yet again to the rescue, and Alice squeezed his arm as she shuffled over on the bench. He grinned at her, and his fingers danced nimbly over the keys in a jaunty intro, and Alice smiled proudly. Woody gave him a nudge and said, "Eh, then, where'd you learn the ivories, youngster?"

"Music hall," George replied. "Me Aunty Gin-Gin were one o' the greats."

"Gin-Gin? Gin-Gin Geneva?" Lionel interjected. "Crikey! I saw her once at the Coronet in Bermondsey. She could sing, by God. The whole hall gave her an ovation when she hit the final high note of *The Boy in the Gallery*."

"Gracious," said Alice. One day, she was going to get George's whole story.

George began to thump the old square's keyboard, and Alice thought the ancient instrument had never, in its very long existence in this drawing room, been played with such gusto. Its very shape, rectangular, though it was called a square, and its sombre ebonised casework, ornately carved, bespoke the Victorian age, and indeed when Alice, as a child, had been sitting upon its bench at her lessons she'd even then recognised the old-world smell of it: oiled hinges and cracked varnish and a dust layer, no doubt, upon its hidden hammers. She wondered the piano could make such sounds as George was wresting from its decrepit carcass, but indeed the drawing room, always a place of solemn quiet, was filled with lively noise. Lionel and Seraphine, then Tupper and Flower, got up to dance, a frenzied effort that Alice thought looked as if the partners had a terrible itch that couldn't be reached. It hadn't occurred to her that people danced to this sort of racket, but it did look like fun, all that wiggling of shoulders and fast footwork. When Serhan held out a hand to her, inviting her to try it, she blushed from her forehead to her bosom, and wondered for a panicked moment if she dared. She glanced at Woody, who was smiling widely, his cheeks round apples, and then at George who called over the exuberant music, "Come on, missus!" And so she allowed Serhan to heave her from the bench and put his arm around her ample waist and then she followed his lead into a quick two-step. Tap, tap, tap, dip. Shimmy-shimmy, shimmy-shimmy. Tap, tap, tap, dip. Shimmy-shimmy, shimmy-shimmy. All her parts jiggled, and she was quickly winded, but good golly it was fun! The others begged off, laughing, and collapsed on the sofa, but Alice and Serhan soldiered on, shimmy-shimmy, and now Woody cut in, taking Serhan's place. Pressed together, elbows out, they tap-tapped and dipped, and the young people hooted and clapped and George thumped extra hard on the keys before bringing the song to a close with a happy tinkle of the ivories. Alice, aware of sweaty armpits and a heaving bosom and barely able to catch her breath, fell against Woody, laughing.

Over his shoulder, framed in the doorway behind him, she saw a small, sun-browned fellow with a scruffy beard and a haversack over his shoulder, and her heart nearly stopped.

"Throckmorton!" she cried, just as he squawked, "Alice?" And she fainted dead away.

*

Alice wasn't a swooner by nature. She was made of much sterner stuff and had never been the wilting flower sort, so she was rather embarrassed to come to with a cough and a sputter to find smelling salts being waved beneath her nostrils. The entire painterly set, not to mention Woody and George, were gathered around, peering at her as if they'd never seen a woman faint before, and she struggled to sit up, though the act of doing so made her woozy. Everyone fussed, and Woody patted her hand worriedly, but she gritted her teeth and told them it was the strenuous two-step that had done her in, and she was, in fact, fine. George suggested they all leave her to recuperate, and even Woody melted away. When everyone had gone, Alice opened her eyes a slit and looked at George.

"Was it *him?*" she whispered, thinking she might have imagined Mr there, like a bad dream.

"Yes, missus, it were," said George, nodding.

"Did he – did he and Woody speak?"

"No, missus. I don't fink no-one else saw him. Once you went down everyone flocked to you like flies to jam, and Mr Isbister, he scarpered. I followed him out, and asked him to wait in the garden."

Alice shut her eyes again and lay still. What did it mean, his returning like this? What about Woody? More pressing, what about she and Woody, as a couple? She felt physically ill, and she thought a headache might be coming on. Perhaps she could ask George to make her excuses, and she could take to her bed. To her and Woody's bed, though, there was the conundrum, and where was Woody expected to go? Where would Mr go, for that matter, since George now occupied his rooms? Good gracious, it was all such a mad muddle. Her world, her perfectly lovely happiness, seemed about to collapse. Why on earth had he come back, anyway? There was nothing for him here. Her eyes flicked open again and focused on George.

"The maid. The one he left with. Is she back too?" There was an edge to her tone. If the maid was back, she'd make them both leave. It was audacious of Mr to expect her to look the other way, as if nothing at all had happened, as if he hadn't abandoned her and taken that impertinent maid with him. She of the red hair and uncommonly blue eyes. Alice's own jaunt to a certain hotel in Nookey Hollow she conveniently put out of her mind.

"Didn't see her, missus," replied George.

"Well, I suppose that's something," Alice muttered. She ruminated for a few minutes, wringing her hands, then said to George, "You wouldn't talk to him, would you, George? See if you can find out what he intends? I mean, what's he *doing* here?"

"Well, don't he live here, missus?" George asked with a puzzled frown.

"Just go and see, George," Alice said, exasperation in her voice. She closed her eyes again, but within minutes Woody had poked his head into the doorway. She could hear the thick sound of his breathing from across the room, and it occurred to her, foul-tempered as she was, that the noise of it was something that would irritate her in years to come. The slight whistle, as if his nasal passages were just a little too small for the amount of breath his big lungs required. And the nostril hairs that required clipping. Why did men have to have such obvious nostril hairs? She sighed. "What is it, Woody dear?"

"Everything all right, love?" he sounded anxious. Her irritation of a moment ago disappeared. He was a good man. A sweet man, even if there was the still-to-be-resolved question of his actual military rank. It hadn't escaped her notice that mail forwarded from Natterjack Hall, as with the records at the lunatic asylum, referred to him as a mere major. Of course, she would forgive him padding his rank to impress her, but she didn't want others to be aware of the truth and she to appear a dupe.

"Just fine, dear heart," she said. "Go on up to bed, why don't you? I'll be along in a while. Don't wait."

"If you're sure, duck," he said, and Alice's heart wobbled. How precious he was, major or lieutenant-colonel. Mr Isbister must not be allowed to ruin things for them.

"Quite sure, darling," she replied. "George is fetching me tea and a bit of cherry tart. It'll fix me right up. It always does."

"Mmm, cherry tart sounds just the thing," Woody said, advancing into the room. His great, round belly strained his waistcoat buttons nicely, and she looked at him appreciatively. Goodness, but he was a handsome devil of a man. She took a steadying breath, and resisted the urge to pat the cushions beside her. This was not the time for that. Right now, she had business to see to. Mr Isbister was waiting. She touched fingertips to temple and frowned, and Woody paused in mid-step.

"I'll bring you some, shall I?" she said, pointedly. And, perceptive as ever, Woody understood that his company was not currently desired. He blew her a kiss and backed out of the room, and she waited until she could hear the creak of the stairs under his heavy tread as he went up to bed, then she swung her feet to the floor, steeled her resolve, and went to find Mr Isbister in the garden.

*

Alice snuck across the garden to George's little greenhouse, lit from within by a flickering oil lamp. She'd decided her best approach would be the offensive, which had always worked to her advantage where Mr was concerned. That she'd bullied him throughout their marriage, she could allow. That he'd never stood up to her was his own fault. And now, at the most important crossroads of her life, she must continue to hold the upper hand.

Strangely, she did not need it. She entered the greenhouse, jaw set, prepared for one of their confounding conversations where she accused and he made excuses, where she tried, with words, to grab hold of him and shake, yet he slipped away as if oiled. Instead, the very look of him gave her pause. Oh, certainly he was the same small man he'd always been, an inch or so shorter than she, but this person no longer seemed inconsequential, and there was a vitality about him that was new, as if something fresh and curious and energetic coursed within him. He had...purpose. He looked fit; his skin burnished from sun and wind, and he'd lost the appearance of a turtle with no shell, although that could have been due to his growth of beard. He smiled tremulously, disarming her, and held out his hand as if to a polite acquaintance, and when she shook it, she noticed that his skin was rough and he had a red leather bracelet on his wrist and, of all things, a tattoo of a potato on his forearm. She was shocked to feel a tiny flutter in her stomach that she recognised as attraction, and wondered what on earth that could mean in its current context.

They spoke, surprisingly civilly – how have you been, well, thank you, I see you've put in an arboretum, down-sized the greenhouse. Neither referred to the months spent apart, the really big issues sitting like several proverbial elephants in the room. Instead, they conversed as if they were barely acquainted. The closest they came to touching on important matters was when Alice said, stiffly, "The maid – I forget her name – is she...here?" To which Mr replied, flatly, "No. Although I heard that Lieutenant-Colonel Barks has been around a lot? I met the

Tracy Kasaboski

Mrses Meake and Mellows at the train station." Alice had the good grace to pinch her lips, and change the subject.

After a few minutes, Mr said he was terribly tired and he didn't like to be a bother but was there a bed he could use, and she, carefully, did not ask if he was staying but instead told him George had his old rooms, if he didn't mind sharing, to which he said he did not. The guest rooms, as he knew, had long been mothballed and the beds put into storage. They'd never entertained overnight guests, so there'd been no need to keep them at the ready. Mr then said he'd remain in the greenhouse a while longer if that was alright, that he'd missed his plants, and Alice nodded and went back to the house alone.

*

Woody slumbered in the big bed, cherry tart forgotten, but Alice couldn't yet entertain the idea of sleep. She sat in the wing-back chair in her bedroom and counted her blessings, insofar as she understood them. Mr Isbister had not railed and ranted, nor had he accused her of any wrongdoing, and she'd not had to defend herself or any of her recent choices. In fact, he seemed very much a visitor, someone who was not staying, and although they'd spoken not at all about the future, either short or long term, she had the distinct impression that he was elsewhere, somewhere other than Sowerby Grange. Indeed, somewhere other than this particular pocket of England. For her part, she'd been magnanimous, she thought, in saying nothing about the maid, or the theft of her purse and the household account monies – although she reserved that trump card should she need it.

The window next to Alice was open; it was a warm night, and the thin white curtain wafted slightly. Through their opaque screen she could see George's little greenhouse. It remained lit, and she could make out Mr Isbister moving about, and another, smaller body following. George, she surmised. The two of them comparing notes, perhaps, on those horrible spiky plants. On the slate roof tiles outside her window, she could hear the patter of a gentle rain, the sound just reaching her over the low, contented snores coming from the mound in the bed that was Woody. How deeply and completely she loved Woody, and, at the same time, oddly, how fortunate she was to have married a man like Mr Isbister, and how grateful she was, in this moment, for both of them.

450

Chapter 42
HAPPINESS

Throck sat on an upturned bucket in the darkness of the old shed, his chin on his fist. He thought about his bland and evasive conversation with Mrs, and he considered what he'd earlier witnessed, Alice – very different from Mrs – dancing with abandon and yodeling as if she hadn't a care in the wide world. In all the years he'd lived with her, he'd never seen his wife have fun. And yet, what a wonderful way to be, if one could. Surely, when one was truly happy, as Mrs had appeared to be, one could dance as she had, as light as a feather on breeze. He'd felt that same feeling himself often enough over the past months he'd been away. Free as a bird. Light as a feather. Happiness was a great elixir.

And then she'd seen him.

So, what did it all mean? What did the future hold for Roderick Throckmorton Isbister? He wasn't certain he belonged here, if he ever had. The only place on this whole property where he felt a connection was this old shed, its darkness and pungent smells like the comfort of an old blanket. Twenty-five years he'd shuffled about Sowerby Grange, wearing flannel slippers within, old wellingtons without, doing nothing much besides padding his frame and losing his hair. Oh, granted, he'd had his greenhouse plants the last several years, and his jaunts with Harold before that, and there'd been many good books that had helped while away the hours, but if he was honest, the most fun he'd had, the most excitement he'd known in his long and rather lacklustre life, had, so far, been these recent few months spent with Eliza roaming the countryside on his Trusty. The knowledge that that was at an end brought him full circle, to the here and now. Himself, sitting alone in the dark in his old shed. What came next, indeed?

The shed door creaked open, and George entered. The boy had grown in the months Throck had been away, shooting up like a weed, Eliza might have said, but the dark forelock flopping down over his eye was unchanged. Now that he knew, from Eliza, that Stephen Vanson aka

Plucky was the boy's father, the resemblance was plain. George stuck out his hand, and Throck stood, and shook it.

"Good to see you, George," Throck said.

"Bit of a shock, seein' you, sar," George replied.

"It did look that way, George," Throck said. "I'm not sure what I'm meant to do, now."

"I guess you'll be figgerin' that out in the next while or two," George replied matter-of-factly.

"Indeed," said Throck, tapping his chin contemplatively. His frown deepened. "Has Mrs Isbister seemed – well, happy these past months I've been gone?"

"As a lark, sar," George answered, and shrugged, as if to apologize.

"As a lark, eh?" repeated Throck. He nodded, and gave George a wistful smile. "I see you've been tending my ocotillo and my bromeliads. And you've prompted my moth orchid to flower. I'd been coaxing it along but to no avail."

George looked bashful at the compliment. "I dunno, sar. Missus says I've got a green finger or somefink. They just bloom for me. I don't fink I do nuffink special."

"Obviously you do, though, George," said Throck kindly. "Give me a tour. Maybe you can tell me what happened to the old structure, if you don't mind." They wandered out of the shed and into the little greenhouse, and Throck heard the awful tale of the deranged Defne Barks, and how she'd tied Alice to her bed and thrown the lamp onto the bedclothes, and then how Alice had escaped that and tracked her out to the greenhouse, where the unfortunate Mrs Barks had been nearly sliced in half by the falling pane of glass. Throck was speechless as George relayed the story, barely able to imagine such horror.

"Missus weren't wanting the greenhouse after that, not even for her mums and pansies," George said with a slight wince, and Throck, noticing his expression, was gratified to know the boy shared his aversion to Mrs' taste in the botanical.

"And yet, you have this," Throck said, gesturing round at the small, but adequate structure.

"Missus is kind to me," George said earnestly. "I dunno why. But I like her, and she likes me. We rub along, as she likes to say. I wouldn't want nobody to hurt her, know what I mean?" This last he said not exactly threateningly, but with a definite admonishment, as if he expected that Throck's presence here would do just that.

They remained in the greenhouse a little longer. The moist warmth was comforting, and it was a joy to press the soil of some of George's plants and feel the damp sponginess under his fingers. The moth orchid was flowering beautifully, and a cutting of something was rooting in a glass jar. Throck peered closer and recognised it as a slip of his crassula succulent, which George had labelled *jucy bugr*. Throck nodded and smiled, and it occurred to him that it would be fun to have a protégé, someone with whom he could share what he knew of the horticultural and botanical arts. There, perhaps, was a purpose for his life. Teacher, mentor, dispenser of knowledge. But even as he considered it, he recognised the idea for the crutch it was.

*

Days passed. Throck spent them in his old apartment. George moved back to his tiny attic room, although Throck had said he would be happy with such a space, an offer that mortified George, unaware that Throck had spent the better part of the last few months sleeping on the ground with nothing but a tatty old rug for a blanket. George seemed to understand that Throck was eager for company, though, so he visited often, and Throck shared his stories while George listened. And as Throck talked he confirmed to himself what he already knew: the times spent on the open road, while often uncomfortable, sometimes frightening, sometimes bewildering, had been the very best of his days. He missed them terribly. He often lost himself in daydreams, remembering laying on that rock in the pouring rain by the muddy lake, almost nose to nose with the bullfrogs, or laughing with Mungo by the campfire, or standing beneath the waterfall with Eliza, fish nibbling his toes. George asked about Eliza, said he'd had letters, although not recently, and Throck replied evasively that she was well, and that he'd given her the Trusty. Of all things, that had impressed George the most, and he'd said, "Corrrr…" in a worshipful tone.

"I'm sure she'll write," Throck said, reassuringly. He hoped that was true, and he hoped she would tell George about Golly, and that they planned to wed. It wasn't Throck's place, he had decided, to share that news. George, for his part, didn't seemed to mind Eliza's absence. In fact, he appeared to take it for granted that she was not coming back, and was happy and content at Sowerby Grange, catering to "missus" and her fluctuating household. Not that Throck ever had contact with his wife's – er – paramour, or the man's son, Serhan, or his artist friends, other than spying them through the gauze of the bedroom curtains if they lunched outside, or the young people appeared on the lawn to play croquet, or to sit at their easels sketching. Through the open window he listened to their laughter with a yearning for their sort of company, but he could not bring himself, yet, to dare a meeting with them, and expose himself to looks of pity, or ridicule, or resentment. And so, he sat in his old rooms, slippered feet on a footstool, reading books, eating food brought on a tray by George, and day by day felt his life reverting to mundane monotony, like the orchid in the greenhouse that would fade to unspectacular dormancy after its burst of bloom.

The weeks trundled by. George continued to deliver Throck's meals on a tray, but George's initial fascination with his stories had waned, and very often the boy did not stay for much of a chat. Throck conceded that he was poor company. He considered borrowing his wellingtons from George and going for a walk in Whortleberry Wood, but in truth the idea held little appeal, and he did not want George to think he must now give back the boots. It seemed best and easiest for everyone concerned if he just kept to himself, and for the time being it suited him to do just that.

One day, a month or more after his arrival back at Sowerby Grange – he'd lost track of the days – he sat nodding in his chair by the open window. It was a sunny, autumn day, and breezy. He'd just partaken of a delicious fish paste sandwich and some dilled cucumbers, and he was considering his tummy and noting that it had begun to take on its slightly pudgy shape of old. As he sat navel-gazing, a thin strip of drool escaped his lip, and puddled, right there, on his dressing gown, next to a tomato soup stain. He stared at the small circle of dampness, and, suddenly and inexplicably, began to cry. He snivelled, snorted, and hiccupped, feeling like a man drowning in melancholia, but the more he listened to himself, the more he sounded like a petulant child whose marbles had been taken away. He clenched the arms of his chair and willed himself to stop. This was no good. It would not do. He drew a deep, steadying breath, pulled a handkerchief from the pocket of his dressing gown, dried his eyes and blew his nose, then got out of his chair. He shed his dressing gown and the rumpled nightshirt beneath it, doffed his slippers and pulled on proper clothing – trousers, held snugly by the leather belt he'd carved himself, a clean shirt and a waistcoat. He put socks on his feet and stepped into some shoes, then he rolled up his sleeves, tied Carlotta's bracelet onto his wrist, and put a flat cap that had seen better days onto his head. He surveyed himself in the mirror. Apart from the red eyes, he recognised the fellow looking back at him. He'd taken life by the proverbial horns, ridden a motorcycle through the countryside, slept in the open air, laughed with a damsel, made new friends and tracked down an old one. He was a man who found life interesting, to whom the world had extended an invitation, and who had only just begun to experience what was on offer. He drew himself up, turned, and went down to the garden.

*

Alice spotted him first, and he saw her mouth drop open as he approached. She wore a bright yellow dress that made her dark hair appear rather more lustrous than he recalled it being, or perhaps she'd put some kind of rinse through it to achieve the same effect. Women did those sorts of things, he knew, although the Alice he'd been married to never would have. She did dress her hair less severely than she used to, even tucking a perky pansy among the strands, and Throck approved of the change, not that she would care what he thought. She stood and hastened towards him, perhaps hoping to head him off before he reached the group, but Throck had no intention of being deterred from his purpose. He called out, "Lovely afternoon!" and everyone swiveled in his direction.

He gave Alice a nod and a smile but breezed past her and went straight to Woody, who was spluttering into his coffee, and scrambling, obviously, to grasp what was happening. Should he expect a punch? But Throck shook Woody's hand, and said amiably, "How have you been,

Woody? Well, I hope. Good to see you." Then, while Woody gaped, he turned towards the young people seated nearby behind their easels, arrayed in a semi-circle. The tall, dark-haired one, exceedingly handsome but with the languid movements of someone who enjoyed rather a lot of leisure time, rose and approached, and Throck knew that this was Serhan, Woody's son, and likely felt obliged to play the role of protector. Throck nipped any unpleasantness from that quarter in the bud, and stuck out his hand. "You must be Serhan. George has told me all about you. Lovely to meet you, and your friends, I'm sure." He gestured expansively to include them in his greeting. "You're artists, I hear. We have a love of art in common, did you know? I profess a profound admiration for Monet, although likely your own tastes run towards something more…abstract?" Over Serhan's shoulder he could see a sketch of what appeared to be a geometry lesson, all circles and squares and trapezoids.

This comment stirred a buzz of conversation among the young artists, and Throck was quickly forgotten. Alice had come to stand dumbly at his side, and Throck turned to her and offered his arm. To Woody, he said, "You won't mind if Alice and I take a short walk?" Without awaiting a reply, he led her away.

"You've changed," he said, when they were out of earshot. And when she pulled away from him slightly, as if to protest, he drew her back and smiled. "I mean that only in the most complimentary way. I can see plainly how you've arranged your life, and I also see it doesn't include me. Nor should it. You and I have never been what one might call a lovesome duo. Not even a contented pair, really. We have nothing in common, and, I think, if we're honest, we'd agree that neither would have chosen the other for a mate, had we been given much choice in the matter. So here, then, is the crux of it. I believe that everyone deserves a chance at a joyful union, if they find it within their grasp. And I also believe that that is what you have with Woodward Barks."

Alice spluttered as if she would deny the statement out of some attempt at propriety, but Throck held up a hand. "Don't dissemble. There's no need. I want you to be happy. And to that end, I've had a bit of an epiphany, because, you see, I want to be happy too, and my happiness does not involve living here, at Sowerby Grange, with you." He smiled kindly at her, to soften the rawness of the words, though they both knew the truth of them. "I'm leaving. Again. Tomorrow, possibly, but I want to arrange things so you are left in the best possible light, from all perspectives, if you understand my meaning." Alice blinked, appearing somewhat gobsmacked, so Throck continued. "You'll recall me mentioning that when I arrived at the Watton Hoo train station, I met – was accosted by, really – the redoubtable Mrses Meake and Mellows, who tripped over themselves to tell me of the – er – living arrangements that had come about in my absence. They suspected that, in fact, Lieutenant-Colonel Barks was making a cuckold of me, and that the story of Woody being a cousin was nothing but a fib meant to cover up your illicit affair. The sisters, I'm sure, fully expected me to express anger and shock, and they practically licked their lips in anticipation of me storming off to take my manly vengeance on the scoundrel and you, my dear, my cheating wife." From the corner of his eye, he saw her flush. "To their own shock and disappointment, I instead confirmed the tale, said Woody was indeed our cousin, had moved into the Grange with my blessing, and further disavowed them of their notion that I'd been in Scotland tending a sick relative. In fact, I told them, I'd been on a research trip for Oxford university, collaborating with Harold Guppletwill. And further, I said, I'd be leaving soon on another. To Cape Town, South Africa." He grinned, remembering. "I wanted to thumb my nose, but didn't."

He let that speech sink in as they walked, their stride matching, unified. Throck supposed it was the first, and perhaps only time he and Alice had been in symmetry. It was pleasant.

"Well, thank you," she said, cowed.

Throck nodded in acknowledgement. "In all honesty, I didn't do it for you. Well, partially. I did want to put the busybodies in their place. But mostly, I did it for myself, to set up a path of escape," he said, surprising himself at his admission.

"Escape?" said Alice. "Oh, from here, you mean. Well, you do look like an adventurer these days. The beard, the tattoo, this strange leather thing on your wrist. Overall, it's rather a bold presentation. It wouldn't be a hard thing to believe, you on some kind of expedition." She glanced at him, as if to take the measure of him. "So, are you? Going, I mean.'"

"I am," he replied. He spoke firmly, as much to convince himself as to convince Alice. He stopped, turned, and took both her hands in his. "Not to South Africa, perhaps, but somewhere. I don't think I'll be back. But you have that story if you want to use it to shield you from the gossips. I'll write, if you'd like me to."

"I would," she said, and Throck was gratified to see her touch her eye. Did she perhaps dash a tear? He thought about planting a kiss on her cheek, such was the moment, but they'd never been a kissing couple, and Woody stood watching them from the other side of the lawn, concern apparent in the spectacular droop of his mutton-chops. Unnoticed by him, the young set had begun a game of leapfrog, cavorting about like children. Throck smiled, and squeezed Alice's hand. Perhaps they'd been friends, of a sort, without even knowing it.

*

The next day, Throck left Sowerby Grange again. This time, George drove him to the train station with the cart and pony. Alice and Woody waved from the front door. It was all terribly civilised, he thought, and would have been exciting, even, had he any idea at all where he was going. In the spirit of adventure, he'd decided he would choose a destination at random once he got to the station and read the schedule. Any town would do. He told himself it was intrepid, and would be amusing, but in fact he felt a bit lonely. He wished he had a travel companion to help make it seem fun.

He had his haversack, freshly kitted out with clean clothes, a stash of handkerchiefs and some food wrapped in butcher's paper – cheese, eggs, bread, apples, the staples. He had money in the Sowerby wallet, and a promise, freely given, from Alice of a small stipend, deposited monthly to his account in Lesser Plumpton. He left his art book behind; Serhan had been glad of the gift of it, and to George he gave *The Illustrated Handbook of English Botany*, extracting both the *campanula patula* blossom pressed between its pages (a memory of Eliza), and a promise from George that he would take good care of the ocotillo and the other plants. The blossom he tucked into the envelope containing Harold's letter, the words of which he'd read so many times since first devouring them on the train ride from Oxford that he could have recited the passage by rote. Admittedly, it was frustratingly short, but it was communication, nonetheless, and he was grateful Harold had thought to write him at all. *Dearest Throck,* Harold had written, *the Amazonian expedition has been the most excellent adventure. I have seen and done things I could not have imagined. Rest assured, I found the giant toad! I know you did not doubt. I cannot wait to tell you all about it when I see you. The conflict with Germany has rather put the kibosh on a proper finish-up here, so I imagine I'll be making my way back to old England soon. All the best, your friend, Harold G.*

George was in a bit of a rush, he told Throck apologetically as they pulled up at the station. He had a nice joint on order for dinner, and the butcher would be soon closing for lunch. Throck climbed down from the cart and pulled his haversack onto his shoulder. He didn't like goodbyes anyway. His throat felt tight and his eyes prickled. He shooed George off with a wave and a crooked smile and the promise to send a postcard, but George halted the cart and turned back.

"I forgot t'say – I 'ad a letter this morning from Eliza," he called, and he fumbled in his pocket, withdrawing a piece of folded paper. "She got married!" He grinned at Throck and shrugged. "Brave fella, I'd wager, marryin' up with my sister. D'you want to read it?"

Throck paused. He looked at the letter fluttering in George's outstretched hand, and he felt the pull of those happy weeks on the road spent with her and the Trusty and his own metamorphosing self. He realised that he'd forgiven her for emptying the wallet, for taking all the money, and if he were to weigh what she'd been to him – companion, friend, partner – against her failings, the scales would tip in her favour. But he knew, too, in that moment, that he didn't need to go back there. Memories were precious because you couldn't go back. He shook his head and without a backward glance, headed into the station.

The schedules board indicated the next train out was heading back the way he'd come, stopping at Oxford. He considered travelling back that way, perhaps visiting Ernest Deverill again, take him up on his offer to read through Harold's reports. But the temptation to continue backwards, then, to find the Kings and Eliza might prove too great, and he wanted new pastures, an open slate, a blank canvas. He studied the route map, and finally decided on a train to Reading that left on the hour. From there, he saw, he could continue on to London, or change and go to Worthing, maybe, or Eastbourne. Or perhaps he'd go to Dover, see the famous white cliffs. They said you could see France on the other side if it was a clear day. A nice seaside holiday might be just the thing, although in truth, the image that idea conjured was less one of excitement than of old folks dozing in canvas deck chairs. But never mind, he told himself. A holiday, like life, was what one made of it. He felt good. He shuffled to the ticket wicket and stood in the queue.

THE END

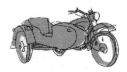

"The tiny, mundane details of these very ordinary lives are brilliantly interwoven with the colossal events and backwash of all-out war that move the story relentlessly, sometimes breathlessly, forward. As in a painting by Seurat, the masses (dots) of information meticulously build up, slowly, vividly, revealing the many personalities and the devastating time." *Globe and Mail*

"Amazingly detailed and moving. ... The quintessential Canadian story." *The Ottawa Citizen*

"The authors' alternating micro/macro viewpoint is thoroughly effective in portraying an entire country in the throes of war. ...A full-bodied, moving story of a battered populace that refused to be annihilated." *Kirkus*

"Not only a family memoir, but a fascinating social history of the time. It's a 'must read' for students of modern history and anyone who grew up in Europe during the Second World War." *Kitchener-Waterloo Record*

"We come to know the den Hartogs so intimately we feel we are seated at the dinner table, sharing their meagre meals." *Vancouver Sun*

"*The Occupied Garden* is a triumphant refusal to accept the silence that erases the past." Rosemary Sullivan, author of *Villa Air-Bel: World War II, Escape, and a House in Marseille*

"Truly gripping. This is intimate history: the writers recover not only the facts, but the tastes, smells, and lived experiences of events that today almost defy belief." *Quill and Quire*

"A dramatic and moving account of the World War II occupation of The Netherlands and the subsequent liberation by Canadian troops as seen through the lens of one Dutch family's experiences *The Occupied Garden* is a fine read." Mark Zuehlke, author of *Terrible Victory: First Canadian Army and the Scheldt Estuary Campaign*

"Already the authors of a well-received family memoir, sisters Kasaboski and den Hartog meet this challenge head-on. …Throughout, the prose is graceful, the research meticulous." *Canada's History Magazine.*

"A true-life family biography that grips the reader with the passion of an engrossing novel. …riveting from cover to cover and highly recommended." *Midwest Book Review*

"The Cowkeeper's Wish is by far, one of the best-written family histories I have seen … a wonderfully written narrative covering nearly one hundred years." Leland Meitzler, *GenealogyBlog*

"This is the family history I wish I had written. …A combination of meticulous and genealogical research and fluid writing make this a book that shouldn't be missed. It is a perfect example of how both standard and unusual sources can be used creatively to allow us to imagine the details of our ancestors' lives beyond the basic names and dates and places." Toronto Tree, *Ontario Genealogical Society*

"What makes this book stand out is the depth of research and the exceptional ability of the authors to weave their various strands into a cohesive account that immerses the reader in a time and place so different from our own." Teresa Eckford, *Writing My Past*

"This book is not only the story of the Jones families, but also the story of London in transition from its gritty and murderous underside." Bobbi King, *Eastman's Online Genealogy Newsletter*

"An excellently researched book, and a very readable one too." *Genealogists' Magazine, Society of Genealogists*

"The Cowkeeper's Wish is like a camera panning across decades of change, the rise and fall of families and the way fate and fortune conspire to create the present and the future." Stephen R. Bown, author of *Island of the Blue Foxes*

TRACY KASABOSKI lives and writes in Laurentian Hills in the beautiful Ottawa Valley, very near the wonderfully nerdy and science-centric town of Deep River. Despite the emphasis on testable hypotheses, or perhaps because of it, this is a place that inspires artists and writers. Tracy is the co-researcher and co-author, with her sister Kristen den Hartog, of two acclaimed works of non-fiction. *The Occupied Garden: A Family Memoir of War-Torn Holland* was a Globe and Mail Top 100 selection and was also published in The Netherlands as *De Kinderen van de Tuinder*. *The Cowkeeper's Wish: A Genealogical Journey*, was praised by *Canada's History* magazine for its powerful blend of meticulous research and superb storytelling. *Mr Isbister's Marvellous Ride* is Tracy's first novel, but rest assured, there are more in the drawer.

Manufactured by Amazon.ca
Bolton, ON

41444303R00273